1917

The Allies continue to press eastward against Axis forces. Nurse Lydia Blackwell-Finney, Doctor Simon Finney, Doctor Marcus Lovell, and their faithful dog Abril make their way back to America, having honorably fulfilled their military service.

Returning to the States, they plan to build their lives in Pittsburgh, where the three spiritual rivers of "faith, love, and charity" will converge. But Marcus must first travel to Rochester, hoping to reconcile with the woman he failed in France, the mother of the daughter he's never met.

As Lydia and Simon start their life together and prepare for the birth of their first baby, Lydia navigates the challenges of a medical system, not yet ready for her battlefield-honed skills. And Simon, still healing from his illness in France, must also learn how to protect his wife and family from unimaginable dangers, on unexpected new fronts.

Knowing the cost, they answer the call to serve those most in need. With rising labor unrest, a dark evil taking root within the family, and the invisible menace of the Spanish flu... not to mention the uninvited ghosts of war which followed them home... it will take their unbreakable bonds of friendship and every ounce of their faith to face the battles ahead of them.

Three Rivers

THREE RIVERS

Book II of *The River Series*
by
Rachael Hiatt

URBAN BOHEMIIA INC

Contents

God is my guide and protector.
   I shall not be confused or lost.
   He places good people to assist me.
   He guides me to my destination and eases challenges...
Yes, though I travel busy roads, crowded with multitudes
   of cars and strangers and challenges, I will fear no evil...

"Psalm for Sunday" in *Cruising at 95*
by Marilyn Downing

These novels rely heavily on the art of written dialogue. In a world where storytelling and shared experiences are increasingly overshadowed by handheld devices, television, computers, and the endless noise of modern life, the art of real conversation is too often lost.

In contrast, these novels rely heavily on dialogue for the expression of feelings, emotions, thoughts, hopes, and expectations. This immersive approach allows readers to step intimately into the characters' lives, experiencing their joys, sorrows, and quieter, more personal moments. Readers be warned; this style of storytelling draws you in deeply. You may laugh. You may cry. Some of the subject matter may be difficult to read.

I personally wept through the last half of book three, *Fishing Creek*, even while writing it.

But then again, I wept through half of *Tributary* as well, so, there you have it.

- Rachael Hiatt

... Chapter Ten: Expecting the Unexpected ...

"Women can actually sleep between contractions," Sister Anne informed Simon. "Amazing, isn't it? How her body can do that? It's really quite remarkable when you think about it."

Simon wasn't immediately impressed with that tidbit of knowledge, but filed it away for later consideration because, before he knew it, his wife clutched his arms, wide-awake again, panting. Her fingers gripped his arms like steel clamps as she screamed.

"The baby is ready, Lydia," Sister Anne said. "Push as hard as you can."

From the downstairs hall, Marcus heard the woman's wail, and his heart almost stopped. He waited for a tiny cry, but none was forthcoming.

Upstairs, Lydia sank back one more time against Simon's chest. "Oh, God!" she cried.

"Dear God," Simon whispered.

Please, God, Marcus pleaded.

"This next one might do it," Sister Anne said cheerfully, waiting for the miracle to unfold.

Pacing worriedly, Marcus held his breath, listening. Lydia's wail flowed down the stairs around him, a maelstrom of pain and effort. He heard Sister Anne and Simon loudly encouraging her to push hard over her own cries. And then, suddenly, there was dead silence... and a thin, tremulous wail filled the house.

Three Rivers

Chapter 1
Across the Pond

PART I

S imon had not lied. The white-crested swells of the ocean had absolutely no effect on his stomach, nor his balance, as they made their way across the ship's teetering deck to meet Marcus, who was no doubt already waiting for them below. Once inside the warm galley, which smelled of breakfast meats and freshly brewed coffee, Lydia envied her husband's ability to enjoy a hearty breakfast while the waves tossed about the formidable naval vessel.

Lydia was not nearly as seaworthy, even when the waves were calm, the ship gliding through the water under the power of its engines. This crossing was notably more difficult for her than when she had first crossed the Atlantic, to volunteer at the front line casualty clearing station... perhaps it was the growing baby inside of her... perhaps the ocean was more turbulent this time. Regardless, she could not hold anything down when the waves were this rough, and today, the sea seemed particularly displeased.

After devouring their breakfasts, Simon and Marcus headed topside while Lydia remained. She sat a long while, nursing a cup of tea, to quiet her nausea. Lydia noticed as one of the few other nurses on board entered the galley. She grabbed something to eat, and spotting Lydia, came straight to her table.

"You look a little green, honey," she said, extending her hand. "Name's Maggie."

Lydia responded in kind, finding it difficult to hide her discomfort. "Lydia—Not just seasick. Pregnant seasick."

"Ouch," Maggie replied sympathetically. "Heading home? I am. Boston."

"Pennsylvania," Lydia responded. "Yes, with my husband. His time was up... two years."

"I was in London. You?" Maggie asked, starting in on a muffin with her coffee, the smell of which turned Lydia's stomach.

"Ypres... at least at the end," Lydia told her, thinking of Charlotte, Nancy, Sally, Gretha, Marlene, Monique... and Doctor Stockton... all of those they had had to leave behind... *still operating, still sleeping on cots, still listening for shells to drop only miles away... and with winter coming...*

"Right at the front," Maggie noted correctly. "Lots of fighting that neck of the woods! We heard, in England. I was supply and troop transfers... What was it like there?"

Lydia stirred her tea. "Challenging to put it into words... I feel guilty leaving the other nurses behind. There were twelve of us, and another surgeon we worked with too. It was hard to say goodbye... after all we went through together—"

Maggie looked shrewdly at her fellow nurse. "Best to put it away for now, honey... you already feel sick. How'd you get pregnant on the front line?"

This last question pulled Lydia back to the present, she smiled. "Oh, the usual way, I suppose," she sighed. "My husband is a surgeon. We just... Well, I suppose it took going to war to find the man I was meant to be with. We met in our casualty clearing station. The baby just, happened."

Maggie laughed. "Well, put that one in the obstetric books under 'just happened'. Suitable reading for students of all ages! Hey, didn't I see you with another man, too? A really good-looking captain?"

"My husband's best friend. They met up the minute they got to Verdun and have been side by side ever since. Doctor Lovell. He's been very good to us, a treasured friend."

"Well, I'll ask you to introduce me." She paused. "I keep asking myself if all this is worth it? So many of the boys we send over never get back home," Maggie sighed. "And it doesn't look like Germany intends to give up any time soon. Can anything good come out of this war?"

Sipping her tea, Lydia nodded. "Finding my husband was good, and our friend, Doctor Lovell. My baby is wonderful of course... and our dog Abril... she was our camp dog, but she kind of adopted me, so she's coming home with us... I couldn't bear to be parted from her." *She saved my life,* Lydia thought to herself, not allowing her memories to surface further.

Maggie sighed. "I didn't get a husband, baby, friend, or a dog. Guess I lost out all the way around. Well, fix me up with that Doctor Lovell, will you? At least for the trip. Be nice to have a companion when they show movies below deck! Maybe I'll get one good thing before we dock in Philadelphia!"

"Do you have family waiting for you, Maggie? At home?" Lydia wondered, finishing the last of her tea and beginning to think she might actually be able to keep a muffin down, herself.

As if reading her mind, Maggie broke off a piece of hers. "Here," she said, holding out her offering. "A mom, dad... couple of brothers. How about you?"

"Mom, dad, and a sister. But I doubt they've gotten any of my letters from the front, telling them that I'm on my way home... with a baby and husband, no less. I hope the shock of me showing up, pregnant and married, doesn't give my dad a heart attack... his heart is weak. Mom will be okay, but Dad... I'm not so sure."

Maggie nodded, she knew all too well how slowly mail moved across the ocean. "Don't you think they'll just be glad you're alive, honey? I'll bet they'll be thrilled," she said reassuringly.

Lydia took a moment to savor the delicious bite of muffin, grateful that it seemed to be staying down.

"While we were over there, my husband was separated from our camp, became severely ill and ended up being transferred, all alone, to the American Hospital in Paris. We didn't know where he was... or if he was even still alive... for what felt like forever... but when he miraculously made his way back to camp... well, I was just so excited that I hadn't lost him! Maybe that's how Mom and Dad will feel about me—"

A sudden thought took Lydia's focus. She worried that the cool, salty air on deck might not be good for Simon's lungs. Rising, she quickly thanked Maggie for the lovely conversation, promising to mention her to Marcus as she grabbed some food to wrap in a napkin and hurried on her way.

Stopping by their little officer's cabin, Lydia first sought out Abril.

"Good dog, Ab," she tenderly patted the animal who was patiently waiting on the metal floor of the tiny cabin. "At least you don't get seasick!"

The dog looked up at her eagerly, perhaps wondering if she would be asked to accompany Lydia topside where she could run, but she was more than satisfied to gobble up the bacon Lydia had smuggled for her, from breakfast.

"Stay, girl," Lydia reluctantly commanded her, as if reading her mind. She would take the dog out in the evening when the other passengers had all retired. She looked tenderly at her rescuer from the trenches, her faithful companion throughout Simon's absence. Lydia touched the dog's nose again. "Good dog," she repeated with genuine gratitude.

Cautiously, Lydia climbed the steep set of metal stairs to the deck, wishing she'd asked Simon for some money to buy a long skirt before they had boarded in England. It would have been more suitable for climbing ladders than the shorter Red Cross uniform, which was now a little snug around her belly anyway.

As she emerged topside, she saw that the sun had broken through the scattered morning clouds. To her relief, as she stepped out, the deck was only a little wet from ocean spray. One of the young sailors on duty nodded to her.

"Morning, Nurse," he said, reaching out a hand. "Need some help?"

"Thank you. I'm going to try to navigate it myself," she offered a less than confident smile.

"You get used to it, Miss," he assured her. "Just takes a few days."

She laughed. "We'll see about that. I'm not so sure."

"Begging your pardon, Nurse, but keep your legs a little farther apart, and it'll help with the pitch... the roll, I mean," the sailor told her from experience. "Or any one of our guys here'll help you out." The sailors enjoyed seeing nurses on board once in a while.

Lydia nodded. "Good advice," she replied gratefully.

The man was right. It did help, but she felt like a drunken sailor walking this way. Though she was only just finishing her fourth month, maybe this would be good practice for when she was full of baby, nearer the end! She'd certainly seen very pregnant women walking like drunken sailors, feet wide apart, when they were almost full term.

She noticed many soldiers in American Army uniforms, also appreciating the warmth breaking through the clouds. They saw the lone woman struggling to find her balance on the deck and indeed looked eager to help, but Lydia managed to stay upright all on her own. She gazed out over the ocean as she made her way. Long, defined shafts of sunshine danced upon the endless waves, the blue-grey water sparkling where they scattered across the broken surface. Rays of heavenly light. It was beautiful.

Lydia soon spotted Simon and Marc just a little farther ahead, leaning rather perilously over the railing at the ship's prow. Had the two men no fear at all? Well, after almost two years of bombs, shelling, and war, perhaps not. Navigating her way around the front artillery guns securely bolted to the deck, Lydia approached the two, wary of slipping and being swept overboard if the ship dipped into a trough of water!

Her inner thoughts narrated her building anxiety. *Well, it's their fault if I do fall in, standing all the way out here like this, forcing me to come find them on a restless sea! They would just have to dive in themselves and rescue me, that is, if either of them know how to swim. I know how to swim, but out here? With sharks?*

Sensing her struggle, the two surgeons turned simultaneously as Lydia approached with her carefully placed, wide steps, trying to keep her dreadfully awkward skirt from blowing up with the wind. She looked like someone trying to balance on wooden stilts while hanging out the laundry. They each reached out an arm, laughing at her discomfiture, and immediately secured her next to them against the railing.

"Okay!" she declared to the two. "You can laugh now, but I'm telling you that if I fall into the deep, you're jumping right in after me... even if there are hungry sharks down there!"

Marcus chuckled, teasing. "If you fall in, your skirt will billow out and buoy you on the surface. We'll toss you that ring over there and pull you right back in."

Simon slid an arm around Lydia's waist as she gripped the cold metal railing. "I thought you were resting! Why didn't you tell me at breakfast that you wanted to come out here? I'd have brought you myself, my love," he reassured her. "And look, Lydia, some dolphins are swimming right below us."

Cautiously, she peered over the rail to where the men were pointing. Sure enough, she could see the sleek, grey forms far below, cruising alongside the ship and keeping pace. Occasionally, they rose to the surface, took a breath, then dove back beneath the waves in perfect harmony. The sight was soothing, almost hypnotizing.

As if he were a seasoned sailor, Marcus added, "If you look out to the horizon, it'll help your balance, Lydia... calm your stomach. The horizon doesn't move."

Giving it a try, Lydia looked out across the curve of the Earth, where the sky met the sea. There were towering clouds that stretched into the distance... seemed to go on forever. She suddenly remembered that the horizon had also looked endless on her crossing before... before Simon and Marcus... before being taken prisoner... before the baby... her before.

She was not the same woman, not the same Lydia Blackwell. Not at all. She was now Lydia Blackwell-Finney, with a file cabinet in her mind full of carefully placed images and memories which had been cataloged under 'to be opened later'... perhaps not for a very long time.

She pulled herself back to the now, leaning against Simon, feeling the strength of his arm around her as she continued to grip the wet railing. Glancing up at him, Lydia was amazed. Her worries had been unfounded. The sea air actually seemed to be doing him some good! His cheeks were full of color. His eyes were sparkling with life, and he seemed to be breathing quite well. Lydia looked at the navigator's watch on her wrist, the one their camp commander had acquired for the station nurses, and was surprised at the passing of time.

"They're already about to serve lunch in the galley, if you gentlemen are hungry," she informed them, already knowing what their answer would be.

The two friends looked at each other happily. The navy fed their sailors quite well, providing a much more satisfying meal than the cook at their camp had been able to concoct with his limited resources at the front. On this ship, meals were something to look forward to.

"Sounds like a plan," Marcus told them eagerly, speaking for Simon. "We can always eat."

"Always!" Simon declared, "And you, my love, must eat for our baby, too!"

Lydia shot a look at him. "I did try this morning. It just wouldn't stay down so I gave up. Anyway, when have you ever turned down an extra meal?" she teased, affectionately. "Certainly not in all the time that I've known you."

"Just getting my strength back," Simon reminded her. "And I feel it. It's really invigorating out here. This salt air will help clear my lungs."

"Arm wrestle later?" Marcus challenged his buddy. "Let's go for sixty percent muscle tone recovery tonight, Simon. And just remember, I was your original surgeon, when that bomb tore up your leg... not those guys in Paris, when you were sick... so, I'll be the judge of your full and complete return to health, as your physician-on-record."

"I would never have chosen for you to have to operate on my tibia while teetering on a bomb crater! That said, I'm sure grateful you did... and kept them from sending me out."

"Hm," Marcus said, thinking back as the group found their way back through the forward guns of the ship. "I never did bill you for that, did I? I meant to. After all, it did require some skill, under only lantern light, with people yelling all around us."

Marcus would never forget the sound of Lydia screaming his name amidst the horrific confusion after that explosion. He had dropped everything to reach her. He had also taken meticulous steps to convince their station commander not to send Simon and Lydia to some remote rehabilitation hospital, where he would have lost contact with them both.

Reaching around Lydia, Simon clapped the other man heartily on the back. "It's okay, Marc, I'd never be able to pay what you're worth anyway, just add it to my tab. You saved my butt more than once and kept Lydia and the baby safe the whole time I was stuck in Paris, thank God."

Marcus regarded the couple walking beside him, these two people were more dear to him than what little remained of his own family waiting back in the States... now just his father, in Pennsylvania. "No, there's no tab," he said casually. "What are friends for?"

Slipping her free arm inside of Marc's, Lydia chimed in, "Speaking of 'what are friends for'... there's a nurse on board who is very interested in making friends with you, Marc. She said she'd be glad to see a movie with you below some evening."

He frowned. There were very few nurses aboard the ship. "Which nurse? The one with the little mustache? Or the one who keeps her eyes down, looking like a nervous schoolgirl?"

"The one with the mustache, but it's very faint and she seems sweet." Lydia laughed.

"I'll pass," Marcus declared. Meeting Lydia had raised the bar for him as far as women were concerned. She was beautiful both inside and out and he would settle for nothing less... and of course there was a slim chance that he might reconnect with Suzie once they were back home... that is, if she would have him.

Lydia found the walk back across the deck, between the two most important men in her life, much more enjoyable than her solo trek had been. They descended the stairs leading to the galley, taking in the amazing smells of the food as they entered. The room was bustling with soldiers and sailors, each grabbing a tray and heading to the serving line. The kitchen staff, working in the heat of the stoves, hastily wiped the sweat from their brows. The galley was mid-ship, and it didn't seem to roll as much as other parts of the ship. Lydia decided she would try to 'eat for two' after all. The sailors were enjoying hearty meals before returning to duty, but some of the army soldiers returning home were not quite as enthusiastic. Some, like her, were a bit more cautious and their expressions of unease helped Lydia feel a little less out of place.

Finding three empty seats amid the men at the tables, Marcus settled in, "You know, I sure am glad we're doing this together. I'd have been lonely crossing back over all by myself. No one to even play chess with at night."

Simon looked up from his tray, his fork already stacked with roast beef. "Not too late to meet... What was that nurse's name, Lydia?... And I'll take you up on the chess, Marc—This is good. Taste the baked apples, my love. I think you'll like them—Did you come over alone, Marc? No others from your hospital or basic training came over with you?"

"Nope," Marcus said, sipping the coffee which swayed slightly in his mug. "I was a big boy. Did it all by myself. Brought a book. At the time, I sure didn't know what I was getting into. Thought it would be a fun adventure doing a residency in the Army, in Europe. I really had no idea what the French Army meant by a 'casualty clearing station'. I just knew I'd be doing surgery. I guess I was bored and looking for... something."

Simon laughed heartily at his friend. "You were twenty-four years old and already bored with the world of medicine, even after jumping ahead in med school the way you did? I find that hard to believe, Marcus."

"How often can someone take an appendix out before getting bored, Simon?" Marcus asked seriously. "I mean really. 'Where is your pain, sir? Oh, in your belly? Maybe it's a hernia. Maybe it's your appendix?"

"You weren't bored when you removed Charlotte's appendix!" Lydia reminded him with a little smile. "As I recall, you were rather enthusiastic about it... and very efficient."

Marcus laughed as he ate. "As I recall, Charlotte woke you and made you come along, to make certain I'd behave myself... I had to be purely professional that night."

"You saved her life," Lydia recalled. "She would have filled with infection. We could have lost her."

"Well, I definitely damaged my reputation as the bad boy of the camp that night," Marcus acknowledged grudgingly.

Lydia reached between their plates and squeezed his hand fondly. "You were never the 'bad boy' to me, Marc," she said, looking directly into his clear blue eyes, thinking of how often he had extended her comfort and safety, even offering to marry her, while Simon had been officially listed as missing in action and then presumed dead by the French command. "Never."

Marcus reddened in sudden embarrassment, focusing on his lunch. "No," he said quietly. "Never to you, Lydia." *Although it had been close, just that once...*

Simon looked at the two of them, with love for them both, his wife and his best friend. Despite Marc's current self-assessment, Simon had witnessed his steady transformation from a womanizer to someone who respected women, and himself, with far more depth than when they had first met. They had arrived together, gone through horrors together, become like brothers, and obtained their discharges from the Army together. They had both become different men than when they'd first reached Europe and were forever bonded. Simon caught Marc's eye, nodding in appreciation.

Lydia had managed to eat her mashed potatoes and apples, plus a bite or two of roast beef, washing it down with a bit of tea. "I think I've done quite well here," she announced, pushing her plate over to Simon, who reflexively finished off her lunch without a word... as she knew he would. "Well, I'm going to go read for a while and see if this stays down." She stood, steadying herself on Simon's shoulder.

Simon noted several heads turning as Lydia stood; the men appreciated what they saw. This attractive nurse had long legs, a direct gaze, and no mustache. So, Simon reached up and patted her little rounded stomach lovingly, a protective gesture. "I'll see you after a bit. Marcus and I have arm wrestling." He flexed his arm and felt, with satisfaction, that the muscle was in fact returning. The push-ups were doing some good for his body, but they also helped him push away the images of the thousands of young casualties he had tried to sew back together. And Marc, after appointing himself Simon's personal therapist, was constantly reminding him that while push-ups would remain a central part of his recovery, they would add jogging when they returned to the States... and possibly swimming, if they were able to find any unpolluted water in the three rivers flowing past the industrial city of Pittsburgh.

Leaving the two men to their highly anticipated contest of strength, Lydia found her way back through the ship's maze of corridors, to their private cabin. Marcus was bunking with the other discharged soldiers, who were either traveling home or heading for extended recovery due to wounds received in their service with the Allies. As Lydia settled into the tiny cabin she shared with Simon, she was greeted by an exuberant Abril. No doubt the dog had caught the scent of the roast beef she had smuggled from lunch, wrapping it in her blue headscarf. Lydia carefully washed the precious square of fabric in the sink while Abril ate with relish, her enthusiasm mirroring Simon's at every meal. Lydia chuckled to herself. Sitting on the edge of the berth, she held the piece of blue fabric in her hand for a long while. Then hanging it to dry, she settled in on the bunk and tried to rest.

Lydia's mind wandered. Gretha had made the blue headscarves for the nurses so their doctors could quickly find them among the countless wounded scattered throughout the station in tents or out under protective tarps. *Alice, Nancy, Monique, Sally, Marlene... they'd all still be wearing their blue scarves... and winter is sure to have set in by now.*

Their last winter had been so frightfully cold. So cold being marched through the snow that one night by the German soldiers, rifles pointed at their backs. So cold while escaping the German trenches later, as they ran through the snow in the darkness... blindly following Abril who had urged her on, despite the pain and terror. She recalled running alongside Charlotte, the two soldiers who had been captured with them and the group of deserting German soldiers, led by Frederick who had been willing to risk his commander's rage to save the four captives and surrender to the French Army. She recalled running away from that steel-eyed commander... *'Such a simple thing I ask of you'*... She remembered the physical pain, the fear, the cold... and she trembled, her eyes welling... a lump forming in her throat, an deep ache in her chest.

Sensing Lydia's distress and sudden withdrawal from the present, Abril whined softly and jumped onto the bunk, drawing near to her human, placing her snout protectively over Lydia's lap. Taking the dog's face in her hands, Lydia laid her head against the blessed creature who had led her back to camp, and to Simon, that terrifying night.

She wept into the dog's fur. "You're such a good girl."

Lydia protectively pulled the blanket over her and sobbed with the pain of memory. It was not something she could share with anyone who hadn't been there. Only Simon knew the whole of it, Marcus knew part. This small, cold cabin was too much like the cold, cramped, underground dirt room in the trench. *'Open your shirt'*...

As Lydia wept, Abril jumped down to the door of the cabin, pushing it open with her snout. Her male humans were on this ship somewhere. She woofed gently at the woman, pushing her front paws up on the bedding, but Lydia was lost in pain, unable to respond. Abril needed to find the man quickly, so she slipped right out the door and went searching the long grey walkways, circumventing the impossible metal stairs.

Enjoying their coffee, Marcus and Simon sat in the now somewhat empty galley. They had much to discuss. Both agreed that they wanted to work together as surgeons, in Pittsburgh. There were several possible hospitals, maybe also a few private surgical practices. The city was a growing, highly populated area with many industries, and the likelihood was high that the services of two experienced surgeons, fresh off the western front, would be needed.

"What's Lydia going to do while you and I are rearranging people's intestines?" Marcus asked, finishing the last of his mug.

Simon looked up in surprise. "She's going to take care of the baby."

Marcus nodded. "Obviously, Simon. But what about before the baby... and then after, when the baby is no longer... a baby?"

Simon hadn't thought too much about that, in the whirlwind of their discharges, saying goodbye to the station, and getting to the shores of England where they had fit in a quick tour of London before finally connecting with the transport back to the States. "Oh, I imagine the little one will keep her busy full-time later on, too," he said casually.

Sighing, Marcus just shook his head at Simon's lack of insight. "You know, Simon, you once told me that I was an idiot, and it was well deserved because I was. Maybe still am a little. But this I know; Lydia is always trying to learn. She loves being a nurse. You do remember they won't allow her to work at the hospitals. A pregnant, married woman. When did you ever see a pregnant, married nurse at a hospital when you were in training? It's not allowed."

Simon thought back. Now that Marcus had him thinking, he realized his buddy was right. Hospital nurses were young, single women. Some older matrons ran floors, but they were never referred to as a "Mrs.", just as "Nurse this" or "Nurse that". Hospital nurses often lived in dormitories at the hospitals where they worked, so they could be ready for duty when needed. Lydia could no longer do that.

What if he and the baby weren't enough? This was going to be a problem. Lydia had told him from the start that she needed to make a difference.

"No, no it is not..." Simon remarked quietly. "You're right, Marcus."

Marcus laughed lightly. "Say that again! It sounds so good, and I don't always get to hear that phrase."

"Why didn't I think of this?" Simon asked his friend. "I should have. I've been so wrapped up in leaving the war behind that I guess I assumed that the baby and I would be enough for her... with a new house... and her family not too far away. I guess, maybe, she'll do a little private duty or something?"

Images flew through Marcus' mind, recalling Lydia running triage, working beside them in the surgery tent, her fingers flying... tying off sutures, helping them resect bowels, finding shrapnel, setting bones, pulling out ruptured spleens, managing her team of nurses. He could not even begin to imagine her being content sweeping the floors or hanging out sheets to dry on the clothesline while bread baked in the oven. Nor could he envision her sitting private duty, at one person's bedside all night. Not Lydia. "Well, maybe I'm wrong," Marcus said thoughtfully. "But I don't think I am."

"No... no, you're absolutely right, Marc," Simon admitted, now deep in thought. "We've all been living on the edge for so long, at such a fast pace. I guess I thought slowing down and just kicking back would be a welcome relief for her. But here I am, sitting with you, planning a busy practice for us to enjoy surgery, and I wasn't thinking about her wanting to stay equally as busy applying her nursing skills."

Marcus watched Simon drum his fingers on the table, as he often did when he was trying to reason his way through a challenge. "Remember that Nurse Baxter, who came from the Red Cross in Philadelphia? Remember how she told the nurses that what they learned in the station would have to stay in the station? That they wouldn't be allowed to use those skills back home? How is a nurse like Lydia, who can do so much, supposed to step back into some restricted role of emptying bedpans and giving pain meds?"

Simon nodded, his expression troubled. His own recent illness and long recovery had clouded his judgment... He didn't like it. He just wanted them all to be together. "My God," he added quietly. "I've got to pray about this... and talk to her about it."

Satisfied his friend would not let the matter go unattended, Marcus sat back and took a deep breath. He set his elbow squarely on the table and extended his hand. "Left one first," he suggested, knowing that it had been the opposite side, Simon's right lung, that had been resected, the ribs and chest muscles stretched and weakened.

Simon readied himself, gladly grasping the extended hand. The two of them struggled for mastery, neither wanting to cede victory to the other. It was Simon who finally took Marcus down, flat to the table. "Not so bad, huh?" he challenged, feeling the thrill of the win.

"Okay, now the right," Marcus suggested with a sly smile.

Simon returned the smile, recognizing the dare in his friend's eyes. "You're on!"

They were fairly matched, but not like the first round... Marcus let himself relax ever so slightly, testing whether Simon could gain the upper hand. He could not. Marcus flattened his arm against the table unceremoniously.

"It's coming," he assured his opponent. "Not there yet, but it's coming. There's real improvement, Simon."

Simon flexed his right arm. "At least I don't need much muscle to remove an appendix."

"Hey," Marcus challenged. "Maybe you can beat me at chess."

They cleared the table and made their way down to where soldier passengers were berthed in rows along the walls of the ship. There, many of the men were reading or sleeping, in bunks and hammocks, trying to pass the time on such a long voyage. Several jumped up to salute Marcus and Simon as they passed, but uncomfortable with formalities, they quickly released the men to their prior activities.

At one end of the room, there was a chess set on a long table which was bolted to the floor. The two men began to reset the pieces. This was Marcus' game and he enjoyed having the edge, while also teaching Simon new strategies to improve against him. But before even making a first move, Marcus looked up toward the door, in shock.

"Hey, Simon, what's Abril doing out here? They give you special permission to let her roam the ship?"

Interested soldiers looked up as well as Marc and Simon headed for the dog, knocking over the chess pieces in their haste. Abril met them halfway, pulling on Simon's trousers with her teeth.

"Lydia—"

"Let me know..." Marc started to say, worried and assuming he knew what troubled Lydia enough for the dog to come in search of Simon. Without the demands of the camp seizing their every waking moment, he suspected that her memories were surfacing.

"I will," Simon said and quickly left with Abril at his heels.

Marcus was more than grateful that their discharges had come at the same time. *They both still need my help,* he thought as a soldier took Simon's place even before Marc could put all of the chess pieces back to their first positions. He played a game with the newcomer before he went to stretch out on his assigned hammock. Marc did not want to live far from Simon and Lydia. Would Suzie be willing to move to Pittsburgh? That is, if she had an interest in them resuming their relationship? They had not parted under the best of circumstances, but he did want to meet his little daughter and make them a family, if given the chance. But Simon and Lydia were already family, along with their baby. Marc would ask Suzie, but if she said no, his course was already laid out. He'd start over in Pittsburgh.

Simon, his mind racing faster than his feet, quickly made his way through the narrow passageways to the officer's cabin. Immediately closing the door behind them, as he and Abril slipped inside, he found Lydia in the berth weeping softly. Not sure if she was awake or caught in a troubling dream, he called to her gently.

"Lydia, my beloved, I'm here," Simon caressed the hair along her face, feeling the wetness of her cheeks as Abril nuzzled up against the woman's clenched hand.

Rolling toward them, in the narrow space, Lydia's eyes opened. "I'm so sorry."

Simon pulled off his boots and suspenders and slid in next to her. "Come to me," he said quietly, taking her into his arms. He kissed her face softly. "What is it?"

"It's nothing... it's everything," she wept. "I'm cold, it's dark, and I'm afraid."

"Oh, beloved," Simon sighed. "I'm here. We're heading home. The baby is safe inside you."

"I can't feel it, Simon," she wept. "I can't feel anything over the noise of the engines, the waves and wind... and everything. Do you think the baby is still okay? How could I even know if anything was wrong?"

"Well, you aren't having any cramping, are you? Just the nausea?" he asked.

She shook her head. "No cramping. My breasts are so sore though."

He chuckled. "Well, that's a good sign! They're growing equal to the task ahead. That's good."

"Were they too small, before?" she asked tearfully.

"No, beloved," Simon assured her, smiling though she couldn't tell in the dim light. "They're perfect. You're perfect—"

"Then maybe you won't like them getting big and full," she wept.

Simon brought her hand to his lips, kissing her fingers. "I will like them whether they are big and full or small and soft," he assured her. "There's nothing to worry about—"

"Simon... what if I'm a terrible mother," she whispered.

He stroked her hair, knowing she was pushing other memories away with this line of questions. "You'll be superb. Our baby is so blessed to have you as its mother. You like to learn. You'll teach our baby to love learning, too. Now, let's try to rest together, you and me... Hey, in the morning, maybe we'll see about getting Marcus together with that nurse you mentioned."

That actually made Lydia smile, just a little. "Maggie, from Boston."

"Ah! Maggie from Boston," Simon chuckled. "Maybe Marc likes chowder and can ignore the little mustache."

"Maybe she'll shave it off for him," Lydia said, wiping the remaining tears from her eyes. With that, Lydia's tormented memories were, once again, filed neatly into her mental filing cabinet. The two fell into a deep sleep, Simon's protective arms wrapped around her and Abril, curled up on the floor beside their berth, a satisfied sigh escaping as she too settled in for the night.

The next couple of days fell into a comfortingly repetitive routine, except for a few light storms which soaked the upper deck from time to time. One evening after supper they took Abril for a walk, topside, in the light drizzle and watched the elusive sun set behind the towering gray clouds. Then, back in their cabin, Simon helped Lydia shed her damp woolen uniform, down to her underthings. She was glad to be rid of the heavy wool jacket and snug skirt, and the tie that completed the ensemble. Climbing into the berth, she rolled onto her side, making room for Simon to join her after he had hung his uniform in their cabin's tiny storage locker. He looked at her, stalling, before sliding in with her.

"Are you leaving those things on all night?" he wondered aloud.

"I don't have to," she admitted. "It stays cold in here on cloudy days... Are you planning on keeping me warm?"

He eagerly reached into the berth, a warm smile lighting his face as he helped to remove her underthings.

"I'll keep you warm," he promised before sliding in and pulling the blanket up over the both of them. He so relished the feel of her bare skin against his own as he pulled her onto his chest. Simon stroked her long, chestnut brown waves, now loose against him, and kissed the top of her head as he wrapped both arms around her. Holding her like this was all of the treasure he ever needed.

"Lydia," he started. "What do you want to do when we set up house together? While you're waiting for the baby to come?"

She rubbed her hand over the hair on his chest. "I don't know," she admitted. "Set up the kitchen and baby's room I suppose. Knit baby blankets?"

"Do you know how to knit?" he wondered, never having seen her do it.

"I used to," she said. "I suppose if I can tie sutures, I can relearn knitting. Or perhaps I could establish our garden, grow tomatoes and zucchini... or roll bandages for the war, maybe."

"Hm. Have to dig a garden then," he admitted. "Marcus says that won't be enough."

"Enough for what?" she wondered, looking up at him. "Zucchini?"

"Enough to keep your inquisitive and talented mind busy."

She laughed slightly. "Oh, that! Well, I can always use it to think of baby names..." She then paused, noticing the intensity in his brown eyes.

"I mean it, my love. Marc is right. We started our relationship with you telling me that you need to make a difference. It has always been important to you to use your skills."

"Our baby is important," she reminded him. "And I'll be nursing for a while."

"Do you want to nurse the baby? Well, good! Yes, that's good. But the baby won't be here for five more months. And I'll be working in an operating theater, and Nurse Baxter told you all that your work will be much more restricted back home."

Lydia nodded, her fingers tracing his ribs and his large scar. "Suzie said the same thing in her letters. She wrote that she was emptying bedpans and giving medication. It paid some bills, but wasn't very satisfying not being allowed to think."

"That's what worries me," Simon said softly. "We're so used to working ten feet apart, in the tents. Now, if I'm away all day at some hospital, and you're... home, I suppose... It's not going to be satisfying for you, if you can't continue to grow professionally."

Lydia didn't answer him. Simon felt her fingers move down his stomach, following the little line of hair down his torso. "You satisfy me," she said.

Simon took that hand running down his body and brought it back up to his lips. "I hope so. I'm not going to be enough though. The baby isn't going to be enough."

"Then we'll have to have a second one," she said, returning her hand to his chest again. Of course, she had been considering options, after the decision had been made to leave the war. She often reread Suzie's letters and shared her friend's belief that nurses were overworked and undervalued. She didn't know what to do with that either... How to make a difference in a country where no shells were falling, and no lines of ambulances streamed in every day. But she did not want to think about this right now. Instead, her hand moved slowly down Simon's chest... and belly...

"I take it," Simon smiled in the dark cabin as he felt her hand, "that this means our discussion about your future is over, at least for the moment?"

She nestled herself on top of him in the narrow space. "Our discussion is over," she whispered, wanting him to meet a need that she knew he could easily meet. "And you're the one who insisted that I take everything off..."

He ran his hands down her back to her bottom, his fingers recognizing her scars even in darkness, holding her to him as her long wavy hair fell around him. "Yes, I certainly did..." he admitted. And as much as he wanted to resolve the other matter, and despite the tiny space available to them, they were soon able to drive any lingering issues right out of their heads.

The next morning, at breakfast, Marcus and Simon were laughing over some absurd story Marc was sharing about his medical school escapades when one of the sailors burst into the crowded galley. "Sirs!" he said, approaching the table and saluting.

Awkwardly, the two men saluted in kind. "Can we help you?" Simon asked the agitated man.

"We're pulling alongside one of the transports, sir. Our medic wants to know—they have a guy on their ship in a bad way—something's wrong with his gut, sir. Sorry ma'am," he nodded anxiously toward Lydia. "But you sirs are surgeons and our medic wonders if... well, he knows you're not on duty or nothing, but..."

"Of course," Simon said. He quickly stood as Marc hastily shoveled a last bite of his eggs and sausage, washing it down with the last of his coffee, in one gulp.

Marc grinned at Lydia. "Never a dull moment, huh? Think I can handle a scalpel with the waves rocking us?"

"I think you can handle a scalpel standing on your head, Marc," she said reassuringly. "Go. Have fun."

"Don't even know where the sick bay is!"

"I imagine he's going to lead you to it!" she smiled.

"You be okay here?"

"I'm fine, Marc. Go! Simon is already half way to the patient!" she laughed, waving him off as he ran to catch up with Simon.

Lydia picked at her eggs and bacon. With the limited space in the galley, the two empty seats were rapidly filled by others. One of the men looked at her, curious.

"Hello, Miss. Red Cross, huh? Going home I assume."

Lydia nodded. "I am. With my husband. Where are you headed?"

"Philadelphia now, then Kentucky. Back to my folks' farm. They have horses. Of course, everyone in Kentucky does, so not unusual. Do you ride?"

"I never have," Lydia admitted. "Just a bike, if that counts for anything."

"Very similar," the man laughed. He had clear blue eyes like Marc's and a shock of hair almost white, although he appeared young. He looked at Lydia closely, and in that look she saw an expression she knew all too well. This man had seen things.

"I'm Lydia," she said, reaching across the table. "Where did you serve?"

"Terry Filbert," he said. "Our unit ended up in Verdun, then kind of all over the countryside. You ever hear of it?"

She nodded because it was all too familiar. "Indeed, I have. Our CCS was there for a while, Terry."

"Ended up with a fake leg. Could you tell? Was in a rehab for a while, but they finished with me."

Lydia looked surprised. "You're just shipping out now, Terry? Verdun was a long time ago. Have you been in a rehab this whole time?"

He laughed lightly. "Naw. Did the rehab till I got used to walking around... like a horse on three legs. Least we don't get put out of our misery like horses that go lame. But after I got back up and moving around alright, I asked for a desk job and they reassigned me to Paris, on base. Did supply, requisitions... stuff like that."

Lydia's eyes showed her amazement. "You could have shipped right out, back home, Terry. You decided to stay on? That's unusual."

He was eating with a healthy appetite. "Well, it's the other guys. Their time wasn't up. I waited so we could get back to Kentucky together. High school buddies. They were still fighting on the front lines. Least I could do was help make sure they got the supplies they needed. They're right over there... tables are kind of full. Can I introduce you to them? We hooked up in Paris when they were discharged so we could go home together."

There were tears welling in Lydia's eyes. This soldier did not want to leave Europe until his buddies were safe. Even if it meant him serving at a different post. "I'd very much like to meet your friends," she said. "They must be terrific guys for you to want to stick around like that."

"They are. The best. People like me, got lucky having good buddies like them," Terry scarfed down his meal and stood, stacking his tray beneath her own and those of Simon and Marcus. He took them over to the wash tub and only then did she notice his long uniform pants hiding the prosthetic he wore on one leg. He was remarkably steady on a moving ship. Terry came right back to her, taking her elbow as she rose from the table. Together they made their way through the crowded galley to a table where six men were sandwiched next to each other. Two of them stood immediately as a woman approached.

"Guys, this is Lydia. She's from... Well, she was Red Cross."

"Gentlemen," Lydia greeted them warmly, noticing some obvious souvenirs of injury some of the men were taking home with them. One had an eye patch, another a folded sleeve, many, no doubt with wounds that could not be readily seen, but were certainly there.

"Ma'am," one said, rising partway while extending his hand to shake hers. "I'm Forrest Dilbert."

Another followed suit. "Jerry Riesinger, ma'am." They went around the table as she perched on the edge of the bench not wanting to take seats away from them. "A pleasure to meet you boys," Lydia assured them.

"Where were you serving, Nurse Lydia," Forrest asked courteously.

"I served with a casualty clearing station, with the French Army," she said. "We were in Verdun, Ypres, up the Meuse to Belgium."

The men stopped eating in unison. "Pardon me, ma'am," Jerry said. "But there's some pretty bad fighting all that way. You're a... you're a wo—"

"A woman? Yes, but a nurse, first," she said. "There were twelve of us in our CCS."

One of the men openly stared at her in disbelief. "Sorry, Miss. It's just, you don't look like someone who should be on the front lines like that. I wouldn't want you up there."

Lydia met his gaze. "You fellas were up there! Someone needed to help patch you boys up. Might as well be me."

Another spoke up. "But, Nurse Lydia, we... that is, some of us... had to get to one of those stations. It was bad. Some of them didn't even have nurses. Lots of medics, docs... and really banged up guys."

Nodding, Lydia explained, "Ours didn't have nurses either until the Red Cross asked for volunteers."

At that, one soldier dropped his face into his hands, momentarily overcome. Instinctively, Lydia reached across the table and put her hand on his arm. "I'm sorry, Rudy. Did my telling you that upset you?" she asked carefully.

He wiped his eyes on his uniform sleeve while Forrest put a hand on his shoulder in support. Rudy finally said, "No, ma'am. It's just... we been talking about going home and wondering how to answer when someone asks us how it was over there. I'm just gonna say talk to one of the nurses. They didn't think it was asking too much."

Terry nodded at the others. If even a woman, a nurse like this one, could be willing to leave her life behind and serve on the front for the sake of their buddies and the French, then that's why he had stayed on at the supply base, unwilling to leave his high school friends behind. It had been a sacrifice he was more than willing to make.

The seven of them talked for hours, even after the rest of the galley had nearly emptied out. Lydia listened to their stories and told them briefly a little about her experience at the station, leaving out the details of her personal hardships... these boys had had enough of their own. She did tell them about the British Christmas party, about Abril finding food for them in the fields when the French Army had lost them in Belgium. And she told them all about Father James, in great detail, and they marveled at the priest who took care of soldiers and who had showed up just in the nick of time with a wagon of food to end their starvation. By the time she left them, she had given them many good stories to tell back home.

Lydia made her way back to the cabin to take Abril out for a brief run on the deck. She loved watching the dog playing in the ocean spray. She also noted that the other troop transport ship, heading for Europe, had moved on, but Simon and Marc had not yet returned... *they must have needed to operate*, she thought. *If so, their patient won't see Europe, or war. At least not yet.* Lydia stared over the railing at the various sea birds occasionally flying past. The earlier discussion with the men in the galley was heavy on her mind. If she couldn't work in a hospital, perhaps there would be some kind of a clinic for returning soldiers, where she could help men find some peace and purpose; she could not just 'grow zucchini'.

Midway through their voyage, Lydia had gained enough confidence to stand at the prow of the ship, by herself. With Abril at her heels, she circumvented the armament, making her way to the railing at the point. The dog loved standing there with the sea wind blowing past her. She closely watched any passing seabirds, waiting for them to descend, ready for the chase, not realizing that they stayed at sea, some soaring for years without coming to land. This particular morning, Lydia let down her hair, inviting the wind to blow through it freely, salt spray touching her face while she marveled at the concept of 'no land in sight'.

She wondered about the depth of the ocean here and what creatures might be dwelling beneath its surface... hidden, yet living out their lives unknown to the world above. Could she become like one of them? Like a whale or an octopus... living out her life in obscurity, fulfilling her days without much in the way of fanfare? Without the demands of traditional nursing? She realized, of course, that she had yet to experience true, traditional nursing.

A movement at Lydia's elbow, broke her reverie. One of the returning soldiers had noticed her at the prow and had decided to join her.

"All by yourself, Nurse?" he asked kindly. "Maybe you shouldn't be up here like this, all by yourself." He had seen her before, talking to a group of soldiers, and was intrigued.

Lydia gripped the railing, suddenly uncertain being alone with him, behind the artillery.

"I'm just waiting for my husband," she said.

He looked disappointed. "You're a nurse and you're married?" He glanced down seeing the hammered pewter ring on her right middle finger. It didn't look like a wedding band to him, so he wondered if she was just saying that to throw him off.

"I'm Ben. Private Ben Arndt. Heading back to Chicago. Ever been there?" he asked, leaning against the rail beside her.

"No," Lydia said. "I haven't been to Chicago. I'm sure it's very nice."

"Great place, lots of culture. You're a very pretty woman," he observed, sliding a bit closer to her. "Be happy to help you pass the time on this trip, if you tell me your name. Be nice to spend some time with a woman like you."

Anxiously, Abril nosed her way between the stranger and her human. Lydia didn't hear Marcus approaching, with the sound of the ship's engines and ocean wind, but Abril did and nudged her leg. Lydia turned her head, still holding fast to the rail for security, and saw, with great relief, that Marcus was coming up behind her. He took hold of the steel bar, wedging himself between Lydia and the soldier on the railing.

"I was looking for you," Marcus remarked. "Simon will be along." He couldn't help but notice her chestnut brown hair flowing around her like a sea nymph, her gaze fixed on the waves and the water. Her beauty was undeniable.

The soldier immediately straightened, giving Marcus, who outranked him, a small salute. "Captain. Um... Nice to meet you, Nurse," the man still had not learned her name. As he left, visibly disappointed, Lydia sagged against Marcus, not realizing how tense she had become.

"You really shouldn't be out here by yourself," Marcus cautioned, watching as the private retreated. "Not with a ship full of lonely men." *Who have all noticed you by now!*

"I'm not by myself," she corrected him. "You're here... and Abril."

"You know what I mean, Lydia," he admonished her protectively. "Is this the same woman who told us we'd have to jump in after her if she fell overboard, just days ago?"

She nodded. "Same one."

"Still," he started, reaching out, pulling the hair away from her eyes as it swirled in the wind. "Don't come out here alone, where you're out of sight, Lydia. Find Simon or me. Please."

"Okay, I won't, Marc," she said, not wanting to minimize his concern. She turned to face him, adding, "Simon said you talked to him about me working."

Marcus nodded. She went up on tiptoe and kissed his cheek, noting that he had shaved and tasting the salt from the ocean spray landing on his skin.

"Thank you." She was truly grateful. "I wasn't sure how to broach the subject with him, but it does concern me. Am I a terrible mother to want to work, Marc? To keep nursing? Most mothers don't work. They do their duty, stay home and have dinner on the table at five and a pair of slippers and the newspaper waiting by the door... my sister does."

Marcus laughed out loud. "A fate worse than death!" he exclaimed. "Although, if you were waiting for me, I'd never be even a minute late. And if I had to be, because I was stuck in surgery, I would bring you flowers."

She smiled, remembering all of the times Marcus had come to her rescue. "Well, I like roses, just a single one, not a whole dozen. And I certainly would understand if a surgeon was late coming home... all kinds of unexpected things come up at a hospital."

"I just assumed you would want to work," Marcus admitted. "Simon will make sure your needs are met. You won't need the income. But no, I don't think you're a terrible mother to want to work. In fact, I'd bet there will be a lot of mothers working, now that three-fourths of the American Army is either already in France or on the way there in those transports we see passing us. Who's gonna keep everything running while the men are away fighting? Someone needs to do their jobs."

Lydia considered this. He was right. Someone would have to do all of the jobs the men had left behind. "So..." she started hesitantly, "I could work in a factory or fix someone's automobile, bale hay... milk cows... like Gretha is going to do when she goes back to her grandpa's farm... give up nursing altogether."

Marcus thought of the skilled nurse Lydia had mentioned, who frequently circulated in the surgery tent, efficiently anticipating what the surgeons would run out of as they operated... like Lydia, always ensuring that they had what they needed before even they realized they needed it. He couldn't imagine either Lydia or Gretha sitting on a stool in a barn, milking cows, or collecting eggs each morning from a cackling hen house while a goat nibbled on their shirts.

"No, I can't see you milking cows," he admitted. "And your tiny little arms couldn't toss a hay bale if a horse's life depended on it—I can't see you giving up nursing, Lydia. What exactly do nurses do, if they aren't working in a hospital?"

"Private duty. Deliver babies," Lydia said. "That's what Marlene Sullivan is planning to do if she doesn't get into medical school. Though I'm hoping that the letters of recommendation you doctors wrote for her will give her what she wants."

"Not so bad, delivering babies," Marcus noted.

Lydia looked at him. "Have you delivered babies?"

"Several, in medical school. Not a single one since. Looked all around the clearing station for a pregnant woman to deliver and couldn't find a single one to practice on since Suzie didn't give me the chance. So don't get any ideas about going into early labor or anything because I'm a little rusty on my obstetric skills. I'd have to pull out the textbook."

Lydia remembered him checking her at the casualty clearing station while Simon was missing in action, when she had started to bleed and panicked that she might lose her baby. After examining her in her tent, Marc had reassured her that all was well with the baby. He had been right. Bedrest had solved the problem, and the symptoms had not returned. He had been very gentle and professional with her. She reached out and squeezed his hand. "I think your obstetric skills are just fine," she assured him.

Marcus remembered as well. He looked away for a moment and cleared his throat, pushing away the memory of that day. He was acutely respectful of the fact that he was the only man other than Simon who had ever touched her in that way. "Nevertheless," he continued firmly, "let's hope we never need to find out if I remember how to cut a cord."

"Okay. Well, in answer to your other question, there is a place called the Henry Street Settlement in Manhattan. The nurse who runs it organized a group of nurses who go out into the community. They teach people how to take better care of their children, eat healthy meals, and take care of sick family members. I heard about them in Philadelphia during our nursing training."

Marcus raised his eyebrows. "Manhattan? Like New York City?"

She laughed and patted his hand. "Don't worry, Marcus, I'm not thinking of going to Manhattan, except maybe to see how they do things. I was just thinking it might be something that has spread to Pittsburgh, since it's another big city with lots of poor workers and immigrants. I think it might be something I'd like to do. Teach nursing care, out in the community."

Marcus looked worried. "Wouldn't that be a little dangerous? Maybe it wouldn't be in the best of neighborhoods. Who knows what you might run into!"

"More dangerous than artillery dropping shells around us? More dangerous than Germans sneaking into our station and taking us prisoner?" she demanded with sudden fierceness as her experiences flashed, uninvited, through her mind. "More dangerous than having someone call you down to his dirty office in a trench to make you—" She stopped abruptly and shuddered.

Not wishing to upset her, Marcus slipped his arm around her shoulders wanting her to refocus on the here-and-now. "No, no, Lydia, of course not. Nothing would be more dangerous than what you've already overcome. Nothing." He pulled her close and kissed the top of her head. "Look at me, Lydia. You're the bravest woman I've ever known. If you decide to do this neighborhood outreach, I'll support you all the way."

Making sure she was seeing him again and not some visage from her past, he waited until he saw her brush a tear from her eye.

"Thank you, Marc," Lydia said quietly. "Now I have to sell the idea to Simon. I'm not so sure he'll agree with you."

"He wants you to be happy," Marcus said. *And we both just want you to be safe...* and that had been a close call, he realized... He also noted that her memory was hovering on the edge of her awareness like the crest of one of the waves around them, the tip of something swelling up from much deeper below the surface. She was not over her terror from the trench, but it had not even been a year since.

Together, they watched the ship cutting through the unending water with no land in sight, making them feel as though they were not getting anywhere at all. A comfortable silence settled over them. Then, while watching the ocean swells, Lydia said, "Marc, you know how much I love Simon."

Marcus nodded, looking at her sideways, wondering what could be coming.

"And I would never want to influence your decisions, after you see Suzie..."

He waited, her grip on the metal railing bleaching the color from her knuckles. "But—" he prompted. "Do I hear a rather loud, 'but'?"

"But," she went on hesitantly, "if you and Suzie work things out, if Suzie agrees to be your wife... and that would be a wonderful thing if she does... but if she doesn't want to leave Rochester, and you think that's best, to not leave Rochester, and... and if Simon has trouble with his lungs... since he's still recovering... and you're way up... you know, in Rochester—would you at least call him, encourage him by telephone, or something... so he—"

Marcus could not allow her to go on stumbling, through baseless fears. He put one hand on hers, gripping the wet railing and cleared the windswept hair from her face with the other. "I will always be there for you and Simon, Lydia. Always," he told her in no uncertain terms. "Suzie left me, without even telling me she was pregnant. I'll have to work through that with her. And Simon and I are brothers. And I will always be there for him, and you, and the baby. Always. I don't know what's going to happen when I talk to Suzie. I just know I need to try. And if she agrees to marry me, I'll convince her to come to Pittsburgh with my daughter. We'll get Simon back on his feet, together, Lydia. We will."

Lydia's cheeks were wet, from sea spray or tears Marcus couldn't tell. He slid an arm around her waist, turning her in the direction of the lower recesses of the ship where she could warm up a bit. "Come on," he smiled. "Let's go find him. When I left, he was talking to the ship's corpsman about medical care on board. Probably has their entire sickbay redesigned by now."

That night, Lydia, as directed, asked Simon to go with her when she took Abril up onto the deck before bed. The two of them stood under the deepest, clearest sky they had ever seen. In the velvet darkness, the stars hung like apples on a tree, near enough to be plucked from branches of the universe, but far enough away to feel encased in a much greater mystery. They admired the stars for a long time, holding each other in silence, humbled by the infinite scale of... everything. The night sky over the camp at their old station had been similar, but somehow, over the sea, the night was even darker, the stars were even brighter, the sense of Heaven even stronger. Overwhelmingly so.

Lydia leaned her head on Simon's shoulder. "Do you think that the soldiers we couldn't save... that they can see us, my love?" she asked Simon, thinking of the souls of the young men who had lost their lives while under their care. "Do you think Heaven is up there somewhere, among all of those stars and that they're looking down at us?"

Simon shook his head. "I'm sure I don't know where Heaven is. Maybe it's a state of being as much as an actual place. Or maybe the stars in the night are just a curtain, or veil, meant to keep it from human eyes. It's certainly here when we come together. It's here, with the baby growing inside of you. But in answer to your question, no, I don't think they are looking down on us. I think that after what they had to go through in the war, they are experiencing wonders even more incredible than this night... and if they are, why would they ever think to look back down here at what's happening in this fallen world?"

She considered this. "When you were so sick, in Paris, thinking you might not make it, did you think about looking back from Heaven, Simon? Did you wish that you would be able to look down here, to see what was happening?"

"I didn't really think about it, beloved," he admitted. "I prayed for you in my lucid moments. I asked God to care for you and the baby... to make sure Marcus was keeping his vow to look after you. I was fighting so hard to get back to you that I wasn't thinking about what it would be like to be on the other side. All I could do was tell God I wasn't ready to leave you." He felt her lean into him.

"I wasn't ready for you to leave us," she said under her breath, remembering how her heart had stopped every time a vehicle had pulled into camp, hoping that Simon had somehow found his way back to her... until, finally, he did.

He leaned down, kissing her lips gently. "Well, we don't have to worry about that now, do we? We have good things to come. The first of which will be to see your folks. I'll send them a telegram when we dock, so they can expect our arrival. That way, we can spend a night in Philadelphia after we arrive. Rest up a bit in a real bed, that doesn't sway, and give them a night to get used to the idea that I'm bringing you home."

"Can we afford that?" she wondered.

"Yes," he replied. "Not the fanciest hotel, but somewhere nice. And Marcus will take his leave of us for a bit, while he goes to see Suzie, in Rochester, so they can figure things out. It'll be good for him to meet his little daughter."

"In Suzie's last letter, she wasn't unwilling to see him. It was a start," Lydia said. "I hope he's not too disappointed if she does turn him away, though. I know she was in a difficult situation when she became pregnant. But she did choose to leave without even asking him how he felt about it or letting him offer to take care of her."

"At that time, I doubt he'd have made a commitment even if he had known," Simon hated the thought. "But since you've done such an amazing job turning that man around, who knows? Maybe she'll see the change. Maybe they'll be able to give it a try."

"Well, if they do, I hope they come to Pittsburgh. I don't want them all the way up in Rochester. We could raise our children together," Lydia said. "Our baby and their Nikki. After all, Marc says he's starting you on a jogging and swimming program... and he says he has a few more chess moves to teach you."

"Don't remind me!" Simon exclaimed. "The man's relentless—"

"Pardon the interruption—" They both started, having been so deep in their conversation that they hadn't noticed the young sailor approaching. "Apologies, but the night watch needs to secure the deck, if you don't mind heading below."

They quickly obliged, Abril running ahead of them and taking the steep steps in a single bound. They undressed and climbed into their berth for the night—their thoughts still swirling... the family with whom they would soon reconnect, the myriad of possible paths for their future... so many unknowns... almost as many as the stars in the heavens.

It had been a long week at sea, but this morning would be their last aboard the ship. Simon was sending a telegram to Lydia's parents, notifying them of their arrival. Lydia and Marcus stood at the railing, doing their best to stay out of the way as they watched the crew ready the ship for docking. They were home... in the States. The naval base of Philadelphia was right beyond the pilings. Lydia knew this was where they would part ways for a time.

"Penny for your thoughts," Marc broke the silence between them. "If I have one. Let's see, what is in my pockets... ah, will this do?" He came up with a stray French coin, placing it in her hand.

The wind blew a stray curl across her cheek. "You're catching a train soon?"

He nodded. "Time to find out where things stand, Lydia."

"I know," she whispered. "I hope it goes well, truly I do, Marc."

"I'll miss you two, you know. You can't arm wrestle Simon, but make him do his push-ups okay?"

She nodded. "He's pretty committed to your plan." She looked up at him, his warm gaze and those clear blue eyes, so different from Simon's. Lydia found his hand and held it tightly. "Marc—"

"I know, Lydia," he said quietly, his heart twisting in his chest.

"I need to say it anyway," Lydia said, her eyes filling. "It very nearly was just the two of us getting off this ship to make a new life together, for the baby... you as my husband."

"Well, thank God we didn't have to do that!" Marcus said in exaggerated relief.

Lydia didn't smile. "Marc, thank you. It would have been an honor to be your wife. Thank you for caring enough about Simon, me, and the baby, to be willing to change your life direction if that had happened. Thank you for being who you are. I love the man you've become."

Swallowing hard, Marcus nodded. He heard her words deeply and with gratitude. "You and Simon have sure had an impact on me. And in a way, the baby has, too. Made me think about what it means to be a family man... to want a home."

Looking at this brave, skilled, beautiful woman, Marcus thought, *not much of a sacrifice. Not for me. She'd have been the one making the sacrifice; I've got to work out a few character flaws to be worthy of someone like her.* "I, uh, well—" Marcus couldn't find the words to express what was in his heart.

"I just wanted to make sure you knew how I felt—" she couldn't find the perfect words either.

"Success!" Simon was running across the deck, eager to join them. Wrapping his arm around Lydia's waist, he offered a quick update. "Telegram is off. Your folks will know we're coming by tomorrow. So, we'll spend the night here to make sure they have time to prepare. It'll be something of a shock, I'm sure, but at least now they'll know that you're married and we're on our way."

Marcus nodded. "I'll send Suzie one from shore. It's a long train ride to Rochester. She'll have lots of time to prepare for the shock of me!"

"It'll be okay, Marc," Simon said with confidence. "Things are different now. You'll see. We'll pray for the best."

"I'd appreciate some help in that department!" Marcus rubbed the back of his neck. "You have stronger prayers than I do."

"It's not about strength, my friend," Simon reminded him of something they'd talked about before. "It's about the doing of it. Remember, it's dialogue, open dialogue."

"With the creator of everything that ever lived."

"Yep," Simon nodded enthusiastically.

"I hear you, Simon," Marcus grinned. "I'll keep working on it."

"Spiritual push-ups, Marc."

They all took a moment to watch as the shoreline drew near. There were many naval ships in various stages of loading and preparedness. There were barges of cargo sitting out in the deeper waters of the river which led to the ocean and even more stacks of cargo and goods waiting on the docks, for distribution. Lydia remembered a little of the city, from her training. Once on land, they would find a telegraph office for Marc and a place to stay along Broad Street, the wide avenue leading up to the town center where the statue of Benjamin Franklin adorned the peak of city hall.

Thanksgiving was approaching and, despite the blistering cold, many people were out, bundled in overcoats, their breath making white clouds in the freezing air. The snow laden ground muffled the sounds of the occasional horse and wagon, and more automobiles than any of them had seen before. Two years away had certainly changed things. Black motor cars lined up along the curbs in astonishing numbers, people scurrying to safely make their way across the streets. Motor cars couldn't match the speed of a train, but they were still quite impressive. Lydia absently wondered if she and Simon would ever purchase such a luxury. Perhaps someday, to see family in Greensburg or West Virginia. Or to see Marcus and Suzie in Rochester, if need be.

The group of four caught a jitney to the train station where they made their incredibly difficult farewells. After working all day and night, side by side for the better part of two years, through multiple battles, trials and tribulations... parting felt like an amputation of a healthy limb. They did not know how to say goodbye.

Simon grasped his buddy by the shoulder. "You have the address for Lydia's folks in Greensburg and we have Suzie's in Rochester. Send a telegram to Lydia's parents when you arrive, and keep us informed on what's going to happen. And keep your wits about you. Don't push! Just be yourself... your new self, I mean! And make sure Suzie knows she's welcome to join us in Pittsburgh, even just for a visit—with Marcie Nichole as well, of course—the welcome mat is always out, or will be, as soon as we have one!"

Marcus shook Simon's hand, holding on to it as he spoke. "Now, you listen," he urged, "keep up the push-ups because I expect you to beat me when I see you next. And don't get too busy with any surgeries until I get there. Wouldn't want you thinking you can run an operating theater without me. I'll be along, before too long, most likely. Like I told you, I'm prepared to find out Suzie's already moved on, with some other guy. I just want to see my daughter at least once. Got to find out if she's got my eyes, or whatever, you know. Probably has her mom's beautiful blonde hair."

"Well, we'll find a little house in the city, with enough rooms for everyone, so we can get established. So don't worry about that, Marc. I'll take care of it," Simon assured him. "You'll stay with us while we get it figured out."

Nodding gratefully, Marcus turned to Lydia after noticing that the conductor had not yet called for final boarding to New York. He saw the tears brimming in her eyes; it felt like a piece of shrapnel was lodged in his heart. He opened his arms to her and she wrapped both arms around him, tightly, the gift of a firm hug to take on the trip with him. She kissed him on the cheek and whispered, "Hurry back, Marc, with or without Suzie. We'll be... we'll be watching for you." It was all she could speak without losing all composure.

Marcus nodded, tears welling in his own eyes, picked up his duffle bag, and pulled his coat tighter around him. "Well, I guess that's it then," his voice husky with emotion. "Guess I'll get on board and find a seat."

Lydia nodded as Simon clasped Marc's hand once more, then Marcus turned away, climbing the steep metal steps into a passenger car while the train's smokestack quietly puffed out steam, preparing to move out from the station. Simon wrapped his arm around Lydia's waist as they watched their friend make his way down the aisle between the rows of seats to settle himself for a very long ride ahead. The final boarding call came and the train slowly gained momentum as it pulled out of the station, heading north. Only after it was well on its way did the couple turn and hail a jitney to take them to a hotel where they would spend the night, with Abril relegated to a close-by garage.

After securing food and a safe place for Abril to weather the night, Simon and Lydia grabbed a quick bite from a corner market where the merchant spoke only Italian. Upon returning to the hotel, Simon approached the desk to get a key for their room while Lydia looked around the lobby. It was a clean place, not too crowded, with simple, but tasteful decorations. Very different from the little French inn in Nancy where they had spent their wedding night. Simon led Lydia up the small, carpeted staircase. The walls were lined with painted scenes of city life. Pushing open the door to their room for the night, he laid their duffle bags on a small stand, and saw that the wash basin, pitcher, and a set of fresh towels were ready for them on the bureau. He slid out of his coat and took hers as well, to hang them where they could dry. Lydia perched on the edge of the bed, looking lost.

"Shall we just turn down the blankets and try to sleep?" she asked him, overwhelmed by the emotions of having finally arrived back on American soil, for the first time in almost two years. So much change... hearing nearly everyone speak American English, and no thudding of artillery outside, no crowded tents of nurses and doctors... she still felt the sway of the ocean moving beneath them, but no sound of the ship's engines constantly laboring... and Marcus was gone.

Simon stood next to her looking down, considering her question. Their room was warm enough with heat coming up through a vent from a furnace somewhere downstairs. He had inquired at the desk about a room with a tub only to learn that there was just one, down each hallway of each floor.

"I think what I want to do," he said gently, "is give you a bath. On board the ship with all those sailors and soldiers, you had to get by with just quick sink wash-ups. There's a tub down the hall, and I'm going to go fill it with hot water."

"I'll come with you," Lydia said quickly, not wanting to be left alone.

Hand in hand, they made the short walk, down the carpet-covered hallway, to the small communal tub room. There was a white, claw-footed tub there, a small chair, and dressing table. Simon sat Lydia on the chair while he patiently coaxed warm water up to the second floor, filling the large porcelain tub. They didn't speak as he undid her buttons and tie, liberating her from her uniform. "We'll get you a couple of pretty dresses in the morning," he told her. "This uniform doesn't accommodate our growing baby very well, does it?"

"Don't bother, Simon. I'll have plenty of dresses I can alter when we get to my parents' house tomorrow. A closet full. Unless they gave them away." She hadn't thought of that before. "Let's save the money."

"If you want," he agreed. "It's up to you. I'm happy to buy you a dozen pretty dresses. Come on, let's get you in the water."

Sinking into the clean, warm water, Lydia immediately and fully appreciated Simon's decision. He wasted no time lathering his palms, to wash her back and arms. There was the white scar of the bullet wound she carried on one shoulder and the stripes across her bottom as he slid his hands over her skin… permanent reminders of the evil behavior of men in war, seeking conquest and control. Simon wondered as he washed her what he would tell her parents, if they should ever see the scars. Hopefully, they would never have the opportunity, but he was exceedingly gentle with her, knowing all too well what they represented. "Legs, please," Simon instructed her.

She obliged, beginning to relax and unwind under his ministrations, perching each foot one at a time on the edge of the tub, letting him wash her legs and feet.

"You are pampering me," she sighed.

"And now the rest of you," he said softly. "Hair, too."

Lydia allowed him to do as he pleased, feeling his love, tenderness, and concern for her. He washed her belly and felt the bump of baby there, lingering over the marvel of life growing, wondering if he might feel it move.

She hadn't told him if she had felt movement since boarding the ship, and, privately, he was a little concerned. She was growing. There should be movement regularly if all was going well. He reassured himself that the rumbling naval transport had probably hidden the delicate fluttering of minuscule hands and feet.

When he was finished, he sat on the chair, drying his hands and watching her enjoy the warm water.

"Better?" Simon asked tenderly.

Lydia nodded. "Yes, so much better. You were so right."

"Now, do you think you can sleep?"

"I do. Thank you for suggesting this, my love," Lydia told him. "You always know what I need."

He looked at her, puzzled... that wasn't really true. He didn't know yet what she needed to fulfill her desire to make a difference in the world. He didn't even know what the options were, but he said nothing and helped her stand when she was ready to dry off. Simon wrapped a robe around her and quickly checked down the hall. It was empty between the tub room and the door to their overnight haven.

"Coast is clear," he said, leading the way to their room where he secured the door and pulled down the coverlet on the bed. He tucked her in under the sheet and blanket.

"Aren't you coming, Simon?" she asked quietly when she saw him standing motionless.

He looked distracted for a minute. *The world is so still*, he thought.

Then he replied, "What? Oh, yes, Lydia, I'm coming..."

He turned down the gas lamp on the wall to a flicker, throwing deep shadows across the room, and removed his clothes. In truth, he was waiting for the planes overhead that would drop the next round of shells. Then, in the darkness, he slid in next to her, into a real bed that wasn't swaying with ocean swells and wasn't a cot in a tent with rainwater dripping on them.

"A real bed," he murmured, lying next to her on his side. "We haven't been in a real bed since the day we got married. It feels enormous."

Lydia nodded. "It feels strange. Do you remember the little French woman who brought us wine and cheese on our first night as, us?"

"Of course," he said, pushing back the hair from her forehead and tracing the outline of her ear with a finger. "And don't forget the woman in the forest village who had the smithy make us our rings... after she absolutely insisted that we eat her breakfast."

Lydia smiled again. It was a good memory.

"And the premature baby that you placed right here," Simon reminded her, lightly stroking the skin between her breasts, "then told the mother to keep it right next to her skin to make it think it was still in the womb, until it grew stronger. Your skills are remarkable. They just can't be wasted."

Lydia snuggled against him now, feeling more like herself as he brought memories to her mind. She really had been able to do a few worthy things in all of the madness.

Simon continued. "And we'll find a way for you to use your skills to their fullest. I don't know where yet, but there's got to be a way. Maybe I'll find a private surgical office for Marcus and me where you can work with us. And if a hospital is our only option in the city, then... we'll go back to West Virginia and take medical care out into the mountains together. Back woods surgery."

"Thank you, Simon," she said softly. "That means a lot to me that you're trying."

Simon leaned over her in the semi-darkness and kissed her lips slowly. He let his hand move over her for the second time that evening, smelling the soap scent on her skin. "A real bed," he murmured.

"And I am extremely clean, thanks to you," she whispered.

He continued to kiss her, breathing in the freshness of her neck, her body. "Yes, you certainly are..." he murmured, caressing the little baby mound of her belly. He moved her legs and kneeled between them, appreciating the luxury of space, the quiet, and all the time they wanted, without the war interrupting them. He could love her now and love her again in the morning if they wished, without a trumpet call for reveille. Lydia gave herself to him with a sigh of anticipation for what he was promising, and Simon did not disappoint her.

Anna Blackwell's unbridled excitement crackled through the telephone line with such intensity that Tommy yanked the earpiece away from his head, trying to hear her better. "Okay, Mom!" he said. "Calm down."

From the living room sofa, Peggy looked up from mending a tear in Steven's little trousers. On the floor, Mary paused her dolls' imaginary play, her eyes full of questions as she looked at her father, who was still waiting for the enthusiastic torrent of words to subside.

"Yes, we'll come over," Tommy replied. "I'll check my work schedule and we'll make time to come... okay, sure... yeh, no problem, Mom. Let us know when they get there... yep... us, too." He returned the receiver to its place and drew a long breath.

"What on earth?" Peggy wondered.

"Your sister is on her way home, from Philadelphia," Tommy told his wife.

The needle pricked her finger as Peggy lost all focus. "Lydia's back? My sister is home from Europe? On her way? Now?"

Tommy nodded. "The wandering nurse has decided to grace us with her presence."

But Peggy was thrilled. "Oh this is great! She's alive and made it back from the war! How about that Tommy!"

"Yeh, Mom and Dad got a telegram from Philadelphia. And... she's bringing a husband with her. Apparently, she got married over there." He bent over and opened the liquor cabinet, pulling out two glasses and a bottle of whiskey. "What a celebration this is going to be."

Peggy jumped, upsetting the contents of her sewing box. "She has a husband? A soldier from the war or something? Did she marry a soldier from the war? And when, Tommy? When are they coming?"

Tommy poured a full glass of the golden liquid, downing it in one swallow, refilling it, then half filling the other glass for Peg. "Not a soldier. Mom says the guy is a doctor of some kind. Must have met him while she was doing her nursing thing over there."

Peg's eyes widened. "A doctor? She married a doctor? Wow."

Steven looked up from the scene he was building on the floor of trucks, animals, little wooden fences, and lead figurines. "I got all kinds of soldiers, Dad, but I don't got any doctors here!" He examined his miniatures carefully, looking to see if any of his army looked like a doctor type. "What's a doctor gotta do over there?"

"Don't have," Peg corrected her son. "A doctor would take care of all the soldiers that get hurt."

"Like you sewing up my jeans, Mom," the boy said, pointing to the task in her hands.

Peg smiled. "Oh, a lot more important than that, Steven! Probably sewing up brave men who were in a bad fight, where the enemy attacked them."

Steven was turning six. He knew about enemies attacking because his lead soldiers had battles all of the time. He and his dad regularly set up skirmishes, amid tiny wooden trees from his play set, to ambush each other... with the occasional demise of a stray horse or cow that fell from the cannon fire of miniature cannons hidden behind toy fences. "You never had to fire a cannon, right, Dad?"

Tommy filled his whiskey glass again. "Nope. Never fired a cannon."

"Dad, how come you didn't go to the war like Aunt Lydia and her doctor guy?"

"Because I have you to take care of, son. I have a family. And I take care of your grandma and grandpa, since Aunt Lydia took off and disappeared over the ocean."

Peggy cut the thread she was using to repair Steven's pants. "Oh, Tom, she didn't just disappear. She took the training and went off with the Red Cross. I think it was a noble thing to do. Maybe I should go back to work and do something noble, too! After all, the children are older. Steve is in school already! And Mary not far behind. Maybe I could get that job at the law office where I worked the first two years we were married, Tom. I could help pay the bills, too!"

"You don't need to work, Peg. You still got the kids to take care of. And Mom and Dad. And me. That's enough for a woman," Tom insisted. "And I make enough to support you."

"My friend Dave's mom works, Dad," Steve said, moving his soldiers around a fence line. "She works at the market. When he goes in, he gets special stuff because she works there! She gave Mom a free bag of oranges."

Tom looked at Peggy. "Why did she give you a free bag of oranges, Peg? You tell her you couldn't afford them?"

Peg shook her head, folding the pair of pants and pushing the needle safely into the red, cloth tomato made for holding them.

"No, Tom, of course not! I just told her they were expensive this time of year, and she gave me some. It was quite generous of her."

Tommy finished his whiskey and filled it again, downing it in one gulp and Peggy looked at him worriedly. It was his fifth glass of the stuff, and she didn't like it when he was drinking one after the other like this. He didn't handle hard alcohol very well anymore. It made him irritable. With relief, she saw Tommy go into the kitchen.

"Mary, run these pants upstairs to Steven's room, please," Peggy asked her daughter.

The little girl jumped up with her doll, took the pants and headed for the stairs. Halfway up she sat down. Her dad was walking back into the living room. He had one of the paddles in his hand, the medium length one. Mary shrank against the railing as her mother looked up in surprise.

"Tommy, what's wrong?" Peggy asked quietly, seeing the dreaded instrument in his hands.

"Come here, Steve," Tommy commanded in a no-nonsense voice.

Slowly, Steve rose from the floor and walked over to his father who was pouring himself yet another shot of whiskey. He pointed to the ottoman by the easy chair. "Bend over, Steven."

The boy's face paled, it was the next-to-biggest paddle. "How come, Dad? What'd I do?" With a passion, he hated the two paddles that hung on the kitchen wall by the basement. They both had holes in them. The one kept in the car did not.

As Peggy started to stand, Tom shot her a look of warning. "Tommy..." she started.

"Did you tell your mom not to take the oranges?" Tommy asked. "We do not take charity."

Steve looked quickly at his mother. "I... they looked good, Dad. We like them."

"Are you proud of your dad for staying home and taking care of his family the way a man's supposed to?"

Steve's head nodded up and down vigorously. "Real proud, Dad," he said in a small voice. "You're a real good dad, Dad. Real good."

"Drop your pants, Steve. How many oranges were there?"

Steve faltered. "Four..."

"Bend over, Steve. Real men don't take charity, so that other people know we earn our keep. Four swats then. One for each orange," Tommy said resolutely.

Steven looked at the ottoman, avoiding looking angrily at his mother who had accepted the forbidden fruit. Slowly he lowered his pants. From the corner of his eye, he saw his mother cross the living room floor, restraining his father's arm. "Tommy, don't. It wasn't his fault," she quietly pleaded with him.

Tommy shook her off. "No, it wasn't. It was yours." The paddle came down on Steven's bottom and the boy caught his breath in pain as Mary gripped the stair railing in fear, sliding slowly up one more step toward safety. The paddle came down again and Steven couldn't help but to cry out. His dad was a strong man. "So, he gets two. Because it wasn't all his fault. Stand up, son."

Embarrassed by the tears running down his cheeks, Steven stood up.

"What's the rule, Steve?" Tommy asked.

"We don't take charity," Steve said in a choked voice.

"Go upstairs," Tommy ordered the boy who grabbed his pants, pulling them up quickly and ran for the second floor where Mary was already closing her bedroom door.

Stricken, Peg looked at her husband. "Tom, that wasn't necessary," she was calm and quiet. "He's a good boy. It was an orange for heaven's sake."

Tommy looked at her and instinctively, Peggy backed up, the alcohol speaking on his breath. "What are you teaching our kids, Peg? That I don't make enough money for you? That we can't afford things? That I don't have a good enough job? I work my tail off for you and those kids. And I come home and then go take care of your mom and dad. I cut their grass, I chop their wood, I take care of their furnace... I fix up our house. That isn't good enough for you? You have to tell people at the market we can't afford oranges?"

Peggy had backed up clear to the kitchen now. "That's not what I said, Tom... I know you work hard and take care of my folks and us, I do!"

"And now your sister is coming back, and you think that's a big deal? Her coming back, married to a doctor? You think that's a big deal, Peg?" he demanded, his words slurring.

Peggy's eyes welled up. "I'm just glad she didn't get killed over there, in the war, Tommy. I'm just glad she survived. It'll make mom and dad happy, and maybe Lydia will help out so it doesn't all fall on you! Right? Maybe it will make things easier on you."

"And now you think you should be working again? At the law office, Peg? Lydia's not even here yet and she's putting ideas in your head that you need to make money for us because I don't make enough?" Tommy took a swig straight from the whiskey bottle he'd grabbed as they inched their way into the kitchen. He was past the tipping point. "Over the table, Peg."

"Tom…" Peg started, dreading his anger yet again. Tommy's 'corrections' were coming all too often lately. When he drank this freely, he wasn't in control. "Tommy, maybe you could get some sleep…"

"You get the other two oranges," Tommy said, swaying slightly, putting the bottle on the kitchen counter and knocking the cups off of the table with a sweep of his arm. One cracked sharply off the hard floor, pieces flying.

When she remained frozen in place, Tom pulled a chair out and pushed her down. Leaning over her to show her the paddle, he said in a thick voice. "Know why these have holes, Peg?"

Tears in her eyes, Peggy shook her head, although she did.

"Obedience. Makes you hole-y," Tom told her. "An' you got a long way t' go, till you're holy." He did not hold back. As with Steven, Peggy gasped in pain.

"Holy," he murmured. "An' a good wife stays home an' takes care of her husband. You wanna work, huh?" Punishment for another orange found its mark.

"No, Tommy," she wept, her skin on fire. "I didn't mean it. I want to be home to take care of you…"

Apparently, in Tommy's head, there were more than four oranges in the bag.

By the time he finally dropped the paddle on the table with a clatter, Peggy was sobbing. He pried her fingers loose from where she clutched the edge of the table. "C'mon."

Dragging her to her feet, he pulled his wife up the stairs to the second-floor bedroom. The children's doors were shut against any sound reaching their ears. Tom put the nearly empty whiskey bottle on the dresser before dropping heavily on the bed. "Your sister's fault... now make me feel good," he said with slurred speech, to a weeping Peggy. Slowly, she shut the bedroom door and did as she was told, her circles of holiness an angry red.

Chapter 2
Reunion

This time it was just Simon, Lydia, and Abril boarding the train. The conductor allowed the animal on after Abril obediently sat beside the metal steps to the passenger car, refusing to leave. Lydia couldn't get on without her, and the conductor backed down, seeing the intense displeasure on Lydia's face at the very notion of putting Abril in a boxcar at the back of the train. He also didn't want the woman to make good on her threat to sit in the boxcar with the dog. When they boarded, Abril lay down on their feet, quietly, patiently waiting for the train to get underway. The chugging of the steam engine and its shrill whistle was of no concern to her, being used to sudden, loud noises, explosions, and artillery fire. She was a war dog, and this noisy train was inconsequential.

As Lydia gazed out the window, the train began its trek westward across the commonwealth, with Philadelphia passing quickly into the distance, behind them. She watched the winter countryside emerge, the white rolling hills, farms, and bare leafless forests, passing by with increasing haste. After a while, Simon pulled her head onto his shoulder, and they dozed together, both tired from a worthwhile lack of sleep the night prior. They woke just in time for lunch on the train before drifting back into sleep.

When they finally pulled into the station at Greensburg, they had to rouse themselves to gather their belongings.

"I hope my folks aren't angry," Lydia said. "I hope they've forgiven me for running off to the war. Do you think they got the telegram?"

Simon kissed her. "No doubt. And I'm sure that they've forgiven you," he assured her. "They'll be glad to see you, beloved."

She wasn't completely convinced, but grasping his hand she followed him down the aisle to the door of the car, Abril right at her heels. After climbing down from the train, Simon hailed a cab hovering close by, hoping for a fare. Lydia gave the driver the address, and the man maneuvered the automobile through familiar streets of the town where Lydia had grown up. They passed the bank where she had been a teller. She pointed out the school she had attended as a young girl. The town already looked so very different to her after being away for so long. Trees were taller, houses older. With the war raging, there was evidence of disrepair in the neighborhood. Times were probably lean for some families, their men perhaps away serving in the army. Simon took Lydia's hand and squeezed it reassuringly, then patted the dog, whose head was resting on Lydia's knee.

Pulling the vehicle to a stop in front of an older home, the driver turned for the fare. This house had a small front porch with two bare trees on either side of a walk leading up to the door. Snow had been shoveled from the sidewalk. There were lights on in the front windows, and a thin trail of smoke drifted out of the chimney. Getting out of the cab, Simon paid the driver, collected their duffle bags, and took Lydia's hand again as she slid out of the back seat with Abril. The three stood, looking at the front door of the house.

"Well, this is it," Lydia took a long breath, nervous. "This is where I grew up, Simon."

"It's going to be fine," he said again and with his arm around her waist, they walked up the few steps to the door.

Lydia reached out for the doorknob, wondering for a fleeting instant if she should knock first. Just then, her mother, who had been keeping watch at the window, swung the door open with a small cry at seeing Lydia in her Red Cross uniform with the tall, bearded, young man at her side and multicolored dog at her feet.

"Andrew!" Lydia's mother called out happily. "They're here!"

"Mom—" Lydia started, but her mother was already throwing her arms around her, hugging her as she wept, holding her tight.

Simon looked on, pleased. He had been right. All was forgiven... at least for the moment.

Lydia's father had come running from the kitchen. He stopped short at the sight of his daughter in her prim navy-blue uniform. He looked at Simon and slowly extended his hand. The two men clasped hands, "You must be Simon, from the telegram we received yesterday. It was quite a shock to her mother to realize Lydia had a husband. She appreciated the forewarning. It's a pleasure to meet you."

"Same," Simon nodded.

"Well, come on in, Simon," Andrew opened the door wider. "You're part of the family now, so just come on in."

Lydia's mother released her daughter at last and Lydia was finally able to properly introduce everyone, "Mom, Dad, this is my husband, Doctor Simon Finney... and Abril, our dog."

As they entered the warmth of their home, Andrew took a moment to look at his daughter, who was so familiar and yet so different. Finally, he embraced Lydia and said quietly, "You scared your mother to death. You could have sent her more than one letter, you know."

Lydia replied, "I did send more than one letter, Dad. I'm sorry it takes so long for the mail to come through the military, but I sent many—"

"Oh, Andrew," Anna exclaimed, anxious for the reunion to go smoothly. "None of that now. She's here, and she's safe, and look at this fine young man she's brought home with her. Who needs letters when she can fill us in in person! Now, come on back to the kitchen. I've been cooking, and I need to stir my pot. Would you like some coffee? I made some coffee..."

"I'd like some coffee," Simon assured the woman, putting his arm around Lydia as they followed her parents through to the kitchen, where delicious smells were emanating from the stovetop. Simon pulled out a chair for Lydia and then took a seat beside her and rested his arm on the back of her chair. He gratefully accepted the cup of coffee as her mother started to hand one to Lydia as well.

"Still one sugar, honey?" Anna asked her daughter.

"Actually, Mom, I'm off of coffee right now. Can I make myself a cup of tea, perhaps?" Lydia asked.

"I'll put the kettle on, honey, of course. Not to worry. Never known you to refuse a cup of good coffee." She took a tea kettle to the sink to fill it, saying, "I'm a coffee drinker, Simon, so I got her fixed on it too early, I'm sure. The only time I couldn't stand the taste of it was when I was pregnant with—" Anna froze. The kettle clattered into the sink as the woman dropped it and turned around to stare at her daughter. "When I was pregnant with you girls... Lydia," she finished in a whisper.

"Yes, Mom, that's why we came home," Lydia said softly.

Anna and Andrew looked blankly at the young couple at their kitchen table. There was dead silence in the kitchen for a moment. Within just twenty-four hours they had had to grapple with learning that their daughter had gotten married, was coming home, and now was expecting a baby!

Andrew looked hard at Simon. "Did she have to marry you, Doctor Finney?" he demanded.

Simon tightened his arm around Lydia protectively. "No, sir," he told the man calmly. "We've been married almost a year and a half, and she's just finishing her fourth month, now."

Lydia looked over at Simon, her eyes filling with tears as she heard the questioned moral judgment in her father's voice. "Simon, I'm so sorry. We should go..."

Simon stopped her. "No, Lydia, it's alright. He is your father, and this has taken him by surprise. He has the right to know if I was an honorable man or not. I understand completely. I asked Lydia to marry me over in France, sir, because I wanted her to be my wife, and we didn't want to wait until we came back to the States. I wish you had received the letters we sent to you. I know this is a lot for you both to take in. But I fell in love with your daughter as we worked together, and we were married in a church, a cathedral, in fact. A priest blessed our union... did everything in the right order. I would never have dishonored Lydia. When we found out she was expecting, we came back as soon as my enlistment was up, when the army discharged me."

Andrew regarded Simon without speaking for a moment, testing his sincerity without saying a word, a contest of truth passing between the two men. "Well, alright then," Andrew finally ceded. "We needed to understand each other."

"Yes, sir," Simon agreed. "We did. There must be no misunderstanding about this."

Lydia's mother looked at her own husband as if asking his permission to feel happy about this news, now that the matter of morality had been cleared up.

Andrew broke into a smile. "Well, wait till your sister hears about this!" he exclaimed. And with that, Lydia's mother assumed that happiness was again welcomed, and she hurried around the table to hug her daughter. Her heart rejoiced in the idea that there would be another grandchild in the family, in the not-too-distant future.

Lydia pushed the chair back and stood up. "Mom, are my clothes still upstairs? I'd like to change, if they are."

"Good heavens, dear, of course. Here, I'll go with you. Of course we still have your clothes. Andrew, will you put the kettle on and make your daughter some tea? Come, dear, let's get you out of that uniform. Looks like it hasn't been washed in weeks..." Anna bustled over Lydia, pouring out all the motherly love she had saved up for two years... now overflowing onto a new son-in-law and a grandbaby!

The two women left the kitchen, heading upstairs, leaving Simon and Andrew alone in the kitchen. Sitting calmly, Simon appreciated the emotional turmoil Lydia's father was experiencing, the storm of emotions with which he was wrestling. He waited as the older man left the stove with its newly filled teapot to heat and again, came to sit at the table, facing him.

"So," Andrew said. "You're a doctor."

"Yes, sir, a surgeon," Simon told him, giving the man space to ask what was most important to him.

Andrew nodded. "I see. And just where were you and my daughter working exactly? We got a letter or two, I believe, in two years, and she never said."

"I think Lydia should tell you the details when she is ready, sir. But we worked together trying to save wounded soldiers, mostly in eastern France and Belgium. The army never allowed us to describe our location in letters sent back home."

"Isn't that where a lot of heavy fighting is going on, Simon?" Andrew asked him, growing concerned. "According to the newspaper reports, it's bad along what they call the western front, along that edge of territory."

Simon nodded steadily. "Yes, sir, there's heavy fighting going on there."

Lydia's father nodded, trying to absorb what he was learning. "And you have seen that? You were there? With my little girl?"

Simon nodded again, confirming the man's assumptions. "We were there."

"And my daughter, my Lydia, has seen that as well," Andrew said quietly, now more as a statement of fact than a question.

Simon nodded a third time. "She has. Lydia is incredibly courageous, sir."

A deep sorrow passed over his face. "She's not my little girl anymore is she, Simon?" It was an awareness of change, a struggle with truth and an attempt to find a way to cross the gulf of almost two years of time, of distance, and of life experiences.

"No, sir, she is not the same as when she left home," Simon said, feeling compassion for the man as he tried to find a bridge. "She's a woman with incredible depth, who has seen more than her fair share of hardship and suffering... and risen above it with grace and dignity. Those wounded soldiers that she cared for received the finest nursing care I have ever seen—"

At that moment, Lydia and her mother returned to the kitchen. In place of her uniform, Lydia was wearing one of her old dresses, a long-sleeved, soft green garment with a modestly dipped neckline, that dropped in pleats from a high waistline, hiding the little mound of her pregnancy in its flowing fabric. Her long, wavy brown hair was loose and fell over her shoulders. She was stunning... and a little shy, waiting for Simon's reaction.

Rising slowly to his feet, Simon beheld her as she hovered anxiously in the arched opening that separated the living room from the kitchen. He had only seen her once in a dress, after their wedding, in the blue garment lovingly made by the other nurses. Simon walked over to her and, heedless of her mother and father watching, he took Lydia in his arms and kissed her tenderly.

"I'm the luckiest man on Earth," he murmured to her, as he had countless times before.

Lydia's mother looked away from the two of them, then turned to her husband while wiping her eyes, tears running over her flushed cheeks. She looked agitated, and her husband came out from around the table to comfort his wife. "It's okay, honey," he said softly. "She looks real pretty—"

"No, it isn't okay!" Anna declared tearfully. "Our little girl is covered with scars, Andrew!"

Andrew swung around; his fists immediately clenched in hard balls as he raised them. "Why, I'm gonna ki—" the man exploded, lunging at Simon.

In one motion, Simon strategically thrust Lydia behind him, heard the dog growl softly—commanded her to stay—even while reaching out to grab the older man's fists in his own hands. The two men stood locked in a stand-up wrestling match, Andrew striving to swing and Simon preventing him from advancing. Simon stood against the man's fury, willing him to listen to what he had to say.

"The German who did that to your daughter is dead," Simon told Lydia's father slowly and firmly. "And I smashed my fist into his face, for you and me, both."

Simon didn't release Andrew until he saw acknowledgment in the older man's eyes that the words had gotten through. He saw his face grow pale, beads of sweat collecting on his forehead from the exertion. "You should sit down, sir," Simon ordered him, remembering that Lydia had told him the man had a heart condition.

Andrew slumped into a winged chair by the fireplace, where Abril took up position in front of the chair, the dog silently encouraging the older man not to move.

Hearing her teapot spitting all over the stove in the kitchen, Anna ran to turn off the burner, while grabbing a kitchen towel and pressing it to her eyes. Coming back into the room, she leaned against the arched doorway for support. There was complete silence in the living room as Simon led Lydia by the hand to the sofa, pulling her close to him with his arm protectively around her shoulders.

"Damn Germans," Andrew said under his breath, his rage barely contained.

Simon looked at Lydia against him. "Only as much as you want to," he told her quietly.

Seeing the pain in her father's eyes, Lydia's heart ached for him. "I'm sorry, Dad," she said. "I didn't want you and Mom to know. I... I forgot... when I was changing clothes with Mom upstairs. I'm sorry for you to find out this way."

Anna moved closer, perching herself precariously on the end of the couch beside her daughter. "You are my baby girl," she said bravely. "You can always tell your mother... anything."

Lydia loved them both and did not want to hurt them further. "Our medical station was five or six miles from the front. It was last winter. The Germans had suffered heavy casualties, and they needed medical people to care for their wounded, so some of their soldiers came at night and took me, one of the other nurses, Charlotte, and a couple of French soldiers."

"Bastards!" Andrew exploded in anger, rising from his easy chair as if to fight an invisible foe. Abril softly woofed and the man dropped back down to his chair.

Lydia shook her head. "No, Dad," she told him. "Most of them were decent men, young men, just following orders. Their commander was... not a decent man. He was the one who..." she faltered, unable to continue. Simon looked at her eyes in concern, searching for tell-tale signs of the trauma that still haunted her.

"Only as much as you want to," he repeated quietly, keeping his arm firmly around her to keep her focused on the present, with him.

"Anyway, Dad," Lydia continued hesitantly. "It was one of the German soldiers who finally helped us escape. His name was Frederick. He and a few of his fellow soldiers helped Charlotte, me, and our two sentries to escape. Simon sent Abril, here, to come find us and she led us all safely back through the snow, in the middle of the night, to our medical camp. The Germans who helped us that night surrendered to the French. It's okay, Dad. It's over."

Abril, having heard her name, left her self-assigned post and returned to Lydia, plopping down at her feet.

"For you, it may be over!" her father exclaimed. "But for your mother and me, we're just hearing this now! It's like it just happened. And I can only imagine what else you aren't telling us. You show up at the door after two years with a husband, a baby on the way, and now we find out that you were injured in the war? Taken prisoner? Why didn't you come home immediately? Why did you stay over there? Didn't you think about making your mother sick with worry? Leaving without a word to her and ending up in the middle of the god-damned war like that? Sending your poor mother a letter that you were gone, overseas, without even saying goodbye? You could have been killed at any time, and she wouldn't have known it. And now this?" Andrew sank back, rubbing his balding head while staring at the floor.

But Anna reached out, taking Lydia's hand in her own. "Andrew, you know you wouldn't have let her go, if she had told us beforehand where she was going. And she didn't get killed, honey," Anna told her husband bravely. "She's come back. We need to focus on that and be happy. And she has married this fine young man, and your own grandchild is coming, so you must try, dear. You must try to be happy for our daughter."

"I'll be happy when I'm ready to be happy," the man said, "but right now, I'm trying to just take this all in, and it's damned hard to do!"

Simon nodded at the man, feeling his pain all too well. "Yes, sir, it's a lot to take in, and there was no easy way to tell it. You'll have many questions, I'm sure. And there will be answers at the right time."

Looking at Lydia with eyes both sorrowful and confused, Andrew said, "Your mother does not need to hear any more of this right now, Lydia. She has had enough for one day. She's making dinner, or was, anyway. Maybe you could help her in the kitchen."

"Of course, Dad," Lydia squeezed Simon's hand, kissed his cheek, and stood, taking her mother's arm in her own to lead her into the kitchen. The men soon heard soft voices, dishes being placed, and pans rattling as they were being stirred. And when they were alone, Andrew forced himself to look Simon in the eyes.

"I misjudged you, Simon, and I regret that," Andrew admitted. "I just saw red and, well, you understand."

Simon stayed on the sofa, calm, and composed. "Yes, actually I do. I almost killed the man myself and was only kept from doing so by... well, that's another matter. The German died regardless, and I was glad when he did. Are you having pain in your chest?"

The man acknowledged it with a nod. "But not the kind a doctor can help. I'm alright," he said.

Simon nodded in return. He wasn't certain Lydia's father was being truthful, but decided not to push it, given the intense emotions of the day so far. As they were called to the kitchen for supper, the conversation lightened under an unspoken mutual decision.

"What are your plans now that you're back home?" Anna asked the young couple once everyone was seated around the table and a blessing had been asked over the food.

"Simon and one of the other doctors from the medical station, who is our very dear friend, are going to be working together, we hope," Lydia told her parents. "He's seeing some family right now, too. You'll meet him soon. Marcus Lovell."

"He may send a telegram here, by the way," Simon added. "We gave him your address until we find a place of our own."

Lydia's mother broached the important question. "You can stay here as long as you like. Your sister and Tommy want to come see you. I called them the very second the telegram arrived! Where will you settle down? Not too far away, I hope?"

Simon passed one of the serving dishes around the table as he answered. "I'm from West Virginia," he told them. "But we thought Pittsburgh would be a good place to set up a practice, or join an already established surgical hospital there."

"Oh, good!" Anna said hopefully. "That's not far."

"Not at all, Mom," Lydia said. "Simon thought that I should be close to you when the baby comes."

Anna let out a sigh. "What a relief! I'm glad you aren't going clear off to Virginia or New York or something. And I'll help you set up house, if you want me to, of course."

"Yes, I'd like your help, Mom," Lydia said, reaching across the table to squeeze her hand briefly. "I'll be looking for work in the city as well. There are months until the baby arrives, after all."

"Do you think that's wise, to work in your condition?" Andrew asked his daughter, pouring gravy over both the heap of mashed potatoes and the meatloaf on his plate. "Your mother never worked when she was pregnant. Your mother never wanted for anything—I saw to that."

Lydia nodded, "That's true, Dad, and I know Simon will provide for us. But I want to work. In fact, I need to work. I watched you work hard all your life, and I think you passed it on to me."

"So, it's my fault, is it?" he asked grudgingly, but without anger.

"I suppose it is!" Lydia laughed lightly. "And I've been working so hard all this time, I'm not sure I could stop even if I tried."

The four of them continued conversing around the table, trying to fill in the missing time with anecdotes and memories that were lighthearted and easy. They carefully avoided any additional discussion of the war, or any topic of a painful nature. Finally, after the meal was over, the dishes were washed, and conversation had slowed down in the living room, they decided to call it a night and go to bed for much-needed sleep. Almost shyly, feeling like a young girl again in her parents' home, Lydia led Simon up the stairs to her old bedroom as Abril settled herself just outside their closed door.

Inside the little second-floor room with its slanted ceiling, Simon leaned back against the bureau and surveyed where Lydia had grown up. "So, I take it yellow was your favorite color?" he suggested, looking at the pale walls, yellow bedspread, and matching bureau runner laced with yellow thread.

She opened the tiny closet door and pointed at the array of colors on the hangers. "Not really, look in here... it's a rainbow."

Joining her at the closet, Simon pulled out a soft, sky-blue dress on its hanger and held it up against her. "Very pretty," he mused. "Reminds me of the one you wore at the party they had for us after we got married. But the green one you have on now is also very fetching. Hm. I see no yellow dresses in here at all." He turned around and closed the closet door thoughtfully. Then he walked over to the bureau, where there was a large mirror over the piece of furniture. Rubbing the beard on his chin, he looked at his eyes and face. "Wow," he started. "I haven't taken a good look at myself for a couple years. When did I get old."

In the mirror, he saw her arms wrapping around his chest, her face peeking around his shoulder. "You're the most handsome man I've ever known."

"More than that Derrick guy you once knew, from here?"

He turned around, surprised to see she'd shed the green dress, which was now lying on a chair. She was wearing a slip and the kind of underthings she hadn't worn the entire time they were in Europe.

"Much more handsome than him... you, my love, are the first man to be in this room," she stated, smiling.

Simon took her hand and turned her all the way around, appreciatively. "I have never seen you looking like this." She really did take his breath away. "Most delightful." He pulled her close to him, feeling her silken slip beneath his hands.

"Remember, this is my parents' house," Lydia murmured in his ear, her arms around his neck. "Their room is just across the hall."

"Also in bed. Probably asleep already! Not... a sound," he whispered, lowering her onto the single bed. "Let's leave your new things on..."

She ran her fingers through his hair and smiled. "All of the new things? Won't that be a little challenging?"

"Almost, all of the new things," he chuckled, enjoying the feel of her in these undergarments, removing just one... and trying hard to make no noise at all.

Simon held Lydia, gently stroking her bare arms and her long hair, glad for the feeling of safety in this small town, in western Pennsylvania. He was still actively listening in the great silence that now surrounded them, still feeling the need to stay vigilant for the arrival of the screeching of trucks or wagons that used to pull him out of his tent, in the medical station.

"It's awfully quiet here," Lydia also observed, caressing his bare chest. "You could hear a pin drop."

"There was a night or two when it was quiet in the camp..."

"One or two, maybe," she agreed. "Does it feel very far away for you, too?"

He looked down at her in the darkness. "It is far away!" he exclaimed softly. "Thousands of miles."

"Do you realize, Simon, that they're already up and probably operating right now?" she mused. "Doctor Stockton is no doubt orienting the new surgeons... Gretha and Monique teaching the nurses what to do."

"Or moving the camp again, now that Passchendaele and Ypres are over."

"I wonder where they'll end up," she said, worried.

"Oh, probably somewhere back in France, following the army. I doubt they stayed in Belgium," Simon sighed, thinking of the endless hours on their feet at the tables in the surgical tent.

Lydia paused. "Sometimes it doesn't feel like it was real."

"Not to me," Simon had a storm of thoughts swirling in his head. "Especially after today, seeing your parents' expressions as they heard even a bit of what you went through. It was a shock for them, but for me, it all came flooding back as if it had just happened."

She nodded against his shoulder, "I really didn't mean to get into all of that. I forget that there are visible scars back there... since I can't see them. I didn't think about Mom noticing, while I was changing."

"I never forget..."

"Well, you have to look at my backside, from time to time—I don't." Her humor was comforting.

"You didn't look in the mirror when you came up with your mother? Not even once?" he wondered. It had been quite awhile since she had been in front of a large mirror.

"I don't want to know what I look like," she admitted. "The scars in my head are enough. All that matters is that you can still look at me without being disgusted."

He tightened his arms around her. "I just showed you again how beautiful you are, especially to me. I want a lifetime together to show you—I'll show you every single day, twice a day!"

"You'll wear yourself out!" she teased.

"Maybe by the ripe old age of one hundred!" he whispered, kissing the top of her head.

Suddenly, Lydia grabbed his hand.

"Lydia, what…" Simon flinched in alarm.

"The baby!" she whispered. "Simon, feel…"

He slid his hand to her belly, gently pressing his palm against its gentle curve. His sensitive hands, trained to feel the pulse of an artery inside a wounded man's belly, felt the flutter of his baby. A wave of relief washed over Simon. Their tiny infant was moving. Leaning over Lydia in the darkness, Simon kissed her belly, resting his head against it, as she ran her fingers through his hair, waiting to see if the tender movements would come again.

"Can I show you again how beautiful you are to me?" Simon asked, overwhelmed in his relief and happiness. His entire purpose in this world was to protect Lydia… and now their baby… to offer Lydia love and happiness, and he was enthusiastic in fulfilling his purpose.

As the train pulled out of the station, Marcus watched as his two friends lingered, getting smaller as the train picked up speed… carrying him away. No matter what happened with Suzie, his life had its direction. Suzie wasn't the only person with whom he needed to mend things. He had a father in Reading who did not know him well… or perhaps, knew him too well. Though, Marcus was no longer the son he once was… and he very much regretted that such an emotional gulf had formed between them. Perhaps they, too, would have a chance to mend their relationship, now that he was back.

While the train chugged along, heading north through Pennsylvania's rolling hills toward the Empire State, he felt... alone. Their group, in the casualty clearing station, had been side by side... working, eating, sleeping and surviving together for so long... never separated. So, on this train, by himself for the first time in what felt like forever, Marcus was acutely aware that he was on his own... and for the most serious adventure of his life... to see if Suzie and their baby daughter and he could become a family. Marcie Nichole was not even a year old, he realized with a start. Not until February, or March? He still had a chance to be the father she needed. And if Suzie was willing, he could be the husband that she needed him to be as well.

When the train pulled in the next day, at the Rochester station, Marcus gathered his duffle bag and overcoat, joining the queue of passengers in the aisle, waiting for their turn to exit the train. The telegram had gone ahead, alerting Suzie of his arrival. Climbing down the steep metal steps of the passenger car, Marcus looked around the train platform for an available cab for hire, someone who knew a boarding house where he could take a room for a couple of days.

Intent on finding a driver, Marcus was shocked when the crowd thinned, revealing Suzie standing on the platform, bundled in a heavy woolen coat against the harsh New York winter. Her blonde hair was tucked under a fur hat... she looked cold... and cautious. But she was there. She had come, in person, in response to his telegram. Marcus crossed the slippery, snow-covered platform, weaving urgently between travelers, finally stopping directly in front of the mother of his child.

Suzie waited for him to speak first. She took in the familiar crystal blue eyes and dark curls, noticing that he had found a way to shave before coming to see her. Unbidden, her heart had jumped a little when she had spotted him getting off of the train, but she dared not allow her feelings to show, not yet. He had hurt her deeply during the war... willing to connect with her physically, when he was in need, but not emotionally, when she was most in need.

Marcus carefully placed his bag at his feet and looked at Suzie as she waited, knowing that whatever he said now would make or break any future chance with her. "Suzie," he started. "I've done a lot of soul-searching since you left the camp. I had to come, to see if you're safe, if you're well, if you'll ever be able to forgive me for thinking only of myself and not of your needs. Thank you for being willing to see me."

She was in shock. Her lips parted slightly, her lovely blue eyes widened. "That's not what I expected you to say," she admitted honestly.

"What did you expect?"

"I thought you'd announce, 'I'm back' with a flourish and expect me to fall into your arms like nothing ever happened," Suzie admitted.

"Good heavens, no!" Marcus exclaimed softly. "I hurt you. And I'm sorry that I did."

Suzie took a moment. "Yes, you did... and I hurt you by not telling you that I was pregnant, when I left. I'm sorry you had to find out the way you did—I should have been the one to tell you."

Marcus stood in front of her, shivering. His cheeks were reddened from the cold, and his hands were freezing even inside his pockets. "Would it be alright with you if we found somewhere warm where we could talk?" he asked.

Suzie responded with a single nod. "Let's go into the station, we can sit on one of the benches. It's not much better, but warmer than this platform anyway."

Grabbing his duffle, he followed her into the train station. Folks were gathered near a coal stove to warm themselves, while others sat, waiting for their designated train to arrive, and others still were milling about the ticket booth to book passage. Suzie chose a bench farthest from the center of activity where there was at least a suggestion of privacy. She knew the people in this town and did not want to inspire gossip, although several were already watching as she took a seat near, but not too close, to the army captain in uniform.

"You look well. I mean, you're still as beautiful as I remember," Marcus fumbled.

"Thank you," Suzie replied. "You're looking well yourself. You look good in uniform. I guess the last twelve months at the station weren't too hard on you?"

Marcus looked down, rubbing his hands to warm them and searching for words. "Actually... they were very hard—"

"I remember you saving Simon when he was hurt in the shelling of our station," Suzie prompted quietly.

Marcus waved his hand as if it had been nothing. "He'd have done it for me. Then Charlotte got appendicitis, and the army lost us in Belgium, the whole camp nearly starved to death, and then Simon disappeared for months—was declared dead—and then showed up missing part of a lung, which had been taken out in Paris, by strangers. And some other things..."

"Sounds like I missed out on quite a lot," Suzie observed gently.

"I think I missed out on more," Marcus corrected her. "You had to go through your whole pregnancy by yourself. I didn't get to help you adjust to coming home or get to be with you at the birth. Did your family help you through it? Or friends?"

Suzie nodded, folding her delicate, gloved hands in her lap. Marcus couldn't see if she was wearing a wedding ring or not. "My family accepted my condition on my return. I think they told everyone who knows us that I was temporarily out of my mind from the trauma of war and, therefore, made some bad choices, but they love Nikki and that's all that matters."

"That's what you call her? Nikki?" Marcus nodded, trying out the nickname for himself. "I heard you're working at a hospital?"

"Yes," Suzie told him. "It is boring, but it gives me a little income."

"I'd like to help too," Marcus said quickly.

Suzie looked at him evenly. "I don't want your money, Marcus."

"That's not what I meant," he said awkwardly. "I mean, well it is. It's part of it, but I want to help... well, I want to be part of your life on whatever level you're comfortable with and I can't imagine someone like you just giving baths and changing bedsheets."

Suzie laughed lightly. "It's not as bad as all that, Marcus. It's still a hospital. Things still come up that are challenging, sometimes. I don't get in any trouble, if I keep my mouth shut and ask for the doctor to come."

"What a waste of a superb nurse, Suzie!" Marcus exclaimed, shaking his head in disbelief, remembering her skilled work assisting in the surgery, triaging patients, and caring for the wounded soldiers in the recovery tents.

"Why, Marcus Lovell!" she said. "That's the first time you've ever said anything complimentary about me as a nurse."

"No..." he started, then added, "really? I never told you that?"

She shook her head, never taking her eyes from him. She had missed him more than she realized.

He sighed, his shoulders slumped. "Well, Simon did say I was an idiot. He wasn't far off. You're a terrific nurse, Suzie, one of the best. I should have told you that, many times, back in France when you needed to hear it."

Suzie brightened upon hearing his praise. "Thank you for telling me, now."

"I always noticed," he reiterated. "And your compassion with the wounded. Everyone respected your ability to think clearly in the most difficult situations. And with me, Suzie, you were always gentle and giving."

Suzie looked down at the floor. "I loved you, Marcus, I really did."

"Do you think," he said, clearing his throat. "Do you think you still might be able to again? It took me far too long to become the man you needed me to be, but in the past year, I've come to realize what it means to commit to someone you love. I'd like a chance to see if you can feel it from me. Unless—you've already met someone who's meeting that need—which I would certainly understand, after so much time."

"I haven't met anyone, Marcus," Suzie said. "It's been enough for me to think about what we all went through over there, and to bring Nikki into the world and enjoy being her mother. She's precious. She was born a little early, but has caught up quickly."

Marcus felt a wave of relief wash over him; they might have a chance after all.

Studying the face of the man beside her, Suzie appreciated his respect for her choice in this. "I named her after you, you know," she said quietly. "Marcie was after Marcus. I wanted to give you that much, at least."

He took one of her hands in his own. "It's quite an honor. A gift." She was so lovely, and he could well remember being with her. Now she was sitting still beside him, watching, waiting, and perhaps wondering the same thing that he was. Hesitantly, he leaned forward and kissed her very softly on her lips, letting them lightly linger. Once, he would have almost devoured her with his need. But now as he touched his lips to her own, reacquainting them, he communicated his caring without any pressure or demand to reciprocate. It was the best he could do.

In response, she put her arms around his neck and met him halfway. Then, they sat briefly in a light embrace, Marcus careful not to pull her too close to him, wanting her to have the space she needed to control what was right for her. When she pulled back, he was elated to see a small smile as if she was remembering their fondness for each other.

"That was nice," she whispered. "Want to get some supper at a hotel?"

"I'd like that, if you have time. I'm starved," he agreed. "And I'd like to hear more about your work at the hospital here."

"And I'd like to hear more about the others from the station," she added, "and about your plans, now that you're back in the States."

Marcus picked up his bag, placing his hand at the small of her back, and they walked together out of the station to her parked vehicle. Driving him through the snow-lined streets to a nearby hotel, she found a place to park just outside. Marc jumped out to open the door for her, offering a hand to help her stand. As they entered, the warmth of the hotel dining room stung at his cheeks. Marcus helped Suzie remove her coat and hat, and he carefully folded them over an extra chair at the table where they were seated. He appreciated her appearance, a lovely burgundy blouse, in contrast with her striking blonde hair. A small chain and pendant hung around her neck. She looked delicate, vulnerable, compared to the woman in rough army trousers and boots, who used to run between tents, through mud and rain, caring for casualties.

"I suppose you wear the white uniforms at the hospital?" he started.

She nodded as they waited for a server to attend to them. "We do, cap and all."

"I can only imagine how difficult that is to keep clean," he said. "Especially thinking back to you changing dressings, covered in blood back in camp."

"It's different now," she nodded. "Even white shoes. No boots on the ground."

"Are you included in any of the medical decisions at all?" Marcus wondered.

"The head nurse is," Suzie replied softly. "She makes rounds with the doctors, not us. We report concerns to her. I'm afraid I've grown rusty with any nursing I did in the camp—but tell me about the others. How are they doing?"

"Marlene applied for medical school… hopes to become a surgeon. Nurse Bertolli went to the British camp where she met a doctor and fell in love with him, David Winston. You might remember meeting him when the British station was overrun, and they came to work with us for a spell."

"That's when Doctor Finney was injured, when that shell exploded in the middle of the camp," Suzie remembered well. "That was a difficult time. Lieutenant Aubert was killed that day and many others. Yes, I remember Doctor Winston. I'm glad Laura found him."

"Some of the nurses, several of them, caught influenza when it went through our station. They were nursed back to health by Nurse Bernstein. They refused to be sent to a field hospital, so the new camp commander gave them the chance to get well with our help. And I took out Charlotte's appendix when she developed acute appendicitis. We moved the station often, to stay close to the front, but not when the nurses were ill. In one move, we crossed into Belgium, and the army lost us. That was rough. We ran out of every provision we had—and medical supplies. Abril would bring back rabbits for Cook, when she found them, to keep us going! A local priest finally heard of our dire circumstances and brought real help, but countless wounded died just because we couldn't feed them and couldn't ship them out. Even the transports didn't know where we were."

Suzie reached out across the table and rested her hand on his. "That sounds horrible, Marcus. I'm so sorry."

"It was all part of the hardships of war that you experienced yourself, Suzie," Marcus said, not minimizing her own experiences from when she had served in the station.

"You mentioned earlier that Doctor Finney went missing?" Suzie pressed him.

She was interrupted by their waiter, who took their order for the house special and left them with two glasses of wine as requested.

Marcus took a sip of the red blend, the first he'd had in a very long time. It tasted wonderful. He nodded, "Yes, Simon was ordered to help at the British CCS when their staff went down with influenza. He contracted it, too, while he was there and was sent to Paris for pneumonia. Had part of a lung removed in a hospital there. No one knew where he was, for months. The French army assumed he'd died."

"You haven't said a word about Lydia, Marcus," Suzie reminded him, knowing his close relationship with the other couple. "That must have been terrible for her."

Marcus took another sip of wine. "She had some rough experiences. It was very difficult for her. Especially because she's pregnant."

Suzie looked up in shock. "Truly?"

"Truly," Marcus admitted. "The three of us came back together, and she's finishing her fourth month now. She said she can hardly wait to see you and compare notes about pregnancy and babies."

"Well, for goodness' sake! Imagine that! Lydia... pregnant! Yes, I'd like to see them."

"And they, you." Marcus looked up as their meals arrived, noting the beautiful plating; the hotel chef was obviously skilled. "This looks delicious."

"So, what are your plans, Marcus?" Suzie said, broaching the delicate subject.

Marcus took a bite, chewing thoughtfully before answering. He took another sip of the wine, looking at Suzie. "First, I wanted to see you, so, as soon as we docked in Philadelphia, I took the train out. For work, Simon and I plan to go into practice together in Pittsburgh. They need surgeons, and the city is rapidly growing. We'll join a group or sign on with one of the hospitals. Simon and Lydia are in Greensburg with her folks, and they're going to look for a place to live in Pittsburgh. I'll probably stay with them until I can get established."

Suzie quietly ate the meal set before her, absorbing this information.

Marcus cleared his throat before continuing. "I, uh, I wanted to see you first, to see if there was any chance for us to—I wanted to see if you were already committed to someone else, but Suzie, I want to be a good husband to you... and wanted to see if you would give me a chance to prove myself."

Suzie stopped eating, putting down her fork. "You would also have to be a father, you know," she reminded him.

"I know! Of course!" he exclaimed. "But it's important to me that you know that I came back primarily for you, not just to be a father to Marcie Nichole. You have to be first—I need you to know that," he said in a rush to explain himself. "And if we would be able to have more children, I want to be with you through the entire thing, to help you through it all."

"Well, well, Marcus, this is a very different kind of talk I'm hearing from you," Suzie admitted with a small smile. "You really have changed."

"I have," Marcus told her. "In more ways than I can tell you over just one dinner."

"Perhaps we'll have several then," she suggested.

Marcus smiled and lifted his glass of wine to hers in a toast. "As many as you're willing."

Chapter 3
Three Rivers

"I'll be back in two or three days," Simon assured Lydia as they sat at her family's kitchen table.

"Simon, you promised," she whispered, her anxiety rising. It felt like she had just found him again. "You promised we wouldn't be parted, and I'm... just not ready to take the chance that something could go wrong. Please take me with you. Please."

They'd had such a long trip returning from Europe and she was just settling in at her parents' house, but seeing her expression, he relented, reaching over to take her hand. "Okay, then, we'll go together. I just thought you might want more time with your folks and sister. I was going to stay at a YMCA or something to look for a position. But you're right. It's not good for either of us to be worrying about each other right now. We'll take the train and go together, if it won't be too taxing on you and the baby."

She looked at him puzzled. "Simon, I'm the same woman who just a few weeks ago was standing all day in the surgery or triaging rows of wounded! Then falling into our cot exhausted, only to get up again and head to the recovery at four. Have you forgotten?"

He shook his head. "Not at all. You shouldn't have had to work so hard then and I don't want you to have to work that hard now. That's all. I'm sorry, Lydia. I need to trust you to tell me when enough is enough as this baby grows. More than anything, I want you healthy and safe. I just don't want anything to happen to either one of you."

She nodded, squeezing his hand. "I'm healthy and safe when I'm with you, my love. That's when I know nothing bad will happen to me. When I'm with you."

"Okay it's settled. We'll catch a train tomorrow and go into the city. I picked up a newspaper when I went to the corner market this morning. I want to show you what I saw in it. And we need to talk about going to West Virginia." Simon looked up as Lydia's mother came into the kitchen and kissed her daughter on the top of her head.

"Did you sleep well, dear?" Anna asked Lydia gently.

"Yes, Mom, very well," she replied. "I hope that you did, too?"

"Your father was up with an upset stomach, but after he settled down, I slept well," Anna explained. "These have been emotional days, you know... good, but... emotional," she hastened to add, not wanting Lydia and Simon to misunderstand. Anna was still getting used to the idea that her daughter was safely back from the war.

"There's hot cereal on the stove, Mom, and bacon," Lydia offered.

"I smelled it from upstairs," Anna smiled. "Your father will be down soon. So, what are your plans for the day?"

"We're looking at the paper for hospitals to visit in Pittsburgh," Simon told the woman as she poured herself coffee from the pot Simon had made for them. "I need to find work as soon as possible, and a place for us to live so that you can come help Lydia set up the house."

"Oh, I'd love to help. I meant it when I offered! I want to see where you'll be living. I wish you didn't have to go so soon," Anna with a sigh.

"We'll be spending Christmas here, Mom," Lydia assured her. "It's already December. Simon also needs to take care of some personal matters in West Virginia, so we'll go see his sister and brother there, but come back here before Christmas."

Anna brought her breakfast to the table, sitting beside them. "I'd love to have both of my daughters home for the holiday," she admitted, her eyes brimming at the thought. "I'm surprised Peggy didn't come immediately. She said she wasn't feeling well enough to sit in the car. Probably when you get back, they'll make it over. I'm still getting used to the idea that you're home myself!"

"So are we!" Simon exclaimed. "No small adjustment for any of us."

"Simon," Anna started, "if you don't mind my asking, why did you want to go to the war in the first place? You were young, with your whole future ahead of you. Why would you take that risk of enlisting in such a dangerous situation before America even joined the war? I mean, I know my daughter is headstrong and adventurous, but I thought she would end up safe in England when she wrote that she'd left for the Red Cross. I don't think she even fully realized what she was getting into, but you're a doctor. You must have had some idea..."

Simon sipped his coffee before answering. "Yes, the army surgeons did their best to warn us. Though even they didn't know the half of it. But long before that, an elderly doctor, who helped raise me, had had some experience with war medicine, back in the sixties. He was very frank about what he had seen during several of the battles that took place in the West Virginia and Virginia territories, where he volunteered his skills to the Union Army. I heard his stories and was struck by how treating the wounded left such a visceral impression on him. I guess I saw the French and German conflict as something equally important. I had a great deal of respect for Doc Albright. I suppose I wanted to follow in his footsteps."

Lydia listened to this part of Simon's life that she had not heard before. She wished she could have known this mentor... met the man who had helped shape Simon's moral character and values. She also wanted very much to meet Simon's remaining family, about whom she knew very little. His sister and brother would help her understand this man she loved all the more.

Anna persisted. "So, was the war what you thought it would be, Simon?"

Simon hesitated before he admitted, "No. It was much worse. Took everything in me, along with my faith in the Almighty, to make sense out of what was happening, from the first battle. Some days, I didn't think I was doing much good at all."

"Oh," Anna replied simply.

"Then, Lydia arrived at the station," Simon continued, reaching for Lydia's hand once more and their fingers intertwined. "When this woman climbed out of the truck and walked into the station wearing army boots and her uniform, I thought to myself, 'now there's a woman I need to get to know.'"

Lydia blushed. "Oh, Simon, you did not know that the minute I arrived!"

He looked at her with a small smile and said softly, "Oh, yes, Lydia, I did. I had to fend off one of the other doctors who had his eye on you, too. And I was prepared to do whatever it took to earn your attention, first."

Lydia knew he was referring to Marcus, but said nothing. She hadn't realized Simon had thought there was a contest between the two men. There had not been one for her. She had only had eyes for the calm, somewhat reserved young doctor sitting in front of her. And now she felt their fingers joined, much the same way as their love was intertwined, and her eyes reflected the same. Anna observed the exchange with great comfort. They had obviously formed a true bond, forged in the fire of war.

When Lydia's father joined them, they informed him of the plan to board the train in the morning. There was an established hospital founded by the Sisters of Charity along the Monongahela River in Pittsburgh. Their advertisement had appealed to Simon. The values it held were in line with his own, and it was a teaching hospital as well. Perhaps the memory of the Catholic priest who had been willing to bless their marriage in Nancy, or the fond memories of Father James, had contributed to Simon's desire to give back to those of the Catholic faith. Regardless, Simon wanted to begin his interviews there... and also look for what nursing opportunities might be possible for Lydia.

Upon hearing the plans, Andrew was visibly displeased with the idea of Lydia going along. He took the cup of coffee, offered by his wife, and the bowl of hot cereal, but paused before eating, turning abruptly to Lydia. "I don't think you should go in your condition," he stated flatly.

"Now, Andrew," Anna objected. "Your daughter is a grown woman. She needs to decide for herself what's best."

"She's never been with child before!" he exclaimed. "Let Simon go walking the streets, trying to find where to go and such. Simon, I think you should just go and set everything up and leave Lydia here, where her mother can watch over her."

Patiently, Anna patted his shoulder, "These are different times, Andrew. She's traveled halfway around the world and seen things most folks will never see. She is not a child. And don't forget that our son-in-law is a doctor? Who better for her to be with if there is a problem with the baby? He can surely care for her better than I, in that regard."

"Better than her own mother?"

"Yes, dear, better than her own mother," Anna said softly.

Lydia looked at her mother with heartfelt appreciation. She was glad, and somewhat surprised, by her mother's active support, having been worried that all three of them would agree she should stay at her parents' home. She was again pleased when Simon himself came to her defense.

"I share your concern, sir," Simon assured Andrew. "I think in this situation, though, it probably would be best for Lydia to be with me. She's interested in finding work and may want to speak to the nursing directors at the hospitals we visit."

"I still think you're unwise to tax yourself this way, Lydia," Andrew grumbled to his daughter. "You just got home, and your mother is scarcely used to you being here, and off you go again and leave her. Haven't even seen Peggy yet!"

Lydia patted her father's hand and looked at him tenderly. "We'll be back soon, Dad. I want to spend Christmas with you, too."

Andrew looked down at his cereal bowl and began to eat. "Good. That'll make your mother very happy." It was all he could manage. "But you can leave Abril with us. Don't need the dog with you in the city."

That afternoon, Lydia made sure to spend ample time sitting with her parents and asking them about the smaller details of the past couple of years... her sister and her children, and the little joys and trials of life. They steered clear of anything related to the war.

After a spell, Lydia excused herself for a short nap—it was likely her parents could use one too. Up in her childhood bedroom, she unfolded the newspaper Simon had picked up, to check in on the news from the front. There was a new battle at Cambria, and Lydia knew in her heart that their team at the French CCS, as well as the British CCS, would be back near the worst of the fighting. She bowed her head in sorrow and prayer for her friends, knowing that they would be in great danger, yet again. A wave of guilt washed over her, knowing that she was safe... and they were not.

Simon found her there, reading the news from the war. He stretched out on the bed and motioned for her to lay against him, where he held her. "We fulfilled our duty... they're there because they choose to be there."

"I know," Lydia said. "But I sometimes feel like we should still be with them, helping them to get through it."

"No," Simon said slowly, "not anymore, Lydia. The baby comes first, and no matter what happens to our friends overseas, we need to focus on building our home together and getting ready for the arrival of our son or daughter."

"Do you care which it is?" she asked suddenly. He had never indicated a preference and she had never asked.

"Hm," he said thoughtfully. "I hope it's a boy so that I can teach him how to be a good man, a good husband and father, someday. Maybe he'll take up medicine, even, and go into practice with me."

"That sounds wonderful," she said.

"And I hope it's a girl so that I can see her beautiful mother reflected in her eyes and watch her grow with love and compassion and your spirit of giving that is still something of a cherished mystery to me."

"Then we have a problem," she said. "You want both! And I'm small enough that I'm sure there's only one in there."

He shifted to prop himself up on his forearm so he could look at her, touching her cheek gently before placing his hand on her stomach, measuring the size for himself. "And how about you? Do you have a preference?"

"No..." she said slowly. "I want it to come out on time, not early like that little baby in the village outside of Nancy. I want it to have every chance to live. And, Simon, I don't want to have it at a hospital. Too many mothers and babies get sick at hospitals. I will have it at home, with you."

Simon looked surprised. "Really?" he questioned. "What if there are complications? It would be safer to be in a maternity ward with a surgery close by."

"You'll just have to deliver our baby yourself and make sure there are no complications." She was decided.

At this, Simon sat up. "You want me to deliver our baby, Lydia?" he asked her. "I can't do that. I couldn't be objective where you're concerned. If something went wrong, I'd lose my mind in the middle of it. You need an obstetrician."

"I don't want another man down there!" There was a tremble in her voice.

"Lydia, it's what they're trained to do," he protested. "Just like I'm trained to be a surgeon."

She couldn't hold back the tears. "And then they would kick you out, and you'll be in a waiting room somewhere with all the other waiting husbands, smoking cigars, pacing the floors, worried sick about how it's going in there! And some stranger will be down there watching me push out our baby and witnessing its first breath! And if they put me to sleep, I won't even see its first breath. Neither will you! I'll have strangers telling me my baby has been born! And what if they get it mixed up with someone else's baby since I won't even see it when it comes out! If we were back at the station, you'd deliver my baby, I know you would!" Lydia rolled away from him, her face buried in the pillow, and wept.

Utterly astonished by her litany of fears, Simon watched her roll away from him, temporarily at a loss for words. Then, he pulled her back over to face him and made her come back into his arms. "Okay, okay," he took a deep breath. "Here's what we'll do. We'll find a reputable midwife who will come to the house and deliver the baby, and I will hold you in my arms while you're pushing, and we'll be there together and watch our baby come into the world and take its first breath. You will look into its little face and know it is your own baby. How does that sound?"

Still sniffling, Lydia's tears subsided. "That sounds reasonable," she said. "Thank you."

Simon held her then until she had quieted. He lay there amazed at her emotional outburst. Of course, she was right. If they had remained in the station, he would have had to deliver the baby... or Harold or Marcus would have done it. There would have been no other option. But they weren't at the station now, and there were perfectly capable doctors and hospitals here, even more in the city... and they didn't mix up infants at birth in the nursery. Surely, she would come to realize that... once they got to Pittsburgh, she would see how modern the facilities had become. Maybe he would be allowed to show her a maternity ward during an interview. She could see for herself how well the new mothers were being cared for. Everything would turn out alright in the long run.

The ride from Greensburg to the Pittsburgh station felt quite short, despite several stops along the route. As the train chugged its way into the city, Simon and Lydia marvelled at the miles of great smokestacks atop factories along the shores of the Monongahela, Ohio, and Allegheny rivers. Rowboats, barges, and some larger ships floated in the water at the various docks. The mountains surrounding the city reminded Simon of West Virginia, not quite as lofty, but still varied and peaked in places, and covered in a blanket of December snow. As the train slowed to enter the station, they bundled themselves into their warm winter coats and hats and Simon gathered up their small suitcase, helping Lydia safely disembark. Their first task was to find a place to stay the night. Simon hailed a cab asking the man what he might recommend. Assessing the man, with his female companion, the driver pointed his cigar at a tall stone building not far ahead of them... a hotel that would do.

As the motor car pulled to a stop, Simon asked the driver to wait for a moment while he quickly checked in, stowing the suitcase with the desk clerk. The spacious lobby with its chandelier glowing overhead was quite impressive, but they would have time later to enjoy the hotel. Simon quickly returned to the car where Lydia was waiting and asked that they be taken across the bridge to where the Sisters of Charity had established their venerable institution.

In person, the hospital made quite an impression rising above the slow moving ice floes of the river it overlooked. Many people came and went through its wide front doors, patients or visitors, in their winter clothes and nurses in white uniforms, wrapped in their protective blue capes. Simon held the door for Lydia to enter the main rotunda where several statues of saints observed from square pedestals. There was an attendant, just inside the door, seated at a small but orderly desk. Catching a chill each time the door was opened, he wore a scarf around his neck which offered him some small relief from the outdoor intrusions.

"Administrative office, please," Lydia said to him. He rattled off instructions: down a long white corridor with tiled floors, toward the eastern end of the first floor... take the third left turn and look for the sign on the door.

Finding themselves at a large oak door, with a brass sign which read, 'Hospital Administration', Simon and Lydia glanced at each other, Lydia giving his hand a squeeze of encouragement. This was it. They opened the door.

Simon introduced himself to the receptionist in the ante-room. Her typewriter clacked away as she worked industriously through a neatly stacked mound of papers on the small desk.

"Doctor Simon Finney," he introduced himself. "And my wife, Mrs. Lydia Finney."

"Well hello, I'm Miss Weston. How can I help you, Doctor Finney?" The woman was cordial.

"We're just back from the war, from serving overseas in the army. I'm looking for a surgical appointment and wonder where to apply," he asked hopefully.

With an encouraging smile, she looked up at him. "I can help you with that. Please, take a seat." She rose, straightened her prim, brown jacket and skirt and turned, quickly disappearing behind a wooden door.

Simon and Lydia saw two chairs next to each other beside a tall window that framed the frozen cityscape, just across the river. After several long, anxious minutes, the receptionist reappeared with an older man beside her, gesturing to the young couple. Extending his hand, he greeted them. "Doctor Finney? Mrs. Finney?"

Simon stood to shake his hand. "Yes, sir."

"I'm Doctor Richard Maloney, one of the administrators here. Please, Doctor, accompany me so we can discuss your situation."

Simon nodded, and with a quick reassuring glance to Lydia, he followed the man who led him to an inner hall and into his private office. Doctor Maloney preceded him, taking his seat behind an unassuming desk.

There were shelves full of medical books and journals along the wall. Simon wondered if the man was still practicing or more focused on administration, with all of these resources at his fingertips.

"Please, sit down," the administrator motioned to a highbacked chair while quickly checking a pocket watch connected to a fob in a small pocket of his suit jacket. "My secretary tells me you've just returned from serving in the army, Doctor Finney."

"Yes, sir," Simon nodded. "Two years assigned to a French casualty clearing station, on the western front. I was just recently discharged from duty."

Doctor Maloney looked surprised. "On the front, you say? I assume you're a surgeon, if you were stationed in a casualty station."

"Yes, sir," Simon confirmed. "I am."

"Tell me about your experience," Doctor Maloney invited him, genuinely interested. The older man sat back with his hands folded in his lap, his eyes never leaving Simon's. He had not yet met a surgeon newly back from the war.

Simon told Doctor Maloney about his enlistment and arrival in Europe. He described the kinds of surgery required of the doctors in the field, some of the challenging conditions in which they practiced, and his desire to continue to do that which he loved doing most, surgery.

"I imagine you're somewhat out of touch with the latest in surgical advances after being two years overseas. You were on the front line of the war, but not the front line of medicine," Doctor Maloney stated. He was not unkind; it was simply an honest observation.

"You're correct, sir," Simon said truthfully. "Although we shared innovations with our British counterparts, whenever we were able to bring the units together, and we occasionally received journals from the States and England, though I'm sure they were dated by the time they reached us. I happened to be in the American Hospital in Paris, within the past few months. Very impressed with the newer anesthesia, equipment, and diagnostic capabilities implemented there. Their physicians were a remarkable team. I realize I may have some catching up to do."

"Tell me more about your work in West Virginia, Doctor," Maloney pressed him further.

Simon looked surprised. "Well, sir, I was mentored through medical school by an old-school, country doctor…" Simon detailed the story of his beginnings, concluding with, "I guess that's why I chose the mobile CCS. It was a way to take the medicine to the wounded, out on the battlefront, where they needed it most."

"A dangerous proposition," Maloney observed quietly.

"Yes, sir… I fractured a tibia when a shell exploded right on top of our station… but since we got to the wounded soldiers right as they were coming off the front lines, they had a much better chance of surviving than if they had to wait and travel by train or wagon across the Red Zone to a field hospital somewhere."

"No doubt many still died… I've seen some of the casualty figures, and they're staggering, the number of dead being reported."

"I haven't seen any reported numbers myself," Simon admitted. "The Army counted, but we didn't. What the reports can't quantify is how many hundreds were saved because they got to us in time. The bravest medical teams in the world are out there on the front, doing everything they can. My wife was part of our team, a volunteer nurse with the Red Cross. We met at the CCS."

Doctor Maloney's eyebrows raised up. "Nurses? On the front?"

"The finest nurses you'd ever want to meet served at our station. We were staffed with twelve volunteer nurses and three surgeons, and some medics. But those nurses saved more lives than I could count helping us in surgery and taking care of wounded in recovery tents."

"Remarkable," the doctor said in surprise. "Women at the front."

"Yes sir, Red Cross trained," Simon nodded. "Amazing women willing to sacrifice their personal safety to save life, under very difficult circumstances."

"Hm," Doctor Maloney said thoughtfully. "That's quite a story, Doctor Finney. I've never actually talked to anyone who served at the front. You could probably teach me a thing or two! Truth be known, I'm not concerned about your need to brush up on more current practices here in the States. Clearly you know how to learn and adapt to surgery in varied conditions.

"What interests me most, Doctor Finney, is your desire to 'take medicine to those who need it'. That's the mission statement of this facility. I'll be honest with you, our institution isn't highly profitable. You'd make a lot more money working elsewhere in the city. It's our mission to serve. You would, however, be given the opportunity to teach medical students the realities of surgery in a variety of settings and broaden their appreciation of what it means to do this work well."

Growing hopeful, Simon said, "I have a close friend, one of the other surgeons at the station, also coming here. We served together for two years and hope to continue to practice together. He's especially talented at delicate vascular surgeries. He saved my leg at the station when it was shattered. I focused on head and chest traumas. Of course, we both took care of whatever came to our tables."

"Is he here now?" Doctor Maloney asked. "I'd be interested in talking to anyone who can do delicate arterial surgeries while bombs are falling around him."

"Not yet, sir, he's visiting family. We just sailed back a week ago from Europe. He'll be along after he has a chance to see them." If there were positions for both Marc and him maybe they would not need to search other hospitals for positions. With Christmas coming, they could just get settled in, start to work, and get ready for the baby.

"I'd like to meet him when he gets to the city," Doctor Maloney said. "We need a couple of surgeons right now. Some of our own have been called to serve with American troops that headed over to France when we declared war. Some of those may very well end up at the hospital in Paris that you mentioned. Are you looking elsewhere for employment?"

"Doctor Lovell and I are considering our options. Can you give me enough to raise my family? My wife is expecting our first child," Simon said. "I want to get her settled into a home and start working as soon as I can."

Doctor Maloney knew the budgetary constraints.

"I believe I can," he stated. "You could make more money at one of the other hospitals, but I think we can be fair."

"Then no, sir, I don't need to look elsewhere for employment," Simon stated, deciding to take the sure bet, while hoping it was the right decision. Marcus and he could always look elsewhere in a year, if they needed.

Doctor Maloney stood up behind his desk and again extended his hand. "Welcome to our staff, Doctor Finney. There is one other matter that I'll at least mention, I think..."

"Sir?" Simon waited.

"There is the matter of your wife. Of course, she's not permitted to work as a nurse in the wards, given her marital status and the fact that she is expecting. That's simply not permitted in the hospital—"

"I'm sorry to hear that, sir," Simon admitted truthfully. "I'll discuss this with her. Another alternative is to return to West Virginia, where Doc Albright's practice was, and she would be able to work beside me, doing country medicine. She's extremely skilled in both surgery and in caring for the sick or injured—"

Doctor Maloney raised a hand to stop Simon. "You misunderstand, Doctor Finney. I was about to say that I'd like to have your wife meet Sister Edwarda, our nursing director, here. She is considering starting a program in the city that would help to meet the mission statement of Sisters of Charity. I suspect your wife may be just the nurse Sister Edwarda has been looking for to help with a project near and dear to her. One of taking care out to the patients in their homes... and we do have a walk-in clinic... perhaps—"

Simon felt a rush of relief. "Really? It would be incredible if my wife could find something that helps her feel like she's making a difference. That seems to be her life's mission."

"Think about how soon you can start, Doctor. We can get you oriented to the hospital routine and put on the surgical schedule."

Hesitating briefly, Simon added, "I need to go home to West Virginia and settle some affairs there, transfer my accounts to this city, and find a place for us to live. Perhaps I could start immediately after Christmas?"

"That would do. It's only a matter of a few weeks," Doctor Maloney agreed as he walked Simon back out to the anteroom where Lydia waited, perched on the edge of her chair. He saw the lovely woman stand as he approached, and now he extended his hand to her as well. "It was a pleasure meeting your husband, Mrs. Finney. He speaks very highly of your nursing skills."

She smiled hesitantly. "That's kind of you to tell me, sir," she told him. "Although I'm somewhat adrift at the moment."

"Understandable given the many changes you've had lately," Doctor Maloney said. "I wish you both a good afternoon." and with that, he turned and left them.

Simon grabbed Lydia's hand. "They agreed to put me on staff, Lydia," he reported quickly. "And he wants to meet Marcus."

Lydia saw the excitement in his face and was happy for him. "I'm glad for you, Simon, really, I am. Dad will be so relieved that we won't be destitute on the streets, living in a tent."

"But Lydia, Doctor Maloney said the hospital might have a position for you, too!" Simon exclaimed softly. "There is a nun here, Sister Edwarda—well, he wants to talk to her about you. I told him about your work at the station, and he said she has something she's putting together. That you might be just the nurse she's been looking for to help her with whatever it is... an outreach program of some sort. He didn't tell me much more... only that he wants you to meet the woman."

"That sounds absolutely wonderful! So I guess we're moving to Pittsburgh!" Lydia exclaimed. Her spirits lifted, she held his arm as they walked back down the long, tiled hallway to the rotunda.

"Let's find something to eat; I'm famished," Simon suggested, the cold wind pricking their faces as they stepped through the wide rotunda door back out into winter. The man at the reception desk shivered, breathing hot air into his cupped hands.

"It's good to know some things never change... food sounds perfect," Lydia was smiling up at him as he motioned a cab to come fetch them.

The day after their dinner at the hotel in Rochester, Marcus got up early, shaved, and went down to the lobby to wait for Suzie to pick him up. The night prior, she had seemed surprised when he simply wished her good night after their meal. Suzie had hesitated slightly when accepting her coat as he held it out for her. Marcus had not presumed; there was too much at stake to make a wrong move. So, he had bundled her up, fastened the button at the top of her coat, kissed her lightly on the cheek, and bid her good night.

All night long, his mind had wandered back and through their evening, every word, every touch, her expressions... at the railroad station and at dinner. The six months they had spent together at the CCS had resurfaced vividly as he lay on the hotel bed alone, and he had not fallen asleep until the darkness had nearly surrendered to first light.

Marcus smiled as Suzie pulled up to the hotel in her black Chevrolet, sliding slightly on the snow. He did not keep her waiting, immediately stepping out into the cold and climbing into the passenger side seat.

"Good morning, Suzie," he greeted her warmly. "Did you sleep well?"

"I was a little restless," she admitted. "There was a lot to think about after last night. You?"

"Same." Marcus nodded. "Took a while to fall asleep. So, what feels appropriate to you today?

"Well, you came right out to the car, so I'm assuming you didn't want to stay at the hotel," Suzie observed dryly.

"What are our options, Suzie?"

She glanced sideways at him from her seat behind the steering wheel. "I told my family about seeing you yesterday."

"Did you?" Marcus said. "That's good... it was good... wasn't it?"

"Seemed so..." She paused, tapping the steering wheel. "I'm going to take you to the house, and I thought it might be better if we didn't show up unannounced," she explained.

It was sudden; Marcus was nervous. "How did they take it? Is there anything I should know?" *Will someone be waiting with a shotgun at the door?* He wondered.

"Actually, they were kind of excited to meet you. I told them everything was tough over there, in France, and that all of us made choices that we probably wouldn't have made under other circumstances. I told them you were eager to meet Nikki, and my folks thought that was probably long overdue."

Marcus nervously rubbed his knee, and to his surprise, Suzie reached over and lightly patted his hand.

"I think it'll go well," she reassured him, carefully pulling out into the snow-lined streets.

She steered the black automobile through quiet neighborhoods where the trees were outlined with a coating of white, befitting the season... tendrils of smoke curling out of every chimney. Finally, she pulled to a stop in front of a large, two-story house with a wrap-around front porch. Marcus imagined her in summer, sitting out on the porch swing, holding their baby. The snow sparkled under the morning sunshine. Together, they walked up the four steps leading to the wide porch. Suzie was first to enter the warm house... and then Marcus.

"Mom, we're here," Suzie called out as she removed her winter hat and coat. "I'll take your coat, Marcus... I see you bought some civilian clothes!" She hung their outerwear in a closet and led him to the back of the house where an older woman tended the baby. "Mom, this is Marcus Lovell."

Marcus smiled, "Mrs. Boyton, it's a pleasure to meet you."

She looked him over, studying him. She did not rise, but her tone was warm. "So, you're little Nikki's father, back from the war? I could have guessed in a heartbeat. She looks just like you. Suzie told us your enlistment wasn't up yet when she had to come back early, and that the army wouldn't let you go."

"That is true, ma'am," Marcus said. "My enlistment just finished in November and it took a bit to get back over the ocean."

"Well, you can call me Vanessa. And here she is," Suzie's mother stood then and lifted the nine-month-old baby to bring her to where Marcus stood by Suzie.

Marcus held out his hands and took the baby into his arms, awestruck at his tiny daughter. She had soft, dark brown curls just like his, not blonde like her mother's, and the bright blue eyes that Suzie and he shared. The baby stared up at him as he held her close, and Marcus was overwhelmed with emotion at the vulnerable innocence in his arms. He looked at Suzie, his eyes welling.

"My God, Suz. She's beautiful," he breathed, in wonder. *This is my daughter!* "I... I had no idea..."

Suzie smiled. "Of course not. I never told you. I saw you in her face every day. Come into the parlor, and let's sit with her for a while. Thanks, Mom."

The three of them moved into the parlor, Marcus carefully navigating his way to the sofa, where he sat with the baby cradled in his arms. There, he marveled over her tiny features as she reached for and caught his finger.

"She's going to be hungry soon," Suzie warned.

Marcus looked up eagerly. "I can feed her if you want."

Suzie smiled. "I don't think you have the equipment," she reached gently for Marcie Nichole, opening her blouse and putting the baby to her breast, where the little one latched on immediately and began to suckle.

Marcus watched Suzie breastfeeding so comfortably in front of him... he was speechless. She was truly beautiful. Marcus saw a chance to create a family in Suzie's decision to allow him to share in this intimate moment. He reached up and touched her face gently.

"You're wonderful with her," Marcus said. "I really do want to take care of both of you, Suzie."

"Okay," she replied simply.

Marcus seemed confused. "Okay?" he asked.

"Okay," she replied. "Didn't you think that I've been hoping this day would come, ever since Lydia sent her letters about you changing and that I should give you a chance? That you were hoping to come see us as soon as you were discharged? Didn't you think I might be waiting for this day?"

Marcus looked at the baby, content against Suzie's breast. *Lydia had had a hand in making this possible?* His eyes welled again, his voice caught in his throat.

"I don't deserve it, but I'm so happy, Suzie. Will you come with me to Pittsburgh so I can work with Simon? Will you come and be my wife there?"

Suzie smiled. "Do I have to wait until Pittsburgh to be your wife?"

"So you'll marry me, after all?" he asked, hoping against all hope.

"Is that a proposal, Marcus?" Suzie laughed lightly.

Marcus dropped down to one knee beside the couch, taking her free hand as she nursed their daughter. "Will you marry me Susannah Boyton... as soon as possible?" he asked more formally.

"Yes, Marcus Lovell," she said, looking into his anxious eyes. "I will. But you'd better ask my father first."

Chapter 4
Into the Mountains

Having found much success during their trip to Pittsburgh, Simon and Lydia boarded yet another train, this time heading southwest, to West Virginia. As the tracks crossed and followed the riverbed, away from Pittsburgh, these snowy forest-covered mountains appeared much taller than those they had left behind. The sky overhead transformed into a clear blue as they escaped the smokey pall which hung over Pittsburgh and crisp air seeped in through the many cracks in the train's windows.

Simon surveyed the landscape with a comforting familiarity and turned to Lydia. "Marcus said this is backwoods, bear country. Said he couldn't see himself living like Daniel Boone!" He laughed lightly, recalling their conversation.

"Did he now?" Lydia countered. "After our rustic conditions in France, I believe we could live almost anywhere!"

"True, but not comfortably—remember, last winter was so bitterly cold, not sure we would have made it without those wood stoves!"

"The mittens the women in England made helped, too... the gifts from the British camp," she recalled.

Simon's eyes lit up at the mention of the British CCS, "I remember dancing with you, to the Victrola that David Winston brought out for their New Year's party for both of our camps. What a time we all had! I hardly felt the cold that night! And I loved holding you in my arms, in front of everyone."

Lydia snuggled against him. "Good things happen when music is playing. That must've been when Laura and Doctor Winston became close. That party was a bright spot for sure... the winter got so much worse when..." She faltered, stopping her train of thought.

Simon kissed her head. "We'll buy a good radio for music in our home. I have some financial things to take care of when we arrive, Lydia," Simon told her. "Doc left me his little house, just outside of town. We lived there for a time when I practiced here. I'll sell that one so we can buy a house outright. Then, there's a cabin on Fishing Creek. I can sell it or continue to rent it out. It's a nice cabin, sturdy, but it qualifies as rustic... outhouse and all. I'd kind of hate to let it go. It could be a nice vacation spot for us in summer. And I need to transfer funds out of my account in town, to a Pittsburgh bank. All of my army pay went into that account, and there should be enough there to withdraw for our new house, until Doc's sells. What kind of house would you like?"

"One that has a bedroom for us and one for the baby," she stated simply.

He laughed. "Okay, what about the other little amenities like the kitchen... Big? Small? Appliances? Things like that..."

"As long as there's no cold outhouse and we have hot, running water, I'll leave it up to you, to know what we can afford. After all, Simon," she continued, "I'm bringing nothing at all to this venture. My small savings from working in the bank paid for me to go to the nursing training in Philadelphia, and I left the remainder with my parents for my room and board there, after high school. I have nothing to contribute since I've made nothing over the past two years as a volunteer."

Simon reached over, lovingly pressing his palm to her belly. "You've made nothing short of a miracle, to contribute to this venture, my beloved wife. I'm happy to provide all the rest—as your father would assuredly say I should."

"Tell me about your brother and sister," she said, eager to learn more about them.

"You'll meet them soon enough. We're pulling into the station now, and someone from the family will be waiting for us." He was a little hesitant to say more, just yet.

They waited for the giant engine to slow, wheels squealing against freezing rails until the long train finally came to a complete stop. Simon took their suitcase and went ahead of Lydia down the metal ironwork steps. He lifted her down the final step to the platform before looking around. Then, he saw his brother hurrying over to greet them. The man appeared to Lydia to be a little older than Simon, perhaps thirty, with a touch of grey at his temples already. It was easy to imagine what Simon might look like as he aged a bit. He had a broad smile, also a beard, and looked like... a Daniel Boone.

"Simon!" the man cried out happily, pulling his younger brother into a bear hug.

"Phillip!" Simon exclaimed, clapping the man on the back. "Good to see you. Really good to see you!"

Phillip looked at Simon carefully. "You're in one piece, after all? Still have two legs? Your letters didn't lie. And this is... Lydia?

She is beautiful! You son of a gun!" Phillip punched Simon in the arm then gathered Lydia up in an equally strong hug till she thought her ribs might break. "Happy to finally meet you! I'm Simon's big brother. We've heard all about you from Simon's letters. Who knew he could write so well? I certainly didn't, until he was thousands of miles away. We've gotten a dozen, probably. You didn't get any from me. I didn't write any! Bet you got some from Rebecca though! She likes to write!" The man laughed. "You two just come with me, now," he continued, taking them each by an arm. "Becky is baking up a storm at her house and is expecting us directly. The whole family will be together, and we'll have a chance to catch up properly.

"Now, Lydia, no matter what he did, or didn't tell you, Simon is the baby of the family and the only one to go into medicine, so we have no idea what he's talking about most of the time. But you can translate if you think you should, that is, if he starts talking about being a doctor over in France. Letters didn't say too much about that. I'm just a coal miner, so I can tell you all you want to know about coal. So just ask me anything, if you're curious!"

The man kept a steady stream of conversation flowing as they got into his truck. He drove them over frozen dirt streets, out of the larger town and through the pristine white countryside to a smaller community with rows of identical houses clustered near the entrance to a mine. Parking next to a bare tree outside of a house, he pointed out the windows with lights and a Christmas tree decorated, inside.

"Rebecca is waiting," he said as he pushed open the front door of the house for them, releasing a rush of warm air until it was securely closed again behind them.

Lydia let Simon take her coat and was grateful when he returned to wrap an arm around her as the woman in the kitchen let out a screech of excitement and called to several children. Bursting into the room, she wiped her hands on a well-worn apron, tears in her eyes, her face smudged with flour, she gripped Simon's face, kissing him on both cheeks... leaving white residue on his beard.

"Well, Simon J. Finney! I do declare you're among the living, after all! You're too thin. Phillip, he's too thin! You wrote that you'd gotten hurt, but here, now, you don't look anything, but older! He's too thin, Phillip, look! He doesn't look hurt at all to me! Does he look hurt to you? Come in, honey, it's so good to see you. Frank? Frank? Where'd you get to? They're here; come meet them! Children, it's okay, come on in, too. And Alice, come away from those vegetables, you hear? You come too. The pies will wait. Come in, Simon. Come on back to the kitchen with your little wife here. It's the warmest room in the house."

Simon steered Lydia through an archway, and into a very large, rustic kitchen with a substantial stove and fireplace—the air was warm and inviting... and smelled incredible.

Rebecca helped Lydia gently into a chair and lined people up to meet her. "Now, I'm Becky, sister to these two boys. And my husband, Frank, well, he's coming—and this is Alice, Phil's wife, and this one is Luke, he's my oldest, and Laura, his sister and my middle child, and Lacie, my youngest, she's three now. Three 'L's so it's easier to remember—And this here, is Wayne. He's Phillip's oldest and Nancy is his next, and then these are Tommy and Theresa, their twins. And where is... well, anyway, you'll see the dog, and if Tiny frets over you, just say so, and we'll put him outside to calm him down. Now, that's everyone. Everyone, this here, is Lydia, your Uncle Simon's new wife. Would you please say hello to her, real polite now?" They did, nearly in unison and Rebecca squeezed her shoulder, turning now to her little brother. "And Simon, you just come over and let me hug you, and you tell me all about yourself. My, it's good to see you home after all this time. I just am so glad we got your letters from time to time... you could have written more often, you know... about what foolhardy things you were doing way over there in France... besides finding a wife!"

Simon looked at Lydia and just smiled as they were immersed in welcome as Becky returned to finish up her pies. The children each came over to Lydia and said hello and reintroduced themselves to her. She asked each one of them something about themselves that she was never going to remember, but she wanted to try. It was truly one big happy family. Little Laura stood shyly next to Lydia and stared at her without saying much while others made themselves known and then went off to play. Laura reached out her little hand and put it on Lydia's small stomach.

"When baby comin'?" the little girl asked plainly, holding a ragdoll.

"Why, in springtime, probably around Easter," Lydia said, surprised that the little girl had somehow sensed her situation.

"Ma, Aunt Lydie's baby comin' Easter time!" Laura called out matter-of-factly, over the hubbub in the busy kitchen.

Becky dropped the mound of pie dough she had been working, with a plop, sending flour flying into the air. She rushed around the table to Lydia, stood her up, critically looking at her stomach while running a practiced hand over her belly, leaving a trail of flour on her brown dress. "Well, now, look at that! You sure are, honey. Easter? Here, Phillip, look! Your brother already got his wife pregnant and see now, she's showing already. Look at this little belly growing. Isn't that just fine now! You're gonna have another little nephew or niece!"

Phillip pretended to punch Simon in the arm for the second time. "You'll never be able to say war is hell again, Simon! Got her pregnant, right in the middle of it all, huh?" He laughed heartily, and Simon chuckled, moving around the table to Lydia to put his arms around her. Phil bellowed, "Frank! Frank break out the whiskey. We're going to congratulate these two!"

"This is exactly why I didn't tell you about them ahead of time," Simon whispered in Lydia's ear, noticing her cheeks were rosy with embarrassment at all the attention. "There is no way to describe a country family from West Virginia. It's just a great deal of life and love. You just have to experience it."

He kissed her in front of them all as Phillip's wife, Alice, made her way over and hugged Lydia tightly. "Congratulations," she said softly. "Don't mind any of them. They just love family, and you'll get used to the excitement around here. Each time I got pregnant they made such a fuss as you couldn't imagine. When the twins came, you'd have thought it was the first miracle God did since the parting of the sea."

Lydia looked around the large, energetic group and took a deep breath. This was a homecoming for Simon that she could never have imagined. These people were so different from her quiet, reserved husband. She could only assume that him being placed into the care of the aging Doctor Albright had played a big part in developing his reserved personality. Yet, his eyes twinkled when he looked at these people. It was clear that he was the adored baby brother, now safely returned from the war. Her baby was going to have quite an extended family, and Lydia knew immediately that she wanted to get to know these people, very well. She was glad she would have a lifetime to do it.

Simon sat down on the chair she'd been using and pulled her down onto his lap wrapping both arms around her. Becky's husband, Frank, came in through the back door with an armload of wood for the fire and kicked off his snow-covered boots beside the back door. He hugged his wife, and she affectionately dotted his nose with a little flour. "You're red as a beet," she said. "Warm yourself right up. Supper's about ready now. Children wash up—you all hear me?"

Supper around this table was a wonderfully noisy affair. The conversation, eating, and passing of bowls and platters of hot, steaming food. Simon ate heartily, and Lydia now realized where his insatiable appetite had originated. This family loved to eat. After they'd finished and cleaned everything, the children went off to play before bed, and the adults gathered around the fireplace in the living room and to talk. Phillip turned to Simon, and suddenly, his entire demeanor shifted.

"Well, brother," he said. "You gave us a real scare with a couple of your letters and what with reading the newspapers. Seemed like you were awfully close to where the action was, and we wondered if you'd be in harm's way. Seems like danger found you with the broken leg you told us about. Looks like that healed up, though? I don't see a limp when you walk."

Becky added, "When you first said something about Lydia here, Simon, I thought, what in thunder is a woman doing over there anyway? No place for a woman to be at all until you talked about the nursing part. That made sense, then. But it couldn't have been very easy for you, Lydia. It sounded pretty harsh."

Lydia nodded. "It was difficult. Simon made it much easier for me. Except for when he was recovering and kept trying to get up when he was ordered not to walk."

Phillip said, "I'd be wanting to stay right there in the bed if it was me. Use that leg as a good excuse for keeping my head down and out of harm's way."

"It was a long six weeks until he could stand," Lydia admitted. "I think he hated it."

"Now, Lydia, couldn't have been that bad if you were his nurse for six weeks in the tent, could it?" Phillip countered. "I think he probably thought he was pretty lucky."

Simon smiled, his arm around her. "She took extremely good care of me."

"I'll bet she did!" Phillip said. "And now, Simon, it's your job to take real good care of her and that baby coming. How many little ones do you want to have, Lydia?"

Lydia looked a little flustered. "We didn't really talk much about that, Phillip. This one actually took us a bit by surprise!"

Phil elbowed Frank, sitting nearby, and said as a loud aside, "And my brother's a doctor, no less! You think he'd gotten that one figured out in medical school!"

Frank shook his head. "Like you planned all yours? I don't think so, Phil."

"No way," Phillip started, "left that up to the Almighty Himself. Life is too short to try to plan out that kind of thing. Take life as it comes is what we live by in the mines, Lydia. You never know when the next cave-in could happen. Gotta live life."

Lydia stared at him, pondering the risk he took daily. She hadn't realized how perilous working in the mines was. But Simon knew. He grew up knowing about life in the mines and the inherent hazards of leaving the light of day for dark, damp tunnels under a mountain where men chopped coal from seams with just their pickaxes and the strength in their arms.

"How's it been for you guys down there?" Simon asked, concerned. "Have they improved some of the safety issues over the past couple of years?"

"Not much," Frank admitted. "Those owners want the coal out. That's all. As long as the mine's producing, they're happy. We've lost some good men down there."

Alice looked at Rebecca, and Lydia recognized the look that passed between the two women. It reflected the same fear she had known; that something bad could happen to the men they loved the most. Every day that their men went below ground was a day of tense waiting for them to reemerge and come home. Lydia immediately felt a kind of kinship with the other two women sitting by the fireplace.

"Was it cave-ins? Or gas explosions?" Simon asked.

"Both," Frank told him. "But we're doing our part in trying to shore up the walls more, and they're drilling air holes for vents. So that's a little better. The shift foremen understand since they're down there with us sometimes. We do what we can. Still pretty good overtime for the risk taken. The overtime helps pay the bills."

Lydia thought of the sight she'd noticed on their arrival to town: the gaping opening into the mountain where the miners went underground. She suddenly realized that Simon could have ended up working underground as well, if he had not been farmed out to the old country doctor who inspired him to go into medicine. What a different life he would have had! And how did these brave wives face every morning wondering if their husbands were coming home by nightfall? Slowly she shook her head, thinking about it. It would be like living at the CCS for the rest of her days, always wondering when the next shell would hit the camp. No wonder these people treasured every minute together and lived life to the fullest!

That night, after the children bedded down, Phil took his family home, just down the street. Simon and Lydia had insisted that they sleep downstairs, on cots by the kitchen fireplace.

"You sure you kids'll be okay on cots with Lydia pregnant and all?" Rebecca asked her little brother anxiously.

"Been our steady companions for two years, Becky," he hastened to assure her. His sister had also amply supplied the two with thick quilts against the cooler air when the fire was banked for the night. And after the house grew quiet, Lydia slid into the same cot with Simon as they'd done countless times before in recent years.

"Much better," Simon said approvingly as she snuggled against him.

She was immediately transported back to the station in winter. This felt so similar to lying near their small stove in the tent, staying warm underneath their army-issued blankets. And true to the memory, the necessary was outside in the snow down below the house. Rebecca had apologized for their lack of modern plumbing, but Lydia had assured her they were no strangers to outhouses.

"This is so like being back at the station, Simon," Lydia murmured as she rested her head against his shoulder.

"Hm," he said, musing. "Even with all those little ones upstairs? And the grown-ups creaking the bed up there? They're sure making a lot of noise!" The creaking continued.

"That's what you call it?" Lydia wondered. "Creaking the bed?"

"Yep. Ah, well, it's good to know my sister and her husband are still getting along so well!" Simon chuckled. "At least there is no danger of shells falling, and there is no cold, snowy air leaking in through the cracks in the tent."

Lydia reached up and stroked his beard lovingly. "I am quite comfortable," she declared. "I like your family. They are so genuine. They're just full of life. Hearts as big as the mountains around us."

"They are good people," Simon admitted. "People who work hard, play hard, and love hard."

Lydia raised herself up in the glow of the embers of the fireplace and kissed Simon on the lips, letting herself linger there. She knew he had been energized by the return to his family beginnings, the power of life here... of living every moment to its utmost. "I get the 'work hard, play hard' part... but tell me more about 'love hard'..." she whispered, tracing his lips with her fingertips.

"I was hoping you wouldn't mind, having all the others upstairs..." he started, pulling her up off the cot, making a mat of one of the thick quilts, on the floor by the hearth. Lowering Lydia down onto it, he pulled the second quilt over top of them. "This is the love hard part..." he murmured, pulling her nightgown over her head and kissing the length of her neck. "Can't do this on a cot like we can on the floor…"

He loved her with an energy that was nearly overwhelming in front of that fireplace, on the unyielding wooden floor beneath the quilt. Perhaps it was from finally being home or from the safety of the similar yet dissimilar feeling of being back at the station in the middle of winter, with the memory of red embers burning that drove his need. He did love her hard, pacing himself until she arched up against him, the banked coals within her sparking into flame. When he finally gave himself to her, they lay exhausted in each other's arms. Lydia rolled on her side and again laid her head on his sweaty chest.

"Okay. I think I understand the loving hard part," she finally whispered, feeling the beads of moisture on his chest beneath her cheek. "Let's do that again… sometime…" The questions she had wanted to ask him had been driven out of her mind completely.

Simon smiled, now very content in the darkness, unwilling to reclaim the cot. They fell asleep that way, wrapped in the quilts on the floor. And that is how Rebecca found them early in the morning as she slipped out through the kitchen to the outhouse with a knowing smile on her face, leaving the outside door slightly open so the cold draft would wake the two up before all the others started their day. It was good to have her little brother home again.

Back in Pittsburgh, Simon was a man with two missions.

"First we find a place to live," he promised her. "Not far from the hospital so I can get home quickly if you need me."

"And I want to meet that nursing director, Sister Edwarda?" she added. "Can we go today? I'm anxious to find out about that idea she has."

He nodded. "We'll go today. Let's check this neighborhood," he suggested, as they got out of the cab. "I like how the houses join up. Keep wind from howling through."

"Look, Simon, they have little back yards. Look down that little archway between the houses. Ab will like a yard." Lydia was peering down the covered walkways between buildings.

"Watch out for those daggers overhead. Those icicles are a foot long!"

"You're the tall one!" she declared. "These are narrow, but three stories! Think your lungs can handle running up and down three stories?"

"My lungs can handle it!" he replied with a little smile. "And digging up a little garden for you out back. I am glad you came with me!" He squeezed her hard through her coat.

Then they came to a house on a corner lot. A tiny yard ran along the side to the back, and a bay window extended from the side of the house, running up two stories. Lydia just knew that a dining room was in that alcove. They saw a small back porch behind a kitchen as they walked around the corner. Lydia looked hopefully at Simon.

"Lydia, look here. There's a sign on the door about its availability." With half-frozen fingers, Simon carefully wrote down the number to call.

Retracing their steps down the block, the two took a trolley across the bridge, icy wind whipping around them. Down below, most of the river was frozen. Only the center passage was kept open by a steady stream of moving ships that defied the ice. Flocks of geese were perched down there, occasionally flying up in large groups when a steamship chugged its way through, parting the flocks.

Men near a bank were cutting ice squares from the river and sliding the large blocks up the banks using rope pulleys and logs. A little farther upstream to the east, huge iron works had been constructed along the river, smoke pouring from great chimneys of industrial mills. It was the bread and butter of the city. Lydia didn't know how many people lived here, but she calculated the human need and knew it must be great.

As they left the trolley, they crossed over the road, avoiding a few vehicles slipping past on the snowy street, and climbed up the steps to the hospital.

"We're taking a cab back!" Simon exclaimed, his cheeks red from the wind despite his beard, hat, and scarf well wrapped around his neck.

Entering the building, Simon sighed. "The heat feels overwhelming after walking in that bitter cold! Open your coat, let it in, Lydia." They returned to the administrative office and inquired about Sister Edwarda. Miss Weston remembered the young couple, the new surgeon coming on staff, and knew where to direct them. Returning to the corridor, Lydia and Simon walked to the end of the hall and up a flight of tiled stairs to the second floor. Going down the long hall, they searched the doors until they found 'Nursing Administration', stepping into a small anteroom, where a nun was working. She looked up brightly.

"How can I help you?" she said. "Other than to give you a chair to thaw out in, perhaps?"

Lydia smiled back, nodding. "It certainly is cold out there with that wind! I'm Lydia Finney. Doctor Maloney suggested I meet with Sister Edwarda when we returned to the city. Might she be available?"

"Sit down, please," the woman nodded. "I'll go and find her. I'm Sister Mary Genevive."

"A pleasure," Lydia said as she watched her leave the anteroom, her feet tapping on the tiled floor as she retreated down the hallway.

"Nervous?" Simon asked Lydia softly as she perched primly on the very edge of the winged chair beside him.

"You bet!" she admitted. "What if they don't like me?"

He laughed. "What's not to like?" he teased her, looking around to make sure no one else was nearby before leaning over to kiss her. "I love you! They will, too."

Lydia grasped her hands in her lap to warm them, and Simon saw it, taking them in his own.

"Yours are just as cold as mine!" she whispered, but she was grateful for his touch.

They separated quickly before anyone saw them, warned by the tapping of multiple shoes getting louder. Both nuns came in, the long skirts of their habits flowing around their ankles as they walked with purpose. Sister Edwarda was apparently a woman who was busy and kept things moving.

Lydia stood and extended her hand. "Sister Edwarda?"

"Indeed," the woman said, her sharp eyes taking in Lydia quickly. She was smiling.

"I'm Lydia Finney," Lydia told her. "And this is my husband, Doctor Simon Finney."

The nun also accepted Simon's outstretched hand where he stood. "You're the new surgeon Doctor Maloney spoke to me about."

"Yes, ma'am," Simon told her.

She looked at the two of them shrewdly. "You are quite young to have gone through the war. I was told some of your history."

Lydia nodded, not certain how to respond to the issue of her age.

"Please," Sister Edwarda said abruptly, "follow me, Nurse Finney."

Lydia did. They went out into the hallway, leaving a puzzled but hopeful Simon behind, and made their way back down the hall and down the stairs at the end to the first floor. There, they returned to the rotunda, but instead of heading to the outer door, they turned left, continuing straight. Lydia saw patient wards behind each door on either side of them as they walked. Finally, they approached the back of the hospital, where a large waiting room was filled with people of all ages in long rows of chairs. It was almost full. Sister Edwarda stopped in the doorway to the waiting room as Lydia beheld the mix of humanity, most bundled up against the cold, some more thinly than others. Most were coughing; some looked feverish. Many were listless. Some young children still moved around, playing on the floor. A man waited nearby with his arm in a hastily fashioned sling.

"They're so ill," Lydia exclaimed. "Out in this cold! Is this a clinic just for the poor, or for anyone sick? Or are they waiting for admission to the hospital? There must be fifty here! How many doctors?"

Sister Edwarda was pleased with the concern on the young woman's face.

"It's a walk-in clinic where people come if they cannot afford a doctor, or their doctor cannot see them in an office. It is always busy here. Our sisters run this clinic and teach healthy behaviors. A doctor is always here, but they do get a bit overwhelmed. Sometimes, people pay a small amount for the care that they receive, but they'll be seen even if they cannot pay."

"With all these people, it would be important to triage the urgent," Lydia murmured to herself more than the nun, trying to determine how the flow of needs was being processed. "Is there a separate area for treating those with coughs from those with injuries? Do they all get seen together? Are there places for the nuns to wash between patients?"

Sister Edwarda nodded. "In the back rooms, there are wash stations," she said. "But at this time, there are so many coming in with illness that it's difficult to separate the injured from the ill. We are trying. But also, many of these should not be out in the cold coming for care. They should not be bringing their healthy young children and exposing them to all the other diseases."

Lydia nodded. "But what's a young mother to do when there is an illness other than bring them all with her? These people don't look as though they have nannies working for them in their homes."

Sister Edwarda smiled. "That's where you might help me."

"Me?" Lydia asked eagerly.

The Sister's eyes twinkled. She had already seen the interest in this young woman's expression and hoped it would soon convert to a commitment to service at the hospital. "Yes, you," Sister nodded. "I need two things. I need someone skilled at triage in this clinic so we can better care for patients. Someone familiar with first aid-type injuries and able to take immediate measures if called upon to do so."

"And second?" Lydia started, waiting.

"Second is something dear to my heart. I want nurses who can go out to the homes so that the mothers do not have to bundle up their little ones and bring them in here when one of them is ill or injured. I foresee nurses going to the homes to check on patients newly discharged from the hospital, perhaps after surgery, illness, or childbirth, to see how they are recovering in their homes. I believe you might have the kind of experience needed to do such independent thinking."

Lydia looked at all the people waiting miserably. Of course, many of them needed to see a doctor, not a nurse. But others perhaps needed to be taught to contain their illnesses, to keep infection from spreading through the family, to safely ride out an illness at home. And visiting someone following surgery would be the same as going to the recovery tent at the station, watching, changing a dressing, taking out sutures, keeping an eye out for infection. She could see the possibilities.

"I would very much like to do something like this!" Lydia exclaimed softly. "It would be similar to the Henry Street Station in Manhattan, wouldn't it?"

"A little. But Miss Wald's endeavors focus on taking nursing to the public schools, and that is not my desire," Sister Edwarda explained. "We can teach people how to reduce infections and recover at home. The pay is nine dollars a week. I envision shared time here in the clinic and going out to homes as families become aware of what we can offer. I'm looking for nurses who can think carefully, recognizing when someone must be brought in, or if they can be safely cared for at home. My vision, God willing, is teams of nurses spread out all over the city seeing people."

Lydia nodded, seeing her future unfolding before her eyes. And a married woman could be accepted doing this kind of work? "You know that I am expecting, Sister?"

"Yes, my dear, Doctor Maloney mentioned it. When are you anticipating the birth?"

"Around Easter," Lydia said, reviewing her mental calculations. "And I have a small problem."

"How can I help?" the nun asked. She was willing to help any way she could if it meant the young Red Cross nurse staying and coming to work for her.

"I'd like to give birth at home, but I don't know any midwives in the city," Lydia said anxiously. Her earlier conversation with Simon replayed in her mind. She still did not want to come to the hospital for the birth of her baby. She wanted to be surrounded by people she loved, not strangers. She wanted Simon there.

Sister Edwarda nodded. "I know women who are quite skilled at home births. Sister Anne comes immediately to mind."

"You don't mind if I work before the baby comes?" Lydia asked.

"As long as you are healthy, I do not," Sister Edwarda declared. "And as your time approaches, you could remain in the clinic instead of going out to homes. By then, I hope we will have other nurses doing what I would like you to help us set up."

"And after the baby?" Lydia almost dared to ask. "Could there be any accommodation? If I breast feed? Or would returning to work be forbidden?"

"We'll see," the senior nurse said with a twinkle in her eye. "There might be a way. Our nuns have been known to enjoy holding an infant back in the exam hall."

Lydia was overjoyed to have found a way to make a difference. She could hardly wait to tell Simon about the reception she had been given and the possibilities being explored.

But that night at the hotel, Simon was less than enthusiastic about her opportunities at Charity. He listened carefully to everything Lydia told him about Sister Edwarda's proposal. He listened over their supper in the hotel dining room. Then he listened as Lydia pondered what kinds of patients would need to be seen in their homes. Certainly, she had the experience. She had treated pneumonia, measles, vision loss, sprains, dislocations, shell shock, amputations, wounds of every single form, complications from infections, and noxious gases. She was skilled at the triage of the wounded and sick who came through their camp. It would certainly demand more than what was now asked of Suzie. Simon could see the eager anticipation in Lydia's eyes of being able to serve as a nurse.

"Are you glad for me, Simon?" she pressed him over their dinner. "Nine dollars a week! I could contribute to our home. And think of the good I can do!"

He nodded. "Sister Edwarda has a powerful vision. I can see why she'd find your background so appealing."

Lydia rested her elbows on the table and grasped her hands together. "I hear a but...."

He put his fork down.

"That looks serious," Lydia said.

Simon nodded. "I have one but…" he started. "Your safety. I'm not worried about you being at the clinic in the back of the hospital where there are people around to help you. But what if you are in a house and something goes wrong? I'd worry about you constantly, and whether you'd make it home in one piece every day. How could I be stuck in an operating theater knowing you were out walking the streets by yourself? And with the baby coming? What if you went into labor early while you were out seeing patients?" *What if some man assaults you, and I'm not there to stop him?*

"You did the same thing in West Virginia, Simon," Lydia objected, "when you did country medicine. Didn't you tell me you never knew what you and Doctor Albright would run into when you got to someone's farm? Didn't you help train nuns to go out into the countryside in West Virginia? How could you train nuns to do this but tell me it's unsafe for me to do it?"

Simon looked hard at her. She had an amazing memory. He had told her a long time ago about some nuns coming to learn country medicine with him before the war. She would have to remember that now and use it in her argument! "Yes, but it was different with me being a man, and they were certainly not pregnant, and they were not my wife!" he exclaimed in protest.

Lydia sat motionless, her hands clasped tightly together, over her unfinished plate. "Simon, this is important to me," she said softly.

He nodded, his brown eyes compassionate, but full of worry. "I know. I don't… I can't stand the thought of you being hurt again. You've been through enough pain and suffering back in France. This is a big city. There are men from all walks of life out on the streets and coming off ships back from the war. There are bars and pubs in every neighborhood where men might be drunk and stupid."

"I'm not going to be out at six o'clock at night when pubs are filling up, my love," she said softly. "And in the city, I'm sure there are policemen patrolling the streets."

"Of course..." he agreed. "Still, I wish you could just be with me in the surgery."

"Well, I can't be with you in the surgery, Simon!" she exploded suddenly. "I wish I could, too! But they won't let me, so that's that!" After the outburst, she withdrew into her thoughts. Simon knew that this was not simply the emotions of pregnancy talking; this was part of her being. The very character trait that had caused her to go to Europe, the same trait that had caused her to bravely jump down from that truck at the station, the day he had first laid eyes on her. The same trait he had immediately fallen in love with. "I'm sorry," she added, embarrassed, lowering her voice, aware of the staring eyes in the dining room.

That night in bed, they agreed not to discuss Sister Edwarda's proposal, though it was at the forefront of both of their minds as they lay in the darkness. Simon pulled Lydia into his arms and stroked her back. He knew, even without seeing her eyes, that she was wide awake, thinking things over. "I just love you and our baby so much," he softly assured her.

"I love you, too," she whispered. "That's not the issue."

"I know," he replied quietly. He just couldn't bear the thought of someone hurting her again. "Just needed to say it."

"When we were at your sister's house," Lydia began, "there was a lot of creaking going on upstairs, remember?" She felt him nod, the hand stroking her back paused for a second before resuming its path. Lydia continued. "You told me they 'work hard, play hard, and love hard'..."

Simon nodded again, remembering their intense night on the floor in the quilts before the fireplace.

Lydia continued. "Well, I talked with Rebecca and Alice about that, while you and Phillip were in town, taking care of your banking matters. I asked them about what it was like for them, with their husbands going down into the mines every day... after listening to you talk about explosions and cave-ins. And they said you were right. Life is hard. They put everything into their children, their cooking, sewing, and their homes. They put everything into making love to their husbands because they never know when sirens will go off. And I know you understand that. Because when Doctor Fortraine gave you the orders to leave for the British CCS, you immediately led me back to the cot in our tent, and made love to me before you left. You packed up your clothes and were gone. You disappeared for months, and I had no idea if I would ever hold you in my arms again. I understand risk."

"And I remember when you didn't come back when the Germans took you prisoner," Simon countered. "I didn't know, night after night, if they had killed you, or taken you to a prison in Germany. No way to find you. I was utterly powerless to be able to save you, though I had sworn to protect you with my life. And you finally returned, bloody and wounded. I vowed to myself to never let that happen to you again, ever."

"Neither of us want to go through any of that again," Lydia said softly. "We both understand the love hard part, don't we, Simon?" She reached up, touching his cheek reassuringly. "We both thought we'd lost this, but we didn't. We made it back to each other. And like your sister and brother, we need to make the most of every day together and hold onto the days like the treasure they are. I know you want me to be happy, and I don't want to worry you. I said in my wedding vows that I would try not to worry you too much or be too headstrong, causing you to be afraid for me. Remember my vow?"

"Every word," Simon said.

"So let me take Abril with me, when I'm out seeing patients. I'll keep her with me. She'll keep me safe from anyone stumbling out of a pub too early in the day... you won't be afraid if Abril is walking right beside me, sitting right outside someone's door."

Simon let out a sigh, releasing a breath he'd been holding for far too long. *Why didn't I think of that?* he wondered in amazement.

"Of course, take Abril with you. She loves being outside, even in winter. She's very protective of you, always has been ever since she lead you back from the German trenches. Abril! Of course!"

"Now," Lydia said, raising herself up on one elbow in the darkness, trying to see his face in the dim lights of the city. "Does that settle it?"

He buried his hands in her long hair, wrapping his fingers in the waves as she kissed his neck. "Yes," he admitted. "That settles it."

"Good," she murmured, kissing his chest, then his stomach, and continuing. "Because I want to try the love hard part again, here, before we return to Mom and Dad's, with them right down the hall..."

Simon just smiled. He was more than equal to the happy task.

Chapter 5
Deck the Halls

Christmas was just around the corner now. Lydia and Simon had returned safely to Greensburg, where an overjoyed Abril was all too happy to have them back under her watchful eye. Lydia was helping her mother finish up the lunch dishes when Simon rose to answer a knock at the door.

"Look, Lydia!" Simon was waving a yellow paper in one hand. "Marc says they're coming!"

Lydia ran from the kitchen, wrapping her arms around Simon. "She must have said yes! I wonder if they'll get married up there, or in the city?"

"Doesn't say. You'll have to wait for all the juicy details, my love," Simon laughed. "I've gotta send Marc an update about the hospital interview Doctor Maloney wants to schedule with him."

"Make sure you tell him that our house has three floors! Lots of room!" Lydia reminded Simon as he took off for the telegraph office, Abril at his side. "Even if there are no beds yet." She called after him.

Lydia closed the door and returned to her mother, who was humming as she readied the house, excited to have both of her children's families home for the holiday. Lydia was excited too;

Simon was taking her to the town's local Christmas dance at the civic center, in honor of the town's brave soldiers—a real dance.

The regular mail arrived while Simon was out, sending his telegram. Lydia thanked the postman, and took the stack of envelopes to her mother, whose hands were full of garlands and mistletoe. "Let your father read through it all," Anna told her daughter from atop a small step ladder.

Lydia seamlessly redirected herself to her father who sat in his chair by the fireplace. "Mail call—sounds like the army!" She cheerfully delivered her bundle, then ran upstairs to change for the evening's festivities.

Lydia carefully considered the dresses in her bedroom closet. *I have just the perfect thing*, she thought, a nostalgic smile lighting her face. She carefully explored their suitcase, finding the flowing, blue wedding dress... with the three-quarter sleeves, a high waist, and slightly daring neckline which Gretha Bernstein had hand-sewn for her in camp. *It's perfect.* She slipped into the dress and ran downstairs for her mother's help to fasten the hook by the nape of her neck.

Happy to oblige, Anna climbed down from her step stool. "It's lovely—you'll need a necklace and earrings," Anna took her hand. "Come back up with me, and we'll take a look."

Lydia followed her mother up the wooden stairs. "Why don't you and Dad come with us," she urged her mother. "It'll be so much fun."

"We used to love the dances," her mother said with a smile, opening the door to their room. "But he gets a bit tired from the exertion now. No, this Christmas Eve we'll dance to the radio, right here in our own living room. Now, let's see—this small chain would be perfect. And oh my, just above the cut of that neckline! How daring!" Anna carefully sorted through the beautiful pieces in her little jewelry box in the top drawer of her dresser. "And two little bobs for your ears. Shall we pull your hair back with a ribbon?"

Lydia looked at herself in their full length mirror. "No, I think I'll leave it down. Do I look alright? Simon's only seen me wear this once, when the other nurses and doctors had a party for us after we were married."

Her mother hugged her. "You look beautiful. Your dress flares just enough, and in the right places... but soon you'll be needing some looser dresses to wear."

"True," Lydia said, smoothing the dress over her belly and looking critically at the results. "The baby has been more active lately. It's such a wonderful feeling."

Anna sighed. "How well I remember!"

"You'll come to our new house when the baby is due, won't you, Mom?" Lydia asked. "I want you to be there to hold your new little grand-something."

"Of course!" Anna exclaimed. "I wouldn't miss your baby!"

"I'm used to caring for wounded men. Tiny babies are a completely different matter. I could use your advice," Lydia assured her, kissing her cheek fondly. They returned downstairs, and Lydia saw her father deep in thought, reading the mail.

He looked up as she twirled, her dress flowing. "Is that appropriate for mixed company?" he exclaimed with a raised eyebrow.

"Oh, Dad, of course it is. These are modern times, you know. And everyone will be having a good time, not paying attention to me. Why don't you take Mom?"

"I don't think so, Lydia. I'm tired, but I'm glad you young people can have a good time." He held out a paper. "Look at this..."

She took the sheet of paper, immediately recognizing the handwriting. The beginning was her own, and farther down, Simon's familiar script took over. The delayed letters were finally arriving. This particular letter announced their marriage, detailing her love for Simon. It also included a passage where Simon introduced himself and described their wedding in Nancy.

The news had finally reached her father—Lydia looked up, relieved. "It's just like he told you, Dad. Everything was done in the right order, just as Simon said when we got here. We did write, you see now?"

"I do," Andrew replied. "And I apologized to Simon for questioning his morals. You weren't in the room, but I did apologize, man to man."

Lydia bent over and kissed his head. "I know, Dad. Simon told me right away."

He grunted. "Don't bend over too far in the dress!"

"Oh, Dad," she sighed, smiling as she went to help her mother with the decorations.

Simon announced his return, letting Abril trot in first before closing the door. The moment he spotted Lydia, his eyes lit up with pleasure at the sight of her.

"I haven't seen you wear your wedding party dress since France!" he declared, delighted. "And you're as lovely in it now as you were the day Stockton walked you from the tent to the mess hall. When I saw you walking in the sun that day, my heart almost stopped." He lightly touched the necklace and inspected the earrings clipped to her lobes. "I will certainly be monopolizing your dance card!" he murmured in her ear.

Lydia's father called out from his chair, "You kids take the Ford."

"Thanks, Dad," Lydia replied as Simon pulled her coat from the closet, bundling her against the cold winter evening. Abril accepted a head rub, while she enjoyed the cold air on the front porch and watched the couple get into the car, disappointed she wasn't going along.

Lydia and Simon made their way to the community center which was ablaze with festive lights around the windows and doors. Taking Lydia's arm, Simon led her through the crowd which was dancing to the lively music of a small band of musicians playing violin, bass, trombone, drum, and clarinet. There were many young men in army uniforms, already twirling or holding young women close to them, enjoying a last fling of freedom. Along one wall, a table of drinks and finger foods was also crowded with people. Small tables had been set up where people were laughing or talking in little groups and tapping their feet to the music.

"See anyone you know?" Simon asked cheerfully as they hung their coats on a waiting rack.

"I can't see a single face with these lights!" Lydia exclaimed. "But if I find any high school girlfriends, I want to show you off."

Simon took her by the hand. "Well, I'm going to show you off first!" He wrapped an arm around her waist, steering her to the dance floor, jostling for position among all the other couples moving to the rhythm of popular songs. He enjoyed the way her blue dress flowed around her legs and how her chestnut hair shone in the soft lights of the decorations.

"Last time you wore this, you had boots on," he said in her ear as she leaned her head against his neck.

"Last time I wore this dress, I also was not wearing any pretty underthings," she reminded him. "Or this pretty jewelry."

"That's true," he told her. "You spin better in these shoes."

She looked up at him and laughed. "And you're just as nimble in your shoes, mister! I do love how you look in that turtleneck sweater. Like a college professor or something. And I do love the feel of your beard on my cheek."

"Hm, was thinking maybe of shaving it off for my new position..." he murmured.

"Don't you dare!" she exclaimed in horror. "I love your beard. You aren't serious, are you, Simon? They won't make you shave your beard, will they?"

Simon laughed out loud. "Sounds like you're afraid of what you'll find underneath!"

She looked into his eyes as he gently twirled her out and then rolled her back into his arms. "I just like how it feels..." she said daringly. Simon didn't miss her meaning.

"That so? Hm. Maybe we should just go home right now..." he laughed, pulling her body closer, and they danced every dance the musicians played without stopping. Finally, the band took a short break and everyone began to find a place to sit for a minute. "Want a drink?" Simon asked her.

"Love it," Lydia replied, just a little breathless.

Simon moved through the crowd over to the refreshment table decked with pine wreaths and candles. There were several neatly pressed young soldiers milling about, talking about leaving for Europe right after Christmas Day. Intentionally eavesdropping, Simon squeezed in beside them at the punch bowl.

"Where are you guys off to?" he inquired.

"New York, then London! Or France, I'd imagine," one of the young men said eagerly. "We're leaving Monday."

"Keep your heads down," Simon said.

One of the young men looked at him curiously. "You been there?"

Simon nodded as he filled two glasses with punch, from the large bowl on the table. "I have. Just got back. Did my two years, to the day."

Now the younger men gathered around him, eager to hear about what was coming their way, from someone who knew more than the newspapers and the sergeant in boot camp could tell them. "Where were you?" one of the men asked. "Did you see any fighting?" another pressed further.

"France, Belgium," Simon said simply. "All over the eastern region."

The men looked at each other, wondering—they'd heard about eastern France. "How'd you do two years already?" one of them asked cautiously. "We just declared war. The army just mobilized this summer."

Simon offered a measured smile. "The French and British have been fighting since fourteen," he reminded them. "I volunteered with the French in late fifteen. Got discharged in November."

"Wow," one of the men said. "You really haven't been back long! There've been reports of some pretty heavy fighting all year. Wonder what we're getting ourselves into. Are they exaggerating? Do you think we'll see any real action?"

"Yeah, well, the reports are accurate," Simon admitted. "But I think the American Army is well equipped. France has lost too many of its young men. It should be better for you fellas."

"Well, parlez-vous!" one man exclaimed. "Sure hope I remember some French words if I run into any of those French women—"

"So, what words of advice have you got for us?" another asked quickly. "The sergeant says we're going to be fine if we keep our boots clean and our rifles spotless."

They peppered Simon with questions as the musicians started to play again. The earnest young men were so eager to go, and also equally afraid... but did not want to show it. Simon took the time to share a few words of wisdom with them while he had a chance. He told them to leave nothing unfinished here at home and to take their faith in God with them. They would need it on the battlefield.

Lydia had found two empty seats for them at a little table. She had also spotted a dear girlfriend from school after all! Lydia called out for her to come sit until Simon returned. The two hugged briefly, exclaiming nearly in unison, "You haven't changed a bit," and "How long has it been?" So much had happened while she was overseas. Lydia was deep into the local news by the time the music was starting up again. As the two friends laughed, Lydia felt a tug on her arm, pulling her up to dance. She finished her thought, and turned to introduce Simon to her friend... but it was not Simon's face attached to the hand around her arm.

"My turn," the man said, placing his other arm firmly around her waist.

"Derrick!" Lydia exclaimed in pure shock. "Where did you come from? I thought you were teaching out in Colorado or Utah... or somewhere out west!"

"You look simply ravishing, as always," Derrick examined her in her blue dress, touching the gold chain that lay against her skin. "I could hardly believe it was you when I caught sight of you! I'm back for the holidays and extremely pleased to find you here, my dear. I see you survived your little stunt, going off to be a nurse in the cause of freedom."

Lydia pulled back, but he held her tightly in his arms, steering the two of them toward the middle of the crowded dance floor, where couples were pressed together as the music played. He breathed in her perfume, his face near her hair.

"Derrick," she protested, "I burned your letter, in a fire in France—and that was the end of us."

"Don't say that, Lydia!" he protested softly in her ear. "You're gorgeous. Now that you're back and got those altruistic notions out of your head, we can pick up where we left off. Things didn't work out with Linda."

"It's not going to happen... I'm married, Derrick!" she exclaimed a little too loudly so others close to them could hear her over the sound of the music. She tried to disentangle herself from his arms.

At just that moment, another man approached, tapping Derrick's shoulder, causing him to loosen his grip ever so slightly, and without hesitation, this bearded stranger used the opportunity to wedge himself between Lydia and her captor.

"I'm cutting in, buddy," Simon said smoothly, sliding his arm around Lydia's waist and pulling her away and into his own embrace.

"I had her first, 'buddy'!" Derrick echoed hotly, his cheeks reddening at the intrusion.

Simon turned to face him squarely, his tone even but palpably intense. "Yes, you did, Derrick. And you gave her up—a fact for which I will be forever grateful. I was there when she burned your letter. And no, there's no picking it up again. Lydia is my wife."

Derrick stood alone on the dance floor, anger twisting his features as Simon moved Lydia safely away from the man. Lydia raised her arms up around Simon's neck, looked into his brown eyes, and kissed him right on the lips in front of the crowded hall.

He held fast around her waist. "So, that was Derrick," he said. "I always wondered what the fool looked like!"

"That was Derrick... and as you can see, he doesn't hold a candle to you, Simon!" she exclaimed, thinking once again how relieved she was to have this man as her husband and not Derrick, who was already pulling some other young woman from a chair to dance. "How did I get so blessed to find you?"

Simon kissed her gently as they danced. His brown eyes twinkling.

"I wondered if he'd show up at some point. Must admit, I was curious," was all Simon said as the musicians started a slow rendition of "Silent Night". Lydia leaned into him, relishing the music swirling around them and the feel of Simon holding her tight.

Exhausted after the dance, Lydia and Simon warmed themselves in the kitchen. At the sound of a car pulling up, Anna jumped up from her seat at the table. Her Christmas wish was fulfilled as Lydia's sister and her family bustled in through the front door. Anna hurried to the foyer to greet them, with Lydia close behind, but Abril waited patiently, wary of the newcomers.

"Oh, my goodness, it's good to see you, Peggy!" Lydia exclaimed, taking her older sister in her arms before the woman was even able to shake the snow from her shoes.

Her sister laughed. "So, you really are back from Europe? Well, I'll be. I was shocked to hear from Mom and Dad about your surprise visit."

"It was only a surprise because the mail is so slow," Lydia clarified.

"Understandable. I hear there's a war on over there," Peggy teased, pulling off her coat and looking carefully at her younger sister. "Well, you at least look like you're in one piece!"

Her husband, Tommy, then came through the door with their daughter in his arms and their son holding his hand.

"Tom!" Lydia exclaimed. "It's good to see you!" She looked down to the boy at his side. "Steven, look how grown you are already. Are you... six?"

The boy looked up at her curiously, knowing she should be familiar, but not recognizing her.

"It's your Aunt Lydia, Steven," Peggy told the boy, bringing him over, to reacquaint them.

He looked withdrawn, but Lydia reached out and shook his hand. "I know you probably don't remember me," she reassured this shorter version of Tommy, "but I'm your momma's sister."

Tommy let Lydia take his coat as he put down the little girl in his arms who pulled off her scarf and mittens, all on her own. "Mary, say hello to your Aunt Lydia," Tommy prompted the little girl.

Lydia knelt beside her. "Hello, Mary," she said softly. "What a pretty baby doll you have! Is she your special doll?"

The four-year-old nodded, but was also reserved, somewhat distant, and clutched her rag doll to her side. It looked well-loved. Lydia looked up to see Simon coming into the foyer while drying his hands on a kitchen towel.

"So, this is the man you married, I assume?" Peggy exclaimed, extending her hand to Simon. "I'm Peggy."

"One and the same," Simon smiled, reaching out in return to shake her hand. And Lydia rose to her feet and slipped an arm into Simon's while continuing the introductions.

Tommy reached around the women blocking his path in the small entryway and shook the other man's hand as well. "So, you're a doctor, huh?"

Simon nodded. "Yep. We were just finishing up the dishes in the kitchen. There's dessert on the table still. And coffee, if you want some."

Peggy looked at Simon. "You washed dishes? Where'd you find this one Lyd—"

"Peg!" Tommy said sharply, but under his breath.

She stopped quickly. "Oh, I'm sorry."

"In France," Lydia said, smiling, picking up the thread of her sister's questioning.

"Figures," Peggy replied, taking her daughter by the hand and leading her into the living room, where little Mary ran right up to Anna. The child was comfortable with her grandmother and eager to see her as Steven greeted his grandfather, who was seated through all of this, in his favorite chair.

Crossing the room, Tommy shook Andrew's hand. "Dad, how do you feel?" he asked.

"Pretty good, son," Andrew nodded. "Good to have you all come for Christmas. Good to have everyone home."

Tommy took a seat on the couch with Steven perching beside him. "You need me to put coal in the furnace, Dad?"

"Not now," Andrew told him. "But later, yes."

Tommy nodded as Peggy joined them on the sofa and Simon pulled in a couple of chairs from the kitchen table. Taking her spot in her easy chair, Anna pulled Mary and her doll up onto her lap. The child was so painfully shy that Anna's grandmotherly heart was always moved by her.

Anna looked around the crowded living room, her joy over-flowing.

"Now it feels like Christmas," she sighed. "Everyone together."

From the sofa, Tommy directed his attention to Lydia. "Last Christmas was tough on Mom and Dad with you in Europe." It was a simple statement of fact, but blatantly laced with disapproval.

"I've no doubt," Lydia nodded. "It was difficult for everyone, being so far away—"

"Taking off like that with no warning," Tommy continued, "nearly gave Dad a heart attack. Worried Mom sick."

Lydia felt her eyes welling up. "I'm sure it was a shock."

Peggy placed a gentle hand on Tommy's arm to stay him. "Now Tommy, please, it's a holiday."

He shot her such a withering look that Peggy immediately withdrew her hand from his arm. Her cheeks flushed. Steven slid off of the sofa to look at the Christmas tree ornaments.

Tommy was on a roll, "Some things need to be said, Peg. It's better to get it out in the open. Mom and Dad suffered a lot worrying about you, Lydia. You left us to help them pick up the pieces and try to hold them together, having no idea if their daughter would survive and make it back home. It was cruel."

At this, Anna quickly intervened, "It's all good now, Tom. When they first got here, we talked about all of that. I understand much better now what motivated Lydia to join up with the nurses. Yes, it was hard for us, but it also was a brave thing for her to do and for such a good cause!"

Simon reached out and took Lydia's hand, for reassurance.

But Tommy had not finished making his point. "Brave or not, good cause or not, you should have said goodbye, Lydia, so they could have had a chance to make sense of it and tell you their concerns. You might have reconsidered and saved everyone a lot of hardship," he insisted forcefully.

Lydia nodded. "That's why I couldn't say goodbye, Tom. It was something I needed to do. So, I wrote to explain while I waited to board the ship and mailed it right as we left Philadelphia... and sent more letters after that."

"We did get a couple letters, Tommy, remember?... But why did you go, Lydia?" Peggy asked her sister mid thought. Lydia knew they had waited two years to ask this. "When America wasn't even at war with Germany yet? American soldiers weren't even over there yet."

Lydia was filled with compassion for her family. She had known this would be hard all along, from her first decision in Philadelphia to board the ship and leave. She had known then, as she did now, that they would not easily comprehend her motivation.

"I went," she said softly, "because there were so many young men dying. And if I could help some of them live to get back to their families, families just like ours, who love each other, then it would be worth it."

"So, you cared more about strangers than your own family—it didn't have to be you," Tommy objected, reflecting the sentiments of so many in the States who objected to American involvement in Europe. "Someone from over there could have done the same thing."

Simon cleared his throat, unable to listen to this in silence. "I volunteered as well," he interjected. "I enlisted, then also volunteered to join the French medical unit in November of fifteen, with two other American doctors. Too many of the French had already died. The French were standing in the gap against the Axis forces—Germany is intent on bringing the war across the ocean, Tom. There were eleven other American nurses who joined our medical unit along with Lydia. We, the doctors, were in awe of their courage because they saw what was on the line and chose to risk their own lives to make a difference."

Her eyes filled as Lydia remembered. "Most of the others are still there, still in the fight, still helping France to stand. Good, talented people helping to hold off a great evil. I don't expect any of you to understand, but I'd hoped that you'd respect me enough to know that I would never have risked pain to my own family unless the cause was truly worthy."

Tommy, was visibly unsatisfied, and shot a look at Peg as she jumped in, interrupting what he was about to say.

"I do admire your wanting to save lives," Peggy admitted. "But the war is still going on, and now our boys are going over, too. Was it worth it, if people are just going to continue to die?"

Lydia looked at Simon, unable to find the right words; he reached out and touched her cheek in reassurance.

"Yes," Lydia said, thinking of the faces of the many casualties that they had helped, the bodies they had sewn back together, while shells thudded against the countryside, close enough to rattle the ground. "Yes, it was more than worth it."

Simon pulled his chair closer to hers, slipping an arm around her. The look between them was beyond comprehension to the others in the room, who had not been there and could not know... but Lydia knew the look of remembrance in his eyes. She squeezed his hand tightly, thankful for the strength of his arm around her. Simon knew. Simon understood. That was enough for her.

It was not enough for Tommy, who had grown deeply resentful of the admiration the couple was receiving.

After everyone had gone to bed, Tommy pulled Peggy out of the house, out to their parked car, under the dull glow of the streetlights—no one else was out on this frigid Christmas Eve. He pushed her into the back seat and shut the door hard behind them.

"Tommy, it's freezing out here!" Peggy whispered anxiously.

"You interrupted me, you disagreed with me, and you mocked me, Peg," Tommy reminded her, pulling her over his knees. "It's intolerable. Just because your sister is back, you don't have the right to treat me like this." He reached down beneath the front seat and withdrew the slat of wood he kept ever near him, no matter where they were.

"I'm sorry, Tommy. Please…" Peg begged him quietly. "Tomorrow's Christmas. I can't be hobbling around…"

"Face down. You already mentioned that it's a holiday after you made such a big deal about that dish-washing doctor," he reminded her, his hands readying her in the darkness of the automobile. "Can't just let that go." It took Peggy's breath away, tears filling her eyes as her hands searched around the car floor for something to hold on to, which was Tom's ankle.

"Please Tom, I'll be more careful," she wept, her face buried in the seat cushion.

"Yes, you will," he agreed. "Damn, I wish I had more room! Isn't gonna be as effective as you need it to be…" Even in the confined space of their car, he wore his arm out. Finally, he slid the wood beneath the seat again, pulling her back across the dark snow-covered yard into the silent kitchen and up the stairs. She longed to just sit in the snow, letting her tears, along with her backside, freeze into numbness.

Pressure from the baby on her bladder woke Lydia. She slipped out of bed quietly to avoid waking Simon and headed to the bathroom, just as Peggy was coming out. She was still in her dress.

"Are you just coming up to bed, sis?" Lydia asked, astonished.

Peg nodded. "We were… Tom wanted to… talk… in the car."

"It's freezing out there!" Lydia exclaimed. "Good grief! What on earth was so important?"

Peggy's eyes looked troubled. "I shouldn't have, well, I disrespected Tom earlier."

Lydia was shocked. "I... didn't hear any disrespect," she was confused.

"Well, he felt it. I need to be more careful what I say," Peg said quietly, moving over for Lydia to get into the bathroom. She bumped back into the door frame and winced; Lydia noticed.

"You in pain, Peg?" she asked quickly. "Need me to check something?"

Peggy brushed it off. "No, no, I'm just tired. I'd better not keep him waiting."

"O...kay," Lydia whispered. "Get some rest then, sis." She went into the bathroom and quietly closed the door, tended to her needs, then returned to her room, rubbing Abril's ears. The dog woofed anxiously. "Lots of strange people, huh, girl?" Lydia then slid back into bed beside Simon who stirred slightly draping an arm over her.

After leaving the bathroom, Peg slid under the covers next to a waiting Tommy. With dread, she felt her gown being pulled up over her hips. He wanted her, as he always did after correcting her, and she didn't want to wake the children sleeping on mats beside them. Tommy pulled her up on top of him. In the back seat, the correction had been lacking so now he gripped her with his fingers as she met his need. Tears spilled from her eyes as Peg endured until Tom was done. As he finally fell asleep, she rolled off of him. She was more than a little worried; this time he hadn't been drunk.

Christmas morning dawned crisp and clear, with a fresh snowfall glittering in the early morning light. Lydia looked out from the upstairs bedroom window, where Peggy and she had played as children, building snowmen and making trails through the cold powder. She and Simon washed up before the others woke. There was no sound yet from Peggy's old room where the family slept. Lydia looked in her little closet for a suitable, comfortable dress to put on for Christmas Day while Simon stretched out again on the bed, watching her choose.

"You handled your family well last night," he observed softly. "Those weren't easy things to hear."

"I knew they wouldn't be able to understand," Lydia told him. "But knowing that you do, makes it alright." She looked down at him gratefully as she reached for her slip.

His hand reached for hers. "Don't put that on yet," he smiled, a playful look in his eyes.

"They'll all be getting up soon. I was going to start breakfast."

"I'm hungry now," he teased her, drawing her back into bed. "And I want to give you my Christmas present."

She frowned. "Simon, we talked about this. We agreed—no gifts!"

Simon pulled her back down. "Yes, we did." He nestled her back into the pillows, positioning himself on top of her. "Because you and our baby are the best gifts in the world, for me. And I intend to be the best gift in the world for you, for a little while here..."

Lydia sighed in anticipation as she felt his hands begin to roam. "Oh, Simon," she exhaled. "You know, just exactly, how to touch me so that I cannot say no to you..."

He always enjoyed waking her body with his touch. "You know," he murmured between caresses, "if you start feeling uncomfortable with the baby growing, I'll get creative..."

She felt her body beginning to melt under his care. "You mean you can be even more creative than you already are? I find that hard to believe..."

"Try this..." he whispered with a little smile, her eyes closing in pleasure, as he offered the gift of himself to her this Christmas morning.

After they held each other for a bit, Lydia broke the comfortable silence, "Someday, when I am earning a little money, I will buy you a real present, one that you can unwrap from under our very own Christmas tree."

He smiled at her and kissed her lips. "So you'll wrap a ribbon around yourself and lay down right on the floor under the branches?"

She touched his beard gently, "No, I'm serious. You gave me the music box last Christmas in the middle of a war; it means so much to me. And I want to give you something in return... but if you give me money to go buy something, it won't mean as much as if I can do it myself."

He rolled onto his side to look at her body, still naked beside him. "Lydia, I don't want for a single thing," he said simply, enjoying the feel of her. "Just knowing I can come home to you everyday, that's all I want."

"Still, one day, I'll give you a gift you can unwrap." She smiled, gazing into his eyes.

"Sounds like you already have something in mind..." There was a hint of curiosity in his voice.

"Well, yes, I do," she said. "But right now, if I've satisfied one of your appetites, I'd like to satisfy another!"

He leaned over and playfully nibbled on her shoulder. "Okay, for now, but they do recommend at least two full meals a day."

She sat up and kissed his lips gently. "You'll wear me out."

"I'm up for the challenge," he laughed softly as she stood and slid into her clothes while he clasped his hands behind his head, watching her.

"Are you coming down yet?" she asked.

"Just taking in the view..."

"Oh, Simon," she sighed happily. "I'll see you downstairs, then."

Lydia ran lightly down the stairs, surprised to see Tommy in the kitchen putting the percolator on to boil. She thought they were all still asleep upstairs.

"Good morning," Lydia said, determined to be cheerful on Christmas.

The man nodded. "When's your baby due again?"

"Sometime around Easter," Lydia said brightly, gently patting her tummy.

Tommy leaned against the counter. "You know, your sister's had two. You could learn from her. She knows how to be a good wife and mother."

"I'm sure she has!" Lydia said, reaching into the icebox for eggs and butter. "You know, Tommy, I do remember when your children were born. Mary arrived just before I left for nurse training."

He nodded. "You were dating Derrick then, working at the bank."

"Mm-hmm," she said, cracking eggs into a bowl and preparing to fry some bacon. "I was."

"Why didn't you stay with Derrick?" Tommy asked. "He would have provided for you."

"Oh, you know how it is, Tommy," Lydia said. "We didn't have that much in common. Anyway, he ended up going off to Colorado or somewhere out west."

"Maybe you didn't know how to take care of his needs," Tommy said quietly. "Maybe you were holding out on him."

Lydia looked up from the pan. "What a strange thing to say! Derrick and I weren't married, Tommy. There was no holding out to discuss."

"Didn't stop your sister," he observed. "She knew better than to say no to me."

Lydia paused, the bacon in her hand only partially separated. "What you and my sister did is a private matter between the two of you, Tommy," she said softly. "I don't need to know about it."

He bristled at her correction. "You could learn a lot from your sister, especially now that you have a man to take care of," Tommy observed. "He really is your husband, right, Lydia? You didn't just make up that whole marriage bit did you? When you got knocked up? Well, regardless, don't you go putting ideas into Peggy's mind about being so independent and headstrong. She knows her place and she doesn't need any new ideas from a wayward little sister."

Lydia's voice was intentionally controlled. "I don't tell my sister how to live her life. I would insist on the same consideration from you, Tommy."

He reached out, gripping her wrist with surprising, unnecessary force. "Mind yourself now that you're home, Lydia. You're too willful for your own good, and I doubt Simon knows how to keep a woman in line. So, don't start filling Peggy's head with ideas she shouldn't hear. You're even more headstrong than you were two years ago. It won't end well for you if you influence her."

Lydia stared at his hand on her wrist until he removed it. And after he had done so, to Lydia's intense relief, Simon bounded energetically into the kitchen.

"Morning, Simon!" Tommy said, suddenly cheerful. "Sleep okay?"

"Sure did, Tom," Simon assured him, coming up to Lydia and slipping an arm around her waist. "Mm. Smells good already. What can I do to help?"

"You did your part, Simon! Keep 'em barefoot and pregnant. I'll go see if Peg and the kids are up," Tommy said with a smile. "Gotta keep on schedule, even if it's a holiday."

As the man turned to leave the kitchen, Abril slid herself in between Lydia and him, woofing at the man softly as he passed. Tommy frowned, looking down at the dog. "Might want to keep that mutt of yours outside on the porch. Not too friendly."

Simon lightly snapped his fingers and Abril came right to his side, sitting obediently, but still watching Tommy. Simon said, "She's well mannered. Just protective of her own."

"Want me to tie her up out back before the kids come down?" Tommy asked Simon.

Something in his tone made Lydia anxious. "She'll stay beside me if I tell her to, Tommy," Lydia said quietly. "It won't be necessary."

"I wasn't talking to you, Lydia," Tommy's reply was icy. Peggy's sister did not know when to keep her mouth shut.

Immediately, Simon intervened. "Lydia is right, Tommy. Abril protects her own. She won't be aggressive unless she sees a threat to her 'pack', which is to say, her family."

Tommy stared at Abril, who held his gaze without flinching... until the man finally left.

Sliding an arm around Lydia, Simon said, "What on earth was that about?"

Lydia just shook her head. "He's a strange guy. I'm not sure why Peggy married him."

"I don't think Abril cares much for him," Simon added thoughtfully. *And that alone is enough for me to watch this guy!*

Christmas dinner turned out to be quite pleasant. It took until the meal was served for Peg to really join in with any family activities and Lydia watched her walking carefully around their mother's kitchen... something was definitely, off... Lydia wondered if she might be in pain... though after dinner was over, Peggy did begin to smile a little. Even Tommy's mood seemed to lighten as evening came. He broke out bottles of wine, offering a glass to Simon and their parents.

"Here, Dad, be good for your heart to have a little," Tommy held out a glass to Andrew who accepted it gratefully. Lydia declined, being pregnant and Peggy was not offered any, nor did she ask for a glass. Tommy drank his glass, quickly refilling it, pulling Peggy over to sit on his lap where he kept a hand firmly on her hips. They listened to Christmas songs on the radio for a time until

Lydia noticed that Abril likely needed to go outside for a quick break. She excused them both and headed for the back door.

"Simon," Tommy said, "want to share a cigar?"

Raising one hand, Simon declined. "Left some of my lungs in Paris, Tom. Think I'd better pass."

"Suit yourself," Tommy replied. Peg jumped off his lap in relief as he headed to the kitchen and out the back door to where Lydia stood on the steps, watching Abril romp in the snow. Seeing the man emerge from the door, the dog quickly bounded back across her own tracks to Lydia's side, sitting on her haunches watching him. Tommy casually lit his cigar, the tip glowing red in the chilly air.

"Still can't believe you got pregnant in the middle of a war," he observed. "Trying to picture that, bombs dropping all around, while you're dropping your trousers."

Lydia moved to rub Abril's ears, cautiously creating distance. "Must you be rude, Tommy? We hadn't planned on that happening."

"Well, at least now, you'll have a chance to set up house and take care of your baby," he nodded.

"I hope to work with the hospital where Simon has been hired," Lydia said. "They might have something I can do as a married woman."

Tom exhaled a little cloud of cigar smoke into the air. "Peggy likes being a housewife. I come home and she's got supper waiting and the kids all set up. The way it should be." He leaned over the porch rail beside her. "I make enough to take care of her, just like Andrew does for Anna."

"I'm glad my sister has a secure home to raise the children," Lydia nodded. "It's okay, Ab, go run." The dog hesitated then took off again across the snow.

"You know, Lydia," Tommy said thoughtfully. "You and Simon could stay with us, over toward Monroeville. Would be an easy ride downtown... for Simon to get to the hospital."

Lydia replied quickly, "He's found us a little house in the city, not far from the hospital. We'll be closing on the sale next week."

"Well, if it doesn't work out," Tommy said, "I'd take care of you. Nice looking girl like you. A man could take care of his wife and her sister both. It's biblical. I wouldn't mind dropping your trousers either..."

Trying to hide her shock, Lydia instinctively edged even further from the man on the railing. *What a horrendous thought!* He slid over closer to her again. "I got more than enough... keep you and your sister satisfied."

Lydia backed toward the door. "You've been drinking too much, Tom. I'm going in. Abril!"

He grabbed her wrist and leaned close enough for her to smell the wine on his breath. "How 'bout if I prove it," he murmured, running a finger over her lips. "Pretty little whore..."

Abril jumped up on the porch and as Lydia jerked back, Tommy stumbled forward, the end of the cigar in his fingers pressing into her wrist.

"Tom!" she cried out softly.

He pulled back his hand and absently rubbed the burn with his thumb. "Oops. Didn't mean to do that!" he chuckled as if he'd made a joke, but Abril's low growl sobered Tommy right up. "Tell your dog to behave, Lydia."

"Abril, stay," she said immediately, backing up toward the kitchen door, while Abril put herself between the man and her human, her teeth showing. When Lydia reached the door handle, she called Abril in with her and fled inside, catching her breath. Quickly she found Simon who was playing a game of checkers with her father. Dropping down on the floor at his knees, she leaned against him, and he dropped one hand on her long chestnut waves.

"Who's winning?" she tried to hide her anxiety, unsure of how to make sense of what had just happened.

"Your dad is," Simon confessed. "I've had to crown him several times already. I'm done for. You're a better player than I am, sir!"

"It's Dad, Simon, Dad," Andrew reminded his new son-in-law. "And I think you let me win just to humor an old man."

Lydia was relieved when her sister's family left to return to their home in a nearby suburb of Pittsburgh, just outside of Monroeville. They hadn't been gone long, when a telegram came from Marcus and Suzie, confirming exactly when they would be arriving in Greensburg... that same day. Together, the five of them would go to Pittsburgh for Marcus to interview with Doctor Maloney and hopefully begin working with Simon at Charity.

While Simon went to pick them up from the station, Anna asked her youngest daughter to stay back, knowing that soon they would all be leaving, and she would have to say goodbye again... even for just a short while. Lydia was grateful for the time with her mother, but found herself sneaking glances out the window for Simon's return.

As they waited, Lydia shared some tea with her mother, while her father rested upstairs.

"I am worried about Dad." Lydia swirled the tea in her cup. "How is his heart? Sometimes he looks too pale, too tired."

Her mother took a sip. "He doesn't complain. But I think he's hiding it."

"Has he been to the doctor?" Lydia asked.

"What's a doctor going to do? Tell him to eat right, lose a little weight, and get plenty of rest?" Anna asked her. "I've already told him to do all of that."

"Of course you have, Mom," Lydia thought carefully of how to proceed. "I just got concerned when Tommy said that Dad nearly had a heart attack. I didn't know if he meant literally or as an expression, to worry me."

Anna slowly dipped and lifted her tea caddy, still coaxing flavor from the leaves within. "That was two years ago. I suppose if his heart hasn't given out on him by now, it isn't going to anytime soon. Besides, there's a baby coming, who he very much hopes to meet."

"I want that, too!" Lydia replied eagerly. She paused a bit before asking her next question. "Mom, were you afraid when you were about to have Peggy?"

Anna looked up at her daughter. "You mean was I afraid of the birthing?"

Lydia nodded.

"Well, I suppose so. Especially as she was my first," Anna admitted. "I didn't know what to expect. Remember that was back in ninety-one, almost the dark ages. What did anyone know about having babies? It was better the second time, when you were born."

"Mom, humans have been having babies for thousands of years. How can it still be such a mystery?" Lydia was impatient.

"No one talks about it, that's how," Anna said, frankly. "My mother didn't."

"Well, then tell me, everything!" Lydia encouraged her. "Tell me what it's like to have a baby!"

"I don't know," her mother said, looking worried. "I don't want you to be afraid."

Lydia took her mother's hand. "Isn't it better that I know what's coming?"

Her mother exhaled deeply. "Well, it's important to remember that labor will finally end and a baby will be in your arms. It's hard to get through the final hours of pushing because your body takes over the entire thing, and you won't have any control over it. It just happens to you. Your body will be screaming at you to get the baby out. When you feel the screams, you know you're close to holding a baby. That's how you get through it."

Lydia stared at her mother, "Really?"

"See there, now I've upset you!" Anna exclaimed. "I've heard tell in the hospital that they give you ether, and then you don't feel anything."

"But then you wouldn't hear its first cry!" Lydia exclaimed.

"That's true. But nowadays, doctors don't want to hear a woman screaming, so they put them to sleep in the hospital—or so I'm told," her mother added. "I stayed home."

Lydia considered this. *All the more reason not to be in the hospital!* she thought. *I don't want someone pulling my baby out while*

I'm unaware of what's happening down there. She realized the irony of her thoughts, considering the countless times she had had her hands inside anesthetized soldiers, who were entirely at the mercy of the doctors and nurses working to save them. It had always seemed a blessing that the soldiers didn't know what was being done to keep them alive.

Just then, Lydia looked up at the sound of a car pulling up outside. She jumped up from the chair in happy anticipation, running to the door just in time to see Marcus, Simon, and Suzie getting out—Suzie was holding her baby.

Without stopping for a coat, Lydia hurried out into the cold, racing down the slippery front steps to Simon and quickly embracing him. Abril dashed around the group in excited circles. Lydia then turned immediately to Suzie, hugging her tightly, but carefully, with little Marcie Nichole still nestled in her arms.

"I can't tell you how happy I am to see you all!" she exclaimed.

Then Marcus opened his arms and Lydia gave him a heartfelt hug. "I'm so, so glad you're back," she whispered in his ear as Abril nosed her way in between them for Marc's attention. He leaned down and rubbed the dog's head affectionately.

"I missed you too, girl," he said, then looked up at Lydia warmly. "She said yes, like we had hoped. And we're coming to Pittsburgh... as you can see!"

"Suzie!" Lydia exclaimed in true delight, so very relieved. "I'm so glad you and Marcus found each other again. And Nikki! She's just beautiful. Simon, isn't she beautiful?"

"Judging by her little face, which is all I can see in that snowsuit, yes, she's very beautiful," Simon laughed. "You're going to freeze out here without a coat, Lydia!"

Lydia nudged Suzie straight up into the house while Simon and Marcus pulled suitcases from the back of the automobile, with Abril still circling them, then bounding up the steps beside them, urging them all inside. Anna came out from the kitchen to greet the new arrivals, fawning over the baby as little Nikki was unwrapped from her outerwear.

"Mom," Lydia explained again, "Suzie and I worked side by side at the medical station. She's a wonderful nurse and has been a true friend to Simon and to me."

"Very glad to meet you," Anna smiled, while watching the dog curiously sniffing the baby. "You also started expecting over there? In the war?"

Suzie nodded. "Things happen," she offered. She looked at Lydia's stomach.

"Yes, things do happen," Lydia agreed, tenderly resting her hand on her belly. "We're proof that good things can come from even the worst—" She then saw the ring on Suzie's finger and grabbed her hand. "You did it! It's official? Congratulations, Suzie!"

She smiled, showing off the gold band. "And he only had to cross an ocean to propose! The longest long distance proposal ever."

Lydia squeezed her hand. "I can't tell you how happy I am for all of you to finally be a family. And that our husbands will be able to keep working together... and we can raise our babies together. It's just all working out so well."

Suzie nodded. "It'll be a change, moving from Rochester to Pittsburgh, but I think that if I could adjust to living in France, I can adjust to living in Pittsburgh."

Lydia agreed. "It's much more familiar than a foreign country, I can assure you, after seeing it myself—but Suzie, wait until I tell you! There's a nursing position for you, too—if you want one."

"Oh, I don't know, Lydia. I'm tired of standing up when a doctor comes into the ward, if you want to know the truth."

"This position couldn't be more different," Lydia hastened to explain. "I'll tell you all about it, but let me say, it's almost like it was custom-made for you and me. We'll be thinking on our feet and for ourselves."

Suzie was more than a little curious. "Really? Somewhere a nurse can use her brain? Do tell!"

"Later, I'll tell you everything. And guess what? It comes with pay," Lydia assured her.

"Okay, I'm hooked," Suzie replied. "Marcus says I can work if I want, but if I don't want to, I don't have to."

"Just as it should be," Anna declared firmly as she listened to their discussion. "Especially with such little ones."

The three women looked up at the ceiling as they heard the two men tromping around upstairs, moving toward Peggy's old room. After stashing the suitcases, Simon and Marc collected Lydia's father who had just risen from his nap. He was interested to meet those who had worked with his daughter overseas. The three men came down to the kitchen, pulling up chairs alongside the women while introductions were made all around.

"So, is there any furniture in this house you're buying, Simon?" Andrew teased. "Or will all of you be needing some blankets to camp out on the floor?"

Simon laughed. "The widow selling the house also sold us several rooms of furniture that she didn't want to have to move to her son's house. Your daughter will not be sleeping on the floor, sir. There's even a dining room table, although I can't vouch for the kitchen."

"And indoor plumbing?" Anna asked.

"Yes, Mom," Lydia assured her. "It's right in the city after all, not too far from the hospital. There's real running water with all the necessary facilities. And a river not far away for beating clothes on rocks, if there's no wash tub in the cellar."

"And three bedrooms plus third-floor dormers," Simon added. "Our friends will have time to find a place of their choosing without having to pay hotel bills. But I do think we need to purchase an icebox, come to think of it..."

Lydia patted his arm. "Don't worry, it's twenty degrees outside. The only thing we'll have to look out for is frozen milk and bottles cracking. Everything will survive quite nicely on the back porch."

"That's true," Simon smiled. "No rush on an icebox!"

After weeks of being apart, Marcus looked at Lydia with concern. "How are you feeling, Lydia?"

She smiled at him. "Everything is fine, Marc. The baby is moving quite a bit. Even Simon feels it now."

He nodded with relief. "That's good." He remembered feeling it move for the first time with her. "What did you do there? Burn yourself?"

Lydia covered the mark, from Tommy's cigar, on her wrist. "Oh, it's nothing."

Marcus rolled his eyes. "You two just cannot get along without me!" he declared. "Simon, did you do a single push-up in my absence?"

Chuckling, Simon couldn't lie. "Almost every night. Ninety-nine percent of the time, Marc. Honest."

"We'll see about that tonight. I'll be counting them off with you," Marcus declared.

"I'm having the baby at home, Suzie," Lydia announced to everyone.

"Are you sure, Lydia?" She was concerned. "You really want to go through all that?"

Lydia nodded. "Every second of it."

"So, you're going to do it yourselves, Simon?" Marcus teased him.

"No," Simon said dryly. "She asked me to do it, but... we're getting a midwife."

Marcus laughed. "Coward!"

"Not at all! If we were back at the station, one of us would have had to do it," Simon reasoned. "You or Stockton would have had to volunteer. But I'm... not objective."

Suzie sighed, holding Nikki against her shoulder. "You would not have wanted to have a baby at the station, Lydia. And I welcomed sleeping through the last part of labor, in a proper hospital—the first half was bad enough. They didn't even let me get out of bed for five days. It was wonderful. Meals served in bed. How did the early settlers ever do it? Have your baby in the morning and go out and plow the field by evening—while nursing. They must have been much stronger than I am—" She noticed Nikki beginning to fuss. "Speaking of that, I'd better go feed Nikki."

Suzie stood to leave the kitchen, baby at her shoulder, and Lydia followed.

They moved into the living room, out of sight of the others. There, Suzie opened her blouse as if there was nothing to it—nursing a baby. Lydia was amazed.

"Do your breasts hurt?" she wondered, noting their fullness.

"They did at first, but then they adjust and make just as much as the baby needs somehow—they know how to keep up with her as she grows," Suzie shared. "I like it. I enjoy feeding her myself. It was especially good for her, coming as early as she did. She was such a little thing. Six and one-half pounds, eighteen inches."

"I was so worried for you," Lydia admitted. "Going through it alone. I was glad when you wrote that your family was supportive."

Suzie settled back as the baby nursed in earnest. "I wasn't the only pregnant girl in town with the father away. There were several unmarried girls in the maternity ward. I just told everybody that the father had to go to war, and then they assumed he was very brave."

"He is very brave, Suzie. And so are you," Lydia told her, thinking back. "You were the one who came to the rescue when Simon almost lost his leg. It was you who showed up in the dark, with a light and instruments for Marcus to operate. You've been there for us in the best and worst of times."

Suzie shook her head. "I don't know about any of that. From what Marcus tells me, you also lost Simon for a while there. I don't know how you got through that."

"Just like you did," Lydia assured her. "You came back home, never knowing if Marcus would survive the war or not. You were there when the shell blew a crater in our camp, you knew there was a chance that he wouldn't make it home, and you lived with that the entire time Nikki was getting ready to arrive. No wonder she was a little early, with that kind of anxiety. I was relieved beyond measure to find out you were both alright."

"Did you ever tell any of the girls?" Suzie wondered then, thinking of the nurses they had served with at the casualty clearing station.

Lydia slowly shook her head. "You asked me not to, so I only told Simon. No one knew why you left. And Marcus figured it out on his own. He cried the whole night when he realized that that must have been the reason. I had never seen him cry. Simon spent hours talking with him that night, Marcus was so upset."

Suzie stared at Lydia beside her on the sofa. "Marcus? Cried all night? The same Marcus sitting in your mother's kitchen, right now?"

"The same," Lydia affirmed. "I think he said something about being such a fool. And I don't believe Simon disagreed with him one bit. He tried to prepare himself that you might find someone else to love, after he had been so noncommittal... we were all just living for the moment, not knowing if or when another bomb was going to drop—literally or figuratively."

Suzie slowly nodded, processing this news as she shifted the baby to her other breast. "That's something to think about, isn't it? I'm sure he was with other women after I left. There were other women before me, so there were bound to be women after me, too. But in your letters, you said he'd changed, and I also saw something different in him when he came to Rochester. Maybe for us, separation was needed to help us figure out what we both wanted most."

Lydia had already decided to avoid the subject of Marcus entertaining other women in France. And Lydia would, of course, never tell Suzie that he had offered to marry her, when they had feared Simon might actually be dead. Lydia thought back instead to all of the times Marcus had plied her with questions each time she received a letter from Suzie.

When the precious mail bags had arrived in camp, he had always wanted to know if Suzie had written—had she asked about him—had she agreed to let him contact her—how was she managing at home. He had been anxious to hear any little detail about her, so he could plan his own future appropriately. Marcus had found his direction, had set a goal to win Suzie back, if he was able... and had made it happen in Rochester.

And now Lydia had them both, as friends forever. The feeling of pure gratitude was nothing short of overwhelming.

Chapter 6
Across the Threshold

This trip, there were four of them taking the train to Pittsburgh—plus a baby and a dog. A festive, pristine coating of snow fell over the bustling city as the train pulled into the station. Simon was scheduled to begin working at Charity on the first of January and he was anxious to get them settled into their house in the short interval between holidays. As soon as they arrived, they hailed a cab to their new home. Unlocking the front door, Simon scooped Lydia up into his arms, carrying her over the threshold.

"Now!" he exclaimed, gently placing her back on her feet in their foyer. "It's official. Welcome home, my love."

Both of them were bursting with excitement but took a tender moment to kiss, locking eyes as they did... before quickly making room for Abril, who bounded in, just before Marcus and Suzie who also rushed in from the cold, with the baby.

Lydia looked around, taking it all in. It was a bit dusty from sitting empty so long. She began by removing the sheets over the furniture in the living room, carefully folding them to keep dust from flying up into the air. Lydia made her way into the dining room, pausing at the bay window, imagining herself snuggled up, reading on a sunny afternoon. *The kitchen*—she would have to make sure they could all eat! As she entered the kitchen, she noted there was in fact, no table—as Simon had thought—but there was a sink, a stove, and plenty of cupboards for dishes she did not yet own.

Simon's first task was to light the furnace—he then ignited the many gaslights, sending a warm glow through the first floor.

Lydia smiled at the warmth of the lights—the house was becoming their home. Opening cupboards, she found that the widow had left several sets of mismatched place settings behind. She then glanced out the kitchen door into the little fenced-in backyard which was filling with fresh snow. *Our child will play out here with Abril this spring*, she thought. There was enough space for a small garden. Lydia had already fallen in love with this house. Simon found her there, looking out the back kitchen door and slid his arms around her waist.

"What are you thinking, beloved?" he asked, leaning her back against his chest.

"I was imagining our child playing out there with Abril. I was thinking about where we might plant a small garden for some fresh vegetables in summer," she turned around and embraced Simon. "I love this place. There must have been some happy times here. It has a good feel to it."

"Come upstairs," he gently pulled her toward him.

Marcus and Suzie were already settling into one of the bedrooms where a four-poster bed remained, a bureau with a slightly faded mirror, and a rocking chair. Ideal for a mother with a baby. Lydia smiled warmly at them as they looked up.

"You look like you belong here," she assured them both. "I hope you're planning on staying a while."

Marcus smiled. "Until you get sick of us, or we find a little place of our own. Whichever comes first."

"We lived ten feet apart for two years. I will never be sick of you," she said convincingly. Crossing the hall to the master bedroom above the dining room, she saw Simon with their suitcases. He was checking their closet for any hangers that may have been left behind. Joining him, Lydia was happy to see that the bay window on the first floor extended up to the second, overlooking the side street. Another four-poster bed was still covered with a sheet, as was a chest of drawers and an easy chair. Simon turned, coming to her.

"What do you think?" he wondered, his eyes twinkling. "Can we make it work?"

She wrapped her arms around his neck. "It's perfect," she said. "We'll need a crib for little Nikki."

Simon nodded. "Marcus is already working on it. I have to get him over to see Doctor Maloney immediately, if he's also going to start working by the first of the year. We'll try to get one on our way home—sounds good, doesn't it, Lydia? We're truly home now."

She embraced him, as they looked out through the large bay window. Below, the city streets stretched out into the distance. The roads were calm and fairly empty due to the snow, but Lydia imagined they'd be bustling once the weather warmed. A lone automobile now slipped over the new coating as it moved past the house. People walking on the sidewalks were bundled up against the weather. Over the trees, the top of the steel mills were visible, from down along the river; their smoke rising into the air. Somewhere below that, the Monongahela wound its way through the city to meet the Allegheny, both coming together to form the

Ohio. Their new life was beginning with family to the east and family to the south, both within easy reach. The City of Three Rivers would be their center.

Simon was eager to introduce Marcus to Doctor Maloney. The way through Charity's corridors was now familiar to Simon, as was Miss Weston. Simon approached her orderly desk as he pulled off his heavy coat.

"Doctor Finney!" she exclaimed. "How nice to see you again! We have you scheduled with one of our surgeons... Doctor Anthony Liskey... on Wednesday, to start your orientation."

"Thank you, Miss Weston," Simon said. "Would you let Doctor Maloney know that Doctor Lovell is with me? He wanted to meet him."

She rose from behind her desk. "Are you the other doctor from the army in France, Doctor Lovell?"

"I am," Marcus said, extending his hand to her.

She shook it, looking quite pleased. "How very nice to meet you."

She disappeared down the hall, returning shortly thereafter. "Doctor Maloney will see you both. You know the way, Doctor Finney."

Simon nodded and smiled his thanks to her. He led Marcus down the hall to the office, where the administrator came forward to shake hands with Marcus and Simon, both. Simon turned to leave, but Doctor Maloney stopped him.

"Please, sit." He motioned them to two high-backed chairs by his desk. "Doctor Lovell, I have already heard good things about you. Doctor Finney tells me you're skilled in vascular surgery and orthopedics."

Marcus nodded. "I've had some experience in both, sir," he assured the man.

"Share your experience with me, if you would, Doctor," Doctor Maloney prompted him.

Marcus was all too happy to share as much detail as possible, while Simon wondered why he was being included in this interview when he would have gladly given Marcus some privacy for it. It took some time for Marcus to cover medical school, and an accelerated residency spent on the front working alongside Simon under intense battle conditions. When he finished, Doctor Maloney smiled.

"I assume Doctor Finney told you that we're down several surgeons. Many enlisted when the United States declared war on Germany, and we're anxious to fill these positions. But not with just anyone. I needed to meet you myself. So, tell me, Doctor Lovell... why Charity?"

"Excuse me, sir?" Marcus was a little confused by this question.

"Why Charity Hospital? There are many, fine medical facilities in Pittsburgh. It sounds as though you'd qualify to work at any of them. So why Charity?"

Marcus hesitated and cleared his throat. "Well, actually, sir, it's to repay a debt," he said.

"Indeed? I'm not certain we can pay you enough money if your debt is sizable," Doctor Maloney frowned. "This is a teaching hospital run by Catholic ministries, not for profit—in case Doctor Finney didn't already tell you."

Marcus leaned forward as Simon looked at his friend anxiously, unsure where Marcus was going with this. He did not want his friend to turn this down due to salary.

"It's not a financial debt I owe, sir," Marcus admitted. "When we went over to the war, things got very bad, and quickly. I made some choices during my time there that I later felt were not the most respectable, in the heat of the moment, with artillery falling constantly. Then, out of the blue, as they say, a priest came to the station, Father James, during an especially horrific battle..."

"...that first visit was during the Somme, wasn't it, Marcus?" Simon interrupted thoughtfully.

"Yes, the same. Anyway, Doctor Maloney, there was something about that man, that priest! He made his way through our small station, ministering tirelessly to... well, I couldn't tell you how many sick, injured, and dying soldiers. He worked twenty hours a day, giving last rites, praying for the wounded. And somehow, he found time for us, for the nurses and doctors, too."

Doctor Maloncy saw Simon also nodding his head, also remembering this event, and he was moved with compassion for these two young surgeons.

Simon interrupted again. "He sure was a good man, Marcus," he agreed quietly.

"He was! Then Father James found time for me. And I warned him his collar might turn a little gray if he spent any amount of time talking to me... but his words started changing something inside me—and Father James camc back again, when we had gotten cut off from the army—"

"...in Belgium... Ypres," Simon interjected again, remembering the timeline. "The French army lost our medical camp... for weeks."

"And we ran out of everything. Seriously, everything," Marcus told the administrator, who was listening intently to his story. "There was no food, no ether, no Dakin's, no supplies. The nurses were tearing up sheets for bandages. The wounded were dying from hunger as much as any injury. The doctors and nurses somehow... we kept going on water and some creatures our dogs caught in fields. But just before the staff started dropping off too, Father James showed up, again, with a wagon load of food. Just out of nowhere. I remember some of the nurses asked him how he found us when the army didn't even know where we were. And Father James just said, 'God knew.'

"Then, there was one last time I spoke to him. Simon, Doctor Finney here, had been missing in action for months. Declared missing in action, many thought he was dead. His wife, who also served at the station as a nurse, was beside herself. I couldn't make any sense out of why such a good man, a good husband, a good surgeon would be allowed to die. And here comes Father James yet again, with Doctor Finney in the back of his wagon.

"That's the last time I talked to the priest, and I asked him to teach me how to get to know his God better. Because his God has had a way of making the impossible... possible. I wanted to find out how to get to know that God. Father James took the time to tell me all about it. You see, Dr. Maloney, I owe that priest a debt I'll probably never get to repay, but I figure serving here, at Charity, is at least a start. This is what he believed in."

There was complete silence in the office as Marcus finished his story. Doctor Maloney allowed both doctors a moment to remain lost in thought. Simon reached out, placing a hand on Marc's shoulder for a minute, clearly revisiting some of the severe difficulties they had endured.

Doctor Maloney took a moment to appreciate the quality of character they displayed, both very different, yet very much alike, and seemingly able to intuit what the other was thinking. He admired their courage, and very much wanted these men to teach the new medical students their values. He cleared his throat, quelling his own emotions.

"I think you'll fit in quite well with our surgical team at Charity, Doctor Lovell. It's an honor to have the two of you joining our staff. If possible, I look forward to you starting with Doctor Finney, in orientation on Wednesday. Can I assume you found a place to live?" Doctor Maloney asked Simon.

"We did, sir. And Doctor Lovell and his wife will stay with us until they can locate a house that suits them," Simon confirmed.

"And your wife, Nurse Finney," Doctor Maloney continued, "I hear that she has agreed to work with Sister Edwarda to help our nuns achieve an ambitious goal to meet the needs of the less fortunate?"

Simon nodded. "She has, sir. Until our baby arrives. She's excited about the opportunity. Doctor Lovell's wife was also a nurse serving at our station on the front lines. They are both remarkable women and nurses."

"Is that so?" Doctor Maloney asked Marcus with surprise.

"Yes, sir," Marcus nodded. "We both found something very good in the middle of that war. Something worth fighting for."

"I'll meet with the two of you again after a couple of weeks to see how you are acclimating to this rather different surgical environment than the one you both just left. I hope it will be less stressful, but just as fulfilling," Doctor Maloney said, rising to his feet again and extending his hand. "Gentlemen, welcome to Charity."

They both shook his hand and left the office feeling like they had just passed their medical exams again. They retrieved their coats from the anteroom, where Miss Weston smiled.

"I knew it would go well," she whispered. "He's been looking forward to this!"

"Thank you," they said in unison, leaving the administrative office wing to return down the long corridor to the rotunda at the entrance to the hospital.

"Have you even seen the operating theater yet, Simon? Are you sure they even have one? Or do we operate on a kitchen table somewhere?" Marcus asked his buddy as he peered curiously down various wings as they passed. "You know, have you had a tour of the hospital?"

"Nope," Simon declared.

"That figures," Marcus laughed out loud. "What have you gotten us into!"

"It won't be worse than the western front," Simon assured him as they bundled up to head back out into the cold. "I'm sure about that."

Marcus clapped Simon on the back. "Did you have to interrupt my story so often, buddy? I almost lost my train of thought—I was so nervous!"

"You did fine, Marcus!" Simon laughed. "Let's go find a crib for Nikki. You know she looks just like you, don't you? It's uncanny."

"Yeh, that whole like-father like-daughter thing is pretty remarkable!" Marcus chuckled.

They continued the light-hearted, easy banter of two very close friends... now with new jobs and able to provide for their new families, in a new city. Life was good for the moment, and they planned to enjoy every minute of it.

Over the dining room table, with their mismatched dishes, their discussion continued well after food was gone. The couples had the luxury of privacy, to reacquaint at their leisure now, reminiscing about war experiences without the uninformed getting upset. They talked about the hospital and Doctor Maloney's interview. They spoke of the clinic, Suzie plying Lydia with questions about the role of a triage nurse, which intrigued her very much. Sister Edwarda had suggested earlier to Lydia that a playpen might be made available under watchful care of one of the nuns in a back office so Nikki could be close and Suzie could continue to nurse her. Lydia had no doubt in her mind that the nuns would love the beautiful baby with her dark curls and crystal blue eyes, just like Marc's.

Mid-sentence, Lydia's eye's lit up. "Now, finally, tell me all about your wedding! I want to hear every detail. Where, when, how...?"

Suzie laughed aloud, spinning the gold ring on her finger. "Well, Marcus asked my father's permission."

"He didn't!" Lydia exclaimed as if Marcus wasn't even at the table.

Suzie nodded. "He did! Went right up to him and said he realized it was long overdue, due to his enlistment and the war refusing to end and all, but that he was there to make it right."

Marcus laughed. "Wayne said 'better late than never!'"

"That's my dad for you," Suzie sighed. "Very pragmatic."

"So that very afternoon, we went down and got the license and the rings," Marcus added, filling in some of the details. "And a week later, we were in front of a minister with her brother and sister, and I had the wedding certificate to prove it was all very official, for her dad."

"Your folks didn't go with you?" Lydia exclaimed in amazement. "I thought..."

Suzie smiled, blushing in front of the other couple. "I didn't want them to. Mom kept Nikki, and I wanted a honeymoon at a hotel."

Marcus reached over, squeezing her hand. "You weren't the only one," he added. "But I wish I could have taken you somewhere elegant like... oh, let's say, the Caribbean or something."

"It's winter, Marcus!" Suzie exclaimed.

"Not in the Caribbean," he corrected her.

She laughed, her eyes sparkling. "Oh, well, that can wait until Nikki is no longer relying on me for her next meal! I'll remember in a year or two, and you can take me to warm sands and deep blue seas!"

"What if in a year or two you have another mouth to feed?" Lydia asked cheerfully.

Marcus raised a hand. "We're going to enjoy reacquainting first. You can produce the next mouth to feed."

"Then, who knows?" Suzie mused. "I think another baby would be delightful." She looked around at the dining room walls. "There is plenty of room on these walls for family pictures, medical school diplomas, wedding certificates. Think of what you two will have hanging here in a few years!"

"Well, family pictures and a medical school diploma for certain!" Lydia exclaimed. "But, Simon, we don't have a wedding certificate!"

"Hm, true," Simon said thoughtfully, suddenly pondering this.

"It was in another country, after all. You probably registered with the local authorities in Nancy, didn't you?" Marcus asked curiously.

Simon shook his head, "No, actually, we didn't. We had such a short amount of time and needed to get back to the station. We just went straight to the cathedral there."

Marcus' eyes filled with concern. "You might want to check on that, Simon. The clerk at the town hall in Rochester asked me if I'd applied for one in France already since they're good for several months. Said the government would honor it if it was registered in another country, but that if I didn't have one already, I needed to get one before we could go to the church... or a judge."

Simon drummed his fingers on the table, hiding his rising anxiety, but Marcus knew the tell-tale sign of his buddy's unspoken concern. He had seen it often enough before.

Lydia wasn't hiding anything. "Simon!" she blurted out, suddenly aware that her secure world might be unraveling... and with a baby on the way. "Aren't we legally married? Here in the States? Are we living in sin?"

He grasped her hand. "Now, Lydia, it'll be fine. There is nothing sinful about our relationship, nothing whatsoever. I'll check on this first thing tomorrow at City Hall." He saw the tears forming in her eyes. "Honest, it's fine! We are really and truly married before God, Lydia! Things are different when people are married in different countries, with different laws. If we need to get it recognized here, we'll find out what to do!"

Seeing Lydia's utter dismay, Marcus quickly added, "You two are more married than any other married couple I know! Suzie and I are witnesses to that. We saw you come back from Nancy, and I even planned the wedding reception for you two! That's how married you were, even back then! Not a single soul in that entire camp doubted you two were truly husband and wife."

Suzie nodded. "I remember that day clearly, Doctor Stockton walking you right out of the tent, to the party. No question in my mind! But even so, Lydia, so what if you need to do it over again here! Marcus and I will gladly stand with you. You probably just have to register it with the government."

Lydia dried her eyes and took a deep breath. "If you say so."

Her voice was shaky, her hand drifting unconsciously to her baby as if protecting it from some unseen threat to its existence, or identity. She did not want to fall into the category of whoredom that Tommy had so viciously described when criticizing her choices in life. It had simply never occurred to her that their vows in front of God's altar in France, with the priest's blessing, were not 'real'. Why, he had even laid his hands on their heads!

Marcus had all of the compassion in the world for Lydia. He knew, even more than Suzie, how important Lydia's marriage was to her... how seriously she had spoken her vows to Simon... how she had waited for those vows, before a priest, to even consider being physical with a man. For her marriage to be illegitimate, here in the States, that could shake her world and would not be good for her or the baby.

"Did I ever tell you all about..." Marcus started storytelling to lighten the mood. With his characteristic humor, he distracted everyone with a tale from his medical school years when bats had gotten into the cardiac ward, and he had had to try to chase them down with a butterfly net before the patients all had heart attacks from fear.

They were laughing till very late, before finally surrendering to fatigue and agreeing to head to bed. They turned everything off on the first floor and all made their way upstairs. Suzie stopped to check on Nikki in her new crib, in the little third bedroom next to their own, with an adjoining door. After everyone had made their rounds in the bathroom at the end of the hall, they settled in for the night.

Lydia was already in their four-poster bed before Simon undressed. "Last one in the bath?" she asked.

"Yep," he said. "Pregnant women and nursing mothers always get first dibs on a bathroom."

"Yes, but what about Marcus?"

Simon pulled off his trousers and socks and peeled back the covers. "I was being a good host. What's this? A nightie for our first night in our own home?"

"Well, you're wearing boxers! And I don't know how creaky this bed is!" she exclaimed.

"That didn't stop us in West Virginia," Simon reminded her.

"Yes, but we were down on the floor, you might recall," she added.

Simon looked around them at the thick braided rug on the floor of the room. "Looks good to me!" he exclaimed. "Should work just as well here as it did there. That little patch of moonlight coming in through the window is quite inviting."

He pulled the blankets from the bed and arranged them on the floor and then picked her up, nightgown and all. "I carried you over the threshold... I will carry you to the floor."

She held on around his neck as he positioned her in the patch of moonlight streaming in through the window.

"I will most certainly have the pleasure of being with my wife on the first night in our new home," he declared softly.

"What if we aren't really married, Simon? What if I'm not really your wife?" Lydia whispered. "What if they say we aren't legal? I wanted so much to do things the right way."

Kneeling between her legs, Simon raised her nightgown up to her waist. The moon made her skin look pearl-like as he revealed her pregnant body. He bent over and kissed her belly with the tiny growing life inside. "We did do things the right way, my love," he murmured. "Just like all the souls in the Old Testament did long before there were city halls and governments. Abraham, Isaac, Jacob, Joseph... all the patriarchs of the faith did it the way we did it, before God and his people. If it was good enough for God, then it's good enough for us."

Lydia absorbed his words like a balm to her soul. She felt the cool night air touch her as he raised the gown over her head and dropped it on the floor.

"My body is changing," she told him, in case he hadn't noticed the obvious.

He gazed at her, draped in moonlight. Her body was preparing for the baby to come, her breasts were firmer and rounded, her belly rising. "You are even more beautiful as your pregnancy develops—"

"I'm getting clumsy and fatter," she whispered, seeking his reassurance that he still wanted her.

He traced the outlines of her body. "You look angelic to me in this moonlight. I can't get enough of you…"

"I haven't had any of you yet," she whispered longingly. "And I want to."

He lowered himself down carefully. "Then how about we fix that right now."

The floor did not creak.

He loved her slowly, taking pleasure in the romance the moonlight created. And afterward, he lifted her back up into their bed, pulled the covers over them, and wrapped her in his arms.

"If we have to get married again," he said softly, "I'll be the luckiest man alive to marry the most beautiful woman in the world, twice."

Lydia nodded, her head on his shoulder. "If we have to get married again, I'll be the happiest woman alive to get married twice to the most wonderful man on two continents."

Simon couldn't help himself. He laughed out loud, not caring a lick, if Marcus and Suzie might hear. "It'll work out. We'll find a way, my love. We always do. But creaking or no creaking the bed, we are not always going to come together on the floor!" His voice was light, but Simon was already quietly hatching plans to make everything okay, to give Lydia's mind solace. He decided Doctor Maloney or the hospital priest at Charity could probably help him find the priest at the cathedral in Nancy. The nun at the cathedral would not have forgotten the American nurse, the Ange de la Miséricorde. There was only one angel of mercy for the French soldiers, a title that had followed Lydia across the French countryside. He would find a way to make their vows legitimate.

The next morning, Marcus and Simon left just after breakfast, to catch a trolley down to the Clerk of Records office in the city. With Marcus as a witness, Simon explained the circumstances of his vows in the cathedral in France to a clerk who appeared overworked and disinterested in his particular situation.

"Just bring the certificate to us from the local church authority there, and we'll register it for the Commonwealth," said the little man, his spectacles perched halfway down his nose.

"But that will take some time to obtain, sending word to Europe with the war still going on and everything in turmoil over there. It could take a while, and we have a baby coming. It's a very difficult situation in eastern France," Simon insisted, his voice calm, but his concern rising.

The man shrugged his shoulders. "You can get a license right away, now. And go to a judge in short order. That would make it legal here, too."

"If we wait for the cathedral to send something, what will my wife's status be, in the eyes of the government, should anything happen to me?" Simon pressed the man. "With the house and my bank accounts?"

The clerk folded his hands on the counter as if the matter were closed. "She is unwed in the eyes of the government. You could get a lawyer and make her a beneficiary of your estate, regardless of marital status. It would at least be something. Or your estate will go to next of kin who, perhaps, would behave charitably toward the woman you are with... and your child. Or you could go to Indiana, where you can spend one documented night of nuptial bliss together and be married by common law in Indiana. The common law would be recognized in Pennsylvania... if you bring proof."

Drumming his fingers on the counter in frustration, Simon turned away from the clerk who had clearly finished providing his best advice. He looked at Marcus in dismay. "This is not good, Marc. This is just, not good."

Marcus shook his head. "Nope. This is not good at all," he agreed, knowing Lydia as he did. With Suzie, they felt no shame in her having their baby long before marriage. They could always attribute it to the passions of war and terms of his enlistment. But both men knew that Lydia would not be at all happy about this.

"How about that!" Marcus added. "I might end up having an anniversary date before yours! Suzie and I will be married longer than the two of you!"

"Don't even mention this—not even a joke—when we get home," Simon muttered. "I'll have to bring her over here right away to get a license, just in case, as a backup."

"I would say so." Marcus agreed.

They waited on the street corner for the next trolley, their breath forming white clouds in the cold air. Simon pulled his collar up around his ears and buried his hands in his coat pockets.

"I wonder why Maloney had me stay in the office for your interview?" he mused aloud.

"I guess you were supposed to back me up on the experiences overseas," Marcus guessed. "Make sure I was telling the truth."

"But I didn't have you, to back me up!" Simon objected. "There must be something else going on in that man's mind. What would he want to ask of two guys recently back from the front?"

Marcus looked up at gray clouds moving in overhead, from the west. "Looks like more snow is coming," he observed. Then he added, "He did mention the teaching hospital thing. Maybe he wants us to teach."

"Teach what? Like how to repair an aorta full of shrapnel, by lamplight, in a leaky tent, in Belgium?" Simon asked, warming his hands with his breath.

"Something like that, I suppose," Marcus nodded. "We could teach the youngsters a thing or two about triage during disasters."

"The nurses did the triage," Simon reminded him. "We'd have to ask them to come in as guest speakers for that lecture."

"I doubt any medical school students would listen to them," Marcus stated dryly. "They're usually riding high on having just been accepted into school."

"Hm. If not to teach, what then?" Simon mused. "Charity Hospital wants to reach out to the community... the under-served. Maybe Maloney has bigger designs."

Marcus pulled his collar up as the cold began to seep in through the gaps in their coats, and saw a few flakes of snow slowly descending around them.

"What... like a first aid station set up on a street corner somewhere in a poor neighborhood?"

"Maybe..." Simon said thoughtfully. "You know, Marc, that's a really good idea! Why not? Lydia and Suzie could assist us again in a little outpatient surgical clinic. I really like this idea! If that isn't what he has in mind, maybe we should suggest it."

"We haven't even seen the nice, modern operating theater at the hospital yet, and you already have us back out in primitive conditions on a street corner in a little clinic? Good grief, Simon," Marcus exclaimed. "Let me at least get used to running water and a sterile field, would you?"

Simon laughed, easing away the worries of the matter of his marital status. "Alright, I'll give you a couple months of getting used to a staff at your beck and call. Then, let's go talk to Maloney about a local first aid center. It could really work."

The trolley arrived, and they gratefully climbed aboard, finally escaping the winter wind.

"So, this is what a real operating theater looks like!" Marcus remarked to Simon, through his face mask, as they scrubbed their hands at an actual sink with hot, running water and surgical soap... and hand and nail brushes. The room was sparkling white.

Simon was also duly impressed. "You look like a white knight, Marcus!"

They were both dressed in bright white surgical shirts, trousers, and caps. In unison, they turned from the scrub sink, where an attendant was waiting, ready with white gowns, attached to sterilized gloves, for them to slide their arms into. Fully garbed, they moved to the table, where a patient was already draped and asleep under the care of an anesthetist at the head of the table. The powerful light above, shone perfectly on the surgical field. Doctor Anthony Liskey was waiting for them.

"Find everything to your satisfaction, Doctors? The changing area? The storage bins?" Doctor Liskey asked.

"Certainly, Doctor Liskey," Simon assured him, assessing the patient. "The patient is already intubated?"

"Yes, anesthesia has prepared the patient. We heard that you have had to perform surgeries under... less-than-desirable conditions, so I wanted to be sure that you have everything you need here. In this theater, anesthesia is our chief assistant, monitoring patients' airways, vital signs, response to treatment, length of surgery. The surgical nurse will follow your exact orders at all times."

"What procedure will you be performing?" Marcus questioned, looking down at the covered man before them. He had assumed that they were simply there to observe...

"Lung cancer has unfortunately claimed this man's left upper lobe—we will be resecting the tumor along with lymph nodes—"

"Any sign that it's spread to other organs or bones?" Simon quickly asked.

"See for yourself," Doctor Liskey said, motioning to a lightboard on the wall where an assistant flipped a switch to back light the films. Simon, marveling at the modern conveniences, carefully moved closer to inspect the images. There was a large white mass in the man's upper chest wall. His right lung looked clean, as well as the lower left. Marcus glanced over as well, but was more anxious to look inside the patient.

"Doctor Lovell, what's the immediate difference for you?" Liskey asked, as he readied a scalpel to make the initial cut.

"The time to consider all of the options," Marcus replied. "Time to consider the best cut, the least invasive procedure, to minimize tissue trauma."

Liskey nodded. "Makes sense. Though time is a consideration here too. We don't want to extend anesthesia beyond what's prudent, but it is a luxury."

"And this," Simon said, holding a new rib retractor he had read about in his journals, "this is a remarkable tool."

"We have the electric cautery ready as well, to minimize bleeding. If we don't have to transfuse, it's preferable. Blood is always in short supply. But, if necessary, it's available. Usually available, anyway. Use it judiciously." Liskey was a polished professional.

Simon glanced at the anesthetist as Marcus and Liskey began the procedure. "What are you using for gas? Nitrous blend?"

"Yes," the other replied while watching his patient's deep and regular breathing. "Reduces the risk of blood pressure dropping, for extended procedures like this one."

The three surgeons worked quickly and carefully. Doctor Liskey relaxed a bit as the operation progressed, allowing the other two to assume more and more control as he gained confidence in their notable skills. These younger doctors were not novices, he quickly realized, not by any stretch. They were unfamiliar with some of the equipment laying out on the surgical tray, but their skill and intuition were on target. They were fast, and they worked seamlessly together. Doctor Liskey offered few suggestions. The operation took less time than Liskey had anticipated, and he was pleased when they looked to him for an indication that they could close. This also was different. Here surgeons did their own closings instead of just packing a wound against infection or asking one of the nurses to do it so the doctors could move on to the next patient waiting in a queue.

The doctors completed the task and moved to the sink to wash, pulling off their gloves for re-sterilization, depositing their gowns into the hamper.

Marcus looked around eagerly. "Where is the next patient?" he asked while immediately seeking a fresh gown.

Doctor Liskey laughed. "You'll get used to the scheduling, gentlemen. The next patient is in an hour, since we got done earlier than anticipated. You have time for a cup of coffee in the doctors' lounge, or cafeteria, if you like."

Marcus was baffled. "And we get paid to do this?" he questioned.

Liskey laughed again. "We do. But not a whole lot!"

"What are the details of the next case?" Simon wondered.

"The scheduler, or a nurse, can fill you in and find you their chart to review. When it's your own patient, it'll be easier. For now, the chart will always be ready for you and any necessary films or other clinical information available," the other surgeon assured them. "How many did you do in a day, before?"

Marcus looked at Simon. "Hundreds, with the help of the nurses and medics," they said simultaneously. Doctor Liskey's jaw dropped.

Marcus and Simon used the remainder of the day to become better acquainted with the surgical staff, routine and rhythm of the operating theater, and the wider range of instruments now available to them. Following the morning's lung resection, they removed an appendix, corrected a hernia, and debrided an infected foot wound. Then, Doctor Liskey declared that the surgical day, at least in the operating theater, was concluded. The two newcomers washed up, removed the surgical garb, and donned the white doctor's coats hanging in the lounge so they could follow Liskey as he made rounds on patients in the surgical wards. They met with nurse matrons on each ward, noting that the flow of nursing care was fairly unchanged from what they had seen prior to their service overseas.

After rounds, the three moved down the corridor to a surgical preparatory wing where tomorrow's patients were being checked in and evaluated. Doctor Liskey knew many of them, introducing Simon and Marcus, as they would be assisting. He was glad when the two new surgeons each shook hands with the patients. A personal touch was critically important at Charity. People were names, not simply numbered cases. And Doctor Liskey thanked both new surgeons at the end of the afternoon for a successful day. Simon made a mental note to review some of the medical literature about the cases for the next day. When he left the hospital with Marcus, he felt confident they would soon be independent in the operating theater, building their own caseload.

As they buttoned up against the cold, catching the next trolley, Simon said, "See? A real operating theater! No kitchen table—I really want to get back to the house, Marc."

"Worried the girls will find something fun to do without us?" Marcus teased.

Simon shook his head. "Actually, I think they were cleaning the house, after it sitting empty so long, but I need to talk to Lydia about the license issue. I told her I was working on it. She starts at the clinic tomorrow, and I just want her to have a good day. Feels strange being away from her all day."

"Separation anxiety?" Marcus laughed lightly. "Suzie and I were apart for a year!"

"I know! I just want to get back to her. You know, Marc, when I was stuck in Paris with opiates clouding my mind, the only thing that made it bearable—when no one could find a way to contact the station—was knowing with absolute certainty that you were looking after Lydia. Otherwise, I would have gone out of my mind. I don't know how I would have managed without knowing you'd be there for her."

Marcus looked at Simon, seated next to him. "I made a vow, remember? Hasn't changed."

Simon's voice had a serious tone. "And I'll do the same for Suzie and Nikki—if it's ever needed. They will never want for anything if something happens to you, Marc."

They shook hands on it, as they rode the trolley home. It was good to have a best friend.

In the morning, Lydia went with them to the hospital so she could start at the clinic with Sister Edwarda. She wore a simple, navy-blue dress with a higher waist to disguise the pregnancy a bit, some patients might just think her to be a little heavy.

"Nervous?" Marcus asked as they boarded the trolley.

She laughed. "Not at all. Excited!" She corrected him. "Right now, patients coming in with injuries are sitting with those who are coughing. Sister Edwarda said I can make suggestions for triage. We'll know how many nurses we need to take care of small injuries versus illness, or who needs to wait to be evaluated by one of your illustrious peers working in the back."

Simon squeezed her hand. "Right up your alley, Lydia. You'll have it running smoothly in no time. Going to use a number system like you did at the station?"

She looked up thoughtfully. "Maybe colors. Red for bleeding, to get in quick. Yellow for nasty infections. And—"

"Green for vomiting all over the floor?" Marcus suggested.

She laughed. "I'll be sure to have someone come get you, to tend to the green group then."

"Not me!" he said, shaking his head. "Not that wild about yellow, either. Keep me in the red. I'll take the simple 'Stop the bleed... Please put my guts back inside of me' cases."

"I'll remember that!" she exclaimed. "And Sister Edwarda is going to tell me more about going out onto the streets for house visits. I can hardly wait!"

Simon frowned. "But only with another nurse... and Abril, remember?"

Lydia patted his arm. "I'll take Abril, at least, until you gain confidence in me, Simon."

He corrected her. "I have tremendous confidence in you! It's the rest of the people out there that I doubt."

"I don't think you need to worry about some dear little old widow who needs her heart checked or a mother with a sick child," Lydia said, thinking ahead. "Just think how nice it will be for a mother to not have to bundle up all of her other little ones and take them out to a busy clinic, full of sick people, when just one of her children is ill. Sister Edwarda has a wonderful vision for how to ease what some are going through."

Simon said nothing, but squeezed her hand again.

"You need a medical bag, Lydia," Marcus said. "To carry whatever supplies you'll need."

"Good idea, Marc! For my stethoscope, some bandages, soap—in case they don't have any—scissors, tweezers, alcohol, thermometers. Oh, yes, a flashlight, of course..." She started checking items off on her fingers, her mind running at full speed about what might be needed. "Tongue depressors for checking throats and tonsils, tourniquets, my blue scarves for covering my nose and mouth if a household is filled with contagion, a small notebook for recording the visit... and a treat for Abril, naturally."

The list was becoming lengthy. Lydia decided she would also talk to Suzie... she would have good ideas, too.

Simon and Marcus walked Lydia down the long corridor to the clinic at the back of the hospital before heading to the operating theater. When they opened the doors, they saw more than fifty people, of all ages, already in the large open waiting area, sitting in chairs, rocking prams—all holding stomachs, aching heads, or clumsily bandaged arms, hands, or feet. There was a nun at a small desk near the back, keeping a list of the names of those waiting.

"Wow!" Simon exclaimed. "It's only eight-thirty in the morning! What's it going to be like by noon?"

"When I was here before, there seemed to be around a hundred," Lydia said, her eyes shining as she anticipated being useful.

Marcus looked around. "Well, the need is certainly real," he said, seeing the light in her eyes, appreciating Lydia's willingness to be of service. "I had no idea what you were talking about when you first mentioned this clinic, Lydia. I see why Sister Edwarda reached out to you. Obviously a diverse mix of patient problems..."

Simon glanced over at Marcus. "Give her a couple of days, and I'll bet this will be all sorted! Just like back at the station. All about priorities. You're great at that, Lydia. You'll spot the head injury coming through the door or the person about ready to collapse. They made a good decision asking you to do this."

"And Suzie will be perfect here, too! She has excellent triage skills," Lydia said happily. "There's a little administrative office, way in the back wing, where Nikki can sleep and play while she's still so small, where the nuns can help watch her." Lydia didn't feel comfortable kissing Simon goodbye in public, but she squeezed his hand. "You two have fun in the operating theater! I'll see you at home later—"

"No, let's meet in the rotunda," Simon suggested. "If I'm done first, I'll wait for you." He wanted to talk to Doctor Maloney after surgery, about finding the hospital priest to help him get in touch with the cathedral in Nancy.

She smiled and quickly headed off in search of the nurse running the hall. Passing benches in the rear, she saw dozens of patients waiting. Lydia found a nun who looked like she knew what she was doing.

"Sister?" she asked, coming forward. "I'm Lydia Finney. Is Sister Edwarda here? It is my first day in clinic."

The robed woman looked up gratefully. "You're the nurse back from the war?" she asked quickly. "May I take your coat?"

Lydia nodded. "I am. Yes, please. Where should I start?"

The doctor in the room looked up from the child he was tending to, the child's mother hovering anxiously.

"I'm Sister Mary Francis," the nun told Lydia. "And this is Doctor Peter Martin."

The doctor leaned over and extended his arm to shake hands with Lydia. "I'm on clinic this month, Nurse Finney. Welcome aboard. Care to assist?"

"Certainly, Doctor," Lydia said. "Where can I wash?"

He nodded approvingly. "Just inside that utility room behind us, there."

Lydia turned quickly, soaped her hands well, and returned to the examining table where the miserable child sat.

"Tell me what you think, Nurse," Doctor Martin said quietly.

"May I?" Lydia said to the mother, who nodded. Lydia pulled out her own stethoscope and turned to the child. She listened carefully to his lungs, then asked him to cough, looked at what he brought out, and listened again. She turned to the doctor and asked, "Have you a flashlight? I didn't bring one."

Doctor Martin reached into his white exam coat pocket and pulled it out, handing it to her.

Lydia looked into the child's throat. "How long has he been coughing?" she asked the mother. "Sweats? Chills?"

"Yes, nights. For three days," the woman said. "He keeps nothing down. No appetite."

Lydia turned to Doctor Martin. "He has congestion in both lungs that does not clear when he coughs. His throat is normal. Sputum is gray green. The sweats and night chills suggest a pneumonia."

Peter Martin looked at her and smiled. "Very good, Nurse Finney. I think so, too. This is what I want you to do, Mrs. Sweeney," the doctor told her. He wrote out a prescription for the cough and handed it to her for the apothecary. "If he gets worse, bring him back and we will check him again."

The woman and her boy left the room, escorted by Sister Mary Francis, and Lydia went to the utility room to wash her hands again, followed by Peter Martin.

"Where did you serve in the war, Nurse Finney?" he asked directly.

Lydia soaped her hands well. "A mobile casualty clearing station on the front: Verdun, Somme, Passchendaele, Ypres..."

"And what did the nurses do there?" Peter asked her curiously.

"Things we aren't supposed to do here," she answered.

He leaned back against the counter, studying her as she dried her hands. "Such as..."

"Surgery assist, post op wound care, triage for the trucks and wagons full of wounded... reduced the spread of influenza, infection, pneumonia, syphilis, measles... burn care, monitored those who inhaled poisonous gases or had concussions from the artillery blasts, fracture care, suturing... a little bit of everything, I guess."

Peter Martin folded his arms across his chest, regarding her carefully. "Wow," was all he could manage—he was trying hard to envision this lovely nurse up to her elbows in burns, fractures, syphilis, and poison gas.

Lydia dried her hands. "I guess."

"Well, I'm glad Sister Edwarda found you! You're just what I need!" the doctor exclaimed. "The month that I'm here in clinic, this is what we'll do. We'll set up a lung clinic, a first aid clinic for small wounds, and a separate area for pregnant mothers and sick infants."

"What about a triage location for those needing admittance quickly to the hospital?" she asked. "We need to get them to an admission ward so they don't get lost in the crowd out there when it gets busy. We need screens for those coughing with influenza or pneumonia, keeping them away from those who just need something like sutures or a joint wrapped—I'll speak with Sister Teresa, out in the waiting area, about what's available."

Peter Martin laughed out loud. "You are a breath of fresh air!" he exclaimed. "Anything is do-able."

"What do you think about isolating people with measles, mumps? Is that something we could consider?" Lydia asked. "Is everyone hand washing often?"

"Of course, to both," he replied. "We have been so incredibly busy that there has been no time to really look at the physical environment here, to map out its better use. That's what Sister Edwarda and I have been discussing during my rotation through the clinic. The timing of your arrival is wonderful, at least for me. Perhaps now we have a chance to improve our practices. Welcome aboard, Nurse Finney. I believe you'll make a very big difference here. We'll sit down with Sister Edwarda this afternoon. For right now, work with me to see these people quickly. If you can screen them ahead of me and give me a quick report, we can get this line of folks taken care of before it stretches halfway around the building."

Now it was Lydia's turn to smile. "That's always been my goal, to make a difference."

He led her out of the utility area to the crowd of people in the clinic's waiting room, so they could start instituting their improvements. Lydia triaged the patients, collected their symptoms, listened and checked for complications, as Sister Teresa registered them. Then the patients were handed off to Sister Mary Frances in the back hall, who kept the exam offices filled for Doctor Martin.

Around lunchtime, Sister Teresa, who was normally out at the desk in the larger waiting room, came rushing back through the inner hall. Lydia saw her coming in haste and immediately left the patient she was examining.

"What is it, Sister Teresa?" she asked quickly.

"Better come quick!" the nun urged her.

They ran back out to the open triage area, where there was a commotion just inside the outer door to the clinic. Several men had their arms around a man slumped between them. They were all covered with blood and grime. Lydia wasted no time.

"What happened to him?" she demanded quickly as they lowered him to the floor. Lydia dropped to her knees and leaned over him, checking his pupils for signs of shock, his clothing was stained with dark blood.

"We was on the street, in our truck and he fell—when the brakes slipped—and tore his self wide open on the edge of a cart—down b'low, miss."

Lydia tore his shirt open and saw the huge gash in the man's abdomen. She could see his bowels starting to spill out of the opening. Immediately, she turned to Sister Teresa.

"Get me a clean, wet towel quickly. Find Doctor Martin," she ordered the other, who ran to find the doctor. "You, please, sit down and get his feet up higher so he doesn't go into shock, too much. And you, cover him with his coat. We need to keep the cold air off him, from the door. What's his name?"

Sister Teresa immediately returned with a wet towel that Lydia folded and pressed over the exposed intestines. "Doctor Martin is on his way," she breathed.

"Thank you, Sister. Please clear the others away from this area, and is there any kind of a rolling cart or litter or something to carry him to the operating theater on? How do we do that here?"

Lydia saw Doctor Martin running toward them from the back hall, as she knelt on the floor beside the prostrate man, her hands pressed against his abdomen.

"Abdominal wound, under his liver, bleeding, intestines eviscerating," she said quickly to the doctor. "And his pupils are changing. How fast can we get him to the operating theater? Is there a waiting list upstairs? How does that work here?" She continued, as she kept her hands on the towel, trying to hold the man together, his blood soaking through as she tried to staunch the flow.

Doctor Martin looked around quickly and saw Sister Teresa coming through the nervous crowd of onlookers. They parted quickly for the nun who was followed by two orderlies pushing a long, rolling cart between them.

"I'll call the operating theater upstairs immediately and tell them what's coming, so they can find a surgeon and set it up," Doctor Martin confirmed.

"Do you want to see the wound?" Lydia asked over her shoulder as she held steady pressure on the bleed.

He glanced quickly down at her while he stood up. "I don't have to, Nurse Finney. You already did," he said and rushed back to the nun's desk to call the operating theater.

"Lift on three," Lydia told the orderlies. "I need to keep my hand in place."

"Yes, Nurse," they said. And on the count of three, the men who had brought the wounded man into the clinic helped the orderlies lift him, in one smooth motion, up onto the rolling cart.

"How far is it to the operating theater?" she asked the hospital orderlies.

"Down the hall, up a ramp to the second floor, miss," one answered.

"Let's go," she said, standing by the table. With one hand pressing a towel against the area around the man's liver, she grabbed the side of the table with her other hand. The three of them quickly pushed the injured patient out of the waiting room, past many anxious onlookers, down the hall, and to the ramp just around the corner. When they reached the top, they made a sharp left into a white corridor on the second floor, where another orderly was waiting for them.

"They're almost ready!" he assured them. "The surgeons are scrubbing now."

"Good!" Lydia exclaimed in relief. "You there, take over for me. Keep the pressure right here, so he doesn't bleed to death."

"Yes, Nurse," the new orderly said quickly, replacing her hand with his own. Lydia stood in the hall, breathing hard, as the three disappeared through a set of doors where she knew the man would receive the help he so desperately needed. Suddenly, the corridor was empty... and quiet. Lydia turned and retraced her steps back down the ramp and into the clinic's waiting room, through those still milling about, in need of care. Disregarding the curious stares, she walked to the back hall, to wash up.

Doctor Martin found her at the utility room sink. "You've got blood all over your dress, Nurse."

"It will wash. I'll find an apron," she assured him. "How remarkable that you could get an operating theater set up just like that! What a wonderful advantage, to have those resources available so quickly! He has a good chance of recovering if he doesn't get infected."

"Yes, they said there were a couple of surgeons available who could take the man immediately. Let's find you that clean apron. Unless you've had enough for one day? Would you prefer to go home?"

Lydia looked up from the sink in surprise. "What ever for?" she asked, astonished. "Didn't you see how many people are still out there waiting for us?"

Doctor Martin smiled warmly. "I'm really going to enjoy working with you, Nurse Finney," he said quietly. "Well then! Let's go see who Sister Teresa has lined up for us next!"

Chapter 7
The Quick and the Dead

I t was late afternoon when the clinic was finally able to shut down. Sister Edwarda, who had joined them earlier, reported that the team had seen over one hundred and ten patients, all meticulously recorded on the waiting room list. Other than the few bursts of heavier arrivals, there had been a fairly steady stream of patients throughout the day. Acute emergencies had immediately been moved to the main hospital for admission. Those with minor sprains and pulled muscles were triaged and instructed by Lydia and Sister Teresa on strategies to treat and avoid further injury, successfully freeing up the doctor's time for only the sickest of patients.

During a quick meeting with the nursing director, before heading home, the three nurses and the doctor began excitedly exploring ways to further streamline patient flow. Coughs and fevers had been the prevailing symptoms of the previous seven hours. The medical staff all knew that with January upon them, this was likely to be the major need of their community. Influenza cases were on the rise all over the city. An obvious priority would be to establish an area where airborne germs could be contained. Sister Edwarda promised to make it so. It was a start, a good start.

Lydia made her way back through the long central corridor, to the rotunda. Tired in body, but not in spirit, she sank down into an empty chair. Standing so many hours had taken its toll on her feet; she needed some sturdier shoes to do this kind of work—her old army boots would have been better. Her mind began to recount and problem solve the challenges of the day: a simple dress, with a long apron to cover it completely, would hold up well. Maybe she should find several more long aprons, so they could be swapped out once soiled. She was still wearing the one Sister Teresa had found for her after lunch, not wanting to put her coat over the dried blood on her dress. She then wondered how the injured man they'd sent to surgery was faring, hoping his intestines were securely back inside, where they belonged.

While pondering such things, Doctor Peter Martin nearly walked past Lydia, stopping abruptly when he realized who it was, bundled up in the chair. Not yet ready to brave the weather himself, he dropped into an empty chair beside her.

"Nurse Finney," he smiled cheerfully over the scarf wrapped around his neck. "Need a way home? Least I can do after all your hard work today!"

She smiled and shook her head. "No, thank you, Doctor. I'm waiting for my husband."

"Your husband?" he asked, openly surprised. "Are nurses at the hospital now permitted to get married? I wasn't aware of that."

"I may be an exception," she admitted. "But then, I'm not working the wards... perhaps that allows for a little leeway, for me... I wouldn't be allowed in the main hospital surely."

He considered this. "Well, however they managed it, I'm glad they did. You did exceptionally fine work today. No way we could have seen so many people without you."

"I was just wondering how the man with the abdominal wound made out. And also what you do with your time when you aren't on duty in the clinic," she asked curiously.

"I'm a general doctor," he replied. "I see those on the wards with diabetes, heart disease... everything that the specialists don't see. In my spare time, I have an office, on the other side of the river, where I see people a couple afternoons a week."

She laughed. "Whatever comes through the door is your specialty then?"

"Something like that," he nodded. "I like the variety. Keeps life interesting. But I did check on our guy, the one literally losing his guts. He'd nicked his portal vein. It's no wonder he was bleeding so heavily. He made it through the surgery thanks to his buddies getting him here so fast... and you being able to size up his situation so quickly. I suspect that's how you managed in the war? Just get right down there on your knees in the blood and gore?"

"There was never time to waste. Hundreds came through during a battle... sometimes for days," she sighed.

Peter appraised her carefully. "And how long were you over there, Nurse Finney?"

"Nineteen months on the front. And in England a little before that," she said softly, remembering.

His eyes widened. "Nineteen months," he repeated. "That's a lot of wounded."

"Too many died," she sighed deeply. "No matter how hard we tried."

"That's rough," he admitted. "I hate it when one dies."

They sat quietly for a moment, an impromptu moment of silence for those who had not been saved.

It was Peter who spoke first. "You mentioned you were waiting for your husband? What department does he work in? Do I know him?"

Lydia looked around, wondering where Simon was. "He just started here, too. He's a surgeon. We met overseas and just got back after his army discharge came through."

Peter nodded. "I see. Well, if you're certain that you have a way to get home, I'll be on my way. I look forward to working with you tomorrow, Nurse Finney—Better not still find you asleep in this chair in the morning!"

"I am also looking forward to tomorrow, Doctor Martin," she replied emphatically, knowing that she had found her niche. She watched him leave the rotunda, pulling his collar up around his ears at the first blast of cold evening air.

It wasn't much longer before Simon appeared down the hall. She had briefly closed her eyes after the long day they'd had, but sensing his presence, she roused herself.

"There you are!" she exclaimed, so very glad to see him. She looked around for Marcus, but saw that Simon was alone.

"Marcus already went home," he explained, seeing her glancing about. "And I stayed to touch base with Doctor Maloney. Ready to go?" Simon asked as she rose from the chair.

"Yes I am, my love!" she exclaimed. "What a busy day! Let's go make supper."

He smiled at her. "I am famished—I'll bet Suzie is starting something delicious at home," he declared. "I want to hear all about your day in the clinic."

"I can hardly wait to tell you!" she said. "How was your day in surgery?"

"Interesting, to say the least!" he declared. "I'll fill you in, but right now, let's button you up!"

The cold air hit them hard. Lydia slid her arm into Simon's as they traversed the slippery steps to the street. The nearness of him warmed her, despite the gusts of wind that found their way up under her dress. She longed for the days of wearing army trousers.

Simon hailed a cab almost immediately—on a night this frightfully cold, he had no intention of them waiting for the trolley.

As soon as they walked in the door of the house, Lydia headed up to the bath. "I won't be long," she told Simon, heading for the stairs.

Suzie called to them from the kitchen. "Supper's soon ready!"

"Smells wonderful, Suzie!" Simon called back through the dining room. "I'm starved."

He hung up his coat and turned to hang Lydia's as well, realizing that she hadn't even taken it off when she had come in from the cold. He followed the savory smells to the kitchen, finding Marcus at the table, already telling Suzie about their day as he bounced Nikki on one knee and played with her tiny fingers, making her laugh.

"It was shades of the Somme, Suz," he was visibly excited. "Guy comes in with his stomach ripped right open, and Liskey asks if anyone knows how to do an emergency wound... abdominal.

Looks at the two of us, as if he knew that we had been chomping at the bit since the call had come up to the operating theater. They had a surgical room up and running in minutes. Soon as we were scrubbed, the guy was already on the table... just bleeding out."

Suzie looked up from the stove. "And? Did he pull through?"

Simon laughed as he took his seat at the table, reaching out a finger for Nikki to grab onto. "Suzie! We could have done that one in France, in the tent, with a flashlight! I'm telling you, Marcus, we should set up a proper first aid center. Maybe near the steelworks, or the docks, where accidents are more likely to happen and may be more severe—You'd help us in a walk-in surgical station, wouldn't you, Suzie?"

"Well, sure," she said. "I'd like that. But I can't take Nikki there, I'd need someone to come stay with her, but even one day a week would be fun."

"One day a week is probably all the hospital would give us anyway," Marcus said. "The pace in the hospital is slower than we're used to, Suzie. So much time is taken to clean the rooms between use. We should just switch to a clean room down the hall and keep going back and forth. We could see more patients that way. Maybe we should make rounds in the wards at lunchtime and then keep doing surgeries later in the day."

"Talk to Liskey," Simon advised. "He seems open to keeping us busy. And I still think Doctor Maloney has ulterior motives regarding us. He reminds me of Fortraine, back at the station."

"At least he speaks fluent English," Marcus observed.

"Oh, Fortraine wasn't that bad," Simon objected. "He got his point across easily enough. He only spoke French when he was angry, and during his tirades, only Monique could fully understand what he was saying."

"Monique?" Suzie asked.

"She came after you, Suzie," Marcus interrupted, careful not to suggest anything that would reveal his rather intimate dalliance with Monique. "She became interested in Fortraine after a bit."

"She did?" Simon exclaimed, surprised. "I missed all that?"

Marcus laughed. "She did. And you did! A lot happened while you were in Paris, donating part of your lung! Maybe those two are still together, who knows?"

"It happens," Simon nodded. He looked up to the ceiling.

"If Lydia doesn't come down soon, I'm eating without her," Marcus declared, grateful for the change of subject. "Suzie, whatever you're cooking in there smells heavenly!"

Simon stood. "I'll go check on her."

He made his way back through the dining room, noticing through the bay window just how dark it had become outside, but knowing that each day was adding a minute or two of daylight now, now that it was January.

He ran up the stairs and made his way to the bathroom, where Abril lay on the floor just outside of the door.

"Lydia?" he called, tapping on it. There was no answer, so he went in.

She was still in the clawfoot tub, head resting against the rim, eyes closed. Her clothes lay in a heap on the floor—coat and all.

Simon smiled, seeing that she had dozed off in the water. He picked up her coat, draping it over the small chair in the corner, then reached for her crumpled dress and underthings.

His smile vanished. His heart slammed against his ribs. The front of her dress was covered in dried blood.

Frightened, Simon turned up the lamplight and woke her.

"Lydia? Lydia!" he called out urgently. He reached into the now cool water, moving practiced hands over her wet, naked belly for signs of bleeding. She roused with the light, and his touch, focusing her eyes.

"Oh, my goodness. The water's cold!" she exclaimed softly. "I must've dozed off!"

Simon looked down at her anxiously. "Are you in pain? Are you cramping?"

She looked up, still waking. "Hand me the towel, would you please, my love? Of course, I'm alright! Why wouldn't I be? Just more tired than I realized!"

He picked up her dress and held it out for her to see. "You're covered in blood!" he exclaimed, alarmed.

Her eyes opened wider and she recognized the source of his concern. "Oh, that!" Lydia said quickly, trying to allay his fear. "That was from some poor guy whose buddies dragged him into clinic with a huge tear just under his liver. He was bleeding, badly, so I applied pressure, trying to keep his intestines inside until we could get him to the operating theater. Sister Edwarda said she's going to get me more aprons, long ones, if I insist on getting on the floor with patients bleeding out."

Simon sat back on his heels in relief, still kneeling beside the tub. He rested his hand on her belly. "Oh my God," he breathed. "I thought it was the baby. You really can't be on the floor in your condition!"

"Simon James Finney!" she blurted out. "What do you mean in my condition! The man was bleeding out on the floor!"

He still looked worried. "Someone else could have done that!" he protested.

"And I could have done it, too! So, I did!" she insisted. "Simon, you need to let me do my work. If it had been something with the baby, if I had been bleeding from the baby, I would have found someone to come and get you immediately, even mid-surgery. You need to trust me."

Simon's brown eyes dropped down to her wet, glistening skin. He stroked her rounded belly. "I do. I'm sorry. Really, I am sorry. I just saw all that blood and I panicked, I guess."

Lydia reached out a wet hand and placed it firmly over his, on her belly. "Simon, I love this baby as much as you do. Oh, my! Feel it, Simon? Feel all that kicking in there? The baby is really moving. It must have heard your voice calling out."

Simon pressed down lightly and felt the pronounced movement against one side of her belly. His mood shifted instantly from anxiety to wonder. "Right there, in that one spot especially. I can feel a little hard knob, kind of. Must be a foot, Lydia, maybe a heel."

"Feels like two feet, from all that pounding going on in there!" She smiled tenderly. "I feel the baby all the time now, my love. It constantly reminds me it's in there, growing. I'm not going to put it in jeopardy. And you yourself told me that the baby is safer inside of me than anywhere else it could be in the world. Even in a war. Remember?"

Simon leaned over the tub, pulling the drain plug, letting the cooled water escape. He leaned over Lydia and kissed her firmly on her lips. "I remember," he said then. "But that was before." He helped her stand up and began drying her off with the towel himself.

"Before what, Simon?" she asked softly as he dried her shoulders, her chest and swollen belly.

"Just before is all..." he murmured. "I can't even explain it right now. I'll fetch your robe. Let's go down and eat, before there's nothing left."

After everyone had shared their stories of the day, eaten their fill and the dishes had been washed and dried, Marcus asked, "So this Doctor Martin is running the clinic right now?"

Lydia nodded, enjoying a soothing cup of hot tea. "I guess the doctors take turns. Doctor Martin and Sister Edwarda have plenty of good ideas for improving the efficiency and safety of the clinic. And he's really interested in our experiences, Suzie. He knows we know how to get things done—asks all about what we did during the war."

Suzie had paid close attention to Lydia's description of her day.

"I'm ready to get in there, just from hearing about it! So much better than just passing out bedpans! Not that that isn't important, too, mind you! But it sounds like this Doctor Martin actually listens, Lydia... and wants to know what you think!"

"He does, Suzie. He asked me all about France. So then, he wanted me to start triaging the patients, and he focused on the ones that I thought he needed to see, while Sister Teresa and I saw the rest. She is very capable, too. It sped things up considerably. And many of these patients just needed a little health education and reassurance."

Simon felt their energy, their enthusiasm and envied them. They were getting involved with the kind of care that had drawn him to medicine in the first place, the unexpected cases that kept the mind sharp and ready for whatever might come, just as he'd experienced in country medicine with Doc Albright.

Finally, glancing at his watch, Simon called the women's attention to the time.

"Ladies, I think we should all be getting some rest soon, don't you?" he asked during a lull in their conversation. "Lydia, you could have drowned yourself dozing off in the tub earlier."

Lydia and Suzie laughed, though fatigue was setting in.

"Yes, I suppose we should," Suzie agreed.

Marcus also nodded and stood to collect the coffee and teacups from the table. "I'll wash these and be right up, Suzie."

"Don't take too long!" she teased. "I'll be waiting."

He smiled at her knowingly. "It's only four cups," he replied with a wink.

Simon followed Lydia up the stairs to their bedroom. Abril was stretched out on the landing of the second floor, monitoring the hallway where everyone slept. She rose for a head rub as Lydia walked by, then settled down again next to their bedroom door.

Simon pulled off his trousers and undershirt in the dim light of the city that crept in through the bay window and into the room. For a moment, he stood there, looking out over the huge city, with all of its many needs. Lydia opened her robe and came up behind him, pressing herself against his skin, feeling the muscles in his back and wrapping her arms around his bare chest.

"What are you thinking, my love?" she asked softly, her cheek against his shoulder blade. She was curious about what had made him so introspective all evening. After a short silence, she added playfully, "Did you know... if I climbed up on a stool, my belly would fit right into the curve of your back?"

As he felt her warmth against him, he didn't want to say what he was really thinking. Not too long ago, he had been the one who had caused the excitement in her voice as they worked together to ensure that the CCS was running smoothly. Now, it was this Peter Martin by her side all day, helping her to best utilize her skills. He missed the days when it had been just the two of them, saving lives in the surgery tent, before going to their own tent for the night. They had been together, 'making a difference', as she was fond of saying. Now, they were both still 'making a difference', but apart.

He wondered if this move to Pittsburgh had been a mistake after all. Maybe he should have reopened his rural practice in West Virginia, where they could have worked as a doctor-nurse team, side by side, taking care of miners and farmers and their families. But then, they wouldn't have had the opportunity to be close to both of their families or to have Marcus, Suzie and Nikki in their lives.

He thought, *Would life always demand these kinds of trade-offs?* So, he didn't answer her, not completely.

"I'm fine," he said quietly, realizing the plain truth... he was jealous of Peter Martin.

"Come to bed," she said with longing in her voice as she ran her fingers through his hair.

"It's going to creak if we do it the way I want," he warned.

"Good," she whispered. "I want the man I love to make it creak."

It was just what he needed to hear. He freed her from her robe, letting it drop to the floor, as she led him to the bed. He lay back against the pillows, watching Lydia as she got into bed, positioning herself over him. "Me, first," she said softly, allowing herself to fully enjoy him until he couldn't bear to wait a second longer. And the bed did creak, but neither of them paid any attention.

The following morning, their group of five set off for Charity, with Suzie cradling Nikki in her arms. For his part, Simon was excited for his appointment during lunch, with the hospital's senior priest, to talk about obtaining the wedding certificate. Miss Weston had arranged it for him, and he was anxious to confirm their options before speaking with Lydia.

Upon their arrival, the two nurses, parted from their husbands to make the long walk down the center corridor to the back of the hospital. Suzie, still holding little Nikki, peered eagerly around her at the various wards, knowing that neither of the married women would ever be permitted to work behind those closed doors. It was just curiosity, as she was very much looking forward to what was waiting for them.

When they entered the clinic, she quickly assessed the patients assembling with their children or other family members...Suzie smiled. This was something she knew... she felt it in her bones... like coming home.

Lydia led her to the back and quickly introduced her to everyone. Then they found the administrative nun at a desk, with a playpen already set up for Nikki.

"So, this is the little darling we've been expecting!" Sister Mary Margaret exclaimed, eagerly rising from the desk and reaching out for the beautiful baby. "Is she crawling yet? Teething? She's just beautiful, isn't she!"

"Little of both," Suzie laughed. "But she isn't a fussy baby."

"I found some soft little toys for her to play with, if you don't mind. Did you bring a blanket?" Sister Mary Margaret added. "Oh, we are going to have such fun!"

Suzie handed the nun a small bag of necessities. "I'll be close by if you need me."

"Now, dear, you just go on out and meet Doctor Martin. We'll be just fine, won't we, my adorable little Nikki." The nun eagerly shooed the women away.

Suzie saw little difference between leaving Nikki with this adoring nun versus leaving her baby with her mother when she had worked at the hospital in Rochester... but this would be much better, not having to pump and store bottles of milk during the day.

"Come on, Suz," Lydia said. "Let's find Doctor Martin. You're really going to like him."

Peter had just arrived at the clinic, and was removing his coat to hang it on a rack in one of the exam rooms. He warmly greeted Lydia and Susannah.

"Ah!" he exclaimed. "The other army nurse returned from the front! I'm already in awe of you ladies from yesterday's experience! Welcome, Nurse Lovell."

He looked at Suzie and Lydia in their long, full aprons and their brown and blonde tresses secured in buns, under matching blue scarves.

"Blue scarves?" Peter questioned. "Is that some kind of code?"

Suzie replied, "One of our nurses made them. We wore them at the station so the doctors could find us quickly in a sea of patients."

"Splendid idea!" Peter remarked. "There is sometimes a sea of patients in the clinic waiting room. I'll look for blue."

Peter leaned back against the counter, folded his arms across his chest, and turned his attention toward Suzie. "Nurse Lovell, would you be good enough to work with me a little this morning so I can see what you're comfortable with."

Suzie nodded. "Very good, Doctor Martin. Shall I stand when you enter the room? Is that also done here, as we did in the wards in Rochester? I don't want to offend you."

"Good grief, no, Nurse Lovell!" Peter exclaimed. "There's no time for that kind of nonsense in this busy clinic. We just keep moving until one of two things happens—we run out of time or run out of patients. The latter almost never occurs, but might just start happening now, with you nurses on duty."

"That's what Nurse Finney told me," Suzie laughed, eyes sparkling. "This is going to be fun." She winked at Lydia as she followed the doctor to the examination room, where Sister Teresa was already queuing up patients from the benches in the waiting area.

Lydia settled into her new station just inside the entry door. She worked with Sister Mary Francis on the priority system. By lunchtime, Lydia had already put slings on several sprains, wrapped bandages around several cuts in need of a few sutures, and advised quite a few patients on how to cover their mouths when they coughed, while leading them to the seats designated for them, behind the room dividers.

It was early afternoon when an older man stumbled into the clinic. Lydia immediately recognized that his color was ashen, instead of red from the cold winter air. He was clutching his chest. She ushered him directly to the exam table inside of the door, helping him to lie down while she quickly asked how long he had been having chest pain.

She motioned for Sister Mary Francis, who came running. "Get Doctor Martin, now!" she exclaimed. "Tell him it's urgent." The nun took off instantly.

Loosening the man's collar, Lydia propped his head up a little to help him breathe. She listened carefully to his chest and heard the extremely slow, irregular beating of his heart. Her warm hand firmly grasped his cold one. "What's your name?" she asked kindly... and calmly.

"Frank," he whispered. "I think I'm dying, Nurse."

She nodded, her blue eyes holding his own. "I believe your heart is very tired," she responded softly.

"I am tired," he whispered. "So, life ends right here, huh?"

Lydia felt the baby lurch in her belly and instinctively reached for her stomach. The man turned his head, noticing her action and protruding belly.

"Having a baby?" he asked.

Lydia nodded. "I am. The baby jumped when it heard your voice."

"Can I feel it?" he asked hesitantly, as his life began to fade before her eyes.

She took his hand and pressed it against her belly. Frank sighed in wonder when he felt the baby moving.

They waited together as Doctor Martin quickly came up behind them with Sister Mary Francis at his heels.

Frank raised his other hand to stop the doctor. "It's okay, Doc, I'm on the way out," he said.

Peter moved around the table, seeing the man's hand pressed against Lydia's abdomen.

"Is it your first, Nurse?" the man asked Lydia.

She nodded, her eyes glistening. Lydia gently touched his forehead while holding his hand against her belly. The baby rolled.

"Well, how about that. Wow! Did you feel that one? It really moved..." Frank managed.

Lydia nodded again, keeping his hand against her baby.

"It really did," she said softly and touched his cheek. "Do you have children, Frank?"

He nodded. "Not here, though. Could you tell them... could you tell them that their dad was thinking about them as he died, Nurse? I'd like them to know."

Lydia's eyes filled with tears, but she smiled at him gently. "I promise you, Frank, I will pass your message along to them."

Peter was listening to the man's heart now, marveling that he was still speaking even as death was taking him away. He saw the tears in Lydia's eyes.

"How about that, Doc?" Frank whispered weakly. "She's got a new little baby in there just when I'm moving on from this world... I guess that's the way it goes, huh... baby can take my place..."

Lydia gently touched his forehead, feeling his skin grow colder. The baby jumped again in her belly. Lydia and Frank both felt it moving at the same moment. He smiled at this, his eyes closing peacefully as he left the world behind.

Lydia gently removed his hand from her belly and laid it on his chest. She quickly wiped away a tear sliding down her cheek. "Say hello to God for me, Frank," she whispered so softly that only Peter and Sister Mary Francis heard her. The nun quickly made the sign of the cross, from her forehead down and across her shoulders.

"Time is two thirty-seven," Peter softly reported to the nun, who recorded it on her paper and turned to call an orderly who would take the man to the hospital morgue.

"May I see you, Nurse Finney? In the back?" Peter asked her quietly.

Lydia met his eyes, noting his concern. She looked to the clinic entrance, where a woman with three small children was standing there, waiting just inside the door. They were thinly wrapped in light coats, without mittens or scarves against the snow and winter air.

"Let me take care of them first, Doctor," she said, motioning toward the small, impoverished-looking family. *We need a box right here, for donated mittens and hats,* she thought... "They look so cold. They cannot wait by the door with the wind howling out there."

"Okay," he said, following her glance. "But then I do want to see you."

When she was able to take a quick break, Lydia alerted Sister Mary Francis that she was going to see the doctor, in the back. She paused for a moment to check on little Nikki, who was napping in the crib under the vigilant eye of Sister Mary Margaret.

Lydia sank down into an empty chair, leaning her head back against the wall, closing her eyes, just briefly. She offered up another quick prayer for Frank's family, who would eventually get the note she had hand-written, conveying his final wishes, the one she had tucked into his hand for those in the morgue to pass along to his next of kin.

Feeling a hand on her shoulder, she opened her eyes to see Peter beside her. Rising immediately, she followed the doctor into an examination room, where he closed the door behind them.

"Talk to me," Peter said to her firmly.

"He stumbled in clutching his chest, gray as a ghost already, not red from the cold, as he should have been," Lydia explained. "I got him on the table and checked his heart immediately, and it was already slow and irregular. His blood pressure was about forty, no higher, and difficult to even hear that. I called for you immediately—"

Peter shook his head, putting his hand up to stop her. "That's not what I mean, Nurse. I know the man had no hope of recovery. Major heart failure. Talk to me about how you are. That's what I want to know."

She smiled sadly, returning his handkerchief. "I'm fine," she told him. "It's not the first man I've seen die, not by a long shot."

"It's the first one here."

"Well... that's true," she admitted.

Peter looked at her for a long silent moment.

"Did I violate a protocol or something?" Lydia then asked, anxiously breaking the silence in the room. "I didn't ask anyone what to do in this kind of circumstance here at the clinic."

"Not at all," he quickly reassured her. "I only wanted to tell you that you gave that man—"

"Frank," she interrupted, speaking the name of the dead man.

"Frank," he corrected himself, "a great gift by letting him feel your baby moving as he lay dying. It was very compassionate, Lydia. And something that many women would never have permitted, to have a strange man touch them like that."

"It just made sense," she said, bringing forward a thought which she had repeated many times over the past several years. "Life and death are two sides of the same coin, at least, they are to me."

Peter slowly shook his head as he considered the lovely woman in the blue scarf before him. "I don't know what to do with you, and you've only been here a couple of days. Thank you for coming back here to speak with me. Are you willing to finish the last couple of hours?"

"Of course," she nodded, her hand unconsciously drifting down to touch the baby which was moving again, inside of her.

"When is your baby due?" he asked her, noticing the small maternal gesture.

"Easter," she told him. "Sometime around there, anyway."

Peter nodded, watching her open the office door before walking back down, past the waiting patients, to the outer room.

Easter. Well, she does have a little bit of a delightful pregnant waddle. Then he got up, carefully folded the handkerchief she'd returned, and tucked it back into his shirt pocket before going to see how the other new nurse was faring, with the patients she was already seeing on her own.

That evening, over dinner, Marcus found himself smiling as Suzie shared how much she'd enjoyed her day. He saw her energy, realizing she had found a way to meet the need for her own professional growth, the same way that Lydia had.

"This weekend, we should do something to celebrate your job," he announced.

"What did you have in mind?" she wondered, passing the mashed potatoes.

Lydia lit up. "I know! Let us watch Nikki, and you two go to a real movie. This city must have several movie houses not too far away. You wouldn't mind that, would you, Simon? Watching Nikki for them for a while?"

Simon helped himself to some warm biscuits Lydia had baked for them. "Not at all!" he replied. "It's wonderful practice for us."

"You two don't need practice, of that I'm quite certain," Suzie assured them. "But it would be fun to go to a movie somewhere, Marcus. What do you say?"

He nodded, digging into a slice of meatloaf. "I'm up for it. Let's go Saturday, then I'll take you out for dinner somewhere nice—Hey Simon, where were you at lunch today?"

Simon spread some butter on his biscuit, watching it melt into the soft bread. "I had an appointment with the senior hospital priest about the wedding certificate. He's sending a letter to the diocese in Nancy on our behalf, Lydia. See what can be done about the paper. In fact, he knows about that cathedral. It is apparently quite an old parish."

Lydia looked across the table to Simon, her eyes hopeful. "Did he think there was a chance of it?" she asked. "It's possible the local priest didn't even make note of it anywhere, since we weren't part of his parish."

"Probably not," Simon agreed. "Father Damien understands there were extenuating circumstances with the war in full swing. He seemed interested in our situation. And since we're, how did he say it? 'One of their own now', he said he would at least try to intervene."

"I want to mail a letter to Charlotte," Lydia told them all, changing the subject before she could feel discouraged. "I want to tell the nurses what we're doing here and offer them some hope that, when they come home, maybe they won't have to give up everything they're learning over there."

Simon nodded. "Ask about Nurse Sullivan when you do, would you? I want to know if she's heard anything about medical school."

"Sure hope she gets in," Marcus agreed. "Damn good at surgery already. Be a shame for that skill to be wasted."

"Do you think Doctor Stockton has left yet? When was his enlistment up?" Suzie wondered aloud, remembering his strong, quiet leadership of their medical group.

"Got to be soon," Marcus replied. "He came after we did, but before all of you nurses arrived."

"Was it just the two of you? Before Doctor Stockton got there?" Suzie asked as she tried to fill in some holes in the timeline. She didn't know much about Marcus' time before she had jumped off that army truck at the station.

Simon shook his head. "No, there were a couple of other doctors who were more than willing to be sent home as soon as possible. I recall asking one of them if he had any parting words. He said, 'just do your best; it won't be good enough', as I recall."

"He was wrong," Lydia told both men sitting at the dining room table. "It was good enough. Both of you men were more than good enough. Doctor Stockton, as well. I hope he gets home to his Tess and gets married right away."

Marcus nodded, thinking back. "Harold is a good man."

At that, Abril came trotting into the dining room and nosed up against Lydia.

"Need to go out, girl?" she asked the dog. "Come on, I'll take you." Lydia pushed back her chair and went to the kitchen, with Abril at her heels. The others heard the door open and felt a quick rush of cold air seep into the warmth of the house. It was just a moment, before Lydia had returned, taking her place at the table again. "The stars are already brilliant... it's a really clear evening. She certainly loves the snow."

"I'm surprised how well she does with Nikki... for not having been around children, she's surprisingly gentle and protective."

"Nikki is just one of her lambs to shepherd," Lydia laughed. "Think about what she'll do when there are two little ones, playing together in the yard."

"Well, sometime in spring, we'll be finding our own place, of course. But that doesn't mean we won't be here for visits and playtime," Suzie said.

Lydia looked at their friends. "I'll really miss you when you go," she admitted.

Marcus placed his fork and knife down on his empty plate. "It won't be until the weather warms," he told them. "Plus, I'm saving money for an automobile of our own too. The small amount that Simon will accept from me every month, for staying with you two, is leaving some extra for me to add to the money the army so kindly deposited into the bank during our two years of service."

"Well, Marcus," Simon interjected. "You have been caught doing the dishes and you are also buying groceries and keeping the lights on every other month."

"Half the groceries," Marcus corrected him. "That's all you said you'd take."

"That's correct," Simon nodded.

Lydia heard Abril at the door again and rose from the table, staying Simon, who had offered to go.

Carrying her empty plate and silverware to the counter by the kitchen sink, she opened the backdoor and stepped outside. Looking for Abril, who had briefly run back out in the yard, chasing some small creature that was scurrying about in the snow, Lydia saw the dog happily bounding back through the drifts. Abril shook the snow from her fur before Lydia noticed that she had a squirrel in her teeth, which she proudly dropped onto the wooden porch at Lydia's feet—just as she would have done at the camp in Belgium, earning high praises from the cook for providing something for the stew pot.

Lydia knelt beside Abril. "Oh, my," she whispered. "Good girl... I think."

Lydia burst into tears.

Abril pushed against Lydia's legs, perhaps concerned that her gift had been misunderstood by her human. She whined softly and looked up at the woman. Out there, in the cold, on her back porch underneath the sparkling stars, Lydia grieved the death of the man, Frank. And in her mind, a sea of faces swept over her like a giant wave… faces of other Franks and so many others who had gone before the man this afternoon.

She heard herself telling Peter Martin that Frank wasn't the first man who had died in her care. And he had reminded her that it was the first one, here. Of course, he was right. Death had followed her here, all the way back to the States. There would not be as many, nor would the deaths occur in such a short period of time. But she still lived with death.

Marcus brought his dishes to the kitchen sink. He saw the back door ajar and heard muffled sobs. He hesitated with his hand on the knob, wanting to go out to Lydia, but thought the better of it. Turning away, he went back into the dining room, caught Simon's eyes, and tilted his head toward the back porch with a look that conveyed his concern.

"Let's go sit by the fireplace before we go up," Marcus said to Suzie. "We can look at the newspaper and see if there is a movie advertised."

Simon rose quickly from the table, following Marcus' prompting, and headed to the back porch. He stepped outside and saw Lydia looking at the dead squirrel with an apologetic Abril at her feet. He immediately wrapped his arms around Lydia and felt how cold she was, tears freezing on her red cheeks.

"Come inside," he urged her quickly. "You'll freeze out here just like that poor creature."

She followed him in, Abril at her heels. Simon leaned back against the kitchen sink and pulled her close, rubbing her arms to warm them. He kissed her face.

"Now, what's this all about?" he asked her quietly. "Thinking about Belgium? Being hungry over there? The squirrel remind you of Abril finding Cook some food to keep everyone alive? What is it?"

She leaned against him, feeling the warmth of his chest through his sweater. "I was doing triage at the clinic today, you know. Sister Edwarda set up a little station for me right inside the door. An older man, Frank, came in, grabbing his chest. I got him down and his heart was almost gone, Simon. And he saw that I was pregnant, and he knew he was dying. Asked me to tell his children he was thinking of them. He asked if he could... well, he felt the baby kicking, Simon, and he was so happy to feel our baby. He died right as he felt the baby kicking. So, I wrote his family the letter and put it in his hand before they took him to the hospital morgue."

Simon nodded, now understanding. "We knew this would happen."

"Of course," she said, her calm returning. "It's what we do. You will lose people in the operating theater, or on the wards, and I will lose people in the clinic or in their homes."

"Yes," Simon said simply. "We will."

"Then, Abril brought that little squirrel, and it turned into memories of so many faces, of the soldiers passing. How many faces? I can't even imagine, Simon."

"We never counted, remember, Lydia? We agreed, all of us, not to do that," Simon reminded her. "It's always been one person at a time. This time, it was Frank. And the way I see it, you were able to give him the gentlest, kindest passage that anyone could have."

"Our baby did that, Simon," Lydia whispered. "Something we created in love was able to give a feeling of love to someone dying, and our baby isn't even born yet. For me, having that feeling of life growing inside of me and being able to share it is such a great gift. You, my beloved husband, have given me such a great gift. You told me once it was your fault that I got pregnant, that you knowingly took the risk. Thank you, Simon, so much for taking that risk. What a wonderful gift you and the baby are to me. I can't even find the right words to thank you."

Simon held her close, her head just under his chin, tight against him. He swallowed several times, trying to move the lump in his throat without success, so he simply said nothing and stroked her hair as she leaned against him at the sink in the kitchen.

Finally, he managed, "Can we go to bed? I just want to hold you and not let you go. Let's just curl up in bed together."

She nodded. They separated long enough to make their way through the living room, where they wished Suzie and Marcus a good night. Marcus looked over anxiously, but Simon nodded slightly. He would fill Marcus in, tomorrow.

They went upstairs and got right into bed, Lydia resting on Simon's chest... his arms around her. They fell asleep, warm beneath the quilts, holding each other while the baby rolled gently within Lydia's womb, apparently unaware of such things as bedtimes.

Chapter 8
Walking a Beat

"Will you please settle down!" Marcus demanded as Simon took an extended time washing and re-washing his hands. "My God, man, you need to focus."

"I'm focused," Simon muttered from behind his face mask as they prepared for a complex surgery. The patient on the table had a tumor growing around his aorta... it was a delicate surgery... to cut the invasive tissue away, before it closed off the man's vital blood flow.

Marcus took a clean towel to dry his hands. "I need you to pay attention here, Simon. She's just seeing some people in their homes—it's not like she's gone back to France."

Simon glanced up at him. "It's a big city out there, Marc, with a lot of questionable types walking around."

"Like worse than the German army?" Marcus countered. "Look, there aren't any bombs falling—no cannons firing—she's got this. And she took the dog, for heaven's sake. Focus, man!" If Marcus was honest, he was just as concerned, but that would have to wait until after this operation, with the man recovering nicely.

Simon nodded. "I'm focused."

They slid into the gowns readied for them and took their places on either side of the table where the patient had been prepped. Marcus looked to the anesthetist, who was already in position.

"How are we doing, Sam?" Marcus asked. "It's going to be a long one. Thanks for getting him intubated."

"I figured," the man nodded. "Saw the pictures. It looks like an octopus wrapped around all those arteries in there."

Marcus looked up at the pictures on the lighted board. "Yes, it does. We're going to buy him some time, but it's going to grow back."

Starting them off, Simon made the incision, and they quickly cauterized the small bleeders as they opened the man's chest and upper abdomen. The assisting nurse quickly passed them gauze pads to staunch any pooled blood.

"Let's retract, Nurse," Marcus said, holding out his hand for the gleaming metal tool.

They spread the man's ribs and carefully looked inside.

"Can we get a little more light in here?" Simon asked no one in particular.

An orderly reached overhead to adjust the ceiling light.

"Wow," Simon remarked softly. "It really is a big one. All around the pulmonary bifurcation..."

Marcus probed the cavity, assessing the extent of the tumor. "Well, let's see what we can do to maybe give him another birthday."

The operating theater grew quiet, the team efficiently passing instruments back and forth as they attempted to remove as much of the tumor as possible, separating the delicate arteries from the fingers of tissue which were trying to strangle them. Both surgeons were deeply focused on the most minute details of their efforts.

"How's he holding up, Sam?" Simon asked anesthesia after a time.

"He's going to need some fluids, Doc," Sam replied, tracking the patient's heart rhythm with his stethoscope. "We've been open awhile."

"Get some running," Marcus said simply as others sped up the intravenous fluids. There was movement behind the table, but Marcus and Simon remained focused on the task before them as Doctor Liskey joined, peering into the incision.

"Hm," he said. "Big tumor."

"Only half of what was in there," Marcus confirmed, carefully cutting away tendrils of tumor... working the scalpel with sure, steady hands from one side... while Simon attended to the other side with the same skilled precision.

Liskey looked at the tray where the specimen was piling up. "Good technique, doctors," he observed. "They said you were good at vascular. They weren't wrong."

"We aren't out of the woods yet," Marcus said. "And we aren't going to get it all. That's the thing about it. It'll start growing again."

"Mr. Bentwood knows that," Liskey said. "He just wants a chance. He's got a twenty-fifth wedding anniversary coming up and wants to spend it with his family. You'll give him that, at least."

"Probably not much more," Marcus said. "Unless the anniversary is next month. But it's always worth a try."

Liskey nodded. "That's right. I'll take your appendectomy coming behind this one. I'll likely be done before you guys are. Just wanted to see how it was going in here."

Neither doctor looked up as the supervising surgeon removed his gown and dropped it into the hamper. Liskey looked back over his shoulder briefly at the two capped heads bent over their task. They were good. Very good. Liskey knew they could handle just about anything. He went to wash up in the next operating theater as he prepared to remove an offending appendix before it ruptured. He would happily update Doctor Maloney later about the new surgeons' progress in acclimating—they were doing just fine.

After several intense hours of operating, Marcus finally looked up at Simon. "That's as good as it gets, Doctor Finney," he smiled, relieved. "Let's close here... and thanks Sam—let him wake up."

Simon nodded in agreement—it would take a long time for this man to heal. They used loose sutures to hold the man together, but also allow for packing underneath. Stripping off their gloves, they went to clean up at the sink. Marcus rubbed his stiff neck. "Glad we had good lighting for that one," he observed as the nurse took his soiled gown.

"It went well," she smiled with her eyes, above her mask.

"Thanks, Nurse Richards. Excellent team here." Marcus replied, and he meant it.

"We're glad you've joined us." Nurse Richards enjoyed her work in the operating theater, the tension of it and the release that followed. She especially enjoyed assisting these two new surgeons who had brought fresh energy and experience with them. Sometimes, change was good. Kept people on their toes.

Marcus and Simon headed for the doctors' lounge to grab some coffee and sandwiches that had been left out for them by the kitchen.

"Dinner and a show!" Marcus said, excited about what had been stuffed between the two thick pieces of bread. "We're so lucky."

Simon sank wearily into the small sofa in the room where the surgeons sometimes took short naps on longer days. "Now, can I please be unfocused for a minute?" he asked.

Marcus nodded his approval. "Yes, you may."

"Good!" Simon took a bite of sandwich, noting how delicious it really was. "Think they could scrounge up another one of these? I'm hungry."

"I think that—once your strength has been restored—you can walk yourself down to the kitchen and find something yourself!" Marcus exclaimed.

"Maybe I'll take a walk downtown," Simon thought aloud. "See what the weather is like."

Marcus laughed at that, seeing through his friend's plan. "Lydia is not going to freeze to death out there."

"She said that she wished she could wear trousers again, and boots." Simon sighed.

"Well that would certainly attract attention from the un-savories you're worried about, Simon." Marcus appraised his friend, "I mean, what's the worst that can happen? Seriously!"

"She could go into someone's house and run into some drunk guy who doesn't have any respect for women. Someone bigger and stronger than she is," Simon's mind began to race.

Marcus' did as well. In a flash, he remembered when he was just that drunk, right after Suzie had left the station in France. It was as close as he'd ever come to being inappropriate with Lydia, who had been beneath him on the ground—the one time in his life that he had been completely inebriated on whiskey, with a lack of self-control that he could still only vaguely remember. The reprimand from Dr. Harold Stockton afterward though, he remembered that quite well. Lydia, though, had never brought up the incident again, and Marcus had taken great pains to make it up to her. She had been... quite discrete.

"Yeah," Marcus said. "Well, at least people don't get drunk this early in the day," he tried to reassure Simon, knowing all too well that the possibilities for danger were many.

Simon crumbled the paper that had been wrapped around his sandwich and stood, grabbing his white office coat. "I'm going to the cafeteria before the next patient. I think we have a hernia repair coming up?"

"Sounds good—I'm going to run down to the clinic and see how Suzie is getting on," Marcus gave Simon another reassuring look as his friend left the lounge. "See you after lunch."

Lydia used the trolley to navigate the neighborhood where she had been scheduled for the day. She had already fit in two patients who lived in close proximity: a sickly baby and a man with a rather large sore on the bottom of his foot. Abril was sitting on the little platform at the back of the trolley, enjoying the breeze blowing through her fur as the trolley transported them to a different section of the neighborhood. Lydia had donned long, thick socks and the extended apron she wore under her coat to try to block a little of the wind while walking—at least it was warmer on the trolley.

On her lap, she held the little satchel which had been filled with numerous supplies and instruments that she and Suzie had compiled in preparation for the day. Lydia reviewed the list of people that Sister Edwarda needed her to see—two already checked off. It was an interesting mix of cases, from children to a post-op patient who had recently been discharged from the hospital. The patients with telephone lines had been called, to let them know that a nurse would be coming, so she had been expected at those houses.

As she stepped off the trolley, they began walking to their next destination, not completely sure if they were going the right way. As luck would have it, a policeman was stationed at the next corner, watching the flow of human activity along the street.

"Hello, Officer," Lydia greeted him.

"Ma'am," he replied, touching the edge of his uniform hat.

"Could you steer me to this address? I'm Lydia Finney, a nurse with Charity Hospital, and I am to see a patient at this address, but I'm new to the city. Trying to follow these directions is proving to be somewhat of a challenge," Lydia reported in frustration.

He leaned over and looked at her paper with the directions. "I know that street," the officer said. "I'm Officer Stevenson. I didn't know you nurses were out walking the beat like me!" he added.

"It's somewhat of a new idea," Lydia explained. "We're trying to reach out to people if they are having trouble getting to the clinic."

"Well, that's real fine," he commented, nodding his head in a show of support. "This is my patrol area, Nurse Finney—you being a young lady out here—you need anything, just call on me or one of the other fellas wearing the blue. We'll help you out. This your dog?"

"It is!" Lydia said. "She's been a steady companion of mine for over a year. You'll never find a better dog than Abril."

"Abril, huh?" the officer said, looking down at the alert animal. "What's that mean, sounds like some kind of a flower or something?"

"It's similar to the French word for shelter," Lydia told him. "She came to me in France, during the war."

"Women in the war? Never heard of that, miss," Officer Stevenson chuckled.

"I was with the French army, at the front," she told him. "With several other nurses. Twelve of us, to be exact."

"How about that now!" Officer Stevenson declared. "I don't know, miss. Don't think a woman should be over in a war like that. It isn't safe, in my opinion. And it isn't always safe for a woman to be alone out here, either, not in this city."

Officer Stevenson looked at the young woman standing in front of him with her dog. Suddenly his eyes lit up with the birth of an idea. He reached up, removing his black whistle on its long black cord, and placed it around her neck. "Now, you just take this. It blows real loud. Can hear it blocks away," he insisted, folding her fingers around it. "You need any help at all—for an ambulance or something else—I'll hear it, or any of us walking our beats, and we'll come running. You just keep it on you, Nurse Finney."

Lydia smiled up at him. "I feel safer just knowing that you gentlemen are on duty, Officer Stevenson. It's so very nice to meet you. I'm sure that we will see each other often."

He touched the brim of his hat again. "I'll look for you walkin' your beat, Nurse Finney," he said with a broad smile as she headed off down the sidewalk, in the direction he had instructed, with her dog at her heels. He felt better just knowing she had his whistle around her neck.

Lydia planned for her next patient, thinking how very comfortable she felt, being on her 'beat'.

In the doctors' changing lounge, Marcus had his feet propped up on the arm of the couch, his hands comfortably crossed over his chest. He studied his buddy, who was chewing on a chunk of kielbasa he'd coerced out of one of the cafeteria staff.

"So... what do you think, Simon? About Lydia still working? Suzie is thrilled with the idea of the independence of these home visits."

Simon was perched on a desk in the room, and considered the question. "I don't think I have much of a say, Marc. She's determined to work right up to the 'very end'—whenever that's going to be, around Easter I guess. If she ends up having a good relationship with the midwife, maybe they can talk her out of being out on the streets when she's nine months pregnant—"

Marcus laughed at that, "Even Lydia isn't that stubborn, buddy. Suzie is already filling her ears with the benefits of time off near the end... when ankles are a little puffy and a woman can't even see her feet anymore."

Simon was hopeful. "Maybe it takes a woman who's been through it to convince another woman to slow down. I can only hope."

The door of the lounge suddenly flew open with a bang. One of the orderlies stuck his head through the opening, "You two, needed immediately, Doctor Liskey says room five, on the double!" He was breathing hard from running, trying to find these two between scheduled surgeries.

Simon and Marcus both jumped to their feet and headed immediately to the fifth operating room where there was a bustle of focused activity. They both headed to the scrub sink and grabbed brushes without delay as one of the surgical nurses came over with gowns ready.

"What happened?" Simon asked, looking over his shoulder at the supine figure on the surgical table.

The eyes showing above the face mask were brimming. "It's one of our own," she said, her voice breaking. "She was walking back to her car after her shift. One of our nurses. Someone... someone grabbed her on the hill, dragged her into the brush and raped her. But that's not all. He shot her in the back. In the back!"

Marc's eyes met Simon's. He also looked over at the table as he donned the sterile gown and gloves. The orderlies had positioned the woman on her belly, a breathing tube already protruding from her mouth as her head lay sideways. She was young.

"What's her name?" Marc asked.

"Leonore Adams," she said quietly. "She's worked for us for years, mostly with kids."

Marcus approached the operating table and noted the sterile drapes being stretched out, leaving the woman's spine exposed. He easily identified the entry wound, confirming that she had been shot from behind, probably trying to flee her assailant. Simon was studying the film on the light board carefully, to find where the bullet was lodged—it was against delicate nerves—Marc joined him.

"What do you think, Marc?" Simon said. "We can get the bullet out, no problem. But it looks to me like the cord is severed."

Scrutinizing the image, Marcus nodded. "Does to me, too. She'll be paralyzed from the waist down, Simon. We won't be able to get that back for her."

"Damn," Simon exhaled. "I know."

"But let's be careful. Maybe it's not a complete dissection," Marcus quietly thought aloud.

"Maybe..." Simon nodded, but he didn't sound too hopeful. Right outside of the hospital? Right back in the bushes? "What's wrong with someone who would go after a nurse like that? Did they catch the guy?"

Marcus turned away from the light board. He had seen what he needed to see. It was more important now to actually get inside. He went to the table and leaned over the prostrate woman, who was already under the effect of the anesthesia. "Leonore," he said softly. "This is Doctor Lovell. We're going to try to help you. So, wherever your spirit is, rest easy. You're safe now. We'll do our very best to make it better."

He straightened as Simon's eyes met his, "Scalpel."

The two men went to work retrieving the bullet and cleaning out the bone fragments from the discs of the spine that had been shattered. She would be in a wheeled chair the rest of her days.

And Lydia is out on those streets, Simon thought, for just a second... pushing the fear aside to focus on what was right in front of him.

Marcus was also planning to have a conversation with Suzie about staying with the walk-in clinic. Maybe, after this, Sister Edwarda would reconsider her plan to expand nursing services to the streets. Maybe the hospital needed to rethink the entire idea.

Lydia paused to look around. It would be getting dark soon. She had just one more stop to make and would have to hurry. Walking would be faster than waiting for a trolley. Heading back down the street, she again saw Officer Stevenson in the distance. He noticed her, and she waved as she made her way to the last patient of the day.

It was dark by the time Lydia came to the corner where her own house stood. There were lights on in the windows, and she knew that Simon would be anxious. She could see movement through the living room window, and as she drew closer, she saw Marcus stand up from having been on the floor and wondered if he had been playing there with Nikki. As Lydia quietly pushed the door open, Abril bounded through the foyer and into the house. Lydia felt the lovely warmth wrap around her like a blanket. Glancing around the door frame into the parlor, she saw Simon on the floor doing push-ups. Marcus was standing over him, counting while Abril looked on, waiting to be acknowledged.

"You're almost there!" Marcus encouraged the man on the floor. "Forty-nine... fifty! Well done! You only lagged behind me by about ten minutes!"

Seeing Lydia come through the foyer, Simon stood quickly, catching his breath. "Yeah, but you did eighty or ninety; I lost count. One of these days, I'll be the one looking down on you!"

"I don't see it happening, buddy," Marcus said doubtfully, "but if it makes you feel better..."

Pulling off her long apron, Lydia folded it, and placed it on her satchel on the little bench near the door. Simon was bathed in sweat from the exertion of the workout the men had been doing, but he quickly pulled her to him anyway. "It's dark out," his tone was serious.

"Just barely," she reminded him calmly.

"You should be home before dark," he said to her, his voice tight as he gripped her arms. *What if it had been Lydia with a bullet in her spine? What if...*

Lydia looked up in surprise. "Simon, are you angry with me?"

"No, Lydia, I'm not angry. I was worried. I don't like feeling afraid, and when you were still out, in the dark... I was afraid of something happening," he said, his brown eyes fastened to hers. His voice softened a little. "I just don't want anything bad to happen to you again."

She was truly contrite. "I am sorry, Simon. I didn't mean to worry you. I'll... do better at getting home while it's still light out. I'm trying to find a way to feel braver myself, to overcome my own fears. I guess I pushed it too far."

Marcus looked over at Lydia. She seemed to be unscathed. He'd had Simon engaged in the push-up competition, knowing his buddy was scanning the windows for signs of her as soon as night had fallen. Better to work off the agitation than let it build up. He saw Simon kiss Lydia and draw a deep breath to calm himself.

"Well, you're home now," Simon acknowledged in relief.

Relief washing over him just as it had over Simon, Marcus wiped the sweat from his own face. "I could have done ten more you know," Marcus observed.

Simon looked over at him. "You could not! Prove it!"

Marcus dropped to the floor and counted them off, then jumped back up to his feet. "There."

"I stopped because Lydia came home, and it was only right to greet my wife and make sure she was safe!" Simon retorted.

"Uh-huh. Save it for someone who will believe that." Marcus turned his focus to Lydia. "Suzie is upstairs with Nikki, Lydia. She's finishing up her bath."

Lydia placed her hands on her hips, looking squarely at both men. She felt guilty for having worried them and there were no good smells emanating from the kitchen indicating supper was ready. Pulling her hair out of its scarf, letting it tumble down over her shoulders, she said, "Both of you should wash up. I'll go make supper." It would be her apology.

Simon nodded, sprinting up the stairs, Abril at his heels. "I'm still faster, Marcus," he called down from the landing, but he was coughing as he reached the top.

Marcus looked up the stairs for a moment, not yet wanting to discuss the case of the nurse. He shook his head. "That man helped me take out an enormous tumor this morning with the finesse of an artist—"

Lydia pointed in the direction of the stairs. "You, too!" she ordered him.

But instead, Marcus reached out and clasped her shoulders. "It's already in use up there. Seriously, Lydia, be home before dark. You worried him sick." *You worried both of us sick!*

"I'm sorry, Marcus, really," she told him, feeling even more guilty than she did a minute ago.

Calmer, he kissed her forehead and patted her belly. "I'm just saying. Before dark."

Lydia nodded her agreement as Marcus dragged a chair back into its place, which the men had moved aside for the push-up competition. Then, Lydia noticed something new on the mantle over the fireplace. She walked over, knowing immediately what it was. There was her small music box, and the white stone with gold flecks in it. Tears sprang into her eyes. She held the stone in her palm, remembering when Simon had pulled it from the Meuse, pledging to protect her always. Not tears of sorrow, but tears of gratitude. Simon had remembered. *We'll put it on the mantle over our own fireplace with a red candle holder.* Now they just needed a red glass sconce for a candle, and it would be complete. Gently, she laid the stone back down next to the Christmas gift that Simon had given her in France, the music box. Yes, of course he just wanted to keep her safe.

Seeing Lydia paused by the mantle, Marcus came over and picked up the music box. "Remember when you got the sign from this? About Simon? You said it went off without you even touching it."

"You remember that, Marc?" Lydia asked, looking up at him astonished.

"I remember everything, Lydia," he said softly, gazing down at her.

"I'll get started on supper," she said, patting his cheek softly. She walked back to the kitchen and began stirring up a meal for the four of them, counting the blessings that were momentarily overflowing. Suzie came down shortly afterward with Nikki in pajamas to help her finish the meal.

"How was the clinic today, Suzie?" Lydia asked her eagerly. "Did you enjoy your day?"

Suzie laughed. "Did I ever!" she exclaimed. "Woman came in, in labor, about to deliver right on the spot! You should have seen Sister Mary Francis run for Doctor Martin! Oh, my, her habit took wings!"

"No!" Lydia exclaimed in delight. "Did she have it right there in the clinic?"

"Indeed she did!" Suzie laughed. "Doctor Martin had his hands full with the head coming out, and the woman screaming, and the nuns shouting. It was marvelous! I got her on the exam table, dropped her drawers, grabbed towels, and Doctor Martin was catching the baby before he could even take his white coat off!"

Lydia laughed, picturing the scene. "I would have just loved to have seen Doctor Martin's face! Boy or girl?"

"Little girl, fifth child, and the mother said the fourth almost fell out on the floor, too, it came so fast," Suzie reached up for some plates from the cupboard.

"I hope mine comes that fast!" Lydia exclaimed. "Wouldn't that be nice!"

"Just the fast part? Or the Doctor Martin catching it part?" Suzie teased. "You need a doctor, you know. Just in case. I noticed you haven't set one up yet."

"Sister Edwarda says there is a nun, Sister Anne, who has delivered a hundred babies. I've asked to meet with her to see if she'll deliver this one, too."

"You should reconsider, Lydia," Suzie said over her shoulder as she headed to the table in the dining room. "Doctor Martin is cuter than the nuns by far! And much more entertaining! Might even do a house-call!"

Lydia just smiled at Suzie's enthusiasm. The two of them were quite different women, yet they were so bonded as friends after having shared so much. Suzie knew how to find the light side of any moment, if there was one to be had.

Returning to the kitchen, Suzie added, "Are the guys upstairs already? Your Simon never skips a meal."

"Isn't that the truth!" Lydia agreed. "Yes, they were having a push-up competition when I came in and were all sweaty, so I sent them to wash up in the tub."

"Funny, isn't it?" Suzie mused. "In the camp, we only had a shower and wanted a bath. Now, we have a bath and might want a shower."

"The camp did get a tub near the end, Suzie! And even a hot water tank for it! Anyway, they'll be down soon, clean and hungry." Lydia tasted the concoction she had thrown together, filled with chicken, egg noodles, chunks of carrots and potatoes and whatever greens she could find in the pantry.

Suzie leaned over the pot. "Sure smells good, whatever you seasoned it with. I'll put out some bread and butter to go with it. How was it out on the streets?"

Lydia glanced up. "The folks were so appreciative that a nurse would come all the way out. And the local policeman, Officer

Stevenson, was walking his beat, even in the cold. He said any of their guys will help us in any way we need when we're out seeing patients. Such a nice man. Saw sick toddlers, casted legs, dressed several wounds, saw an elderly man who was a recent amputee—did his dressing."

"Wow," Suzie said softly. "Sounds a lot like being back in the recovery tent!"

"Yes, it did feel a little like that... and you really need to be able to problem solve on your own."

"Same way in the clinic when Doctor Martin says to call him if we need him, then he just lets us go off and take care of people," Suzie chimed in. "This is what I was missing in the Rochester hospital. I really missed working closely with the doctors like we did in camp—when they'd pull us all together and ask us to come up with suggestions. Marcus, Simon, Harold Stockton... they really valued us."

"They certainly did," Lydia agreed, grabbing a tureen for the rich soup she was ready to serve. "And here come two of them now, trying to beat each other down the stairs, I think, from the pounding—like two brothers."

Suzie laughed. "They certainly are."

The following day brought with it frustrating news for Simon. Father Damien had finally received word that the Church could not endorse the marriage in Nancy since the bishop could not approve a priest performing a ceremony for a couple who were not already confirmed Catholics. The hardships of the war actually had nothing to do with it. The dioceses held the position that even if the priest in Nancy would be willing to vouch for having blessed the marriage, they could not produce an official document that would satisfy the government in the Commonwealth, according to law. The only recourse left to Simon and Lydia was to get married again. Simon left Father Damien feeling utterly defeated. Lydia had become a little more emotional as her pregnancy progressed and he had so hoped for a better outcome to report back to her.

Meeting Marcus, who had already changed into his surgical garb, in the doctors' lounge, Simon shared the outcome of his conversation with the priest.

"Could be worse," Marcus assured him.

"How could it possibly be worse, Marc?" Simon demanded. "Her own father asked me point blank if she had been forced to marry me because of the pregnancy."

"Did he now?" Marcus asked, casually stretching his legs over the arm of the divan as Simon began to dress. "Sounds like he was just protecting his little girl from living in sin."

Simon pulled on a pair of white pants over his boxers. "So, what now. Do I go ask him for permission to marry his daughter, now, like you did with Suzie's father? Or do we just do it and spring it on her family? Leave them out of it twice?"

Marcus said, "You know what? I really miss having my softball to throw up in the air sometimes. Wonder whatever happened to that?"

Simon grunted, pulling a white surgical shirt over his head. "You hit me in the back with it once, when I didn't tell you that Lydia had taken a bullet in her shoulder."

"Did I really? I don't remember that..." Marcus said. "I remember that you removed the bullet for her, but not hitting you with my ball—I think I loaned it to you when I suggested bedrest—with your leg in the splint—do you still have it?"

"It was not a suggestion. You ordered them to keep me on six weeks of bedrest, said I wasn't allowed to move. Felt like imprisonment!" Simon protested, remembering when Marcus had saved his life after the bomb had exploded in the middle of their camp.

"Well, everyone should be so lucky to be imprisoned—with your beautiful wife as your private duty nurse—giving you sponge baths, in a private tent," Marcus observed dryly. "Hate to think how you suffered, Simon."

Simon paused, thinking back. His mood lifted. "Yeah, that was pretty nice..." he admitted with a small smile. "She gives a good cot bath."

Marcus folded his hands over his stomach, having nothing else to do with them. "So, you could have a housewarming party with her family and your family so they can finally meet each other and ask some minister to show up and do it over again with everybody there, just because they all missed the first one. Bless the house, bless you... bless the whole crowd. They don't have to know this will be the one that's truly legit for that clerk down at the courthouse."

Simon looked over at Marcus, both amazed and relieved. It was a good idea. One that just might give Lydia a great deal of pleasure instead of distress. "She'd probably go for that," Simon said. "Thanks for the suggestion, buddy."

"I live to serve," Marcus said, jumping up. "You finally ready? We have a gallbladder full of stones to remove."

"Yes, I'm ready— and I'll buy you a softball," Simon said, clapping his friend on the shoulder as they headed to the operating theater.

That night Simon talked to Lydia about the idea of a wedding ceremony for the families. They were talking quietly, after supper, sitting on the sofa by the fireplace. Marcus and Suzie had already gone up for the night. Wrapped in his arms, Lydia watched the wood embers turn to gold and then red, finally collapsing in upon themselves as they burned down to ash. Abril was stretched out on the stone hearth, also listening to the crackling of the wood.

"We could have our families come, since they couldn't be with us in Nancy? It's about time they at least meet each other, don't you agree?" Simon offered.

Lydia nodded against his shoulder. "They should. But they're probably going to come see the baby when it's born, too. Two trips in such a short time might be hard on them."

"It's not that far," Simon reminded her. "We'll need to find a minister willing to marry us."

Lydia frowned, although he couldn't see her face as she leaned against him. "But if we have a minister, it's like saying the first time when the priest heard our vows didn't count," she protested softly. "I don't want a minister taking that away from us."

"We can just go to a judge then," Simon told her. "It's legal, and it will satisfy the government that you are really and truly my wife. That's all we really need anyway, to satisfy the courts."

Lydia frowned again. "But then it's a meaningless piece of paper just for some agency in the city. Why are they making us do this?"

"Because I didn't think back in Nancy that this would happen. I wasn't thinking ahead to what it would be like when we came home," Simon confessed. "I wasn't even thinking that we'd make it home from the war. I was only thinking about being with you and making my commitment public."

She slid her fingers inside his shirt and touched his chest. "You weren't thinking about a wedding night?"

He kissed the top of her head. "Oh, yeah, I was certainly thinking of a wedding night. We waited a long time for that, didn't we?"

"How ever did you convince Lieutenant Aubrey to let me go with you to Nancy anyway?" she wondered, feeling the hair on his chest between her fingers.

"I told him that I needed the angel of mercy, as the French were calling you, to be an ambassador of goodwill, so to speak, and that you could speak French much better than I could," Simon chuckled. "He had to give in because we needed those supplies so badly. But if that hadn't worked, I would have come up with something else. I wanted you to be mine, no matter what it took."

"Let's go upstairs." She caressed his face and kissed him. A long, full kiss, relishing the perfectly interlocking puzzle of their lips.

"Oh, yeah," he murmured in anticipation. "Go on up. I'll let Abril out once more and be right there," Simon assured her as Lydia climbed the stairs ahead of him.

Simon let Abril out the back door for a minute while he tidied up the house. He hung Lydia's coat in the front hall closet. Then gathered the satchel she had carried with her to work, with the apron folded on top, and placed them on the little bench in the foyer. As he picked up the apron, something dropped to the floor from its large pocket. Puzzled, Simon reached down and picked up the black object on a long cord—he recognized it immediately as a police whistle. Simon froze, holding it in his palm. What was Lydia doing with a police whistle? Where had it come from... and why hadn't he been told about it?

He heard the dog at the back door and quickly let Abril back into the house. She waited for Simon to go up the stairs with her before dropping down at her post on the landing, where she protected the entire human population of the house. During her night watch, no danger would get past her.

Simon checked in on Lydia, curled up under the covers in their bed. He walked down the dark hall to the bathroom to wash up before going to her—he was troubled. When he at last made it to the bedroom, he could see in the dim lamplight that she had already fallen asleep, her hair tousled about her face. He carefully slid in under the covers and pulled her protectively toward him. She snuggled into him, but didn't awaken. Simon sighed. *I can always count sheep,* he thought, *maybe ten thousand of them.* It took a good long time, but Simon finally dozed off into a restless sleep, filled with shadows and police whistles blowing into the darkness. *Who had given her such a thing for protection?*

The next morning, at the breakfast table, Lydia was full of regrets. Simon had been very quiet this morning. "I'm sorry, Simon," she said softly, knowing she'd fallen asleep too soon to meet either of their needs—and he was probably still upset about her coming home after dark.

Marcus looked up from his eggs and bacon. "Apologies at breakfast?" he observed, overhearing. "That's not a good way to start the day."

Simon looked at Lydia and smiled softly. "It's okay, Lydia," he smiled.

Marcus looked back and forth between the two of them. He knew that Simon had planned to talk to Lydia about getting married again and assumed that it had been a difficult matter. It really was no big deal to Marcus—just putting icing on a cake that was already baked, in his mind. Given the tension at the table, he wondered if Lydia had been upset about the steps needed to meet the legal letter of the law.

"Can we go register at the clerk's office first thing?" Simon asked Lydia.

She nodded. "I guess we'd better. I want the baby to have your name on the birth certificate. Sister Anne says she will fill it out. I guess she has the ability to do that for the city, as a midwife." Lydia looked ready to cry.

"Oh! I'm glad she agreed to do the delivery," Suzie looked up from her own breakfast. "One more detail taken care of. How many people are you seeing today, Lydia?"

Lydia looked up, glad to divert her thoughts. Recalling what was written on her assignment sheet from Sister Edwarda, she said, "Five, I think."

"Where are these five?" Simon asked quietly, thinking of the nurse who had been attacked. He would check on her today in the women's ward.

"Between the river and Fifth Street. Not as far as the hill district. I can take the trolley to two of them to save the walk. Abril loves sitting on the back platform, watching things fly by."

Simon nodded. "So, all are fairly close? And Sister Edwarda knows everywhere you're going?"

Lydia nodded in return. "Yes, Simon. She keeps close track of these assignments, and they call everyone who has a telephone ahead of time, with reminders from the clinic. Should be very few surprises."

Simon was thinking of the black whistle that he'd carefully tucked back into her apron pocket. "Okay," he said, drumming his fingers on the table.

Marcus looked at the both of them. "We know you're enjoying this work, ladies," he interjected, trying to downplay their collective worry about the girls being out on the streets.

Suzie smiled at him while feeding Nikki. "Very much!" she said. "But I also love the pace and variety of cases in the clinic!"

Lydia agreed. "Sister Edwarda says they're going to try to find more of us to go out into the homes. I wonder if some of the other girls from our station would move here and work with us? Charlotte would love this kind of job. If not, maybe Nurse Baxter in Philadelphia could put the word out to the nurses returning to the States. I should write to her. What do you think, Suzie?"

"Maybe you'll hear back from Charlotte soon and get an idea of when they're all calling it quits over there. I would think they'd all be coming home soon," Suzie offered. "Get our little group back together again for a reunion."

Lydia smiled, her mood lifting, but still watching Simon's expression with care. "Wouldn't that be nice? Marlene, Gretha,

Charlotte, and Nancy? I wonder if we could find Linda and Alice. Maybe Doctor Stockton and Tess, if he's left an address, that is."

Simon was still so quiet. She knew that he had wanted her very much last night... with walking all day and caring for the patients as she was doing, she would have to find a way to save some energy before bed. Lydia never wanted to disappoint Simon.

Marcus had stopped talking too, not wanting to put a damper on the enthusiasm of the two women at the start of their day. *That nurse will be paralyzed for the rest of her life,* he couldn't stop thinking about it or wondering if the police had caught the criminal yet. They all finished breakfast and cleared the table.

Suzie gathered up Nikki and her baby bag and left for the hospital with Marc, while Lydia and Simon caught a trolley to the government offices downtown. Simon held Lydia's hand the entire bumpy ride, and she quietly leaned against his shoulder. She didn't want to discuss last night, not in public.

They entered the pristine government office, its gray stone front looking quite official, with its metal swinging door and austere square windows. The young couple made their way along the wooden floors of the hall to the clerk's office. With the heat system seemingly on full power, Lydia slipped out of her coat, fanning herself in the warm air.

"Do you feel okay?" Simon looked concerned, as they sat in two wooden chairs, in the hall, waiting for their turn at the clerk's desk. Her cheeks were flushed.

"Can pregnant women have hot flashes?" she asked. She was a little nervous, but didn't want to show it. "If not, then this is a first."

Simon squeezed her hand. "It'll be alright," he said quietly.

Soon enough, they were being called up to the desk. "We need to apply for a marriage license," Simon informed the woman behind the desk and immediately regretted his choice of wording.

The older woman glanced up as they approached, immediately judging Lydia's enlarged stomach. "Hm. So I see," she said abruptly and turned to her file cabinet, retrieving the necessary application from one of the drawers.

Lydia's eyes immediately filled with tears at the implied judgment in the woman's eyes. *I am not ashamed; we thought we did everything right!* She wanted to scream.

Quickly, Simon corrected his mistake. "We were married in France, during the war, but it is not recognized here in the States," he confirmed for the older woman.

"Of course," the woman replied. It was irrelevant to her. She had heard every excuse imaginable. "Fill out this form and bring it back to me with the fee."

Simon led Lydia back to the wooden chairs as someone else took their place at the municipal desk. He filled out the paperwork, and they both signed their names at the bottom. "Stay here, Lydia," Simon told her, not wanting her to have to endure the woman again. "I'll go pay her."

Lydia wanted to sob, but took a deep breath, closed her eyes and clasped her hands. This was all so cut and dried. Nothing like the spontaneous joy and fulfillment they had experienced under the vaulted ceilings of the cathedral with the awe and holiness of it all. This was just all wrong to her.

Then, the baby rolled in her stomach. That simple maneuver reached through Lydia's anguish and restored in her a sense of purpose. She could do this for the sake of the tiny life inside of her, so that it would have Simon's name in the eyes of the law. The baby was worth all of this.

She opened her eyes as Simon returned. He helped her to stand, kissed her cheek and led Lydia back out of the government building. He had the application that would legitimize their future in his pocket, good for a finite interval of time in which they would need to finish the rest of the tasks required.

They had to part ways at the trolley station, Simon heading off to the hospital where he had surgeries waiting for him, and Lydia off to the neighborhood where she had patients waiting for her.

"Please be careful. Stay alert. Do not be late. In before dark, remember?" Simon urged her yet again. "Wait, you don't have Abril with you."

"It's okay," she said softly. "Have a good day." She kissed him as she climbed up the step to the trolley, with a little more effort than she was accustomed to, and turned to wave to him as he stood there, waiting for his ride, in the other direction. The best thing she could do was get busy taking care of her patients. Her work always encouraged her.

Lydia got off at her stop and soon spotted the policeman walking his beat. She waved and went over to him, greeting her newest friend. "Good morning, Officer Stevenson!" she called out, approaching him. "Going to snow today a bit!"

"Got your mittens, Nurse Finney?" The big man smiled down at her. "I have mine, and my wife made me wear a scarf under my coat. Not exactly uniform, but it sure is warm."

"I should knit one for my husband," Lydia smiled back. "He would like that."

"You be careful, miss," he told her. "Some union unrest going on. People are a little riled up around here."

"Union unrest?" she questioned.

"Yeah, about pay and safety and all that," the police officer noted. "Sometimes things get a little heated when unions argue over money. Not everybody is a Carnegie, you know."

Lydia nodded, realizing she would need to learn who Carnegie was and why he mattered to the unions and the people of this city. Simon's brother had spoken of the mine owners in a similar tone as the policeman did of the unions. Perhaps there was a link. She would pick up a newspaper and talk to Simon about it.

"You have a good day, Officer Stevenson," Lydia yelled over her shoulder. "Stay warm!"

"Where's Abril?" He called as she turned away. "No dog to-day?"

"Had an errand to run this morning," she called back. "Had to leave her home, but I have my whistle!"

Lydia found her first patient and was well received to change a dressing on an elderly woman's leg. She called the doctor using the woman's phone on the wall, to give him an update on the status of her healing. He thanked her and asked her to call again. Feeling a bit more herself, Lydia made it through her next two stops and by the third, she was feeling perfectly normal, the needs of the present pushing aside the problems of the morning.

Completely by accident, she wrapped up her day with the shortest walk back to the house. As she was heading to her final stop, in her own neighborhood, she looked up to see Abril, bounding down the sidewalk toward her.

"Abril!" she cried out, bending down to hug the dog. "How did you get out of the yard? How did you find me? I missed you this morning!" And she realized she really had missed having the dog at her side while she worked. Abril happily stood on her hind legs, her paws up on Lydia's stomach, glad to be back on the beat.

"Come on, girl, got one more to see and then we'll go home," Lydia said cheerfully. They walked down the sidewalk to the desired street, greeting others as they went on their own errands, and passing the local butcher shop, where Abril always took time to sniff around the front door. The butcher saw them through the window, waved, and motioned for her to stop. He came out with a small piece of sausage for the dog and wished them a good afternoon. Everyone liked Abril... and the nurse, who was out tending to their neighbors.

Their last stop was a man with a failing liver. Lydia stopped at the door and the wife answered. "How is Mr. Waring doing today?" she asked.

"Awfully confused, Nurse," Mrs. Waring replied. "It's like he doesn't know what day it is or something."

Lydia followed her to the bed where the man was resting. She saw how distended his belly was from the fluid building up from liver failure. Even in the dimmer lighting of their bedroom, she could see just how yellow his skin and eyes had become. Lydia pulled out her stethoscope and flashlight to listen to his heart and check inside his eyelids. That's when she saw the variety of pills strewn over the bedside table.

"What are all of these?" she questioned.

"Oh, no! Bob, what did you take?" the wife demanded, shaking her husband.

Immediately, Lydia felt for the man's pulse in his neck and grabbed her stethoscope. "Call an ambulance, Mrs. Waring," she said. The patient was scarcely breathing.

"I... I don't know how he got all these!" Mrs. Waring wept as Lydia waited to hear a siren approaching the house—hoping they would arrive in time. Or, perhaps, the man had planned it so they would not. Before long, the patient was being loaded onto a stretcher and carried out to the waiting vehicle. Lydia did not think he would survive the short trip.

She grabbed her coat, leaving the house as the sun dropped below the city buildings and the houses, the shops... everything was closing for the night.

"Okay, Abril," Lydia told the dog. "It's time for us to go home and quickly!"

They walked rapidly. Lights in the windows of the houses were shining out onto the snowy ground. It had gotten even colder—the sun offered what little warmth it could during the shorter January days, but nights were brutal. Lydia marveled at how the city quieted as the day wound down. Even the sound of the steel mills softened toward suppertime. She liked the change in rhythm.

Rounding a corner, Lydia realized she'd taken a wrong turn into a less familiar neighborhood. Abril balked at the turn, sensing that they were off track. A group of men were coming down the street from a pub, arms around each other's shoulders, singing a boisterous song of solidarity. They were clearly unwinding after work, just as Lydia was anxious to do. Lydia stepped aside to give them room. They passed while tipping their hats to her in unison.

Then, one of the men turned. "You lost this neck of th' woods, miss?"

"No, thank you. I'm just on my way home," she quickly replied.

He came over to her. "I'll walk you home…" he offered, slurring his words.

"C'mon, Hank," the other two called out. "You can't hardly even stand up."

"I'm fine, really," Lydia told the man, and she continued on down the street with Abril on high alert.

The man followed her, the other two calling after him. "Hey, Hank! Come on, man!"

"Jus'sa minute," Hank yelled back. "C'mon pretty lady. Muss be meant to be, meeting like this."

The man stepped in front of her, pushing her back against the brick wall of the building alongside the sidewalk. Abril growled. Fast as lightning, the man swung out with a steel-toed boot and kicked Abril in the stomach. The dog flew against the wall and dropped limply to the ground. Horrified, Lydia felt the man's wet lips slobbering over her mouth as she fought against his weight, pinned against the bricks.

The other two men took off running into the night, down to the end of the street, where they disappeared around a corner. The drunken man pulled her coat open and groped her as Lydia struggled. She was trying to get inside the bodice of her apron where the whistle hung.

Now exposed, when he had pulled her coat open, her fingers found the long black cord. In the split second that he used both of his hands to reach for the hem of her dress, Lydia grabbed the whistle, put it to her lips, and blew into it as hard as she could. The police whistle shrieked into the twilight. Lydia blew it again. In only seconds, a policeman came running around the corner from the direction of the pub and shouted to her.

"Hey, you there! What's going on!" The policeman yelled, seeing the woman pressed up against the wall. The drunk man let go of Lydia and took off running. But as the officer started after him, Lydia pulled on his arm.

"Help me! Please, help me!" She sank down next to Abril in debilitating fear.

Hesitating, wanting to go after the man, the policeman paused, heeding her pleas. "Alright, miss. Are you okay?"

She nodded. "He kicked my dog, hard. Please," Lydia begged. "Help me get her home!"

The brawny man scooped Abril up into his arms. "Where do you live, Miss?"

She rattled off their house address. The man quickly strode down the street carrying the dog, Lydia wiped her face with her coat sleeves, following right behind until the house on the corner mercifully came into view. As Lydia pushed open the door, she saw Suzie on the floor by the fireplace, playing with Nikki. Marcus was sitting on the sofa, reading the paper. He jumped to his feet at the sight of the police officer holding Abril.

"What the—" Marcus exclaimed, running to the door.

"Marc, help her!" Lydia begged.

Suzie scooped up Nikki and rushed to the kitchen, flinging the newspaper onto the table as the police officer gently laid the animal down.

Marcus looked at the uniformed man. "I'm a surgeon," he explained, as he ran his hand along Abril's belly, feeling a bulge forming in her stomach. "Suzie, I need—"

Suzie placed Nikki into the policeman's arms and ran to the front hall for Marc's medical bag. Lydia had already turned up the lights and gotten her flashlight and a bottle of antiseptic from her satchel. Suzie took the baby back from the officer, who watched, fascinated, as Marcus swiftly opened Abril's abdomen and located the bleed. Lydia staunched the flow with the towels and held the flashlight so Marcus could suture the artery that had been ruptured.

Abril didn't move, her eyes remaining closed. They rinsed out the dog's belly wound, and while Lydia spread her fur apart, Marc wove her skin back together with neat, careful stitches. Lydia looked up at Marcus, terrified. Running his hands over the dog's head, he felt a small lump there as well.

"What happened?" Marc demanded quietly.

"Some drunken fool kicked her," Lydia said tearfully. "Into a wall."

"She took a hit to her head," he said quietly, checking the dog's eyes. "We'll just have to wait and see if she wakes up. Go get... no, never mind. I'll go." He turned and ran upstairs, grabbing Abril's blanket pad, coming right back down to cover Abril and keep her warm.

Then, the policeman said, "If you're okay, miss, I'd best be going. Where'd you get the whistle?"

"Officer Stevenson gave it to me," Lydia explained, now trembling a bit. "We are nurses—caring for people in their homes."

"Good thing! I heard it straight away. Keep it on you," he nodded.

Walking the policeman to the door, Suzie thanked the man profusely for bringing the two of them home.

Picking up the dog, wrapped in her blanket, Marc carried Abril to the living room, placing her on the floor next to the sofa. Lydia rolled up the soiled newspapers from the table and wiped it clean before making her way into the living room.

Exhausted, she sank down onto the cushion beside Abril, where she could watch over her. Lydia suddenly surveyed the room. "Where is Simon?"

"An emergency surgery came in, that he had to take. He'll be along in a little while. What the hell happened out there?" Marcus demanded, turning his full attention now to Lydia, anger masking his fear.

Lydia had never seen Marcus quite like this before. It was disconcerting to see his clear blue eyes darken like this.

"We were on our way home, and some guys had come out of a bar and passed by. Abril growled at one of them, and he kicked her. They all ran off," Lydia said tearfully. "She was just protecting me."

"That is what she does," Marcus said. "But you're okay? They didn't hurt you?"

Lydia nodded her head. "I'm okay. I was so frightened when he kicked her. He had been drinking too much. They just came along... singing."

"Must have been doing more than just singing to make Abril go after him," Marcus said, knowing that she had not told the entire story.

"I need to change," Lydia said. "Then I'll come back down and watch her."

"We left supper for you and Simon in the kitchen, Lydia. I'll come up too and put Nikki to bed," Suzie said, following Lydia up the stairs. She put her daughter in her crib and came into the bedroom with Lydia as she slid out of the apron and dress and put on her warmest nightgown and robe.

"I need to go to the bathroom." Lydia announced. She needed to wash the man's grubby memory off of her and brush her teeth! When she came back, Suzie was waiting on the bed.

"Spill it," she ordered.

"He was just drunk," Lydia told her friend.

"How far did he get?"

"Just his hand, groping."

Suzie stood and hugged her friend. "You okay?"

"I'm okay, but I won't be if Abril dies," Lydia admitted.

Suzie nodded in understanding. "What's with that whistle?" she asked.

"It's a police whistle. One of the officers walking the beat gave it to me, for us to use when we're out on the street. It's for calling for an ambulance, or help, or whatever—if we need one of them."

"Apparently, it works!" Suzie declared. "I want one!"

"We'll share this one until we can get another one from Officer Stevenson," Lydia nodded in total agreement. "If I'm in the clinic and you're out... you wear it. It seems to travel quite far."

"Will do... Oh, not to change the subject, but did you get the license application filled out this morning?"

Lydia nodded. "Yes, first thing. The woman looked at my stomach and made it obvious she did not approve of me already being pregnant."

"Stupid woman. There's a war going on. Hasn't she heard?" Suzie replied. "Ignore her."

It was Suzie's turn to do her own washing up as Lydia headed back downstairs. Lydia curled up in her robe on the couch, to wait beside Abril until Simon got home.

Having calmed his inner turmoil, Marc's voice was more gentle this time. "You want me to wait up with you?" he asked.

"No, Marcus, but thank you so much for taking care of Abril like that."

Lydia was glad to see the dark fire was gone from his eyes.

He kissed the top of her head. "Any time. Call me if you need me," he whispered and made his way up the stairs, to Suzie.

Lydia lay on the sofa hugging a pillow, dropping her hand down onto Abril's head to rub her ears. It was becoming difficult for her to get up from the floor, so she stayed on the couch. But she spoke to her faithful dog, reminding her of all the times they'd shared together. Then, she retrieved the water bowl and food dish from beside the kitchen door and laid them next to the animal in case Abril woke and needed them. Lying back down on the sofa, Lydia waited for Simon, finally nodding off.

Marcus was fuming as Suzie told him what Lydia had confided in her. He wished that the officer had caught the bastard and bashed him with a nightstick for even trying to touch Lydia like that. He thanked God the man had not had a gun, thinking of the paralyzed nurse. Suzie, still, had said nothing about the attack near the hospital... the matter was apparently being kept quite confidential.

As he lay there, the house quiet, Marcus heard the night terror starting, even from upstairs in bed with Suzie, where he lay keeping one ear open, listening in case Abril took a turn for the worse.

Slipping out of bed, Marc padded barefoot down the stairs. Lydia was sitting bolt upright on the sofa, staring into the dark. Marcus already knew that her mind was elsewhere, she was not seeing the living room around her. He had seen this look on her face before, but it had been a long time, and he had hoped her terrors from the German trenches had disappeared for good. The events of the afternoon must have reawakened them.

Her hand was slowly moving as if trying to push something away. She was terrified.

Images were flying through her unconscious. Images of a cold night, wet mud walls, and soldiers' faces lining the trench. They leered at her as she stumbled down the slippery wooden plank walkways. The German commander was calling for her; her heart sinking in dread and fear. She knew what was coming as he took his crop from his waist. "I can't... no..." she begged him, tears running down her face, but her memory unfolded involuntarily in terrifying images.

A strangled sound came from Lydia's throat as Marcus approached and knelt on the floor beside Abril and her, both.

"Lydia," Marcus called to her softly. "It's Marcus... come back, my dear. You're at home. You're in your living room. The commander is dead."

She winced and flinched, whimpering in pain, no doubt hearing the crop whistle through the air... Marcus knew something about what she was remembering. His heart ached for her seeing her tears flow. He kept his voice soft.

"Lydia, my dear, hear my voice. You're safe now…"

It was cold, the desk was cold, her skin was on fire and he wouldn't stop… "It's my fault… it's my fault…"

Marcus touched the tips of her fingers. "Lydia, it's over. You're home. It's Marc… I'm right here…"

He heard the front door open and felt the cold draft and knew Simon was coming in quietly, trying not to disturb the house. He raised a hand as Simon came around the foyer into the living room and saw Marcus in his robe, kneeling on the floor at Lydia's feet as she stared into the night.

She whimpered again in terror and grabbed her belly, shielding the baby with her hands, bending forward in re-membered pain.

Letting his coat fall, Simon dropped down, kneeling beside them. His eyes met Marc's in confusion. The dog was lying still and silent on the floor, Lydia in terror, with Marcus engaged in an attempted rescue.

"Simon is here now, Lydia," Marcus said softly. "Come on back…"

Simon came closer, but didn't touch her yet. "I'm here, beloved. Just open your eyes and see me. You're safe now. The commander is dead."

Her lips trembled, his familiar voice was reaching her, though her eyes still stared down the dimly lit trenches. Simon looked anxiously at Marcus, seeking answers.

"Abril is right here, Lydia," Marc reassured her. "She's right at your feet. Everything is okay now, you can touch Abril."

Simon took her hands now. "And I'm right here, beloved," he reassured her again. She felt his touch, then suddenly gripped his hand fiercely as pain split her skin. She cried out in agony as Simon's eyes filled. "It's over, Lydia. Everyone is safe, my love... wake up."

After what felt like forever, as his voice pulled her back, she blinked several times—the veil broken. She felt Simon's hands. Her eyes began to focus as she saw Simon's face, with Marcus beside her. She felt her large abdomen, the baby still safely within her. Then, she saw Abril still on the floor and started to sob, falling forward into Simon's arms. Marcus leaned over to check the dog. He felt the beating of her heart and that her temperature was good. There was no bleeding from the careful stitches he had made along her belly. He rubbed her head.

"Come on, Abril," he urged the dog. "You can do this."

Simon took it all in, bewildered. *What on earth happened today?*

By some miracle, the dog whimpered, trying to move, but was unable. Her dark eyes opened at last. And Marcus smiled. "Look, Lydia," he exclaimed softly. "She's waking. Abril is looking for you."

Lydia lifted her head, her eyes wet, but clear and present. She slid to the floor and gently embraced the dog.

"Oh, Abril, you didn't leave me behind," she said gratefully, holding the creature's head. The dog gazed up at her with pure trust and love. The tip of her tail moved slightly against the floor, but she didn't try to stand, somehow knowing she shouldn't. Lydia moved the water bowl close and encouraged her to drink.

Lydia turned to the two men, "Help me up... please," she begged.

They did, lifting her to her feet, then Simon helped her to the sofa.

Marcus stood as they settled in, not able to reveal what he was feeling for them.

"My work here is done," he said softly. "Glad you're home, Simon. I'm going back to bed."

Lydia thanked him, her eyes full of gratitude as Marc returned upstairs.

"We need to talk, I think," Simon declared. "The first night I come home late from work—"

Lydia told him everything. Almost.

Simon gently carried Abril up to sleep on the floor of the landing where she liked to be at night. He had thought it might be less stressful for her to be in her preferred spot, close to them all. He marvelled that Marcus had been willing to open her up. To Simon's knowledge, Marc hadn't done any veterinary surgery, at least not since medical school, if even then. And he was grateful beyond measure to the dog for trying to protect Lydia from the drunk man on the street.

Simon took her in his arms. "I'm sorry Abril got hurt. It woke up old memories, didn't it?"

Lydia lay against Simon in their bed and simply nodded. She also needed to clear up the troubling matter still on her mind from the morning. She didn't want to go to sleep with that unfinished between them. "I fell asleep last night, before we could be together," Lydia confessed to him. "I'm so sorry, Simon. You were upset this morning, and I felt terrible about it all day."

He held her in the darkness of the bedroom. "But Lydia, I wasn't upset that you fell asleep!" he exclaimed softly. "Good grief! You're allowed to be tired. I will never be upset about something like that! A little frustrated maybe... perhaps... well, probably, depending. But never upset."

"Then why were you so very quiet this morning? Was it still from me coming in late?" she asked him, touching the beard along his chin, tracing the line it made around his ear, still trying to suppress her earlier ordeal... keep the feeling of being groped out of her awareness.

"I'd picked up your nursing things last night to put it on the foyer bench," he explained, "and a police whistle fell out onto the floor. When I saw it, I wondered why the police had given it to you. Why you hadn't said anything about someone giving you something like that. I needed to talk to you about it, but there wasn't time. That's why I was upset."

"I hadn't given it a second thought. Never thought I would need it," she admitted. "I thought Officer Stevenson was just being kind."

Simon cleared his throat. "Yesterday, Marc and I took a bullet out of a nurse," he said quietly. "She was raped and shot on the street. She'll live but she's paralyzed."

"Dear God!" Lydia whispered, horrified. "Oh, my God, Simon."

"That's why we've been... a little edgy about you going out alone," Simon said. "When I saw the police whistle, well—did you use it today?" he asked. "When the drunk guys came around?"

She nodded. "I did. A policeman heard it and came running."

"And that is all the drunk man did? Kick Abril into the wall?" Simon insisted.

Lydia hesitated for a second as the feel of his fingers resurfaced. She didn't want to upset Simon, but it only took that second of hesitation for him to notice. He leaned up on one elbow over her. "What else happened, Lydia?"

Quietly, Lydia said, "He pushed me against a wall and... and he felt the baby. But when he moved his hands down, I was able to blow the whistle."

Simon sat up and swung his legs over the bed, sinking his head into his hands, his worst fear realized. He stood up and hit his fist into the wall as Lydia struggled to sit up, freezing when heard the sharp thud from his fist making contact.

Finally, he sat back down on the edge of the bed. "I can't do this, Lydia," he said angrily. "I'm sorry, but I can't."

He laid her back on the bed. "No wonder you had the night terror with that in your mind," he added, pure grief taking over. Holding her tightly in his arms, he said forcefully, "You are only mine! Only my hands belong on you!"

Lydia nodded again, realizing he was talking to the universe, not necessarily to her. She had seen him this way once before, when soldiers had pulled her away from him, outside of Nancy, and he had felt like he couldn't protect her. She recognized the tone of his voice and knew already what he intended to do, as he had done before on a bank along the Meuse.

He touched her face. "Look at me, Lydia," he insisted. She was already watching him intently, but he didn't want her to slip backwards into memory. He pressed his lips against hers, and she immediately yielded to him, wanting his touch to be the only thing she felt. He fiercely, passionately reclaimed her, but when he joined himself to her, he was incredibly restrained and gentle, as she knew he would be.

Simon took his time using his body as the instrument to drive out the events of the day from their minds, the anxieties, the images of past and recent present. Lydia trembled beneath him, fully surrounded by his protection. There were no other hands or faces or images able to intrude her awareness. She saw and felt only Simon and his fierce love filling her being. Finally, he met his own need, released her, and dropped panting beside her, holding her tight.

"You are mine to protect."

"Yes, my love." She felt the safety of his declaration. And nothing more was said as they fell asleep in each other's arms.

Lydia wasn't the only one with an unsettled unconscious mind. During the night, Marcus tossed and turned. His dreams were filled with horror as he found himself back in the camp, in the darkness.

Lydia was screaming his name. Oh God, she's hurt! She's hurt! Where...? He was running in the dark, leaving the hanging lantern over the makeshift surgical table. Everyone was running in every direction. The shells... shrapnel. "Marcus!" Lydia screamed again. Heart pounding in fear, he ran straight toward the terror. When he came to the hastily erected tarp, the Belgium surgeon turned to him with the bone saw in one hand and a bloody leg dangling in the other. "It was the only way to save his life," he declared. Marcus looked in pure terror to the table where Lydia was bent, sobbing over the patient... it was Simon... his leg was gone. Lydia reached for Marc in agony. I wasn't in time, Marcus despaired. Oh God, I wasn't in time...

Marcus was covered in sweat as he woke from the nightmare. Carefully sliding out of bed, he felt the cold floor, glad that he had two feet to touch it. Suzie remained asleep, for which he was grateful. Grabbing a robe, he quietly went down the hall to the bathroom and washed up, knowing it was somewhere around four or so and he'd have to get up in an hour or two anyway. Padding down the hall, he headed for the stairs, as Abril softly woofed at him. Marc checked her quickly before going down to the kitchen.

Simon heard the dog woof, immediately going on high alert, given the earlier events of the night. He slid out of bed as well and grabbed his robe to find out what had awakened Abril and to see if she needed anything. While he was checking the dog, he heard a sound in the kitchen below and ran down the stairs quietly, cautiously assessing the light glowing there. Coming into the kitchen, he found Marc reaching into the cupboard for a glass. At the sight of Simon, Marc reached for two. Opening the inner kitchen door, he grabbed one of the milk bottles between the storm and kitchen doors, flipped off the lid, and poured them both a glass of very cold milk.

Together they moved into the living room, and Marcus handed one glass to his buddy. He grabbed an afghan before taking the easy chair and ottoman. Simon grabbed another and dropped onto the sofa, but before Simon could spread it out, Marcus quickly counted his legs.

"Glad you still have two," he said in relief.

"Did when I went to bed anyway," Simon nodded. "Did one of them go missing on you, Marc?"

Marcus shuddered. "Yeah, you could say that."

"Isn't this supposed to be warm milk, if you want to sleep again?" Simon asked kindly.

"Not going to happen, Simon. Anyway, it's probably four o'clock. I didn't see for sure," Marcus said, pulling the afghan over himself. "We'll have to get up soon, regardless."

"May not be worth it to get two more hours in?" Simon asked his friend.

Marcus lifted the glass. "Here's to two working legs, regardless!"

Simon gave him a salute. "Here's to two more hours of sleep, if we can!"

"Yeah, okay, we'll go with that," Marcus agreed, draining the glass. He knew that Simon understood. That was all he needed. His eyes closed again as he laid his head back on the chair, with the afghan over his robe.

Simon watched Marcus tenderly. Well, cold milk or not, he would go back to sleep, too.

He put down the empty glass and pulled the other afghan over his own robe, as his eyes closed. He started thinking about babies needing milk before bed to sleep. Then he thought of his baby, knowing Lydia wanted to nurse it—thinking of Lydia—her lovely, full breasts caring for their child. Any harmful thoughts were instantly dispelled by the image of Lydia, nursing their baby, while he held her.

In the morning, Suzie came down the stairs looking for Marcus, wondering if he'd headed to the hospital early. She immediately saw the two friends asleep in the living room and felt a little pang of jealousy. *Sometimes it seems like he's closer to Simon than he is to me*, she thought.

But then, she thought of the atrocities they had seen after she had already returned home. No doubt that the bond would have deepened with every day they were in that camp. It was probably good that they had each other's companionship, in case, just in case, her own life took a different direction. Quietly, Suzie went back upstairs to complete her morning routine and wake Nikki. They all had a full day ahead.

Chapter 9
Let These Be Joined

They were changing in the doctors' lounge for surgery when Marcus noticed Simon's hand. "You know," he remarked. "You really need to take it easy on that hand. That's the one that smashed up the German... and... now a wall, I think?"

Simon hadn't yet noticed his bruised knuckles. "It still works," he said, wincing slightly.

"What did you two decide?" Marcus actually had many questions for his friend, but had decided that spreading them out, might be wise.

"She's talking to Sister Edwarda. She'll be home every day before the sun is even low against the buildings," Simon said.

Marcus nodded. "That sounds reasonable. But I was asking about the marriage ceremony."

"Oh, right." Simon took a deep breath. "She doesn't want another minister doing something, before God, that we've already done. It makes sense. The government wants this, so we will go to a government official. And have a party afterward. You did say you'd stand with us, you and Suzie? Still have to have a witness co-sign that we're legitimate."

"Absolutely!" Marcus assured him. "Wouldn't want to miss such an auspicious occasion."

"Good. Next week, then." Simon placed his hand on Marcus's shoulder. "Thanks, Marcus, for helping last night."

"No problem, buddy," Marcus replied as they headed for the operating theater. "By the way," he added, almost as an afterthought. "How's the wall?"

It was late afternoon when Lydia arrived home, after a shortened day, sanctioned by Sister Edwarda. Abril was sleeping soundly by the fireplace, where Simon had carefully laid her for the day. Lydia set about making some fried chicken for dinner, flouring the legs and breast pieces and rotating them in the frying pan, until they were just the perfect golden brown. She laid them out onto a rack, letting the oil drain. It was her grandma's recipe and the smell filled the entire house, just like it had when she was little.

Sensing movement at the door, Lydia turned to see Abril, limping gingerly, in from her makeshift recovery. Overjoyed, she dropped down, gently hugging the dog.

"There you are, my beautiful girl!" she exclaimed. "You're up! What a good dog you are."

Lydia awkwardly rose from the floor, pulling herself up with the help of a chair. She broke off a tender piece of chicken for Abril, who eagerly accepted the gift. "And your appetite is coming back too! Good girl!"

When Simon, Marcus, and Suzie with Nikki came through the door, Lydia had the table set and ready for them. She quickly lit some candles and prepared for the second fry, so the chicken would be nice and hot.

Simon came straight back to the kitchen and took her in his arms, kissing her firmly... very much wanting this evening to go better than the one before.

"Oh! You have flour in your beard!" she teased, quickly flipping the chicken breasts in the hot skillet.

He kissed her again, not at all worried. "Now you know how I'll look when I start turning gray," he remarked, stroking the hair on his chin.

"You will be as incredibly handsome as you are right now," she assured him.

"Are you okay? Hurt at all?" He knew that he had been a bit, energetic, with her the night before.

She smiled up at him, kissing his lips softly. "Not even a little. You are always gentle with me, my love, even when you are being my knight in shining armor."

"I'm glad you got to come home early," he whispered into her ear as he wrapped his arm around her waist and lovingly stroked her stomach. Bending down, he kissed her belly.

"You know, I am too! I'm not nearly as tired," she admitted. "Now, go wash up."

Over dinner, they planned the details of the celebration for their extended families. It would be after the appointment with the judge where they would finally have the crucial wedding certificate duly signed and administered by the courts. The party would take a bit more effort and planning, but Simon and Lydia were looking forward to their families meeting. The when, was the only remaining question.

They decided to write letters, offering a few weekends for the families to consider. Marcus and Suzie offered to take a hotel for the weekend, but Lydia absolutely refused.

"You are family," she declared. "You must be here, or I will cancel the entire thing!"

Marcus held up a hand. "Heaven forbid! We'll be here. Now, what about next week when you go to the judge? Will you want new rings or something? Other than us standing with you, what can we do to make it special?"

"I can't think of a thing," Lydia said, and Simon agreed. "Just stand with us—Nikki as well."

"Standing we can do," Marcus said.

Over the next few days, work was steady but manageable, for everyone. More importantly, Abril was healing remarkably well. They filled their days with work, dinners together, playing with little Nikki and, of course, plans for the family gathering. After the respite of a rather unremarkable, but very good week, the big day had finally come.

It was snowing as they stepped off the trolley, with Nikki in tow. Little Nikki was fascinated by the delicate flakes gracefully drifting to the ground and lifted her tiny mittened hands to catch the larger ones. It was a quick walk to the courthouse door, but their shoulders were coated in white as they stepped inside. There were already several couples in the hallway which led to the judge's chamber. The group joined the queue, doing their best to leave the snow at the door, not wanting to make any slippery puddles on the wooden floor.

Lydia was nervous, fearing the judge would notice her condition and form the wrong opinion. She wondered if she should just stay bundled in her coat. While Simon and Marcus signed them in with the judge's secretary, Suzie took Lydia's arm. "Now, listen to me," she said in support. "I got plenty of... looks... when I came home pregnant, so I understand what you're feeling. You just need to ignore anyone who hasn't got a heart and wants to think they are holier than everyone else."

Lydia was surprised at how deeply comforted she felt. Suzie had indeed come home very pregnant, and unwed, to face the social scrutiny of people who seemed to live to judge. "You're right, I know. Thank you, Suzie. I'll remind myself of that."

"And anyway," Suzie continued. "You've got a splendid man over there wanting you to be legally bound to him. Without that license, if anything happens to Simon, you get nothing—not the house, not the money in the bank, none of it. Simon wants to make sure it goes to you and your baby, if anything should happen to him."

Lydia felt a pang of anxiety. "Without Simon, I don't want any of it," she said, speaking foolishly.

"Don't be ridiculous," Suzie admonished. "You have a baby coming very soon and you must always think of what is best for your child. When Marcus came back and offered to take care of the baby and me, I didn't worry myself about anything that had happened between us—I jumped at it. And guess what? We're still quite compatible and care about each other... and he loves Nikki. And maybe we'll even have another child. I'm his legal wife! So you just let the state give you everything you and your baby are entitled to!" Suzie finished with a flourish of self-satisfaction, just as Marcus and Simon rejoined them.

"Should I take off your ring and then put it back on you?" Simon asked Lydia, taking her right hand in his own while considering the pewter band on her finger.

"It hasn't been off my hand yet," she smiled. "I'm not taking it off today either! Do you want me to put your ring back on your finger?"

"Mine hasn't been off either... it stays put."

Marcus groaned. "I don't believe you two!" he exclaimed. "You're hopeless romantics, the both of you. You do realize those are pewter and are going to wear thin or crack and fall off one of these days. That's why people get gold."

"When they fall off, then we'll worry about it!" Lydia laughed.

"I'd be happy to get you a gold ring, Lydia," Simon was suddenly very thoughtful. "And a diamond ring, too."

"Don't you dare," she threatened. "I don't have the money to buy you one and it wouldn't be fair. What we have has meaning. At least to us."

"And the grandmother in the village," Simon said, remembering.

"The smithy she found at the last minute—" Lydia recalled.

"After the night in the barn in the hay—" Simon said, pulling her to him.

"With the cow and the rooster..."

Marcus and Suzie groaned at the same time. "Should we wait outside in the snow? Give you some privacy?" Marcus teased.

Lydia laughed, remembering those first nights together after going to the cathedral. She had felt different, changed, spiritually joined to Simon as her husband. She had felt very married. She was very married. Today changed nothing.

Finally, it was their turn to enter the judge's chamber. He looked up from the blank certificate on his bench.

"Ah, which two are the couple to be married?" he asked, seeing one woman pregnant and the other already holding a small child. He didn't want to make a mistake by guessing.

Marcus and Suzie both pointed to the other two.

"I see," the judge said, looking up over his spectacles. "Well, this is a short but solemn occasion of your nuptials. So, I will read to you the ceremony, and you will respond when I indicate."

"I want to say my own vow," Lydia voiced firmly.

The judge looked surprised, but said, "As long as you repeat after me exactly what I tell you to say, you can add anything else that you like."

He began intoning the words from the paper that he'd already used many times that same day... and knew by heart. The court secretary stood by, mentally calculating the size of Lydia's belly; she had certainly seen this many times before. *Some things never change,* she thought. *People slip up and need to decide what to do about it, for the sake of the child.*

When it was time for the vows, Lydia carefully repeated what the judge told her to say—there could be no question whatsoever that this legal rite was binding. After reciting the official vow, she took Simon's hands in her own and looked up into his loving brown eyes as she spoke loudly enough for everyone in the chamber to hear.

"Simon, my love, when we stood before the priest in France and said our vows at the altar in the cathedral in Nancy, I had no idea what would happen to us over the next year and a half. The Germans tried to tear us apart by dropping a bomb on us that nearly took your life. And thanks to God, and Marcus, you pulled through and stayed beside me. And the Germans tried to tear us apart by taking me prisoner in the trenches. And thanks to God and many others, I pulled through and got back to you. And the army tried to tear us apart by sending you away to serve with the British, and you went missing for months. And thanks to God and to Father James, you healed from illness and came back and found me again. So! We are strong enough to remain together through all the 'for better and worse, sickness and health' that this world can throw at us. And now our baby is coming. And I will still be standing beside you, no matter what comes, and for as long as I live. This is still my vow."

Everyone stood in stunned silence. The astonished judge sat speechless, forgetting to move on to the part involving Simon. His secretary had to close her mouth, which had fallen open in awe, as Lydia's words hung in the air of the judge's chamber.

Suzie felt her eyes brimming with tears... this was the first she was hearing... *prisoner in the trenches*?

Marcus quietly renewed his own vow to himself, *this is why I will always strive to be a better man! I want to be worthy of that kind of love and faithfulness!*

The judge cleared his throat, but Simon stayed him with a hand and gazed into Lydia's eyes, so filled with love and memory.

"I am just a man who fell in love with the most amazing woman almost two years ago, across the ocean, on a whole other continent—had to go to the front, in a war, to find you. I never thought my life was incomplete, until you came into it. And yes, we went through all those hardships in the Army, but found incredible joy together too. You are so important to me, Lydia, that I would go through the hell of war all over again—the bombs, the Germans, the hunger, the hardships—I would do it all again, just to have the chance of having you as my wife.

"Today, we're making legal what was already sealed in Heaven, long ago. It is necessary to do this today, but it is not our beginning. Our beginning cannot be undone by anything on this side of Heaven. I vowed to protect you, and cherish, and love you before God in the church in France. This is still my solemn vow to you and our baby."

Removing his handkerchief, the judge blew his nose and the secretary wiped the tears from her cheeks. Suzie and Marcus glanced at each other with a knowing look.

The judge cleared his throat. "May we now complete this formality? You do have to repeat these words after me…"

"Yes, sir," Simon held Lydia's hands, repeating the necessary phrases verbatim… never taking his eyes from hers. Lydia was radiant; it was pure joy coming from her soul. She liked very much that the judge had used the word 'formality'… that he had at last recognized this ceremony for what it really was.

"I, em, now pronounce you man and wife in the eyes of the Commonwealth of Pennsylvania, which is privileged to have conducted this ceremony in this chamber, thus formalizing the union you have declared. You may kiss… your wife!" The judge concluded and waited while Simon took Lydia's face in his hands and kissed her softly. The judge then shook each of their hands gratefully, and his secretary pressed forward and shook their hands as well, and also those of Marcus and Suzie.

As Marcus pumped the judge's hand, he declared enthusiastically, "You know, I was there for the whole army thing in France... we all served together over there... every single thing they said is true."

"Then it is a good thing you are signing as a witness today, isn't it?" The judge handed Marcus a fountain pen with which he signed his name, with a flourish, then passed the pen to Suzie for her to sign as well.

The air was uncommonly warm for February as Lydia walked the street with Abril at her side. Today, the dog's curiosity was especially piqued, with the breeze carrying an array of new scents from the city at every turn they took.

"We have some interesting patients today, Abril," Lydia told the dog while reading her detailed notes from Sister Edwarda. She looked up to see Officer Stevenson at the next street corner. He raised his hand in salute as she came closer.

"Morning, Nurse Finney," he called out. "Beautiful day, isn't it?"

Abril ran ahead to the familiar policeman, who reached down to rub her ears. She liked this man and looked forward to his greeting whenever Lydia made her rounds in the neighborhood.

"How's Abril doing? She looks well enough to me. I heard what happened—you're keeping your whistle on you, Nurse Finney? How many patients you got today?" Officer Stevenson asked the woman in rapid succession, amazed that she was still out doing her duty despite the pregnancy, and her recent run in.

"She is much better! And yes, it's right here around my neck. And only four today," Lydia told her policeman friend. "Lots of people getting the flu, it seems."

Officer Stevenson frowned, "Just don't you get it with that little one coming along in there."

"I cover my mouth and wash up well," she confirmed. "Makes it harder for the germs to get through."

"Ah," he nodded. "Is that what the blue scarf is for around your neck then?"

Lydia nodded, looking up at him and shielding her eyes from the sunshine. "Do you have any symptoms?"

"Healthy as a horse," he assured the nurse as he pounded his chest in a show of strength.

"Very well then, good to see you this morning!"

Lydia looked at her list as they began walking. "Okay, Abril, who is next? We have someone with gout who was supposed to show up at the clinic, but never made it in... has a doctor concerned about him taking his pain medicine. You'll never get gout, girl, thank goodness. At least, I don't think dogs get gout!"

Lydia looked back toward Officer Stevenson, waving once more, then headed down the street. She could have taken a trolley, but it wasn't that far... and the sun felt so warm and inviting on her cheeks.

While searching the door numbers as she passed each house, they crossed paths with a woman walking a baby, bundled up in a pram. Lydia stopped to fawn over the infant. The woman noticed Lydia's pregnancy beneath her winter coat and happily began talking about her baby's unique talents. *I get paid to do this wonderful job,* Lydia thought in delight as they finally parted.

It was just a bit further when she found her destination and asked Abril to stay. The dog plopped down in the sunshine on the top step to wait.

"Mr. Randall! Mr. Randall?" Lydia called, periodically knocking. "It's the nurse."

The door opened slightly. "I wasn't expecting anyone," the man said. "Who sent you?"

"Doctor Sims over at Charity. He said your gout was advanced, and he's concerned that you might be in a lot of pain since you missed an appointment with him at the clinic. May I check your foot?"

"Okay," he said, opening the door to let her in. He had a small, dim, one-room apartment, and as she walked in, Lydia saw only sparse furnishings and a few half-eaten cakes on a table by the bed. She turned at the sound of the man locking four locks on the door, stacked one on top of the other. She heard the series of clicks with concern, but kept her voice calm.

"Now, can you tell me what you take for pain, Mr. Randall? Gout is so painful, and Doctor Sims would like you to be as comfortable as possible," Lydia asked the man.

"I want a girlfriend," the man stated oddly.

Lydia appraised him carefully. He seemed to be listening to some internal debate. She was not aware of any history of psychiatric illness reported for this man, but these days, one never knew. It was something people rarely discussed, even with their own doctor and this man was obviously fearful of going out around other people.

"It's hard to feel lonely," Lydia said. "Have you been out to see anyone this week, now that the weather is warmer? Gone for a walk, perhaps, or talked to your neighbors?"

"You could be my girlfriend," he told her simply, looking at her in the dim light of the room, not with evil intent, but looking hopeful.

"I am a nurse, Mr. Randall, and I can help you get to the Community Center to make some friends, when your pain is under control," she said firmly.

He sat on the bed, the only place to sit in the room, and put his foot up. "Not with this foot. It hurts pretty bad." He pulled his sock off, showing her that the top of his foot and his great toe was red, hot, and swollen. It had to hurt terribly. Lydia gently checked for circulation in the foot.

"I can see how painful this would be walking," she exclaimed softly, carefully putting the sock loosely over the offending toe. "We must really get you to the appointment at Doctor Sims's office to see how we can get the swelling down in your foot. It's not enough just to have a pain syrup with it being this red. That's a lot of inflammation. I imagine it interferes with your sleep!"

The man stood and looked out the window while Lydia edged over to the locked door of his little room.

"You're having a baby," Mr. Randall told her as if she was not aware. "I don't mind."

"Would you like to meet my dog, Mr. Randall? She's just outside, a really terrific animal," she said cheerfully while calling sharply through the door. "Abril!"

In an instant, Abril picked up on the edge in Lydia's voice as she called through the door. Without hesitation, she took off at a full run down the sidewalk, retracing their steps until she found Officer Stevenson walking his beat just a few blocks away. Stopping short in front of the man, Abril woofed. Then, she ran off ten feet, turned, went back to the man, and woofed again.

Officer Stevenson said quickly, "Where's Nurse Finney, Abril? Where's the nurse?"

Abril woofed again and turned, running, but stopped to look back once, waiting on him. "I'm coming, Abril," Officer Stevenson said, picking up his pace. He followed the dog down the street and straight up to the house, where Abril put her feet up on the door.

"Oh," the policeman said. "I know this house, girl." He rapped his nightstick sharply against the door. "Ah, there, Mr. Randall, it's Officer Stevenson. I need a word with you, sir." He saw the curtain move at the window.

Randall turned to look at Lydia, "You called the police."

"No, Mr. Randall, I came to check the gout in your foot for Doctor Sims," Lydia assured him steadily. She watched the man look cautiously out through the window again while she stood up and moved slowly toward the door once more. "I think we should open the door for Officer Stevenson, Mr. Randall. It would be best."

He looked at her, confused. "Why won't you be my girl-friend?"

"Because I am the nurse," she told him. "I'm concerned about your foot."

There was another sharp set of raps on the door. "Mr. Randall, I need a word, just for a minute," came the police officer's muffled voice through the door.

Lydia stayed by the door as Mr. Randall released one of the four locks with his keys.

"What day can you come in to see the doctor?" she asked. "I'll tell the office to expect you so he can get that swelling under control."

He was so near her that she could smell his odor and feel his apprehension, but she needed to stay by the door. He opened the second lock.

"I'll come Tuesday," he finally said, putting the key in the third lock and turning the bolt.

"Good," Lydia told him. "I'm glad you're going to go in. It's best to get that checked out."

The man put the key in the fourth lock, and Lydia gratefully heard the mechanism give way. He opened the door a crack, and Officer Stevenson immediately put his boot in the door, wedging it open to peer inside.

"Oh, Nurse Finney?" He exclaimed in feigned surprise. "Are you in there too? Well, we wondered where you were because someone has fallen flat down on his face around the corner, and I need you to come check the poor guy. He's all banged up.

"Sorry, Mr. Randall, I thought she might have come to check on you because I saw her dog out here. Apology for having to trouble you, sir, but I need to borrow the nurse for a little bit. You understand."

As Randall opened the door wider, Lydia quickly slipped out. She turned and said, "Now, remember, Mr. Randall, I'll tell the doctor you'll come on Tuesday. He'll be expecting you."

"Yes, Nurse," Randall said plainly as he watched the police officer take the nurse's elbow and lead her down the few front steps to the sidewalk.

Abril growled softly.

"I'm fine, Abril," Lydia assured her and turned to the big policeman. "Thank you."

"Thank your dog," Stevenson said. "I know this man. He hasn't been right in his head for a while. Lives like a hermit. When you walk the beat, you get to know people. I'd have gone in with you if I'd known which house you were going to. Now, any time you have a doubt, Nurse Finney, you just take me with you. I'll patrol right outside the house and give the person inside something to think about. Where are you going to next?"

"A woman with four children, all with coughs," Lydia said as her heart resumed its normal rhythm in her chest. "Nothing to worry about there."

"You've still got the whistle, right?" Officer Stevenson asked.

Lydia patted her chest where it hung beneath her apron. "Right here."

"If Abril hadn't been here, you would have blown it, right?" It was an order, not a request.

"I would have if the man had not opened the door," she assured him.

He nodded, satisfied. "Good! Can hear those whistles right through a wall."

"Yes, sir," she smiled, patting the black whistle again. It was a comfort having it. She turned down the corner, where she was glad to see that there was no poor fellow lying on the sidewalk after all. Officer Stevenson made sure she was safely on her way and returned to his beat.

It was early March by the time the housewarming party came around. Lydia and Suzie had cleaned the third floor and readied the two extra dormer rooms for guests. The widow, who had sold them the house, had left behind some simple furnishings, which would work perfectly for Simon's family, whoever could make it from West Virginia. Nikki's crib was moved into Marcus and Suzie's room, freeing up a bedroom for Lydia's parents on the second floor.

Lydia was nervous about the two families finally meeting. She hoped everyone would get along. This gathering would be her chance to make up for them not being included in their wedding. She also knew that Marcus was preparing a toast, and she half-feared what he might say, knowing his sense of humor as she did.

She could hear Simon climbing the stairs. After a quick look around, he exclaimed. "Wow! Sure is a lot of space up here. Wonder how many kids the widow lady had!" He peeked into a little closet. There was a small space beyond. Crouching to reach inside, he pulled out a wooden truck and remembered that the widow had mentioned at least one son—perhaps this had been his room as a boy. Simon stood up again, careful not to hit his head on the sloped ceiling.

Lydia had already moved on to the next room to help Suzie. Curious, Simon went to the small dormer window in the back; looking out, he could just make out the tops of the steel mills and a glimpse of the river, through the treetops. And below was his own little backyard, where Abril was currently sniffing at the base of a tree. Investigating never grew tiresome for her.

Simon headed to the front room, where Lydia was making the bed. He showed them the wooden truck and then helped Lydia tuck the sheets under the mattress. They heard a muffled voice, from the first floor.

"Up here," Simon called down the stairs.

A series of pounding footsteps, and Marcus appeared through the opening to the third floor, pulling on the handrail to check its strength... finding it to be solid. "Any bats lurking up here?"

"Not a one," Simon laughed.

"Whew," Marcus said with relief. "I don't have a butterfly net on me. Got the rest of the groceries though... and bottles of both white and rosé and a couple of champagne. And I picked up a set of eight more plates, just in case."

Suzie nodded. "That should do it. I think we have everything."

With effort, Lydia stretched her back. "I've had enough for now," she declared. "Feeling it in my back."

Marcus approached, touching her stomach. "Probably overdid it. It won't be long now."

Lydia smiled down at her belly. "I can no longer see my toes."

Suzie laughed. "You're in the home stretch when you can't see your toes," she remarked. "And you'll need a size bigger shoe for your swollen feet."

"Lydia, are your feet swelling?" Simon asked in concern. He hadn't been paying any attention to the fit of her shoes.

Lydia waddled over to him, kissing his cheek. "Sister Anne said that my feet are just fine. Now go downstairs ahead of me so I don't miss a step and roll down like a boulder."

Simon quickly maneuvered in front of her and slowly descended backward, anxiously watching her take each step, one at a time. They stopped at the second-floor hallway, with Lydia heading to their bedroom. "I'm just going to rest for a few minutes. You all go on down without me."

Lydia eased onto the mattress, exhaling as the weight lifted from her lower back. The twinges, likely just muscle strains from pushing too hard while cleaning, nagged at her briefly before settling. Simon had followed her in, silently sliding a pillow beneath her legs as she tried to get comfortable in their four-poster bed.

"Feeling alright?" he asked, hovering. "You've been working too hard."

"My back is sore, just the muscles cramping up a little from the lifting..." she sighed. "And from being big and heavy and fat."

Simon frowned. "You are not fat. You're pregnant. Very pregnant. And doing too much. Enough for today. We'll do the rest."

"Would you rub my back for a second?" She begged him.

"Absolutely. Roll over." He sat down on the edge of the bed, considering her long dress. "This won't do," he said, standing to go close their door. When he came back, he slid off her dress and lifted her slip. "That's more like it."

He began to massage her back, kneading the muscles into submission. "You know," he observed, "from the back, you don't look pregnant at all. You're carrying the baby all in the front."

She sighed, feeling his hands working through the knots in her muscles. "Tell me about it..." she murmured. "Oh Simon, that feels wonderful. You could do massage with those hands if you ever give up surgery."

"Higher or lower?" He asked, moving his hands experimentally in both directions.

"Lower," she breathed. "Sister Anne says it's normal for my size to have a back strain, even my tailbone."

"Your elastic is in my way, then," Simon observed and lowered her underthings. The white scars across her skin tore at his heart. He hadn't told Lydia that he and Sister Anne had spoken about them. He had wanted the nun to be prepared in case of any questions about them, or any emotional needs Lydia might have during the pain of childbirth.

Now, he very tenderly massaged her low spine and then down her buttocks.

She took a deep breath. "Um, Simon, that's a little lower than my back, you know."

"Is it?" He asked, his hands continuing to massage her skin, her hips, and even her thighs.

"And that's not my tailbone..." she suggested, feeling herself slipping into a dreamy state of pleasure. "You might want to stop right there..."

"Why?" He murmured, watching her eyes close as a tender smile formed on his lips. "Why would I ever want to stop massaging you?"

Her voice was a whisper. "Because I am very pregnant... and fat and awkward... and round... and soon there won't be any way for you to even find me."

He chuckled at that. "I will always be able to find you. And I will always want to find you. You're a very desirable, beautiful, round, and awkwardly pregnant woman," Simon said, smiling. "And we've always found a way."

Simon lay, curled up behind Lydia with his arm over her, his hand across her belly. She was dozing after they had indeed found a way to come together, and now he held his palm against her abdomen, feeling their baby rolling, turning, and stretching its tiny arms and legs. He didn't know if their coming together had stimulated the baby's actions, but he marveled at the movements he felt under his hand. It was as if he and the baby were having their own playtime. He pressed tenderly, feeling a response coming from inside of her womb. Pressing again on a little, knobby protuberance, he again felt movement as if in reply. It was a miraculous exchange between himself and his child.

Laying there, holding the two of them, Simon suddenly realized that Lydia had been completely right about the birth. He was already bonding with this tiny life inside of her. It was his responsibility to be right there when this life emerged, for him to hold and protect them from the very beginning. Tears stung his eyes as he realized her wisdom.

With less than one month to go, Sister Anne had already assured them that things were progressing nicely. Simon knew that the baby had turned, he had felt its head was down, preparing to make its entrance. *Oh Lydia, my wife, you know me so well. I do need to be with you through it all. Lord, let it be so. Let me be there for them. Don't let her go into labor without me,* Simon prayed, hoping that his petition would be acceptable to God and would be heard.

It was a beautiful Saturday morning, the air warm and clear. As his family arrived, Simon studied the little caravan of automobiles, from their living room window. It turned out that the entire group had made the trip: Rebecca, Frank and their three, and Phillip, Alice and their four, in multiple black Fords now parking along the side street. There were pieces of furniture tied to the roofs of the cars. There would be children sleeping all over the living room tonight!

Simon stepped outside as his nieces and nephews tumbled out and ran to the house. He was glad beyond measure that they had all decided to come. Lydia's parents were already settled in up in Nikki's room, and her sister, Peggy, and Tom had insisted on getting a hotel room. They were 'having a vacation', in Tom's words, and had also planned to see some of the sights of the city with young Steve and Mary.

Simon's family stampeded into the kitchen where Lydia and Suzie were cooking. Phillip's presence immediately filled the house. He leaned over and hugged Lydia warmly, then held her shoulders and looked at her closely. "You're going to have that baby any time now, aren't you, Lydia!" He exclaimed. "Well done, Simon! Well done!"

"I'm not doing much at all," Simon protested. "Lydia's doing all of the work."

Lydia smiled at her brother-in-law. She was truly glad to see them all again. "All of you, come in! We're blocking the door here, Phillip. At least, I seem to be blocking the door."

Becky was next to enter, leading little Lacie, and hugged Lydia as well. Becky ran her hand over Lydia's swollen abdomen. "Hm, three weeks to the day, I'll bet. You're down. Look, Alice and Frank! Look, she's down. She's about ready."

Frank looked over Alice's shoulder and scrutinized Lydia. "Yep, you're right, Becky. She's down, alright. That baby's getting ready, Simon," he said with the authority afforded him from having already had three deliveries in his marriage.

Phillip called out over the group. "Frank, I recall you passing out during one of your births. Right in the living room. And you didn't even have to watch twins arrive, like I did."

Frank flushed. "I didn't pass out! It was hot in the house, is all," he protested. "And I'd worked all day! I just closed my eyes a minute!"

Becky patted his arm fondly. "It's a bit much for any man to watch a baby come out. I didn't blame you at all for that, honey. And, anyway, you came to, when Lacie popped her head out... even if your head was over a bucket."

Phillip put his arm around Simon's shoulders. "Now let me tell you how you do it, Simon. When they start really hollering, you just go pour a whiskey and take it into the room. Works every time... makes the labor easier, I'll tell you."

Simon looked puzzled. "I don't think Lydia should drink alcohol in the middle of a delivery, Phil," he disagreed.

"Not for her... for you!" Phil laughed heartily.

Lydia watched the two men move off into the living room, where Marcus was about to be inundated with adopted-relatives, and she smiled. Simon would have to fill her in later, on the men's collective wisdom on home birthing. She sincerely hoped they didn't scare him off right after he so recently relieved her worry by admitting that she was right about him needing to be part of it all. She didn't fully understand the change in his thinking, but she was grateful for his newfound support.

Lydia really wanted everyone to get to know each other; she pulled Suzie and her mom away from their meal preparation, urging them to go meet the Finneys.

With eleven more people suddenly in the house, there was much jostling for space and moving from room to room. In the foyer, Frank and Phillip stood, looking up the stairs.

"Third floor, you say?" Frank asked Marcus. "Just had to be the third floor?"

"Closer to Heaven, Frank," Marc assured him, holding his hands palms-up, as if to say he wasn't the one who made the arrangements. Frank and Phillip started climbing the staircase with their belongings. There would need to be several trips made.

Looking around at the bustling house, Marc hoped that Lydia wasn't overdoing it again. He noticed two new faces who he could only assume were Tom and Peggy coming in through the kitchen with their little ones, just as Nikki came scooting through the room, to find him. He scooped up his daughter to introduce her to everyone, who all exclaimed how 'adorable' the toddler was.

In the kitchen, while Lydia washed some tea glasses so they could be used again, she noticed Tommy coming around the table, toward her.

"Nice little get together," he said. His tone of voice actually sounded fairly pleasant to Lydia's thinking so she grew hopeful this would go well. He did not smell of alcohol, which was also a relief to her.

"Thanks for bringing everyone over, Tommy," she said. "It was overdue getting our two families together and to have everyone meet."

"Kinda surprised you associate with the lower classes," Tommy said, leaning against the counter beside the sink.

"Excuse me?" Lydia was confused.

"The miners. Simon's family are coal miners, right? Not doctors, not lawyers. Common miners? And you associate with them." Tom crossed his arms over his chest as if amazed that she would do that.

Lydia carefully put the glass she was rinsing in the dish drainer. "They are wonderfully fine people, Tommy," she resented what he was implying. "They're a very loyal and loving family. Simon is the youngest of the three."

He stroked his chin, his gray eyes pierced hers. "Too bad you couldn't be a little more like them, then—the loyal and loving part."

Lydia took the dish towel and wiped her hands. "Oh, Tommy, must we do this?" She wondered aloud. "This is supposed to be a happy celebration."

"Is it? All that self-righteous stuff about being married in a cathedral in France! Didn't count for anything, did it, Lydia? Or did you just make it up to cover for coming back here pregnant and unwed, living with a man? You're just a whore who got caught getting pregnant and had to get hitched."

Involuntarily, her hand flew up in the air toward his face, and quick as lightning Tommy grabbed her wrist, holding it mid-air. His face was very near hers. "You... are... a... whore," he breathed, running a finger down her neck with his free hand. "And you don't know how to obey."

Turning on his heels, he left the kitchen to join the men in the living room, leaving Lydia stunned at the sink, staring at her own hand. She had almost struck Tommy across the face! She had almost hit her brother-in-law! What on earth was wrong with her?

Quickly, Lydia stepped outside onto the back porch and took a deep breath. She was filled with emotion. If she had struck him, it would have been all downhill from there. She simply had to be more careful.

In the living room, Becky cheerfully hugged Anna and Suzie. "We brought Lacie's crib and playpen. Don't think the good Lord is going to be favoring me with any more children! Unless, of course, you already brought them the same baby gifts?"

Anna replied, "We brought them a stroller from her sister, Peggy, and a highchair, so they should be set now, I'd say. Although maybe she could use a little set of drawers for the baby's clothing? We'll get one while we're here. There's got to be a Sears around here somewhere."

Re-appearing through the back kitchen door, Lydia joined the conversation. Forcing a smile, she said, "No shopping! I just want everyone to relax and have a good dinner this evening. Tonight is about everyone getting to know each other. This is not only a baby shower, but also the family wedding reception we never got to have."

Her mother slipped an arm around her large waist. "I want you to tell the whole story to everyone at dinner. How you met and all. It will be just as if we had been there."

Dinner was a production indeed. A dozen adults squeezed around the dining room table and seven children around the kitchen table, with Nikki in a highchair next to Suzie. The wine was freely distributed to those who could consume it. At the end of the meal, Anna disappeared into the kitchen and reappeared with a cake she'd hidden. It was white and decorated with flowers of icing. On the top were Simon and Lydia's names written in flowing script. It was a lovely gesture, and Lydia was completely surprised by it.

Marcus rapped on his glass and called everyone to attention as he passed another bottle of wine around to top off the glasses on the table. Lydia and Suzie were both drinking apple juice. "A toast!" Marcus exclaimed. "To the best friends in the world." All eyes looked to the end of the table where Marcus took a dramatic stand, his glass lifted high.

"Some may think it's a little late to raise a glass for the marriage of Simon and Lydia Finney. I say it is never too late to have a glass of champagne in someone's honor, and God willing, we'll be raising a toast to the happy couple on each anniversary, for fifty years to come."

Phillip said, "Hear, hear!" as Simon smiled at Lydia, wrapping an arm around her shoulders.

Marcus continued. "As you all know, my buddy here had to travel thousands of miles to find his wife. Now, no one should assume that was because there wasn't a single woman in West Virginia who would have him. I'm certain there were many beautiful West Virginian women left with broken hearts in the mountains back home."

"More than a few!" Frank called out from the other end of the table. "Especially after he got his doctor practice going."

Marcus nodded. "I'm sure!" he exclaimed, "but I also recall when a certain lovely nurse threw a letter from an old beau into the fires of France where it was duly destroyed, a loss that suitor will likely regret to the end of his days."

Andrew called out, "He wasn't worthy to marry her, I say!"

"Indeed!" Marcus agreed. "However, the truth of the matter is that these two people were simply meant to fall in love and marry each other, even though they foolishly decided to do it in the middle of a war, which did its level best to separate them at every turn."

Heads nodded around the table as Marcus continued. "It's these two and the unfailing love they have for each other that showed me what commitment means, what love is really supposed to be about. Made me a better man. So, with this somewhat stretched out, better late-than-never, wedding toast... I lift my glass to you both and wish you a long and happy life!" He lifted his glass in salute, as others around the table clinked theirs together.

Simon nodded to his best friend gratefully, and Marcus lifted his glass to Simon a second time as he resumed his seat at the table.

Phillip stood next.

"Not to take away from such a toast as that one was... but I also have a word to say."

The many faces around the table looked up expectantly.

"Wish Dad and Mom were here, little brother," Phillip started. "Wish they could have seen this day and met Lydia. But since they can't, I'll just say in Dad's place... It's about time you got off your rear and settled down with a woman willing to put up with you and your medical talk... someone who can understand what the heck you're saying... and finally bringing another baby into this family that will carry the Finney name—if you have a boy, that is. So, let's hope you knew what you were doing and created a son in that little wife of yours. And if not, well then, we'll just welcome another little girl into the family! And you'll have to try again for a boy."

Phillip drained his glass and took his seat, pleased with the laughter at the table.

Then, to Lydia's dread, Tom stood up. Raising his wine glass, he said, "Here's to the couple who elevated the family a notch in social circles, who raised the bar so our kids won't be content with just getting by, but will be pushed to new heights. To people who show that you get what you deserve!"

Those around the table looked at each other, a little puzzled. It was... maybe... a complimentary toast? They couldn't be sure, but as the wine and champagne were flowing freely, it was at least an excuse to take another celebratory drink.

Deciding it was his turn, Andrew looked around at his newly expanded family. He pushed his chair back and stood while a new bottle of wine was uncorked and passed around the table.

"I suppose," Andrew began as he looked straight at Lydia, "the father of the bride, so to speak, should also say something. Now, when this young man came into my living room, I have to say I gave him a bit of a rough time. After all, we didn't know yet about the vows back in France, and we found out when my daughter walked in that she was already pregnant, so we didn't know exactly what was going on here. I may have, just may have, made some questionable assumptions about this relationship of theirs. But," he continued, raising a hand to stop the disapproving murmurs from Simon's family, "I will tell all of you assembled here that I realized quickly that her mother and I have been honored, having this young man join our family as Lydia's husband... and the father of her child. He has demonstrated his desire to be a loving and devoted husband to her... and a loving and protective father to my grandchild—boy or girl I do not care—and he even lets me win at checkers... and I am pleased to call him my son-in-law. Well done, Simon and Lydia!"

There was a round of applause at this apologetic, welcoming, honest-hearted toast.

Lydia looked around the table. "Can we cut this beautiful cake now?" She asked, not wanting any more toasts.

"Finally!" Yelled multiple, small voices from the kitchen, where they had quickly tired of the speeches. Simon stood to cut the cake.

After the table had been cleared, they gathered around the radio in the living room. Marcus found a lovely music station and the men pulled the sofa into the hall and the easy chairs to the corners of the room. Couples started to dance together to the happy music. Holding Lydia in his arms, Simon moved slowly with her to soft strains of orchestral pieces. It was a little more difficult for her to rest her head on his shoulder with the baby between them, but he loved to dance with her, regardless. Periodically, Phillip bellowed out the word 'switch' for everyone to change partners. After one such call, Phil cut in on Simon and took Lydia on a slow, gentle spin around the living room. He wasn't as jovial as usual, and his light banter had quieted.

"I'm glad you found my little brother, Lydia," Phillip told her softly as he swayed with her between the other couples, trying not to trample the young cousins who had also paired up. "He loves you a lot, I know."

Lydia looked up at the man, so like Simon, just older. "I am, too. And I'm very glad your family came for the weekend."

"My family?" Phil questioned. "No, our family, Lydia. We're all family now. You need anything at all, you got family, ready to help. It's what we do. We're only a couple hours away, after all. And I hope you feel welcome to drop in often with your little one as soon as you're fit to travel. With or without Simon. And Abril is welcome too. Real nice dog, that one. I spent a little time with her on the porch—she's a good dog."

Lydia nodded. "She's been with us through thick and thin."

"How bad was Simon hurt in the war, Lydia?" Phillip asked quietly as they danced. "He still has trouble breathing."

"It was really bad for a while, Phil," she admitted. "He came back, though. He never complains about pain. Still has a cough... gets winded easily."

"Okay. He's a little thinner, though," Phillip said. "Gotta get a little more meat on him."

She nodded. "I'm working on it, believe me! He does like to eat!"

"Just remember, you got us to lean on," he said again.

Simon cut back in on Phil and gently twirled Lydia as the music wound around them. "My brother giving you marital advice?" he teased, his eyes twinkling.

Lydia smiled softly. "Your brother loves his family so much. He was just making sure that I knew I'm a part of it now—I really like them, Simon. They are good people. I feel their wholeness when we're with them."

He smiled, pulling her close despite her belly. "We can still dance, can't we," he murmured appreciatively, breathing in the scent of her delicate perfume. "You are the most beautiful woman in this entire room."

"Have I stepped on your toes yet?" She asked, her cheeks blushing.

"Not once," he assured her. "But I'm watching out, since you can't see them."

Over the music and the voices chattering away in the room, Phil again bellowed out, "Switch!" and everyone dropped their hands, turning to someone beside them. Lydia now found herself with Tommy. She felt incredibly awkward with her sister's husband after their private encounter in the kitchen, but she was determined to be cheerful.

"I'm very sorry about earlier in the kitchen, Tommy," she told him quietly, trying to make things smoother between them. "I guess the pregnancy is getting to my emotions a little. I am glad you and my sister could come and meet everyone. It means a lot."

He had an arm around her waist tightly, steering her off to a corner of the living room, his other hand gripped hers securely in his own. "Wasn't going to come, to tell you the truth. But I've been thinking on things. You're a bad influence on your sister. You don't know how to control yourself, and that doctor husband of yours doesn't know how to make you listen. Since you've been home, Peg hasn't been as easy to get along with and I think it's because of you, Lydia."

Lydia looked up at him quickly. "I'm a bad influence? I didn't mean to hurt anyone, Tommy, don't you know that? And my sister is a strong woman in her own right, an excellent mother, and I've always looked up to her. I don't tell her what to do."

He glanced down at her. "You could set a better example of how to be a dutiful wife. You need a real man to teach you obedience."

"I don't need to be taught obedience, Tom," Lydia stated. "And neither does Peggy."

"Simon lets you have your way all the time," Tom said under his breath. "He should be the head of the house. But you don't think about those things, do you, Lydia?" He tightened his hold on her, keeping her at the periphery of the crowded room. "Dad is the head of his house with Anna. She knows her place. But Peggy is less agreeable since you've been home, filling her ears with talk about your job at the hospital. Don't go putting ideas in her head. A disobedient wife is a stubborn mule who needs hit on the rump frequently to keep it going the right direction."

His words stung Lydia even as his hand slid down too close to her bottom.

"I think the world of my mother and sister both. They're wonderful women," Lydia said, wishing Phillip would call out 'switch' again, but at the same time knowing that she had to face this with Tom. She added quietly, "I'm going to give you the benefit of the doubt and assume that you're angry because you love my parents and my sister, and just want to protect them."

"I'm angry," he said just as quietly, "because my life, and what I wanted to do with it, got pushed clear out of the picture because of you. And the life I should have with Peggy has been messed up because she watched you go off to war and all. Everything is 'Lydia this' and 'Lydia's baby coming' and 'Lydia's doctor husband' while I'm working my butt off trying to take care of your family."

Lydia stopped dancing, trying unsuccessfully to pull her hand from his, to back away from the man. "I'm sorry, Tom," was all she could say as he held her tight.

He forced her to move again, saying, "Don't make a scene, Lydia. Behave yourself in front of all these people. And one 'I'm sorry' isn't good enough," he warned. "You'll have to do a whole lot better than that. You owe me, Lydia. Big time."

As Phillip finally, lightheartedly, called out the cue to 'switch' again in a lull between songs from the radio, Tommy finally released her waist and looked for Peg. "Time to go. Peg, get the kids," he called over to his wife.

Lydia followed Tommy toward the foyer where he was pulling coats out of a pile on the bench by the front door. She didn't want her sister to leave with an angry Tommy, but Peggy came immediately to the door at his summons.

"Oh, Tommy," Peggy said very softly to her husband, "I'd love to stay. We're having such a good time. And the children are having a great time with the other kids. How about just another hour or two?"

There in the foyer, Tommy stared at his wife, furious at being questioned. "You are just begging to get paddled aren't you," he hissed at her as Lydia looked on shocked, the man's 'stubborn mule' metaphor coming to life. Lydia saw her sister pale and instinctively moved protectively closer to her as Tommy shot her a warning look.

"No, no, Tommy," Peggy said quickly, under her breath so only Lydia caught it. "No, please, I'm so sorry. You're right, Tommy, of course. I just thought…" Peggy handed her son his jacket and helped Mary into her coat.

"You shouldn't think," Tommy muttered. "Makes for a sore rear end, doesn't it?"

"I'm glad you came, Peggy," Lydia told the children and her sister, frightened by what she'd just overheard. "Thank you for coming and for loaning me the stroller and highchair. I appreciate them."

"No problem, Sis. We really were having a nice time with the whole family. I'm sorry we have to leave," Peggy told her quickly, now quite anxious to get out the door.

"I heard that, Peggy. Start moving." Tommy's tone was cold, as he waited at the door listening. "Steven, get over here."

Noticing Tommy at the door and Peggy bundling up the kids, Simon, Andrew, and Anna all made their way to the foyer to say their goodbyes.

Anna hugged her oldest daughter. "You have to leave already?" she said sadly, glancing at Tom glowering nearby, his hand on the doorknob.

Peggy nodded anxiously, glancing at her husband. "Afraid so, Mother, Dad. It's been a long day. Thank you for dinner, Lydia. We'll see each other again. Take care, Simon."

The sisters hugged. "Please, please, be safe," Lydia whispered. It was all she could think of. She was afraid of how angry Tom was, and his whispered threat to beat Peggy was stuck in her head.

"Have a good time tomorrow in the city, Tom," Andrew told his son-in-law.

"Will do, Dad," the man cordially replied to his father-in-law. "Ought to be interesting."

Turning, he walked out the door as his wife and children followed dutifully after him.

Lydia stood in the doorway, watching their automobile pull out and disappear down the street. She felt terrible about them leaving this way and she was frightened for Peggy. Did Tommy truly beat her sister? Her mother stood beside her as they watched them leave, shaking her head.

"I don't know," Anna said regretfully. "They're having a rough spell."

Lydia nodded. "I can see that. I'm afraid I may have made it worse. I'm so sorry. Tom is so angry and controlling."

Anna turned her daughter around and looked at her firmly. "Their problems started long before you left, Lydia. Don't take any of it on yourself. They put up a good front for a while. Your dad tries to talk to Tommy from time to time. Tries to settle him down. And when he drinks, he gets upset easily."

"Oh, Mom, I didn't realize," Lydia said softly. "Peggy never said a word."

Simon stood nearby, realizing he had missed something important transpiring in his own living room. Now, he joined the women, just outside the front door. "Can I help in any way?" he asked.

"Yes," Anna answered directly. "Just keep being the good and loving husband my daughter deserves. That's all I ask. Hold onto what you two have... I can see it's real. Take care of Lydia and the baby, just as you've been doing, Simon."

Simon wrapped an arm around Lydia's waist. "You have my solemn word, Mrs. Blackwell."

"Mom," Anna corrected him. "Please, Simon, it's just Mom."

"You have my solemn word, Mom," he repeated, using the requested familiarity.

In the hotel room, Tom was livid. Peggy quickly took off the children's coats and found them some books to read or color, to entertain themselves quietly.

"You challenged me right in front of your sister," Tommy stated furiously.

"I just... we were having such a nice time, Tommy," Peg said quietly.

"You challenged my authority in front of your sister," he said, his voice like steel. He went to the suitcase. "Bend over the bed."

Peg backed up. "Tommy, the children are right here," she whispered.

"If you keep disobeying me, you won't be able to sit for two weeks instead of one," he said, drawing out the flat rectangle of wood from the suitcase. "I said... bend over the bed."

Frightened and ashamed, Peg looked at her children as Mary fled to a corner, burying her face into the wall. Expressionless, Steven took a seat on the chair by the window. He knew his father did this to help his mother learn. He didn't know why it was so hard for her to learn how to behave.

Tom's voice was low, but filled with rage and alcohol. "Mary's got to learn a woman has to obey her husband. Steve needs to learn the man is the head of the house and the woman's gotta obey him. He's old enough to learn a man's gotta do his duty," Tom said, a thin white line forming around his mouth.

Mary covered her ears with her little hands at the first sound and even Steven winced. His father never hit Mary or him this hard, but he did everything possible to avoid getting paddled. Then with morbid curiosity, Steve turned to look over at the bed, watching his father. The boy's face had no expression at all as the instrument of correction rocked the bed along with his mother as she buried her face in the blanket.

Then Steven remembered hearing his dad say that there was a lesson here that he was supposed to be learning. Not wanting to be found disobedient himself, he joined his father. His mother had only herself to blame. If she just listened, and didn't talk back, his dad wouldn't have to do this. Steve never talked back. It was his mother who provoked his dad all the time, making him mad. Suddenly, the boy felt an anger rising toward his mother.

Tommy looked down at Steven watching. "I don't enjoy doing this, son," he told the boy. It wasn't true; he was imagining this was Lydia after she had nearly slapped his face. It was giving him considerable satisfaction.

"It's okay, Dad," Steven said looking on in morbid curiosity. He wondered if the sound was traveling through the wall to the next hotel room. It was so loud! "The man has to make his wife listen."

As Mary wept in the corner, Steve wished she would be quiet. It was distracting.

"I want you to teach me to be a strong man, Dad," he said, hoping it would make his father happy with him. "How does a man know how hard to hit?"

"When the pain of correction is worse than the pleasure she gets from being disobedient... then it's hard enough," Tommy taught his son through clenched teeth, waiting until Peggy's pain subsided so it could be made fresh again. "A man's gotta be obeyed, no matter what it takes. If it's not hard enough to make her cry, it's not working. You have to keep going."

Peggy's fingers dug into the coverlet over the bed, her knuckles white, so people in the next hotel room would not hear her as Tommy tried his level best to crush her soul.

"She's crying now, Dad, so... how do you know when she's learned her lesson? When your arm wears out or something?" Steven asked. He feared but also admired his dad's strength. "How's a man supposed to know how many swats it takes? Or which paddle to use?"

Tom didn't answer, taking a moment to rub the muscles of his upper arm. "Who's in charge of our house?" Tom demanded, leaning over Peg.

"You are, Tommy," Peggy moaned, her hands flying backwards to stop more injury.

"Then do what I say. And get those damn hands out of my way! Thank me, that I care enough to correct you," he demanded.

Slowly, Peggy moved her hands, choking out the words, "Thank you... for caring enough... to correct me."

His anger spent, Tommy tossed the slat into the suitcase. *She'll remember this one alright, tomorrow, walking around the zoo, and sitting the whole way home in the automobile afterwards.*

Tommy pointed to Peggy, on the bed. "That... is how you know it's enough, Son... when she thanks you for correcting her. Now, get your sister in bed and get her quiet. Peggy... bedtime!"

Clutching the headboard, Peg dragged herself to her feet as Tommy turned the lights down while throwing her a nightgown and putting his pajamas on. Steve immediately went to Mary with her own nightie.

"Stop crying. Put this on, Mary," Steve ordered his sister. "Get in bed."

Terrified, the girl immediately did what she was told, climbing in beside her brother. In the dark shadows Steve saw his dad moving on top of his mother as she wept. Apparently, this was part of the process of obedience training. So, he tried moving on top of Mary too.

Then the dark room was quiet, except for muffled sobs. Steven lay awake in the dark, wondering what he should be feeling, because he felt absolutely nothing. He wondered why his mother would still be crying, when it was she who needed to learn and she had thanked his father for the correction. Just before falling asleep, he pondered how being the man of the house carried a great deal of responsibility.

By Sunday afternoon, the house on the corner was back to normal. The two remaining couples sat quietly in the living room enjoying the fire while Abril thumped her tail happily on the floor and played with Nikki as she crawled and toddled around on unsteady feet. Nikki loved Abril, who tolerated her attentions patiently.

Simon and Marcus were bent over a chessboard on the coffee table next to the sofa. Suzie picked up the book she had been reading, tucked herself into one of the easy chairs, and found her place in the story. Lydia pulled her feet up on one end of the sofa and rested.

She was exhausted from the two days of preparation and entertainment, and was still troubled about her sister and Tommy. She had never appreciated how different family relationships could be until she had found Simon. And now, as she watched him stroking his beard as he considered his next move against Marcus, she was grateful for the quality of their relationship. It was one her own sister obviously did not enjoy.

"Hm," Simon muttered. "I'll take your knight, then."

Marcus studied the board from his position, sitting cross-legged on the floor next to the table. "Why did you do that?"

"Why'd I do what?" Simon protested.

"You just gave me your bishop," Marcus showed him and swiftly took Simon's bishop captive.

Simon sat up, staring at the setup. "Ouch," he admitted.

"Yeah, ouch," Marcus agreed. "Now your queen is in danger."

Simon leaned over the board, seeking a path of escape for his queen. "Well, we can't have that now, can we..."

There was silence except for the happy babbles of Nikki talking to Abril and a low murmur in the dog's throat as if she were talking back. Lydia closed her eyes, grateful for the peace in the room.

Simon sat up again. "Not if my knight moves right here and there. The queen is saved," he triumphed.

"Yes, but now your king is in check," Marcus said slyly. "Didn't see that, did you, Simon! Got to always be thinking two or three moves ahead."

"I thought I was thinking two or three moves ahead," Simon said regretfully. "Apparently not."

"Are you going to surrender? Or do you want to go through this brutal and humiliating defeat?" Marcus wondered. "If you must put yourself through the pain, I will be happy to oblige."

Simon tipped over his king. "No, I stand, or rather fall... I am defeated."

"Yet again," Marcus reminded him. He set the chess board up again for a new game, at another time. "I like your family, Simon," he added. "Really nice people. Not too sure about your brother-in-law though. He seems like a loose cannon." He scooped up his daughter, who was beginning to look sleepy, and stretched out on the floor with Nikki lying on his chest. Abril, deprived of her default playmate, happily settled in beside the couch.

Simon lifted Lydia's feet onto his lap as he took his place on the sofa beside her. He looked at Marcus lying on the floor by the fire, with little Nikki starting to doze off laying on her father's chest. "Yeh, Tommy's rough at that."

"It was my fault," Lydia said, suddenly growing sad.

Simon looked at her shocked. "What are you talking about, Lydia? You aren't responsible for that man."

She sighed heavily. "This time I am. I made him really angry in the kitchen."

Going on high alert, Simon stared at her. "What happened in the kitchen, Lydia..."

"I almost slapped him," she confessed. Marcus shot a look up at her from the floor, trying not to disturb Nikki. Suzie also put down her book in surprise.

"If I hadn't done that, he'd have stayed calm... I think..." her voice trailed off because she wasn't sure about that. Tom might have been angry anyway, just looking for an excuse to show it.

Now Simon was on edge. *In my own house?* "I need to know what happened," he demanded.

"He called me a whore. Said the only reason we got married now was because we got pregnant. And I... I don't know what happened. My hand just flew up and he grabbed it, thank goodness, before I hit his face. I know I set him off. I'm just afraid he took it out on my sister," Lydia confessed, her eyes tearing up at the thought.

Suzie snapped her book shut, tossing it aside. "Men like that don't deserve to have a wife and family."

Simon was furious. The man had insulted Lydia in his own kitchen? "I wish you would have told me immediately, Lydia!"

Lydia sighed. "I was afraid of making a scene. And he would have taken it out on Peg, I know it. I thought it was better to try to keep him calm."

"Keep him—" Simon started. He would have beaten him enough the man wouldn't have touched another living being. "Next time—never mind! There won't be a next time. That man is never coming back into this house again. Your sister can visit. Not Tommy."

Lydia looked over at Simon and recognized the look in his eyes. She nodded.

"Well!" Suzie softly exclaimed. "Looks like someone is asleep." She got up and gently scooped Nikki from Marcus' chest. "Bedtime, sweetie," she said, kissing the little toddler and putting her over her shoulder to carry her up to bed.

"Think it's time for me to wash up," Simon chimed in, wanting to vent his anger without letting Lydia see it. Before going upstairs, he went to the closet and pulled something out of his coat pocket. Returning to the living room he said to Marcus, "Heads up!"

Marcus turned, catching a baseball. "Seriously, Simon? You got me a baseball?"

Simon nodded. "Owed you one," he said, running up to the bathroom where he would let off some steam. There was room for push-ups in the bathroom, too, and he intended to do many!

It grew quiet in the living room as Marcus tossed the leather ball in the air a few practice throws, his own thoughts kept private. *The man called Lydia a whore? Lydia of all people?*

Lydia felt the baby rolling over. "Gracious," she exclaimed softly. "Marc!"

Looking over quickly, he saw her abdomen changing shape. Lydia motioned for him to come over, and he did so immediately, now distracted from his own anger. She laid his hand on the baby, and he felt it rolling within her. To him it felt like a little shoulder rose and fell. Lydia moved his hand under her ribs, and he felt what seemed like feet kicking against her taut skin.

"It's amazing the baby still fits in there, upside down," he breathed in wonder. "I am amazed I can almost tell which part of the baby it is... a shoulder here... and that's probably its little bottom right there..."

Lydia laughed softly. "Remember those first flutters we felt? I sure keep stretching as it grows, don't I!"

"Is your stethoscope in your bag?" Marcus asked suddenly.

She nodded. "Of course, by the front door. Why?"

He jumped up and retrieved her bag, taking out the stethoscope as he returned. "Have you heard the heartbeat?"

"Marcus, how could I hear the heartbeat of a baby?" she asked. "The heart is the size of a pea!" But she lowered her waistband enough to let him try to listen, even though she was doubtful.

"A walnut," he corrected her. Marcus placed the bell against her abdomen and listened intently in various places across her abdomen. "Listen to this," he said then. "It's the sound you are making pushing blood through the cord, feeding your baby." He held the bell in place and offered her the earpieces, which she eagerly accepted.

Lydia heard the steady, rhythmic swooshing of blood moving through the cord, and her eyes widened. "That's my blood going through the cord?"

He nodded, enjoying her wonder. After a moment, he took the earpieces back and listened again, moving the bell lower across where he suspected the baby was positioned with its back against her skin. Then, Marcus smiled broadly, his eyes twinkling. "Want to hear the heartbeat?"

Speechless, Lydia took the earpieces again. She listened carefully and heard the soft, rapid tapping, steady and persistent, only fading when the baby moved. "That's my baby's heart?" she breathed, enraptured.

He nodded. "That's your baby's heart, Lydia. Beating about a hundred twenty times a minute."

"It's so fast!" she softly exclaimed, tears forming in her eyes. "Why is it so fast?"

"Very tiny heart!" he offered, smiling at the expression of sheer joy on her face. "I can't believe you haven't listened yourself, with or without Simon."

"I didn't know I could hear my baby's heartbeat!" she breathed in awe. "Oh, dear God, it's my baby's heart... your godchild's heart is beating in my ears..." A tear slid down her cheek, and Marcus reached up and wiped it away with his finger. They sat for a time, listening to the baby's heartbeat, finding it again when the baby turned, enjoying the miracle of life which was soon to emerge into the world.

"Oh, Marcus," Lydia said. "Thank you! Even Sister Anne didn't try to find the heartbeat. I guess with the baby being so active, she assumed she didn't need to, and I really didn't know you could hear something so tiny."

He nodded, understanding. "Makes sense. I didn't get to be part of any of this with Nikki. It means a lot to me that you've shared this pregnancy with me, Lydia."

"Since almost the beginning," she said, thinking back to his support early on and especially throughout Simon's absence. "You've always been there for us. And you and the baby must form a special bond."

"Why do you think I haven't moved Suzie and me out of the house yet, Lydia?" Marcus said. "I've moved many times in my life gladly. This is the one time I regret ever having to leave anywhere. I will be here until your baby is safely delivered."

Her eyes filling, Lydia reached out her hand and grasped his. "I can't think about that right now, Marcus. Really, I can't. Please don't speak of moving away. I love Simon with my whole heart, you know that. But I can't think of you leaving just now." Marc was the one keeping Simon on track healing his damaged lungs and body. He struggled to breathe just climbing the stairs sometimes. Simon's life depended on Marc.

He got up, leaving her with the stethoscope. "Then don't," he said, kissing the top of her head. "Because I'm here. And I promised Simon I will always be here if you two ever have a need... and I will keep that vow. Good night, Lydia."

Chapter 10

Expecting the Unexpected

Part II

Lydia stood in the nurses' back office, patiently listening to Sister Edwarda. Her voice was firm. "I think you should remain in the clinic from now on," she stated, noting the size of Lydia's abdomen. "It looks as though the baby has dropped. You mustn't be out seeing patients this close to your delivery."

Lydia knew better than to argue with the formidable woman. "Very well, Sister," Lydia replied. "I'll stay at the clinic, but I do want to continue working as long as I can."

"You may, but only because this is a hospital and if you go into labor, we can assist you," Sister Edwarda was decided. She had grown quite fond of this young woman and wanted to leave nothing to chance.

Lydia gently rubbed her belly. "My husband will be relieved... being right upstairs and all. He's also uncomfortable with me going out, I think."

"I'd imagine so," Sister Edwarda nodded. "Very well. You are back on clinic... and I will go inform Doctor Maloney as well, in case one of his rising star, young surgeons fails to show up for the operating theater, one day soon.

"Thank you." Lydia smiled warmly, deeply appreciating the sister's wisdom and guidance.

As Sister Edwarda left the room, Lydia reached for the long apron, laying it over her swollen belly. It helped to hide how far along she really was. Hearing footsteps coming down the hall, Lydia looked up as she pulled her blue scarf around her hair. To her astonishment, it was Peter Martin who came into the room.

"Doctor Martin!" Lydia exclaimed in surprise. "How very nice to see you! Are you back in the clinic already? You just finished a rotation."

He nodded, smiling as she tucked her long brown waves up into a bun under her scarf. "One of the other doctors is taking time off to see family out of state, for Easter. I'm covering until he gets back."

"That's lovely!" she exclaimed, genuinely pleased. "Sister Edwarda has confined me to clinic."

"Lydia, please don't do any on-the-floor, emergency-type maneuvers. Please call me instead."

"Yes, Doctor," she smiled. "I promise."

"Good," he said, watching as she made her way down the hall. She did indeed have a bit of a waddle... and it was beautiful.

"Sister Teresa?" he called into the next little office down the hallway.

"Well, good morning, Doctor Martin! Welcome back!" The nun was always so cheerful.

"Can we please have a birthing setup on hand—just in case Nurse Finney decides to bless us by having her baby here?"

"Already done, Doctor Martin," Sister Teresa said, pointing to a bundle of sheets around a basin in a corner of her office, with all of the contents required for a sudden delivery. "Sister Edwarda had us pull it all together, after our last unexpected clinic delivery."

"You're all truly amazing. Well, let's get to work then."

The next couple of days in the clinic passed rather uneventfully. Patients arrived in their usual bursts with lulls in between, affording Lydia short breaks to elevate her feet on a stool in the office, under the ever-watchful eye of Sister Mary Margaret. Suzie was out seeing patients in the community, with the police whistle safely around her neck. Doctor Martin had been looking for an opportunity to take a break himself so he could ask Lydia about her experiences visiting patients.

"So, what's it like for you nurses to be out making house calls?" Peter asked. "I mean, doctors have been doing it forever... but it's got to be a little different for nurses."

Lydia nodded. "For the most part, patients are just so grateful that we come. And when I call a doctor's office to report, most of them are also appreciative of the clinical information we gather. Then, they can advise if they want something else checked, or want us to go back again... or have the patient come into their offices."

"Have you run into any problems out there that we should resolve... before we hire more nurses to go out into the neighborhoods?" Peter was understandably concerned for the nurses' safety.

Lydia considered his question carefully. She wanted more nurses to come despite the risks she had already encountered. "We need to offer them training—there are some differences that should be discussed to help them be safe and successful."

"Such as..." Peter encouraged her.

Lydia didn't answer; she winced as a cramp moved from her back straight across her abdomen. She let slip a light gasp, holding her belly. Peter immediately felt her stomach for muscle activity. "What did it feel like?" he asked quickly.

"Sharp, tight..." she said. "It's passed—was that a contraction?"

"Probably what we call false labor. There was no matching change in the muscle tone of your uterus. Usually, labor contractions start mild and steadily increase, instead of starting out sharp and tight and dropping off," Peter observed cautiously, wondering if he should send her home to rest.

"Well, it's gone," Lydia said firmly. "I'm fine now. I want to go back out."

Peter looked worried. "If you have another one, tell Sister Mary Francis to help you get back into the examination room right away... and to find me."

"I will," Lydia assured him. The pain had taken her by surprise, being so sharp and starting in her back like that. "Thank you, Doctor."

The issue of nurse safety out in the community had been sidelined, for the moment. She waddled back down the hallway and made a mental note to call Sister Anne as soon as possible to tell her what had happened.

As Lydia was preparing to wrap up for the day, an urgent message arrived: Sister Edwarda needed to see her in the administration office. Without hesitation, Lydia washed up and checked out with Sister Teresa before swiftly gathering her belongings. As she was making her way out, Peter stopped her briefly.

"I've been summoned," Lydia explained, offering a hurried smile.

"Do you want me to walk you over to the office?" he offered.

She smiled. "No, thank you, I'm fine. I didn't feel anything else today—just a little backache."

Peter nodded. "That, too, can be false labor."

"Does false labor turn into true labor?" she asked anxiously.

"Maybe?" he offered. "Maybe not?"

"You are no help at all!" she teased, smiling. She fully appreciated the guesswork in all things medical. She would ask the midwife. Sister Anne, who would know for sure. "I'll see you tomorrow, Doctor."

"Maybe," he called out after her. "But maybe not!"

Lydia walked down the long hall to the front rotunda, turned right, and went down the other long corridor to the administrative offices, at the far end. She was a little out of breath by the time she got into the anteroom and approached the receptionist.

"Miss Weston... Sister Edwarda called me... to the administration office—" she started.

"Nurse Finney, yes, please follow me." The woman quickly rose to her feet, motioning for Lydia to follow.

Lydia was led back to Doctor Maloney's office, where she was surprised to see both Simon and Marcus already seated. Immediately, Simon stood, offering her his seat in one of the high-backed chairs. Lydia was grateful to rest after the long walk.

Doctor Maloney rose and reached across the desk to shake her hand. "Nurse Finney, thank you for joining us," he said cordially.

Lydia could not begin to imagine what this was all about. Apparently equally perplexed, Simon and Marcus exchanged confused glances between them.

Doctor Maloney settled back into his seat. "There is another joining us," he remarked. The sound of Sister Edwarda's rapid footsteps echoed down the hall, a testament to her boundless energy. Marcus rose from his seat, a gesture of respect for the senior nurse. He offered her his high-backed chair, which she accepted with a polite nod, perching primly on the edge of the cushion.

"Will he be much longer?" Doctor Maloney asked Sister Edwarda.

"He is on his way," the nun replied.

Doctor Maloney turned to Lydia, "Nurse Finney, I've been talking with our newest surgeons, reviewing their first couple of months here. Our staff has found your husband and Doctor Lovell to be exceptional additions to the hospital."

Lydia glanced at Simon and Marcus warmly. She did not need the administrator to tell her that they were excellent, but was glad to hear that the hospital had recognized their merit. She simply nodded her agreement with Doctor Maloney, knowing that her biased opinion did not need to be voiced... and again, wondering why on earth they all had been summoned.

Breaking a moment of quiet, Sister Edwarda spoke up, "We have also been discussing you, and Nurse Lovell, who unfortunately could not be here, due to her house visits and needing to get home to the babysitter. Doctor Lovell, incidentally, I must say that Nikki is a most beautiful, well-behaved toddler when she is here. The nuns thoroughly enjoy it when she is in clinic. We're tremendously pleased with the work the nurses are doing."

Now, Lydia better understood the reason for her presence in the crowded room. "Thank you, Sister Edwarda. It's a blessing to work here—I know I speak for Nurse Lovell as well. The doctors and staff have been incredibly kind and supportive. This has been a wonderful opportunity for us."

Doctor Maloney then took the floor. "Not that it hasn't come without cost. You're a dedicated group! We've been wanting to give something back, and when a need was made known to us, for a couple of you at least—well, we hope this is a welcome surprise for you—"

A light rap sounded at the door, and yet another person arrived. Simon's face lit up with recognition as a portly, older man entered the room. Although Lydia did not know him, she instantly recognized the black clothes and white collar of a priest.

"Ah, Father Damien," Doctor Maloney greeted the man.

"Doctor Maloney, Doctor Finney," the priest greeted them in kind. "Is this Mrs. Finney?"

"My wife, Father," Simon said, resting his hand on Lydia's shoulder as he stood protectively beside her.

"I hear that congratulations are in order, Nurse Finney—and soon, I rather expect?" the priest added, noticing the size of her belly.

Lydia's body no longer felt like her own; it seemed to have become everyone else's business. She patted her belly gently. "Yes," she smiled at the priest. "Sometime very soon. Easter, we think."

"What a splendid time to give birth, with our Savior's sacrifice and resurrection!" he exclaimed with delight.

Doctor Maloney impatiently cleared his throat. "Well, Father Damien?"

The priest redirected his focus. "Oh, yes, of course." He turned to Simon and Lydia. "Doctor Finney, in early January, you approached me about a delicate matter regarding your marriage at the cathedral in Nancy. As you know, I did write to the diocese there, after speaking to the bishop here."

"Yes, Father Damien," Simon said. "We appreciate all your efforts, sir."

"Well, I've received a correspondence which I've been asked to convey to you." He reached into his inner pocket and pulled out an envelope, handing it to Simon.

It had been previously opened, as it was addressed to Father Damien. Simon stared curiously at the man, who motioned for him to open the letter. Simon removed the contents to find a small note written in French, which he could not translate, as well as a folded paper which was written in both French and English. He quickly scanned the document, and in astonishment started reading aloud for Lydia and Marcus, "*...and on that date, and in so much as I myself was present and bestowed a blessing on their spoken vows... the witness below... these two in the sight of... worshipful pledges consistent with principles of Holy Matrimony... vows in good faith of that of man and wife... signed Father Andrew Paul... Sister Joanna Mary Rebecca, Diocese of...*" Simon's voice trailed off to a whisper. He stared at Lydia in amazement.

Taking the letter with trembling hands, as if it were a sheet of the purest gold, Lydia read it again for herself! Someone had finally and truly acknowledged the sanctity of their vows made at that altar! It was all she needed and worth more to her, even if not official, than the license issued to them by the government.

"It is not an official church marriage certificate, mind you," Father Damien apologized. "But Father Andrew obviously felt strongly enough about the events of that day that he wanted you to have something to honor what he had witnessed when you knelt before him."

Lydia passed it to Marcus, her expression radiating her deep peace and happiness.

Marcus also read the small note, in French. He recognized a few words: *Ange de miséricorde.* "Do you know what this note says?" Marcus asked Father Damien. "Can you translate it? Nurse Finney is most certainly the angel he is referring to."

"It says he is happy to reward a great kindness done in the midst of war. I suspect you understand this somewhat cryptic remark," Father Damien replied.

"Indeed, I do. And it's well deserved." He reached over to squeeze Lydia's hand, recalling when she had risked her life to retrieve a soldier who had been left behind on the battlefield. For that act, she had received not only a bullet in her shoulder, but also her heroic nickname from a grateful group of French soldiers.

Simon bent to cup her face tenderly in her hands. "Now, my beloved wife, someone has properly acknowledged our vows at the cathedral in Nancy!"

She rose awkwardly from the high-backed chair and, precariously standing on tiptoe, kissed the priest on the cheek. "God bless you! This is a precious gift, for us and for our baby," she whispered. She would have the letter framed for their wall!

"It was a very great pleasure, my dear," the priest replied.

Before dawn, Lydia felt a real cramp. She slipped out of bed, padded down to the bathroom at the end of the hall, and turned up the gaslight. She checked herself but there was no bleeding. *I wonder...* she thought. *Is this it?* She decided not to wake Simon just yet, and instead drew a bath. If it was labor beginning, she wanted to be clean. No one else was up, so she decided to linger for a bit in the comforting water of the tub. Leaning back, she felt extremely large as she beheld her belly, so swollen with life. *If you don't come out soon, I may explode,* she told the baby telepathically. For a moment, she felt fear for what was to come, but then remembered the words her mother had told her: the screams from her muscles meant the baby would soon be in her arms. *I can do this*, Lydia reminded herself.

Carefully stepping out of the tub, Lydia dried off and slipped back into her nightgown. If the baby was coming, there was no sense in getting dressed. She drained the tub and faced herself in the small mirror above the sink. "So, this might be the day... almost Easter..." she said to her reflection. "You'll be a mother by tonight, I hope." Lydia turned at the sound of a soft tap on the door. Still barefoot, she went to open it quickly, so as not to wake the house.

It was Marcus standing at the door, hair tousled, still half asleep. "I saw the light. Everything okay?" he asked as he tried to will himself awake.

"Two cramps," she reported.

His eyes flew open. "Is Simon up? Should I do anything?"

She laughed softly. "Two cramps, Marcus, just two. It could be hours before there are more."

His eyes traveled over her nightgown. "That is not how this works, Lydia! Two will be three, and then a hundred before you know it. I should stay home today and keep Simon calm."

Suddenly, she winced, holding her belly as pain washed over her abdomen. Marcus immediately reached for her. Slowing her breathing, she reached for his arm. "Make that three! Nonsense, you go to the surgery and tell Doctor Maloney that Simon is staying home, and then you just get home as soon as you're done. I do want you to be here for Simon, so he doesn't go crazy with anxiety, but if you get held up, that's fine too."

"Are you absolutely sure you don't want to go to the hospital?" Marcus asked her for the hundredth time.

"And put Simon and you out in the waiting room? No, Marcus," she was emphatic. "He helped create this situation; he's going to suffer right through it with me."

Marcus smiled. "It might keep him from ever wanting to create a situation again! Are you certain you want to take that risk?" he teased.

She quickly countered. "Are you ever going to risk it again with Suzie?"

"That's different," he protested. "She lets them put her to sleep."

Lydia stopped short at the thought. "Oh, that's right. She does. Well, I want to go through this like all the women in the Bible did, with a midwife. I want to know what it means to bring life into the world and not miss a single minute."

Marcus took her by the arms and kissed her forehead. "You're wonderful," he said. "I'll get back as fast as I can!"

He watched her waddle back down the hall to her bedroom, shaking his head. *Dear God, don't let anything go wrong*, he prayed. He felt the familiar pang of regret that he'd missed all of this with Suzie. Next time, he would be there with her, unless he was out in a waiting room, not permitted to be part of the birth, like most men.

Lydia slid back into bed, feeling clean and as ready as she could be. Simon stirred as she slipped back under the covers next to him. Even in his sleep, he reached for her, so she nestled in against his chest, drawing strength from him as she waited for another cramp to come—just some twinges. She fell back to sleep against Simon's shoulder, lulled by the soft, steady sound of his breathing, interrupted only occasionally by a wave of pain.

With the first rays of morning sun, came a cramp that was quite a bit more pronounced. She anxiously felt her stomach. Simon entered the room as she was rubbing her belly. He immediately dropped down beside her. "What is it? Contraction?"

"I think so," she replied. "I've been having them off and on, but fell asleep again. I do feel wet. I think I lost the mucous plug."

"Why didn't you wake me?" Simon demanded, kissing her head.

"What, so we could both lose sleep?" she teased. "I thought I should rest a bit longer, so I did."

"I'll stay home, of course," he reassured her. "And I'll go ring Sister Anne straightaway."

"Thank you," she said, kissing him lightly.

Lying back down on their four-poster bed, she waited. In the quietness of the house, she soon heard the voices of the two men talking downstairs and knew Marcus and Simon were discussing how to get through the day ahead. She was hopeful that Simon would be able to gain the reassurance he needed, that all would go well. Suzie's softer voice also reached her ears, though her words were unintelligible. Lydia relaxed, knowing Suzie would get the men pointed in the right direction, and that she didn't need to go down. She decided to try to doze off again, knowing that the rest of this was already in motion. In and out of sleep, Lydia kept track of her contractions.

Simon attempted to read a medical journal in the easy chair by their bay window. On the surface, he appeared his usual calm and reserved self, but beneath that composed exterior, anxiety raged within him as they awaited the arrival of Sister Anne... who had needlessly assured him on the telephone that *'These things take time'*. He was a doctor; he knew it could take time. She had told him she would be there after checking on a few of her other patients. So there Simon sat, unable to relax, waiting for the nun.

The medical journal in his hands was from obstetrics. He hadn't shown Lydia, but for the past two weeks he had been reading and re-reading the latest cesarean procedures. He recalled his preparation with Marcus... *"Here, Marcus, memorize this,"* he'd said one evening after dinner. Marcus had taken the journal in surprise.

"You can't be serious, Simon! Here? At home?"

Simon had nodded. *"Just in case. I mean, the hospital is just across the bridge, but what if something happens!"*

Marcus had shaken his head. *"A home cesarean is not something I would even remotely consider."* But to humor Simon, he had taken it, promising to commit the procedure to memory.

Lydia was now frequently getting out of bed to walk down and back along their upstairs hallway, to help 'speed things along'... or to wear her out so much that she wouldn't care about the pains seizing her abdomen. Lydia finished her walk, returning to the bedroom.

This time, the contraction was much stronger. She uttered a little gasp, holding onto the bedpost. "That was a good one!" she exclaimed... still thinking, *I've got this!* "This baby means business!"

Simon looked up from his journal. "How far apart?" He closed his journal, placing it on the windowsill.

"They're getting stronger—every ten minutes or so. Maybe you should check me, Simon," Lydia suggested.

Sister Anne still hadn't arrived.

"'Or so'?" he asked, deciding to keep track of the timing on his own watch. After all, the pain might cloud her accuracy. He ran down the hall and washed his hands as if going into surgery.

Lydia lay on the bed and pulled up her nightie, bending her legs as Simon felt for her cervix. His eyes widened. "My God, Lydia, you're already about five centimeters dilated!"

Relieved to hear that she was making progress, Lydia nodded. "Good! It's good to know it isn't false labor."

His soft brown eyes couldn't hide his worry. "Things may start moving very quickly."

"She'll be here, Simon," Lydia assured him softly. "I didn't plan this so that you'd have to deliver our baby. She knows what she's doing and she'll be here. First babies take time."

"Well, there's no need to rush this, so let's not continue the walking!" he ordered, before taking his seat again and turning to the same page of the obstetrics journal he had been on for the last hour.

After a time, he glanced up to see Lydia checking her wristwatch again, noting that she was doing so more regularly now. He checked his own watch. *Just past noon... this is taking forever!* His anxiety was growing. He had only tended to women who had arrived at the hospital well into their labor. He also thought back to the occasional mare or cow he'd helped deliver in West Virginia, but that was so very different.

His stomach in knots, Simon did a mental inventory of his own supplies tucked away along the far side of the bed. In his bag, he had a small bottle of ether and a mask, surgical tools, lap sponges, and sutures, just in case something went wrong. It was ridiculous of course to even consider a cesarean at home... and it was better that Lydia not know that he was thinking about it, but he needed to feel prepared. What was taking Marc so long to get back? He couldn't do a cesarean by himself! Luckily, Sister Anne had helped Weyland's obstetricians do them in the hospital. But here at home? It would take at least two surgeons, and Marc swore he would be here—

A knock at the door broke the silence. Suzie opened the door for the midwife. *Sister Anne is here!* Relief flooded over him! He jumped from the chair and ran down the stairs to welcome her. Both women recognized the anxiety in his eyes.

"Now, Doctor Finney," Sister Anne reassured him. "We have been expecting this, you know. It's going to be fine. The baby is turned, in a good position, and Lydia is strong and healthy."

"I'm just glad you made it," he uttered with the utmost sincerity.

Sister Anne led the way up to the bedroom, greeting Lydia warmly. "Ready to do this, my dear?"

Lydia held her belly in the middle of a contraction. "Don't think I have much choice in the matter, Sister Anne," she groaned. "My mother said my body would take over and I wouldn't have any more say in it."

"Wise woman. Your body knows what it needs to do," Sister Anne reminded her. "At this point, it will be relentless until the work is done. Your job is to go along with it and not fight the inevitable. You'll want to fight it, I mean, when the pain is strong. Don't. You must go along with the pain and make it your friend."

Lydia breathed a sigh of relief as the contraction passed. "Pain is my friend, is that it?"

"That's it," Sister Anne said. "Let me check your cervix." She walked to the bathroom and washed her hands for a good, long time. When she returned, she was still wiping them on a towel. As she donned her gloves, she looked as if she was ready for surgery herself.

Lydia was glad for the woman's experienced presence, remembering the countless number of babies she'd already brought into the world. Sister Anne exuded a sense of calm control and shared it graciously with those around her.

"Wonderful progress! Your cervix is becoming paper thin!" Sister Anne declared, withdrawing her fingers. "I can feel the head. You're starting to crown. This baby will be here before suppertime."

From the bedroom door, Suzie called to Simon, "Simon, I put Abril out back in the yard. She may not do well if Lydia is in pain."

Turning to Lydia, who was holding her belly, she added, "You've got this!" Suzie was grateful that she had been put to sleep during Nikki's birth and hadn't felt the pain Lydia was about to endure.

Simon was clearly having some difficulty with all of this. It would be better now that the expert had arrived. Sister Anne had already taken the easy chair and was pulling out knitting needles and a ball of yarn while Simon pulled a rocking chair into the room.

Suzie headed back downstairs to wait it out, while keeping little Nikki occupied.

Lydia leaned over the bed, holding on to the bedpost as the pain began in earnest. She sent a silent message to her mother. *I think the screams might be coming, Mom. Just don't know if it's going to be my body screaming or me... make friends with the pain... make friends with...*

"Ohhh!" She stood up straight and turned to walk the upstairs hallway, all the way to the bathroom then turned back to do it again.

"Shouldn't she be in bed?" Simon asked Sister Anne softly, but with urgency.

Sister Anne smiled calmly at the doctor. "Let her go," she advised. "Let her do what she needs to do." Her knitting needles were tapping rhythmically as they slid the stitches back and forth between them.

They heard a heartfelt cry from the hallway, and Sister Anne raised a hand to restrain Simon. "Keep breathing, Doctor Finney, slow and easy, in and out through your nose. Don't hyperventilate," she reminded him, now for a second time, as she continued her knitting.

After an hour or so, and several more trips walking the hallway, with contractions coming closer together and accompanied by cries of pain, Lydia returned to the bedroom. "I think you'd better check me again, Sister Anne," Lydia said. "It feels kind of heavy down there."

With Simon's help, she got into the bed and Sister Anne checked her. "You're almost fully dilated. Almost ten centimeters. Totally effaced. Lots of hair. Splendid!"

Lydia gritted her teeth as a searing cramp moved across her belly. "Oh... my... God...!" she cried out. "Simon, sit behind me, please, hold me up! I can't lay so flat!"

Climbing up behind her, he supported her between his spread knees. She gripped his arms. Calmly, Sister Anne began to move the sheets and newspapers into position beneath Lydia, then laid out the tools of her trade for cutting the cord and such. She brought a basin of fresh water from the bathroom at the end of the hall and carefully placed it nearby. Everything was ready and waiting... Now it was up to the baby.

Marcus had arranged to borrow an automobile, just in case they needed to make it back to the hospital quickly—and jumped into it directly after his last patient. Putting it in gear, he screeched out of the parking space and over the bridge, to their little street. He threw it into park in their alley and jumped over the low back fence rather than stopping to open the gate. Abril came at a run, anxious to get into the house where she could hear Lydia through the upstairs windows. "I know you won't understand, but stay, Abril," Marcus told the dog as he ran up the porch steps and into the house. Abril dropped down right outside the door and anxiously woofed her frustration, but she did feel a bit better, knowing that this human was also home, now.

Running into the house, Marcus spied a note on the dining room table. "Took Nikki to the park. Getting intense up there." It was from Suzie. *Probably a good idea, for both of them,* Marcus thought. He was at the base of the stairs, one hand on the newel post when Lydia let out a scream. He leaned against the banister, unsure of how he was going to help Simon get through this.

"Simon, I'm home!" he called up the stairs. He could hear the midwife's voice, calmly talking Lydia through the contractions and his breathing eased, knowing Sister Anne was up there too. He could hear his buddy trying to be reassuring.

"Marc!" Simon called back with an intense sigh of relief! *Another surgeon is in the house!*

"I... can't... do... this!" Lydia cried out, her fingers like a vice around Simon's arms, her voice easily carrying down the steps as pain rolled over her like a fire ball.

"Yes, you can," Marcus heard Simon tell her. "You can do this, Lydia."

Marcus looked up, anxiously pacing in the foyer. He did not think Simon sounded the least bit convincing.

"Aghhhhhh!" Lydia screamed.

Now Simon was able to focus on Lydia fully; if he had to do an emergency cesarean, he wouldn't have to do it alone.

But Sister Anne clearly wasn't worried about a surgery at all. She was on a kitchen chair right beside the bed, while Simon held Lydia's legs up, holding her against his chest. "Lots and lots of hair! This baby is going to come out needing a haircut, Lydia."

"If... it finally... ever... comes out!" she cried and fell back against Simon, her eyes closing as the contraction passed. Too soon, another equally powerful contraction seized her and Simon prayed to God this would be over quickly... he didn't know how much more he could take, let alone Lydia! He anxiously wiped the sweat from her forehead, not knowing what else to do. He checked to make sure Lydia was still breathing as she had suddenly grown so quiet.

"Women can actually sleep between contractions," Sister Anne informed Simon. "Amazing, isn't it? How her body can do that? It's really quite remarkable when you think about it."

Simon wasn't immediately impressed with that tidbit of knowledge, but filed it away for later consideration because, before he knew it, his wife clutched his arms, wide-awake again, panting. Her fingers gripped his arms like steel clamps as she screamed.

"The baby is ready, Lydia," Sister Anne said. "Push as hard as you can."

From the downstairs hall, Marcus heard the woman's wail, and his heart almost stopped. He waited for a tiny cry, but none was forthcoming.

Upstairs, Lydia sank back one more time against Simon's chest. "Oh, God!" she cried.

"Dear God," Simon whispered.

Please, God, Marcus pleaded.

"This next one might do it," Sister Anne said cheerfully, waiting for the miracle to unfold.

Pacing worriedly, Marcus held his breath, listening. Lydia's wail flowed down the stairs around him, a maelstrom of pain and effort. He heard Sister Anne and Simon loudly encouraging her to push hard over her own cries. And then, suddenly, there was dead silence... and a thin, tremulous wail filled the house.

"It's a boy!" Simon exclaimed. "Lydia, it's a boy! We have a son!"

Lydia was crying. "A boy...?"

Marc wiped the tears from his cheeks with a sleeve. *They have a son.* And right then and there, he re-committed to his vow before God, the vow he'd made to Simon while overseas, that if anything were to happen to Simon, Marcus would take care of Lydia. Now, he made a renewed promise to God, *I swear before you that I will also look after their son if I'm ever called upon to do so. I swear it.*

Almost before he'd finished the prayer, Marcus looked up to find a hot and sweaty Simon walking down the stairs with a tiny, wrapped bundle in his arms. Simon dropped down on the landing step above his best friend and sat staring at the wrinkled newborn in his arms.

"Marc... look..." he breathed. Their eyes met.

"Congratulations, dad," Marcus rested a hand on his friend's shoulder. Simon, without words, just looked with awe back at his closest friend in the world, thankful he could share this moment with him.

Sister Anne's voice reached down the stairs. "Simon, come back up here right now," she said with a measured urgency.

Simon nearly dropped his newborn son into Marcus's arms and jumped up. He ran into the room, noting that a pool of blood was spreading over the newspapers and sheet beneath Lydia. Lydia had dropped back onto the bed in exhaustion.

"Part of the placenta has torn," Sister Anne told him calmly, but quickly. "It's not intact. There is no time. I must go after that piece or else..."

Simon nodded, understanding. *Or else she will hemorrhage.* He already knew.

Sister Anne bent Lydia's knees. "Doctor Finney, get behind her. Hold her legs tight. She isn't going to like this."

Dread filled Simon's heart. He wrapped his arms around Lydia and held her legs firmly, holding her against him. "Please forgive me, Lydia..." he murmured, knowing what was coming.

Sister Anne reached one hand inside of Lydia's body. "Oh... my... God! Stop! Stop it!" Lydia screamed.

Her cry ripped Simon's heart, but he held her still as Sister Anne carefully felt around inside the womb until she found, and removed, what she was seeking. Lydia suddenly slumped back against Simon.

Something's wrong! Marcus held the precious newborn close to him, prayers flowing from his heart. *Don't take her, please God! Not now*, he begged the Almighty, terrified when he heard the bedroom go still. He looked down at the tiny baby's face, its wet hair was brown just like its father's. The infant was actually looking at him, blue eyes like Lydia's, not brown like Simon's, squinting up at him in this new and strange world. Marcus felt his eyes filling. "It's going to be alright," he whispered to the puzzled newborn.

"There now," Sister Anne said finally, satisfied after comparing the matter in her bloodied glove to the missing portion of the placenta on the newspaper. "It happens sometimes, Doctor Finney. It'll be okay now, I think." She began folding the red, soaked newspapers around the afterbirth.

On the stair landing, Marcus carefully stood with his tiny godson in his arms. He had not held a newborn since med school. Climbing the stairs, he cautiously approached the door of the bedroom and stepped inside. He was shocked by how much of Lydia's blood had been lost, and in such a short amount of time. He handed the infant to Simon. "Put him to her breast, Simon," Marcus reminded him, his voice unsteady. "It'll help."

Sister Anne looked up at Marcus, "Oh, that's right!" she said cheerfully, continuing her cleanup as if nothing was amiss. "You're a doctor, too. Thank you, Doctor Lovell, you're quite right. It will help her stop bleeding."

Supporting Lydia from behind, keeping her against his chest, Simon held the baby against her breast as the midwife finished her tasks. Sister Anne then helped the infant to get its tiny mouth properly latched onto Lydia's nipple. Marcus rested his hand on Simon's shoulder in encouragement.

Marcus leaned down and kissed the top of Lydia's head, concerned at the white pallor of her face. Once he realized there was little more that he could do, he returned downstairs to wait for Suzie and Nikki to come home. He was glad after all that he hadn't seen Suzie when she was giving birth. But in his heart, he knew without a doubt that it had been necessary for him to be here today. He would not forget what had happened or the promises he had made. He was to be this baby's godfather and had been there at his first tiny breath. Returning to the back kitchen door, he allowed Abril to come inside and watched her bound up the stairs to Lydia's side.

Leaning back against the headboard of the bed, Simon held Lydia and watched as the baby nursed. Sister Anne was massaging the uterus, to help it shrink back down and stop the bleeding, as Abril swept into the room. She was a war dog and used to the smell of blood, so that did not concern her, but she nosed herself against Lydia, who weakly stroked her head.

"I'm okay, Abril," she whispered. The dog sat at attention next to the bed, not sure if Lydia could be trusted on this matter. Abril cocked her head to one side, seeing the small bundle attached to the woman... she sniffed at the newborn.

Sister Anne, satisfied that her work was complete, washed up in the bathroom and returned to offer her final instructions. "You must knead her uterus hourly at first, Doctor Finney, to help it contract until there is no more bleeding. I do expect some, so keep some fresh newspaper under her. Stay in bed, Lydia, for tonight, then you must get up and walk around. Ice your bottom, if you can get some from the iceman. You didn't tear, but it will help with the pain and soreness. I'll be back tomorrow to check you."

Lydia reached out her hand for the nun. "Thank you, Sister. I wouldn't have made it without you."

"I'm glad I could be here," Sister Anne replied gently. "What are you going to name your son?"

"James Marcus Finney," Lydia whispered. They were the names of the most important men in her life.

Simon kissed her cheek, his eyes shining. "That's a great name! A strong, good name. How long have you been thinking that one up, my love?"

"Since the day you went missing in France… if it was a boy," she whispered, staring down at her baby, feeling her uterus cramp as the infant sucked.

"Well, I like it!" he exclaimed, adding softly, "and so will Marc." He bent to kiss her several times while watching their son at her breast.

"I'm glad you were here through the whole thing." Lydia barely squeezed Simon's hand. "I know it was hard on you too."

Simon's eyes filled with tears. "I can't even begin to imagine you going through this alone, my beloved. I would never have forgiven myself if I had been off, sitting in some waiting room, apart from you."

"Just remember that for the next time we have a baby," she said, closing her eyes even while he held their newborn son against her.

Astonished, Simon gazed down at his wife and baby and shook his head. He couldn't believe she could even think of a next time after what she had just been put through. But that was Lydia. He shouldn't be surprised. After a time, Simon slid out from behind her, laying his newborn son in his bassinet, right beside their bed. Then, Simon sat on the edge of the bed to press his hand over her uterus and massage it gently, willing the arteries to close off in the contracting organ.

"That hurts," she whispered, spent from the birthing.

"I know," he said. "At least, I assume it would, but it is necessary."

"Okay, but," she grimaced. "Tell me why, later."

"Let me look between your legs," he told her.

"They feel heavy," she said.

Simon moved her legs for her. There was still bright red blood, with clots, coming out. He pulled the top layer of newspaper out from under her and wrapped it up, placing a fresh layer beneath her. Abril was on the floor beside the bed, refusing to leave the room. Simon wondered if dogs could even remember giving birth to their puppies, as Abril had done in the medical camp. Simon kissed Lydia's forehead. "I'm sure they do." He stood to take the newspaper outside. "I'll be right back. You must drink and eat something. I'll be right back."

He ran down the steps, soaked newspaper in hand, legs trembling as if he'd done a marathon. Marcus was waiting at the kitchen table, drinking a cup of coffee while something cooked on the stove. Simon was wishing he had gotten that whiskey that Phillip had advised that he have on hand for the birth. His normally steady hands were shaking, and he looked quickly to Marcus.

"How's she doing?" Marcus asked.

"White as a ghost," Simon reported. "Scared me half to death. But, oh brother, was I ever glad you got here when you did. I thought I'd have to open her up there for a minute. What've we got that she can drink? She lost a lot of blood."

Marcus nodded. "Give her a glass of milk, at least. I'm cooking some oatmeal. And we'll scramble up some eggs. Get something substantial in her."

"Okay, thanks, Marc. Where's Suzie?" Simon added as he took the newspaper out to a burn barrel in the back yard. He came back in quickly and washed his hands before pouring a glass of milk from the ice box and breaking off a chunk of ice for her bottom.

"She took Nikki out in the stroller when things got really intense up there," Marcus replied. "I'm sure they'll be back soon. Women can sense these things, I think. But if she had been here to hear all that, she'd probably never let me touch her again!"

Simon thanked Marcus as he pulled out a pan to scramble some eggs for Lydia. "Hey Marcus, did you hear Lydia say what she named him?"

"No," Marcus replied, pausing as he cracked eggs into a bowl, waiting expectantly.

"James Marcus Finney," Simon said with a big smile. "My little Jimmy! My son!"

"No kidding?" Marcus said, his eyes wide, jaw dropping in astonishment. "That's a... a pretty big honor, Simon."

Simon nodded, the smile never leaving his face. "And well deserved! She said I wouldn't even be here to see my son if it hadn't been for you saving my life." Milk in hand, he left Marcus, stunned beside the stove, as he headed back up the stairs.

Simon had to wake Lydia for the milk and helped her lift her head. To Simon's amazement, she drank the whole glass without taking a breath.

"I'm so tired, but I'm starving," she breathed. "You'll have to call Mom. I'm too worn out. I don't think I can make it down the stairs."

Simon laid her back down on the pillow as he tucked an ice pack against her bottom. "You aren't going anywhere near those stairs! I'll call your mom," he assured her softly. He looked at the baby, who was sleeping, wrapped snugly in his blanket. Simon went around the bed and laid down on top of the covers, beside Lydia, brushing her hair from her face and noting how pale she had become. He kissed her lightly on her lips. "Can you ever forgive me?" he whispered, suddenly troubled.

"For what?" she murmured, her eyelids heavy.

"For all of the pain," he admitted.

"We have our son," she whispered as she dozed off again.

It was Marcus who woke them as he came upstairs, bearing eggs and oatmeal, with juice. They all hoped that Lydia would be able to get some of it down. He paused at the bassinet, looking at the tiny, wrinkled newborn lying within it. *My godson, James Marcus Finney*, Marcus thought, humbled by their choice of names. "Here, Simon," he said softly. "Suzie is home if you need a break."

Simon nodded. "Did you bring her up to speed?"

"A little," he said. "Didn't tell her the whole thing, though. Suz might not want to ever get pregnant again."

"The thought already crossed my mind about that!" Simon exclaimed softly. "Thanks for this, I'll stay with her. Are you as worn out as I am? Childbirth is exhausting!"

Marcus looked at Lydia then back to his friend. "There has to be a better way to bring a kid into this world. We would never, not in our wildest dreams, put a surgical patient through that kind of pain, wide awake!"

Simon chuckled, pointing toward Heaven. "You have to talk to Him about that!"

"I've already tried... only got 'that's the way it is'."

Simon just shook his head. "We'll make a true believer of you yet, Marcus."

"I'm getting there," he answered. "I just don't understand why some things have to happen the way they do."

Simon looked up from his place beside Lydia, who was already dozing. "He never promised to tell us the why, Marcus. He only promised He'd be there, with us, through it."

Marcus slowly nodded his head, considering the wisdom in this statement. "Well then, I think He was here today."

Simon nodded, "I know He was."

Marcus turned, "Call if you need something. Um... can I—?" He motioned to the baby.

Simon nodded and Marcus tenderly picked up the newest, wrinkled, little member of the human race and left the room with Jimmy cradled in his arms. Simon woke Lydia to help her eat and to knead her uterus again, as ordered. He then took her in his arms and they both drifted off to sleep.

Chapter 11

When Pain is a Gift

As evening fell, Simon moved methodically from one wall sconce to the next, a warm glow spreading through the rooms. Knowing Lydia was too weak to make it downstairs to the telephone on the kitchen wall, Simon took the responsibility of assuring her mother and father that she was recovering, while sparing them the details of the complicated afterbirth.

Instead, he focused on the wonders of their tiny son, the wrinkled, helpless, marvelous, new addition to the family. Simon's brother, Phillip, congratulated him heartily for carrying on the family name through a son and promised that one day soon, he and Rebecca would drive up, just the two siblings, to meet little James M. Finney for themselves. Simon appreciated their sensitivity in not bringing the family en masse at this particular time. He didn't believe that even he could handle a house full of guests, family or not. Becoming a father was something to be processed intimately, with Lydia first.

Relieved that Suzie was upstairs, spending some time with Lydia and the baby, Simon sat with Marcus at the kitchen table, reflecting on the day. Each man was lost in his own thoughts as they quietly finished some leftover wine from their recent family gathering. After a time, Marcus reached across the corner of the table and clinked his wine glass to Simon's. "Cheers! You're a father!... I love my daughter. Would love to also have a son one day."

Simon finished off his half-filled glass, then refilled both with the rosy, pink wine. Marcus did not protest. Simon's voice faltered, "I was afraid... for a fleeting moment... that I'd be a widower father. God Almighty, Marcus. I thought I'd have to do a hysterectomy on the spot... if she hadn't stopped bleeding. There was so much blood on the newspapers! Sister Anne didn't seem too worried. Maybe it's not that uncommon after childbirth? But if one of my patients had lost that much blood, I'd have been calling for a unit to be brought over without a second thought."

"I would have helped, too." Marcus assured him.

Simon drummed his fingers on the table; the wine not yet dulling his anxiety. "I have a duffle bag of medical equipment hidden up there, under the bed. Ether, sutures, retractor, everything... just in case it's needed. Didn't let Lydia see it, of course. I'll get it back over to Charity when I go in."

Marcus smiled. "Good planning ahead, Simon! Most people are buying booties and cigars to hand out. You bring ether and a retractor! Make sure to move them before she sweeps the floors again."

Simon nodded. "Just wanted to be prepared for anything. Can't tell you how relieved I was that you made it back in time... I couldn't have cut her open myself."

Neither could I! Marcus thought, keeping it to himself. But he knew it wasn't actually true, for either of them. If it meant saving her life, they both would have picked up the scalpel... just as he had when Marcus had cut into Simon's leg to save it. They were doctors; instinct always kicked in when required.

Simon was somber. "Marc—" he started, then paused before continuing. "What are we doing in medicine, keeping fathers out of the birth? Can you imagine if both of us had been pacing the waiting room while someone was working on Lydia, doing all that to her in the back of the hospital, and we didn't know what all was going on and just had to wait to hear? Can you imagine her placenta tearing like that while we were just reading magazines in the waiting room, hoping someone would come out soon to let us know if it was a boy or a girl? Why do we keep the men out? What are we afraid of?"

Marcus took in Simon's question along with another substantial gulp of wine, finally feeling his nerves settling from its warmth. "Lots of men wouldn't go back into the birthing room, not if you paid them. You know that. Remember your brother-in-law said he fainted dead-away when one of Rebecca's was arriving. And that was apparently without a complication!"

"Yes, but at least he was there!" Simon declared. "Head in a bucket or not, she knew Frank was there. If Lydia had had to go through that alone... well, I never would have been able to forgive myself! She's been through so much already. The least I could do is be there, finishing what I started with her."

"Anyway," Marcus added, not disagreeing, "It's different for us. We've, you and I, we've seen a few things. It doesn't hit us the same way it would one of those steel mill workers or the local grocer. We like to be in control, even when the world is out of control. We stop the bleeding. We set the bones. We take out the offending organ. It's what we do. Not always on someone we love, but it's in our nature to want to know what's going on."

Simon looked just plain miserable, leaving Marcus confused. He leaned over, "Okay, buddy, out with it."

Simon gazed down as he swirled his wine, ashamed. "She may never be able to forget what I did to her up there, Marc."

Raising his eyebrows in surprise, Marcus quickly asked, "What on earth are you talking about, Simon?"

Simon cleared his throat, "I was the one holding her steady when Sister Anne retrieved the placenta fragment, Marc. I took her in my arms, held her legs, and forced her to endure that pain while she fought it. She already has so many bad memories, but at least I wasn't part of them. You know, the night terrors. Now I am. I never wanted to be part of her pain."

Nodding, Marcus understood what he was trying to say, but his assumption was flawed, and Marc quickly tried to correct it for Simon. "You saved her life, Simon. There isn't any other way, short of a surgical curettage in the operating theater, to remove a torn placenta. Period. Lydia will understand that, if she even remembers it."

"How could she not remember it? She screamed like we were trying to kill her!" Simon demanded of his friend. "It is certainly seared into my memory. The sound just about ripped me apart."

"I know," Marcus said, remembering how her strangled cry pierced his own heart, as he sat on the landing holding his new godson. "But it's a strange thing about the birth of a baby. You ask women later, and they say they don't even remember the pain. It's almost like there is something in the biology of it all that makes them forget. Suzie says she remembers that she was in labor, but doesn't really remember what it felt like. Only that it was getting harder, so she told them to put her to sleep. I don't doubt that Lydia will forget. And even if she doesn't forget the pain, she'll remember that you saved her life... and that it was hard for you to have to do that. She knows it cost you something. That's automatic forgiveness, Simon."

Simon took a deep breath. "I hope you're right, Marcus. I sure hope so. Did what happened up there today make you think twice about Suzie getting pregnant again?"

Marcus nodded. "Sure did," he admitted. "But I also know that the risk of complications, in the span of things, is reasonably low. How many times have you delivered a baby where the placenta tore? I mean... never, right? And the second child, usually, is a little easier than the first, or so women say, unless they tell us that just so we won't hold back and not let them have any more. Suzie is already thinking about another one. I know it. She's been watching Lydia get ready for this birth, and I see the want growing in her, now that Nikki's turned one. She's probably up there holding Jimmy right now, counting fingers and toes and making all kinds of baby sounds for him."

"What do you think? Are you going to do it?" Simon asked curiously. "You said you wouldn't mind having a son."

"Don't know. I guess I should have a house first, so the kids can have their own rooms. Got an automobile... still need the house."

"Have you been looking?" Simon asked carefully, not really wanting to hear the answer yet; he didn't want them to leave.

Marcus nodded, glancing sideways at Simon. "Sort of. Well, sure. The problem, my friend, is that I want one on this block. None have come up for sale yet. You two just can't seem to get along without me. So, I figured I'd better be somewhere at least within walking distance to keep you out of trouble."

Simon relaxed at that, intensely relieved that his friend wasn't thinking of heading back to upstate New York or even across the Ohio or Allegheny rivers to the southwest foothills of this huge city. He appreciated having his chess partner close by. "I'll keep my eyes open!" Simon exclaimed. "If I see so much as a sign in a window, I'll let you know."

Simon stood and rinsed his wine glass, placing it on the counter to dry. He didn't know how to say what he was thinking. "You know, Marcus," Simon finally managed, "a man couldn't ask for a better friend." Then he turned, pushed in his chair, walked around the table, briefly resting his hand on Marc's shoulder before heading back up the stairs to help Lydia for the night. Marcus finished his wine and settled into a chair in the living room to wait for Suzie to come down. He was anxious for her to fill him in on how Lydia was doing up there. *Good grief, he has ether and sutures up there? Thank you, God, we didn't have to use them! No, I don't want to be far from these two, well, three now! It's hard to fulfill a vow if you're too far away.*

In their room, Simon kept the lamplight to a low flicker so that he could see the baby and check on Lydia often. He was worried to see that Lydia was still passing clots of blood. Earlier, when he had carried her to the bathroom, her knees had buckled, unable to stand or walk down the hallway. Unable to sleep, he roused her around midnight again to knead her uterus. The baby hadn't stirred. Simon knew what had to be done.

"Sorry, my love, have to check you again," he whispered to Lydia.

She didn't roll over. "I'm too sore..."

"I know," he said regretfully, but rolled Lydia onto her back anyway. Massaging the fundus in her abdomen, he saw her grimace, but she didn't make a sound, he assumed in an attempt to not upset him.

"Must you really keep doing that?" she murmured wearily.

He nodded, intent on the task ahead. "Let me see if you're still bleeding."

Checking, he found much less blood, but still strings of smaller clots. Simon just nodded his head. "Yes, I'm afraid I do," he said decidedly. She bit back the moan of discomfort, knowing he wasn't deliberately trying to hurt her.

"You lost more blood than I expected," he explained. "That's why you're feeling so played out."

"I don't remember exactly what happened," she admitted. "I just know it hurt. Whatever Sister Anne was doing, really hurt. It felt like she was ripping me apart inside."

Simon continued his massage. "She was taking care of the placenta. A piece was stuck, and you needed to pass it, to stop bleeding."

"Thank you for helping me through that, my love," Lydia said gratefully. "I remember feeling your arms around me, holding me up, so that I would feel safe. I would probably not have been able to endure it without you. You're so good to me, Simon..."

With that, Simon realized that Lydia really did not remember his own role in that pain. He felt an intense wave of relief. If only he, too, could forget her ordeal. It had shaken him badly, and at this very moment, he wondered how he would ever be able to risk her becoming pregnant again.

"Will you let me sleep tonight?" she asked, exhausted.

"We'll both sleep on and off, of course, depending on the baby.... who, for the moment, seems rather content. If you can go back to sleep right now, you should do it."

"Lay with me, Simon. I'm cold," she whispered. He moved around the bed to get under the covers beside her. "Not like that," she said, feeling that he was still in his pajamas.

"Lydia..." he murmured doubtfully. She looked so pale, so drawn.

"I want you next to me," she said. "Please. Just at least open your pajamas so I can warm up. You're a furnace." Her voice was weak, filling him with deep compassion. Unbuttoning his pajama top, he slid in under the sheets alongside her and she immediately curled up against his chest. She shivered, needing his body heat. Simon held her in his arms and kissed her softly. Resting her palm against his chest, she quickly fell asleep, connected to him that way. Simon remained awake, experiencing her touch. Had she sensed his need to be connected to her? It seemed to Simon, as he lay in the twilight, that in Lydia's mind, nothing had changed in the least between them, after the birthing. Simon did not understand how that could be, but was profoundly grateful. He drifted into a light sleep, only to be pulled back all too soon—it was time to knead her belly again. As Simon tended to Lydia, in the bassinet, on his first day of life, their infant son slept.

The next morning, Marcus and Suzie quietly slipped out of the house for work, with little Nikki in tow. Roaming the house,

Simon made coffee, fixed Lydia a proper breakfast, and was just about to carry it upstairs when he heard a light rap on the front door. Setting the tray on the little table in the foyer, he opened the door, relieved to find that Sister Anne had come to check on her patient.

"How did she manage the night?" the midwife asked Simon without ceremony as he took her coat, folding it over a chair in the foyer. "Ah, egg on toast? And milk? Good. Help her get her strength back. I was concerned about her last night."

Following the nun up the stairs, Simon reported, "She's pretty weak. Clots."

"To be expected." Her soft words reached him as he trailed behind her with the breakfast tray.

Gently waking Lydia, Sister Anne smiled, "I must check you this morning, my dear. I see a splendidly beautiful little angel sleeping in the bassinet. Doctor Finney, I trust you'll keep an eye on the cord for any signs of infection, so I needn't wake him just now?"

Simon nodded. Of course he would. While waiting for the nun to return from washing her hands, he stroked Lydia's hair.

"Now, let's take a look," the midwife prompted. "I spoke to the obstetrician on duty at the hospital last night, Doctor Franklin, just to alert him that we had a little setback yesterday."

"They feel like lead," Lydia said quietly. "My legs. They're so heavy."

Simon helped her get positioned so the midwife could examine her tissues. "You didn't tear," Sister Anne observed in relief. "But there is considerable blood and clotting here. Simon, if you would be good enough to get a basin of warm water, we'll clean Lydia up and see what we can see."

Lydia waited, too tired to protest, for him to return with the supplies. By the time the nun was satisfied that she had clear visibility, the water in the basin was a dark red. Sister Anne retrieved a flashlight from her bag to take a closer look. Feeling inside, she was satisfied that the cervix was closing, but a small rush of blood followed her fingers as she removed them.

"It is much better," Sister Anne said cautiously, noting the woman's pallor. "But I remain concerned. You must continue to massage your belly and nurse your baby to help the healing process. And you must eat meat, eggs, and fish to strengthen yourself. Make sure you are drinking water and milk. You are very brave, my dear."

Shaking her head, Lydia said, "I don't think so, Sister Anne. I was frightened..."

"Of course you were," the nun replied. "We prepare but cannot foresee every possibility. It is up to our Lord to look into the future. We are only called upon to handle today. Rest and eat and walk to the bathroom, only with Doctor Finney's help, of course. Enjoy your infant. What was the name again that you decided on, for the birth certificate? I have the required paperwork with me. I must be sure it's written correctly."

"James Marcus Finney," Lydia said softly, spelling it for her.

"May I inquire what this name means to you?" the nun asked. "Names interest me."

"They are the names of my husband and of Doctor Lovell, who will be his godfather," Lydia told her. "We wanted to honor

Marcus... he saved Simon's life twice in the war." *And saved me in many ways.*

"Very good then," Sister Anne said. "Of course, James is the name of our esteemed Saint, the Apostle. And Saint Mark helped found the early Church while writing Peter's memories. These are two very strong names. They will be a strength to your infant. A very good choice. I shall leave this certificate with you and register the first with the city, Doctor Finney."

The nun leaned over the crib and gently touched little Jimmy's cheek. "Welcome, little James Marcus Finney," she whispered. Straightening and turning back to Lydia and Simon, she said, "I will see you tomorrow. Don't bother walking me out, Doctor Finney. Stay with Lydia and call if there are any changes at all."

"But how will I know when to feed him, Suzie?" Lydia asked her friend after Suzie had returned from her shift at the clinic.

Suzie laughed, "He'll let you know. If he fusses, if the diaper is dry, if he's warm and bundled but holding him for comfort isn't enough, then put him to your breast. He'll let you know very quickly that that's what he wanted all along."

"But I don't have milk yet," Lydia said sadly. "Just this thin, clear water."

Suzie nodded, "That's the way it comes out at first. The milk will come in a few days, and you'll have more than enough."

Lydia looked down at her chest. "They're already feeling tight."

"That's good," Suzie reassured her. "Your body will figure out how much to make soon enough. It's not so different from figuring out what a grown man needs."

Looking up at her friend, Lydia asked, "You surely don't mean that it's the same checklist?"

Straightening the bedclothes, Suzie chuckled, "I certainly do! Men aren't that different than this precious little baby boy in what they want most! Hold them, feed them, comfort them. And yes, offer them a breast once and a while, and they seem content enough."

"They are deeper than that, Susannah!" Lydia protested.

"Not much, in my book," her friend objected, shaking her head. "Keep them happy in bed and you will stay wed. That's the old saying."

Lydia let out a deep sigh, "I suppose that, whether old or young, keeping them happy can be harder than it looks."

Suzie nodded. "That's why only women give birth and run a house," she informed her friend. "Men wouldn't stand a chance. Now, you finish eating while I hold your little son. You're as pale as those sheets beneath you. I'll get some clean newspaper." Suzie was worried. She had not needed frequent newspaper changes like this after having Nikki. Something wasn't right.

Lydia dutifully ate her dinner of fish and rice, surprised at how hungry she had become. Abril sat up for a piece of fish, much to Suzie's dismay, when Lydia offered the dog the morsel.

"That fish was for you to get your strength back!" Suzie protested firmly. "We're feeding Abril. Don't think she's being deprived. Because she isn't, no matter how she begs!"

Lydia looked sheepishly at the dog. "Couldn't help it, look at those eyes."

"I'm looking at these eyes instead. Blue, so blue, aren't they! He has your eyes. And all this hair! How is it he doesn't have Simon's brown eyes?" Suzie marveled. "He's a sweet little thing. Just look at those tiny little toes. Just holding him makes me want to have another baby! Oh, how I've missed the smell."

Lydia smiled, "If you get started now..."

"Hm... I must talk to Marcus about that. He does love Nikki a lot," Suzie sighed. "He's a good father to her. He did mention maybe having another, at some point."

Nodding, Lydia finished her food and took her baby from Suzie. She looked tenderly at his sweet little face. "You were inside of me just hours ago, and look at you now, all wrinkly and precious. Little Jimmy."

Suzie looked at the two of them. "You named him after Marcus, too," she started. "That's an honor. Marc was thrilled."

"As was Simon," Lydia murmured, taking the infant's fingers in her own and marveling over how perfectly formed they were. "Marcus saved Simon's life twice, Suzie. I wouldn't have my husband without Marcus! Or he would have been hobbling around on one leg or dead from the blood infection. I could have been a widow. And it's Marc who keeps working on improving Simon's lungs and stamina too. Anyway, Marcus is going to be Jimmy's godfather when we have him baptized. It's just so fitting since Simon and Marc are truly closer than brothers."

Suzie considered this. "Yes, they certainly are," she said softly. "Sometimes, I think Marcus tells Simon things he doesn't even tell me."

Lydia looked up. "Our husbands do have a special bond... maybe from the war, maybe it's a doctor-to-doctor thing? Or perhaps it's just that they both have to put up with strong and independent women. We are, you know, Suzie. Strong and independent. No doubt we give them lots to talk about."

Suzie laughed. "I thought Simon confided everything to you."

"Most things, he does tell me, I think. But there are times when I see them together and they just have this unspoken understanding. I think France did it, forged that bond. After all, look how they operate together. They don't even have to talk about the plan; they just get to work. Suzie, what about Jimmy's cord? It's so long. When does that come off?"

Suzie studied the protrusion from the baby's abdomen. "Oh, that will dry up and fall right off, in about a week. It's supposed to look like that. Then he'll have a nice little belly button."

"Last time I saw a baby with a cord was back in nurse training. Seems like a lifetime ago," Lydia admitted. "Thank God you're here, Suzie. I'd be full of questions with no one to ask, unless I called my mother and ran up the long-distance charges."

Standing, Suzie stretched, "If you're okay, I'll go make supper for the boys, although I suspect Simon will bring his up here. Check on you later."

"Thanks, Suzie," Lydia was unable to take her eyes off the baby in her arms. She touched his cheeks, wondering if one day he would have a beard like his father. Then touched his arms, wondering if one day he'd be on the floor doing push-ups with Simon. She touched his tiny legs and prayed he'd never go through the hardships his daddy had. "I only want you to be healthy and strong," she whispered.

The baby whimpered a thin little cry, his tiny lower jaw trembling.

"Alright, little one. Are you dry? Are you warm enough? Do you just want to be held? Or are you hungry? We'll try all the above... until I learn how to read your little mind..." she said softly.

It didn't take Simon long to make his way back upstairs to check on Lydia and the baby. As Suzie had guessed, his dinner was in his hands and some fresh water for Lydia. Laying the baby in the bassinet, he sat down beside her. "On your back, please," he said, reaching his hand out to knead her belly. "Your mother is coming in the morning so I can go back to work. She rang while you napped. Plans to stay a couple weeks."

"Are you okay with Mom being here that long?" Lydia asked as Simon settled into a chair to enjoy his meal.

"Absolutely!" he assured her between bites. "I was worried about leaving you, but I know the hospital expects me back sooner rather than later. Somehow, people just keep needing surgery, no matter what else is going on in life."

"Remember when Sister Anne asked you to go get the basin of water this morning?" she asked.

"Uh-huh," he nodded as he took a drink of water and motioned for her to do the same from the cup on her nightstand.

"She told me 'no intimate relations', for several weeks!" Lydia paused. "She said that in the Old Testament, a man was defiled if he was intimate with a woman who was bleeding."

Simon almost choked. "You have got to be kidding! Who would want to... well, I can't imagine any man being so selfish as to want to... after what you went through?"

Lydia smiled. "Well, I certainly hope someday you'll want to be with me again! And she didn't say we couldn't do other things while my body recovers."

"Want to walk to the bathroom? Are you willing?"

She nodded, as he draped her robe around her shoulders. Standing in front of him with her knees against his, she let him help her to find her balance. The room moved in a circle, but she didn't lose her vision. Leaning against his chest, Lydia realized just how weak she had become, finally saying, "That's not so bad."

Holding her securely, he murmured, "If we had music, we could just stand here and sway... pretend we're dancing."

Lydia looked down. "My feet are back!" she exclaimed.

Laughing lightly, Simon looked at her. She was as white as the sheets on the bed, but he stayed focused. "They certainly are back! Take a few steps?"

Feeling shaky, she began slowly, walking to the bedroom door, not the bathroom, and immediately returned to the bed with Simon's arm around her. Being flat in bed again reduced the light-headedness, and she lay back with a satisfied sigh. "Maybe the bathroom later. Sister Anne will be so pleased!"

Their infant stirred in his crib, making thin mewling sounds. Lydia opened her robe to receive him and was astonished, at the feeling of the milk coming in. "Simon, look at me!" she exclaimed in wonder as pearls of milky fluid appeared on her nipples at the sound of the baby's plaintive cry. "It's like we're still connected somehow..."

Simon rested the baby in Lydia's arms and she put the infant to her breast. He immediately began to suck, with little effort. "Suzie told me to put his belly to my belly for the best position."

"Little known facts of motherhood," Simon smiled, watching her. "Something only you women would really know." He reached over and touched her waiting breast, as a drop fell from it as well. "I think you're simply beautiful."

"I'm saggy and baggy..." she said, dismissing the compliment.

He leaned over and kissed her. "You are simply beautiful. And I won't have to massage your belly when Jimmy is done. That's the best part. The nursing is doing it already."

The hours passed into evening, and with the baby asleep again, Simon pulled Lydia to himself for a while. He stroked her breasts, marveling at the way her body was meeting their son's needs, the miracle of her motherhood. He kissed her forehead and stroked her hair. She was still too pale for his comfort, but she had walked to the bathroom several times. Then he felt her hand slide down under the sheets.

Simon sighed. "I love you touching me..." he started, "make no mistake! But we are not going to do anything. You do know that. I didn't need a midwife to stop me, either."

"No," Lydia whispered. "We aren't going to do anything, but I can at least hold you. It takes very little energy on my part to rest my hand here, unless you don't like it..."

"I do like it, but you will save all your energy for healing," Simon ordered her.

"Well, I don't intend to move my hand. So, unless you plan to sleep down on the couch, be quiet and at least kiss me..."

She didn't have to ask twice.

"Now, listen," Simon was saying as he dressed, getting ready to go into the hospital. "Stay in bed until your mother arrives. Jimmy is right here. You have juice and breakfast... let's see... Abril is right here on the floor. We've just gotten you to the bathroom... there are diapers here... hmm... what am I forgetting...?" He ran his fingers through his hair, agitated. "I know I'm forgetting something..."

"We'll be fine. I'm sure they'll be here within the hour, and they know to come right in," Lydia assured him. "It's going to be fine. You go to the hospital and take care of all those people who need you. We both love you."

Turning to Lydia, with the bassinet right beside her, he gave it one last shot, "Are you absolutely, positively, sure? I can stay until they get here. I really don't mind."

"What, and tell the poor person with the ruptured bowel that his surgeon can't make it in because of his wife? Not a chance! You need to go," she insisted.

Simon kissed her softly, then the baby. He made his way to the bedroom door but paused, turning back to kiss her once more before leaving. "Just don't do anything foolish... please, Lydia. Wait for your mother."

"I'll be safe. We're fine." She smiled to encourage him.

Unable to help himself, he came back one last time, lifting the covers. "Spread your legs for me, let me check you one more time..." She did. Satisfied that she wasn't bleeding any more than a few bright red spots on the cloth pad beneath her, he kissed her a third time and tucked her back in. "Okay, tell your mom to ring the hospital right away if you need me."

"Go!" Lydia ordered him, pointing to the door.

Simon briefly hesitated at the top of the landing. Then, Lydia finally heard the patter of his feet descending the stairs, and the familiar sound of the door opening and shutting as he left.

"Now," Lydia said bravely to Jimmy and Abril, "what shall we do today?"

In the clinic, Suzie was in triage. The winter weather had broken, and when the doors were opened, a fresh breeze blew in with each new patient. She considered the waiting areas with concern. There were increasingly more people coming in with symptoms of influenza, and the area behind the special curtains was rapidly filling.

During a lull in the flow, Suzie walked back to the exam rooms where Sister Teresa enjoyed working the most. A new doctor was on duty this month and had come in late from rounding on the wards. She wanted to meet him. "Sister Teresa," Suzie called out. "Did the doctor show up yet?" Before she could even turn, she heard a deep voice saying, "Yes, Nurse, the doctor is here!"

Turning, she looked at the man walking through the door. He was smiling broadly, looked to be about her own age, was tall and blond-haired, and acted as though he already knew her.

"You are Nurse Lovell," he exclaimed, extending his hand in greeting.

"I am... and you are..."

"Mike Franklin, at your service," he offered. "I've heard all about you from Peter Martin. He couldn't say enough about the beautiful blonde nurse, returned from Europe. Said you're excellent."

Suzie was a bit flustered at the greeting, but enjoyed the high praise. "Well, I'm certainly glad he's found my work acceptable!" she exclaimed. "But please remember while you're in the clinic that we're a team. I value the sisters we work with, with the exact same enthusiasm."

He laughed again, studying her. "And he said you are direct, honest, and smart. Correct on all three counts. I hope to earn your respect this month! And are you the nurse with the baby here, in the playpen?"

Suzie smiled. "She's hardly a baby anymore. She's one."

"Still a baby! Beautiful girl. Apparently having babies is the new trend," Mike said. "Peter said that another nurse was expecting?"

Sister Teresa chimed in at this. "Nurse Finney just delivered her child, Doctor Franklin, a boy. We can hardly wait to see him when she returns from her maternity time."

"Prolific little community." Mike Franklin had donned his white exam coat and already washed his hands. His stethoscope was curled up in his pocket, and he now turned to the two women. "Bring me up to speed. Peter said you ladies have made significant changes to improve this clinic. Tell me everything I need to know. Show me around out front, Nurse Lovell... and then Sister Teresa, would you fill me in on the examination procedures back here? I'm all ears."

Suzie nodded and turned to head down the hall toward the outer waiting area, the doctor falling into step at her side.

"Some doctors have told me that clinic duty can be rather dull and something to get through... until one can get back to the in-hospital wards. I suspect the truth is closer to Peter's description. He said anything can happen, and probably will, and that the clinic is good medicine for all concerned." Mike smiled, keeping pace with the lovely nurse.

"Doctor Martin is right! How new are you, to the hospital?" Suzie wondered.

He nodded enthusiastically. "Hired on a couple months ago, upstairs. I'm actually in obstetrics. But I've been looking forward to clinic, not the least of which, working with a nurse who can think on her feet and knows what she's doing. Peter said you picked up this kind of work in the war?"

"Yes, Doctor," Suzie replied. "I served over there."

He proceeded carefully, trying to picture this beautiful, blonde woman on a battlefield. "I'm impressed," he said. "I was in Italy. Just got back."

She turned and looked at him, amazed. "Really?"

"Yes, really? Why so astonished? You're the one who doesn't look like she has any business being in the army. Don't I look like I could serve?" he laughed.

Suzie backpedaled. "No, it's not that at all. It's just, I haven't run into anyone else who knows what it was like. That's all. Other than my husband and two close friends... we all served together."

"We'll have to swap tales sometime. I'll treat you to lunch, and you can tell me how you changed the face of the war," he said. "Now, what are we dealing with out here? Teach me!"

Suzie smiled, excited by the task of teaching this man, who so clearly admired her experience.

Anna Blackwell could hardly wait to see the little house on the corner. She fervently wished Andrew would drive a little faster, but he maintained that forty was fast enough and would get them there in one piece. So, she fussed and watched the countryside pass by as it exploded into spring greens and blossoms.

When they arrived at the house, Anna ran up the stairs of the two-story building, with her suitcase, leaving Andrew to follow at his own pace, due to his heart. She dropped the case in the hallway and rushed into the bedroom, bending over Lydia, hugging her firmly. Abril nosed up to their new guest immediately and then went to the landing to watch Andrew slowly ascending the steps.

"You look too pale, my dear daughter!" Anna exclaimed, holding Lydia's face in her hands. "You're white as a ghost."

Lydia embraced her mother. "I'm so glad you came! Simon and the others are at the hospital. I almost couldn't get him out the door earlier, he'll feel so much better now that you're here!"

The bassinet beckoned Lydia's parents like a magnet. Without hesitation, Anna scooped up the newborn and pressed him to her.

"Oh my, oh my, oh my..." Anna murmured, her heart overflowing with matriarchal love. "Look at this dear little precious boy. Oh, Andrew, look at this dear little precious boy! Our grandson!"

He peeked over her shoulder and saw the tiny face, well bundled.

"Can't see much of him yet."

"Lydia, he's too precious," Anna said, taking a seat in the easy chair by the bay window, holding her newest grandson tenderly as Andrew made his way to perch on the edge of the bed.

Hugging Lydia lightly, Andrew said, "How's my girl?"

"Doing fine, Dad," Lydia smiled bravely. "As well as any could expect, I'm sure. Simon and I really appreciate you being able to spare Mother for a time, the hospital is so busy. He was home the past two days, of course, but they needed him today."

Andrew settled into the rocking chair, and a soothing, back and forth cadence. "So, you really did it? Had the baby here at home?"

Lydia nodded contentedly. "We did. Sister Anne, the midwife, got here well before I delivered, and Simon was right here with me the entire time. I couldn't have done it without him. He says now, he wouldn't have wanted it any other way." She dropped her hand over the bed to rub Abril's head as the dog returned to her spot, faithfully beside the bed.

Andrew looked doubtful. "Hm, I'm not so sure it's a man's business to see that. Don't know how a man can look at his wife the same way afterward. But if you say so, I won't disagree. Just as long as things turned out okay."

Reaching out a hand for her father, Lydia nodded. "They turned out okay," she said, and she was telling the truth. Her strength was slowly returning. "But I welcome Mom's help. I've never cared for a newborn. Suzie has been answering many of my questions, but there's nothing like having your mom."

In the easy chair by the window, Anna had scarcely taken her eyes from the baby, having already retrieved one of Jimmy's wrinkled hands from inside the blanket, grasping the tiny fingers. The baby stirred and opened his blue eyes, looking up at her, and her latent maternal instincts fully resurfaced, as if she'd had her own babies only weeks ago.

Lydia turned her attention to her father. "How are you feeling, Dad?" she asked. "Are you having a lot of pain in your chest? Are you taking care of yourself? It was a long ride from Greensburg. Would you like to lay down a while?"

He rocked, shaking his head. "I'm fine right here. When your mother gets over her oohing and ahhing, I hope to hold my grandson a bit."

Reticent to release her new charge, Anna stood and crossed the bedroom, bringing the baby to her husband and placing him in Andrew's arms. The man looked down at little Jimmy and his eyes filled with tears.

"What did you name him?" Andrew asked.

"James. James Marcus Finney," Lydia said, remembering what Sister Anne had told them about these two strong names. "James is Simon's middle name, and we'll call him Jimmy. And Marcus, a saint in the early Christian Church, of course. I suppose God knew we needed a son because here he is, after all. And I owe Marcus my husband's life from the war."

Nodding, her father gently held the baby's little hand. "You could have named him Moe for all I care. Just look at him! He's a fine little guy," his voice was husky with emotion. "I'm real proud of you, girl. Bringing me and your mother a new little grandson. It's real nice to see the family growing. We should stay around to see Simon, but I want to be home before dark."

"Don't go, Dad. Spend a night or two," Lydia urged him. "You and mom can have Nikki's room, and you can go back later. Don't go home today, Dad. I'd like to spend time with you." She really wasn't ready for her father to leave.

Perched on the side of the bed, Anna took Lydia's hand. "So, are Marcus and Suzie staying for a while yet, with you two?"

"I certainly hope so!" Lydia exclaimed. "They bought an automobile, which is wonderful getting us back and forth from the hospital and to the grocer's market. Marcus is looking for a house for them but said they haven't found the right one yet. And Suzie has been a great blessing during the last two months of my pregnancy. She's done so much to help keep things going, with cleaning, cooking, laundry. We've been able to share the work... after coming home from work! It's wonderful to have such close friends."

As Andrew gazed down at the baby, Jimmy wriggled his other hand from the swaddle and began to tremble, a thin cry emerging from Jimmy's tiny mouth.

"That's my signal to hand him back!" Andrew exclaimed.

Anna took him and held him to her shoulder, gently patting his back. When that didn't calm him, she turned to Lydia, "Is it feeding time?"

Lydia smiled. "We're still trying to figure that all out, but let's try."

Andrew stood. "And that's my signal to go downstairs!" He squeezed Lydia's hand and made his way back down to the living room, where he found a copy of the newspaper. He even dozed off after a little, the news being far less interesting than what had happened upstairs over the past couple of days.

Anna gently placed the baby in Lydia's arms as she opened her robe to nurse. The baby latched on immediately and Lydia winced, feeling the pull, not at her breast, but in her womb as it continued to respond to the nursing and do its work of healing. Anna noticed.

"You're still quite sore, I'm sure," Anna observed softly. "Was it too frightening, dear? Did I scare you too much by telling you what to expect?"

Lydia looked up from the baby at her breast, "Actually, Mom, your advice was terrific. I kept telling myself that the pains meant the baby would soon be in my arms. You helped me so much, to know it would be difficult but that it was worth it."

Breathing a sigh of relief, her mother said, "I'm so glad. I was afraid, you know, that I'd said too much. It's hard to know the right amount of information for things like this. Did you have any trouble?"

"I lost some blood, but Sister Anne says I'm doing well. She'll be here again today. She says I must eat well, and I'm not allowed to walk to the bathroom without help, so I'm very glad you came, Mom. I need you."

Anna's eyes filled with tears. "I'm happy to hear that. A mother still needs to be needed, even when her children are grown. As you will find out... many years from now. Well, I will make you lunch after Jimmy is done with his own."

Lydia switched him to her other breast. "How is Peggy, Mom?" Lydia asked. "I've been worried about her since they were here at the party and left so suddenly like that."

Anna sighed. "I don't know for sure. They haven't been over for a while. Tom drinks too much and, I think, gets easily frustrated when he does. The children are so quiet. I don't know what's going on. I'm worried about them, too."

"Can Daddy have any influence on Tom? They seem to get along."

She nodded. "Tom is usually respectful to your dad, that's true. I don't know. I wish Tommy would let Peg work. She was so much happier when she was working."

Lydia held her newborn protectively, as if there were a threat in the room. "I think Tom beats Peggy, Mom."

Anna paled. "What makes you say that?"

"There have been other things as well, but at the party, as they were leaving, Peg told Tom she was having a good time and wanted to stay. He asked her if she was begging for a paddling... and said she was disrespecting him."

"Oh my," Anna sighed, her eyes filling with worry. "Really? I know some men do... paddle their wives. But... oh my. When Tom is drunk and angry, he might be too harsh. He's a strong man. But surely his wife, he wouldn't hurt his own wife... surely."

Lydia's voice was a whisper. "Do you think I should tell Dad what I heard?"

Anna shook her head. "Not with his heart the way it is. No, I'll find a way to let Peg know she's welcome to move back home if she needs to. Somehow."

"Well, don't let Tommy hear it," Lydia begged her. "Especially if he's drunk."

"No, no! Definitely not when he's been drinking. Of course not," Anna agreed.

The women then turned to talking about other important matters like diapers, care of the baby's bottom, and precious knowledge that mothers have passed along since the beginning of time.

Marcus, Suzie, Nikki, and Simon returned from the hospital late in the afternoon. Simon jumped right out of the car and sprinted through the backyard to the kitchen porch, before Marcus had even turned off the motor. Dropping his jacket in the foyer and calling out a quick hello to Andrew on the sofa, he immediately ran up the stairs. Turning left, he entered the bedroom and saw Anna in the rocking chair, Lydia dozing in the bed, and Jimmy asleep in the crib. Simon stopped in his tracks, breathing very hard, and made himself relax. Everything looked just fine.

Anna waved to the young doctor and smiled. "She ate lunch and walked to the bathroom. And the baby is feeding well."

Simon squeezed the woman's shoulder gratefully. "Thanks for coming, Mom," he said. "It was hard to leave her this morning." He went around the bed, leaned over Lydia, and kissed her lightly on the lips, glad to see her rouse, looking more alert and a bit more rested. Simon sat on the edge of the bed. "How are you feeling, my beloved?" he asked tenderly.

"Fine," Lydia reassured him, holding his hand.

"Mom," Simon started, looking at Anna. "Would you mind giving us a moment?"

She rose from her chair, laying Jimmy back in his bassinet. "Certainly, Simon," she left the bedroom, closing the door, and returned down the stairs to greet the others, happy to see little Nikki again.

"Now," Simon said when they were alone. "How are you really, Lydia? I could hardly concentrate all day. Good thing I was just doing some gallbladders and hernias with Marc today."

Lydia cupped his face in her hand. "I'm fine, Simon, really. I think everything is going okay."

"Let me be the judge of that," he declared, pulling down the covers and loosening her robe.

Obediently, she let him examine her. He felt her abdomen and kneaded her uterus. Checking between her legs, he saw a sizable clot emerge. Hiding his concern, he rolled up the newspaper beneath her, replacing it with a fresh layer.

"Do I pass inspection?" she asked.

"You are beautiful!" he exclaimed, kissing her lips again as his eyes traveled over her. She was too pale. Reluctantly, he pulled her robe back around her.

"Whew. It's been a long day waiting to get home. I'm glad your mother is here. It'll make it easier to go in tomorrow." Leaning over the crib, he picked up his son. The baby opened his eyes, looking up at his father. Simon gently touched his face, traced his tiny ears, and put the tip of his finger into the tiny little hand. In awe, Simon sat on the edge of the bed, holding the infant. "Hello, son," he murmured, raising the baby to kiss his little forehead. "You smell of milk. Has he been eating okay, Lydia?"

"Like he was born to nurse," Lydia reassured Simon.

Simon smiled broadly. "That's my boy!"

Abril approached, sniffing little Jimmy as Simon held the baby. The dog was ever so gentle, just as she was with little Nikki. Another welcome addition to the family, Abril decided. Sitting beside Simon, she watched every move as he showered attention on the tiny human in his arms.

"I'll be right back," Simon said, taking Jimmy with him and leaving the bedroom. Lydia heard him tromping down the stairs.

There were exclamations of delight from below as Lydia sighed, momentarily feeling a bit left out. She was determined to get up and move soon, not wanting to miss a moment more than she had to. She pushed herself up to a seated position on the side of the bed and gingerly found the floor with her feet. She felt solid enough to try on her own. Bending down to retrieve her slippers under the edge of the bed she saw the medical bag. "What on earth is..." she whispered to herself. Reaching under the bed, Lydia pulled out the bag of surgical tools, the small bottle of ether, a cone for administering it, *and operating room towels, no less?* Obviously, Simon had been planning ahead.

For a moment, it gave her pause. Simon had truly been afraid that something would go wrong. Her decision to have the baby at home had caused him that much anxiety. Carefully, she closed the bag, replacing it in the exact same spot, underneath the bed. Again, Lydia was flooded with appreciation for Simon and his faithfulness. Despite his worry, he loved her enough to support her wishes. She didn't fault him for wanting to be ready, knowing as she did that he liked the ability to restore order to chaos. It was part of what made him a great surgeon. It was his nature to be in control and prepared.

Her head swam as Lydia stood at the side of the bed, hanging onto the bedpost for support. Standing upright, she felt a strong cramp in her pelvis and instinctively grabbed her belly. Holding onto the wall, she slowly made her way down to the bathroom and carefully sat down to relieve herself. She felt a significant pressure. When she managed to stand again, the lightheadedness returned. Looking down, she noted a rather large blood clot in the bowl where she had been perched and quickly sat back down again, head spinning. *So, you're still cleaning things out in there, are you?* she asked her body. *Well, you can just be done with that now.* She would be careful, resist sharing her meat with Abril, and nurse her baby often... which would also minimize how often Simon massaged her tender belly. It would be fine. But as she stood, the room made circles.

She grabbed the sink, then the wall.

As Lydia slowly made her way back to the bedroom, Simon ran briskly back upstairs, without Jimmy, who was now nestled in Andrew's arms again. He saw her wavering in the dim hallway and immediately came to her side, chiding her thoroughly.

"What on earth are you doing, Lydia?" he quietly demanded, reaching for her. "I was coming right back up! You need to wait for me!"

Lydia took his support, letting go of the wall. "Now, Simon, I must try to do things, you know," Lydia objected. "I need to get my strength back."

"I agree, but with me! Or your mother!" he admonished her. He wrapped an arm gently around her waist and lifted her, carrying her the distance to the bedroom. Lowering her carefully onto the bed, he spread her legs to examine her, his chest tightening at the sight of the bright red stain on the cloth beneath her. He covered her protectively and began massaging her uterus. "You're not my rosy-cheeked girl just yet," he caressed her cheek in concern. "It's only been three days, Lydia. Give yourself time—give me time. Let us help you. Please."

Lydia thought of the bag beneath the bed. "Okay," she sighed. "I just felt left out with everyone downstairs sounding so cheerful and happy."

He took her in his arms, holding her tight. "You'll be strong soon enough. I know you. You always come back stronger." He lifted her chin, kissing her softly. "I missed you so much today.

And last night, I felt guilty... feeling you holding me... when I should be just holding you."

Lydia smiled, comforted by Simon's attention, his caring and his belief in her. "It makes me feel less infirm if I can comfort you a little. Okay. I love you, Simon. Go back downstairs and enjoy the others, and I'll rest... but I'm so cold. Would you find another blanket?"

Simon kissed her again, letting it linger a bit longer as she closed her eyes. He retrieved another blanket, tucking it around her, then went to the bathroom to clean up.

Washing his hands at the sink, he happened to glance at the toilet. His heart stopped. There was a very large clot. He flushed it quickly. The walls seemed to be pressing in around him as his fingers drummed anxiously against the edge of the sink. He made his way back to the bedroom to check on her again, considering her pale face, resting against the pillow. Despite her assertion that she was cold, Lydia felt a little too warm to him.

Deep in his thoughts, he returned to the group downstairs, motioning for Marc to follow him into the kitchen.

"What's up, buddy?" Marc quickly read the look on Simon's face.

Simon was rapidly tapping his fingers on the kitchen counter. "I don't know, Marc. She just passed a large clot. She's warm to the touch. Should she be having large clots? On the third day? I don't like this."

Marc didn't like it either. "Um. You could call Sister Anne."

"She's already scheduled to come by today," Simon said. "Maybe it's normal. Sister said Lydia didn't tear. This has to be from inside."

"We'll keep a close eye. I'll go to the market. We'll make up liver and onions tonight," Marcus offered. "You still have ice on her, right?"

Simon looked up in near shock. "Ice! I forgot ice today!" He immediately reached into the ice box and ran back up the stairs.

Giving Lydia a chance to rest, the men of the house chatted quietly in the living room. Simon sat in one of the easy chairs by the fireplace, cradling Jimmy in his arms. Abril had also joined them, eager to play with Nikki. The patient dog allowed the little toddler to grab at her tail and crawl around, trying to catch her, playfully exercising Nikki's toddling muscles. The table was soon set and the women in the kitchen called out that the food was nearly ready to be served.

Marcus quickly ran upstairs to his bedroom. As he made his way back toward the stairs, he stopped at Lydia's door, poking his head inside. She seemed to be asleep, so he went to the side of the bed to check on her. She was breathing softly, but still looking very pale, only her cheeks were flushed. Understanding Simon's concern, he bent down to kiss her forehead. She stirred.

"You didn't forget me," she murmured, still drowsy.

"Not for a single second," he reassured her, stroking her hair. "Feeling okay?"

She nodded. "Tired. This mother thing is hard work... in bed all day and then nursing a baby when he says it's time... such a strain, you know."

Marcus chuckled. "Ready to go out and push the plow, huh? Shear those sheep? Milk those cows?"

"I have enough milk for two cows, I think," she sighed. "I'm leaking all over the place."

He laughed. "Suzie says it'll slow down. Even cows don't leak all over the place. Or so I'm told, anyway. I've never asked a cow, so I don't know for sure. Two nursing mothers under one roof! By the way, it's nice that your mom and dad came. I wish Nikki had been born before my mother passed away... and my father doesn't even know her yet."

Lydia took his hand. "I'm glad, too. Nikki is just wonderful. I hope little Jimmy has the same easy temperament. They're going to be so close, growing up together, Marc. Everyone enjoys Nikki so much, even at the clinic. It was nice of you to come up and see me in my isolation."

"My pleasure. You rest now, and we'll bring you some dinner when it's ready," Marcus said gently, feeling her forehead again. It did feel warm to his touch, but her fingers were cold.

"I am tired, but resting is all anyone will let me do!" she protested softly, her eyes already closing. He pulled one of the chairs closer to the bed and sat with her for a moment, watching her sleep... wishing her strength would return to her.

The dining room buzzed with conversation and the food was plentiful. The meal felt like a celebration, a tribute to the enduring cycle of life. But just as the meal was winding up, they were startled by a loud knock at the front door. Curious, Suzie rose from the table to go answer it. When she opened the door, she was met by a policeman. She recognized him as the same officer who had carried Abril home, the day Lydia had been assaulted while coming home from her house visits.

"Ma'am," he started, visibly agitated.

"Can I help you?" Suzie asked quickly, seeing his patrol car waiting at the sidewalk.

"Is the doctor at home?" he asked with urgency, looking past her into the house.

"Yes..." She turned and saw Marcus, already coming into the foyer, after hearing a man's voice at their door.

"Officer?" Marcus asked. "Come in!"

The man stepped just inside the door. "Sorry to bother you, Doc, but when I was here before, you said you was a surgeon... when you was sewing up your dog?"

Marcus nodded. "Yes, that's right. Do you need help?" Marcus turned as Simon now joined them as well.

"Yes, Doc, or rather, someone does. There's a fire down at the mill, on the river. Real bad. Some fellas getting hurt down there, and I was wondering..."

"Of course," Marcus exclaimed. He looked at Simon. "You still have that bag upstairs, right?"

"I do," Simon assured him. "I'm coming with you."

"Stay with Lydia, Simon," Marcus responded quickly. "She's not out of the woods yet."

Simon locked eyes with Suzie, knowing that Marcus shouldn't be going into a bad situation alone and that Suzie was a skilled nurse, more than able to handle Lydia's needs.

"Go," she whispered. "I'll feel better knowing you're with Marcus. I'll take dinner up to her."

Simon ran up the stairs, then quietly entered the bedroom. Lydia was asleep. He reached under the bed, grabbing the smaller of the two medical bags and, turning once to Lydia, decided not to wake her. He quietly closed the door behind him and ran back down the stairs.

"Be careful!" Suzie urged them both as they ran out the kitchen door and through the yard to jump in the automobile.

As Marcus pulled out of the alley, sirens were now wailing from various points in the city. They caught sight of flames clawing at the evening sky, rising above the trees down by the river. It was easy enough to know which way to turn down the city streets. They followed the red glow and the fire trucks careening around corners in their haste to get to the scene. Marcus fell in right behind one of the ambulances en route and, racing along with it, covered the distance quickly.

When they reached the steel mill yard, an inferno was raging within one of the massive brick structures, flames roaring through shattered windows. The two surgeons felt the heat well before stepping out of the automobile. Nearby, an ambulance driver opened his door, and just froze, staring at the blaze until his colleague barked at him to grab the litter from the back. They quickly dropped it onto the ground, bracing for the first casualty to be brought out. More ambulances sped in, forming an expanding semicircle. At a safe distance, a cluster of mill workers watched anxiously, their faces lit by the fiery glow they had just escaped.

Simon quickly approached a firefighter who was wrestling with the hoses, positioning them to battle the surging flames.

"We're doctors!" Simon shouted over the incredible noise, hoping to be heard. "Anyone still in there? Are any of those guys over there injured?"

"Don't know yet," the man shouted back over the roar of the fire. "We just got here ourselves. Go ask that cop over there! He looks like he's directing traffic."

Simon and Marcus made their way toward a group of several policemen, who were gesturing and pointing as they worked to assess where help was needed most.

"We're doctors," Marcus shouted out to them as the heat from the fire stifled his breath.

One of the officers looked over and nodded. "Wait here a minute. I think some guys are hurt... over by the forge." A thick cloud of smoke came rolling toward them out of a lower window, then rose up sharply, caught up in the swirling wind created by the fire itself. A shower of sparks fell around them like a glowing, red-orange rain. Marcus glanced at Simon. They knew what they were getting into.

The medical bag firmly in his grip, Simon spotted an officer farther down the slope, waving them over. Signaling to Marcus, he led the way through the ash as it swirled in the searing air before settling on the gravel beneath their feet. Step by step, they maneuvered around scattered debris and massive pieces of yard equipment until they reached the waiting officer.

"He must've had something fall on him," the officer shouted over the sirens and roaring flames. "I think he's alive."

Dropping down to the ground, the two doctors quickly examined the injured man. The fire was still growing.

"Yeah, he's alive," Simon shouted back. "Tell the ambulance guys to bring the litter down here."

The officer shook his head. "They won't come this close. Our guys'll have to carry him out."

"Watch this leg," Marcus warned the officer, motioning to his right leg. "It's broken."

"Got it," the officer nodded as he signaled orders to two uniformed men who lifted the worker from under his arms and knees, mindful of the one leg and began carting him off, up the slope, toward the ambulances.

Marcus' eyes scanned the chaotic scene, locking onto a worker stumbling out of the inferno. The man's legs buckled, and he crumpled to the ground. Without hesitation, the two doctors sprinted to his side. His skin was burned, his hair singed, and his shirt clung to his scorched back. Marcus shouted over the flames for two of the other officers, who came running. "Tell the drivers to step on it with this one!" he yelled. "These are serious burns. They've got to make it to the hospital, and quick! Do not try to pull his shirt off! He can't wait."

The officers nodded, their faces already black with smoke and ash, as they quickly lifted the man, one on either side of him.

Just then, two firemen ran past and into the building. One of them quickly ran back out and straight over to the doctors, shouting over the roar of the flames, "There's a guy pinned in there. Leg is under a girder. Can't lift it up. Can you take his leg off?"

"We going in?" Marcus shouted to Simon.

"What do you think?" Simon shouted back, and they nodded in unison.

Opening the medical bag, Simon reached inside and pulled out the bottle of flammable ether. Handing it to Marcus, he closed up the instruments again as Marc threw the bottle as hard as he could into the farthest section of the burning building... where it exploded.

Following the fireman to the door of the building, the heat and smoke took their breath away. Pulling off his shirt, Simon ripped off both sleeves, wrapping one around his face to cover his nose and mouth, and quickly passing the other to Marcus. Staying low, they followed the fireman through the smoke and into the next room, where they found another fireman kneeling by the pinned man, both dripping in sweat.

Screaming in fear and pain, the injured worker cried out, "Get me the hell out of here!"

"They gotta take your leg to do it, man!" the fireman shouted. "You want 'em to take your leg?"

"If they don't, I'm dead already!" the man shouted back. "Take the damn thing off!"

Simon nodded, grabbing the scalpels while wishing he had packed a bone saw. He had not anticipated needing a bone saw for Lydia's delivery. Marcus was already whipping off his belt to secure a tourniquet above the man's knee.

"Gonna hurt like hell!" the fireman warned the man.

"Punch him out!" Marcus shouted, sweat pouring down his face and neck.

The fireman hesitated, then planted a right hook into the man's face; he went limp. Simon and Marcus simultaneously began cutting away the man's trapped lower leg, the blood flow restricted by the belt. Taking the leg just below the knee was the easiest way they could cut through ligaments and release the imprisoned man. They didn't even notice when another fireman came running up to them, staying low to the ground, beneath the smoke. The heat was searing.

"You guys gotta hurry up and get out of here. That brick wall behind you is bulging. It's gonna go!" he yelled.

Working quickly, the two surgeons severed the man's lower leg, tying off blood vessels, leaving his calf and foot trapped beneath the steel girder. Simon wrapped the remainder of his shirt around the stump and yelled to the firemen, "Go!" They retrieved the injured man and carted him off, stumbling through the debris.

Quickly, Simon grabbed his instruments from the ground, hastily throwing them back into his bag. He and Marcus jumped to their feet as they heard a loud boom. The ground shook beneath their feet. Horrified, Simon saw Marcus go down, disappearing into a cloud of dust and black smoke. Choking, Simon fell to his knees, feeling around in the darkness. Finding Marcus' foot, he followed his friend's body all the way up to his arms. Crouching on the ground, he reached under his buddy's shoulders and wrapped his arms around Marcus's chest, hauling him backward with all of his might. Simon prayed to Almighty God that he was heading out of the flames and not deeper into them. He couldn't see, and was struggling to breathe in the heat and smoke. A pile of loose bricks on the ground sent the men tumbling. Simon crashed hard onto the blistering mill floor, dropping Marcus beside him.

With every ounce of strength he had, Simon got back onto his feet and found Marcus' body again. Clenching his hands together around his friend's chest once more. Simon thought he heard shouting and tried to follow the sound through the roiling smoke. After an eternity of dragging Marcus over the fallen bricks, Simon pulled him out through the rapidly decaying entry and out into the yard where firemen helped him carry Marcus to a small rise where they stretched him out on the grass. Simon bent over him, checking him for injuries, finding a gash on his head where falling bricks had struck him. Assessing his friend's eyes, using the red glow of the fire, Simon saw with relief that Marc's pupils were still equal.

"Can you get him up, into better air?" Simon shouted to the firemen who nodded their confirmation. Looking back down the slope, he saw another fireman carrying out another wounded man slung over his shoulders. Running back down the slope, Simon helped him get the worker to higher ground before laying him down and also checking him quickly for injuries.

"He still alive?" the fireman shouted.

"Not by much," Simon yelled, not seeing burns. "Probably breathed in too much smoke. Get him to an ambulance."

The fireman nodded, calling for help to carry the injured away. Then Simon and the fireman looked around for more workers to emerge, but instead seeing that the outer brick wall of the building was giving way. Shoving the surgeon ahead of him up the slope, the fireman ran right behind, bricks falling hard, scattering in every direction. A huge tongue of fire split the air over their heads as they ducked. Covered in dust and smoke, they made it to the top of the slope where the hoses sprayed arcs of cold river water over them and into the conflagration. Mist from the water fell around them, streaking the dirt that covered them as they crouched down, breathing very hard, trying to fill their lungs with cooler air.

"Hey Doc," a policeman shouted. "Got one more over here..."

Wearily, Simon rose. He followed the officer to where a couple of workers sat on the ground, heads in their hands. Checking them both, Simon continued to render first aid to the injured until the fire gradually came under control and there were no more casualties requiring his attention. Then he returned to Marcus who was on the ground at a safe distance waiting, now sitting up and holding his throbbing head.

Dropping down beside him on the ground, Simon thanked God that Marc was awake again.

"Glad to see you woke up for the ending. Have you had enough fun yet?" he asked his friend. "Want to go home?"

"You mean back to the States?" Marcus asked, checking his hand for blood from his scalp.

"We're already back in the States, buddy!" Simon exclaimed, worried suddenly that his friend was disoriented from the head injury.

"Doesn't feel like it!" Marcus continued, "I thought for a minute that we were back in France, with shells dropping around us! Man, I have a headache."

Then absurdly, Simon started to laugh. Marcus was alright after all! "Good! If you feel the pain that means you're alive! Come on," he said, pulling Marcus' arm around his bare shoulders and dragging him to his feet. "You don't look so good! This time, I get to drive."

Pulling the car into the dark alley behind the house, Simon got out first and went around to help Marcus get out of the passenger side. Opening the fence to their backyard, he saw light stream out across the grass from the kitchen door which swung open for their arrival.

"Don't feel too steady yet," Marcus said quietly, still coughing up the smoke that had filled his lungs despite the make-shift bandanas they'd used, trying to filter the air. He draped his arm over Simon's shoulder and let his friend help him stumble up the walk. Flying out through the kitchen door, Suzie ran down the steps to meet them, pulling Marcus' other arm around her own shoulders as they helped him climb up the porch steps and into the kitchen. There he dropped heavily into a chair at the table while Anna and Andrew looked on, in shock.

"Got hit by a wall of falling bricks," Simon told Suzie quickly.

Immediately, Suzie grabbed a bowl of water and some towels and turned up the kitchen light to start washing the cut on Marc's scalp. Grabbing her hand, Marcus pulled her down to kiss her and she touched his face gently.

"You're a mess," she teased tearfully.

He smiled, looking up at her. "Got a headache," he repeated.

"Okay, you can use that excuse once tonight," Suzie told him, her intense relief that he could speak coherently, clearly evident in her voice. Marcus just laughed.

Simon looked up, shocked. Lydia had somehow stumbled her way down the stairs and was now standing in the kitchen doorway, looking even more pale than she had before he had left the house. She looked stricken with fear and he immediately darted around the table to her. Despite his bare chest being covered in sweat and dirt and smoke, Simon pulled her to him and held her tight. Pressing her head against his shoulder, he stroked her hair, comforting her, kissing her forehead. As she began to sway in his arms, Simon scooped her up and carried her into the living room, placing her gently on the sofa, kneeling beside her, still caressing her face.

White as a ghost, Lydia reached up feebly and touched his beard and his lips, looking at him with her very soul reaching through her eyes, but saying nothing. Lowering his head, Simon placed his mouth gently against hers, breathing in her presence. She tasted the smoke from his lungs, and felt Simon kiss each of her eyes, her tears spilling over, though she didn't make a sound.

Simon gathered the salty wetness on his lips, regretting having caused her such dismay after having just given birth. He raised her head from the sofa just enough to wrap his arms around her and then he kissed her hard, driven by the emotions of the harrowing experience just behind him... and she, driven by how close she had come to losing him, responded. She felt much too warm to his touch. Perhaps it was just a stress response from the ordeal of the fire... he feared it was something more...

Chapter 12

Rising From the Ashes

Simon had taken it slowly while helping Lydia back up the stairs. After gently tucking her in, and again finding a large clot on her pad, he had kneaded her uterus for a while. More than aware of the need to clean himself up, he kissed her forehead before joining Marcus in the bathroom. Both men were quiet, focused on their efforts to rid their bodies of the smoke and ash, unable to scrub away the memories of the heat, the danger or images of the injured. Simon marveled at how quickly they had managed to sever the pinned man's leg. He prayed that the worker had survived the trip to the hospital, not to mention the inevitable surgery needed to clean the stump and create a skin flap to cover it.

Pulling Marcus from the flames now seemed as though it had taken no effort whatsoever. Simon felt stronger and more capable than he had since losing a section of his lung. He was exhilarated, relishing the energy of the rescue, so reminiscent of the challenges they had faced during the war. He welcomed the urgency, the demand on his focus and skills. It felt incredibly rewarding.

Despite the thorough bathing, the faint smell of smoke followed Simon as he joined Lydia in their bed. She nestled up against him, unable to shake a visceral sense of terror. Seeing Simon and

Marcus in the kitchen, streaked with smoke and ash. She wasn't sure how to sort it all out. What if the fire had claimed either of the men, or worse, both? What would Suzie have done?

What would she herself have done, now with a newborn to care for? She'd almost lost him three times already during the war, but now that they had little Jimmy... She felt Simon's chest, her fingertips lingering in the curls of hair, feeling the muscles over his ribs. Now, more than ever, he had become her rock. *What happens if you lose your rock?*

"You're still awake," Simon noted softly, stroking the arm she had draped over his chest. He felt her head nod against him. "What are you thinking about, Lydia?" he asked gently.

"You are my rock," she said simply, voicing her thoughts.

He was glad. He felt strong and wanted to continue to be so, for her.

"What are you thinking about?" she countered.

He bent one arm back behind his head and stared up into the darkness. "I want to talk to Maloney about starting a walk-in surgical clinic, in the community... where people with lacerations, boils, wounds, foreign objects... whatever... can stop in and get fixed up. Maybe near the river by the mills, where workers are more likely to be injured. Or near the factory district... I don't know. Marcus and I talked about seeing if we could take a day each week to run such a clinic. Or a couple of afternoons, when the surgeries drop off over at the hospital. Treat whatever comes our way. It would be a lot like what you and Suzie do in the clinic."

"Sounds like you've given it a lot of thought," she said. He wasn't thinking at all about almost dying or leaving her alone with the baby. She felt him shift beneath her. He turned onto his side, his eyes glittering in the faint streetlight that spilled over the windowsill.

"What do you think about the idea?" he asked.

"It sounds like something you would enjoy, something out of the routine, something challenging," she admitted quietly. "I can see you doing it. At least it wouldn't be in a tent."

"Good," he exhaled deeply. "I'm glad you like the idea."

"Will Marcus be okay?" she asked anxiously.

He nodded. "I sewed him up. He has a hard head. It was a worthy gash that he can brag about for years, but it's closed now and should heal well."

"He said you dragged him out of the fire, unconscious... you were inside the burning building..."

"Just for a little, while we took a guy's leg. Fastest amputation in history, I can assure you," he said with satisfaction.

"You saved lives today, Simon," she said. "You saved Marcus."

Simon paused before answering. "It's about time. He's done it too often for me."

She nodded, utter weariness overcoming her. "Yes. You've saved each other."

Simon kissed her. "Are you okay with all this? I know it scared you when we came in all messed up like that."

"As long as you're safe now, that's all that matters," her voice was a whisper from the emotional strain. "That's the only thing that matters."

He leaned over her, kissing her cheek again, then her neck. He cupped her breast in his hand. "I wish I could love you the way I want to. Tonight, more than ever."

"I love you, Simon. Soon..." she whispered, exhausted... already drifting off, as she uttered the words.

Suddenly, Simon jerked awake. He wasn't sure why or what time it was... it was still dark out. Lydia was sleeping on her side. Jimmy was sleeping there too, tucked inside her robe, at her breast. *She must've fallen asleep nursing him,* he thought. *And I slept through it!*

Simon slipped out of bed, gently lifted the infant, and nestled him back into the bassinet beside their bed. Slipping back under the covers, he reached an arm around Lydia. She was burning with fever. Startled, he jumped from the bed and turned the lamplight up to a soft glow. Even in the dim light, he could see that her pale cheeks had turned an unnatural crimson. It was barely the fourth day after the birth. If there was an infection, it would be peaking now. Childbirth mortality rates had dropped so much in the past ten years that Simon had not been too concerned about infection, but with her complication, perhaps he should have been.

Simon made his way down to the kitchen, wondering if they had any salicylic acid for the fever. He searched the cupboards. quickly growing frustrated. No apothecary would be open at this time. He might try the hospital. Running back upstairs, he quietly gathered clothes and lightly tapped on Marcus and Susannah's door. Suzie got out of bed and opened it, surprised to see Simon in the hall, fully dressed in his street clothes.

"What's wrong?" she asked quickly as she stepped out into the hall, trying not to rouse Marcus from his sleep.

"Lydia has a fever," Simon reported.

Suszie followed him across to the other bedroom. She placed a hand on Lydia's forehead. "Wow!" she exclaimed softly. "She's hot, alright. Is it mastitis? Is it her breasts?"

Simon stopped in his tracks. "I didn't think to look." He was embarrassed to admit it, immediately opening her robe. He saw no redness or signs of inflammation in either breast. "I don't think so. Got to be her uterus."

"What are you going to do?" Suzie asked, now just as worried as he.

Simon ran his fingers through his hair, considering their options. Not as familiar with obstetrics, he assumed that most of the time people let a postpartum fever run its course and tried to maintain fluids. "I... I'm not sure... Suzie, I'm not sure!"

"Look," she advised. "Go to the hospital, get some salicylic acid, and while you're there, talk to someone in maternity. Maybe they'll have an idea. We can take her over to the hospital today if you think it's best."

"What about the baby? What about Jimmy and feeding him?"

Suzie placed a reassuring hand on his arm. "If I can't get her to nurse him, I probably can make enough for two. He won't take that much from Nikki. We'll deal with that."

He nodded, running briskly back down the stairs and out the back door, to the automobile parked in the alley.

Simon deftly maneuvered the dark, empty streets, made his way across the bridge to the hospital, parked and ran inside. Deciding to go straight up to the maternity ward, he pushed through the door, into a dim room save one lone light illuminating the night nurse's desk, in the back corner. Quickly crossing the ward, he approached the woman on duty.

"Nurse," he started in earnest, "Doctor Finney, from the operating theater."

She looked up, startled. "What can I do for you, Doctor?"

"My wife, she had our baby at home, and now she has a high fever," he explained, keeping it brief and to the point.

"Does she have mastitis?" the woman asked.

"No, I don't think so. At least no obvious signs of it," he said, suddenly remembering his main task. "Do you have salicylic acid... to bring the fever down?"

She nodded, grabbed keys from a drawer and disappeared into a utility room, where he heard a cupboard door open and then close. She returned with the medicine, and some advice, "I think you should talk to Doctor Weyland. He's sleeping in the doctors' room, waiting for one of our women who is nearly ready to deliver. It's outside of the ward, just to the right and down the hall."

Simon took the little envelope of the antifever medication, thanking her profusely.

"And, Doctor Finney, you know you can't bring her in here. We can't risk an infection spreading through the new mothers," she warned.

"Of course not," he assured her. "That much I do know."

Leaving the ward, Simon turned down the hall as instructed and rapped on the door of the on-call room. A tousled, half-asleep obstetrician answered the door with a quick, "Is she here—" before realizing that it was a man in street clothes standing at the door, in the middle of the night, not a nurse coming to get him for a delivery.

"Doctor Weyland?" Simon asked quickly. "Doctor Finney. How do you do? Listen, I need your advice."

The man rallied himself and focused, having grown accustomed to being summoned at all hours of the day and night for deliveries. This, though, was a bit out of the ordinary, encountering an agitated, unknown doctor... during night hours, no less. "Talk to me," he replied.

Rapidly, Simon described the events of the birth, the complication, the midwife, Lydia's symptoms, and her current fever.

Doctor Weyland grew visibly concerned. "While it's less common for puerperal infections to occur, they remain a serious complication, Doctor Finney, as I'm sure you are already aware. But it may not be that. You are certain that all of the placenta was removed by the midwife?"

"I saw her compare the piece she retrieved to the incomplete placenta, and she seemed to match it up pretty close, at least to my eye," Simon was drowning in self doubt.

He nodded. "Who was the midwife?"

"Sister Anne," Simon confirmed.

"Oh," Weyland nodded. "She's good. I know her. Still, it's possible a piece remained. Is your wife still bleeding?"

"She's still passing sizable clots. I didn't check her tonight, though," Simon admitted, feeling as though he had failed in his duty to her. "If there is an infection in the uterus, can anything be done?"

Doctor Weyland paused. "Not much for infection, but if it's still the placenta, we can do a sharp curettage. Can you get her in here? Not to the maternity ward, but to the general surgical ward... we can clean out the uterus."

"I can get one of the operating theaters set up and bring her over. If you could—"

"Certainly, Doctor Finney. I have a woman coming, in labor, but we'll work around it."

"I'll assist you," Simon said firmly.

"I don't think that's wise. There can be complications for your wife, Doctor," the obstetrician objected. "Your judgment is clouded."

"There have already been complications, Doctor Weyland," Simon asserted. He turned and hurried down the hall. The procedure for an emergency surgery after normal hours was familiar to him. Finding the surgical ward charge nurse, he started the process with the staff on duty, then drove back to the house to get Lydia.

Suzie was waiting up for him. "What did they say?" she asked, following him back up the dark stairs to the quiet bedroom.

"I talked to one of the obstetricians, Weyland, and the surgery team—they're setting up a room for a curettage."

Suzie was surprised. "A curettage?"

"Yes, her placenta tore." Simon began to gather anything Lydia might need. "And either she is infected, or some bit of tissue is still stuck in there. Sister Anne tried to remove it, but perhaps she wasn't completely successful."

The woman's eyes were round. "She never said anything. I didn't realize she'd had a problem."

Simon wrapped Lydia securely in her robe and looked down at his son in the crib.

Suzie followed his gaze. "I'll call Sister Edwarda and let her know what's going on. I'll stay home. Don't worry about the baby, Simon. I'll nurse Jimmy."

Simon lifted Lydia in his arms and carried her down the stairs. Abril followed them out the kitchen door and into the backyard. "Stay, Abril," he commanded the dog, who went as far as the little yard fence and then obediently sat to wait. As Simon placed Lydia on the automobile seat, he did not turn and beckon for her. So, the worried dog sat just at the fence, determined to wait there for their return.

As the early morning sun broke through his window pane, Marcus slowly woke himself, feeling his scalp... the night before had not been just some terrible dream. As the world came into focus, he was shocked to see Suzie sitting on the edge of the bed as the sky steadily brightened. She had the newborn at her breast, feeding him.

"Am I hallucinating?" Marcus exclaimed, confused, propping himself up in the bed. "Or is that Jimmy?"

"You are not hallucinating." Suzie declared. She was amazed that Jimmy had latched onto her breast so easily, as if he were her own infant. He felt so tiny and vulnerable compared to Nikki now. It was delightful holding him in her arms.

With that realization, Marcus was instantly alarmed. "Where's Lydia?"

"At the hospital," Suzie explained calmly. "Simon took her in for an emergency curettage."

"My God, what happened?"

"High fever," Suzie said, looking tenderly at the tiny infant in her arms. "I want another one, Marcus."

This was the farthest thing from his mind at the moment. He sprang out of bed and headed to the bathroom to wash up before Anna, Andrew, and Nikki woke. When he returned, still toweling himself off, he quickly dressed.

"Just where do you think you're going?" Suzie demanded.

"Why, to work, of course," Marcus said. "Been doing it every day."

She shook her head as she shifted the baby to her other breast. "Don't you think you deserve a day off... with stitches in your head?"

"Naw," he said, kissing her cheek. "Just a little flesh wound. Not enough to even worry about. And I don't use my head to do surgery. I mean, I do, but not in that way, anyhow."

"Hm," she mused. "I don't think it's wise, but you didn't ask my opinion."

"Tell you what," he said, now kissing the top of her head. "I'll make it a short day and come home early. Soon as I figure out if Simon's patients need to be covered. How's that sound?"

"Better," Suzie relented. "Oh, and Simon took the automobile."

Of course he did. Marcus thought quickly. *I'll catch a cab or the trolley.* He hurried downstairs, skipping breakfast and instead heading right out into the street toward the trolley, since there were no cabs in sight. On the corner near the trolley stop, Officer Stevenson was starting his early morning neighborhood patrol.

"Doc, how are you this morning?" the police officer called over cheerfully. The officer was now well familiar with their household which had become an integral part of his beat.

"Got to get to the hospital right away!" Marcus declared.

"Hop in then," Officer Stevenson said, pointing to his black patrol car parked nearby.

Even better! Marcus thought. "Many thanks, Officer!" He climbed into the passenger side and heard the siren begin to wail. Officer Stevenson tore through the streets, glad when others immediately moved out of their way upon seeing them. Being a beat cop, he didn't always get to use his siren. He sped across the bridge in mere minutes and delivered Marcus to the front entrance of the hospital. Once inside, Marcus immediately ran up the stairs to the surgery, throwing on scrubs from the stack in the doctors' lounge. He noticed Simon's clothing piled haphazardly on the sofa. He ran to the operating theater, pushed the doors open, and quickly scrubbed.

Simon and Weyland were both at the operating table next to Lydia, who had now been put under anesthesia after blood work had been drawn and a radiograph taken of her abdomen. She was already slumbering under the watchful eye of the anesthetist. Marcus approached the head of the table, noting the sharp curette and speculum among the surgical tools prepped and waiting on the metal instrument tray. Simon looked up, surprised at Marcus's appearance at the hospital after the wound he'd sustained.

"Shouldn't you be resting?" Simon asked.

Weyland glanced over at Simon. "Should he be here?" he nodded toward Marcus.

"He's family," Simon replied, then added to Marcus, "thought you'd take the day off after last night. Did Suzie bring you up to speed?"

Marcus nodded, touching Lydia's flushed cheeks. "She's still pretty hot."

"This is Doctor Weyland, one of the obstetricians here," Simon told Marcus. "This is Doctor Marcus Lovell. Also a surgeon."

Weyland, now perched on a stool between Lydia's legs up in stirrups, looked up at the two. "I wasn't aware this was going to be a teaching procedure. Wait. Aren't you two the new surgeons back from the war? You probably didn't do much obstetrics in Europe."

Marcus was abrupt. "Just help Mrs. Finney!"

"Wait a minute. Finney. Is this Nurse Finney from the war, who took our walk-in clinic by storm?" Weyland asked, suddenly gaining a profound understanding of the patient in front of him.

Simon nodded. "My wife, yes. The nurse."

"I've heard about the two war nurses down there doing great things. Didn't realize that's who your wife was, Doctor Finney. Sorry about that," Weyland added.

He studied the blood work on a piece of paper as a nurse held it in front of him for review. He let out a whistle. "We need to get a unit of blood in her. She's pretty low. Must have seen a whole lot of clots, Doctor Finney. Get a unit up here, Nurse."

Simon nodded. "I'll put an intravenous in—"

Marc gently moved Simon aside. "I'll do it, Simon," he said, reaching for a tourniquet to tie around Lydia's arm. In moments, he had saline running while they waited for the blood to arrive. No doubt she needed the fluids anyway.

Looking back to his patient, Weyland instructed the assisting nurse, "More light down here, please. And get me a catheter."

She reached for the overhead light for repositioning.

"Better," Weyland nodded. "Okay, doctors, let's see if we can find the problem," he said as if he were instructing medical students. Inserting a speculum, he widened it with the corkscrew, looking inside the woman's body with an experienced eye. "Cervix looks okay. Obviously, this is unfortunate post-delivery, but at least she's asleep and won't feel what I'm doing. Curette please, Nurse. There are still clots in here, Doctor Finney. She's bleeding somewhere," Weyland continued with his instructive tone. "You know the risk, Doctor Finney, perforation after childbirth with the uterine wall already thinned," he continued. "But... we're only going deep enough to remove residual placenta, not attempting to remove invasive tumor tissue or the like, so it is slightly less of a hazard. How's her pressure?"

The anesthetist said, "Ninety-eight over forty-six. Heart rate one-ten."

Simon stood by, filled with anxiety, trying to force his surgical mind to track the procedure, unclouded by emotions. "And...?" Simon said after only a few brief moments.

"Give me a moment to do this, Doctor Finney... if you would, please," Weyland said calmly, already having anticipated the man's anxiety about the entire procedure and appreciating Simon's restraint. "There are several, large clots..."

The circulating nurse accepted the blood upon delivery, handing it off to Marcus who immediately started infusing it. Simon held Lydia's hand beneath the drape covering her abdomen and thighs. He prayed to Almighty God that the curettage would not perforate her womb, that this would not turn into an emergency hysterectomy. For a brief second, Simon was afraid that she would never be able to have another child. He could accept the possibility, but knew that she would struggle with it terribly. He looked at her closed eyes, grateful beyond measure that she was under anesthesia while the doctor worked.

"There it was," Weyland reported with relief, having retrieved a large clot of tissue. "Way up at the fundus. No wonder the midwife didn't find it.

"Your wife should recover. I think the fever is from the attached tissue, not infection. I see no signs of necrotic tissue or purulent drainage, but it was a sizable area of wall still bleeding from the placenta there. Nevertheless, I'll irrigate the uterus with antiseptic, preventive I think, with this having been sitting in there the past several days. The diluted solution is not toxic to the healthy cells or bloodstream, if absorbed."

Simon nodded as he watched the nurse already bringing the required equipment Weyland had requested. "Go ahead. Whatever it takes."

"You can let her start coming up now," Weyland instructed the anesthetist, then looking up briefly to Simon. "We can admit her to the general surgery ward for post-op care."

Simon shook his head. "I'll take her home. She'll want to feed the baby, and she'll heal faster there."

"Since you're a physician, I'll allow it," Weyland replied. "But otherwise, I certainly would not. Can't imagine she'll feel up to breastfeeding, but encourage her to try so her breasts don't get engorged. I want to see her in my office in three days, regardless. I'll tell my nurses to fit her into my Monday schedule."

Simon nodded, leaned over, and kissed Lydia's forehead through his face mask. "She'll be there," Simon assured Weyland in no uncertain terms.

Doctor Weyland finished the procedure and then allowed Simon and Marcus to lift Lydia onto a waiting gurney, which was headed for the empty recovery room. Marcus walked alongside Simon, with an operating room tech pushing the cart down the hall. There were hospital staff arriving for morning duty in the operating theater and the corridors were getting busy. "I've got two cases this morning after rounds. I'll look at your schedule too," Marc informed his friend.

Simon nodded. "I'll stay with her in the recovery for a while. It won't be busy there first thing. The nurses can finish the blood transfusion and watch her for a couple of hours. I don't mind scrubbing in for my cases before taking her home, what with the operating theater right down the hall. I'm worried about Jimmy, though."

"Don't be," Marcus told him. "Suzie was feeding him as I left... and told me she wants another baby now."

Simon looked at Marcus' head covered by its surgical cap. "How's the headache? Did you sleep? Are you okay to operate?"

"Feel fine. I have a hard head, remember? I figure I bled out, not in. Must be okay. And yes, I slept. What a night, huh?"

Simon nodded. "Yeah, what a night!"

Marcus clapped his hand on Simon's shoulder. "She's going to be okay now, Simon. Tomorrow is Saturday. Starting today, when we get home, we aren't going to do anything other than eat and sleep and watch women feed babies for the next two days, even if three steel mills go up in smoke!"

"Sounds good to me!" Simon exhaled, his fear for Lydia now diminished to a smolder, like the pile of rubble that was once a mill along the river.

Lydia began to stir as the effects of the anesthesia lifted. There were bright lights overhead and the walls were a sterile white. Panic took a hold of her. She tried to lift herself, but was too weak to do so... and one arm was strapped to an intravenous board.

"Where am I?" she whispered to the large room, her voice sluggish.

Simon leaned over her, still dressed in his surgical garb. "You're at the hospital, beloved. At Charity, in the recovery."

"Where's my baby?" she asked.

"Jimmy's home with Suzie and your mother. He's fine," Simon reassured her, tenderly stroking her hair and cheek. "They had to do a procedure on you, on your uterus. It's over now."

Lydia reached down to her belly. There was no dressing. "Did they cut me open? Did they remove it?" she asked, suddenly fearful.

"No, beloved. Doctor Weyland went inside, removed a piece of placenta still stuck there. Just scraped it clean," he reassured her. "You were asleep, and I was there with you the entire time, not in the waiting room. I was right there holding your hand. In fact, Marcus scrubbed in too, for your intravenous. You weren't alone."

"I'm sorry, I didn't tell you, Simon," Lydia said tearfully. "I was still passing big clots. I didn't think it was that unusual."

He kissed her lips softly. "It's okay, you're going to heal now. You've had a unit of blood. You'll feel better."

She grabbed his hand. "I don't want to stay here, my love."

He nodded. "I thought not. I've already made rounds on the wards. I've got one more case to do, and then I'll come back and take you home."

Groaning, she thought of the baby. "My breasts are huge."

Simon smiled. "Remember you have a live-in wet nurse at home, and Jimmy didn't mind since Suzie was his only alternative. He'll be fine till I get you home, and then he'll be very glad to have you back."

Seeing Lydia awake and talking with Simon, one of the nurses came over to the bed. "Are you in pain, Mrs. Finney?" she asked gently.

"I'm cramping but it's okay. I don't want anything. This is my husband. He'll be taking me home to feed my baby in a little bit," Lydia told her, trying to stay positive.

"I need to check you for bleeding, then you can rest," the nurse informed her, pulling a rolling screen around the bed for privacy. The nurse looked at Simon in his surgical garb, questioning how to proceed. She knew him, of course, as one of the new surgeons. And as he gave no indication he was leaving, the nurse decided to lift the covers just enough to do her duty. She pulled the screen back again when she was finished and smoothed the sheet over her patient.

"Let me know if I can do something for you," she added softly.

"Listen, beloved," Simon told Lydia then quickly. "The sooner I get this last patient taken care of, the sooner I can take you home. So, I'll leave you here now, just for a bit."

"Okay," she said with a little apprehension as Simon left her for the operating theater.

She didn't want anything else to go wrong and thought of Jimmy. Lydia lay there with nothing to do but think. She felt flushed but not uncomfortable. The previous evening was a little hazy for her, but she pondered the birth, what she recalled of the fire... and being in the hospital as a patient for the first time in her life.

She wondered if her father had gone back to Greensburg. It was certainly different being the one in the bed, just laying there thinking, unable to get up and leave whenever she liked... waiting on someone else to do things for her. She didn't want to be a difficult patient for the nurse on duty. Her eyes were so heavy and she drifted into sleep.

When Lydia came to again, it was Marcus, in street clothes, sitting in the chair next to her bed.

Seeing her eyes opening, he took her hand and kissed the top of her head.

"I'm done in surgery, Lydia," he said. "How are you feeling?"

"How is your head?" she countered. "I know Simon stitched you up."

He laughed. "My head's okay, hard as ever. And you're okay, thank God."

She gazed up at him anxiously. "Are you really alright, Marcus?"

"Really am!" he assured her. "Simon saw to that. Last thing I remember, we were in the building, the ground shook and then a loud boom, and I was down. Next thing, I was out on the grass slope in cooler air... with quite a headache. Simon had pulled me out."

Clutching his hand, Lydia chuckled, "I don't think you'll be able to tease him about being strong enough to do push-ups anymore... And the last thing I remember was nursing the baby and then I was waking up here." She paused for a moment, lost in thought, then noticed the nurse walking by, with raised eyebrows at the sight of a different man at her bedside. Ignoring the nurse's gaze, Lydia became more pensive.

"You know something, Marcus," Lydia said at last, "Simon's sister, Rebecca, and Alice, Frank's wife, you know, they watch their husbands go off every day into the mountain... down into the mine. And they never know if their men will come back out at the end of the day. They live with that, day in and day out."

Marcus nodded, listening.

She continued. "When I saw you two coming into the kitchen covered in smoke and grime from the fire, I imagined what it was like for Rebecca and Alice. I'm very grateful that you and Simon don't work in the mines. It's hard enough, doing what you do. I don't think I would have the strength to live with that kind of daily uncertainty."

"But we did it in France, Lydia, all of us living one-day-at-a-time, never knowing if the Germans would overrun us or another shell would drop on us," Marcus reminded her gently.

She nodded. "I know, that's what puzzles me. What's changed? I should feel even more secure now, but I don't. I think I'm just so scared of losing everything we have now. I think there's something wrong with me."

Shaking his head, Marcus smiled with deep compassion. "There's nothing wrong with you. It makes perfect sense to me. We'll talk more later. I've got to finish up so we can all leave early."

He stood, and when he leaned down to kiss her head, his own began throbbing. He was just grateful that she wasn't as flushed now. And Lydia was left to ponder life briefly, then dozed off yet again.

Lydia was next awakened by a strange man at her bedside, wearing a white exam coat and calling her by name. "Mrs. Finney," he said. "Can you wake up for me, please?"

She roused herself. "Who are you?"

"I'm Doctor Weyland," he said. "I operated on you early this morning. Let's check you out and see how well I did!"

"Is my husband here?" she asked warily, not recognizing this man, and glancing around the recovery ward for any sign of Simon amid those milling around the various privacy screens in the room.

"No, I'll get a nurse, though." He motioned for the duty nurse, who came over to the bedside and rolled a privacy screen over to her bed.

"Do you need a speculum, Doctor Weyland?" the nurse asked.

He shook his head. "No. I'll see her in the office Monday for that. Mrs. Finney, I'm going to check you for bleeding and infection."

He opened her patient gown and pressed down on each of her breasts, squeezing the nipples gently, milk coming as he did so. "No pain?" he asked and saw her shake her head. "This is good."

"Only that they are very full," she said quietly, wishing he had not done that.

"You have no redness and no signs of mastitis," he told her. "It was one of our concerns regarding your high fever last night. You should be able to nurse without difficulty. Please roll over so that I can see how much blood is under you. It has a way of hiding."

Gingerly, she rolled. The doctor's eyebrows raised, and he glanced at the duty nurse but said nothing.

"Alright," Doctor Weyland told her. "I'm going to feel your uterus and make sure that it isn't soggy. Nurse, would you please?"

The nurse bent over Lydia. "Let's just raise your knees up."

"Can we wait for my husband?" Lydia said weakly. "He is coming soon."

Doctor Weyland looked down at her, kindly. "I need to examine you now, Mrs. Finney. The nurse will stay beside you."

Lydia closed her eyes, feeling the man enter her with one hand while he pressed on her abdomen with the other.

Is there no part of my body that belongs to me anymore?

The doctor was careful to be gentle and talked to her throughout the exam. "I had to go through your cervix in the procedure, but it will close now after the birth of your baby. Your uterus feels firm enough… and I don't see any more clots emerging after applying pressure. I believe that your bleeding has stopped. You'll recover quickly now." He withdrew and washed his hands in a nearby sink, then returned as the nurse covered Lydia again with the sheet. Lydia gripped the edge of it tightly, pulling it close to her body. She couldn't help but feel invaded.

"Thank you, Nurse," Doctor Weyland said. "Please leave us."

The woman nodded and turned away, passing out of sight, behind the rolling screen.

Doctor Weyland pulled up the same chair that Simon and Marcus had used earlier. "In my line of medicine, Mrs. Finney, I see and hear many things from women. Not all of them are pleasant, like the birth of a healthy infant."

Lydia froze in the bed, her anxiety climbing, although she did not know why. "Is there something wrong with me I don't know about? Will I not be able to have any more children? Oh, my God, please say that isn't so! I should have told Simon I was still passing clots, but I didn't know that it wasn't normal, right after a baby."

Doctor Weyland raised his hand to stop her. "Don't upset yourself, Mrs. Finney. You'll have more babies if you choose to. Your uterus didn't rupture. It's healthy now, or will be when it finishes recovering from this baby... in four or five more weeks."

"What is wrong then?" Lydia pressed him.

Doctor Weyland said very gently, "Who is beating you, Mrs. Finney?"

Her eyes clouded in confusion. What was the man talking about? Did he have her confused with some other patient? Then she realized... the scars that haunted her life... There was movement at the privacy curtain, Simon and Marcus coming into view, having finished up and eager to tell Lydia that they were taking her home.

"Simon," Lydia cried in dismay, trying weakly to sit up and reach for him.

He took the last five steps to the bedside as one. Taking her outstretched hand, he bent over and kissed her forehead.

"Simon, this doctor has just examined me," Lydia faltered. "He wants to know about... about the scars."

Simon gripped her hand securely and stood up, calmly looking down at a concerned Doctor Weyland seated by the bed. Simon gestured to Marcus and Lydia.

"We three all served in the war together, Doctor Weyland," he told the man evenly. "In the same medical station on the front, in France. My wife was taken prisoner by the Germans during the war, and she was injured by one of them while being held captive. Those are the scars you saw."

Marcus nodded, as if verification of his friend's story was required.

Doctor Weyland slowly inclined his head as understanding came. "Ah," he said. "I see. Forgive me, Mrs. Finney, but in my work, many women come to me who are living in difficult situations about which they are reluctant to talk. It's my duty to try to intervene for their safety, whenever I can."

Incredulous, Marcus chimed in, "And you wondered if Sim—Doctor Finney did that? To her?"

"It's my duty to protect," Doctor Weyland replied firmly.

Simon bent down over Lydia and caressed her cheek softly. "And mine as well," he told Lydia, offering her reassurance. "Are you ready to go home, beloved?"

She nodded quickly, one arm reaching up for him. "Oh, yes, please... if I can have this tube pulled out?"

Doctor Weyland's energy had shifted, "Of course. I'll write your orders."

"Then I'll go change out of these scrubs and be right back," Simon said, returning her arms to her sides.

"I'll be here," she said with a fragile smile.

Simon hurried out of the recovery, but Marcus lingered. Turning to Doctor Weyland, Marcus pulled him aside, "That's one of the finest men who ever walked the earth."

"I have no doubt... now," Weyland assured him. "I'll always seek the best welfare for my patients. As, I'm sure, you do also."

Content now that Simon's reputation as a husband was untarnished, Marcus replied, "Indeed I do."

He looked around for what he needed, to remove Lydia's intravenous. Marc really wanted to go home... his head was throbbing.

By the time they arrived home, Lydia was already improving, and quickly. Over the weekend, she was up and walking, her appetite grew, and she was able to go up and down the stairs with some confidence. Lydia fell into a comfortable routine of eating, sleeping, and feeding her baby. It wasn't long before she felt nearly back to normal... except for the distressing loss of muscle tone in her abdomen.

After her father had gone home, Anna stayed on, running the kitchen, rocking the babies, and mopping floors as needed. She insisted on also keeping Nikki home while Suzie worked. Anna adored the toddler and treasured this time with her tiny grandson. They took many walks in the stroller in the balmy afternoons of late spring.

By Monday morning, Lydia was gaining strength quickly. Simon kissed her goodbye before reluctantly leaving for the hospital. "Now remember, I'll be home to get you for a two o'clock appointment with Doctor Weyland, at his office."

"I feel fine, Simon," she protested. "I don't think I need to be seen."

"Yes, you do," he said firmly. "I'll be here at one-thirty to get you."

"But—"

"No buts!" he stated. "Not taking any more chances." His face had a don't-argue-with-me look, so Lydia said nothing further.

After lunchtime, Lydia washed up at the sink and nursed Jimmy once more. Knowing that Simon would be coming to pick her up soon, she tried on a light blue dress. Brushing her hair, she tied a light blue ribbon into it to keep it from blowing in the breeze. The dress was tight at her bust line from the changed dimensions of a nursing mother, but none of her dresses fit right anyway, so she decided to make the best of it. Anna took the baby up to rock him to sleep for an afternoon nap, joining Nikki who was already resting in her own crib.

Lydia decided to get some fresh air and wait for Simon just outside their front door. He had planned to borrow the automobile again from Marcus who was still in surgery. It was a warm day, with yellow and red tulips blooming along the house. She enjoyed seeing what the widow had planted in the yard, green shoots emerging... It was fun to try to guess what they might grow into. She was already planning a small vegetable garden for the backyard. The tree out back was in leaf. It was a maple and would provide much needed shade from the summer sun.

Simon pulled up to the sidewalk and jumped out of the car to open the door for her. He took one look at her in the sky-blue dress and whistled. "You look lovely," he said, admiring her. He leaned in to kiss her, "Voluptuous curves... you are quite impressively filling out that dress."

She looked down anxiously. "Should I go get a sweater?"

He laughed. "No, I'm just admiring the view."

"Oh, Simon," she sighed. "My waist is not at all what it should be."

He closed the door after she was safely settled in the passenger seat. "Everything about your body is beautiful. It has just given birth to my son."

In silence, Simon drove them through the busy streets and across the bridge. He glanced at Lydia, sitting quietly beside him, then turned toward a separate building near the hospital where some of the doctors had their medical offices. Finding a spot in the parking lot, Simon quickly went around the car to open the door for her. He wasn't sure she should even attempt to get out of the automobile on her own. Sure enough, as he opened the door wide, she looked up at him.

"Do I really have to?" she asked, not moving.

He reached in for her hand. "You really have to."

Supporting her firmly, Simon led her into the foyer of an office which smelled of antiseptic and alcohol.

"Lydia Finney," Lydia told the woman behind the desk.

"Hello, Mrs. Finney," the woman welcomed her. "Someone will take you back momentarily. Please have a seat."

Lydia looked around her. There were pregnant women, women with infants, and some men too, waiting for their women to return to them. One of them very courteously stood, motioning for her to take his seat. It looked as though Doctor Weyland was a very busy obstetrician. Too soon, a woman in a white nurse's uniform came to the waiting room and called Lydia's name. Simon stood with her, noticing the shift in the nurse's expression as he did so.

"I'm sorry. Men aren't permitted in the exam rooms," the nurse kindly informed Simon.

Lydia turned in the opposite direction, toward the entrance. "Then I am leaving," she declared. "I'm sorry for the inconvenience."

"Mrs. Finney, wait!" the nurse called in dismay.

Simon reached for Lydia's to stop her. "Lydia, you've met the man. It'll be alright."

"It's silly and foolish, I'm sure you'll both say. But I won't go back there alone," Lydia declared. "Did Doctor Weyland say that my husband can't go back there?"

"Doctor Weyland is detained at the hospital in a delivery. His associate Doctor Franklin is going to see you," the nurse explained in a reassuring voice.

Lydia pulled against Simon's hand as she headed toward the exit. "Well, I certainly haven't met a Doctor Franklin! I am going home now."

"Lydia, no," Simon insisted firmly. "You may not leave."

The nurse looked at Lydia anxiously and decided to give them a moment and take someone else into the examination hall instead.

Simon took both of her arms. "I'm not taking any chances that everything is okay," he told her. "We can't just leave, Lydia." He saw her eyes brimming with tears.

"Well, you just have an evil man hurt you down there, and you have a drunk man grab you down there, and you have a strange doctor put his hand inside there and squeeze your nipples, and then you tell me that I have to go in there, alone!" she declared fiercely under her breath, not wanting the other women in the waiting room to overhear as her tears threatened to rush down her cheeks. "You don't understand, Simon. Everybody else claims rights to my body. It's not that I won't do this... I can't do this! I can't. Not alone."

Simon held her fast. "Okay," he said, coming to a decision and raising a finger. "You won't have to. Do not... do not leave this office, Lydia!"

He headed for the receptionist desk, "I want to speak with this Doctor Franklin for a moment. Tell him it is Doctor Finney from Charity."

"Yes, Doctor," the woman said quickly, reacting to his authority and having observed the couple's exchange from afar. "I'll be right back."

Lydia waited, still standing, eyeing her escape route through the front door, her arms folded protectively across her tight bodice, wishing she had brought a shawl to hide herself.

A moment later, a tall, blond-haired young doctor emerged from the back hallway. He spotted Simon immediately, as he was the only male standing there, waiting expectantly. "Doctor Finney?" he said, approaching with an outstretched hand. "What can I do for a fellow Charity colleague?"

"A moment, if you would, please," Simon said, returning the handshake.

"Of course," Doctor Franklin said, leading the way into the back hall, the door whispering closed behind them as Simon mouthed the words to Lydia again: *Don't leave!*

Simon came back into the office, this time alone, and gently took Lydia by the arm. "We're going back now... it'll be okay," he said, leading her through the door. A nurse met them in the hall and led them to an examination room, where a gown lay on an exam table and a silver tray was prepped with bright, shiny instruments. The nurse handed her the gown and looked at Simon.

"Thank you, Nurse," he said, taking the gown from her himself.

Lydia stood motionless. They heard a tap on the door. The tall, blond doctor came into the room. "Please, Mrs. Finney, sit down."

She took the only chair in the room, and the doctor pulled a rolling stool nearer to her while Simon stood with his hand on her shoulder, keeping her focused.

The doctor took the lead. "I'm Mike Franklin, a new doctor to this practice," he informed her. "And you have just had a baby, congratulations. A boy, I think it is?"

She nodded, "Yes, a son."

"That's good. I'm happy for you both. I understand from Doctor Weyland's notes that you had a bit of a complication after the birth? And a procedure on Friday?"

She nodded. "I feel much better now," she admitted. "I'm not passing clots anymore, and there is just some light pink on my pads. I don't feel nearly as weak anymore."

He nodded. "That's all very good to hear. Are you eating and drinking enough for your milk to come in?" he asked.

"Yes, I believe so. I have lots of milk. The baby seems to get his fill when I nurse," Lydia confirmed.

"Also good," Doctor Franklin assured her. He chuckled. "You know, I'm glad to be back helping mothers and babies!" he declared. "It's so much better than doing battlefield surgeries over in Europe."

"You were overseas?" Lydia asked, surprised.

"Yes," he replied. "Southern France and Italy. Two years. I'll tell you, it's a miserable way to practice medicine with soldiers shooting at each other every day. Even worse for an obstetrician. There weren't very many babies to deliver along the battlelines."

Lydia looked up at Simon. "We were there, too!" she said softly. "I'm a nurse."

Mike Franklin appraised her steadily. "Wow," he said softly. "Bet we could swap some stories then. I met a nurse in the clinic, a blonde, Nurse Lovell. She said she'd been there too, along with her husband. Do you know her?"

"Why yes," Lydia said. "She and Doctor Lovell were in the same unit with us. They are very close friends. Doctor Lovell and Simon work together in the operating theater at Charity."

Mike's smile radiated compassion and calm. "And now, here we all are, trying to adjust to being home, trying to be normal. On top of that, you're adjusting to the birth of your son and dealing with complications. Isn't that just the way things go..."

She nodded, feeling as though he truly understood.

"Well," Mike said, "after all you've been through, I imagine this isn't the easiest thing for you, to be on the other side, being the patient. I'm sure you know how serious the placental tear was. My concern is that no infection sets in. I don't want an experienced nurse, with a newborn at home, to become infected. Doctor Weyland said he did an irrigation of your uterus. Probably not unlike what you did with wounds over there. I'd like to examine you and irrigate your uterus once more. Do you think you could allow me to do that?"

Lydia looked up at Simon. "Can my husband stay with us?" she asked.

"Of course!" Doctor Franklin said. "I don't expect any surgeon who has served at the front is likely to pass out in this office. It would probably help you if he could steady you, don't you think?"

With a rush of relief, Lydia suddenly let down her guard. "It would help me very much," she said, then gestured to the gown. "I hope you understand..."

Doctor Franklin glanced up at Simon who had just told him about her having been taken prisoner. Mike nodded and stood, "Yes. I think I do understand. I'll step out now while you put the gown on. Would you like a nurse to assist you?"

"That won't be necessary," she said softly. "Simon is here."

"Very good," he said, leaving the room and pulling the door tightly closed behind him. Only then did Lydia undress and accept the gown Simon was holding out for her to drape over her trembling body. She felt naked, even with it on.

Simon stayed beside her as Doctor Franklin talked her through the procedure. The doctor showed Lydia the speculum with its corkscrew handle. "Did you know that a French midwife named Marie Boivin actually invented the speculum for her practice, Mrs. Finney? I find that nurses often know what's best for patients. You're going to feel me insert it now so I can see better."

Lydia glued her wide, round eyes on Simon, who squeezed her hand reassuringly while he nodded to Franklin to proceed. He saw tears glittering in the corner of her eyes. *Better to get this over with as soon as possible*, he seemed to be saying without words as she looked up at him, feeling a bit helpless.

Doctor Franklin said, "Your cervix is still a little open from the birth. Even so, you're going to feel me insert a very small irrigation tube. The solution is room temperature."

Lydia's breathing quickened as she felt panic rising in her throat. "Sim—"

Simon took her face in his hands. "Look at me, beloved," he said softly. "Look right here."

When Mike Franklin finished the irrigation, he said, "The return fluid is mostly clear with just a little pink, sloughed tissue, but no bleeding. I'm removing the tube now. I think you're out of danger of any infection at this point. Have you had any fever since Friday, Mrs. Finney?"

She shook her head, somehow unable to speak aloud, so Simon assured the other doctor they had not noticed additional chills or fever.

Doctor Franklin nodded and stood. "Now, one more thing, Mrs. Finney, as I press on your fundus, you may feel some of the irrigation fluid come out." He stood and pressed her abdomen, feeling her uterus for firmness. "I'm finished now. I'll leave you to get dressed, and then I'd like to speak to you once more."

Again, he stepped out of the room, closing the door behind him.

"Simon, can you find a towel or something for me to wipe off with?" Lydia asked. "I'm all wet."

Simon looked in the cupboards and found a stack of clean surgical towels. He helped her reassemble herself and held her tightly in his arms for a moment. "You did great," he said softly, reassuringly.

Fully dressed again, she sat back down on the chair to await the return of the doctor.

Doctor Franklin tapped on the door before entering again. He pulled the stool up to Lydia, "I'm very sorry you've had the extra burden of all of this during an otherwise happy time. So, now, what I want you to do is go home and enjoy your baby. I don't anticipate any other problems. If something unexpected comes up, I'll be happy to see you again, Mrs. Finney, if you'll trust me to do so."

She looked at his honest, open expression and nodded. "It may be easier next time," she admitted. "But I hope I don't have to come back."

He laughed. "That's the great thing about surgery and obstetrics. We hope we do a good enough job that it puts us right out of business."

Leaving the office, secure in the knowledge that Lydia's health was improved, Simon felt immense relief. They got into the automobile and Simon started the motor. He paused briefly. "I have a quick stop to make before taking you home, if you don't mind."

She nodded, "As long as I'm with you, I don't care where we go, for a little while. But I do want to get back before Jimmy needs to nurse again."

He reached over the seat and squeezed her hand, turning down a busy street in the shopping district on Fifth Avenue. He carefully pulled the automobile into a space in front of a store called 'Feldman's'.

"What is this place?" Lydia asked as he helped her out of the car once more.

"You'll see," he told her, smiling. He took her hand as they entered the store. Lydia saw a maze of low glass showcases filled with beautiful baubles of glittering gold and shimmering gemstones.

"Simon," she whispered. "We said we wouldn't get rings just yet, remember?"

He looked into her eyes. "We have rings," he reminded her. "But you need this."

Simon approached the man at one of the counters. "Mr. Feldman, good to see you again," he said as if they knew one another.

"Ah, Doctor Finney, have you decided then?" The older man's tone was friendly as he looked up from arranging articles of jewelry in one of the showcases.

"Yes, sir," Simon told him. "The one you showed me with the sapphire set in the center."

"An excellent choice," Mr. Feldman nodded approvingly, though Simon thought the man would likely approve of any purchase he was about to make. He reached into one of the cases, pulled out a chain with something hanging from it, and handed it to Simon.

"Hair up," Simon ordered Lydia. She lifted her long waves from her neck and Simon fastened the necklace at the nape of her neck. The jeweler handed Lydia a round mirror. It was a gold locket with a central blue sapphire set within a star design on the lid. Seeing it against her chest, Lydia carefully pried it open, revealing the empty space within.

"Why?" Lydia asked Simon. "Why this lovely gift?"

"I want you to have something for a little lock of Jimmy's hair, or maybe even mine, or both, to keep us close to your heart. It's for the mother of my son."

Lydia handed the mirror back to the smiling jeweler and threw her arms around Simon's neck. "It's a lovely gift. Thank you, Simon. And thank you for being there for me today." She kissed him right there and then, right in the store, and only then did Simon agree to drive her home.

"But it's her first baby, Tommy," Peg said quietly from the kitchen sink where she was washing dishes. "We ought to be there for the baptism, don't you think?"

"No, I do not," he declared from the table, the steam from his hot coffee spiraling up into the air. "Don't need to hear some preacher spouting off the thou-shalt-nots as it suits them."

"What are you talking about, Tom?" Peg asked. "Rules are meant to help people live better lives, to be better people. That's all."

Tom took a drink, eyeing her carefully. "That so?"

"I think so. It wouldn't hurt to take our children to church once in a while," Peggy said. "Mom and dad took Lydia and me. You were taken as a child, weren't you?"

He folded the newspaper he was reading. "Yep. Every Sunday. Learned a lot about how things are supposed to be done."

Peg turned as she rinsed some plates. "See what I mean? It helped you grow then. I could be a good godmother for Lydia's baby."

"So, you would try to teach the kid how to live a godly life or something?" Tom suggested, taking a sip.

Peggy rinsed some silverware, placing it in the drainer. "I would! How to be kind to others, help take care of people who are going without."

"Charity," Tom stated.

"Well, not in a bad sense anyway. Charity really means loving, I think. You know, acts of charity are acts of kindness. Not acts of just giving away something for free."

"Churches never give anything away for free, Peggy," Tom declared. "They hand someone a hot cup of coffee and there's this little paper, goes right along with it about avoiding the fires of hell. Ulterior motives all the time. We'll give you a warm place to stay in a shelter as long as you listen to what a sinner you are."

Peggy carefully removed her apron and hung it on a rack to dry by the sink. "Is it so bad to want to save someone's soul?"

"Who's to say someone's soul needs saving?" Tom countered.

"I suppose only God can," Peg admitted. "But you can tell by someone's actions whether he's on the right track—"

"He?" Tom asked, his eyebrows raised. "You talking about me?"

Peggy quickly sat down at the table. "No, no, of course not Tom. I just meant the average person on the street."

"So, my actions are on the right track then?" Tom questioned her.

She hesitated. "Well, I suppose we all have room to grow, Tommy. I know I do."

"And where do you suppose I need to grow?" Tom asked, eyeing her critically.

"I, um..." Peggy started, suddenly feeling nervous. "Oh, hi, honey. What do you need?"

At that very moment, Steve came up to the table, by his father. "Hey Dad, would you help me later with a school thing?" the boy asked. "We have to make a castle, with a bridge that opens."

"Sure," Tommy told him, rubbing his hair. "Say, son. Do you think your dad is a good man? I ever treat you wrong?"

Steve looked up quickly, catching the inflection in his father's voice. "Never! You're the best, Dad!" he replied immediately. This was dangerous territory, and he knew it.

"Do something for your dad then," Tom said evenly. "Get the paddle off the wall. The long one."

Steven froze, wondering what he had said wrong. "O...kay, dad. Sure." The boy went to the wall by the basement door, pulling it off the wall where it hung by a little rope next to its companion. He took it back to the table and carefully put it down in front of his father. Both had holes, but once, this longer device had left long rows of round circles all the way across his butt that lasted days. He avoided this one at any cost. The smaller one used more often wasn't quite as bad...

Tommy picked it up. "I ever hit you with this one, unless you needed it, son?" he asked.

"N... no, dad," Steve stammered. "Only if I was really, really bad." He shot a look over at his mother, seeing her eyes wide with anxiety.

"And why is a good paddling a good thing, son?" Tommy pursued the matter.

Steve said quickly. "If a dad doesn't correct, then he's not a good dad."

Silence filled the kitchen as Tom examined the paddle in his hand carefully, blowing air through the holes as if dusting it off.

Steven said quickly, "Did I... did I do something really bad, Dad?"

Peggy said quickly, "No, Steven, you didn't do anything bad. Go work on your project."

Tom flashed a look at Peggy. "Who asked you, Peg?"

"Uh... no one, Tom," she stammered. "I just, he just needs to finish it..."

"And you think you could be a godmother to a baby? That you could teach one how to be good, how to obey the rules? To know right and wrong?" Tom chided her.

Peggy's face flushed. "Well, I think, for a baby, there are different rules, you know? Babies just want love, Tommy. That's all. I can love Lydia's son."

"Your son already knows how to be obedient better than you do," Tom said evenly. "You already got a son to love."

"I do love our son," Peggy said quietly, feeling the tears already coming.

Tommy looked at Peggy. "In the last half hour, do you know how many times you contradicted me, Peg?"

Peg flushed. "We were just talking, Tom. We weren't arguing."

"Nine," Tom said. "Nine times. I counted."

Her words failed her.

"Nine," Tommy repeated matter-of-factly. "You got nine coming. Get ready."

"Oh, Tom," Peg whispered. She grabbed the edges of the chair.

"Then ten. Depending on what you do next," Tom said, coming around the table to her.

Her eyes were already filled with tears... Peggy thought even nine would put her in the hospital if he made good on his threat.

The time in the hotel was awful, when he was drunk. Now, Tommy wasn't even drunk… for some reason that scared her even more.

"Tom, please. It took forever for the blisters to heal the last time," she whispered growing frightened, watching him move his coffee over to the counter so if the table moved it wouldn't spill. She was very much afraid Tommy was going to make the table move. Steve shot a look at his mother. Why didn't she just agree with his dad? Obey him right away? His dad might have been willing to settle for five like last time.

"You see, son, your mother still has trouble being obedient. For some reason, she still thinks she knows best. Or maybe she just enjoys being punished. You can leave now, son. So, then it's te—" Tommy started and slowly Peg did what she was told, the sob catching in her throat as Tom flexed his arm muscles. "You can blame your sister for this. Asking you to be a godmother when you aren't ready for it. Well, let's just get down to business now. Nine."

Tommy held nothing back, the air whistling through the holes in the long paddle.

From halfway up the stairs, after the first swat, Steve wondered how his mother could have managed to disagree nine times in just a half an hour. It seemed like a lot and his dad was taking his time with the correction. Number two hung in the air and Steve cringed, thinking about what it would feel like when it landed. His dad must love his mom a lot to try so hard to make her behave. His dad said it was a solemn obligation that he himself would have to do someday. She shouldn't have talked back to his dad.

"And why is it wrong for you to disagree with me?" Steve heard his dad ask.

Steve almost missed the muffled answer. "Because you are the man, the head of the house, and you know what's best."

After the second, his dad refreshed his mom's memory about how this was good for her soul. Aware that his father was not going to compromise, Steve knew there were still seven to go. Steve had to be man enough to do the same thing when he grew up. So, he went upstairs and found a frightened Mary holding her doll close to her chest.

"Put your doll away, Mary," he told her in her bedroom.

"Why?" she asked, clutching it to her.

"Because I said so, and I'm the man," Steve told her, waiting to hear number three from the kitchen.

"You aren't the man yet," she whispered. "You're still a kid."

Steve looked around and saw a ruler on her drawing table. "Bend over, Mary," he told her. "You disobeyed. You want me to tell Dad you disobeyed?"

Through the open bedroom door, Mary heard judgment being delivered and turned pale. "No," she whispered in terror. "Don't tell Daddy, Steve."

"Then do what you're told." And Steve repeated his dad's words. Stricken, Mary obeyed, bending over the bed where Steve pointed. He brought the ruler down on her hard, not knowing how to judge his own strength. He felt powerful delivering the correction as Mary whimpered. Keeping pace with his father, Steve hit his sister until she had red lines across her skin and tears like their mother.

Downstairs, Tommy appraised his wife. "You sure test my patience, Peg. Did you count? One more if I counted right. Next time, think twice before you listen to your sister over me."

Steven and Mary both heard their mother right through the floor.

Still holding the ruler in his hand, Steve shut the door part way, seeing his father dragging his mother, stumbling, tear streaked, upstairs to the bedroom.

"On the bed," Steve heard his dad tell her across the hall. "Now, thank me for stopping at nine. I'm feeling merciful."

She obeyed in a whisper. It had been ten.

Steven looked through the slit in the door, studying what his father told his mother to do next.

As soon as she could walk again, Peg stole away to the police station speaking quietly to an officer behind his tidy desk. She clutched her pocketbook in her hands trying to muster her courage.

"I'm sorry Mrs. Franklin, but the police do not interfere in domestic affairs of this nature between a man and his wife. Men have been correcting their wives since the beginning of time. It is their duty in most cases," he told her dispassionately.

Her voice faltered. "But... he is so strong. And it's cruel," she said in a small voice. "Don't I have the right to leave with the children?"

"You can leave, I suppose," he said. "But don't count on taking your children. He could just come and take you all back. Have you talked to a lawyer?"

Peg's eyes filled. "No. I don't have the money for a lawyer."

"Well, he hasn't broken any bones, right? You haven't needed any stitches, right? A few swats on nature's padding are an acceptable form of punishment under the law. My advice is go home, make him a nice dinner, bring him his paper, and show him that you love him."

Devastated, Peggy stood, leaving the police station to catch a trolley back to the house.

As the door closed behind her, the policeman picked up the telephone and placed a call.

"You'll never guess who just left the station, Tommy... Yeh, can you believe it?... I know, I know... I didn't think so either, Tom... Well, just thought you ought to know."

Tommy returned from work that day armed with this information. He kissed Peg hello on her cheek as she stirred supper on the stove. He laughed and joked with the children through the meal and suggested they listen to a radio program before bed. Sending them upstairs he reminded them to brush their teeth and told them to have good dreams. And after tucking them in, Peg returned to the living room where Tommy sat in his easy chair reading the paper. She saw the bottle of whiskey on the end table next to him, the large glass beside it already half empty.

"You tell your sister we aren't coming yet?" he asked her, glancing up at her over the edge of the paper and taking a drink.

Peggy nodded. "I called. Told them I was sick and we couldn't make it. Sent our regrets," she said quietly and headed into the kitchen to put away the dry dishes and make sure the kitchen was spotless before she went to bed. Suddenly the kitchen lights went out. Tom was right behind her at the kitchen counter. He put an arm on either side of her, pinning her against the cabinetry. She could see his face in the dim light coming from the living room.

"So," he started. "What did you do today, Peg?"

"Oh, you know. Errands. Cleaned a little. Made supper," she answered quickly.

"And went to the police station," Tom said, the alcohol thick on his breath. "What's it gonna take, Peg, huh? To teach you how to be respectful to me? You just don't get it."

She couldn't say a thing. He took her by the hand and pulled her out onto the dark back porch where a cool spring breeze whispered through the neighbors' backyards. Lights flickered from kitchen windows and back porches on either side of their house. Voices could be heard from open windows, cracked open to allow fresh air into the homes which had been long closed to winter. Stepping just inside the back door, he grabbed the longer paddle from the wall and returned to her outside.

"You made our business public," Tom said. "So, let's make it public business everywhere, Peggy. Just the way you want it."

Pushing her over the porch rail, he said, "Make as much noise as you want. Hell, let the entire neighborhood know! Let them hear you and look over here and see you bent over the railing getting what's coming to you. You want the world to know our business? Then we'll let the whole neighborhood see."

She was still blistered from the ten. The next-door neighbor sitting on his back porch, smoking a cigarette, looked over in the darkness as Tom started. Peggy tasted blood on her lip from biting down in an attempt to hold in her terror.

"You okay over there, Tom?" the man called out from his porch.

In shadow, Tom held up the paddle. "Just a little correction, Bernie. She forgot who's head of this house is all."

"It happens," the other man called back as his own kitchen door opened and his wife stepped out to see who had come by.

Following her husband's gaze, she saw Peggy just fifteen feet away, covered her mouth, horrified, and quickly slipped back inside the kitchen.

"No apology yet, Peg? For embarrassing me with Jack?" Tom demanded.

Gripping the wooden railing, Peggy hid her face in the bushes lining the porch as she heard another door open then bang shut. Bernie called over to the concerned newcomer, "Tom's just getting his house in order, Parker. A little family discipline. Nothing to be concerned about."

The man grunted, reaching over his own railing to accept a cigarette Bernie offered and let the man light it. They blew smoke up in thin streams that dissipated gracefully into the cool air. As Peggy let out a cry of pain, the two men nodded at each other knowingly. It wouldn't take but one more like that to get the neighbor's wife in line.

But Tommy said again, "I'm waiting, Peg. Don't hear any apology yet..." A window flew open.

"Everything okay down there?" a male voice floated down from a second-floor window of the house to the other side.

"It's just Tom's wife, Ricco," Bernie and Parker pointed. "Got out of line."

"Hey, Tom, might want to ease up a little there," Ricco called down in the twilight, the sound reaching the second-floor window. "Don't kill her for Pete's sake. You're gonna draw blood there, man!"

Tom raised the paddle. "You discipline your way and I'll do it mine," he called back, his voice now raised in drunken anger. "'Less she apologizes, she's gonna have to feel it."

"Geeze, Peggy," Ricco called to the neighbor woman whom he knew well through his own wife. "Apologize already, girl! What's the matter with you?"

Tommy was furious at Peg's silence. The wood railing creaked and there was blood on the paddle now, unseen in the darkness. Peggy had lost consciousness from the blistering pain. The neighbors slipped back inside their houses, shutting their doors, as Tommy unleashed his drunken rage.

Finally, Tom went into the kitchen and tossed the bloody paddle in the sink. She could clean it in the morning. He took a big swig of whiskey from the bottle before heading back outside to drag Peg into the house and drop her over a kitchen chair. Jaw clenching in fury, he stared down at her before heading upstairs to wash up and change his clothes. She hadn't told him that he was right and she was in no shape to be dragged up to bed for the customary apology.

Unsure of the time, Peggy roused, finding herself in the kitchen, alone, in the dark. She reached back and felt the sticky blood, already drying. Too weak and exhausted to do anything, she downed the remaining whiskey herself, straight from the bottle on the kitchen counter and stumbled into the living room getting as far as the sofa.

She had not apologized. It had almost cost her more than she could pay. But she hadn't told Tommy she was sorry... and she didn't intend to. She would have to see the doctor in the morning. At least the doctor would not tell Tom that she asked for help.

For efficiency, the baptism was scheduled during Andrew Blackwell's return visit to Pittsburgh, to see his wife home. Simon and Lydia had visited several of the small churches in and around their neighborhood. It seemed to them that each section of the city had its local pub, church, and market as if the city designers had planned some kind of checks and balances system for people to find a place to get food, pray, and unwind after work.

After meeting with several church leaders, they had decided on a small church that opted not to preach the customary fire and brimstone, did not demand a life-long membership to perform a Christian baptism, and requested a donation rather than charging a fee to the church treasury.

After discussing the baptism with Father Henderson, Simon rang his brother and sister, asking them to come and stand with Marcus, two godfathers and one godmother to guide baby Jimmy's immortal soul in the right direction throughout his life. Because of the distance between them, only Marcus could have an in depth meeting with Father Henderson, before the ceremony. Marcus had told Simon that he wanted to go alone.

After a hectic day at the hospital, Marcus walked into the quiet church, taking in the surroundings. The church was not large, but had a stained-glass window, behind the altar, depicting Jesus carrying a lamb in his arms. Along the walls of the church, there were candle holders between smaller stained-glass windows, depicting other scenes. Marcus was not quite sure who the people were, but most had halos over their heads. He assumed they must be biblical figures of great significance. The pews were wooden and cushioned. A prudent idea to give people comfort, he thought, in the event of a long-winded sermon. Father Henderson met Marcus as arranged, and they sat in the front pew where they could talk.

After introducing himself to Marcus, Father Henderson surprised him by asking a single, direct question. "Doctor Lovell, do you want to be this child's godfather, or did you agree to it out of courtesy, being a family friend?"

Marcus leaned forward, a little anxious about the pointed nature of the question. "Actually, Father, it's a little more complicated than that."

"Tell me," Father Henderson said, pausing as he waited for an answer.

"We, all three of us, served together over in Europe, in the war," Marcus explained. "Some things happened to my friends that resulted in me making a vow to God that I would always take care of Lydia, and then later, when she found out she was pregnant, to take care of their baby as well. I mean to carry that out regardless of whether I'm one of the baby's godfathers, or not. Simon's brother will also be one. But I took a vow, at any rate. I wouldn't even think of undoing that, and anyway, I imagine God would strike me dead or something if I even thought about breaking it."

Father Henderson smiled. "I don't think our Lord would strike you dead if you changed your mind. But it's commendable that you want to keep your promise, given that you're no longer in the war and circumstances have changed considerably."

Marcus folded his hands together. "It's a little surprising even to me. You see, I was never really much of a religious guy. I didn't have that kind of upbringing. But in the war, things take on a different meaning, if you know what I'm talking about. A lot of life and death to deal with. So, I'm a little new to... all of this." Marcus gestured toward the stained-glass windows and the altar in front of them.

"We all have to start somewhere," Father Henderson offered.

Marcus looked up over the altar. "Hm, indeed. Well, I started with a Catholic priest in Europe, who was able to help me understand the basics of it."

"Such as..." Father Henderson was curious.

"This whole thing of everyone sins and does things offensive to God. And since we can never make it okay, He did it for us. It's like when people come to me with an abscess in their belly or something ruptured inside. They can't do surgery on themselves... they need me to take it out for them. So, I'm the one that gets my hands in there, surgically speaking, to get it all cleaned up. Then, hopefully, they take care of themselves a little better. Or I suppose they come back for more surgery. There was probably more, but we got discharged, so I didn't get to talk to him again."

"So, you were starting to figure some of this out, and Doctor and Mrs. Finney asked you to be their baby's godfather?"

"Yeah, that about sums it up," Marcus nodded. "Lydia, Mrs. Finney, told me she wanted me to be the baby's godfather. Made the baby's middle name my name... which was pretty amazing, actually, to do that."

"Ah, the name of one of the early saints in the Church," Father Henderson said.

Marcus nodded. "So I'm told. A lot holier than I am, I'm sure."

Father Henderson looked as though he was about to tell Marcus a secret. "You know, as the baby's godfather, your role is to help the child grow in faith in God."

Marcus seemed taken aback. "Whew. Tall order."

The other man laughed out loud, seeming almost out of place right there in the front of a church. "It's not as hard as you think, Doctor Lovell. A child's faith is more straightforward than that of an adult, if it's encouraged early on. Children naturally assume there is a God out there. And if they have loving parents, they naturally assume God is a loving being as well. And if their parents encourage the child to come to them if they mess up, which they will, and the child sees the parent loves them anyway and will help them to get things right, then they naturally assume that God will love them and get them back on track as well, if they mess up later in life."

Marcus looked doubtful. "It sounds like you're saying the baby is going to be teaching me a thing or two about God, not the other way around."

"It is often a two-way street," Father Henderson observed. "Do you speak to God, Doctor Lovell?"

Marcus nodded. "We've been having some rather lengthy conversations lately about how things have been going, much to my wife's dismay, I'm afraid. She doesn't share that inclination right now, but tolerates me reading the Bible and things like that. Simon, Doctor Finney, told me that God doesn't promise to tell us why things happen, only promises to be there with us through it. That kind of made some sense to me. I can't tell one of my patients why they have a tumor growing in their chest, but I can tell them I'll help them get through the surgery and recovery."

"Did Doctor Finney say that?" Father Henderson mused. "Then I think you won't be guiding this baby into an understanding about God alone, godfather status or not. Doctor Finney has a good grasp of faith, it seems."

"I'll say he does," Marcus agreed. "Lydia, too. They are miles ahead of me. But at least I think I'm walking on the same road as they are now."

"Is your own daughter baptized, Doctor Lovell?"

Shaking his head, Marcus confessed not. "My wife and I haven't talked about it yet. After this, we're likely to bring the subject up, but I imagine it would be met with some reluctance. I don't think Suzie would like the idea very much."

Father Henderson stood and offered his hand to Marcus. "If I can help you and your wife understand baptism, I'm at your disposal. But I believe you're the man for the job, as they say, for Jimmy. You'll be the godfather that this child needs."

Marcus also stood up, assuming his interview, if that's what this was, was over. "So, I guess I'll see you at the baptism?"

"Indeed, Doctor Lovell, you will," Father Henderson called out as he turned to leave.

Peggy had indeed sent word through their mother that she was unwell, and that her family would not be able to attend the ceremony for little Jimmy. So, when the Sunday of the baptism arrived, it was Lydia's parents, Simon's brother and sister, and Marcus and Suzie, who were present to attend. They all walked together to the little church on the corner, not far from their house. A congregation was gathered within for the morning service, during which the baptism would take place. Marcus was wearing a suit and tie, which did nothing to hide his very apparent nerves. Suzie tried to reassure him that he would be just fine, thinking the whole event was rather unnecessary. Marcus took his cues from Simon, who appeared to be his usual calm, reserved self. Both Rebecca and Phillip had been present for many baptisms before, with each other's children, and seemed completely at ease and familiar with the entire process, down to the crossing of oneself and when the amens were due.

Father Henderson sat quietly as the congregation sang hymns and a deacon read passages from the Bible for those assembled. Then, everyone took a seat on the padded pews. In a conversational tone, Father Henderson began telling the group a story about a man who had had two sons, one of which was a dutiful man who helped his father, and the other, a son with a somewhat rebellious nature who ended up becoming destitute, but then decided to come home after all... where the father received him joyfully.

Marcus listened to the story, intrigued. He wasn't completely certain that he would have forgiven a son, after wasting so much of his life and resources. Then he heard Father Henderson say that the father had put his own ring on the wayward son's hand, and that act protected him from being disgraced, or worse, and that God does that for anyone who goes astray but returns to Him. Something about the story struck a chord within Marcus' soul. As Marcus joined Rebecca and Phillip at the baptismal font, standing with Simon and Lydia to repeat the words that Father Henderson asked them to say, he found himself contemplating a return to this church. Perhaps, he thought, he'd sit in the back and listen to more of what this man was teaching.

Simon was holding the baby. When it was time, instead of handing Jimmy directly to Father Henderson, Simon looked at his buddy and handed the baby to Marcus first. Marcus looked down at his tiny charge, thinking of the promises he'd made. He then handed the baby to the waiting priest, who sprinkled water over the infant's tiny head, three times, while saying prayers that Jimmy would never remember. He said the baby's name, James Marcus Finney, announcing it clearly to the congregation. *God, help me do this right,* Marcus found himself praying. *I don't want to make a mess of this godfather business.*

After the baptism, many people in the congregation approached Lydia and Simon to admire their son, congratulate them, and wish them well. Anna and Andrew Blackwell seemed quite happy and repeatedly thanked Father Henderson for planning the ceremony so that they could be in attendance while in town. While the others were engaged in conversation, Father Henderson handed Marcus an envelope.

"Give this to Doctor Finney if you would, please, Doctor Lovell," Father Henderson asked of him. "It's the baptismal certificate."

In turn, Marcus reached into the pocket of his suit jacket, retrieving an envelope of his own. "And please put this in the church account, or whatever, for doing this for all of us... By the way, really good story earlier, Father. Something I seem to be able to relate to somehow. Certainly worth thinking about a little more."

"The Bible has a way of doing that," Father Henderson smiled, hoping this young doctor would frequent his parish again in the future.

Marcus nodded with a new understanding that the story wasn't of Henderson's making. "Ah, you didn't write that little anecdote?"

Father Henderson laughed. "No, Doctor Lovell, our Lord wrote it. He's a much better storyteller than I am. But I do enjoy passing his stories along to others and I tend to do it often."

"Well, I'm sure you know many more. I'll have to come back," Marcus said.

Father Henderson shook the man's hand with a firm grip. "I certainly hope that you do, Doctor Lovell. Should you have any questions, I also have office hours, much like you doctors enjoy."

As the crowd began to disperse, Lydia took Jimmy back into her arms and softly kissed his tiny cheeks. Her heart was overjoyed to have family, with Marcus and Suzie, present for this occasion… though it was sad that Peggy had taken ill. She would call her sister on the telephone later, to check on her.

They all thanked Father Henderson and bid him farewell before beginning a leisurely walk back to their house. Abril, who had patiently waited just outside the red door of the church in the warm spring sunshine, joined them. Back at the house, Suzie finished setting out the special meal they had prepared, and they all took pleasure in being together, cherishing the rituals of life that gave it added meaning.

In the kitchen, Lydia took Marcus aside for a moment to thank him for his willingness to embrace his new role in Jimmy's life. "I'm so glad you didn't refuse," she told him gratefully, searching his eyes and noticing the thoughtfulness within them.

"Was that even an option?" Marcus asked her, confused. "I didn't think refusing was even on the table! Didn't want to offend God! And sure didn't want to offend you, Lydia!"

She quickly kissed his cheek. "It wasn't. But I'm still glad you didn't say no."

Marcus looked at her, his eyes glistening. "I'll do my best, Lydia. I will."

"I know," she said softly. "That's why I wanted you."

With that, they happily rejoined the others. Everyone made the most of the evening, enjoying the precious time with each other before heading back to their own busy lives.

Chapter 13

Building the Scaffold

"Goodbye, my dear," Anna Blackwell embraced her daughter, not knowing how the visit could have passed so quickly. "I wish I could stay longer, but I know you are in good hands."

Simon, cradling little Jimmy in his arms, stood by the door with Andrew, who was waiting patiently for his turn to hug his daughter farewell. "Take care of our girl," he ordered Simon, reaching out a hand. Simon nodded, shaking his father-in-law's hand firmly.

The house was going to feel so very empty. Marcus and Suzie had already left for a week, taking the train to Rochester, so Nikki could spend some time with the Boytons.

"Drive carefully, Dad," Lydia hugged her father as Abril sat dutifully by her side.

"Not to worry, dear," her mother assured her. "We won't go any faster than forty. Your father will see to that. I will ring you when we get home."

Lydia descended the porch steps, following her parents as far as the fence, waving as they began their trip home. Simon was just behind her, gently transferring Jimmy into her arms, then checking his pockets for trolley fare. He had waited to go into the hospital until the in-laws were safely on their way.

"I'm off then, too. Promise me you'll be alright," he said, kissing her cheek. "You can call me for anything, Lydia. Anything at all. They'll find me."

"I think we'll go for a walk today," she said. "It's lovely out and Abril seems anxious to be outside. Maybe we'll walk over to the hardware store and get some seed packs for the garden."

He nodded, kissed the baby, kissed Lydia, and hopped behind the wheel of Marc's automobile and headed for the hospital, thinking one of these days he should really purchase one of their own.

As Simon turned the corner at the end of the block, Lydia turned to Abril, who was waiting expectantly.

"Shall we walk now?" she asked the dog.

Abril thumped her tail loudly against the floor.

"I'll take that as a yes."

Lydia bundled the baby in a blanket and gently placed him in the stroller. She grabbed a light sweater to drape over her shoulders before stepping out of the house. As she walked down the neighborhood sidewalk, Abril trotted faithfully at her heels.

It was a beautiful, sunny day and many were out walking in the neighborhood. Maintaining a steady pace, Lydia hoped that the exercise would aid her in getting back in shape. They made it to the end of the long block and then turned right, toward the local stores. Seeing Officer Stevenson out on patrol, Lydia changed course to intercept her friend. When he spotted her, he stopped traffic at the corner so she could safely cross, along with a few other pedestrians who were going about their daily tasks. He then joined her on the sidewalk, excited to meet the neighborhood's latest arrival.

"Well, now, Nurse Finney, very good to see you and Abril out and about! And let me see the wee one. Ah, a boy, is it? That's just fine... look at him!" Officer Stevenson leaned over the stroller, utterly captivated by the infant. "Can I hold him then?" he asked. "Got four of my own, you know."

Lydia smiled at the officer. "I did not know that! Congratulations!" With care, she gathered Jimmy from the stroller and placed him into the big man's arms. "His name is James Marcus Finney," she proudly announced.

"Jimmy boy, it is then." Officer Stevenson said, looking oddly comfortable, holding the little baby, in his official blue uniform and cap. "Well, now, how about that? He's a fine boy. I'm glad for you and the doc." He looked down at the baby tenderly, adding, "You know, my own Mary Anne just loves the little ones. Ours are all in school. If you'd consider it, she might be very happy to watch little Jimmy... if you need someone. We don't live but a few blocks and around the corner."

Lydia hadn't yet considered finding someone to care for Jimmy if both she and Simon were working, but the realization struck her now... plans would need to be made soon.

"I'd love to talk with your wife about it," Lydia said, thinking of how she might be able to stop and nurse the baby between patient visits, perhaps. If the policeman's wife was anything like her kind-hearted husband, she would surely be a wonderful choice.

As Lydia took Jimmy back into her arms, Officer Stevenson placed a hand on her arm. "I heard you used the whistle, Nurse

Finney. Good girl! Glad you kept your wits about you and had it on you. Makes me feel much better!" He reached down and affectionately patted Abril.

"And glad Doctor Lovell fixed up your dog. You're a good dog, Abril," he added. "Say, did I hear right that Doctor Lovell and your own husband were down at the big steel mill fire?"

Lydia nodded. "They were."

"Brave men," he offered. "Look for the fire chief to be stopping in on you one of these days."

Lydia was glad. She already knew that they were brave men of course, but enjoyed knowing that others also recognized their merits. "They both served as surgeons in the war, in the army, you know, in Europe. They really are good men."

Officer Stevenson gave a little salute, his fingers to his hat as if Simon and Marcus were standing right there. "Well, keep it between us for now, Nurse Finney. Just don't be surprised if he stops in on your household soon. We stick together, us police and fire crews. Yes, we do... and take note of brave men and women."

She nodded, rising on tiptoe to kiss his cheek. "So do I. Have a very good day, Officer Stevenson. Say hello to your Mary Anne, from Jimmy and me."

Lydia set out again on her errand, leaving the officer to return to his patrol, whistling as he strolled down the sidewalk, twirling his nightstick. Along the path to the hardware store, they passed the butcher shop and she asked Abril to wait a moment. The dog sat dutifully just outside of the door, looking hopeful. The butcher spotted her there in short order and came out to them with a morsel for Abril.

"Ah, Nurse Finney! Abril! Good to see you out," the man exclaimed, peering into the stroller. "You had your baby, I see! Well, isn't that fine! Here you go, Abril. And you just wait right here, Nurse Finney." He disappeared back into the shop and reemerged with a wrapped paper package. "Here are some chops for you and Doctor Finney, for supper."

"Thank you, Mr. Johnson, you're very kind, but..." Lydia said in protest.

"Now, you helped my Sarah with her swelled-up legs... it's the least I can do," he insisted.

"Give her my best, please," Lydia said. "Tell Sarah it's a boy. Jimmy."

The butcher repeated the name so he would remember it. "I'll do that. Take care of yourself now."

By the time they returned to the house, Lydia was too tired for planting, and the baby had begun fussing... a sound she now recognized as hunger. She dropped the seed packets into a kitchen drawer and took Jimmy out the back door to sit on the porch swing where a great rhododendron spread its glossy leaves almost to the porch roof. Cradling him in her arms, she felt him seeking her breast, and her body responded instinctively. Settling into the swing, she watched as he latched on and began nursing contentedly.

"Such a good appetite!" she whispered. "You'll grow up to be as tall as your daddy, eating like this!" The warm breeze touched her chest as she fed him, and her hair blew lightly around her face. The newly turned soil from the garden bed smelled of potential life.

Lydia realized that, at least in this moment, she was completely at peace, for the first time in many weeks. She had been filled with joy at giving birth, and giving Simon a son. The temporary disruption of her complications was behind her now and her joy had returned. Her parents' baptismal visit had been relaxed and healing, erasing all guilt Tommy's anger had once imputed to her. Simon was thriving in his work at the hospital and would soon be walking through the door. Spring and summer were seasons of renewal, and in this moment, sitting on the porch swing with her baby at her breast, Lydia felt reborn. She thanked the Lord for the gift of the moment.

After his last patient, Simon straight drove home... he was energized. He'd had a good day in the operating theater, the cases coming through so smoothly that he had taken some of Marcus' cases in his absence. He felt productive yet was eager to get back to his family, knowing that Lydia and the baby had been alone all day, for the first time since Jimmy's birth.

As Simon drove, he replayed moments from the day. He thought of an encounter with Mike Franklin, in the hall outside of the surgery, after he had performed an emergency hysterectomy. Doctor Franklin had asked after Lydia, and Simon had happily reported that everything seemed to be going well, now. Taking advantage of the unexpected opportunity, Simon had thanked the doctor for his sensitivity to Lydia's needs.

"You were very good with her," Simon had told the man gratefully. "She had no lingering aftereffects emotionally, after you saw her in the office. That's a skill, Mike, to have that kind of sensitivity to women who were hurt like she was."

"*Thanks to your quick thinking,*" *Mike had returned.* "*I had no idea the nurses in the war up north had been on the front lines and exposed to so much hardship. The nurses in our unit were always back in the field hospitals. I think your wife is remarkably courageous.*"

Simon had nodded his agreement. "*I wish she never had to think about any of what happened there, it's bad enough for us just remembering how many bodies we tried to put back together—*"

"*And often failed,*" *Mike had sighed.* "*So many didn't pull through... or came back only partially whole. Did you know that Dixmont, up in the northwest, over on the Ohio, is taking a lot of the boys coming back with post-traumatic stress from the war?*"

Shaking his head, Simon had asked, "*Inpatient psychiatric care?*"

"*It's kind of in the country, a farm atmosphere. Hopefully, a healing environment for those who saw too much over there. Of course, the place is named after a nurse. Gotta tell you, Simon, we owe a lot to the nurses.*"

"*That we do,*" *Simon had readily agreed.*

Curious, Mike Franklin had added, "*I would've been out of my mind knowing my wife was taken prisoner by the Germans.*"

"*I try not to think about it,*" *Simon had said truthfully.* "*Occasionally, she still gets night terrors... I have to talk her down... bring her back.*"

"*More than understandable,*" *Mike had replied.* "*No wonder she gets frightened when men, even doctors, need to mess around down there. Let's meet for lunch sometime, Simon. I appreciate that you actually understand what it was like over there. I'm still getting used to the routine here at the hospital. And there are times that I have complicated abdominal surgeries from uterine cancer tumors or tubal pregnancies. It would be good to have a surgeon to call on in a pinch."*

"Glad to help anytime," Simon had assured the other. "Lunch sounds good this week. Right now, though, she'll be looking for me to get home."

Simon had taken an instant liking to this young doctor, who had much in common with Marcus and himself. The three of them would have to get together, maybe have him over to the house sometime.

Simon realized that he had arrived home and parked on the street. Running up the walk and gently closing the front door behind him, he found the house was as quiet as a tomb.

He started anxiously up the stairs, but stopped abruptly, realizing that the kitchen door was open, a nice breeze flowing through the house. He headed for the back porch.

Quietly opening the screen door, he saw Lydia on the swing, her blouse open, the baby at her ample breasts, the breeze moving through her long brown hair. She was humming a little tune for their son. Simon stopped, taking it all in, wanting to preserve this image of her, securely in his mind, before interrupting the moment.

She had a soft, contented smile on her face, as she gazed down at their son, and a much healthier glow to her cheeks, for which Simon was more than grateful. Abril looked up, acknowledging him, from her spot on the wooden boards of the porch where she was stretched out, relaxing. Simon ached for Lydia with every fiber of his being. The many weeks of abstinence had built to this moment, right here on their back porch, as she sat nursing their son.

Closing the screen door behind him, Simon leaned over and kissed her as Lydia looked up at him. Her eyes were warm and completely at peace. Simon dropped to one knee beside the swing.

"He's sleeping?" he asked softly, touching the baby's little cheeks. Jimmy was still loosely attached to her nipple, sucking reflexively with his tiny eyelids closed.

She nodded. "He just finished up and dozed off."

Simon tenderly took the baby from her. "Let's go in," he said, his voice catching in his throat.

Lydia nodded, pulling her blouse together.

"No, Lydia, leave it open," Simon requested softly, with a little smile. He ran a finger lightly over her breast. "It's most becoming."

Lydia's heart began to race with a new hope.

Together, they went in through the kitchen, and as Simon glanced back at her with her open blouse, Lydia followed him up the stairs of their quiet house, to the bedroom. Simon placed the baby gently in his bassinet. Lydia's heart was pounding just from Simon's earlier glance. Then he turned from Jimmy and gazed at Lydia standing there before him. He reached for the open blouse and caressed her breasts.

"How I want you," he exclaimed, softly taking her into his arms.

"It's not safe yet, is it?" she asked, hoping he would say that it was.

"I can make it safe," Simon replied confidently.

She took his bearded cheeks in her hands and kissed him. "I can't even take a bath yet for three more days."

"Then we'll stand in the tub and wash each other," he suggested, leading her down to the bathroom. He set the water running in the tub until some steam emerged, gathering soap and sponges.

Lydia waited. After the birth, after all of the medical procedures, after her body not belonging to her, after months of everything being obstetric and clinical, she just wanted Simon to simply be her husband. "No more medical things, my love, no more home doctoring," she pleaded. "Just be my lover, Simon. I just want... you."

Simon shed his clothing, removed hers, then took her hand as she stepped into the tub. "I promise to just be your lover," he agreed.

They stood in an embrace, lathering each other with warm, soapy water, reconnecting with sensual touch, rinsing with water from heavily saturated sponges. Lydia took her time washing Simon in an encouraging way until he smiled at her with deep longing, but shook his head.

"Oh, woman, there's nothing left... except for the lover part," he said with a little smile, leading her, still damp, from the tub to the bedroom... their clothing, still in a heap on the bathroom floor.

Simon picked Lydia up, laying her gently on the bed, her breath catching in her throat. As he embraced her, he didn't need to say how he would make it safe. The restraint he exercised only fueled the ache within her. Hovering over her, he tenderly gazed down at her body. Hearing her sigh of happiness as he gave himself to her for the first time in weeks made his heart rejoice. Now nothing hindered their joining except caution for her continued healing.

"My beloved wife," he murmured in her ear as he moved ever so gently.

"...oh... Simon..." she suddenly cried out with her arms around his neck.

Simon knew Lydia would still be tender after her delivery, but he did not have to be cautious with his lips and was not restrained in using them. Smiling, he gazed at this precious woman beneath him, thanking God for the privilege of giving himself to her.

Simon brought Lydia supper in bed. Finding leftover chicken, grapes, thick slices of bread with butter, he carried the meal up to her on a tray. It was a warm evening, and she was resting, still naked on top of the sheets, right where he had left her. Simon gazed at her, not wanting to awaken her just yet.

Pulling the easy chair next to the bed, he watched her, while the curtains in the window moved gently from the late-day breezes. His life was full... complete. He thanked God again that he and Marcus had both made it safely out of the mill fire, that Lydia was healing, that the baby was healthy.

When she stretched and awakened, she saw him sitting there, watching over both her and their son.

"Don't get up yet," he told her. "I'm enjoying the view."

Lydia laughed softly, teasing him. "You've certainly seen it often enough. Aren't you getting a little tired of it?" Nevertheless, she paused, luxuriating on the bed as the warm breeze flowed over her skin.

Simon leaned forward in the chair, touching her ankle. "Tired of this?" he asked. He moved to the edge of the bed, working his way up her leg. "Or are you thinking I'd be tired of this..." he added, now sitting on the bed, pursuing his quest to find out exactly what she thought he'd grown tired of.

Lydia laughed again, feeling like her body had been restored to its rightful place as his wife and lover. "You were very gentle with me…"

Looking relieved, he stretched out beside her. "That was the idea," he said, kissing her belly, as he had countless times before.

"No baby in there anymore," she noted. "And still a bit loose."

"I reserve the right to kiss you anywhere I want," he murmured. "Especially after six weeks and three days, fourteen hours, twenty minutes, and twelve seconds of waiting for this. Being beside you in this bed, night after night, not being able to—"

She interrupted, "Heroic restraint to be certain."

Sliding up over her, Simon kissed her neck. "You have no idea…" He moved further down. "Hm. Appears that you're getting ready to feed our son soon—"

She looked down at herself, "I don't think that was from Jimmy needing me, my love. I think you did that."

His hands explored her curves. "There's still a little time for us, before he needs you."

Her eyes widened. "Really?"

"I'm just going to lay to rest any concerns you may have had that I'm 'tired of the view'," he smiled. "Let me enjoy making you happy," he added as he reached for her with a gentle hand.

Having returned from their trip to Rochester, Marcus, Suzie, and Nikki were getting settled in, up in their bedroom. Lydia had made a pot roast to celebrate. Bathed in juices and surrounded by carrots, celery, onions and potatoes, it was a hearty meal for some healthy appetites. On his way home, Simon had picked up a loaf of fresh bread from the bakery as well. Lydia walked the yard, picking some of the gorgeous spring blooms and crafted a bouquet for the center of the dining room table. She paused for a second and surveyed the scene, satisfied. The windows were open, inviting a warm breeze to flow through, carrying the aroma of the pot roast to every corner of the home.

In no time, Marcus was bounding down the steps and into the dining room, stopping to kiss Lydia on the cheek. "Does that ever smell wonderful! You've outdone yourself!" He appraised her in her flowing summer dress. "Are you the one who had a baby not even two months ago? Can't be the same woman! Look at that tiny waistline!"

"The very same," Lydia smiled.

"Beautiful as always," he said appreciatively and she blushed, to his delight. "I'm hungry. Hurry up, everybody!" he called out to the others.

"Simon is getting a bottle of wine for you two, from the porch," she informed him.

Suzie briskly entered the dining room, her blonde hair pulled up to help keep her cool in the warm evening air. She was wearing pants and a tucked-in summer blouse.

"What on earth have you got on?" Lydia exclaimed in delight.

"Got them for horseback riding in New York. I love them," Suzie stated, turning around so that Lydia could see her new outfit.

"I want some!" Lydia declared quickly. "Even if they aren't legal!"

Marcus ran a hand along Suzie's hip as she took a seat beside him at the table. "They do fit rather well," he observed. "Better not wear them out on the street, though, or you'll stop traffic better than Officer Stevenson. That's why they're illegal. You'd mess up the order of morning traffic, create accidents galore, distracting all of the drivers."

Suzie smiled and kissed the top of his head. "I only need one man distracted by me."

Marcus raised his hand, volunteering, just as Simon stepped through the kitchen door, Abril trotting by his side and a bottle of wine in hand. He passed the bottle to Marcus, then gave Suzie a low whistle. "Wow! Susannah! You look fantastic. Pop the cork, Marc!"

They began passing the plates to Lydia to serve up the meal.

"Load me up," Simon requested. "I'm starving tonight and it smells wonderful."

Both women just smiled at him. "You starving is nothing new!" Lydia declared, filling his plate and then turning to Suzie, "I want to hear all of the news from Rochester. How was the visit? How is your family? Did it take forever to get there?"

Suzie recounted the highlights of their adventure to the Empire State and her home, making memories with family and old friends from school. Suzie's folks, Vanessa and Wayne Boyton, had understandably declared the visit not nearly long enough.

Watching as Lydia listened enthusiastically to their stories, Marcus was pleased to see that her energy was back to its normal level and her cheeks were now a healthy pink.

At a lull in the stories, Lydia pushed back her chair and stood. "That's my cue." She placed her napkin on the table.

"What—" Simon started, looking up from his plate of seconds.

"It's Jimmy," she said.

"I didn't hear anything," Simon said... then added, "Oh, now I do. How does she do that?"

Marcus shook his head. "They have a gift," he said, helping Nikki mash up the potatoes so her little spoon could better corral them.

Kissing the top of Simon's head, Lydia went up to get Jimmy from his bassinet. She brought him down to the living room, where she could feed him and still overhear her friends, not wanting to miss out on any of it.

Sweet little dear, she thought to herself, looking at her son, whose newborn wrinkles had already smoothed into gentle plumpness along his tiny arms and legs. Lydia got comfortable on the couch while Abril settled at her feet. Lydia put the baby to her breast and listened to the conversation from the other room.

"I talked to Maloney about the idea of the surgical clinic," she overheard Simon telling Marcus.

"What did he think?"

"Liked it. Said it could set a precedent in the city for bringing care to urgent situations. He wanted to know how to word the description for a potential newspaper ad, to make sure people understood they couldn't show up for a ruptured spleen or something."

"Local police might appreciate a place like this, too, and firemen," Marcus said thoughtfully.

Suzie interjected, "Let's try to avoid massive fires! What about near the docks, along the river?"

"Has to be on a trolley line." Simon thought aloud, imagining how people would access it from multiple areas of the city.

"You know," Marcus said, "this would be good experience for the medical students. Get them comfortable with quick interventions and minor surgeries."

"True," Simon added. "And taps into the teaching goal Maloney suggested to us, on hire. Are you still in to help us out, Suzie?"

"Absolutely. I miss doing surgery," she said enthusiastically. "Have to run it past Sister Edwarda, but you know that she's all about taking the care where it's needed most."

Lydia listened to them talking with so much energy... in full problem-solving mode. She was content to nurse her baby and let them hammer out the details, knowing just how much thought Simon had already put into the idea. The baby began to relax. He was staring up at her with his blue eyes fixed on her face. She noticed that he often stared at her while nursing, after the first frantic suckling had been satisfied. "What do you think, Jimmy?" she asked him softly. "Should your daddy teach medical students all about emergencies and doing stitches? He's really very good at it. He sews even better than mommy does."

In that instant, Lydia noticed Abril's ears perk up and her body go on alert. The dog was making quiet, repeated woofing sounds, at the door. Lydia hastily pulled her bodice shut and buttoned it. With that kind of warning, the subsequent knock on the door didn't surprise Lydia. Baby in arm, Lydia got up to answer it, with Abril close at her side. She pulled open the door and almost fell backward in shock.

"Oh, my goodness!" Lydia cried out.

Simon heard her from the dining room, threw his chair back from the table, and rushed to the front door. As soon as he could see the door, he stopped dead in his tracks. "What the—?" he exclaimed so loudly that Marcus leaped from his chair and dashed to the door.

"Well, I'll be!" Marcus said under his breath, skidding to a halt, nearly colliding with Simon, who remained frozen in the foyer.

Standing in the doorway was Harold Stockton. With him, was a woman they could only hope was Tess, along with Marlene Sullivan, Nancy Mitchell, and Sally Winfield. They were all beaming with huge, excited smiles... all fully aware that their planned surprise had been a complete success. They tumbled in through the front door to the foyer, not waiting for an invitation from their stunned friends.

"We brought champagne!" Harold exclaimed with a wide smile, holding out two bottles. "Not that some of you can enjoy it, I see!" He gestured to Lydia with the baby in her arms, adding, "So this is who you were incubating over in Belgium, I see! Congratulations to you both! Simon, it sure is good to see you! Marcus! Can't believe you're here too! Tess, this is Simon Finney and Marcus Lovell, the doctors I've told you about. And Lydia, a nurse from our station."

"Marlene, Nancy, Sally!" Lydia said in a rush, trying to hold the baby and embrace all three of them at the same time. "I can't believe it! I can't believe you're all here! How did you find us? Doctor Stockton, Tess waited for you after all?"

"She did," Harold happily replied. "Even though many of my letters never made it to her. But your letter made to us, Lydia! Remember, you wrote us in France. Everyone read it at least three times, so your whereabouts were no great secret."

Lydia took the hand of the woman standing at Harold's side. "Tess, it's wonderful to meet you. That man pined away for you the entire time we were in France and Belgium! Are you two married then?"

The woman, Tess, held out her left hand with a gold band on it. "We are," she said. "And believe me, I've heard stories about you folks many, many times."

Just then, coming up from behind, with Nikki in her arms, Suzie joined the unexpected reunion. Harold recognized her immediately, "Well, how about that! Nurse Boyton, if my eyes don't deceive me."

Marcus wrapped an arm around his wife, pulling her toward him. "Now Mrs. Lovell, Harold," Marcus proudly announced. "And this is Nikki, our daughter."

Harold paused. "Well, I'll be!" he wondered aloud. *No wonder Suzie had gone home. It's all making sense now.* "She's a beautiful little toddler. Looks just like you, Marc."

Marlene, Nancy, and Sally looked at each other in an unspoken understanding, nodding in agreement. The older baby was the spitting image of the only man who could be her father.

Nancy quickly chimed in, "Looks like our visit is long overdue! It appears we have some catching up to do!"

Marlene looked down at the dog who was sitting alertly by Lydia's side. "Lydia, this cannot be Abril? Abril is still with you?"

At the sound of her voice, Abril stood on her hind legs, affectionately laying her front paws on Marlene's waist. Abril knew all of these humans, except for Tess. And she was as excited to reacquaint as her humans were.

Harold knelt down, taking the dog's face in his hands. "Good to see you, girl."

Simon warmly invited them into the dining room.

"Come in, come in—there is room at the table. And possibly some pot roast left, if you're hungry."

Marlene headed for Suzie, extending her arms toward Nikki. "May I?"

"Sure," Suzie replied as Marlene gently took the child. "What's her name again?"

"Marcie Nichole," Suzie replied. "We call her Nikki—"

"So, tell us, Marlene!" Marcus exclaimed. "What's the good news about you? Are you in?"

"I'm in!" Marlene replied, eyes sparkling as she admired the dark curls on little Nikki. "I actually started in January, in Baltimore! And I'm happy as all get out... taking biology and chemistry and physiology. They are teaching us where everything is... the liver and the spleen."

"Which you've seen a thousand times, from the inside out!" Marcus exclaimed. "You could teach it yourself. That's great, Marlene... truly! Really glad they accepted you to medical school."

"So! You're really going to be a doctor, Marlene," Suzie was thoughtful. "I've got to say, you always had the highest aspirations of any of us nurses."

Marlene kept her eyes fixed on the little toddler and slowly shook her head, as the group settled in at the dining room table. "I don't know about that. Seems like your own aspirations were on the high side too. Married to Marcus now, and already having this beautiful daughter. That's about as good as it gets in my book."

Laying out the last container of leftovers he could find from the icebox, and resuming his seat at the crowded table, Simon turned to Harold. "What about you, Harold? What are you doing these days?"

"Tess and I have settled in Maryland, near Hopkins," Harold reported while handing a dish to his wife. "In general surgery. Far cry from operating in a tent with rainwater dripping into open patients!"

Nancy interjected, "Or by flashlight without any other power available. Lydia, we all read your letter about starting work in the city and the clinic at the hospital. Do you really like what you're doing, going out in people's homes like that?"

"My goodness, yes," Lydia told her enthusiastically. "We're allowed to think for ourselves and use our own judgment, and that's remarkable given the current climate for nurses. Suzie is working there, too, and if Simon and Marcus open their walk-in surgery clinic, we'll be able to help there, too. Assuming Sister Edwarda, who runs the community outreach, approves."

Nancy looked at her wistfully. "Any chance she would hire another nurse?"

Suzie shot Lydia a hopeful look. "I'll bet she would, wouldn't she Lydia?" Suzie asked. "She wants to expand the program. Would you want to move here, to the city, Nancy?"

Nancy nodded, "I'm tired of waiting for a charge nurse to tell me what to do... every minute! What about you, Sally?"

"I'd consider talking to someone about a job like that. I like the idea of seeing patients in their homes... or in a busy clinic. Why? Are you thinking we could share an apartment somewhere, Nancy?"

"We shared an eight-foot tent for two years! Why not?" Nancy laughed.

Delighted, Lydia jumped in. "Sister Edwarda says she appreciates nurses like us, being able to think on our feet as we do. Out in patient's homes, we never know just what we'll find as we walk through someone's door. We can help you both get established, can't we, Simon? We would need to get them over to meet with the sister."

Simon nodded, smiling at her. "Our house is open to anyone from the clearing station. We've got a couple unused rooms on the third floor. All of you can stay now if you want to spend a few days with us. The more, the merrier." Simon reached for the baby, "Lydia, let me take Jimmy so you can finish your own supper!"

Surveying Marcus now holding Nikki again, and Simon with his little baby, Harold marveled. These young surgeons, with their families, gave him a great deal of satisfaction. They had both made it home, in one piece, after the war and their lives were moving forward. It was so gratifying.

Lydia looked around her full dining room table with a happy smile. Everything was coming back around full circle, and she wanted it to last as long as possible.

As the evening drew on, Harold Stockton decided they'd had enough champagne and that it would be wise to spend the night. They retrieved their overnight bags from the automobile and four of the guests climbed up to the third-floor rooms, while Nancy volunteered to sleep with Nikki in her room. Lydia loved having the house full of loved ones again. They ended up talking late into the evening, long after Jimmy and Nikki had gone down for the night. It was a time for reminiscing about the war stories and the battle of Cambria, which the station had endured after Simon, Marcus, and Lydia had left for home.

"Is anyone from our original group still over there?" Suzie asked Harold.

He nodded from his spot on the floor near Marlene and Tess. Abril was lying with her head comfortably resting on Marlene's lap. "When we left, Charlotte Stein was still there with Mary Atkins and Alice Miller. Gretha Bernstein made it home to the family farm, and Linda Trent left at the same time. Of course, you knew Linda Bertolli left us to go be with David Winston at the British CCS. We lost contact with her after that. They all may be home by now. Everyone took down your address, Lydia, so you may hear from them before the rest of us do. Our replacements arrived near the end of December and Fortraine got them acclimated to the routine. We took off when it was bitter cold again. Really nice to be back... with real furnaces."

"And hot running water," Sally agreed.

Suddenly, Lydia thought of the beautiful French nurse who had come to replace Suzie, jumping right into the surgery eagerly. She asked, "What about Monique?"

Nancy smiled knowingly. "She stayed with Fortraine. Do not quote us on this, but we're pretty sure she was pregnant when we left!"

"No way!" Suzie exclaimed. "Three babies coming out of that war? Is that even possible?"

Nodding, Sally said, "She didn't come right out with it. But she certainly seemed very pregnant, all the symptoms. I guess Doctor Fortraine and Monique hit it off pretty well. Their baby will be born crying en français."

Taking a gulp of the wine, Marcus tried to slow his pounding heart. *It can't be possible!* he thought anxiously, quickly piecing together the timeline. He had ended things with Monique when Simon went missing. It was... it was September, when Marc had turned his full attention to helping Lydia make it through Simon's absence. *Could Monique have concealed four months of pregnancy... until January?* Of course, the nurses hadn't known Suzie was pregnant at four months when she had left either. *No... no. It couldn't be! But, at least, France is far away.* And by all accounts, Monique was with Fortraine now. And Marc was married to Suzie. His heart thumped so loudly he was afraid the others could hear it, Marcus drained his wine glass, refilling it immediately.

Simon sat on the floor, leaning against the sofa, resting his arm on Lydia's knees. "How bad was Cambria, Harold? We saw it in the newspapers last winter after we had come back."

"Ended in December sometime," Harold said. "Lots of tanks... over seventy thousand killed, some say. It was more of the same, Simon. War doesn't change too much. The new guys who replaced you and Marcus in November got the hang of things quickly."

Marcus looked around the group. "Well, there's no choice but to get the hang of it quickly, that's for sure. With Verdun, there wasn't any time to waste. Constant bedlam from the minute we got to the station. The brightest spot in the entire war was when you nurses showed up that spring. Looking back, I don't know how we ever got through Verdun without you."

"Verdun was still going when we got there," Suzie recalled. "That was our introduction to nursing on the front. What an eye-opener."

"Not nearly as many casualties, with Cambria, compared to Verdun or Ypres," Nancy observed. "Though, even one is too many in my book. It took a while to get used to being home and it being quiet all night... not waking up to the sounds of planes and shells. I think the silence was the hardest for me to adjust to."

Sally looked down at her hands. "Not for me. The hardest thing for me was getting used to sleeping at night. We got so used to being up for a four o'clock shift in recovery that sleeping in short snatches became normal. I still find myself waking up every four hours and not knowing why I'm up. So, if you find me roaming the hall in the night, I'm just wondering who needs a dressing changed or something for pain."

Nancy patted her arm. "It's only been five months, girl, give yourself time to readjust. It'll happen. But if not, you can always work night duty somewhere!"

"What do you think I'm doing now?" Sally exclaimed. "That's why I volunteered for it at the hospital. If I'm up anyway, I might as well put the insomnia to good use."

The little group fell silent, remembering the station each in his or her own way, both the victories and the nightmares.

"It was easier for me, coming home to start medical school," Marlene admitted. "The demands of school were welcome distractions, and I can still feel like I'm doing some good when I get to round with the doctors on staff. You all know I want to be a surgeon, so I spend as much time as I can in the operating theater, even watching from the gallery, just seeing how things are done here. Talk about modern!"

Nodding, Marcus agreed. "That's what Simon and I thought, too. Just getting used to the anesthesia, the equipment. I gave up all the shoestrings in my pockets and I've even learned how to operate wearing gloves!"

Simon laughed at that. "You almost took them off more than once when we first started at the hospital... Marcus said he couldn't feel the arteries as well with them on, as he could with bare fingers. I think they threatened to transfer him to housekeeping if he didn't keep the gloves on!"

"You've complained enough yourself, my friend!" Marcus countered. "You also said the gloves were slippery."

Simon laughed again. "I don't think I said that."

"Well, if you didn't, I was thinking it then," Marcus admitted. "Or else it's the champagne talking."

Harold glanced over at Tess. "Speaking of champagne talking, I want to go to bed while I can still make it up two flights of stairs. What do you say, Tess?"

"I'm ready," she admitted. "Although it's quite interesting to hear all of you talking about your war experiences. I admire all of you so very much."

"Forgive us, Tess, for not asking sooner," Lydia said before the couple went up, "but do you work somewhere?"

She stood and smiled. "I do. I'm a history teacher. So I enjoy hearing your stories. One day, they will be the history worth repeating for students who weren't there. I make mental notes of everything I hear. Right from the horse's mouth and all that, you know."

Marcus looked up at her from his comfortable spot on the floor. "Just forget the housekeeping thing okay? That wasn't true. They didn't threaten me with a mop-and-pail transfer."

She smiled kindly. "Already erased from the blackboard. Not to worry."

"Well, good night, then," Harold said, joining his wife. The other three nurses also stood and stretched, adding their good nights, deciding the day had been long enough and the champagne good enough to warrant their waiting beds.

"I'll go up with you, Nancy," Suzie told her friend. "In case Nikki wakes. She's a pretty good sleeper, though. She probably won't even hear the door opening, but if she does, I'll roll her crib into our room."

They all quietly ascended the stairs to ready themselves for bed while Lydia, Simon, and Marcus remained behind in the living room. Abril made her way over to lay at Lydia's feet, beside Simon. Marcus remained stretched out on the floor, and Simon remained against Lydia's lap as she stroked his hair.

"You boys both need haircuts," she noted, running her fingers through Simon's brown locks. "Tomorrow, I'm shearing you both, on the back porch. Plus, I want a curl from each of you for my locket."

"I saw your new locket when we got back. Very pretty," Marcus observed quietly. "Well done, Simon! You have very good taste all the way around. Sure is good to see the others again."

"And good to know they got home in one piece," Simon observed quietly. "We didn't lose anyone close. That's pretty amazing when you think about it."

"It is amazing, alright," Marcus agreed. *We didn't lose Simon to sepsis, or Lydia and Charlotte to the German prisoner of war camps either...*

Lydia was thinking, *and then we almost lost both of you to a fire at the mill...* wishing that the thought hadn't jumped back into her mind again so easily.

"Sounds like things have settled down up there. I'm going to take a quick bath," Simon announced after a bit, getting to his feet and kissing Lydia on the top of her head. "See you upstairs, soon."

She nodded. "Bring Jimmy down, would you, Simon?" she asked. "I'll feed him before we go to sleep."

He nodded, disappearing upstairs then returning with Jimmy, who was still dozing but would awaken soon for his next feeding. Lydia took the baby into her arms and rested him in the crook of her elbow, stroking his fine, gossamer-soft hair.

"Thank you, Simon," she said tenderly, still in awe of her son. Simon kissed her again and went back up the stairs to quickly claim the bathroom.

Marcus and Lydia remained, comfortable in the living room. He had something he really needed to ask her, but did not know how to start.

Jimmy stirred when his minuscule internal clock woke him. Putting the baby to her breast, Lydia was happy he immediately began to nurse. She had something she wanted to ask Marc, the question from the recovery room that was still unanswered.

"I remember," Marcus said, in quiet reverie, still stretched out on the floor, "feeling his first movements inside of you, the miracle of him fluttering that night in the tent when you shared it with me. Didn't I say that he was going to be a boy that night? With that first over-the-goal kick?"

"That was the first time I knew it was the baby and not indigestion from something the cook had served us in the station," Lydia said gratefully, with a tender smile toward the man sprawled out on the floor. "Marc, you promised me weeks ago, in the recovery room..."

"...that we would talk?" he finished for her. "I remember."

"You said there wasn't anything wrong with me," she reminded him.

Marcus looked up at her from the floor, where he remained, relaxing. "There isn't, Lydia."

"Then why is it that someone can be more afraid after something is all over than during it?" she wondered. "I don't understand."

Marcus put his hands behind his head and stared up at the ceiling. "Well, I suppose in the middle of things, you just try to focus on how you're going to get through it from one minute to the next, like we all did over there, especially while Simon was missing. The sense that everything important might be gone, any second, was all around us, and we knew it... so only each minute counted. We didn't think about how to feel about the future because there might not be one."

Lydia stroked her baby's cheeks, enjoying the soft sounds of him feeding. "But later, when the danger has passed, or I think it's passed, why am I still afraid of losing all of the good things in my life... instead of just being grateful for having them, now?"

Marcus paused. "What are you afraid of losing, Lydia?"

"I'm not sure... everything I guess," she admitted. "Maybe I'm afraid that this is all too good to be true. Other people endure so much loss and pain. Why shouldn't I also have to endure loss and pain as so many others have? Why would God allow me to keep things so wonderful... when others have lost everything...

arms, legs, loved ones? I shouldn't be the only one spared. And the longer I hold on to the good, the harder it feels it would be to have to let it go, if ever I'm asked to.."

Now, Marcus sat up, cross-legged. "I don't think you were spared pain and suffering, Lydia. You've had more than your share." *And some things worse than the rest of us.*

She assumed he meant when Simon was missing. "But that was different because I was carrying his child, and I knew there was a part of him that would remain, that I could hold onto if he never returned. And you were there for me every step of the way, Marc, letting me know I wasn't alone. We all went from death, and shelling, and danger, and hunger to... all of this. Comfort, warmth, jobs, this house, marriages... dear little Nikki, and this precious baby boy. It could all be taken away in a heartbeat." *Or in a fire...*

Getting to his feet, Marcus sat on the sofa next to her. "Yes, it could. And you were thinking of that when Simon and I went down to the mill fire, weren't you?"

Lydia looked up, tearful. "Yes," she whispered. "When you two came back all covered in smoke and ash, and your head was bleeding... knowing that both of you could have been killed, instantly, when the wall collapsed... and I still wasn't well from the birth. I felt so helpless. I wouldn't have survived if I'd been asked to give everything up that night. I wouldn't have, Marc."

Marcus put his arm around her shoulders. "You would have survived it because you are a strong woman with a strong faith that God has a plan for your life. And then every single minute of good you've collected in memory would have given you comfort. Remember how you got through the trench? When Abril brought you Simon's identification medallion? It wasn't the metal tag that got you through, it was every single moment of what that tag represented that got you through it. It was the reminder of how much Simon loved you. Or that white stone on the mantle over there... Simon told me that he pulled it out of the Meuse for you when you were on your way back to our station from your marriage in Nancy, and were facing more danger and hardship. He said that it represents his commitment to protect you and care for you. You see, Lydia, that each one of the moments adds up to something that can sustain you. The good moments in life become planks for the scaffold inside of you... to hold you up while you do repairs if hardships come."

Lydia looked down at the baby at her breast. Tears slid down her face, and Marcus wiped them gently from her cheek.

"Simon and I have many things in common," Marcus reminded her. "One of them is to give you as many good moments as possible so that your scaffold is strong."

"I... I want to do the same for both of you," Lydia whispered, looking up at him. "But I feel like I am leaning on both of you too much lately and not giving enough in return."

Marcus stood, smiling gently. "You have already given us more moments than we have a right to, Lydia."

They were quiet, both looking at the little baby in her arms. Then almost as an afterthought, and before he lost all of his courage, Marc cleared his throat nervously, "Uh, can I ask you something personal, Lydia?"

"Certainly," she nodded, surprised he would ask a question that way... after all they'd been through together. Something deemed too personal, for them?

"Um, did you... were you aware if... that is, I mean, did Monique say anything to you, directly... you know, before we left the station, to suggest she might have... been pregnant?" he asked, anxiously stumbling over his question.

Immediately, Lydia assumed the reason behind him asking. Of course, she knew that Marc had spent time with Monique. "She did not tell me that she was pregnant, Marc. And I didn't see any signs of it," she told Marcus gently. "There were no whispers among the nurses either. No rumors. Were you with her right before we left?"

"No. I, uh, I stopped spending... time... with her completely when Simon went missing," Marcus confessed. "When they couldn't find Simon, I only wanted to try to help you get through it all. You and your pregnancy became my sole focus. Monique was a live-for-the-moment-in-case-we-die relationship that I certainly regret now."

"I understand. I think chances are slim that she was pregnant when we left, Marc," Lydia reassured him tenderly. "Simon was missing so long we thought he wasn't coming back, remember? I think I would have been told if Monique was pregnant. Just like I knew about Suzie."

His shoulders sagged. The other nurses had indeed confided in Lydia as their leader. If Monique had not suggested anything to her, maybe it was all okay. *Maybe I'm not the father of her baby after all.* "You must think I'm a horrible guy right about now, Lydia. I'm so sorry."

She was still cradling Jimmy against her but reached out a free hand to take his. "Marcus, I think you are a wonderful man. I understood then why you were doing what you were doing with the other girls. I know you wrestled through things with Simon. When I see how you've grown, the husband you are to Suzie, the strong love you have for your daughter, I'm in awe of the man of principle that you've become. You were just starting the journey back then. And we're all on the journey together now, aren't we?"

"I think you've arrived. You and Simon," he said, his eyes filling.

"No, I have not arrived, Marc. I have a long way to go until the anger and... and something even more... is gone from my heart. You know I still struggle with what happened to me and how I feel about the German commander. I'm not sure how to... well, my soul isn't in the right place about it. I don't even see the way out of this yet."

He glanced at her, nearly overwhelmed by the compassion in her eyes as she looked directly into his own. She really didn't think he was a lost cause! And he was grieved to his depths that she was still suffering. "I'm so sorry, Lydia. How I wish that any of us could have taken that pain for you!"

"And I wish that you will let go of any burden about Monique's baby. It's unlikely and anyway, what's done is done. Doctor Fortraine and Monique have formed a relationship. And we must leave it at that. Let them build their family without interference or speculation."

He nodded, truly accepting her advice. "Well, then, I think I'm going to let Abril out and then head up. Are you ready to sleep soon?"

"I am," she said, putting Jimmy to her shoulder as she stood. Leaning up to hug Marcus, she kissed the stubble on his cheek. "Good night, Marc. Thank you, for being you. I'm so grateful that God gave you to Simon and Jimmy and me."

"Good night, Lydia," he said and, turning to Abril, added, "C'mon girl." Before turning in himself, he headed to the backyard with the faithful dog as Lydia went up the stairs to find Simon waiting for her in their bed.

"What was that all about?" Simon asked her quietly as she settled Jimmy into his bassinet, and he heard the back door closing and Marcus' footsteps finally coming up the stairs. Lydia turned off the lamp on the wall and slowly undressed in the ambient light from the windows. She did not reach for her nightgown. He saw her locket still hanging around her neck. Simon pulled back the bed sheets for her as he watched her and waited, hoping.

Lydia sat on the edge of the bed by him, touching his chest gently. "Simon, what did you do with your identification tag?"

"It's in the footlocker with your blue dress," he assured her. "With my discharge papers and the rest of the—"

Interrupting him, she nodded. That was all she wanted to know. "Good," she sighed. "I'm glad it's safe." She slid in next to him and snuggled her head beneath his beard adding, "Marc was worried that Monique's baby might be his. He asked if any of the girls had said anything to me before we left Europe."

Simon's eyes widened in the darkness. "Oh, man. Again?"

She nodded against his chest. "It sounds like it could be a close call. I have no doubt he'll talk to you about it, but I suggested that he let it go... let them build their family free from any rumors... but he may need his friend to help him figure this out."

Stroking her long hair, Simon held her close to his chest. "His choices keep catching up to him, don't they? I'm so grateful we did things the way we did."

"Yes," she whispered, keeping her voice low so Jimmy would remain asleep. "Little Jimmy is so very ours. And I am so very yours. And you, my love, my precious husband... are about to become very much mine... again."

Lydia took one of Simon's hands in her own and turned it palm side up. Bringing it to her lips, she kissed his palm and each one of his fingers in turn, and his body reacted immediately. Taking his other hand, she repeated the gesture. Lydia began inching her way down his body and Simon hungered for her.

"Got something on your mind, my beloved?" he murmured happily.

"I certainly do," she whispered. "I intend to give you a... special... moment." Her moment very nearly consumed him as her locket dropped cool against his skin.

"Lydia," Simon groaned softly after a short while, his body aching. "You need to come up here to me..."

"Do I?" she whispered, lingering a little longer, delicately increasing his desire.

"Oh... you do!" he returned, matching her tone, pulling her up to him and rolling her onto her back... hovering over her as his lips found hers. She ran her fingers down his spine as Simon kissed her deeply. They joined together in one intense, enduring moment... time... fully suspended. Simon froze, just gazing into her eyes looking back at him in perfect trust. She was so beautiful. She was his heart and soul.

"I love you, Simon," Lydia whispered, her arms wrapping around his chest and down his body to caress his hips. "Have you any idea how much I love you?"

Moving gently, Simon pursued her until Lydia's breath caught. He leaned on his elbows over her briefly, watching her enjoy her moment, stroking her hair, kissing her neck, her cheeks, her lips. Then Lydia wrapped her legs around his hips and whispered, "I want more, my love..."

He was happy to oblige. He was breathing hard as they found that place of joy together. Then resting his forehead against hers, Simon whispered, "I'm not exactly sure what this was all about tonight. But whatever it was, I'm grateful for it... and you!"

"That's exactly what it was all about," she murmured, content... secure in the knowledge that she had just helped his own scaffold grow a little stronger.

Over the next few days, their guests continued to stay at the house, taking in some of the sights of a city, the museums, zoo, and historical sites... which pleased Tess no end. Sally and Nancy had also secured an interview with Sister Edwarda regarding the expansion of Charity's clinic and community outreach services. There was a promise that the hospital budget would be reviewed to assess the availability of positions to strengthen the program. Sister Edwarda had wanted teams of nurses, and suddenly here was another team! She seemed enthusiastic about trying to make it work.

It was late afternoon when Lydia began working on dinner for everyone. Simon was entertaining Jimmy in the living room, when there was a knock on the door, yet again.

"I'll get it," Lydia called to the others, wiping her hands on her apron as Abril joined her in the foyer to open the door. Swinging it wide, Lydia was not the least bit surprised to see the fire chief standing outside of her home. Officer Stevenson had prepared her for this visit, which, as promised, she had kept secret from Simon and Marcus. Reaching out to shake his hand, she welcomed him, "Please come in."

"Are Doctors Lovell and Finney about?" he asked her, his uniform cap in hand.

"They are," she smiled. "I am Mrs. Finney. They're both home," she assured him happily, knowing exactly what was coming next.

"Who is it, Lydia?" Simon called, preparing to gather up the baby and come to the door.

"Fire department," Lydia said, leading the way into the living room as Marcus and Simon shot looks of concern across the room at each other.

It must not be an emergency, they both thought, since Lydia didn't look alarmed in the least.

Getting to the visitor first, Simon extended his free hand. "I'm Doctor Finney. What can we do for the fire department?" he asked curiously.

"Chief Watson," the man returned, shaking Simon's hand heartily. "May I speak to you men in front of all of the others here?" He gestured to their guests.

"Certainly. This is Doctor Lovell," Simon said as Marcus approached curiously, extending his hand to the chief.

"Sure hope there isn't another mill on fire!" Marcus exclaimed suddenly.

The chief laughed. "Not at all. But it's just that, that brought me here."

"Do you know how the man did? The one who lost his leg?" Marcus asked.

"He's recovering, thanks to you two," Chief Watson said. "Unfortunately, the man who was badly burned did not pull through, or the one with such bad smoke inhalation... he didn't make it either."

"Sorry to hear that," Marcus said regretfully. "I'm sure the hospitals did everything they could."

The man nodded. "Well, let me get right to it. I am here to extend an invitation from the mayor and fire department to see both of you men at the mayor's office on the first of the month at four o'clock. The city would like to formally thank you for your help."

"Oh! That isn't necessary," Simon assured him. "We were glad to do it."

The chief nodded. "I appreciate that. Nevertheless, you've been invited to the mayor's office the first of the month at four o'clock, your wives too. We certainly hope you'll show up, so the mayor isn't standing around waiting for no reason."

Simon and Marcus exchanged glances. "Of course," Simon said. "Please let him know that we'll be there, but thanks is not necessary from our end. In fact, Chief Watson, we'd rather talk with you about a logical location for setting up a walk-in surgical clinic for men or women with minor injuries who might not need to go all the way to a hospital. We've spoken with our administrator at Charity about locating a clinic near the docks or the factories or wherever injuries are most likely to happen for our city's workers."

The chief looked surprised. "Really? That'd be real good for the crews. I'll share that with the mayor. Maybe he could spare a few extra minutes that same day for you to explain what you're thinking of doing."

"We appreciate it," Marcus added.

The chief returned his cap to his head. "Then I'll be on my way. Dinner will be waiting for me, too. Yours smells mighty tempting. If I stay any longer, I'll steal a seat at your table."

Lydia walked him to the door, thanking him for his time. She returned to the living room where Simon was still standing, an odd expression on his face.

"You weren't at all surprised by the chief's visit, were you, Lydia?" Simon asked.

Her eyes twinkled. "Not at all," she replied. "Knew all about it. Sworn to secrecy."

Suzie got up to help Lydia plate the meal. "She didn't even tell me!"

As the group gathered at the table, Marlene spoke up, "I think there's another story that needs telling! I'm totally in the dark, but very intrigued that our two doctors are being recognized by the city?"

Harold nodded. "I'm curious too—not surprised though... not with these two."

Reluctantly, Simon and Marcus told the tale, leaving out some of the details, which Suzie was happy to fill in. And Marcus couldn't help but enjoy the group's reactions when he recounted the bit about the wall falling down around them.

Nancy looked around the table. "Looks like we're going to have to move here just to keep an eye on everyone, Sally. Apparently, there's a lot of excitement going on in this city!"

"And plenty of things to see. We didn't even scratch the surface this trip," Sally agreed. "I have no doubt we'll do lots of interesting things here, if Sister Edwarda finds room for us in the budget."

"If there is a way, she will," Lydia assured them both. "This is her passion, reaching out to the city. She wants teams of nurses going out."

"We're a team already!" Sally exclaimed, gesturing to Nancy.

"Have you ladies ever been nervous about going into people's houses?" Nancy wondered.

Lydia looked at her friend across the table. "You can ask that, after what we went through in France? Nothing compares to that!"

"Well, sure. But we had each other, after all... living, eating, and breathing each other's air."

Appreciating that there were differences, Lydia explained, "True. We've found here, though, that help is only just around the block. We've built a good relationship with the police and, as you've seen, the fire department. The neighborhood people appreciate what we offer them. Before my time off, I had some German families who felt ostracized, with the war going on... afraid even to go to the clinic. Bringing the care to their homes made a world of difference to them."

Nancy looked surprised. "It's not their fault the Germans are at war in Europe."

"I know," Lydia agreed. "I feel the same way. But they're getting associated with the enemy. It's quite sad actually."

"Wouldn't surprise me if they have extended family over there. People are often first or second-generation citizens here. I wonder if they know people fighting—" Simon added.

"Or people who died…" Harold said quietly. "How would word ever reach them here?"

"I imagine it doesn't," Marcus asserted. "America is helping France push them back though, so maybe the war will be over soon. I doubt our guys will have to serve as long as we did. Six months maybe, tops."

Harold had been thinking the same. "Agreed. I think we were there during the worst of it. Maybe, soon, everyone will be able to get along again, if the German army can see its way to a surrender."

"Meanwhile," Lydia continued. "We're just going to take care of anyone who needs us, no matter where they're from, just like we did at the station.

"Tess, I remember the first time a German boy came into the surgery tent. It was your husband who operated on him. He only saw a young man, whose spleen had been nearly obliterated… who would have died without immediate help. Harold left what he was doing right away… without hesitation."

Beaming with pride, Tess squeezed Harold's hand. "One of the things that attracted me to Harold was his compassion. He didn't go into medicine for status or glory. Where we grew up, he was the kid on the block always helping others… those who fell out of a tree or flew off the swings. But I didn't know your station took care of German wounded as well as the Allies, Harold. Of course, it makes sense, being on the front line as you were. I just never thought much about who would have been coming through your camp. Were civilians there, too?"

Harold shook his head. "Civilians were farther from the front lines. Their villages were already in ruins by the time we took the ground. Most of them had barely a wall left standing. The countryside is littered with craters and abandoned machinery from both armies. In some areas, not a single tree remains. There will be a huge need to rebuild when the fighting ends."

Tess listened intently. 'I wonder if the world will come together to help them rebuild. Where will Europe stand in twenty years, by the time another generation has grown up... when our children come of age?"

Sally sighed deeply. "In a better place, I certainly hope. Meanwhile, Lydia, we left our addresses with Sister Edwarda, and also told her she can reach us through you. Make sure to ring us right away if you hear anything that sounds like a job offer!"

"And if we do get the go-ahead, please come and stay with us until you find a place you want to rent," Lydia assured Sally and Nancy. "Our door, as Simon says, is always open."

Chapter 14
Making a Difference

"You aren't going unkempt!" Lydia exclaimed. "So come out here and just sit down. And Marcus, you're next, so don't you dare disappear on me."

Simon obeyed, following her out to the back porch, where she was waiting beside a kitchen chair, hair scissors in hand. Sitting as directed, he stayed still, allowing her to wrap a towel around his shoulders. "I do love it when you cut my hair," he admitted. "It's just that Marcus and I are drawing up plans for the surgical clinic... trying to figure out a budget for the equipment and the cost to rent a space."

Lydia took a comb in one hand, smoothing his hair in preparation for the shears waiting in her other hand. "All very important, I realize. But, goodness, my love, you're meeting with the mayor of Pittsburgh!"

"He's just like the rest of us," Simon tapped a finger on the arm of the chair. "Well, maybe with a little more authority, but still, an elected official, representing the rest of us. In my book, Officer Stevenson does a more important job, keeping our neighborhood safe... especially when you're out there with Abril."

Lydia ran her fingers through his hair, lifting it so she could taper the sides behind his ears. "Speaking of which, I do want to go back to work, Simon."

Having dreaded but anticipated this moment, he closed his eyes. "I figured you'd bring it up sooner than later. Do you really think you're ready, Lydia? You went through a lot. It wouldn't hurt to take just another month off, would it?"

He heard the scissors snipping away and felt the small hairs tickling his neck as they fell. She brushed them away on the early summer breeze giving him a shiver.

"Hmmm, there's a good one," Lydia murmured. "Hold still while I cut off that little wave."

"Just one?" he asked, puzzled.

"For my locket!" she whispered. "It's perfect." She showed him the small curl of brown hair and placed it in his palm, closing his fingers over it. "Don't let it blow away."

"I suspect there's more where that came from, beloved," he observed dryly.

"But I like this one, so please just do what I ask," she smiled.

"Yes, ma'am," Simon murmured as she trimmed along the back of his neck, chills running down his spine. Suddenly he forgot all about his equipment list and budget—

"Spread your legs, please," she instructed him, now moving to stand between his legs to tend to the front and even out his beard.

Simon breathed in the scent of her as she stood so close to him. "You realize if you stand there long enough, we won't make it to the mayor's office at all. You smell of perfume, and baby milk, and everything womanly," he murmured, his eyes closed. "The baby milk is a surprisingly nice addition…"

"The meeting is not until tomorrow, my love," she said softly. "Lift your chin for me, your beard is next."

As she took her scissors to his cheek line, he lifted his chin, relishing her touch, and slipping into a dreamy state. "That's exactly what I meant. I could keep you busy... all day... night... straight through till tomorrow—"

She laughed softly. "I doubt it! You have that budget you're drawing up for equipment for the clinic... and designing the space for..."

He reached up and took her hands, mindful of the scissors. Pulling her closer, his gaze leveled with her blouse, he nuzzled his face against her and teased, "Wanna bet I couldn't keep you busy all night?"

She leaned in to kiss him gently. "I'm sure I'd lose. You have a wonderfully insatiable appetite. Now, let me look at you." Lydia pulled away and walked around him. She appraised her handiwork with a critical eye, snipping here and there, making sure it was satisfactory. Then, she reached for the new Gillette she'd purchased. "Don't move, I'm shaving your neck and don't want to nick you."

"I thought that was supposed to be one of those new safety razors?" he asked, but remained still for her anyway.

"Behave!" she admonished him, then finally brushed the loose hairs from his neck and shoulders with a towel. "I'm pleased. You're the handsomest man on two continents! Now, you're ready for the mayor."

Simon rose to his feet. How had a haircut, in her hands, become such an intimate experience? He pulled her to him, kissing her longingly. When their lips finally parted and his eyes met hers again, he could see that he had rendered her breathless.

"Either you pay very well for your haircuts... or that was quite a tip!" she exclaimed. "I'll put you in my book for two weeks from today, same time, same porch."

He headed back into the house as she called in through the kitchen door, "Marc, you're next!"

Marcus passed Simon, saying, "I added a counter along one wall for clean instruments and another for dirty, so we have a dedicated area ready for procedures. Take a look at it when you get a minute, will you?"

"Sure. But you won't be thinking about much of anything after a minute out there," Simon warned him, glancing over his shoulder to where Lydia stood waiting with her scissors.

Marcus' hair was much wavier than Simon's, and he had no beard to trim. "You're certainly overdue for a cut," Lydia observed. "With these curls of yours. Now just hold on, I'm going to wet your hair first." She slipped into the kitchen and filled a small bowl with warm water, then returned to the porch. Dipping her hands in it, she ran her dripping fingers through his hair, wetting it down before combing. "That's better. I don't want this coming out lopsided. I know you like it a little longer than Simon does..." She moved around behind him and ran the comb through his dark brown curls, finding the length she thought he would want. Then, she trimmed the arc around his ears before tapering the back to fit.

"Where did you learn to cut hair?" Marcus murmured, quickly falling under her spell, as all thoughts of the clinic evaporated from his mind, just as Simon had said they would.

"Long time ago, doing my own and my sister's hair... even my friends," Lydia paused briefly, lifting his chin. "Marcus, you're acting like this is the first time I've given you a trim!"

He sighed deeply. "I just appreciate when you do it rather than the barbershop. When you were resting from Jimmy, Simon and I both went over to that place on Fifth Avenue. It's just not the same, believe you me. Bunch of guys talking politics and football... smoking cigarettes... not anything like this."

She snipped away at the side of his head, layering the curls after wetting his hair once more. After a few moments of quietly shaping his hair, Lydia broke the silence, "I'm starting back again, Marcus."

"Where? The clinic or people's homes?" he asked.

"I think the clinic at first, if I can, so I can still easily nurse Jimmy," she said thoughtfully. "Have to speak with Sister Edwarda about it. But if you men don't want to go back over to the barbershop, I'll make sure there's always time for your haircuts here at home. You can leave your two bits in my cup."

"Hmmm," he said, his eyes closing again.

"Make some room, please," she said, stepping around to stand in front of him. He obliged, sitting still as she carefully styled the curls framing his face. Tilting his chin upward, she surveyed her work with a satisfied smile. "With this breeze, the back is already dry again. Let me make sure I didn't miss anything."

She moved around behind him to run the comb through, then took one more snip of curl. This one was going to go into the locket with Jimmy's and Simon's. She blew away the stray hairs after shaving his neck and brushed them from his shirt. "You look splendid!" she exclaimed, happy with the outcome. "Ready to be the center of attention at the mayor's office with Simon. I hope someone takes a picture of you two. If they do, I want a copy to frame."

Simon and Marcus had left work a little early to be able to make it to City Hall by four o'clock, as Chief Watson had instructed. Both wore suits with vests, looking quite handsome by any account. The invitation had been for the families to attend as well, so Suzie and Lydia chose two of their fancier dresses for the occasion. Lydia wore her locket with the small snips of hair inside, each carefully tied with a different color of thread. The women even decided to snap on earrings, for this celebratory meeting with the mayor of Pittsburgh.

In the late afternoon sunshine, Marcus expertly maneuvered the automobile between police vehicles, delivery trucks, and other cars ferrying people to City Hall on official business. He found a parking spot close enough to the Mayor's office and all six of them hopped out of the automobile and made their way toward the large, impressive entrance.

The building was an enormous stone structure with ornate gas lamps flanking the door. The door to the office was half glass, with the word "MAYOR" in large black letters across the frosted glass window, marking their destination clearly as they walked down the tiled corridor among people of every background, all headed to their various destinations.

"Nervous?" Lydia asked softly as Simon ran his fingers through his hair before opening the door.

"A little, I think," he said, now a bit disheveled.

"Come here," she said, running her fingers through his hair, smoothing it back into place.

"Simon, relax," Marcus reassured his friend. "It's not an interview! We've already got jobs!"

"Just don't need all this attention for what we did, that's all," Simon muttered. "We didn't go down there for attention. We did it because it was the right thing to do."

"Yes, of course. But sometimes doing the right thing results in recognition..." Marcus replied, understanding fully. "Which inspires other people to want to do the right thing, too. And that can't be a bad thing. Think of this as a public service, buddy."

Simon looked at Marcus. "You do the public talking."

Suzie smoothed Marcus' tie. "You are so good at public speaking," she reminded him. "Be glib."

"Be glib?" Marcus asked, looking at Simon with the question.

"Be glib, she says..." he repeated, turning the doorknob for them to enter.

Inside, the group was pleased to see the familiar face of Chief Watson, already present in the spacious office. Beside him stood several policemen, one of whom was the officer who had come to their door asking for help on the night of the fire. Another had been the one in charge at the scene. Several members of the mayoral staff were milling about, and in a room toward the back, a man sat behind a large desk, undoubtedly the mayor himself. He looked up as the group entered and motioned for them to come into his office, with Chief Watson leading the way.

"Mister Mayor, may I introduce Doctors Finney and Lovell and their wives and children," the chief said, introducing each of them individually. He then proceeded to introduce the office staff to the group of honored guests.

"Mrs. Lovell, Mrs. Finney, please... take a seat there with your little ones," the mayor said, gesturing to a line of green leather chairs positioned along the wall beside his wide desk. Lydia noticed a man standing by the office door, leaning casually against the wall. He held a camera with a large flash attached, waiting silently for his moment. Lydia nudged Suzie's arm as she settled Nikki on her lap, so she would take notice. The women looked at each other. *We might just get a photo out of this afterall!* Lydia thought excitedly.

"One of the gentlemen of the press," the mayor informed Simon and Marcus. "I understand that both of you doctors are relative newcomers to our three rivers?"

"Yes, sir," Marcus confirmed. "We moved here at the first of the year, to take positions at Charity."

"And do I understand correctly that you both served overseas in the army? At the western front?" the mayor wanted to clarify an earlier report he'd been given about these two men.

Marcus nodded. "Yes, sir... all four of us served... two years in France, primarily, and Belgium, with a casualty clearing station."

The mayor nodded, appraising the group. "Splendid. We appreciate when citizens such as yourselves choose our fair city for work and to raise your families. A city is only great when there are good people living and working in it, bringing their talents to address the needs of the people in the community... as you two have so recently done... and at no small personal risk."

Marcus spoke up at this, "There are others who have been serving the needs of the people in this community for many years before we arrived, Mayor. We work at a hospital whose entire mission statement is to offer health care to those in need, regardless of their ability to pay. Charity has devoted years of service to Pittsburgh... we're just fortunate to have had the opportunity to join such an excellent team."

"I thought you might say something like that," the mayor responded, looking up to one of his aides. The aide stepped out of the office briefly, returning after a few moments with none other than Doctor Richard Maloney in tow, who softly patted little Nikki's head as he entered the office, breathing hard from having just rushed through the corridors.

"Sorry, Mister Mayor, there were no parking places out front," Doctor Maloney apologized. "Ah, Doctor Finney, Doctor Lovell! Good to see you. And ladies, of course, it's always a pleasure to see you as well."

Another aide approached, carrying two framed certificates, and handed them to the mayor. Taking them in hand, he turned toward Simon and Marcus.

"The people of Pittsburgh would like to thank you doctors for coming to the aid of the workers at the mill during the lethal fire that took place. For offering your service with courage beyond the call of duty. These certificates are to honor your dedication to your profession and to this city. Doctor Finney and Doctor Lovell... from our grateful citizens."

Handing Simon and Marcus each one of the certificates, the mayor shook hands with each of them, holding on long enough for the photographer to snap each of their pictures in turn. Then, he turned to Doctor Maloney. "Would you be good enough, Doctor, to stand with your two surgeons and myself as we would also like to recognize Charity Hospital in all of this."

"Certainly, Mister Mayor," Maloney said, joining the group in front of the mayor's oak desk. "We're honored that they signed on with our exceptional team of doctors at the hospital."

"Yes, indeed, Doctor Maloney," the mayor said. "I'm very much aware of Charity's reputation for attracting qualified people. Chief Watson mentioned that there is one other matter that you doctors wanted to talk about? Something concerning a surgical walk-in clinic?"

Simon cleared his throat. "Yes, sir," he said. "The mission of Charity is to get care out to those who need it most, to make medical care accessible to the people of the city. A walk-in, minor surgery clinic is what we have proposed to Doctor Maloney and the hospital administration. We wanted your opinion, Mayor, about a possible location to best serve those injured, who often need quick access to care."

The mayor looked over at an aide. "Maybe they should meet with Lou over at city planning, he tracks where the most ambulance calls are made and where the greatest concentration of workers are. We can help you evaluate neighborhoods with a risk and needs assessment. After being told about your idea, I've also spoken with the owners of the mill where you intervened. For saving many lives that night, they would like to offer some assistance, perhaps financially or by way of donating a location for such a clinic—to show their appreciation for what these men did that night."

Doctor Maloney looked at Simon and Marcus, who both nodded. "Absolutely, sir. Let's make it happen. Hospital administration is at your disposal."

The mayor then turned to Lydia and Suzie, shaking Nikki's tiny hand. He asked Lydia if he could hold Jimmy for a moment, and admired the baby while another set of photos was quickly snapped by the photographer, not wanting to miss a potential campaign moment for their archives. Mayors and babies were always well received.

"And is there anything that the city can offer the wives of these two fine surgeons?" the mayor asked Lydia.

"Yes, sir," Lydia spoke up immediately. "An actual photograph of our husbands together! That would be wonderful."

The mayor laughed. "We can do that!" he exclaimed, motioning to the photographer, who pushed Simon and Marcus side by side and told them to shake hands with each other. The flash bulb went off one more time, to Lydia's deep satisfaction. Simon and Marcus would get their clinic, she had no doubt about that now. And the women would have a framed photo of their handsome husbands.

Upon returning home, Simon outright refused to put the certificate up on the dining room breakfront. He maintained that God had called him to be a surgeon, and if God's name wasn't on the certificate, then it didn't need to be on display.

"Credit where credit is due," Simon told Lydia as he set the frame aside to store it up in their room, likely in the footlocker.

"Well I already knew that you are incredibly brave, and I'll give you credit for that any day of the week." She wrapped her arms around his waist, kissing him. "Anyway, you're my hero, many times over."

"That's enough for me," he replied. "Let's get some supper on the table."

Lydia heard Jimmy begin to fuss. "Give me a minute and I'll take care of it."

"Go ahead, Lydia," Suzie told her. "I'll get it while you take care of the baby."

Marcus followed Suzie into the kitchen and leaned her back against the counter. He kissed her passionately. "How are you feeling?" he asked. "Was I glib enough?"

"You were!" she exclaimed. "You were very smooth, I thought!"

"Suzie, I've been thinking..." he started.

"What about?" she said, pulling an apron from a drawer to wrap around her waist.

"I want to go to church on Sunday and listen to that preacher from the baptism."

Suzie stopped, mid-tie. "Well, you certainly don't need my permission for that, Marcus," she told him softly. "If you want to go, then go."

"I'd like you to go with me," he prompted in earnest.

Suzie shook her head. "I'll stay home with Nikki. She's a little young for that. And I'm not really into that kind of thing, but you go ahead, if you think you should."

Marcus nodded as he watched her start the supper. "Let me help," he said. "I know how to cut up lettuce and tomatoes!"

"Using a knife, not a scalpel?" she teased, turning to the stove and pulling out a pot.

He opened a drawer and found a suitable kitchen knife. "Why not?"

"Why not what?" she countered, focused on their dinner.

"Why not go together?" he asked.

She stirred the contents of the pot and turned down the flame to a blue glow. "I just don't think in those terms, Marcus. I just don't feel that I need a god in my life. That's all."

Marcus nodded slowly. "Does it change anything for you, if I do want God in my life?"

She turned to look at him, curious. "Look, Marcus," she smiled. "You're a good husband and provider... and a great father to Nikki. Anything else you do beyond that is fine with me, as long as you're satisfied with it... if it's something you want."

"Okay," he said, feeling suddenly troubled. *Good husband... great father...?* "Just thought I'd better talk to you about it, Suzie."

"Oh, remind me to tell you about a book that my club is promoting," she said as she turned to the stove again.

Marcus continued chopping the tomatoes.

A few days later, after their shifts, Marcus and Simon returned home from the hospital. Marcus parked the automobile and hopped out, a newspaper clutched in his hand. Suzie had already come home from making her house calls and had scooped Nikki up off the floor, where she had been playing with her bear and blocks. Lydia was lost in some writing with Jimmy on the sofa beside her, the baby waving his feet in the air, trying to capture them with his little hands.

Coming in through the back door, Simon rounded the corner into the living room, bent over and kissed Lydia, then picked up Jimmy. He kissed the baby and put him up to his shoulder, carrying him around as he got himself a cup of water from the kitchen.

"What are you writing, Lydia?" Marcus asked, putting his keys on the foyer table. He grabbed a spot on the sofa, curious.

"It's a letter to Jimmy," she held up the paper, appraising her progress. "I'm trying to write him a letter every month that he can read when he's all grown up. Reminding him of all the little 'first moments' in his life."

"So, by the time he's ten years old, there will be one hundred twenty letters for him to read?" Marcus added, doing the math. "It'll be a whole book."

"Hm. Maybe I'll change it to yearly! Make it a Christmas letter!" Lydia exclaimed. "It just seems like he discovers something new every day right now. It's amazing to me."

"He's making wrinkles, in that tiny brain," Marcus nodded. "Building nerve connections and new cells and storing all that love that you and Simon have for him, right there in his mind."

"I certainly hope he knows how we all love him!" she exclaimed.

"Well, if being contented is a sign of him knowing, then he's alright. He is one contented baby."

"So is Nikki," Lydia said. "She's played with her bear all day, and Abril, and her blocks. She's really smart, Marcus, matching block shapes already. Her vocabulary is growing. I'm glad I could watch her while I've been off and Suzie working. It's also good to see what Jimmy will be doing in a year."

Marcus laughed. "Got the newspaper. Wait until you see it!"

Lydia looked up, excited. "Is it the mayor's office?"

He nodded. "I was supposed to be the 'glib' one, remember? But get this headline, *'The mission of Charity...'* They used Simon's entire little speech to start it off! Not mine! A lot of this is stuff from Chief Watson and Doctor Maloney, thank goodness. Simon will appreciate that we didn't blow our own horns too much."

"Let me see!" Lydia eagerly reached for the newspaper where the article continued, *two local surgeons responded to the mill fire tragedy...* With a great photo of Simon, Marcus, the mayor and Doctor Maloney! Her eyes quickly read the entire article. "Oh, wow," she breathed. "This is well written, Marcus. And it gives a lot of appreciation to Charity and the work that the hospital is doing for the city."

"That's why I told Simon something good can come out of a little appreciation," Marcus said, reading over her shoulder. "The hospital got good press, and people will recognize how hard it is for people trying to make a living here when things like a fire happen at one of the factories. It's a good thing all the way around."

"That's a great picture of you boys with Doctor Maloney and the mayor," Lydia said. "And look here, they made mention of the idea of the surgical clinic, too! Maybe when the clinic opens, they'll run another story!"

"Maybe," Marcus replied happily.

Just then Simon burst into the room with Jimmy still on his shoulder. "Look how he's holding his head up, Lydia!" Simon exclaimed. "He's looking all around."

"That's wonderful! And look at this, Simon!" Lydia said, pointing to the article. "It's a really good picture of you both with Doctor Maloney."

Simon bent over the picture briefly. "Nice haircuts," he said. "Those guys have a great barber."

Lydia feigned hitting him with the newspaper. "Good grief," she said. "I'm proud of you, both of you. You're putting your God-given talents to good use and look what's come of it! More people being served. You're making such a difference! And I'm keeping this newspaper, so don't you dare throw it out when you two are done reading it!

"In fact, buy another copy, will you? Even better, buy ten! I want to send one to Mom and Dad." *And maybe one for Marc's father in Reading... That man should get to know his son again!*

Simon bent over her, a hand cupping the baby's head to keep Jimmy from falling, kissing Lydia's cheek. "You make a difference every single day, my love. To all of us. More than you could possibly imagine."

He didn't want her to forget that taking care of Jimmy was equal, in his opinion, to what had happened at the steel mill.

Suzie, having heard the excitement, joined them in the living room. Lydia handed her the paper. Suzie took a seat, reading the article, smiling broadly. Then she flipped through some of the other pages, looking for something else.

"Well, how about that?" she said softly.

"What?" Lydia asked.

"Our little writer's group, the book club people. One of them got a little article written in here, too," Suzie mused. "An opinion piece."

"Really? Which one?" Lydia asked curiously.

Suzie handed it to her, pointing to the spot. "That one... on the rights of women and the vote."

"Wow." Simon leaned over Lydia's shoulder and skimmed it. "Good writing. Good opinion piece."

Suzie nodded. "There are a lot of really good writers in our little group."

"That so?" Simon asked. "Is that a once-a-month thing? Every other week?"

"Weekly, right now," Marcus added, from what little he knew about Suzie's new hobby.

"Just for fun," Suzie declared. "There is a whole world outside of medicine, you know."

The other three just looked at her.

"I'm just saying," Suzie added, heading out to the kitchen with Nikki on her hip and literature on her mind.

Lydia was grateful to find the nuns waiting to welcome Jimmy, upon her return to the clinic. Sister Edwarda had also come down to see the baby... exclaiming over his cheeks and tiny smile. Lydia carried the baby back into the examination offices, where the crib was positioned safely beside Sister Mary Margaret's desk. Lydia handed him to the nun, who immediately held him to herself.

"What a fine young son!" she said, appreciating this new little life. "He's so healthy and strong. How old is he now, Nurse Finney?"

"Ten weeks," Lydia told her. "He's like his father, calm and even-tempered."

"Ten weeks, and he's already looking around, so aware," Sister Mary Margaret marveled. "Look, Sister Teresa, look how he looks around so. He's so attentive!"

Sister Teresa held out her hands for Jimmy. "What's his full name again, Nurse Finney?"

"James Marcus—" Lydia began.

"Oh, that's right, after Saint James and the saint of—"

"… Peter's helper," Lydia finished, laughing. "That's right! I'm told by Sister Anne that it's a very good and strong name. It will serve him well in life."

Sister Teresa looked at Lydia, still holding the baby in her arms. "We were all praying for you, Nurse Finney, when the doctor brought you in during the night just after the birth. The word spread quickly that you were having difficulties, and we got up and prayed for you straight away."

Lydia put her hand on the woman's shoulder. "Thank the sisters for me, that means so much. I guess that kind of complication doesn't happen all that often, it was difficult. Doctor Weyland did the procedure and was kind to me."

"Doctor Martin was very concerned as well. He asked often for updates on how you were doing," Sister Teresa added.

"Next time he's on rotation, we'll show him how healthy everyone is now!" Lydia assured the two nurses. "I'm glad to be back in the clinic. What have I missed? Which doctor is on duty today?"

"Doctor Thaddeus Trent is on this week. He's one of the doctors on the Fourth Ward."

Lydia knew that many cancer patients ended up on the Fourth Ward. It was probably a nice change of pace for the man to be removing embedded splinters from swollen fingers or looking at tonsils, instead of treating life threatening tumors in patients with six months to live.

They began updating Lydia on the clinic's activities and what had changed since summer had arrived. There had been the usual mix of work-related injuries, fractures, chickenpox, the occasional measles, bee stings, mumps, and upset stomachs. As Lydia had anticipated, lung-related illnesses had significantly decreased, thanks to fresh air circulating through homes and people spending more time outdoors walking or taking children to parks, to play outside. In the clinic's waiting area, the enclosed section reserved for coughs had become much smaller, as more space was now being prioritized for fractures, breaks and other injuries.

Lydia happily donned her long apron and headed to the front, taking her place at the little desk by the door. Whenever the door opened, a welcome breeze flowed past. Lydia quickly fell back into the rhythm of triage. It was also a blessing being able to go to the back office to nurse Jimmy whenever he needed her. Just after one of the feedings, Doctor Trent stopped by to introduce himself. He was a bit older than some of the other doctors who had come through the clinic rotations, but still tolerant of the arrangements that had been made for the new mother and her baby.

At times, Lydia would fetch Jimmy just to spend a few precious moments with him, strolling through the clinic or stepping outside to soak in the sunshine and get a little fresh air. To her surprise, Simon even came down from the operating theater during his lunch break, eager to see her and cradle the baby for a while.

The scene didn't go unnoticed—patients in the waiting area glanced curiously at the man in his surgical gown, carrying a baby around with ease. Lydia saw a few people pointing in Simon's direction with more than just curiosity. After he had left the clinic, a small group came up to her desk.

"Was that one of the doctors from the newspaper?" they asked excitedly. "He looked like one of the two doctors that ran into that fire and saved that man who was trapped inside the steel mill."

"Yes," Lydia confirmed. "He is one of them."

"Took a lot of courage to do something like that," one observed.

"Could've gotten killed, even," another added.

"They must have good doctors here," said one woman.

"He looked so sweet holding your little baby," a woman chimed in. "Some men won't."

Lydia smiled at the group of women, then turned to the door where a new woman holding a child had just come through the doors. Lydia greeted her warmly.

"How can we help you today?" she asked.

The woman looked quite anxious. "My little guy got a... bean... up his nose," she admitted. The toddler had been crying. It probably hurt the delicate nasal passages, Lydia thought. Using her flashlight, she saw some light red drainage in his little nose.

"We'll get him right in with Doctor Trent," she assured the woman, assigning him a priority number, in case his nose began to bleed again. They took a seat right near the clinic hallway which led back to the exam room. As Lydia was finishing the intake paperwork, the child suddenly went limp; his mother letting out a small scream. With scarcely a thought, Lydia rushed to pick up the child and threw him, head down, over her knees. She whacked the center of his back and the bean flew out of his throat and across the tile floor. A thin cry rapidly gained steam as the toddler expressed his dismay over being hit between his shoulder blades.

"What just happened?" The mother looked at Lydia, astonished.

"The bean had moved down and blocked his little throat," Lydia explained quickly. "Luckily it flew right out. Look, here it is." She bent down and retrieved the offending object from the floor to show the mother.

Doctor Trent had arrived just in time to see the whole episode unfold. "Good job, Nurse Finney," he applauded her. "You opened the airway. Who taught you to do that?"

"It just made sense," she replied, a little surprised herself. "He probably just sniffed it right down into his airway."

The doctor was visibly impressed. "I'll take him back, and we'll watch him for a little to make sure there's no additional bleeding. Thank you, Nurse Finney," The child and his anxious mother followed Doctor Trent down the hall into an exam room, where Sister Teresa would keep an eye on the child.

Grateful the toddler was safe, Lydia returned to the desk by the door. As the day, which had been successful in her book, ended, Lydia headed back to nurse the baby once more before leaving. She sat with Sister Mary Margaret in the little office and put Jimmy to her breast, where he latched on eagerly.

"Jimmy was delightful today," Sister Mary told Lydia. "Let me get all my work done and let me hold him, too. Since I never had children, it's a blessing to hold such a little guy. Just like little Nikki. I love it!"

"I know your service to God is rewarding, Sister," Lydia said. "But does service like this make up for not having children of your own?"

The nun shook her head. "Sometimes I miss not having had the experience of a life growing within me," she admitted. "But I've never known the feel of a man, nor have I gone to South America, or seen the pyramids... or a rain forest either. No one can truly say that he or she has done it all... there is always more to do. I'm glad to do my part, whatever it is that the Lord gives me. It's enough."

Lydia looked up at the woman, amazed. "That's so wise. Thank you for sharing that with me. I write these little letters to Jimmy, about his early life. I'll put that piece of wisdom into my letter tonight... that there will always be more in this world that can be done. Just be glad to do your part."

"Our Doctor Finney was in the mill fire, wasn't he?" Sister Mary Margaret said, changing the subject.

Nodding, Lydia stroked the baby's little head tenderly. "Yes," she said softly. "Doctor Lovell and he both went in—"

"To save the man pinned in the fire," Sister Mary added.

Lydia nodded, thinking of how terribly it could have gone.

"When you're doing what the Lord gives you to do, you need not fear the flames, Lydia," Sister Mary Margaret said softly as if she was able to intuit the other woman's heart.

Lydia's eyes flew up to meet the compassionate look from the nun sitting across from her. Suddenly, her eyes filled. Lydia swallowed hard. "I will..." she started, clearing her throat, "add that, too."

The nun smiled, nodding her head in return. "See you tomorrow." She gathered her belongings and left the office while Lydia finished nursing Jimmy, changed his diaper, and gathered up her own bag.

With Jimmy in her arms, Lydia left the office and found Doctor Trent also finishing up for the day. He had just finished washing his hands, tossing the towel into a hamper.

Turning to Lydia, he asked, "This was a good day in the clinic! All set to go home?"

Lydia nodded. "Yes, Doctor, time to go make supper."

The older man smiled at her. "May I?" he asked, holding out his arms.

She handed little Jimmy to the doctor then removed her apron. He took Jimmy and comfortably cradled the baby in his elbow as they walked the long corridor to the rotunda at the front of the hospital.

"Handsome little guy," Doctor Trent observed as they walked.

"I think so," Lydia replied. "Biased, quite a bit, as I am."

"I have a granddaughter myself. Hoping for a grandson when my daughter delivers in a few months," he informed her.

Curious, Lydia looked up at him. "Are they nearby? In the city? I hope you get to see them often."

He nodded. "Not far, just across the border in Ohio. An easy drive in good weather but terrible in winter."

Lydia laughed lightly. "I should imagine it is!"

The man looked down at the baby and touched his little chin. "You have a very special mother," Doctor Trent told the baby.

As they entered the rotunda, there were two men waiting, watching them. Lydia approached one and kissed his bearded cheek.

"Ah," said Doctor Trent. "Must be the father. Doctor Finney, I presume?"

"The same," Simon said, extending his hand in greeting.

"Thaddeus Trent... Fourth Ward usually," Doctor Trent accepted his handshake. "And you must be Doctor Lovell, then? I saw your picture in the paper with Doctor Maloney. Well done!"

"I am, sir," Marcus said, also accepting the older doctor's handshake.

Doctor Trent handed the baby back to Lydia with a small smile before turning to the two young surgeons. "Good to know that some men like you are coming up through our ranks to replace us older doctors."

Looking flushed despite the beard, Simon said, "No, sir, experience can't be replaced. Just shared."

Doctor Trent looked at Simon. "As I learned from my mentors as well, Doctor. Have a very good evening, all of you." And he left them in the rotunda as Simon reached for Jimmy and put the baby to his shoulder before they all headed out to the car.

"Seems like a nice enough guy," Marcus observed as they all got into their automobile. "Was he in the clinic today, Lydia?"

Lydia nodded as she settled into the back seat. "For just a week. Seems like they can't get by without him too long, the cancer patients. So he only takes a week for his turn in the clinic."

"You know, I like the idea of everyone taking a turn there. When do we get a turn, Simon?" Marcus asked.

"Guess they don't think we have enough experience to handle it just yet, Marcus," Simon smiled.

"I can do splinters, heart attacks... sprained ankles!" Marcus insisted.

"How about a bean in a windpipe?" Lydia asked from the back seat.

The two men both turned to look at her. "A bean in the windpipe?" Marcus repeated.

Lydia nodded. "Flew out six feet with one hit between the shoulder blades!"

"Little out of Trent's realm of cancer treatments!" Marcus chuckled.

Lydia just smiled. So, Simon added knowingly, "Trent didn't do it, did he, Lydia?"

She just looked out the window of the vehicle at the other staff getting into their autos to go home for the day.

"It—" she started.

Marcus and Simon finished together, "—just made sense!" They both laughed as Marcus drove out of the parking lot, across the bridge, and toward their neighborhood.

Marcus turned down a side street to avoid a small group of protesters holding signs on sticks, clustered on one of the corners. They could see a policeman standing nearby, talking with them. It looked peaceful enough, but Marcus was anxious to get them all home and he was hungry, so he turned and took a street that ran behind their house.

Suddenly Simon shouted, "Stop! Marc! Stop."

Marcus hit the brakes hard, glad they were going slowly in the first place. "My God, Simon, what is it?" he demanded. Anxiously, he peered out over the hood of the automobile, afraid there might be a body lying in the road.

Simon jumped out of the passenger side of the auto, still holding Jimmy in his arms, and came around while Marcus nervously jumped out as well, searching the paved street, afraid of what he would find crushed beneath the front fender, but Simon grabbed his friend's arm.

"Marc," Simon insisted. "Look!"

Marcus followed the direction of Simon's finger. "Well, I'll be!"

By now, Lydia had also slid out of the back seat to join the men, quickly taking the baby from Simon and searching for anyone in peril of life or limb.

Marcus grabbed her and hugged her. "Look, Lydia. I think God might have actually heard me talking to Him after all! Way up there! Wherever He is!"

"What on earth are you talking about?" she demanded, heart pounding, enormously relieved that no one was wedged beneath their tires.

Marcus and Lydia followed Simon, who was writing something down. "There's a sign in the window. It's for sale."

The house was much like their own, but sandwiched between two others. It was two stories with dormer windows at the top and a porch in front. There was a narrow, arched walkway along one side, leading to the backyard.

Simon looked at them with a 'should we?' look on his face and headed back through the small arch to the backyard, wanting to see the rear of the house. Marcus and Lydia followed. When they emerged into the back yard, Lydia could scarcely believe her eyes... and ears. She heard a familiar bark and saw Abril standing up on their own back fence, paws resting on it, wanting to jump over when she saw the three, but knowing she wasn't allowed. Their own backyard was caddy-corner to this one, across the small alley winding its way between the backyards of all the houses on the block.

Elated, Marcus took Lydia's face in both of his hands and kissed her on the forehead. Simon threw his arm around Marcus's shoulder in relief and joy. "Right behind! Well, almost right behind anyway!" Simon exclaimed happily. "Right here! Same block, Marcus!"

Marcus grabbed the paper Simon had used to take down the number, from the sign in the window. He tossed the automobile key to Simon and ran across the yards to their own house, greeting Abril as he hopped up on the kitchen porch to call the sellers that very minute.

Simon wrapped his arm around Lydia and the baby, beyond excited that a house had become available so very close to them. "He wanted the same block, Lydia. Didn't even wait to see the inside! Sure hope it's livable. We've seen it a hundred times from our own back porch," Simon said as he led her back through the little archway to the front to retrieve the automobile. "Who knew?"

Lydia laughed. "In the words of Father James, 'God knew'," she smiled as he got behind the wheel and drove them around the corner to park under the maple tree, Abril leaning on the fence to greet them. Entering through the kitchen, they heard Marcus in the foyer, still on the phone, most certainly talking with the seller of the house across the alley. He was asking questions, but as Lydia placed Jimmy in a playpen in the living room, what she overheard was less about the features of the house and more about its price and availability. Marcus seemed anxious to complete the purchase as quickly as possible.

As the were preparing for dinner, with potatoes cooking away on the stove, Lydia checked on the salmon baking in the oven. Marcus and Simon bound into the kitchen, full of energy. Simon kissed her cheek and they headed for the back door.

"Now where are you two off to with dinner nearly ready?" Lydia exclaimed in protest.

"We're going for a run," Marcus said with a mischievous smile.

"You're going for a what?"

"A run." There was a twinkle in Marcus' eyes. "You know, one foot in front of the other at a rapid pace."

She swatted him with her hand towel. "I know what a run is! But Simon, you don't just... run. Your lungs—"

"I realized after the fire that I need to build up my legs, and my lungs," Simon said cheerfully. "We'll be back before Suzie gets home."

Marcus nodded at Lydia and added a smile for reassurance. "It'll be good for him."

Doubtful, she relented, "Well be careful. Don't hurt yourself." And she watched them bound out the back door and thud down the porch steps, taking off with Abril at their heels. At least the dog would enjoy keeping them company.

The two friends jogged down the block at an easy pace, Marcus aware of Simon's breathing.

"Now, how far are we going to go?" Simon asked Marcus curiously.

"Around the block, so we can see my new house from all angles," Marcus said easily. "Then, we'll see."

"Okay," Simon breathed in deeply. "Around the block sounds good. The 'we'll see' part is a little... disconcerting."

"Come on, Simon. We've been standing at an operating table all day. Breathing hard is good for us."

Simon shot a sly glance at his friend. "I can think of better ways to end up breathing hard!"

Looking back at him, Marcus laughed heartily. "Get your head out of the bed, my friend."

"Wait. You're telling me to get my head out of the bed? Me?" Simon asked, astonished. "And Suzie says you're trying to get her pregnant? What's wrong with this picture?"

Marcus led them up through the alley, running along the houses on their block. They turned left for the sidewalk, doubling back along the street side of Beech which paralleled Maple. "This is a nice street! I like it! Good little houses, neatly organized, nice little yards. Yep, I can see Suz taking our kids for walks around this block."

Simon was already breathing hard. "Kids. I heard kids. You are trying then, aren't you?"

"Thinking about it," Marcus nodded, paying as much attention to his friend's endurance as he was to where they were heading.

Simon was panting so they were silent for a moment, jogging down the cross street. "You know, you have to do a little more than think about it, if you're going to make it happen, buddy," he puffed out the words.

"Well, let's just say, if it happens and it makes Suzie happy, then so be it. She still breast feeds Nikki at night, so we'll see," Marcus said evenly as they came up to the little park they enjoyed visiting. Abril ran on ahead of them, knowing the area well. She headed straight for a little creek that flowed through it and took a drink from the clear water, then ran back, circling around the men. "Abril is doing great! But you sure need some work! Sit down on the bench here and catch your breath."

Simon did. He rubbed his face. "You were so right! Boy, I'm out of shape! If we're going to be running into emergency situations, I need to fix this. Look at you. Hardly even panting."

"I have all five lobes of my lungs, though," Marcus said, dropping down on the bench beside Simon. "Makes a difference."

"Glad I quit smoking?" Simon laughed lightly.

"Glad you never started. You never did, did you? Like before the war?" Marcus asked suddenly.

Simon wiped his face on his shirt. "Oh, I suppose I picked one up. One, anyway. Then Doc Albright showed me a piece of lung tissue a miner had hacked up. Said, 'See this, Simon? Cigarettes or the mines. Both will do this.' I figured maybe I should avoid both."

"Wise decision," Marcus said.

"Where's Suzie this evening?" Simon wondered.

"At her book club meeting after work. Said she'll be home by six," Marc said casually.

"So, is it everything you hoped it would be?" Simon asked suddenly.

"What, this little jaunt?" Marcus asked, puzzled.

"No, being with Suzie and Nikki," Simon said plainly.

There was silence between them for a moment. "Yes and no," Marcus admitted. "Yes, because I love them both and am trying to show them, in all the ways they can feel it... hear it. But Simon, Monique being pregnant... it could... she could... that is... it's possible—"

"That it's yours," Simon finished the labored thought.

Marcus stared at the ground. "Yeh. I didn't tell Suzie. I'm not even sure I should... don't even know how I would."

"That's a tough one," Simon observed. "How about using those same words?"

"Well, I could. But Suzie... well, Suzie already isn't very happy with me right now."

"What makes you say that?" Simon asked, resting his elbows on his legs and leaning his chin on his clasped hands.

"I don't think I'm enough for her, Simon," Marcus admitted. "She needs more. And I don't want to make things worse by telling her about Monique. Suzie needs the clinic at the hospital, the comradery of the staff, the stimulation of her club members. Suzie would never be content if we were stranded on a deserted island, even with Nikki... and plenty of coconuts. That's the difference between us and you and Lydia. You two could be stranded on an island—now with Jimmy—and still be content watching the sunrise over the water."

"Don't forget plenty of coconuts for us too. I'd be starved." Simon attempted to lighten the mood. "Better have a good banquet table on that island for three square meals, or I wouldn't make it one day."

"Okay, full course meals then, Lydia, and Jimmy... and you'd be content, and so would Lydia," Marcus said.

Simon considered his friend's predicament carefully. "Oh, I don't know about that, Marc. You know Lydia. She always needs to be making a difference, somewhere. Her life's mission is also bigger than just us."

"Understood," Marcus nodded. "But on the island, you and Jimmy would become her mission. Suzie would tire of me being her mission... and quickly. She'd be searching for the first ship to break the horizon."

"Think that's why she wants another baby?" Simon wondered, his heart aching for his friend.

"I do, which is why I'm not working too hard at making it happen," Marcus confessed. "Don't know how much she'd have left over after another baby. But I do adore Nikki. That little girl just fills my heart right up when she runs over and grabs my leg and it's, 'Dada, up.' Brings tears to my eyes thinking I had something to do with creating her little life." Marcus continued slowly. "And Suzie doesn't want to go to church with me. Said I can go if I want to, but she doesn't need God in her life. And even before this thing with Monique, I've realized that I do. I've got a lot of soul-searching happening... and you keep telling me that souls are God's domain."

Simon winced at hearing his friend's fear that Suzie might run out of love for him. "You're a good, moral man, Marc... a good husband and terrific dad. You've already changed so much for the better," Simon said, placing a reassuring hand on Marc's shoulder. "And you're the best friend God ever made. I'm glad you're on this journey... and, hey, someday Suzie may be, too. And there's also a chance that Monique's baby is not yours and she's quite happy with Fortraine, but if she ever shows up at your door with a baby in hand, well... we'll deal with it together. But if we don't go home soon, and Lydia's dinner burns, neither of us is going to be welcome, on any island."

Marcus laughed out loud at that. "You are so right! Ready?"

Simon took a deep breath. "I am. It's only, what... six blocks. I can do six blocks... maybe at a walk though?"

"We'll do this again in a couple of days, and you'll do seven," Marcus assured him. Simon's lungs really were dreadful! The push-ups were good enough for tomorrow, though. Give him a day off and work up slowly to running. The two of them had delayed strengthening Simon's lungs for far too long.

Two days passed like a brisk summer breeze. It was a fine afternoon when Lydia stepped through the front door after finishing up at the clinic. Nikki came running right up to her on her stubby, little legs, her arms extended. "Iddy! Iddy, up!"

Beaming down at the toddler, Lydia scooped up Nikki in one arm, giving her a quick kiss on the forehead before greeting their capable housekeeper.

"Was Nikki good for you, Mrs. Gilbert?" Lydia asked, resting Jimmy in the playpen.

"She's an angel," the woman exclaimed. "Doesn't cry, doesn't fuss, and she ate her lunch without complaining... and some teething biscuits too. And she sure does love that dog of yours!"

"Ahh, I should have asked you if the dog behaved as well!" Lydia laughed. "Nikki usually gets along with everyone, but I know Abril can be protective."

The woman looked at Abril. "I like dogs," she admitted. "This one seems to know if someone is here for a good reason. She stayed in when I asked her to and walked right alongside us when I took the little one for a walk in the stroller."

"Oh, did you get out then?" Lydia asked. "I'm glad. It was a nice day, wasn't it?"

Mrs. Gilbert nodded. "Until those union boys got it into their heads to march up and down the streets with their signs again."

"Oh," Lydia said. "They're back? What is that all about?"

Gathering up her purse, the woman was happy to share what she knew with Lydia. "After that fire, they're letting the bosses know they want some safety improvements... and more pay if they've got to work in dangerous places."

Lydia nodded, with more understanding for the group they had seen standing on the street corner the other night... and the presence of the police officer they'd seen speaking with the men. "They looked peaceful enough the other day."

"Sometimes!" the woman exclaimed. "Things can get heated real fast where the unions are concerned. Carnegie, well he's not real popular at the moment. Check the paper if you can get your hands on one. Probably has a write-up about the rumblings at the mills."

Lydia bounced Nikki on one hip as the toddler looked curiously at her locket. "I certainly know a bit about the fire down there. It must have been terrible on the men working there... two died, and many injured."

"Well, just stay out of union business, I say! Will Mrs. Lovell be needing me tomorrow again?" Mrs. Gilbert asked, pausing at the back door.

"Yes, please. And thank you so much for watching little Nikki here," Lydia waved goodbye as she closed the screen door behind the older woman.

Marcus and Simon were the next to come through the door. A quick kiss from Simon and he was bounding up the stairs to change and wash up. Marcus, though, headed straight for the telephone on the wall to place a call to the seller of the house on the alley. The moment he hung up, Lydia turned to him eagerly, ready to press for answers.

"Well?" she asked. "What did you find out this time?"

"It'll be available in three weeks, when the family moves out. The guy got another job across the Ohio River, and they're moving. Lydia, it's perfect!" Marcus exclaimed. "I've been holding off on moving. Told Simon I wanted something on this block too... well, you know! To be close by and all. And here it is, right across the alleyway. It's just right! Wait till Suzie gets home! She'll be so happy."

Lydia laughed, placing Nikki into her father's outstretched arms. "You haven't even looked inside yet!" she exclaimed. "What if there's something wrong with the place or all of the walls are painted red, or something?"

"Red can work... okay, red is not good at all! But whatever might be wrong with it, can be fixed surely," Marcus admitted, refusing to let anything dampen his spirits. "What would not be fixable, would be ending up across the river or somewhere far away from all of you. Anyway, look at you two, still living with the widow's old furniture."

"Those are heirlooms!" Lydia exclaimed, laying a hand on his arm, then adding, "I told you right after the baby was born that I couldn't bear to think of you leaving."

He leaned over and kissed her forehead. "Can you bear this move, Lydia?"

Her eyes were sparkling. "Across the alley? I think I can bear it across the alley. Oh, Marcus, I am truly grateful that I'm not being asked to give you all up yet. My 'scaffold' just got another level added to it. I can hardly wait until Suzie gets home to hear the news."

At that moment, Simon came down the stairs having changed into more comfortable clothes. He stopped to check on Jimmy, safely in the playpen, then headed for the kitchen. "Your turn to change, Lydia, I'll keep an eye on our son."

Lydia headed upstairs to freshen up, leaving the men to talk.

"What did you find out?" Simon asked Marcus.

Upstairs, Lydia gathered up a change of clothes and headed down the hall to the bathroom for a quick wash before starting dinner. As she did so, she heard Suzie coming in through the front door, greeted excitedly by the men downstairs.

Lydia's relief was palpable. *Simon's lungs are not getting better... Marcus will still be close by, to keep helping him get stronger...*

Over dinner, their conversation circled around from the picketers, to the new house, and back to the steel mills and the plight of workers in the city... before returning again to the house.

"Did you even ask how many bedrooms it has?" Suzie questioned Marcus. "Does it have a fireplace or a basement or an icebox or stove... anything?"

Marcus dove into his dinner with enthusiasm. "Suz, a family is still living there for three more weeks! Naturally, they have appliances like a stove and icebox! They have to eat!"

She shook her head. "I'm just saying they might take all of that with them, along with the furniture."

"Then we'll buy furniture, and a new icebox and whatever else we end up needing." Marcus was unstoppable in his problem-solving.

"And we need a real bed for Nikki. She's growing so fast, she'll need a bed of her own soon," Suzie added.

Lydia nodded. "Look at her holding her little spoon there! Seems like just yesterday she was rolling over, and now she chases right after Abril on her own two feet. It'll be hard keeping Abril in the yard if she sees her little playmate just across the alley."

Simon passed a bowl of green beans around the table again for anyone wanting seconds. "Abril's smart. She'll learn to jump the fence... just for them, especially if Marc or Suzie calls to her. She knows we're all her family—"

"And we'll need a nursery," Suzie said, accepting the bowl of green beans from Simon.

"But Nikki is..." Marcus started, but quickly looked up at her. "Do we need a nursery, Suzie?"

She smiled serenely, nodding. "We do."

Marcus wrapped his arms around Suzie, kissing and hugging her tightly. "When? When do we need the nursery?"

"Certainly not in three weeks!" she assured him as Lydia had also excitedly come around the table to embrace her friend. "How about by February sometime?"

Simon reached over the table and shook Marcus' hand heartily. "Congratulations! Well done!" he exclaimed. "You two are apparently on the two-year plan!"

"Another baby," Lydia sighed happily. "I'm so happy for you both. What wonderful news to come all at once. A house and a new baby on the way. Wait until Sister Anne hears this! And your baby and Jimmy will be about a year apart, just like Nikki and Jimmy. Oh, this is too perfect!"

Suzie raised her hand at even suggesting a home birthing. "Now, now... a midwife may have worked for you, but it won't work for me. I'll be at the hospital and knocked right out. They can surprise me when I wake up and tell me what I had. I'm not into feeling the pain, like you did. Nor do I intend to work right up until the end, like you! I'll be home, knitting baby blankets and arranging the nursery."

"Nevertheless, the nuns at the hospital will be overjoyed. They've become quite delighted with their shifts with the babies. Sister Mary Margaret particularly has said she enjoys the opportunity to be with Nikki and Jimmy, both," Lydia assured her. "Oh, can't you just see Nikki with a new baby?"

Gazing at Suzie, Marcus appreciated that this time he could share in her pregnancy... every stage. If he couldn't share the birth, so be it. He would be there for all the rest. He fleetingly wondered if they could get Nikki baptized before the new baby came. *What if we have a son?* he thought... And it occurred to him that he had never seen Suzie's body transform with third-trimester fullness or known how she had coped the last time with the changes as they took place.

It would be a new experience for them both. His life was falling into place.

That night, after everyone had retired upstairs, Lydia stood at the bureau and reached for her hairbrush, loosening the bun she had worn during her long hours at the walk-in clinic. Across the room, Simon unbuttoned his shirt, carefully hanging it in the closet.

"Simon," Lydia started. "This will be so different for them... to share this pregnancy."

He looked over at her in surprise. "I hope it brings them closer together."

Lydia pulled the tie from her hair, letting the tresses fall around her shoulders. "Do you think it will change anything for Nikki? She's the center of attention right now. I wonder how she'll adjust."

Simon came around the bed, taking the hairbrush from her hand.

"Let me," he said, counting in his head, as he ran the bristles through her long waves for the one hundred strokes she did each night. "Are you wondering about Nikki? Or more about Suzie and Marcus, as a couple?"

She nodded, melting as he stroked her hair, smoothing out the tangles.

"If I'm being honest, I'm thinking more about our next pregnancy. The next time we have one, it won't be an accident or under such complicated circumstances. I can just picture you coming to bed, saying, 'Let's make a baby tonight!' And then, together, we'll get to wait and see if it happens!"

"Well, I just lost count of my strokes!" he teased, before continuing. "And if it doesn't happen right away, we'll get to try again, and again, and again."

Lydia laughed in turn. "What a chore!"

Simon pulled her to him. "Forget the hundred strokes! Now my mind is completely occupied elsewhere."

She turned around. "And where is your mind, Simon?"

He opened her robe and slid his hands inside of it. "I can tell you... or I can show you."

Lydia took his bearded face in her hands and pressed her body against his. "Is that so?" she murmured. "Our anniversary is coming. And I have something to show you, too."

Simon looked down at her. "Is that so?" he mimicked her.

"Come to bed," she ordered him as she reached up to the lamp on the wall, turning it down so only the glow of the streetlights found their way through the window.

"What can you show me in the dark?" Simon asked curiously, laying down.

She slid into bed, snuggled up against his shoulder, and draped one of her legs over his hip.

"That's a great start!" he whispered. Simon reached down and pulled her thigh tighter to him, suddenly sliding his hand down her leg.

"What have you done?" he exclaimed, thoroughly aroused, pushing her onto her back and sitting upright in the bed. He ran his hand down to her ankles.

She stretched out, luxuriating under his touch. "Gillette safety razors..."

"Your legs, my love, are as smooth as Jimmy's little bottom!" he exclaimed softly.

Lydia smiled at him in the darkness. "You like it?"

"Do I like it?" he murmured, in complete delight. "Let me explore a bit more and I'll let you know..."

Chapter 15

Social Unrest

"What's that, Mom?" Peggy asked, her curiosity piqued as she dried the last supper dish and settled into a chair beside her mother at the table.

Anna looked up, placing her cup of tea on its saucer. "I grabbed the mail before we left home to come see you. It's a letter from your sister, honey."

"No, I meant the photo… the newspaper photo," Peg said, pointing to the newspaper her mother was reading.

Anna sighed, "Ah, you are not going to believe what those two men did!" She handed the paper to Peggy.

"Wow," Peggy exclaimed, taking in every printed word. "Geeze."

"We were there that night, your dad and I. It was right after Lydia had given birth, which is not mentioned in the article, of course. Those two came in all black from the smoke. Marcus even had a big gash in his head from a brick wall falling."

Just then, Andrew and Tommy came in from the yard, arms full of firewood. Andrew carried only a few small pieces, while Tommy had a dozen or more, balanced in his arms.

"Who has a big gash in his head?" Tommy asked quickly.

"Marcus did," Peggy replied, still reading, astonished.

"Marcus who? The doctor? Lydia and Simon's friend?" Andrew asked, dropping his small load of wood into a basket near the door.

Peggy nodded, still reading, perched on edge of the chair. "Listen to this!" She read aloud an excerpt about the two surgeons, running into the burning building to amputate a man's leg, saving him from dying where he lay, pinned, surrounded by flames. "Can you just imagine the courage it took to run right into the fire?"

Anna nodded. "When they came home that night, they were joking around like it was no big thing at all. Simon sewed the gash closed right in the kitchen, didn't he Andrew? Right there, he stitched him right up at the kitchen table. Didn't even go to the hospital."

"Nope," Andrew sank heavily into one of the chairs, catching his breath. "Lydia ended up at the hospital, not Marcus. Those two... I'm telling you. Cut from the same cloth, those men."

Peggy looked at her parents, wide eyed. "I cannot imagine what those three days were like for all of you. Must have been amazing... Lydia has the baby. Those two run into a fire, heroically saving the workers' lives, and then Lydia ends up with a horrible complication... It's all too much!"

"What complication?" Tommy asked, joining the rest of them at the table.

"She was bleeding too much, a complication from the birth," Anna reported. "Needed to have a procedure done to stop the bleeding."

Andrew raised his hand, not wanting to hear anything more about female matters. "What's important is that she made it, and they made it... and apparently a whole lot of steel mill workers made it, because of those two. No wonder the mayor of the city wanted to recognize them."

Peggy tapped her pointer finger on the photo. "It's a good picture... I bet Lydia cut it out to put in her Bible or something, for safekeeping!"

Anna laughed. "I'm sure she did. She is very proud of him."

"It was brave. First the war, then that," Andrew nodded. "Good men."

Peggy picked up the letter her mother had handed to her and skimmed through it. "Baby's growing fast. Look at what she wrote, Mom. Geeze, she really started back to work, already?"

"With the baby no less! Says the nuns watch him while she's on duty." Anna called over to her husband, "Andrew, we need to get over there to see them again, soon. Been too long since I held my newest grandbaby."

"She'll work herself to death," Andrew said worriedly.

"Don't worry, Dad. She was used to working hard in the war. And with a doctor husband, she's got built-in house calls. It'll be okay," Peg reassured her father.

Steve and Mary joined the adults at the table, Mary climbing up onto Peg's lap. She had a drawing in her little hand. "A picture, honey? Let mommy see," Peggy's face lost a shade of color. "Wow, look at all that detail—"

"Something for Grandpa's icebox, Mary?" Andrew asked eagerly, his love for the little girl always evident.

"It's... not quite finished yet," Peggy replied, doing her best to hide her panic that someone else might see it. She scanned the picture of a tall man hitting a woman bent over the bed, with two children watching. "I'll help you finish it and then we'll give

Grandpa and Grandma their own picture for their icebox, how about that sweetie?"

Mary looked up and nodded. She was clutching her doll tightly to her chest.

"And we're going to make a new dress for your doll today," Anna assured the little girl. "Maybe something in yellow. Would you like that?"

"Dolls are for babies," Steve said, hovering next to his father. "Aren't they, Dad."

"Mary is still young yet, son," Tommy said. "She's practicing, for being a mother, that's all. No higher calling than being a mother of a man's child, son. Wives honor their husbands by having their babies."

"And this mother is very happy to have a son and a daughter," Peggy said, gently brushing Steve's hair from his eyes. "I was blessed to have one of each. I wish I could have had a dozen!"

"Why didn't we get another brother, Mom?" Steve asked. "Why is it just Mary and me?"

"Just the way it worked out, honey," Peggy said. "I just didn't get pregnant again, that's all. That happens sometimes."

"I also only had two, Steven. Remember?" his grandmother chimed in. "And I didn't even get to have a son. Still, I'm glad my daughters got married and I got to have two sons-in-law. And I got you for a grandson. That makes you very special."

Steve flushed, feeling praised. He liked being special. Now there was another grandson though. He didn't want to lose his special status.

"I'm worn out," Andrew said. "Time for bed, for me."

"I'll go up with you, dear," Anna told him, wanting to help if his heart was troubling him. "Let's get you comfortable. Come on, Mary. I'll help you brush your teeth for bed."

Peggy watched her dad get up, slowly. Anna and Mary helped Andrew head for the stairs. Her father was definitely slowing down and Peg was quite worried.

"Are you going up soon, Tommy?" Peg asked.

"Yeh, after they're all done up there. You head on up, too, son," he told Steve who obediently headed straight for the stairs.

Peggy stood. "I'm going to bring up some jars for lunch tomorrow. I think I'll make a green bean casserole. We have plenty of canned beans left."

She headed for the cellar to fetch tomorrow's meal. Holding the handrail down the wooden steps, she made her way across the dirt floor to the shelves of preserves and canned goods. Peg began to sort through the various sizes of jars, grabbing the ingredients she sought. Standing there, she was suddenly plunged into total darkness as the bare bulb hanging from the ceiling went out.

Frightened of tripping over something on the dirt floor, she froze for a moment. Just then, she heard the lock at the top of the steps slide shut. Carefully, she placed the glass jars back on the shelves, cautious not to drop them in the darkness. Calling for help would do no good—no one would hear her from the second floor, all the way upstairs.

The cellar's darkness seemed to press in around her. A shiver ran down her spine as if something was crawling on her—perhaps something was. Arms outstretched, Peg shuffled toward the steps, only to collide with the wringer washer, her knee striking it sharply. At least it gave her a sense of direction in the blackness.

The stairs would be to her right. She felt the wall until her foot reached the bottom step. Resigned, Peg sat there and took a long, measured breath. It was going to be a long night.

What have I done this time?

Hours later, Peg stirred. The scrape of the latch sliding open at the top of the steps jolted her awake. The light flickered on. It was blinding after being in total darkness for so long. She looked up to see Tom filling the door. Quickly, Peg stood and started up the stairs—apparently, she had been down there long enough for Tommy, but then he started down the stairs, closing the door behind him. Peggy backed up quickly. At the bottom of the steps, he studied her, but didn't say a word.

"Tommy," she started, apprehensive. "I want to take you to bed..."

He nodded. "That would be good."

She drew closer. "You've had a long day. Wouldn't a nice massage be relaxing?" She reached for the buttons on his shirt and opened the top two. Peggy was relieved when he reached for her dress. He opened the long row of white buttons, sliding her dress over her shoulders. It dropped onto the dirt floor.

Tommy said, "We'll start right here."

"In the cellar?" she asked, looking around.

"Why not? Won't disturb your parents this way. There's my workbench," Tom said.

In just her slip, Peggy shivered a little. "It's kind of chilly down here," she said softly. "Let's not take too long. I want to get you in a warm bed, rub you down."

His expression began to change. "All that talk, about those two doctors... how brave... how courageous... how noble. You didn't have one single thing to say about me."

Peg looked around nervously. "Well, it was just that newspaper article, you know, that Lydia sent. I mean, you can't blame us all for being amazed at what happened. You know, Tommy? It just brought up the subject."

Involuntarily, she backed up a couple of steps; the look in his eyes had changed. She knew this look. Tom was right. Being down here in the cellar would not disturb her parents up on the second floor. Her eyes filled. "Maybe a hot bath, Tommy..." she pleaded quietly now. "I'll wash you myself. It will feel good. Then, we can do... other things you enjoy."

The rage had found its full force, his eyes narrowed. In two steps, he was beside her. He picked her up and placed her on the workbench. There were tools hanging from the cellar ceiling, but Tommy paid them no mind... a pile of wood was within reach. Peggy watched him gauge the thickness of one slat, her heart sinking fast. He cast that one aside and looked for another.

"This is better," he said under his breath. "Face down."

"Oh, Tommy..." She was already weeping.

He ran his hands over her bare skin. "Your sister this, your sister that, her husband so brave! You couldn't say one good thing about me."

Her hands were already searching for something to hold on to. The workbench was set into a small indent, with the cellar wall running along three sides. The open edge of the bench was rough and full of splinters. The smell of sawdust was already in her nostrils with her face pressed against the wood surface.

"There are so many good things I could have said about you, Tommy," Peg wept.

"Yeh, but you didn't," he said, experimentally running the slat over her. "You just don't seem to learn, Peg. It's your sister's fault, bragging the way she does. Makes you get all caught up in her life. You just don't get it. I don't leave scars... but maybe you need a lasting mark after all... to stay focused on us. Hm... yes, maybe you do at that... somewhere you can easily see it."

Peggy knew it was morning when she heard the lock opening again and saw a gleam of light dart down the stairs. His footsteps were heavy as he stomped down the stairs. He was carrying a clean dress for her and brought it over to the workbench where she was shivering severely.

"Roll over," he told her, checking her backside; she winced. "You have some splinters there. We'll pull them out upstairs. Show me the front. Hm. Well, you made me do that. Can you see that easily enough, Peg? Is it a good enough reminder?"

She nodded. It would stare back at her, right in the mirror.

"Time for breakfast," Tommy told her, pulling her off the workbench. "Your folks aren't up yet. You have time to wash up in the bathroom downstairs before making breakfast."

Her knees buckled and he propped her up against the bench, dropping the dress over her head and smoothing it out. "There," he said. "You need to wash your face and arms. Get the sawdust off."

Numbly, Peggy nodded as he pull-pushed her toward the stairs. She stumbled as she climbed the steps, her legs refusing to obey her. Tommy put his hands on her, propelling her forward... she gave a yelp of pain.

"Yep," he said. "You won't forget this one... but then, I thought that the last time, too."

I wish you were dead, Peg thought, grasping the single rail to help pull herself up the steps into the kitchen. The sounds of the night still rang in her ears, as present and real as the pain she felt now. She avoided looking in the mirror over the sink in the bathroom as he came in behind her, shut the door, and turned on the water.

"Wash your face," Tommy instructed. Peggy obeyed, filling her hands with the cold water, scrubbing her face and arms, to rinse away the night on the cold workbench.

"Bend over the toilet," he commanded.

Her heart sank. Silently, slowly, she obeyed, willing herself to move. Peggy felt the washcloth. The soapy rag stung, but she welcomed the soothing cold water.

Then he fished around in the little mirrored medicine cabinet and got down on one knee. "Hold still," Tommy grunted. In the dim light of the bathroom, he pulled out several splinters with the tweezers. Peggy bit her arm to keep from screaming as the tip of the tweezers probed her raw skin.

"Bet that feels better!" he announced cheerfully, showing her one stubborn sliver of wood, pinched between the tweezer tips.

Peggy stared at it, then nodded.

"You know, I think we should invite the neighbors over for a cookout on the back porch!" he said as if it were just another routine morning. "What do you think about that? We haven't seen much of them... not since they saw a good bit of you bent over the railing... well, at least Bernie, Parker, and Ricco."

Peggy's cheeks burned with shame. She had been completely avoiding everyone in the neighborhood.

"Whatever you want, Tom," she whispered. Maybe he would beat her to death before the charcoal grill was even lit.

He smiled broadly. "That's being a good wife! Maybe you did learn something after all."

They left the bathroom and turned the corner to the kitchen where Anna was already at the counter, washing some fruit. She turned at the sound of them coming. "Well, good morning you two. Honey, you look exhausted. Didn't you sleep last night?"

Peggy accepted her mother's hug. "I'm just a little achy this morning," Peggy managed.

"It's going around!" Anna exclaimed. "Your dad is having trouble getting moving this morning, too. He'll be down in a minute with the children. I'll help make breakfast."

"Thanks, Anna," Tommy said. "Sit down at the table, Peg. I'll make the eggs." He pulled out a chair from the table and sat her down in it, firmly... Peggy's face went white. She needed to lie down and be off her bottom.

"Thank you, Tom," she said in as strong a voice as she could muster. "That is so nice of you. You're so thoughtful."

"Well, you're welcome!" Tom said cheerfully.

"Yes, it is!" Anna said in surprise, looking at Tommy who rarely cooked. "I didn't know you cooked, Tommy!"

"He helps with meals all the time, Mom... He's wonderful helping me in the house," Peggy added, hearing her husband's words echo in her mind. *In the morning, just think of all the good things you're going to tell your folks about me. You'll have all night to think about it,* Tommy had told her during her correction in the cellar.

"I'm so glad to hear that!" Anna exclaimed, delighted. Maybe her daughter and son-in-law were finally working things out. *Wouldn't that be a blessing?*

"Morning, Mom. Morning, Dad," Steven said, running downstairs and into the kitchen. He looked at his mother curiously. She was sitting at the table and his father was at the stove cracking eggs? Something wasn't right. "Need help, Dad?"

"Sure son, make some toast for everyone," Tommy said, roughing up the hair on his head. "You're a good boy to offer."

Steven's face flushed. That was good to hear! He was on his dad's good side this morning. A great way to start the day. "Hey, Dad, I'll help you clean up the yard today after Pop and Grandma go home."

"Sounds good, son," Tommy nodded. "That storm last night sure blew a bunch of branches off didn't it?"

"Lots of thunder and lightning cracking all over the place!" Steve exclaimed.

Oh. So, there was a storm last night? No wonder no one heard anything from the cellar, Peg thought miserably.

"Everyone on the block likes the way Tom keeps our backyard, Mom," she said for everyone to hear. "They walk by and admire it all the time."

"I'll bet they do! It is well landscaped, Tommy," Anna praised her son-in-law. "Oh, hello, dear! Did you smell something good cooking?" She hugged Andrew as he entered the kitchen. "You sit down. I've got a fruit salad."

"Smells great, Tommy," Andrew said, taking his seat. "Turning into a chef, huh?"

"Just helping out, Dad," Tom replied. "Peg didn't sleep so well."

Andrew sat in a chair across the table and looked at his daughter with concern. "You do look a little peaked, Peg. What's the matter?"

"Just a little achy, Dad. It's nothing much," Peggy said through tight lips. Her bottom was screaming as she wondered if there would be blood on her dress when she stood.

Anna looked anxiously over her shoulder. "I hope you aren't getting the flu, dear."

"I'm sure I'll be alright in a few days, Mom," Peggy replied softly.

Tommy came up behind Peggy, placing both hands on her shoulders. "She can spend some time resting in bed today after you folks go home," he said. He was well aware that he had gone without his after-correction apology during the night.

"Well, then, we should leave after breakfast," Andrew suggested to his wife. "Let her sleep."

They ate breakfast while talking of the week ahead. Tommy scooped a serving of eggs onto Peg's plate. She managed a few bites... offering the chef sufficient praise.

Anna and Andrew were soon gathering their things and saying their goodbyes, promising to have the family over to their house in Greensburg, soon. They all waved as the older couple drove off down the street. Once they were out of sight, Tommy turned to the children. "Find something to do, kids."

"You bet, Dad!" Steven said, watching his father pull his mother up the stairs to the second floor. He recognized that way of walking that his mom was using. She must have been bad again last night after the rest of them had gone to bed. Well, at least his dad was helping her get back on track.

In the bedroom, Tommy pulled down the sheets and took off Peggy's dress and slip, pointing to the bed. "You can get in, Peg," he told her, and gratefully she sank onto the bed. But this time rolling on her stomach did not help with her pain. Seconds later, she groaned, feeling Tommy climb on top of her. "Time to make amends," he told her. "Look, Peg, these are right where you can see. Think they'll help you remember to be respectful?"

"I'll remember," Peggy whispered as he lowered himself, rocking against her until she cried out from the pain.

"Feels good, huh, Peg?" he said, breathing hard in her ear.

Peggy forced herself to say what he wanted to hear. Maybe she could find a way to poison him or... steal money from his pockets and take the car and drive to... to... Boston or St. Louis... somewhere he could never find her. As he used her for his purposes, she comforted herself by thinking how far away she could get. *Or maybe he'll just kill me one of these times.*

But Tommy was thinking something entirely different. *That sister of hers, needs to be knocked down a few pegs... bragging about her husband like that!* The more he tried to correct Peggy, the more disobedient and willful she was becoming—all because of Lydia bragging and showing off. It was making Peg ungrateful. Tommy started imagining that he was correcting Lydia... with red welts, bringing her down a notch... teaching her her rightful place, in submission to a man... that's what the woman needed. He would find a way. He would show Lydia what she was really good for... nothing more than satisfying a man's needs. Maybe then Peggy would settle down and finally behave.

The dockside clinic had finally opened, nestled between a towering steel mill and a bustling district of garment factories. Rows of workers' homes lined the busy city streets nearby. To the south, the river flowed steadily, while to the north, wholesalers and butchers kept the city supplied with essential goods. Between the generosity of the mill operators and a few of Pittsburgh's benevolent, wealthy citizens, the money had come together for a small building, equipment, and the supplies needed, with little expense to the hospital. Doctor Maloney had agreed that the medical students would benefit from the hands-on experience of real-world medicine. Between an announcement written up in the newspaper and the sign over the front door, word got out quickly that mild surgical issues could be addressed close by, with little waiting, and considerable expertise from the exceptional doctors on site.

Simon and Marcus were grateful that other surgeons from the hospital team had also generously volunteered their time and expertise. During their shifts at the clinic, each kept a meticulous log, clinically documenting procedures including stitches for hands, heads, and arms injured in the workplace; mild lacerations from barroom brawls; sprains splinted from overexertion; puncture wounds caused by sewing machines; children tumbling off bicycles and tearing tender knees; and butcher shop mishaps, where slippery cleavers occasionally went astray. For many, the clinic on the corner was just a short, convenient walk away.

It wasn't long before return visits were being scheduled, as patients came back for follow-ups such as suture removal, wound assessments, or treatment for infections—an ever-present risk among the hard-working, hard-living population. At the front of the clinic, on the check-in counter, sat a wooden box with a slot in the top. Patients could drop in a few coins or a dollar, as they felt inclined. For now, the clinic operated on donations alone—those who could pay did so, while those who couldn't were treated anyway, in line with Charity's mission. Men, women, and children... all received care.

Suzie thoroughly enjoyed assisting the doctors with the light surgical duties. The variety of conditions and individuals they saw was stimulating. Work ebbed and flowed, but they found that lunch hours were particularly busy as people seemed to come in for help when they had a break. Nikki played in the back in her playpen, happy with the periodic attention from her mother who stopped to play, read a story, feed her, or settle her for nap time mid-morning and also in the afternoon.

This particular day, Suzie was working alongside Simon, while Marcus was operating over at Charity. During a lull, as they cleaned the counters after their last patients, Suzie couldn't help but notice that Simon seemed to have something on his mind.

"What do you think, Suzie?" Simon began. "I think you're a natural at this. You're good at all of it—assessments, quick interventions, knowing what someone is going to need, dressings and washing out wounds... and you remembered how to suture! It's like you were born for this kind of work."

Suzie laughed, her eyes sparkling and full of enthusiasm. "I do love it here!" she openly admitted. "It's the best of both worlds... I'm not limited at all and I can have Nikki here with me. I know she needs other children, too, so we'll spend time at the playground and such. But she also seems to like just playing in her playpen and reading her little books to Bear."

Smiling, Simon nodded. "She's so bright! I think she really believes that Bear understands the story. Who knows? Maybe he does! You and Marcus read to her a lot, don't you?"

"Every day," Suzie confirmed. "Although, some of what Marcus reads to her... well, I'm not sure about it."

Puzzled, Simon glanced at the little toddler napping in the other room. "What on earth could Marcus be reading to her that you'd be concerned about? He's not teaching her the inner workings of the intestines or how to repair an aortic dissection—?"

Shaking her head, Suzie raised a hand to stop him. "No, no, nothing like that. No medical stuff, as far as I can tell! Honestly, Simon, it's the religious stuff he reads that worries me."

"Religious stuff," Simon pressed, thoroughly confused.

"Yes, like baby Moses in the basket, and the sheep and shepherd, the lion's den... stories like that. They're bound to fill her little mind with all sorts of strange ideas," Suzie explained while carefully wrapping the instruments that had been soaking in alcohol, drying each one on a clean surgical cloth.

Simon leaned back against the counter. "What kind of strange ideas are you worried about, Suzie? I doubt little Nikki is going to run into any real lions. Although she might see some sheep in a field when you drive up to Rochester. There's no harm in knowing that a good shepherd watches over them, is there?"

Placing the bottle of alcohol back up in a cupboard, Suzie shook her head. "No, there's nothing wrong with that, of course. But there's a potential harm in teaching her that she can't rely on herself, on her own best judgement. Those tales seem to teach that a person must rely on something outside of themselves to get by in life. That's what's risky, in my book. Sets a precedent for weakness. I want her to learn to be confident with herself and her decisions."

Now Simon was the one who nodded. "So, if Nikki thinks there's a God up there helping her, she won't develop her own strength of conviction? Is that it?"

"Worse than that, Simon," Suzie added. "If she thinks her daddy believes he has to ask an invisible being, somewhere up there, for help all the time, then she'll see him as a weak man!"

Gently, Simon pursued the idea. "Suzie, do you think Marcus is weak for trying to figure out what God is, for him?"

She just shrugged. "I guess I do. I mean, he used to be so bold and irreverent. No holds barred. He just lived for the moment... and made the most of it. I loved his sense of humor, the irreverence. Now, he's always got to plan ahead, think about the future, all that. He's much more serious."

"Hm," Simon said, crossing his arms as he carefully navigated his thoughts. "I wonder if some of that is just natural... from him being a husband and father... and with a second child coming now. Men like us, who lived in the moment during the war... well, now we're nearly forced to start thinking about the future, kids in school, earning a living to support our families. Just normal adjustment to life stuff really."

Suzie rolled her eyes and sighed in frustration. "Simon, he actually asked me to pray with him the other night. My god, what was he thinking!"

He was thinking about my God, Simon thought, happily realizing that his friend was growing in his faith. "So, what did you tell him?" Simon maintained a casual tone.

"I told him, 'If there's such a thing as an all-knowing God, why would I need to set aside a time to talk to him? It's like telling someone something they already know, over and over.' Sort of pointless, in my book, anyway."

"You do realize that I talk with God regularly, right?" Simon asked her curiously. "That Lydia and I pray together?"

"Of course I realize that, Simon... but that's you guys!" she declared. "You've always been like that, with the religious stuff... the whole time I've known you. The getting married to Lydia, the doing things the conventional way. You've never shied away from your beliefs. But this just isn't Marcus. It just doesn't fit his personality. Frankly, it makes me a little uncomfortable."

Simon was concerned about the impact a growing spiritual divide could have on his friends' marriage. Wanting to find a way to help her understand Marc's emerging faith, he offered a suggestion. "You know, you're more than welcome to go with us on Sundays to see what it's all about, Suzie. It's not just telling God things He already knows. It's building a relationship with a creator who knows what we're capable of and wants to see us fulfill all our gifts, our talents... kind of like, as parents, we want Jimmy and Nikki to be everything they are meant to be."

Suzie dismissed the invitation. "I just want Nikki to be all she wants to be. That's enough for me. And I wish Marcus would focus on what he can see around him, instead of trying to find something invisible... if it's even real. Not to offend you, Simon, but even you can't see this god-being, literally... my book/writer's club people get it. They think as I do, discussing social issues and the world right around us. It's why I enjoy going to our get-togethers so much."

Simon was formulating his response when they were interrupted by a man who rushed in, bleeding from an accident with a lumber mill saw. He wanted to tell Suzie just how many times he'd seen the direct hand of God at work in his life... how he saw God working through Lydia's own eyes when she looked at him in that special way, reserved just for him. Maybe Suzie would be open to talking about it again sometime, or maybe with Lydia. He prayed they would be given another chance.

July was proving to be downright stifling. The temperature had risen dramatically, it was humid, and there wasn't much of a breeze blowing. A tension hung in the air that was difficult to define, but easy to sense. Lydia went about her business in the clinic, attending to the influx of patients, all of whom seemed visibly on edge. Having never experienced a big city in the summer, she realized that she had no idea what to expect when life, quite literally, heated up for a large population living in close quarters.

Peter Martin was back in the clinic for the week, and Lydia had been glad to see him coming through the doors earlier that morning. She was also pleasantly surprised when he approached her at the little front desk, between patients. He quietly pulled her aside.

"A word, Nurse Finney... I saw your handsome little son back in the exam hall, with Sister Teresa."

"Was he fussing?" Lydia asked in alarm, not wanting the special arrangements for the baby to interfere with anyone's work.

Peter smiled, "Not in the least. In fact, your little one seemed like he was trying to communicate something incredibly important to Sister Teresa with his little sounds."

Relief washed over Lydia. She knew the little babbles he was referring to, when Jimmy tried to imitate the grown-ups around him. She was sure that, in his own little mind, he was expressing something deeply profound—perhaps a truth familiar in heavenly realms, one that young souls could intuit far better than adults. Listening to him attempt to form words at this tender age was utterly captivating.

"That's good to know!" she exclaimed. "I mean, that he wasn't fussy, that he was not distracting Sister Teresa. Did Sister Mary Margaret take him back?"

Peter smiled. "She did. She seems to just adore James Marcus—I heard all about the auspicious name you chose! But Lydia, that's not the only thing I wanted to talk to you about."

"What can I do for you?" she asked quickly.

Assessing the flow of people, Peter spoke from experience, "Just be careful, Lydia. Tempers are flaring in the city as the Americans help the French push back the Germans. There are many of German heritage in this city and some groups have become a little hostile towards them as the war drags on and our own soldiers are being killed. The war has taken on a more personal tone than it had when we weren't involved directly, as a country. Plus, there's still union and labor unrest brewing. As the weather gets hotter, so do tempers. Add sickness or injury on top of all that, and it can be... well, tense. Just let me know if you sense anything coming to a head in the triage area so I can help."

Lydia nodded in agreement. "I'll keep my eyes open. It's such a shame... those who are worked up likely can't even fathom what real fighting looks like. If they had witnessed the war themselves, all they would want is to live together in peace."

Peter locked eyes with the nurse. "You saw some of the actual fighting, Nurse Finney? Even from the safety of the medical station?"

She nodded. "We were five miles from the front, Doctor Martin. Bringing the wounded in from the field was... well, there were a lot of wounded. And Simon, Doctor Finney, was almost killed when a shell dropped right on our camp. And one night German soldiers came right into our station after dark, during the winter... they took some of u—" Lydia shuddered. *What on earth am I thinking... blurting out such a thing here, and to Peter Martin?* She shook herself, then looked around the waiting area, refocusing on the here and now... on the needs in front of her.

Peter was shocked. Immediately noticing her anxiety, he gently placed a hand on her shoulder to steady her. "I'm sorry," he said softly. "This wasn't the right time or place to bring up the war. I truly apologize, Lydia—I never meant to cause you any distress."

"What?" she clarified. "Oh. We have to take life on its own terms, sometimes. They're just memories now. That's all. Just some... memories—I'll get you immediately if something looks out of the ordinary."

"That's all I ask," Peter said as he walked back to the examination hall. He recognized well the veil that had come down over her eyes, and deeply regretted triggering it. She must have seen a lot. What had the Germans taken that she couldn't even finish the sentence? Prisoners? More than concerned, he wrestled with whether or not he should mention this to her husband.

Their shift progressed smoothly, with Lydia savoring the quiet moments spent nursing Jimmy during the occasional lulls between patients. Even now, weeks later, she marveled at her body's ability to provide exactly what he needed to thrive and grow. After lunch, she settled him down for a nap in the dimly lit office. Sister Mary Margaret assured her that the low light posed no hindrance to her work. Still, Lydia couldn't help but wonder if the nun ever drifted off herself while the baby slept soundly.

As Lydia returned to the triage area, she considered the concerns Peter had raised. Nancy and Sally had been working for a few weeks now at Charity. What were they encountering out there, seeing patients in their homes? Were they wearing their whistles, in case Peter was right about tensions rising in the city? She would have to catch up with her fellow nurses and see how they were adjusting to their new jobs.

Lydia walked around, speaking with several of the waiting families, assuring them that they would be seen shortly. She knew how difficult it was to wait when loved ones weren't feeling well. As she made her way back to the desk, a young mother anxiously burst through the door, holding her baby.

"Help!" she exclaimed, terrified. "He's yellow all over! Something's terribly wrong!

Lydia rested the baby on the exam table next to the desk, where there was sufficient light. She looked into his little eyes and mouth.

His skin was indeed a dark shade of yellow. It was possible his tiny liver was failing, but that would be unusual. "Is he eating well? Drinking fluids well?" she asked.

"He has a huge appetite," she assured Lydia. "I put him on real food because he doesn't get enough with just my milk."

"What are you feeding him?" Lydia asked, knowing the impact diet could have on little ones.

"Just what they said, strained carrots, sweet potatoes... he loves carrots."

"What about peas and applesauce and cereals?" Lydia questioned further.

"No, he's still just on those vegetables," the woman assured her.

Lydia smiled to ease the mother's fears. "I think his color is from the carrots and sweet potatoes. Orange vegetables can make children's skin turn a yellow-orange color. It will fade away, over time, if you start giving him a balanced variety of fruits and vegetables, as long as they can be mashed up easily. Doctor Martin will see him... I think he'll also reassure you that it might just be time to add more variety to his diet. Otherwise, he's a very strong, healthy-looking baby!"

Every inch of the woman visibly relaxed as she took a seat to wait for Doctor Martin to confirm Lydia's assessment.

Just as Lydia was about to retake her seat at the triage desk, she paused, standing again to greet a family at the door. Several of the children were covered with a rash. The mother hovered over them, distraught, as she tried to stop the children from scratching their irritated skin. She spoke broken English and the father appeared to speak no English at all, just looking apprehensively around the waiting area. Lydia smiled reassuringly and quickly went to them.

"I can help you," she offered. She pointed to the rashes with a questioning look.

The mother nodded and followed Lydia to the triage desk, where Lydia asked for their names. The woman seemed to understand the request, answering and touching each head, "Greta, Franz, Frederick, Wilhelm... please help..."

Lydia nodded and bent to the children with her flashlight, indicating she wanted to see their throats. As she made her way down the row, a group of men came through the door carrying a man between them who was favoring his leg, unable to put any weight on it.

"Nurse!" one of them shouted as they came through. "Our buddy needs help."

Lydia nodded. "Sit him right there in a chair, and I'll be right with you." She resumed her examinations of the children's throats.

One of the men pushed his way past the family to get to Lydia. "Our buddy needs help now!" he said urgently, angry at having to wait. "Can't you see these kids later?"

Lydia replied calmly, but firmly. "I'll be with your friend in just a moment. Just as soon as I'm finished with this family."

The father of the children moved cautiously around them as the mother grew visibly fearful. He spoke softly to her, calming her.

"They're German!" the angry man exclaimed. "No dirty German kid gets treatment before my buddy does, who is an Am-er-i-can cit-i-zen!" he yelled, punctuating each syllable with force.

Lydia noticed the German father's fist curling protectively, and she quickly stepped between the two men. "These are just sick little children who need attention. It won't take me but a moment. I promise, we will help your friend."

The man glared down at her. Lydia turned swiftly, her focus on guiding the German family to safety. She never saw the fist coming. It struck the back of her head, spinning her into the wall where it met the edge of the door. As she fell, her head hit the sharp edge with a sickening thud... the world dissolving into darkness.

From her odd position on the floor, a flurry of feet came into view as Lydia's vision returned to her. Confused, she felt the back of her head... it was throbbing. One of the nuns was on the floor next to her, trying to say something... maybe about waking up... but it sounded so very far away and not like something she wanted to try to understand. She closed her eyes again, hearing a tumult of yelling... she couldn't sort out any of it. Some of the feet moved away. She felt arms picking her up from the floor and carrying her somewhere, dimly aware that they belonged to Peter Martin. She slipped away one more time... it was so comfortable in the darkness.

Lydia realized it was quiet. She opened her eyes briefly and saw the white ceiling overhead. Her neck and the back of her head ached. She knew that she was laying on one of the examination tables in the back... Sister Edwarda was in the room beside her.

Peter Martin's voice pierced the silence, "Nurse Finney? Lydia? I'm just checking your eyes." She squinted against the bright light as she felt her eyelids being opened. "Do you know where you are?"

She nodded.

"We'll send her upstairs—we need pictures of her head and neck—make sure there is no fracture," Doctor Martin informed the nun. *How could this have happened?* He found himself repeating the question over and over in his mind.

"Yes, Doctor Martin," Sister Edwarda replied, also worried.

Lydia felt the room start to sway until she realized that she was on one of the hospital carts being pushed down a long corridor. The movement made her nauseous. When it finally stopped, she felt like her body kept on moving a distance. At least the world was getting brighter again, her vision more focused. Someone told her to hold still... she gladly complied. Then, the rolling cart swayed again, back down the corridor once more until she was back in the clinic's examination room.

"Jimmy," she managed to whisper to Sister Edwarda.

"He's fine," the nun assured her. "Just in the next room. Rest a moment. Doctor Finney will be down to take you home after they review your radiograph and make sure that you are alright."

Lydia nodded. It was so simple to obey the woman. Then, she heard Simon's voice nearby, angry and alarmed. "What happened?"

"Doctor Finney, come with me a moment," Peter Martin spoke steadily as he pulled Simon into the hallway, aiming to reassure and calm his distressed colleague.

"What happened?" Simon demanded again.

Peter quickly explained. "Racial tension between a German family and some angry factory workers, who chose that moment to try to solve the war between two countries in our waiting room. Nurse Finney got caught between them. Sucker punched to the back of the head, then into the wall unfortunately. I cannot believe this happened to her, in our own clinic! I need to look at the film being developed to make sure nothing is fractured, then she can go home."

Simon nodded. "You go; I'll stay here."

Peter Martin ran down the hallway, hoping the films would be normal. Simon re-entered the examination room and lowered the lights. He took a flashlight as Sister Edwarda moved out of the way and looked into Lydia's eyes himself. "Lydia," he said quietly. "Tell me where you are."

"I'm at the hospital, Simon," she replied. "Things are clearing up a little. But I have an impressive headache—"

"I'll bet!" he softly exclaimed, relieved that she sounded coherent. "I'm supposed to worry about you when you're out on the street, not here at the clinic... squeeze my hands... now follow the light with your eyes."

"I'm sorry," she whispered, closing her eyes again after completing the exam. "Can we go home?"

He caressed her cheek. "Soon. Marcus is coming down shortly from the operating theater. He's changing clothes now. And Doctor Martin will be right back... he's reviewing the film they took. I'll help you and Marcus will take Jimmy."

"I know what he'll see on the film, Simon..." she sighed.

"What's that, my beloved?" he asked, kissing her forehead.

"Stupidity," she murmured, closing her eyes to wait.

By the time they arrived home, Lydia was able to walk into the house under her own power. She rested on the sofa with Jimmy close by while Suzie made supper. In her aching mind, she pondered how she could have handled the situation differently.

Simon crouched down beside her, his expression calm, masking his concern that she might still develop a bleed.

"Will you let me know if your headache gets worse or you have any trouble seeing or if you feel nauseated?" he asked. "I'll help you upstairs a little later."

"I will," she assured him. "You can drill a burr hole in my skull, like you did for that soldier in France. Take the clot right out."

He stroked her long hair. "You remember that burr hole? Guess your long-term memory isn't damaged, but I'd prefer not to have to shave away your lovely hair or drill a hole in your head," he smiled tenderly.

"I just wanted those little children to be out of the way in case the men started a brawl," Lydia admitted, thinking back. "Why were those workers so angry at that family for simply being German? It just doesn't make any sense... such hatred."

He caressed her face. "People tend to judge and live in their emotions when they don't understand something. It makes hateful actions easier to justify, in their minds."

She sighed. "I am still eternally grateful to those special Germans who saved me from a truly terrible fate."

He nodded. "Frederick. There was no language barrier with our handshake. I think he understood what I was trying to say too."

"I know he did, my love," she said, a lump in her throat. "He was ashamed of what his commander had done. That's why it's so sad to me when people pass judgment on all German people who are just trying to live their lives, do their best, raise their families and go to work. They aren't responsible for the Kaiser or his subordinates."

Simon's gaze was tender. He loved this about her, her ability to appreciate people of all walks of life, all heritages and backgrounds. She really didn't see differences as much as she saw commonalities. She did not know how to hate. "I'm going to wash up before supper," he said, kissing her forehead.

She nodded, watching him run up the stairs.

Jimmy began to fuss in his playpen. His little cries were becoming more lusty as he grew stronger, expressing his opinions about things.

Hearing the baby, Marcus came into the living room. "Someone seems to want you," he said. "Are you up for it, Lydia?"

"If I'm not, it seems Jimmy will make sure the whole neighborhood knows," she said softly. "I'll get him."

"No need," Marcus assured her. "Let me." He reached into the playpen, scooping up the baby and laying him beside her on the sofa. Lydia rolled onto her side and pulled the baby to her breast, where he immediately latched on.

"So, what was that all about at the clinic?" Marcus asked her, peering into her pupils to ensure that they were equal in size.

"I forgot to never turn your back on the enemy," she admitted honestly. "And at that moment, Marcus, the day laborers that walked in were the enemy, not the German family. I saw the father making a fist, moving in to protect his children. All I could think of was to get them behind my desk and put distance between the children and the workers who were so angry. I really didn't see a fist coming at the back of my head."

"I guess not! The man was a coward, hitting you," Marcus was seething beneath his practiced bedside manner. "Follow my finger..."

Obediently, her eyes followed Marc's pointer finger as it traced the invisible pattern. Then, she gently touched Jimmy's soft little cheek as he nursed. "He didn't mean to hit me. I'm sure of it. He meant to hit the German father. They were just sick little kids needing care. I'm sure the injured man needed care just as much, but if they'd just given me two minutes, I would've been able to get to him, too."

Marcus reached over, feeling the back of her head for the lump which was emerging through her long waves. "I get hit by falling bricks. You get hit by an angry man. I wish I'd been there. He wouldn't have come near you."

"I know," she said.

"Look at me," he insisted.

"Don't worry," she assured him. "Simon has a flashlight. He's been checking."

Marcus nodded with certainty. "No doubt! No, what I want to ask is whether today woke up... other things in your mind?"

At that, Lydia did look up at him. "A bit," she confessed. "It'll be okay."

"Hm," was all he said. "I'm going to help Suzie set the table. Stay focused on Jimmy and us, and make sure you say something if you're struggling," Marcus insisted.

After just a few bites of supper, Lydia decided that she wanted to go to bed with Jimmy. As Simon walked her up the stairs to help her get ready, she paused to appreciate that he had mounted a few family portraits along the wall leading up to the second floor. They were nice reminders, before bed, of all of the people they loved. He'd also hung some pictures of France. They were images of the unspoiled countryside, peaceful fields, and wholesome pastoral scenes of sheep and farms. It was important to see the good in the world... the *before* images. The images of what could be again, given time and healing.

Lydia slipped out of her clothes and, without the warmth of Simon's body next to her, wrapped her robe around her nightie. Simon tucked Jimmy into his bassinet and turned down the covers of their bed so Lydia could climb in. Tucking the blankets around her, he kissed her softly.

"I won't stay up late," he reassured her. "I'll come up soon and read up here, with you two. Just need to talk to Marcus about a couple of things first and do some push-ups." They would not leave the house to go jogging this evening.

She nodded, laying her head back on the pillow, but not finding it particularly comfortable, she quickly rolled onto her side. Sleep would be good if she could relax into it. To distract herself, she wondered what Marc's father had thought of the newspaper article she had mailed to him. Hopefully he was proud. Maybe he would reach out to his son soon... especially with a second grandchild on the way.

Downstairs, Simon and Marcus sat by the fireplace. Suzie was also upstairs getting Nikki down for the night. Simon drummed his fingers on the arm of the high-backed chair in front of the fireplace as Marcus skimmed through the daily newspaper for an update on the war in Europe, thinking that there must have been something in the news that triggered the anger in the workers at the walk-in clinic. The American army was making major advances with the Allied forces as troops continued to arrive. He didn't envy them. Marcus noticed Simon's fingers drumming and folded the paper again, laying it aside.

"No way to prevent stuff like this from happening, Simon," Marcus stated, breaking the silence.

Simon nodded. "Troubled world."

"Let's buy that island. Only for us. Somewhere in the Caribbean where there isn't too much risk of hurricanes. Put up hammocks... pick coconuts..."

Simon considered the idea. "Do the whole Robinson Crusoe thing?"

Marcus nodded. "Sure! Why not? The girls could run around half-naked in grass skirts, and we could get tanned in loincloths and spear fish in the shallow water."

This made Simon smile. "And swim with the sharks, over coral reefs?"

Marcus sat back comfortably, legs crossed, "Naw, skip the sharks. Sea turtles, yes... I'll outlaw sharks at our island. We'll be the only apex predators."

Together, they dropped down, doing their push-ups in tandem. Simon quit long before Marcus, who, this time, did not insist that he keep going. When Marcus finally gave in, they rested there on the floor, silent for a moment.

"All the paperwork in order, for the house?" Simon asked at last.

Marcus nodded. "Met with the lawyer. It's all taken care of. Waiting for it to be empty, is all."

"Are they leaving the icebox and stove for Suzie?" Simon asked.

Marcus laughed. "No! And I'm glad! They were pretty outdated. I have new ones being delivered as soon as we're able to go in.

That'll make Suzie even happier, to have new ones. She can set up her kitchen to suit her taste."

"She told me she was questioning the direction of your personal growth. Over at the surgical clinic... we had some downtime," Simon said after another pause. "It's the first time she's mentioned anything even remotely religious to me. I was glad she felt like she could bring it up."

Marcus sighed, "I wish we could do this together, Simon, I really do. Maybe if she could have talked to Father James like I did, he could have reached her like he reached me."

Simon paused, thinking about this. "Father James reached you because you wanted to be reached, Marc. You were ready to accept what he had to say."

Marcus got up, moving to sit on the sofa. "You're probably right. Though, it was more like he listened and let me find it myself. As if he was the road sign, but I had to walk the road. He simply said 'it was something worth pursuing'. Father Henderson is a little like him, you know? I listen to him, and it's like he's saying stuff that I kind of already knew, somewhere in the back of my mind, but never really stopped to think about."

"You are growing," Simon observed, sitting upright as well.

Marcus sighed. "Yeh, well, this thing about Monique is a set-back. I know God can't make time go in reverse—"

Simon laughed softly, "Well, He did do that once, during a battle in the Old Testament."

Looking up with wide eyes, Marcus exclaimed, "He did? Made time go backwards?"

"Stopped it anyway so that the battle could be won," Simon nodded.

"You need to show me where that one is!" Marcus added. "Sounds interesting. But no, seriously, what I did with... other women. I know it can't be undone. But I'm ashamed of it, Simon. I mean, how many kids do I have out there? When I think of how I was—"

"You need to read something, Marc. About a guy in the New Testament named Paul. Talks about how he does the things he doesn't want to do and doesn't do the things he wants to do. Killed a lot of people for believing the messiah had already come. Then God grabbed hold of him. Turned him around and what a turnaround it was!"

"I might have something in common with that guy," Marcus admitted. "I still have to live with my past though, Simon. Whatever might come of it."

"At least God didn't have to strike you blind for three days to get your attention!" Simon smiled. "I'm glad my son shares your name, buddy. And I'm really glad Lydia asked you to be Jimmy's godfather. It's great hearing you grow your faith in God. What Suzie doesn't realize is that it's that growth in you that made your relationship with her even possible. I'm not sure you'd have ever settled down with anyone, without some soul searching."

"Lost cause, huh?"

Simon shook his head. "You were never a lost cause, Marc. Maybe a work in progress—and there were times I wanted to throttle you when I first met you—but never a lost cause."

Marcus laughed. "Don't take it personally, Simon, but it was really Lydia that started this soul searching."

"Was it? I'm not surprised," Simon countered with a little smile.

Marcus nodded. "Yeh, well, you know I admired her, just like you did, right from the start. But she chose you... and because she chose you, I decided to become the kind of man someone like her would see as worthy. That was you. So, I started watching how you responded to things, how you handled the war... all the death... the uncertainty... you still found it in you to see something good in me, even when there wasn't much there to see. I wanted to understand what kept you going... what kept you steady. I remember you asking me once if I wanted something more, with her. And I did... but not to take her from you, Simon. You are my best friend, and I've always been happy for you. What I wanted, I guess, was to earn her respect... her full trust."

Simon chuckled. "She does tend to draw that out of people. She did with me, for sure. And yes, I may have been worried about your motives for a moment, the day I asked if you wanted more of a relationship with Lydia, but if I had died over there, I knew you would at least try to love her the way she deserves to be loved."

"Maybe we've both come a long way?" Marcus offered.

"Yeah," Simon agreed. "We've both grown. And Lydia truly sees only the good in both of us. And she's so happy that you're finding yourself and your place in God's grand plan. I really hope that Suzie joins you in it as well, so you can grow together. Because what happens next, Marc, is we get all of eternity to keep getting to know each other in God's kingdom. We don't ever have to say goodbye."

Marcus stood and stretched as he glanced up the stairs, it was time to call it a night. "I do like the sound of that! I was one of the lost sheep, huh?"

"More like a ram," Simon laughed, placing a hand on his buddy's shoulder. "Good thing you'll be right across the alley, Marcus. You've always said you have to keep an eye on us, but I think it maybe goes both ways."

Marcus smiled as they headed for the stairs, suddenly turning to Simon with a matter of more immediate concern. "Oh, one more thing, Simon. Lydia said today did trigger some bad memories... German family and all that."

"Thought of that, too."

"I'm sure you did," Marcus replied as they quietly climbed the stairs, hoping not to wake the others.

Simon gently closed the bedroom door behind him and settled into the easy chair by the bay window. He flipped through the latest medical journal to the articles he had marked for reading. After skimming through a few, his eyes grew too heavy. He dimmed the lamp and slipped beneath the covers, snuggling in beside Lydia. She still had her robe wrapped around her. He debated helping her out of it, but, as much as he wanted the feeling of her body next to his, he thought better of it. Maybe in the night, she would take it off on her own when Jimmy woke for a feeding. She was lying on her side, so he curled up gently behind her. After a bit, he drifted off into a restless sleep, pondering the miserable lack of compassion in this world.

Lydia glanced back at Charlotte... was she pregnant?... or was she Susannah? Somehow, Lydia couldn't tell the two women apart, their features merging into one... but Susannah shouldn't be in the trenches. Her friend was following right behind her, called to the commander's office with Lydia... but that wasn't right, either. She wasn't supposed to be in danger. I have to protect her, no matter what. As they entered the small office, the commander looked different, big and burly, more like the factory worker at the clinic. He came out from behind his desk, walking toward them. "One of you will lose your baby. You choose." The Susannah-Charlotte woman cried out. Lydia heard herself telling the commander to let her friend go. Simon would understand. Suddenly, she was alone with the commander, face down against his desk... and terror set upon her like the hounds of hell as his crop came down... she screamed in fear and felt him punch her in the head to quiet her...

Then, Lydia fought. "Never again!" she screamed. "No!" She kicked her feet at the man she hated. He tried to pin her arms, but she struggled against him with a surge of strength, hitting him with her fists to save her baby. She tried to kick him away, but he caught her in a bear-like grip against the desk she hated, sneering as he threatened, "Then I will take your friend's baby." He was on top of her and... she began to beg him now. "No, take mine... please leave her alone... please..."

"I told you I could make you beg me to hurt you."

"I hate you..." she whispered, knowing that she was firmly in his trap. "I hate you... I hate you... I hate you..."

Simon had just fallen into a deep sleep. His first awareness that something was wrong was when Lydia screamed out into the darkness, waking Jimmy, who immediately began to wail. Abril was frantically barking outside of the bedroom door, scratching at it to get inside and protect her. Lydia's terror also woke Nikki, who began to cry across the hall. Marcus and Suzie both jumped out of bed, thinking the house was under attack, like in the war. Suzie ran into Nikki's room to scoop her up, quickly coming to the realization that all of this traced back to Lydia, caught in a nightmare.

Marcus rushed across the hall, throwing open the other bedroom door. Leaping past him to get inside, Abril was confused when there was no intruder within. Grabbing the baby, Marcus moved Jimmy to safety, holding him against his chest, soothing him as Lydia inadvertently kicked the bassinet. Grabbing her flailing arms, Simon steadied Lydia, wanting to keep her from hitting her head again on the headboard or throwing herself onto the floor as she fought the very real enemy that none of them could see.

While Simon held her, he spoke to her, trying to guide her back to him, but this was different from the night terrors he had witnessed before... he couldn't reach her. He protected her injured head as she began sobbing and suddenly stopped fighting, surrendering to her fate, realizing she was trapped.

"Run, Suzie!" she cried out through the commander's underground door, her voice garbled with sorrow and terror. "Run!"

Simon was breathing hard, trying to contain her in his arms, as Marcus looked on, grief stricken, still sheltering the baby.

"Lydia, Suzie is safe... you're safe," Simon called to her. "You're home, no one is going to hurt you. Lydia, listen to my voice... no one is going to hurt Suzie... or you..."

He released one of her hands as she stopped fighting, and she protectively grabbed her belly. Simon understood instantly. "The baby is safe, Lydia, Jimmy is safe... it's okay, beloved." He wept for her as tears also streamed down her cheeks.

Still carrying Jimmy, Marcus moved over to the wall by the door and turned up the lamp. Meeting Simon's eyes, Marcus saw the pain in his friend's face. Simon was afraid to let go of Lydia until she was fully awake and cognizant of where she was.

As tiny Jimmy began to calm against Marcus's chest, the room grew quiet. Placing the baby back in his bassinet and tucking him in securely, he turned to see Lydia opening her eyes.

She stared around the room, recognition coming to her steadily.

"Simon..." she wept. She saw Marcus and reached out a hand for him. "Marc, did Suzie escape?"

Marcus gently touched her face. "Suzie is just fine, the baby is fine. Everyone is safe, Lydia."

"Thank God," she whispered, her eyes closing in relief. "Thank God. Thank God. It was a dream then... oh my God... oh God..."

Marcus exchanged a silent glance with Simon, his question conveyed without words. Simon's subtle nod was all the confirmation he needed. Without a sound, Marcus slipped out of the room, crossed the hall, and closed the door to his bedroom behind him. Inside, Suzie was waiting for him. She had already nursed Nikki briefly to calm her and had settled their daughter back into her crib. Marcus slid under the covers.

"What on earth was that all about?" Suzie demanded in frustration. "The entire neighborhood's probably awake by now, wondering if they should call the police or something!"

"Nightmare," he replied unnecessarily.

"Well, for heaven's sake!" Suzie exclaimed in a whisper. "What on earth would give her a nightmare like that? She's got a great home, husband, job, and a beautiful son. She's got everything."

"It's from the past, Suz," Marcus closed his eyes.

"Well, we all went through the war, Marcus," Suzie said, settling herself back down against the pillow. "It's not like the rest of us didn't see horrible things, too."

Marcus realized that Lydia must have never told Susannah about the trenches. *That's right*, Marcus thought to himself, thinking back. *Suzie had already gone home. She didn't know. And Lydia must not have said anything to her! Wow... but it's not my place to say.*

"She went through a little more than we did," was all Marcus could manage.

"You could have at least put on a robe before you ran over there," Suzie said as she rolled onto her side, closing her eyes.

Oh! Well... whatever. He dismissed the issue of his lack of attire and thought back to the timeline. Susannah had already returned to the States when Lydia was captured, when they starved, when Simon was missing in action... For whatever reason, Lydia hadn't told her... and it would remain in her control to reveal the details. Marcus held his peace and tried to go back to sleep, a somewhat futile exercise as he lay there listening for Lydia's soft sobbing to stop.

Simon put Jimmy to Lydia's breast, knowing that being close to the baby would reassure her of his safety and help to ground her to reality. He was right. The tangible experience of the baby nursing helped her to focus, driving away the fear as she held Jimmy, soothing them both. When the baby was done, Simon took him and changed his diaper before tucking him in and returning to their bed. He realized that Lydia had lost her robe at some point.

"What can I do, my love?" he asked. "What would help you most?"

"There's only one thing that helps... leave the light on, so I can see you."

Simon nodded, getting under the blankets with her. "Are you sure?"

She nodded, her eyes still glistening with tears. "Make me yours again, please, Simon. Drive him away from my memory, get him off my body... out of my mind."

He set everything else aside, focusing solely on tenderly kissing her and offering comfort. Simon gently brought her back to the night of their marriage in Nancy, and the following night when they came together in the hay stacks in the small stable, in the little French village. He reminded her of both moments, those joyous times of connection and togetherness.

And, just like the last time she had been transported back to her captivity, Lydia sought him out with an all-consuming passion that always surprised him. Rolling on top of him, wrapped in his arms, she drove out her demons by filling every corner of her awareness with only him. Holding fast to his eyes in the dim light of the room, she clung to him so there was no presence, but his. His touch was healing. And as Simon held her against his chest, he stroked her hair and her back, still marveling that they had been given the gift of each other, for both joy and comfort, restoration and healing. It was an incredible gift.

Lydia lay there, her head resting against his chest, feeling the steady rhythm of his breath. *Something has to change,* she thought. *I have to do something about these memories. There must be some hate in me after all... and it cannot be allowed to remain.*

Chapter 16

Dixmont

With Suzie, Nikki, and Marcus all moved into their new home, Suzie threw herself into the décor. The new appliances had been installed to her satisfaction and the dining and living room sets had been delivered and set into place. To their pleasant surprise, the walls of the house were not bright red after all, so there was little painting required.

Abril acclimated quickly, anticipating when she might find Nikki, with either of her parents, out in their little yard, just across the alley. When given the invitation, Abril would enthusiastically jump the fence for some playtime in her newly extended domain. She always allowed Nikki to chase her with abandon, while keeping the little toddler safely far from the alley.

Lydia and Simon were thankful to still feel connected to their friends. From their kitchen, they often caught glimpses of the lights turning on and off in the house across the way. Jimmy had been moved into his own proper little nursery. The four-month-old didn't seem to appreciate the privilege of having his own room, other than to fuss a bit louder for attention, during the nights.

With summer in full swing, Lydia's small vegetable garden was producing volumes of tomatoes, zucchini, onions, and lettuce...

the staples of any respectable backyard garden. She enjoyed watching Jimmy on his blanket, trying to roll over, as she pulled weeds from between tomato plants or caterpillars from the broad zucchini leaves.

Simon and Marcus still drove in together whenever they were both scheduled in the operating theater. Lydia or Suzie would often join them, depending on how their own schedules aligned, but today, Lydia had the day off and two errands to cross off her list.

Lydia finished the weeding, then gathered Jimmy up in his blanket and headed back into the house. On the back porch, she passed Abril, who had settled into the perfect spot, enjoying a gentle breeze that offered some relief from the warm summer sun. Lydia went upstairs to wash up, find a nice dress, and change the baby. Then, the two of them headed out.

Lydia boarded the trolley for her first destination, stepping off just outside Feldman's Jewelry Store. Cradling Jimmy in her arms, she pushed the door open, triggering the cheerful jingle of the bell overhead. It rang once more as the door drifted closed behind her.

In no time at all, the jeweler emerged from behind a curtained-off room just past the counter. "Ah, Mrs. Finney! How very nice to see you! Is this your son?"

Lydia smiled warmly and nodded, gently turning Jimmy to face Mister Feldman so he could admire the baby's chubby cheeks and endearing smile. True to form, Jimmy reached out for the man's beard, just as he always did with his own father's.

"How did it come out?" Lydia was anxious. She had saved up all of her pay to buy the perfect anniversary gift for Simon, and now held her breath, hoping it would live up to what she had envisioned.

The man smiled, peering over his half-spectacles. "Wait till you see," he held up a finger. "I think quite well."

Reaching beneath the counter, he pulled open a drawer and retrieved a small envelope, placing it gently on the countertop. Then, with a warm smile, he extended his arms toward the baby. "Allow me," he offered.

Lydia handed Jimmy over to the man, who cradled him with practiced ease as Jimmy reached for the man's white-flecked beard. Lydia carefully opened the envelope and drew out a fob and chain, revealing the pocket watch she had dreamt of giving Simon for so long now. With a click of the button at the top, the back sprang open. Inside the back cover, she read the carefully engraved, delicate script: "Simon, man of God, my rock. Lydia. 1918."

The jeweler noticed the tears welling up in Lydia's eyes and felt a quiet sense of satisfaction, knowing that she was truly pleased with the work.

"Doctor Finney will love this," Lydia exhaled slowly. "Thank you so much, Mister Feldman."

"How many years is it?" he asked kindly.

"Two," she confirmed. "We missed our first anniversary, having to be apart for a time... over in the war. So, this one is very special to me."

"I will find you a small gift box, then." Mister Feldman handed Jimmy back to Lydia before disappearing into the back for a moment.

Lydia gently bounced Jimmy on her hip. "Your daddy is going to be very happy with this."

After paying for the gift and carefully securing it in her pocketbook, Lydia thanked the jeweler again and left the little shop. Once outside, she hailed a taxicab to take them across the Ohio River, to the northwest part of the city. She had an appointment at Dixmont.

The taxicab drove them up a long, winding road until, at last, the impressive three-storied stone structure, with its towers and arched porches stretching across the front, came into view. Lydia noticed some patients outside, walking the paths or sitting in the shade of the trees. These were residents of the facility who lived there while receiving their treatments. Through the window of the taxicab, Lydia observed a number of them on crutches, navigating cautiously, many balancing on just one leg. Also scattered among them were staff, dressed in white, engaging in quiet conversations or strolling alongside the others.

On the surface, it seemed like a peaceful place, yet Lydia sensed that by nightfall, the corridors were likely teeming with restless ghosts or demons, drawn to the shadows of night—invading the dreams of those who slumbered within. She handed the fare to the driver and stepped out, her gaze shifting to the imposing entrance. Ignoring the lump in her throat, she offered Jimmy a reassuring smile before settling him at her shoulder. With resolve, she began the climb up the steep steps that led to the front porch and door.

Once inside, she asked for directions and was instructed to turn right down a long corridor that ran along the exterior porch. The windows running along it held her reflection, which like her memories, followed along beside her as her footsteps tapped against the linoleum tiles.

Reaching the office, she stepped inside and offered her name to the woman who greeted her warmly from behind the outer desk. After a short wait, during which she entertained Jimmy with a cloth book she had brought along with them, a tall, lanky man, wearing a white coat, came out to greet her.

"Mrs. Finney, I'm Doctor Sheldon Reese. Please, come in."

She followed him into his office, where he gestured toward a surprisingly comfortable, high-backed leather chair. Taking his place across from her in a matching seat, he crossed his legs and reached for a legal pad and pen, neatly positioned at the corner of his spacious oak desk.

"I'm curious what brings a woman with a small baby in to see me? You may have noticed that we don't have many mothers with infants on our grounds."

Lydia nodded, her mouth was dry... her words stubbornly refusing to form as she acknowledged him silently.

"How old is your son?" he asked, trying to put her more at ease. "Looks about... what, four or five months?"

"Four," she managed.

"And you are married to..." he asked, writing on his legal pad.

"My husband's name is Simon... he's a doctor... a surgeon, over at Charity."

He made another brief notation. "I assume you are neither seeking employment nor admission to Dixmont? As you might know, our beds are full. That being said, how can I help you, Mrs. Finney?"

"I'm having nightmares... they have to stop."

He nodded. "I see. How long have you been having nightmares, Mrs. Finney, or may I call you Lydia?"

"Yes," she replied simply. "For over a year."

"Do you know what caused you to start having these nightmares, Lydia?" Doctor Reese asked, his voice calm and low.

She nodded.

He said nothing, his gaze steady as he watched her, patiently waiting for her to speak.

"I, um, that is... my husband and I served together in the war, in France, mostly... on the front. With the French army."

Doctor Reese nodded again, his pen poised to take notes, but he appeared absolutely unhurried.

"I was a volunteer nurse, and Simon, my husband, had enlisted as a surgeon in the army. Our medical station was managed by the French army. Simon and I met over there... at the station."

"How long were you there, Lydia?" Doctor Reese was already piecing together an understanding of the many possible factors leading to her recurrent nightmares.

As she felt Jimmy drift off to sleep in the calm of the office, Lydia shifted him down from her shoulder to her arm. "Close to two years... from when I left Philadelphia to coming home again."

"That's a long time," the psychiatrist observed.

"We married over there, and when Simon's enlistment was up, we came home, in November. Jimmy was born this past Easter."

"Tell me something about your experience there... if you can," he prompted her.

Lydia cleared her throat. "We served in a mobile unit. What they called a casualty clearing station. Always within five or six miles from the front. Moving often, of course, as battle lines shifted. There were always shells falling... not far from us... hundreds of wounded soldiers coming through, sometimes days on end... Verdun, the Argonne, Ypres...”

Doctor Reese stopped taking notes, setting his pen and paper down on the desk before resting his hands calmly in his lap. These were places with which he was quite familiar. Many patient stories had these locations as their backdrop.

“Difficult work.”

Lydia looked up, picturing the camp in her mind... the tents, trucks, wagons, horses... the people. “It was rewarding to help those soldiers, demanding... exhausting at times. There were twelve nurses, three surgeons... and hundreds of wounded, day after day.”

“The nightmares didn’t start until you came home?” he asked.

She shook her head. “Actually, they started over there, in the camp.”

“Understandable, considering.” He had heard countless stories from soldiers. He was less familiar, though, with the experience of the nurses serving at the front.

Lydia took a moment, studying Jimmy’s face, his even breathing, his tiny mouth. She was hesitant to speak. “A year ago, in winter... we, um, one of the other nurses and I, and two of the sentries on duty... it was a really cold night... we were taken by Germans.”

Doctor Reese’s expression was steady. He watched her and listened and waited.

“... they took us, we had to—actually, we walked the five or six miles at night... to their trenches, where they had soldiers of their own who needed help... wounded.”

The silence in the office deepened.

"Simon didn't... our station didn't know we were gone right away. It was awfully cold."

While looking around the room to steady herself, Lydia saw that Doctor Reese was still calmly listening; she was grateful. She did not have to take care of his feelings as she did when she didn't want to upset Simon with these memories. Doctor Reese was in full control of his feelings. Her voice faltered, so she took a deep breath to give it strength. "At first, we cared for their soldiers, but they didn't give us any food, you see. The, uh, the German commander—well of course he was German—he finally gave me some food for the others, if I did... what I was told." She stopped.

Doctor Reese watched her carefully, gaining more insight into what had brought this young woman to his office. He didn't want her leaving in a distressed state of mind, especially with her baby. Now he intervened.

"Lydia," he said, calling her attention back to himself and the present. "It's common for people to have nightmares, even a long time after an event has occurred. That's why it's called post-trauma syndrome. You said this was a year ago last winter since it happened. And cold. Not like today's hot, summer day."

His reminder of the length of time that had passed helped Lydia to stabilize her emotions. He was right. She could distance herself from it a bit again with that reminder. And it was warm today.

The doctor continued. "I appreciate you helping me to understand why the nightmares are coming. I can help you with them if you want me to. I'm not able to put you into a group with soldiers who were also there, who would understand firsthand. But I'm willing to work with you individually, if you are able."

With relief, she looked into his eyes. She saw he was not afraid of her memories, not the way she was. "Okay," she said. "The nightmares have to stop."

"Would you consider bringing your husband with you next time?" Doctor Reese asked. It was hard to imagine this lovely, young, mother and nurse in the middle of war. "It would help you if he were a part of this. If you can't, then I can work with that, but I'd prefer you have someone with you, your husband or a friend, for when you leave my office."

Lydia nodded. "I'll have to... well, you see, I didn't tell him yet that I had made this appointment. I didn't know what to expect... or if—"

"Or if you would even come back?" Doctor Reese finished the thought.

Nodding again, Lydia felt as though she should be apologizing for causing him some offense, but he was smiling softly.

"It's not uncommon for people to wonder if they'll come back, Lydia. I hear it often. Sometimes I even get fired one week, then rehired the next."

Now, she was the one smiling. "I won't fire you, Doctor Reese. I need to figure this out."

The doctor rose, nodding. "Then speak to your husband and call me after you do. I'll have Martha set up an appointment for you before you leave. If everything goes well at home, then let me know that you'll keep the appointment."

Slowly standing, Lydia lifted the sleeping baby to her shoulder and rested her pocketbook over her arm. "Oh, I need to call a taxicab."

"Martha will help you with that as well," he assured her as they stepped out of the office together.

"Thank you, Doctor Reese, sincerely."

"It's what I'm here for," he said as he watched her leave, the weight of her pain lingered in his thoughts, fueling his determination to guide this young woman toward healing... and hope.

Marcus and Simon had enjoyed a good run this evening, covering nearly half a mile before Simon's lungs gave out. Slowing their pace, they walked the rest of the way home.

Just about a block from the house, Simon suddenly broached the subject which had been on both of their minds. "I don't know how to help her with these dreams, Marc."

Marcus nodded. "I know. Suz thinks it's a lot of fuss over nothing... but then, she doesn't know what happened."

"I do know... and I still can't help her. It's like she's still there... in that underground dungeon."

"Maybe it's a good thing she's starting to, kind of fight back, you know? Maybe that means something."

"All I know is that I feel helpless. I'm a doctor, and I don't know how to help her, Marc. Not with this."

Marc rested his hand on his buddy's shoulder. "Just keep loving her, Simon. You'll figure it out."

As they neared the house, Marc wasn't sure he even believed what he had said.

With Jimmy peacefully tucked in for the night, Lydia climbed into bed and curled up against Simon, resting her head on his shoulder... feeling the safety of his strong arms as they wrapped around her. This was her favorite bedtime ritual. The city was quiet tonight. The windows were open, a refreshing night breeze swirling gently through the room. There were sounds of train whistles in the distance. Too warm for sheets, they lay uncovered, allowing the soothing air to drift over their bodies, cool and comforting.

Abril lay sprawled on the floor, also enjoying the fresh air. With Jimmy now sleeping in Marcus and Suzie's old room, the bedroom doors remained open during the night, so she moved freely through the upstairs, checking on Jimmy and then coming back to stay close to Lydia, always listening for any sounds beyond the familiar creaks and murmurs of an older house.

Simon had a slight cough that worried Lydia, but as she rested against him, she listened closely and heard no rattle in his lungs.

Lydia's fingers traced the muscles of Simon's chest. "Simon," she started softly. "Can I tell you something? Or are you already half asleep?"

"I'm awake, my love," he murmured, pushing away the haze of drowsiness as his focus shifted to her. "What's on your mind?" He stroked her hair.

"Well, tomorrow is our anniversary—"

"Indeed, it is," he kissed the crown of her head. "I know we missed last year... with me... well... not there for it, so I want to make it up to you this year. Do you have something special in mind?"

"Yes, actually, I do. I wonder, can we stay home after work? I don't want to go anywhere. I just want to be in our home."

"Well, that sounds just about perfect to me," he sighed with pleasure. "I've got to warn you, though, I did get you a little something."

She smiled in the darkness, thinking of the little box in her pocketbook. "Then I must warn you that I also got you a little something... with my own money."

He kissed the top of her head again, gently. "How's your head feeling tonight?"

"I'm fine," she said. "And I am well aware that you already know that since you've stopped shining that light in my eyes twice a day."

He laughed softly. "Was I overdoing it?"

"Just a bit!" she declared.

"Well then."

She paused. "But that's not what I really wanted to talk to you about."

He rolled onto his side so they were facing each other, and tenderly brushed her hair past her shoulders so he could see her figure in the dim light. He slid his hand down the slope of her shoulder, her waist, and up over the curve of her hip, where he lingered. "So, tell me..."

"I went to Dixmont today, Simon," she nearly whispered.

His hand stopped moving. "Did you, now? How did that happen?"

"I saw Doctor Sheldon Reese. He's a psychiatrist over there... working with soldiers with trauma."

Simon wished he could see her face more clearly. "Makes sense, being at Dixmont."

"I took a taxicab. I... I didn't tell you at first because I didn't know if I would have the courage to go through with it... and if

I did, I wasn't sure I would ever go back. And I didn't want to disappoint you… if you got your hopes up and then I chickened out."

"Disappoint me? I'd have gone with you… taken you myself… had I known… regardless of if you ever went back."

She nodded, resting her hand on his cheek. "I was hoping… that is, Doctor Reese suggested that you come with me to my appointment next week. He thinks he can help stop the nightmares… and I want to try, Simon. It scared me the last time, when I realized that I was fighting you in my sleep. I don't want that to happen again."

His hand started moving again, slowly tracing her curves. "Whatever it takes, I'm willing."

"Thank you, my love," Lydia whispered, relieved. This had gone better than she'd dared to hope—he didn't think she was the least bit crazy. Her finger traced his lower lip, following the familiar, smooth line where his beard began.

Simon gently stayed her hand, intertwining his fingers with hers. "Is there anything else we need to talk about?" he asked, rolling her onto her back and propping himself up on one elbow beside her. He was certainly awake now.

She shook her head. "No, that was it… well, there is one more thing."

Simon waited.

"I sent Marc's father a copy of the newspaper article about the fire," she confessed. "He gave me the address—said it probably wouldn't make much of a difference, but that the choice was mine. So I went ahead and sent it. I told his father what a wonderful son he has… and family."

"Hm. Well, then. It's good that we cleared that up." He was a little surprised, but confident that she had thought this through and felt it had been a necessary effort. Simon snuggled in closer to Lydia, pulling one of her legs up over his own and stroking her silky smooth skin... her new razor really was a marvel... he found it next to impossible to resist the feeling. "You are such a beautiful woman," he breathed. "Inside and out."

"But, Simon, what about tomorrow?" she whispered as he stroked her inner thighs making her shiver with anticipation. "I want us to be together on our anniversary."

He laughed softly. "Tomorrow is a long time from now," he teased as he leaned over her. "Far too long to wait. And we can make time for us tomorrow as well."

"Just promise you won't ever get tired of us..." she trembled, his hands now fully exploring her body.

Simon laughed again. "I waited twenty-five years of my life for this... for what we have. That's a quarter of a century of waiting. That's... let's see... nine-thousand, one hundred and twenty-five days... give or take a few. I waited so long for you that it would probably cause me physical damage to hold back now."

"Oh," her heart was racing, under his persistent, gentle caresses. "I certainly wouldn't want to cause you 'physical damage'..."

"I should think not," he murmured, hearing her breath catch, excited to be the source of her pleasure tonight... and again, tomorrow.

Marcus brought the automobile to a stop at the bridge, letting it idle at the crosswalk for a group of people crossing the street. "So, you think this is a good idea? For her to see this guy at Dixmont, this Doctor Reese?" he asked as he and Simon watched an elderly couple carefully making their way across the street, their canes tapping softly against the pavement.

Simon nodded, noticing that the morning sun was already warming the metal of the car door where he rested his arm through the open window. "I think it was really good that she thought of it and called for the appointment herself. Psychiatry is an area of medical expertise all its own, you know."

"Yeah, but..." Marcus hesitated. "What if talking about all that stuff actually makes it worse? I mean, it's not like a fractured bone that can just be set."

"I guess... there could be a chance... but this guy has probably heard just about every story imaginable... with all the soldiers with post-trauma memories being treated over there. Maybe if she talks it out, she won't have to process it in her dreams."

As the older couple finally made their way safely to the other side, Marcus gave the automobile some gas, moving them forward over the bridge. "You're probably right. You know, I didn't realize Suzie wasn't aware of what all happened over there."

"Is that so?" Simon asked. "Lydia never told her? Have you?"

"Nope," Marcus confirmed. "Figured it wasn't my business to tell. Leaving that to Lydia."

Simon nodded, gazing out the window. "I suppose you're right." His eyes traced the vast river stretching beneath the bridge, where tugboats deftly maneuvered barges in every direction. On shore, trains hummed along the tracks with impressive precision. "You sleeping okay in your new place?"

Marcus waited for an ambulance to pull around the corner near the hospital before he eased forward to make the turn. "It's pretty quiet compared to your house. Somewhat predictable. Wake up. Go to work. Come home. Eat supper. If luck allows, be graced by a certain neighbor's presence for a chess match and a round of push-ups. Then, off to bed—Hey, wait a minute. Isn't today your anniversary?"

Simon laughed. "Sure is. And since I missed the last one... while also losing a lung... I have to make it up to Lydia this year."

"And just how are you planning to do that?" Marcus pulled into a spot and turned off the engine.

"It's a tall order. She already gave me a gift, just last week."

The two men got out of the automobile and headed in the direction of the hospital. "Oh, yeah? What was that? New tie or something?"

"No, buddy, she shaved her legs! Completely. Smooth as silk. The new Gillette safety razor."

Marcus coughed, a sudden rush of memory catching him off guard. Beatrice, the French woman with silken legs, flashed through his mind, from the medical train outside Paris.

"Good grief, man!" Marcus exclaimed. "Why didn't you call out sick?"

"Believe me, Marcus," Simon smiled. "I'll be going home as early as possible."

"Damn!" Marcus exhaled, pushing the memory of Beatrice out of his mind, refocusing on the day ahead of them.

After finishing her house calls, Lydia picked up Jimmy from Mrs. Stevenson's and headed home. She fed the baby, cleaned up a bit and set about preparing dinner. She had decided to make a pot roast, Simon's favorite, and loaded the roaster with vegetables to steam in the flavorful juices.

Lydia had moved Jimmy's playpen into the dining room so she could keep a better eye on him. She began setting the dining table with a little extra care, folding napkins at the place settings and arranging some beautiful flowers in a simple vase for a centerpiece. The small box from the jeweler was wrapped and waiting in the center of Simon's plate.

Abril was tethered to the kitchen, not physically, but captivated nonetheless by the promising aromas of the roast. She looked up, imploring Lydia for a taste, each time the human returned to the kitchen. As Lydia left once again, the dog let out a soft exhale, patiently resting her head on the cool floor.

As Lydia reentered the dining room, she stopped suddenly... staring into the playpen.

"Didn't I lay you on your back?"

Jimmy was definitely on his belly, trying to push up with his little arms. Lydia rolled him onto his back again and paused, watching. Jimmy arched his little back and, sure enough, managed to roll himself over onto his tummy again, looking up at his mother with the most adorable smile—rather pleased with himself.

"Well, I'll be!" Lydia exclaimed, delighted. "Wait until your daddy sees you doing push-ups just like him! What are you going to do when you want to lay back the other way, hm?"

She shook her head, smiling as she made her way to the cupboard, to retrieve two wine glasses. Just for tonight, she thought they might enjoy a tiny bit with dinner, to mark this milestone. The table looked beautiful, the house smelled amazing... She could hardly wait for Simon to come through the door and see what she had done. *Two years together*, she thought. *Two years. Incredible.*

It wasn't long at all before Simon did swing open the door, and he was beaming. Lydia went to greet him, kissing him right in the doorway, and noticed that he had a shoebox tucked under his arm.

"You got me a pair of shoes? For our anniversary? What a thoughtful husband! No wonder I love you so much!" She took his free hand. "Come in and see what your son has done today!"

"Did you have a good day?" Simon asked, following her into the dining room, where he spotted the playpen.

"I did indeed. Now look at this!"

While Simon pulled a chair from the table to watch, she rolled Jimmy onto his back again... in no time at all, Jimmy had rolled himself back onto his tummy and was reaching eagerly for a teething ring, which he didn't really need yet, but about which he was undeniably curious.

"Whoa!" Simon exclaimed, delighted. "Look at our little guy trying to push up on those arms. He must be watching me do my push-ups every evening."

"He's following right in your footsteps, Simon."

Simon sniffed in the direction of the kitchen. "Smells sensational. Pot roast? Love it." He pulled Lydia down onto his lap and took her face into his hands, kissing her tenderly. "Happy anniversary, my beloved Lydia," he murmured. "Just you wait until after supper."

She stroked his beard suggestively. "Just you wait until after Jimmy goes to bed..."

The dining room table quickly filled with delicious food and wine... and laughter as the couple talked and lightly clinked their wine glasses in honor of the occasion.

"I wonder if the wine goes through my milk?" Lydia voice took on a tinge of concern. "I sure hope not."

"If it does, he'll just sleep a little more soundly tonight. And anyway, with all that rolling around, he'll wear himself right out anyway."

After clearing his plate, Simon reached for both the shoebox and the small gift from Lydia. He handed her the shoebox, resting her gift in his palm, unopened.

"You first," he insisted, his gaze steady, yet filled with anticipation.

She untied the ribbon, lifted the lid and gently pushed aside the tissue paper, revealing red cut-glass which sparkled in the light of the gas lamps.

"Oh, my goodness!" Lydia gasped, her fingers trembling a bit as she lifted the crimson sconce from its wrappings. "Where did you find this, Simon?"

He had promised it long ago, to go with the candle on their fireplace mantel, a reminder of the cathedral in Nancy where they had spoken their vows. It looked just like the sconce that glowed in the alcove of the cathedral, above the railing where they had knelt together, as the priest had blessed their union.

Her eyes shone as she looked up at Simon. "You didn't forget," she whispered, leaning in to kiss him. "It's perfect. Thank you."

"You're very welcome," he was relieved and thankful that it had made her so happy.

Lydia pointed to the little box still in his hand. "Your turn," she prompted him, not wanting to wait another minute.

Simon removed the blue wrapping paper and lifted the lid, revealing the pocket watch lying inside. An eagle, majestic with wings spread wide, was engraved on the front. The other side displayed Roman numerals elegantly lining the face. "This is really nice, Lydia," he said, his voice thick with emotion.

"Open it," she smiled.

Simon pressed the release on the winder, and the back flipped open. His breath caught as he read the inscription etched inside. He swallowed hard, then again, unable to find the right words.

"If I am the rock..." he managed at last, his voice unsteady. He cradled her face in his hands, kissing her deeply... passionately. "I don't even know where to begin—"

She pressed a finger to his lips. "Don't say anything. Let's go sit outside on the swing until it's time to take Jimmy up."

Abril padded along with them through the kitchen and out onto the back porch. Simon draped one arm around Lydia while cradling Jimmy in the other, as they snuggled together on the large swing. As the sun dipped behind the rooftops, they watched as the shadows stretched and melted into the evening.

With the evening breeze growing crisp and Jimmy sound asleep from the gentle motion of the swing, they decided to head inside and get him settled safely in his nursery. Simon took Lydia's hands in his and led her to the bathroom, where he lit candles on the windowsill, sink, and chair, bathing the room in a soft glow.

He helped Lydia undress while the tub filled with warm, soothing water. Holding her hand as she stepped into the tub, he began leisurely washing her with a soft sponge, letting the water run over her body, her skin sparkling in the flickering candlelight. He enjoyed watching her relax into the moment, eyes closed, while he tended to her. When the water began to cool, her eyes fluttered open and she smiled, gesturing for a towel. He reached for one, his gaze never leaving her as she stood, the shimmering water cascading over her form. He wrapped her in the warm towel and led her back to the bedroom, scooping her up to lay her on top of the bed. He began to undress himself.

"I will be right back," he announced. "Don't go anywhere."

Returning to the bath, he quickly washed himself and pulled drain in the tub, grabbing a fresh towel to dry himself as he made his way back down the hallway.

In the dim light, he found Lydia standing in front of the bay window, looking down their street as the lamp lights lit in succession. She turned and took his hand. Simon took a seat on the cushion in the bay window, turning and pulling her to him so she was seated between his legs. His arms wrapped around her, he began kissing her neck and shoulders, feeling her shiver with anticipation. Lydia found him... it was her turn to tend to him now. In no time, Simon was sighing from the very depths of his toes, his fingers deep in her hair.

He whispered in her ear, "Lydia, we have got... to go over to the bed..."

"Is that so..." she murmured. "But I like it here... don't you?"

"I most certainly do," he pulled her up into his arms and led her to the bed, where he laid her back onto the pillows. "But I made you a promise that I intend to keep..."

Simon brought her to the edge again and again, stopping each time just before she found release. When she could hardly breathe for wanting, she clutched him, "Simon, if you don't take me now... I am going to lose my mind..."

He gave himself to her the moment she cried out. He loved hearing her lose herself, because of him. He loved knowing he could please her this much. He loved how she loved him in return. And as they lay there, entwined, her legs still wrapped tightly around his hips, he kissed her over and over as they caught their breath.

"Happy anniversary, my beloved wife."

"Do you know how much I love you? Can we do this again tomorrow?" she exhaled deeply.

He laughed at that, so delighted with her. "We can do it again... in a couple of hours maybe... I hope anyway..."

Simon and Lydia sat in two high-backed chairs, across from Doctor Reese who remained seated behind his desk.

"You believe that if Lydia talks it through, she won't have to work it out in her dreams anymore?" Simon paused for confirmation.

"Yes," the psychiatrist nodded. "From what you've observed, the night terrors of reliving the event have changed now... to nightmares where her unconscious mind is trying to fight back, trying to win, so to speak... a battle of good over evil. If she can speak it consciously here, then half the battle is already won—but it can be exhausting, draining... and I don't want her going home alone after these sessions."

Simon nodded. "How can I help?"

"It sounds, from what Lydia has already shared, that you're doing everything possible to help her. Now, it is up to her to work through it. If she can do it here, in this office, then she might be able to leave it here... not carry it home."

Simon turned his attention to his wife. "Lydia, I'll take Jimmy... if you're ready."

She nodded, a tinge of fear in her eyes.

"I'll be right outside," he reminded her, infusing his voice with as much confidence as he could summon.

As Simon pulled the door closed behind him, Doctor Reese addressed Lydia. "Ready?"

She nodded. "I think so."

"Okay. Start wherever your mind tells you to start."

Lydia hugged her knees. "When I had the baby, there was a complication. It was a home birth with a midwife, but the placenta tore... and I bled. After a couple of days with a fever, Simon took me to the hospital... the doctor there did a procedure, a scraping."

Doctor Reese nodded, "The curettage," he said, curious to see how this would fit with memories of a war, thousands of miles away.

"Yes, I don't remember it. They gave me anesthesia... I woke up in recovery. The doctor came in, and he... he checked inside of me and had me roll over, you know, to look for bleeding. And he said... he asked, if Simon was beating me."

The psychiatrist waited, knowing the connection between this and the German trench was coming soon, if she did not retreat from it.

Lydia paused, afraid she might be swept into the memory again. "The doctor, when I rolled over, he saw the scars made by... made by a German commander who had... who always had his... had a crop in his belt."

Doctor Reese sat quietly, masking his ah-ha moment, just watching this young nurse who had survived the war. He stopped taking notes and simply listened.

Lydia gripped her hands in her lap, rocking herself slowly. "You see, Doctor Reese, I always said he couldn't make me hate. I told myself... that I forgave him. Now... I'm not so sure. Because in the nightmares, I do hate him for making me do what he wanted...or for wanting me to do what I couldn't do."

"And did you do what he wanted you to do?" the psychiatrist asked carefully.

Lydia faltered. "No... not always" she whispered. "But I told him, at first, that I would. I said I would do whatever it took to make sure the others could eat. He said they could eat the rats if I didn't. So, I told him I'd do anything he wanted."

"But you didn't."

"At first, I did. He told me to take down my hair. Something easy to do. Later, he told me to... to open my shirt. He had a little box of food. 'That wasn't so difficult now, was it... I ask such a simple thing, really,'" Lydia recalled the commander's words, starting to slide into the trench.

"Lydia," the doctor directed her. "Stand up."

It took a moment for the directive to reach her consciousness, but when it did, she stood, waiting for instruction.

"Look around you. Touch things, feel things. See where you are. You are free to walk around the room."

She stood and walked behind the chair, placing it between herself and Doctor Reese's desk—a welcome barrier.

The psychiatrist followed her gaze, seeing the fear creasing her face as she stared at the desk. Lydia's fingers brushed the chair's leather cushion, grounding herself in its texture. Then, forcing herself forward, she moved closer to the desk, only to retreat again, back behind the chair.

The motion reassured her that she was not trapped.

She was drawn to the sunlight streaming through the tall window and focused for a moment on the figures outside. Patients in wheelchairs, staff in crisp white uniforms, figures moving through the courtyard in quiet routines. The sight steadied her... a reminder of where she was. She was safe, at a hospital.

She took a deep breath. "The, uh, commander... one night told me to take off... and he, he took off his own... he was, um... you know... ready. He wanted me to hit him... with his crop. But I couldn't... I threw it on the ground." She paused, the memory of that that night still so vivid. "Even though I said I would do whatever it took..."

Doctor Reese watched, alert for signs that she was losing herself beyond a point of no return. "You couldn't do it," he prompted her. "You couldn't strike him, so you threw it away."

Lydia made herself focus on this man in front of her, in his white coat, sitting there, steady and composed in his high-backed chair. She realized that nothing she was saying seemed alarming to him. Maybe she could move safely through this memory...

Lydia reached out one hand, her fingers landing on the doctor's wide desk. "So he hit me with it instead. He said, 'You force me to hurt you. Just take the crop and hit me and it's over...'" Lydia's voice trailed off into a whisper as she quoted the commander from the trenches. "'What a pity. You're bleeding now. What a pity. You're making me have to keep doing this, again an—'"

Doctor Reese picked up a soft handbell from his desk and rang it gently. Its beautiful, melodic tone hovered in the air, instantly breaking through the memory. Lydia startled, hearing the bell in the man's hand. It was so out of place, in her memory... such a soothing tone. She didn't yet notice the tears tracing her cheeks.

"I hated myself... for making him do that," she said finally. "And when he let me stand up and pull my pants back on, my blood was... smeared on him..."

She ran her hands along the smooth desktop once more, then Lydia turned from the desk and sat down. "I didn't fight back," she informed Doctor Reese, adding, "and I hated myself for not fighting back. The nightmares began soon after we escaped the trenches."

The psychiatrist paused before asking. "Lydia, do you consider yourself brave?"

She looked puzzled. "It's not brave to do something you have to do."

"Are you certain?"

Lydia now paused, considering this follow up question, "Quite."

"Why?"

"Well... because... if it's something you have to do, then you just have to do it. It has nothing to do with bravery, or courage of any sort, because it's mandatory. Bravery requires choice... a decision."

He nodded. "Say that again, Lydia."

"Bravery... requires choice... a decision."

"And what did you choose, in that moment, back then, Lydia? What decision did you make?" Doctor Reese pursued.

"I... I chose not to hurt him even though... even though he told me to."

"Then wasn't that brave?" he asked her, then raised his hand. "Don't answer that. I only want you to think about it."

Lydia was confused. Considering the doctor's question drove everything else from her mind. She didn't even hear when Doctor Reese called Simon back into the office.

Simon was visibly anxious, not at all his usual, reserved self. He quickly noted the puzzled expression on Lydia's face, but also was relieved to see that she was present, not trapped in her memories.

She met his gaze and reached for Jimmy, cradling the baby against her shoulder. Slowly, she shifted her weight from one hip to the other, a gentle, instinctive motion that steadied her as much as it soothed him.

Doctor Reese addressed Simon. "She did very well today. Come back next week, please. Call me if there is any problem you need to discuss with me, Doctor Finney."

Simon nodded, considering the many problems this could cause between now and next week. He wrapped a protective arm around Lydia's waist and walked her out of Dixmont. He was prepared not to get much sleep tonight.

"Simon, do you mind if I nurse Jimmy while we drive? I can cover up with his blanket, once we're in the Ford," Lydia offered.

Simon opened the passenger door and helped her settle in with Jimmy on her lap. "I don't mind at all. If we end up stuck in traffic, some fellow might glance in the window, but while we're moving, I don't see the harm." *Perhaps this will help to steady her,* he thought.

He drove down the long winding road, leaving the hospital and making their way back over the river to their side of the city. They had rolled the windows down to allow the warm breeze to flow through. Lydia opened her dress buttons and cradled Jimmy as he latched on, hungrily.

"Someone worked up an appetite!" Simon exclaimed.

"He's just like his daddy," Lydia smiled. "Always starving."

Simon smiled, watching the road but also focused on Lydia. She seemed alright—not too distressed. A flicker of hope stirred within him. Perhaps this doctor truly could help her. He would wait to share any of his remaining anxieties with Marc, during their chess game tonight.

By their third visit, Lydia wasn't nearly as afraid to step into Doctor Reese's office. After a brief exchange with Simon and her together, Simon once again stepped out with Jimmy. Right away, Lydia noticed that the chairs had been rearranged. They no longer faced the doctor's desk—instead, they faced the outer door. She wondered about the change but said nothing, settling into her seat as the psychiatrist took his.

Her gaze drifted past him, landing on the handbell. It was comforting to know that she could hear it, no matter how far into her memories she went.

Once again, Doctor Reese began with, "Start wherever your mind tells you to start."

"My mind wants an answer to the bravery question."

The doctor smiled. "Well, what have you come up with so far?"

"You're the doctor here... you're supposed to have the answers," she stated honestly. "Like with Simon... patients say, 'Doctor, my belly hurts, what's wrong with me?' And he gives them the answer."

Doctor Reese raised his eyebrows. "Ah, that's it, is it? But I don't have the answers, Lydia... you do."

"If I had the answers, I wouldn't be here. But I think that I was right when I told you bravery involves choice."

"You thought about that..."

"I did."

Again, he waited patiently, allowing Lydia the space to find her way.

"My mother saw the scars... by accident," Lydia admitted suddenly. "When Simon and I visited my parents, I went upstairs with her... to change for a dance. I'd forgotten how visible they were. Of course, I can't see them, and I won't look in the mirror... they're so ugly."

She exhaled. "But my mother saw them. And she was horrified. When she told my dad, he immediately assumed Simon had beaten me. If Simon hadn't handled it so well, my father might have had a heart attack on the spot. Simon called me courageous... he made a point to let my dad know."

Lydia was getting used to the psychiatrist allowing the space for quiet, to him patiently listening... not saying much other than an occasional guiding word. She was realizing that she was the one who had to come to some kind of an understanding with her unconscious mind, both about how things had been and, now, how they should be, in the future.

"Sometimes, I see the trench, in the nightmares. The dim lights along the muddy wall. It was terribly cold... and slippery. One night, a dog just jumped down into the trench... came right up to Charlotte and me. Some of the soldiers laughed at that. But we knew it was Abril right away, our dog from the medical clearing station... we couldn't believe she had found us. After we had gotten to the dug-out room, where they kept us, I ran my hands through Abril's fur and felt a chain around her neck, hidden by her fur..." Lydia remembered the feel of the chain, the surprise of finding it and what it had meant to the captives.

Doctor Reese listened intently.

"Simon had put his identification tag around her neck... hidden so the Germans wouldn't see it." Lydia clenched her fist, remembering that incredible moment. "I knew Simon had sent her to find us. So, I put the tag in my pocket and just cried..."

Lydia wiped her eyes. Doctor Reese silently handed her a handkerchief.

"The German commander promised that eventually I would beg him to hurt me. Isn't that an odd thing to say? Who would ever beg someone to hurt them? Was there some demon in him... that wanted to feel pain? Some twisted kind of self-punishment at someone else's expense...?"

Again, the silence took on weight. Of her own volition, Lydia got up to walk around the room, stopping to look out the window, the late afternoon sun shining across the grounds, casting shadows from the trees.

She continued, slowly, "And that was hard... because while waiting for him to call me to his office the next night, my mind... I thought of a thousand ways he could make me beg. None of them very nice. And I did that to myself... wondering, trying to guess how he was going to make me beg. The waiting was horrible. I even wonder if he intentionally skipped a night just so my imagination would run wild with all those terrible thoughts.

"He asked me if it hurt. Did the crop hurt... as if the blood wasn't enough, you know? And then, Doctor Reese, I felt guilty. I felt sorry for him that he had to hit me so hard, because he made it seem like he didn't want to, as if he regretted having to do it but that I was the one forcing his hand." She slipped right into the memory. "'Such a pity... does it hurt you? I'm so sorry you insist on this.' Oh God, yes it hurts! It hurts!" Lydia uttered a sharp gasp, holding onto and leaning over the psychiatrist's wide desk.

Doctor Reese's hand hovered just over the handbell, but he hesitated... waiting.

Her voice was strained. "I heard the whistle of his crop before I felt it... expecting the pain made it worse. He stood right behind me, hitting me... always where he had hit me before... but so apologetic." Lydia was whimpering now. "I'm sorry... I'm making you... I didn't obey... it's my fault..." Lydia was at Doctor Reese's bare desk. She pressed her hands down on top of it, feeling the cold, smooth surface. *'Lean over the desk'...* she heard the commander's voice as if he was right there again.

Doctor Reese didn't move from his chair, watching, on alert.

"I have Simon's medallion... he'll understand... he'll love me anyway... no matter what, he'll still love m—"

Moving quickly around the desk, as if to try to escape, she grabbed for the chair but missed, dropping to her knees on the floor. "Oh God... oh God..." Lydia cried out, remembering what had happened next.

She crumpled into a ball.

The sound of the handbell reached her, the waves of sound flowing into her head. She dropped her head to the floor and wept, her heart broken.

Doctor Reese was kneeling beside her as the door flew open.

Simon had thrust Jimmy into the arms of the woman at the outer desk before rushing in... he knew that particular sob all too well.

He dropped to his knees with her, then gently lifted her head and shoulders from the floor. She fell against him, wetting his shirt with her tears. Simon stroked her hair and held her to him. "You survived. You're with me," he said again. "It's all that matters. It's the only thing that matters."

"Oh, Simon," she wept. "I'm so sorry. The crop hurt so bad that I didn't feel... I didn't remember..."

Simon stroked her hair, kissing the top of her head. "You're with me, Lydia, and I love you."

"He's dead, right? You're certain, aren't you, Simon?" Lydia pleaded, her voice trembling.

"I'm absolutely sure, beloved. There's no doubt—Harold pronounced him dead." Simon's voice was steady, resolute. "That man will never come near you again. Not in this life. Not beyond it. He'll rot in hell."

Lydia clung to him. "Now I understand... why it's haunted me... what was missing. And I know—I know you would never..."

"God Almighty, no, I would not!" Simon swore fiercely, stroking her hair, pressing kisses into the crown of her head.

He lifted her chin until their eyes met.

"The only things that matter are you and me... our baby... our family, our friends. Nothing else matters. Look at me, Lydia." His voice was firm yet full of tenderness. "You are my beloved wife. I would give everything I have just to keep you by my side... forever... and remember this, nothing God has sealed in this life can be undone. You and I, we are one before Almighty God."

He wiped her tears with the fabric of his shirt, then helped her to stand, steadying her before easing her into one of the chairs.

Lydia gestured toward the open door, to Jimmy, sitting in Martha's lap.

Simon nodded in answer to her unspoken request. Lifting the baby from Martha's outstretched arms and bringing him into the office, he placed Jimmy into Lydia's embrace. Then, he knelt beside her chair, looking into her eyes. "Jimmy is the visible evidence of our being one, Lydia. When you look at our son, you are looking at our oneness, which cannot ever be broken."

Lydia leaned against Simon, Jimmy sheltered against her chest, completely ignoring Doctor Reese's quiet observation.

Simon turned to the psychiatrist. He held out his hand. "Thank you, Doctor," Simon said, "for helping my wife find what she needed to find so she can heal. I couldn't... help her find it. I'm grateful that you could."

Doctor Sheldon Reese gripped the other man's hand in return. "Healing is what we're about here. She must come back. It's critically important."

"We will," Simon promised.

Shifts at the remote surgical clinic were always unpredictable, but today, a new medical student had been assigned to Suzie and Marcus. He shifted nervously, but seemed willing to learn and they were in no real hurry. Nikki was content in the playpen and everything they needed was prepped and organized, including snacks, toys, and books for the toddler. Fresh air drifted through the open doors, bringing a sense of calm. Wiping down the counters with alcohol, Suzie took satisfaction in the clinic's pristine state. She enjoyed the rhythm of the work, methodically lining up instruments on a silver tray, covering them with a surgical towel to keep them clean.

The medical student was happily shadowing Marcus. "What made you want to do this, Doctor Lovell?"

Marcus leaned back against a counter with his arms comfortably crossed. "There was an obvious need and it was in keeping with the hospital's mission statement. And truthfully, it's just fun to see what walks through the door, isn't it, Nurse Lovell?"

The medical student glanced at the nurse... blonde, beautiful, and visibly pregnant, she carried herself with an effortless grace that captivated him just as much as the work itself.

She nodded. "Just like the clinic at the hospital. It keeps you on your toes, David. Adaptability makes a good doctor. You've got to be ready to adjust, in the moment."

"What do you do here, Nurse?" he asked.

She laughed, "A little of everything!"

By early afternoon, David was reviewing the logbook. "Five lacerations with sutures, three sprains, a couple of splinters or embedded industrial nails, an eye abrasion—"

"And a partridge in a pear tree," Marcus laughed. He glanced out the window and immediately stiffened. "Anyone order twelve drummers drumming?" His jovial tone had vanished. "Suzie, stay inside, shut the door after me and keep Nikki in the back."

Marcus stepped outside, and Suzie closed the door behind him as instructed.

On the street, two groups of men were closing in on each other. One side held picket signs. The other, raised fists. Shouting had already soured into threats.

Marcus took in the scene, fully aware of the potential for imminent violence.

"Hey, gentlemen," he began. "This is a corner medical clinic. Looks like you guys are planning to give us some business."

"What's it to you?" one man snarled in response.

"I'm a surgeon. Just want to make sure we have enough sutures and splints to take care of the wounded when this is all over," Marcus replied smoothly.

He took a quick head count of the crowd and calculated the numbers. "When you guys are done with each other, just come on in... one at a time, and we'll do our best to get you all fixed up. We might have enough supplies, and I've got a medical student helping me today, too. Unless you need to go to a hospital... we'll have to telephone for an ambulance—"

"It don't need to come to that!" a man with a sign shouted out. "We're just walking over to the park for a meeting with the factory owners—wanna tell them how many guys are getting hurt on the job."

"When we get hurt, can't work... our families are out of luck... we don't get paid enough," others added.

The opposing group answered back.

"You're marching in our neighborhoods now! Keep it away from our houses," yelled an older man.

"Come on down to the mill. You guys'll see what real injuries are!" The men were shouting over each other, fists raised.

Marcus stepped between a few of them. "I understand the getting hurt part! In the mill fire, we had to run in and take a guy's leg off to save him! That fire never should've happened. Not like that."

One of the men stepped closer to Marcus. "Hey!" he suddenly shouted over the noise of the crowd. "This guy is one of the docs that went into the mill fire!"

Murmurs burst out as the men shifted their focus to the doctor. Another man called out, "You're right, Rudy! His picture was in the paper. He's one of 'em, alright! This guy is here lookin' out for us!"

The men carrying the signs lowered them slightly, as the man closest to Marcus exclaimed, "Yep, it's one of the two doctors that ran right in and saved that fella who was trapped! We don't wanna give you no trouble, Doc... not here at your clinic."

The men had found a common ground upon which they could at least pause their hostility.

Marcus shook hands with many of them, from both sides. They all wanted to thank him for helping the workers in the fire and Marcus made sure to tell each of them, "If you guys need help... you ever get hurt, you come on over here and we'll fix you up. That's what we're here for."

The responses came, one after the other—gruff, relieved, grateful.

"Thanks, Doc."

"Good to meet you."

"You take care now, Doc."

"Have a good afternoon, Doc."

"Appreciate you looking out for us, Doc."

The men dispersed in every direction as Marcus waved goodbye and stepped back inside.

David greeted the doctor, just inside the door and blurted out, "What was that all about, Doctor Lovell?"

"Just some guys with strong feelings," Marcus assured him. "Hard-working guys who reached an understanding."

"I thought they were going to take you out with them," David exclaimed, shaking his head.

Marcus just laughed. "They just needed help communicating."

Suzie was quiet. She wished Marcus hadn't involved himself in something that truly wasn't his concern... especially with Nikki in the back. Still, she held her peace.

Lydia didn't sit immediately when she entered Doctor Reese's waiting room for the next appointment. Simon was busy in surgery at the hospital, so Marcus had offered to drive her over this afternoon, while Mrs. Stevenson was keeping Jimmy a little longer than usual.

When the psychiatrist stepped out to greet Lydia, she introduced Marcus as their closest friend—the one who had *been over there*... who had *gone through it all* with them.

She knew he would stay nearby in the waiting room, just as he had promised.

Marcus offered Doctor Reese a skeptical glance before settling into his seat.

"Your friend out there is quite concerned about you," Doctor Reese observed as he closed the door behind them and watched Lydia make her way over to the office window to look outside.

She nodded, turning to the psychiatrist, who remained standing on the other side of the large desk. "When the army pronounced Simon officially missing in action and presumed dead, he offered to marry me and raise Jimmy. I said, yes. He would have loved us both... still does, in a way. As do I..."

Doctor Reese did not show any reaction, just continued to listen, as she had come to expect of him. "Simon had been missing for many months. I was already pregnant with Jimmy. Marcus—Doctor Lovell, was a great source of strength for me during that terrible time. He knows all about... things. I trust him implicitly."

The room was quiet.

Then, Lydia protectively crossed her arms, "Why did you say it was important for me to come back? And... please don't just ask why I think it's important..."

Doctor Reese smiled softly. "How's this, then? What do reporters do when they're writing a story? What questions do they ask?"

She leaned against the windowsill. "That's easy. Who, what, when, where, why."

The psychiatrist waited patiently.

Lydia nodded. "Ah, I get it. I have the when. I have the where. I know some of the who. Although, I never knew the commander's name, and I didn't ask Doctor Stockton to see the death roster." Her voice drifted off. "I didn't want to know his name."

She returned to the high-backed chair and sat... on the edge, smoothing her skirt over her knees. "I suppose now I know the *what*... at least, I hope there's no more *what* hiding anywhere... so that leaves—"

Doctor Reese took his seat as well and comfortably crossed his legs.

"The *why*, naturally... but that's easy. He had something evil in him," she waited for Sheldon Reese to give some indication she'd hit the target, but he did not. "So, it's not that easy?" she asked. "And without this, it's not done?"

He shook his head. "No, not that easy. And you're right, it's still not done."

"Oh."

They sat quietly. Lydia pondered his words as her gaze drifted to the window. She considered the patients at this facility, much worse off than she.

"Why are they left with one leg... one arm... or in rolling chairs... or blind. All those young men outside... missing something."

When she found her voice again, it was faint. "Am I missing something?"

It was a rhetorical question. "What am I missing? Okay... so maybe the German commander never had anyone who loved him, as a child?"

"Does that matter?" Doctor Reese challenged.

She refocused on the doctor, in his chair. "Does it matter if no one loved him as a child? Well, yes, I suppose. If it explains the *why*."

The doctor's tone remained steady. "Lydia, you're focusing this question of the *why* on *him*."

She lifted her chin slightly. "Who better?"

He met her gaze. "Who, indeed?"

"Me?" Lydia asked. "Is the *why* about me? Did I bring it on myself? Is there something inherently wrong with me? Was he right? That I made him do it?"

"You sound angry," the doctor observed.

Her cheeks flushed. "Well, yes... I guess I am!" she exclaimed a bit too forcefully. "I didn't ask him to hurt me! No, wait. Yes, I did. Me—rather than Charlotte or our sentries. I did put myself in that position. The *why* is about me. I didn't want him to take Charlotte. And... he would have..."

She rose abruptly, striding angrily past the desk, back toward the window, before addressing the doctor, who remained in his chair. "Well, why not me? Look out there, Doctor Reese! They all suffered. And think of all the hundreds of thousands of families whose sons died over there. Every last one of them is still suffering. They didn't deserve it!"

Her breath caught, but she pushed through.

"I couldn't bear for him to take Charlotte. And he would have killed our sentries. So I told him... as long as the others were taken care of, he could have me... and... and he did..."

Doctor Reese's voice was careful, deliberate.

"Did he...? Have you?"

Her lips trembled.

"Yes..." she whispered, teeth pressing into her bottom lip. "And no..."

"Lydia, take the tablet. First, write down what he took."

She hesitated, looking down at the yellow pad on the desk. "I don't want to see it in front of me."

Doctor Reese's voice remained steady. "It's already in front of you... put it outside of you."

Slowly, she picked up the pad and pen, the weight of the request pressing against her.

She wrote one word: *taken*.

Then, others followed.

Dignity... privacy... peace... sleep... safety...

Then more came, unspoken truths taking physical shape in ink.

The absence of pain.

The certainty of knowing the right thing to do.

He had taken those, too.

Lydia set the pen down. Looking away from the words, she slid the pad across the desk, toward the psychiatrist.

"Now, circle the ones that are still... *taken*," he requested, pushing the paper gently back toward her.

Lydia drew a deep breath, steadying herself. "With Simon, I have my dignity back. My privacy... my safety... I am absolutely safe with Simon... and Marcus."

She exhaled softly. "Pain? I'm not in pain now."

Her voice was quiet, but firm. "That's the best I can do."

He nodded. "Now, to what was *not taken*," he said. "What was he unable to take from you, Lydia? What didn't he get?"

She hesitated.

This was harder.

Lydia tapped the pencil against the desk, the rhythm filling the space between her thoughts as she let them flow. She began writing in earnest:

He did not take my desire to protect my friends. He did not take Simon from me. He did not make me question God. He did not make me think all Germans are bad people. He did not make me enjoy the pain. He couldn't make me hit him. He did not make me beg him to hurt mc...

Lydia stared at the paper. *The thing he had wanted most... he did not get from me.*

She looked up at Doctor Reese, who watched intently.

"In the trench, in his little office, I never begged him to hurt me—the thing he wanted most.

"But in my nightmares, I do. I beg him. Better me than someone else. Because I can get through it. I have faith in God. I am loved. I can endure... but... it was not my fault. Not my failure. It's on him."

The psychiatrist stayed with her, patient, unwavering, letting her think it through.

"Write down the last thing you said."

Lydia put pencil to paper. *It was not my fault or failure. It's on him.*

"Doctor Reese, I need Marc," she said softly.

He nodded and went to the door, opening it. "Doctor Lovell, would you join us, please?"

Marcus nodded, quickly jumping up from the waiting room chair. He entered the office, anxiously appraising Lydia for any signs of distress.

"Please," Doctor Reese said to the man, gesturing to the empty chair beside Lydia.

Pulling the chair close to her, Marcus sat on the edge of it, visibly concerned.

Lydia reached out, grasping his hand. "Marc, do you remember when those German soldiers brought Charlotte, me, and the sentries back to our camp... and they surrendered?"

He nodded. "Of course, Lydia." That night was indelibly engraved in his mind.

"And in my nightmares at the camp, when Simon was missing..." Her voice wavered. "Did I fight you then, Marc? Like I fought Simon in that last nightmare at the house?"

His hold on her hand was steady, "No, Lydia. You didn't fight," he said gently. "You were frightened. You were sad. But you didn't fight." His voice softened further. "I only tried to help you remember that you had escaped."

"I've been trying to escape ever since, rather than fight back," she sighed as he waited, holding her hand. "Marc, the day the commander died, was it the same day that Simon punched him out? Did he die the exact same day?"

Marcus nodded. "After he grabbed you in the triage, Simon decked him and then came back to the surgical tent with us. Harold asked him what was going on, and someone brought the guy over by the surgery because he was bleeding from his battle wounds."

"...and because Abril had bitten him," she nodded.

"Yes, and because Abril had bitten him, but Harold didn't know that," Marcus said. "The orderlies dropped the man outside the tent and wanted to know what to do with him. Harold went out and told our orderlies to take him over to wait under the tarp... that's where he died. Harold said his wounds had been too severe... Simon didn't make that decision."

"Simon didn't decide?" she asked, relief softening her voice. "And you didn't have to decide anything?"

"No, Lydia," Marcus said, squeezing her hand securely. "The decision was Harold's. And when Stockton made the decision, he didn't even know who the guy was. He was just another unsavable wounded man."

Lydia hesitated, her eyes filling. "Marc, were you ever ashamed of me... for not fighting back in the trench?"

"Ashamed? My God, no! I thought you were so incredibly brave! And anyway, Lydia, there are many ways to fight back. It's not always a physical fight. Father James told me once... sometimes, fighting the internal battle is more fierce, more defining, than swinging with a fist."

Lydia studied Marcus, surprised at the depth of his words. "Our Father James told you that, Marc?"

He nodded. "You made a decision, in the trench—to treat the wounded German soldiers."

She held his eyes for a moment, then nodded, the memories surfacing. She could still see them—men laid out on little more than planks of wood... Charlotte beside her, working in the bitter cold to save them.

"Why did you decide to help them, Lydia?" Marc asked gently.

"It was the right thing to do, Marc. You know..." she replied without hesitation. "They were hurting. They were suffering."

Marcus nodded, his voice steady. "Even held hostage, in the trench, you chose to ease their suffering."

She met his gaze, the answer simple and resolute. "Well, sure, Marc. Of course. Just like we did in the camp. If a German came in who could be saved, we saved him."

"That's another way of fighting back, Lydia." Marcus poured every ounce of love he had into his next words, willing her to truly feel them. "If you can do good in the midst of evil, then you've already fought, and won, the real war."

Lydia stared at Marc, her eyes now riveted to his face. "Marcus, say that again..." she inhaled deeply.

He repeated it word for word, watching her expression. "If you can do good, Lydia, in the midst of evil... then you've already fought, and won, the real war."

"Then I did fight back didn't I, Marc?" Lydia exhaled again. "I fought back by doing good in the midst of his evil."

He nodded, Marc's clear blue eyes penetrating her own, hoping that he had helped in some small way.

Without hesitation, Lydia threw her arms tightly around Marc's neck, holding him close. "Thank you, thank you," she whispered in his ear.

Then, turning to the psychiatrist, her voice steadied with newfound certainty. "That's it, Doctor Reese. That's the *why*. I won the real war."

He nodded, "Yes, Lydia. I believe you've found your *why*."

She exhaled once more, feeling the weight lift—not all of it, but enough to breathe more freely than she had in quite some time.

As Lydia and Marcus left Dixmont that day, they had yet to learn that WWI had also found a resolution.

On June 28, 1919, the final treaties defining a new world order were signed, by men who had never stepped foot on a battlefield... never seen the horse-drawn carts of wounded and dying.

The Allies now controlled Germany. Peace had been restored and the world could begin to rebuild, hopefully for the last time.

Yet, even as a fragile hope emerged, the shadow of a new, invisible enemy loomed. A virus had rapidly begun waging its own war, sparing no nation, recognizing no treaty. A merciless pandemic no one knew how to defeat because neither side could even see it.

Chapter 17

Epidemic

As autumn settled in, an unease rippled through the staff at Charity. The influenza that had emerged the year before was gaining momentum with the shift in seasons. Each day, the walk-in clinic was swarming with hundreds of patients, coughing and feverish.

While Simon prepared for the day ahead, his worry wasn't for himself; the operating theater was kept clean, and everyone there was masked and gowned. He knew that he was better protected than most. But the others weighed on his mind—Lydia and the other nurses, out in patients' homes, tending to those too sick to reach a physician's office.

He had been relieved when Suzie announced that she wanted to stop working, now in her third trimester. She was more than ready to stay home, regardless of the flu... Marcus, however, was down with a fever. It could be nothing, but then, it could be this disease, hitting far too close to home.

Worried, Simon crossed the little alleyway and slipped through the back door, taking the stairs two at a time. He found Marcus lying in bed, a rare sight. Warming the bell of his stethoscope in his hands, Simon pressed it to his friend's skin, focused on his lungs and heart.

Marcus stirred in the bed, his eyes still shut. "I'm fine, Simon. You shouldn't be here. Don't breathe."

"I'll be the judge of that," Simon replied through his surgical mask, listening carefully for irregularities or congestion. "You're still hot. Make sure you drink everything in that pitcher Suzie left for you." He poured a glass of juice and carefully helped Marc lift his head to take a sip. "I went through this once, remember? With the British? A wonder we all escaped it last winter."

Marcus nodded, eyes still closed as his head sank back into the pillow. "I feel for you. All over again—my head's pounding."

Simon looked down at Marcus with compassion. "I'll check on you again after surgery tonight," he said softly.

Marcus waved him away feebly. "Don't. You'll catch it again... and you're already missing a lobe."

"I don't miss that lobe at all," Simon assured him with a faint smile before heading down the hall. He washed his hands thoroughly, then stepped out the back door, pausing to tell Suzie he'd return later.

Simon passed Abril, who was waiting patiently along the yard's fence. He paused to scratch her behind the ears, earning a soft wag of approval, before climbing into the Ford and steering it onto the street, toward the hospital.

As Simon drove through the quiet neighborhoods, he caught sight of a hearse just a block away. Its back door was open, waiting to receive a body whose soul had likely departed only moments earlier. It was happening more often than Simon cared to admit.

His worry deepened.

Lydia had promised that she would cover her dress with a long apron and wear a mask in anyone's house. She also had a bottle of rubbing alcohol in her bag for her hands. He suddenly realized that she hadn't taken Abril along on her calls today—the dog was still in the yard. *Hmmm*, Simon thought as he parked the Ford. *I wonder why...*

Passing through the hospital rotunda, Simon noticed that few people were on duty. No doubt some were home caring for loved ones who had fallen ill. The hospital may also have reduced any ancillary staff to lessen the potential for exposure... likely a futile effort, given that people were contracting the disease just as easily at the market as they were at the hospital.

As businesses and schools shuttered under government orders, the only places that remained operational were hospitals and funeral homes. There really wasn't much anyone could do for those afflicted. Try to get fluids in them, try to keep headaches under control, try to get fevers down... followed by a slow road to regaining strength.

Simon headed to the doctors' lounge and reached for an exam coat to cover his clothes, but thought better of it. Why risk taking anything home on his clothes? He changed into surgical scrubs, tucking his clothes into a locker. His first task was checking on post-op patients in the wards... removing sutures, assessing wounds, and checking fevers. He would send anyone home who was stable enough to go, an effort to keep hospital beds open. Entire wards had already been shifted to care exclusively for influenza patients. Asymptomatic medical or surgical patients had been consolidated into a single ward, where every possible measure was being taken to keep the epidemic at bay.

"Good morning, Nurse Bristol," he acknowledged the head nurse on duty. "How are you? How is everyone doing this morning?"

She glanced up from her desk, where she was already preparing a chart for him, noting temperatures and blood pressures recorded earlier that morning. "I'm fine, Doctor. These two at the top of the list have fevers; you might need to look at them first."

Simon nodded. "I will. And if he's healed well enough, I want to take the stitches out of Mister Whitcomb's leg today. We'll also pull the drain from Mister Barto's abdomen."

"Very good, Doctor," the nurse replied. "Is everyone alright in your family?"

"Doctor Lovell is down with fever. Checked on him earlier. Everyone else seems to be unscathed... I've seen hearses out all across town, though. Disconcerting, to say the least."

Rising from her desk to accompany him on his rounds, she added, "It's touching everyone, isn't it. Many families will not have a very pleasant holiday season... empty seats at the table and all."

"It's a difficult time of year to lose someone, I agree," Simon said. "Especially for those who don't have faith in a life beyond this one."

She considered Simon thoughtfully. "I've seen you in this ward every day for nearly a year now, Doctor Finney. Not much seems to get you down. Share your secret with me? Whatever it is, I want some of it!"

Simon smiled at the older nurse. "God has given me a belief that He knows best, a wife who loves me wholeheartedly, a son who makes me smile no matter what else is going on, and a friend who has become a brother. It doesn't get better than that, Nurse Bristol."

"No," she agreed softly. "I guess it doesn't. Well, let me fetch a suture tray for you."

Simon nodded as he gathered the charts of Marc's surgical patients to review their conditions. He flipped through the pages carefully, updating himself on their progress. He stopped at several bedsides, before the nurse returned, carrying a small silver tray with a cloth draped over the necessary instruments. Together, they moved down the row of beds, working methodically. Within the hour, Simon was heading back to the operating theater.

As Simon scrubbed his hands, an orderly found him at the sink. "Doctor Finney, can you spare a minute?"

"Sure, what's up?"

"Doctor Franklin is in the next theater and wondered if you could stop in? He's run into a problem."

Simon called over to his anesthetist. "Can you hold him, Sam?"

"Sure, he can sleep maybe fifteen or twenty, if you need it. Let me know as soon as you can, though," Sam replied. "I'll let him come back up to twilight."

Simon nodded and walked briskly to the adjoining operating theater, scrubbing his hands again, before accepting a gown and gloves offered by a nurse. As he approached the table, he noted it was a female patient under anesthesia.

"What've you got, Doctor Franklin?" Simon asked.

Mike Franklin looked up quickly. "Something quite unexpected, Doctor Finney," he said quietly. "I thought it was an ovarian tumor, but it's much worse... and now there's a significant bleed. The placenta is actually feeding right off the femoral artery... quite literally sucking the lifeblood out of her leg. Need to save the artery."

Simon peered into the open abdominal cavity, his gaze steady. "Clamps. Electric cautery," he ordered, his hand already outstretched. Without hesitation, the instruments were placed into his grip.

Meanwhile, Mike worked quickly, turning his attention to the tiny fetus, lodged outside the woman's uterus, where it never should have implanted. Every move was precise and urgent. The two surgeons quickly began cutting out tissue and closing off bleeders.

"Are we keeping this ovary?" Simon asked. "It's awfully close to everything."

"Nope, take it, she's got another one," Doctor Franklin responded tersely. "It'll take too long to try to reconnect the tube... and the scarring will likely block it anyway. Better to just take it out... but that femoral..."

The risk was obvious. Simon nodded.

With the umbilical cord clamped, Mike carefully lifted the fetus in its sac—barely more than three inches long—from the woman's groin. He passed it to Simon, who gently placed it on a metal tray held out by the operating room nurse. Simon saw one of the tiny arms waving helplessly and noticed the tears in the nurse's eyes as she bore the tray off to a counter.

"Must have been causing the mother a good bit of pain," Simon observed.

"It's siphoning blood straight from her leg   look how tightly it's wrapped around the artery. The placental tissue kept reaching for more supply. Her leg was going numb, and she had no idea why. Radiographs only showed mass displacement... but she's over three months along." He took a breath, steadying his hands. "Can you get in where that—"

"I see it... I've got it," Simon said, working quickly with clamps, staunching any bleeding and cauterizing small vessels. "I think maybe the femoral isn't too compromised."

They worked efficiently; the silence broken only by their requests for instruments. Then, finally, Mike Franklin exhaled a deep, exhausted sigh. "That might do it," he murmured. "Can you check her foot for pulses for me?" He shook his head, the weight of it all settling in. "My God, I'm glad this doesn't happen but once in a lifetime."

Simon nodded, moving to assess the circulation in the woman's foot. "She's got a pulse and quick blanching," he reassured the other surgeon. "Her leg has blood flow."

Mike nodded. "Thanks. Damnedest part of all this? She's Roman Catholic. If I tell her she was pregnant, she'll wish she had died instead of the baby. But if I tell her it was a tumor or something else, I'm lying to her."

Simon met Mike's gaze, understanding fully the weight of his dilemma. "You'll find the right words, Mike."

"Thanks, Simon. Usually, both of my patients survive. I'm not used to losing half of the pair..." His voice faltered briefly. "I can finish up here."

Simon nodded, heading to the sink by the door. As he reached for the faucet, his gaze lingered on the motionless, tiny figure resting on the tray. While relieved that he had not had to make this call, he was acutely aware of the toll it would take on Mike

Franklin. Quickly, he washed up and returned to his operating theater... and waiting patient.

The fetus lingered in Simon's thoughts—its fully formed ears and arms, delicate fingers and toes, and a heart no larger than a tiny pea, already beating. He knew there had been no choice. If the femoral artery had ruptured, both mother and child would have died in unimaginable pain. Saying a silent prayer for all involved, Simon scrubbed in again, accepting the fresh gown and gloves offered to him.

With his patient once more under anesthesia, he turned his focus to the next task at hand, carefully removing a bowel obstruction.

After his shift, Simon cleaned up and stepped out of the hospital, the weight of the day heavy on his mind. The crisp autumn air did little to ease the gravity of what had transpired. He wondered if Father Damien might send one of the priests to speak with the young couple, who had yet to realize that the woman had been pregnant... and whether the priest might also find time for Doctor Franklin.

Back home, Simon washed up once more before kissing his wife and scooping up Jimmy. He perched his son on the edge of the kitchen table, where the baby babbled eagerly, his tiny sounds tumbling forth in an enthusiastic attempt at conversation.

Smiling, Simon recounted the better parts of his day, his words slow and gentle. Jimmy stared, fascinated by the movement of his father's lips, reaching out with tiny fingers to grab hold of his beard.

"...And then we took out the nasty, twisted portion of the bowel," Simon said in a singsong voice for the baby, "with very little blood loss and sewed the man back up with retention sutures... and the patient is expected to fully recover in time for the holidays..."

Lydia stirred some sizzling sausage and vegetables in a pan, the warm scent filling the kitchen as she listened to Simon recount his day for the two of them.

"And what did mommy do today?" Simon asked, still in his falsetto voice. "Did she help people get over their coughs and fevers and all that bad stuff that happens to people when the influenza gets worse as winter comes?"

Over her shoulder, Lydia replied, "Don't expect me to sing my day to you! Suffice it to say, Mrs. Stevenson has completely fallen in love with our son. She thoroughly enjoys staying home with him while her own children are in school. Although..." Lydia paused, stirring the fragrant mixture thoughtfully. "She thinks the school will be shutting down for the rest of the year now."

"And did Mommy have any trouble out there today?" Simon cooed to Jimmy. "Because Daddy noticed that she didn't take Abril with her... and we wondered why, didn't we, Jimmy?"

Lydia began setting out the plates and silverware on the table. "Because it was cold, and we were running a bit late to get over to the sitter... and Abril wanted to play in the yard. She deserves a vacation, too, you know, from time to time, just to chase squirrels."

Simon supported Jimmy as he practiced standing, balancing him on his tiny feet. "But Abril doesn't even know what a vacation is, does she, Jimmy?" Simon half-sang the admonition. "And Daddy likes it when Mommy is safe on the streets so he can focus on what he's doing because he loves her very much and worries when she's alone out there." He shifted Jimmy slightly, keeping him balanced. "And Daddy wants to go check on Uncle Marcus, too..."

Jimmy babbled eagerly, his bright eyes locked onto Simon's moving lips. His tiny mouth trying to mimic the shape of the words.

Lydia felt Simon lean into her touch as she passed him, laying a hand on his shoulder and kissing the top of his head.

"I checked him when I got home. He's still lethargic... with a headache, but he drank everything Suzie gave him. She's there now and said her book club thing was cancelled. Too many people sick. I asked her to ring us immediately if he needs you to go over."

"Well, Daddy will go over tonight before bed anyway, just to be on the safe side, because Uncle Marcus doesn't get sick very often and it's a worry," Simon sing-songed to Jimmy. "And now, son, it's time for you to go in your playpen so Daddy can grab Mommy as she walks by and give her a kiss she'll remember till bedtime..."

Lydia smiled as Simon settled Jimmy into the playpen beside the table. The rich aroma of onions, peppers, and sausage filled the air. As she stirred, Simon stepped up behind her, wrapping one arm around the small of her waist. His other hand tracing a slow, affectionate path over the curve of her hip to her bottom.

"Hmm," he murmured in her ear. "I am starving."

Lydia laughed softly, shaking her head. "Supper's coming right up!" she said lightly, knowing precisely what he meant. "You will be well fed!"

He nibbled at her neck. "This is a good start..."

"Our baby is wide awake... and watching," she scolded, lightly.

"And he's learning what it's like to love a woman who means the whole world to a man." Simon pulled open her blouse just enough to gently kiss her from her neck to her shoulder.

Lydia turned and slid a piece of sausage into Simon's mouth.

"Delicious," he said while chewing. He drew her backside firmly against him.

Lydia set the spoon down and turned, wrapping her arms around his neck. "Oooh, you are indeed hungry," she exclaimed softly, pressing closely against him. "And I'll bet there is more to your day than what you just sang to our son..."

He swallowed, nodded, then kissed her fully, leaning her back against the countertop. "Second course..."

She sighed deeply. "You certainly know how to whet a girl's appetite, my love... but dinner is ready."

Reluctantly, he released her, taking his seat at the table as Lydia placed a steaming platter beside their plates. Simon said a brief prayer over the meal, and for Marcus to heal fully and soon, before dishing up the meat and vegetables.

"I'm at the remote surgery clinic tomorrow..." Simon announced between bites. "Suzie is going to work with me... her last shift till the baby comes."

"Good," Lydia replied. "Is it still working out with Nikki?"

He nodded, taking a sip of water. "Suzie's trying to keep Nikki away from other children, with so many ill. We'll take her with us and keep her in the playpen."

"I'm glad Jimmy is the only baby Mrs. Stevenson is keeping right now. You know, I stop in to nurse him at lunchtime, and then again as soon as we come home. He has such an appetite!" Lydia laughed.

"He's got my blood running through his veins, alright!" Simon declared, watching the baby playing with a soft washcloth in his tiny hands. "How is Suzie feeling? Any symptoms of her own today?"

"Said she was fine," Lydia replied between bites. "She's been sleeping in Nikki's room."

"Marcus must hate that!" Simon shook his head and chuckled.

"Or he's been too sick to care." Lydia pushed her food around on her plate, worried.

"Hm. Well that's not good," Simon remarked. "I will go check on him, right after supper."

"It certainly wasn't his choice. It was hers, Simon. She's afraid of getting sick... with the pregnancy. This flu is spreading so easily."

He wiped his mouth, placing the napkin on the table and headed for the foyer to grab his coat. "Be back soon," he called out, kissing her forehead as he passed back through the house. "Save room for dessert!"

Lydia gathered the dishes and carried them to the sink, pulling Jimmy's playpen closer to the counter so he could see her. As she washed, she sang him a washing-the-dishes singsong, continuing the cheerful mood from earlier. Jimmy cooed in response, his tiny fingers grasping at his toes, kicking excitedly.

Simon knocked on the back door as he pushed it open, not wanting to startle Suzie with his arrival. The house was quiet, leftovers from supper still piled by the sink in the kitchen.

As he hurried up the stairs, Simon secured a mask over his nose and mouth. He reached the bedroom door and tapped lightly, waiting for a response. Down the hall, the bathroom door was shut, but he could hear Suzie's voice as she spoke to Nikki beyond it.

Simon pushed open the bedroom door and peered inside, stethoscope in hand. "House call," he announced cheerfully. "You don't look nearly as much like death warmed over tonight!"

Marcus, still lying in bed, managed a weak smile. His fever had eased, leaving him gaunt, but not nearly as drained as before.

"Death warmed over..." Marcus managed wearily, coughing. "What a weird expression that is. Whoever thought that up had a sick sense of humor..."

"Everyone misses you at the hospital. You know... 'where's the other surgeon? The good looking one with the quick wit and great sense of humor? We're stuck with the boring one!'" Simon assured him. "Roll over so I can hear your lungs."

Marcus rolled onto his side, grumbling as he obliged. "Just don't say 'turn your head and cough' or I'll start worrying about where your finger is going next."

Simon chuckled, relief evident in his voice. "That's the very surgeon they keep asking about. Your sense of humor returns—an excellent prognostication for a full recovery."

"If I don't get better, Suzie won't come back to bed with me." Marcus murmured.

Simon shook his head, adjusting the stethoscope as he listened carefully for congestion. "Can you blame her?" he asked incredulously. "She's pregnant, for goodness' sake!"

Marcus nodded. "I can. I'd be a lot better, a lot faster, if she was in bed with me. That's the medicine to cure me!"

Simon smiled. "Well, I will not give you a prescription for that! Not even if you beg! I happen to agree with her precautions... in her condition."

"I'd wear a mask... I'd settle for a bed bath!"

"Not a chance," Simon said firmly. "I know what that would lead to, buddy. No, you must remain celibate, for now. Think of it as a time for quiet reflection, soul-searching... pondering the origins of the universe. As I had to do for months in Paris. I survived and so will you."

"You're a much stronger man than I am," Marcus sighed.

Simon laughed again. "This from the guy who prides himself on beating me at push-ups every time I challenge you. Well, now I challenge you to two weeks of bedrest and celibacy!"

"You are an evil doctor," Marcus muttered under his breath.

Simon stood. "Lydia will be so pleased to know you're getting better. 'Evil doctor,' huh? I've been called many things in my years practicing medicine, but that's a first. Not sure I want to live up to that title."

He tucked his stethoscope into a coat pocket, tossing a glance over his shoulder as he headed for the door. "Get some sleep, buddy. I'll check on you tomorrow—might even bring a pitchfork, just for you."

Simon tromped down the stairs, out the back door and across the alley, the cool night air greeting him as Abril trotted up to the fence, just like clockwork.

He crouched down, giving the dog a fond pat. "You look just fine to me," he murmured, affectionately. "Hope you enjoyed your little vacation, because tomorrow, it's back to work for you!"

Abril looked up at Simon as if she had no clue what he was referring to and followed him back into the house.

Simon slung his coat over a chair and scrubbed his hands clean before heading into the living room. Lydia sat on the sofa, cradling Jimmy as he nursed, his tiny eyelids fluttering with drowsiness. Soon, he'd be fast asleep.

Simon went upstairs, quickly gathered some quilts and returned to the living room, where he built up the fire again and turned down the lamps until the room glowed in the warm, flickering light. As Jimmy nodded off, Simon scooped him up with practiced ease, settling him gently into the playpen and tucking a blanket around him. Then, he laid a quilt before the fire, pulling Lydia up from the sofa and easing her down onto it. He pulled off his shirt, drawing her head to his shoulder as he draped the quilt over them.

Stroking her hair, Simon broke the silence, "Mike Franklin called me to scrub in with him today."

That was unusual.

"What happened?" Lydia asked softly.

"He thought his patient had a tumor, ovarian. Turned out there was a fetus growing in her groin, feeding on the femoral artery... would have killed both of them," Simon paused. "I've never seen a three-month old fetus like that..."

Lydia stroked his chest and waited, listening.

"It was so perfect, Lydia," Simon continued. "Perfect little arms and legs, fingers... a beating heart... I could see right through its chest wall. It was a living baby... and we had to take it out."

Her fingers paused for a moment on his chest. "I can't imagine how difficult that was... for both of you."

He stared at the flames undulating, rising from the glowing logs. There was a hiss as the wood released moisture, the fire turning it into a little burst of steam.

"There was no other choice," he stated. "But we ended its life."

"It doesn't make it any easier, when there is no choice," she said, kissing his hand.

"No." He fell silent.

She tilted her head slightly, gazing up at Simon's profile as he stared into the fire. "Are you regretting that you helped Doctor Franklin?" Lydia finally asked him softly.

"No. I'm glad he felt he could call me in for help... and I'm glad the mother was saved," Simon admitted to her. "But when I saw Marcus at the house just now, he called me an 'evil doctor'—"

"He called you a what?" Lydia blinked, clearly astonished.

Simon looked down at her. "Not for that. I haven't told him about today's surgery yet. He was just joking... frustrated... because I told him he had to be celibate for a couple weeks to keep Suzie from getting sick. And, by some cruel coincidence, today was also the day that Mike and I ended the life of that little baby... to hear Marc use that term, even teasing, was just odd."

He looked at his hand, resting on Lydia's shoulder. *The same hands can end a life as easily as they can save one*, he thought. "I've never intentionally caused someone to die, at any age... until today..." he murmured.

Lydia propped herself up on one elbow, as she gently turned Simon's face to look at her. "You didn't end that little life, Simon. God did. That baby was not created to grow in its mother's groin. It was impossible for it to survive there. And very wisely, God led them to call you in to help save that woman's life. Don't think for even one second that a loving God didn't just take that little infant soul to Heaven where it can grow up there, strong and healthy, surrounded by the angels. Remember He said to let the little children come to him and forbid them not."

Simon held her gaze. "Yes, that's true. He did say that."

Lydia nodded, wishing she could mend his heart, unaware that, with her timely words, the healing had already begun. She leaned over him and whispered, "I love you, Simon."

Letting her lips softly brush over his, she kissed him tenderly. Simon untucked her blouse from her skirt and slipped his hands up inside the soft fabric, pulling her closer so he could nuzzle against her. The comfort of her touch as her long hair descended around him was like a veil blocking out the rest of the world. He nearly lost himself in the moment, then abruptly stopped and rolled her onto her back. She waited, watching him.

Drawing back the quilt, Simon raised Lydia's skirt. The glow of the fire illuminated her skin with a soft orange-yellow glow. Life and death intermingled as the same hands that had helped end a life earlier that day now explored his wife, bringing her to life, now.

He gladly heard her utter, "Oh my goodness..." and when he continued to focus on her, instead of turning to his own needs, she whispered, "I love you, Simon... I don't think I need anoth—"

He kissed her, pausing just long enough to say, "Yes, you do..."

As the fire crackled beside them, he stoked the flame inside of her again, then joined her as a shower of embers exploded and drifted down inside the hearth to settle in a crimson glow for the remainder of the night.

Christmas came quickly, winter frost edging the windows in delicate patterns. The days had grown shorter and the air more crisp. Both houses were adorned for the holiday, their living rooms brightened by small evergreens, draped in handmade and delicate blown glass ornaments, cherished baubles sure to become a yearly tradition.

Marcus had recovered, back on his feet and back at the hospital. Lydia's parents had come down for the weekend, with gifts for both families, as they were eager to include Nikki and wanted to get a glimpse of the house Marcus and Suzie had settled into.

Lydia, her mother, and Suzie, filled Suzie's kitchen with their laughter and lively conversation. Jimmy, nestled in Anna's lap, soaked up her affection, while Nikki giggled as she played with Abril on the kitchen floor.

"Suzie, with the shops closed over this flu, were you able to find something for Marcus, for Christmas?" Anna asked curiously as she rolled out biscuits on the table.

Suzie nodded. "I found a chess set for him to have here at home so Simon doesn't have to keep bringing his over. They start a game and then come back to it later, you know, so Marcus keeps insisting that Simon shifts the chess pieces around whenever he resets the board to continue playing."

Lydia laughed, jumping in. "Not intentionally, of course! That's a perfect gift, Suzie! What about you, Mom? Did you find something for Dad?"

"Well, he has everything known to man, including fifty ties and every tool ever sold in a hardware store. We stopped buying each other things long ago. Now we're just glad to have another Christmas to share in front of the fireplace."

Anna looked into little Jimmy's face as he watched the movements of her mouth. "Of course, you've given us the best gift ever with this little guy. There's nothing better! My dear little grandson. Suzie, will your parents come down at some point?"

"We'll probably head up to Rochester after this flu eases up," she told them, brushing flour from her hands over the sink before sliding the tray of biscuits into the oven. "At least for a weekend. There's just as much influenza there as here in the city. So, if we do see my folks, we won't visit anyone else. I don't want Nikki to get sick or Marcus to come down with it again. Once was bad enough! He's still not a hundred percent."

"Simon is calling down to Rebecca's. If none of them are ill, we're going there... for a day or two anyway," Lydia said. "Probably at New Year's. But if they've got it like everyone else, we'll stay home. I worry about Simon, with part of his lung already gone. My hands are chapped from rubbing alcohol on them every chance I get."

"It's curious that he didn't get sick from Marcus, considering how often he came to check on him," Suzie remarked.

"A blessing," Lydia nodded. "He was bathed in prayer, Suzie..."

Suzie shot her a skeptical look. "I guess you weren't praying for Marcus, then!"

"Oh, yes, I was!" Lydia assured her. "That he'd be back on his feet in no time... and that the experience wouldn't be wasted on him!"

The sound of the men, laughing in the living room, caught their attention.

Lydia pushed back from the table and wandered into the other room, where she noted that the new chessboard was already in play. Her father, to everyone's surprise, was thoroughly besting Marcus, who was rarely defeated in the game.

"You see now, son," Andrew told Simon. "That is how it's done!"

"But how did you know that five moves ago?" Simon demanded. "I couldn't follow the strategy you were using."

"You're young," Andrew said with a hearty laugh. "Give yourself time."

A sudden fit of coughing seized him. He reached for the glass in front of him, taking a small sip of wine before shaking his head with amusement. "Laughing takes its toll on us old men."

Lydia sat on the arm of the sofa, placing a hand on her father's shoulder. "You okay, Dad?"

He patted her hand. "Just fine. Having more fun than a man my age should be allowed. I'm real glad you men are such good friends and live close by like this. This kind of friendship is a gift."

Lydia glanced at the two younger men, catching the shared look between them, then turned back to her father.

"Well, if you're ready, Dad, we can head back home. You and Mom can turn in early, so we're all rested for church tomorrow."

"Sounds like a plan," her father agreed, glancing out the window. "And we got some snow for Christmas, too."

"We get snow for two solid months every winter! The ground stays white until February," she laughed. "Abril loves it. So do I, as long as we have warm quilts at night."

Marcus pushed himself up from the floor, his defeated king lying toppled on the board. Crossing to the living room window, he gazed out at the quiet street. Sure enough, snowflakes drifted down, catching the glow of the streetlamps.

"The tree you put up is lovely," Lydia said, coming over to check on him. "Are you really feeling better, Marc?"

Nodding, Marcus drew her gaze out the window. "Another hearse is sliding its way through the snow," he said quietly. "This is lousy..."

She placed a hand on his arm. "We're all grateful you made it through."

"A while back, Simon told me I should ponder the 'origins of the universe'!" Marcus exclaimed. "I guess I did enough pondering, so I was allowed back up again. Even so, I wonder why God in Heaven puts up with us. Well, me anyway... you're a different story. You already qualify for sainthood, in my book, Lydia."

I think that's something Father Henderson will touch on tomorrow," she said. "That whole 'why God came down to Earth, and walked among all of us fallen creatures' thing."

He was still looking out the window. "Suzie isn't going, Lydia. She says I'm not the man I used to be. Not the one she married," he said quietly.

"I know," Lydia said softly. "She told me. And she's right, Marcus. You aren't the man you used to be. You're a wonderful, caring, strong man, learning how to become all that God wants for you. Just like the other notable men in the Bible."

Marcus turned his gaze to her. "Am I really so different now, Lydia?"

She searched his eyes. "Yes, and no. Yes, you've become a man I admire deeply. And no, you're still the man who planned the reception for Simon and me in an army mess tent. You haven't lost anything in my book, but you've gained so very much. And someday, Suzie will see that. And God-willing, someday, she will see a need for God to touch her life, too. It just takes some people more time than others."

"What, so Rome really wasn't built in a day?" Marcus said more lightly now. "I'll be patient. It took me a long time, with more than one person helping me along the way."

His thoughts swirled. *I've become a man she admires? Lydia just said that? Then... I am becoming a little more like Simon, after all this time.*

Lydia nodded and turned to see Simon already bundling Jimmy into his blanket and little hat. After saying their goodnights, they made their way back across the alleyway, through the lightly falling snow which always made the sounds of the city so much softer... more gentle. Stamping the snow off their boots at the back door, they were glad for the warmth of the house and went up to prepare for bed.

After finishing up in the bathroom, Lydia settled Jimmy into his crib, closing the door halfway behind her. She saw her parents laying out their night clothes on the bed in the spare room which used to be Nikki's.

"Do you need anything, Mom? Dad?" Lydia asked.

Anna came to the door and hugged her. "Not a thing. Get some good sleep, dear."

"You too," Lydia replied, opening the door to her room. "Love you both."

Closing her bedroom door behind her, she slipped off her dress, hanging it in the closet before wrapping herself in her robe and reaching for her hairbrush. Simon entered a moment later, taking the brush from her hands to complete the familiar ritual... one hundred strokes before they got under the quilts.

He rested his head on her chest and she traced his temples, running her fingers through his hair, along the line behind his ears, and down the curve of his neck. She felt his body relaxing, giving in to her touch.

"Nancy told me that so many died at the hospital this week. She said that even in the clinic... that some folks barely made it through the doors, never even reached the ward," she spoke softly. "I was thinking, maybe they didn't want to die alone at home, and somehow got themselves there just in time, so someone could be beside them."

"You lost patients in their homes, too, though," Simon reminded her gently. "You found a couple of folks already gone, didn't you?"

She nodded, softly caressing his face. "One older woman... she didn't even know her husband was gone. She thought he was napping. It was heartbreaking to have to tell her he had already passed. He didn't have any heartbeat at all... this flu hits the older people hard."

Simon shifted position, settling his head on the pillow beside hers. "Are you okay, my love?"

"I am. Another woman was dying. Her two daughters had arrived just in time, along with the family priest. He administered last rites. I couldn't hear a heartbeat, and she was already turning blue—but Simon, you wouldn't believe it. She sat up and thanked the priest for taking such good care of her family. Then she turned to her daughters, thanking them for being so faithful to her through the years. And then, just like that, she laid back down on the pillow and simply died... I... I couldn't believe it. One moment she was thanking them, and the next... she was gone."

"Wow," Simon exhaled. "That is remarkable."

Lydia nodded. "I thought so, too. She had such strong faith. Roman Catholic."

"Sounds like she was at peace with God and her family."

"I think so," Lydia agreed. "Her daughter called her death 'beautiful'. Interesting word choice. A 'beautiful' death... When you were missing, that was the hardest part... the thought of not being there if you got sick, or died... not being there with you, to hold your hand and whisper how much I love you as you crossed over to the other side. I prayed every single day that, wherever you were, you felt my love right there with you."

Simon cradled her face in his hand. "Let's not think of that now, not on Christmas Eve. Let's listen for the angels singing instead, my love. Especially since I'm right here beside you, now."

"Can I ask you about something, Simon?"

"Of course."

"At one of the homes there was a woman, about my age... she has heavy cramps with her monthly. She started seeing a doctor who says..." Lydia paused.

Simon waited a moment, kissing her hand softly. "Who says...?"

"She told me he sees her every week and touches her, on his table, the way you touch me, to make her feel... the way you make me feel. He says it will relieve her cramps, if he does it regularly. Is that... is it an actual thing doctors are doing?" she faltered, wondering how she had even managed to ask such a thing.

If true, she knew she would never set foot in a doctor's office again. She couldn't imagine Doctor Franklin doing that to women in his office, but if it was standard practice...

Simon's brown eyes couldn't hide his surprise, but he kept his tone even. "Well, of course, as a surgeon that's a little out of my area. But I cannot imagine that... medically speaking... Well, I can ask Mike about it."

"Would you, please?" Lydia implored him. "I didn't know how to advise her because she feels a little like she's betraying her husband. I can tell you now that if it is an established treatment for cramping, I will never go back to one of those doctors ever again, even if I get pregnant again. Not even if it's Doctor Franklin. I don't want anyone who does that for his patients touching me..."

Simon pulled her into his arms. "No one will ever make you feel that way except me, beloved. I promise... however, if you're having any cramping right now..."

"I'm not even ovulating. Remember? The whole breast-feeding thing?"

"Then it should be even better, shouldn't it?" he teased.

"Does regular... does what we do, if we do it regularly, benefit a man?" she wondered aloud. "For health?"

Simon chuckled. "Oh, yeh. My health down there is definitely better when we do it regularly... so just go ahead and put it on the calendar, my love!"

She hit him lightly on the arm. "I'm being serious, Simon! It was a real question!"

"And this is a real answer," he said, nodding. "My body says it will become ill if I do not have you, right now. So, what should we do about this?"

"Well, I don't want you falling ill," she said, wrapping her arms around his neck.

He kissed her deeply. "I'm feeling better already..." he murmured.

Christmas morning had drawn quite a large congregation to the church. Candles were flickering in every window, illuminating the stained-glass scenes. Father Henderson took his place behind the pulpit by a large nativity scene, readying himself to address those gathered together for the joyous holiday, but as his gaze swept over the congregation, his heart sank. So many dressed in black. So many in mourning.

The Father noted that Doctor Lovell was seated with the Finneys near the front, his presence becoming a familiar sight among them. The young doctor had come a long way since the day they first met to discuss little Jimmy's baptism—no doubt a little closer to heavenly reality than he had been. Father Henderson also noted that his wife had not come, but his daughter was there on his knee... and an older couple had also joined them today. The woman looked so similar to Lydia that the priest assumed it must be her mother.

The choir led the congregation in familiar Christmas hymns, melodies so well-known that most voices rose effortlessly, even through the third verses, without glancing at a hymnal. After the final notes faded, Father Henderson stepped forward as the congregation settled into their seats, ready to receive the message.

Even though they had just sung it moments before, he began by reading the words of the hymn "Silent Night", then paused, before beginning his homily.

"You know, that night was not silent, and things were not calm and peaceful in Jerusalem. Just as things now are far from calm and peaceful, as many of you who are grieving know too well. My hope, in these few words of instruction, is that you'll hear why the angels could praise God even in the midst of worldly troubles, why they called their message a tiding of great joy... even in the midst of deep sorrow. For that is what we're promised in the birth of the infant in a stable..."

Lydia took Simon's hand, holding it tight. Marcus held Nikki, who leaned back against her daddy, quietly watching the flickering candles. Anna Blackwell held Jimmy against her shoulder, gently patting his back as she pondered the baby in the manger.

Andrew Blackwell sat in silence, a sharp pain twisting through his chest, climbing up his neck, into his jaw, and down his arm. He focused on the candlelight flickering, the warmth of his family beside him. This was the moment he wanted to carry with him—the memory he would hold when his eyes closed that night, not to wake again in the morning. It would be alright. He knew Simon would care for Lydia and the baby, faithfully. And Anna—she had known for some time, hadn't she? She had been especially tender, watching him more closely these past months, as his strength had faded.

Andrew was ready. He was ready to rest. Ready to meet God.

In Greensburg, Andrew's funeral was well attended. Town-folk who had known the Blackwell family for years came to pay their respects, yet few lingered. The ever-present threat of influenza kept visits brief. They paid their respects to the family and quickly left.

This funeral was just one of many the week between Christmas and New Year. With so many succumbing to the flu or other illnesses, the town was weary with loss. There was no customary meal in the church hall and only immediate family returned to the Blackwell house. They sat quietly in the living room... Andrew's chair by the fireplace, left empty.

It was obvious to everyone that Peg and Tommy's relationship was strained beyond the weight of current circumstance. Tommy was aloof and irritable. Peggy kept Mary and Steven out of his way, occupying them with books and toys to avoid giving him any excuse to be frustrated. Tommy accepted a glass of wine from his mother-in-law, who had offered it to everyone, to ease emotions, then commandeered the bottle for himself.

"You can come and live with us, Mom," he announced abruptly.

Anna replied quietly, "Thank you, Tommy. I do appreciate the offer. My friends and community are here... this house is all I have left of Andrew and our years together. I'm not... I don't want to leave all of our memories."

Tommy nodded. It meant he would have to come more often, to take care of things in Andrew's absence, but he kept his annoyance to himself.

"You could come weekends, Mom," Peggy offered. "If you just want to spend time with the children. Anytime."

"I might do that." Anna took a deep breath and addressed the group, "You children need to realize that I knew your dad wasn't well... for a long time. I knew this was coming. I'm glad he had a good Christmas. In some ways, I'm glad he passed Christmas night. It was somehow the right time. As if he had chosen it."

"That does happen, Mom," Lydia nodded. "I've seen people wait for loved ones to come home... or to leave... as if they have some choice about their passing."

Anna dabbed her eyes. "Your father had a good, long life with no deep-seated regrets. He was a good, loving husband and father. We should all live our lives like he did, being ready to cross over whenever God says it's time, without regret."

Abril trotted over to Lydia, who sat on the floor beside Jimmy, watching over him as he lay on his blanket. The dog cast a quick glance at the door. Lydia stood, gently passing Jimmy into Simon's arms.

"Come on, girl, I'll take you out."

They headed through the kitchen to the back porch, where Abril wasted no time, bounding out onto the snow-covered back-yard. Lydia turned her gaze up into the crisp, clear night sky. The stars were so bright.

The Dipper was hanging there... and Simon's North Star. Despite the ache in her heart, she smiled, thinking of when she and Simon had gazed up at the stars from the French medical sta-tion—remembering the moment in the surgery tent when he'd asked her, *"How many stars are in the sky?"*

Bringing her abruptly back to the moment, she heard the back door opening behind her and turned to see that Tommy had stepped out onto the porch.

"Needed some fresh air? There's plenty of it out here." Lydia studied Tommy. "How are you holding up?"

He leaned on the porch railing and looked up into the night sky. "Yeah... it happened pretty suddenly... so, they spent Christmas with you two in the city, huh?"

She nodded. "They wanted to see our friends' new house and went to church with us Christmas morning."

"And you couldn't tell that Dad was in trouble..."

Lydia answered, cautious. "Dad didn't say a word, Tom. He seemed to really be enjoying the music, the service, the time together... he even beat Marcus at chess—"

"So much for you being a nurse and Simon being a doctor," Tommy criticized. "You're so smart but didn't see your own father having a heart attack."

Lydia replied slowly, "Tom, we've spoken about this often. Dad knew his heart was getting very weak. His legs were swollen with fluid, a telltale sign of heart failure, and it was hard for him to breathe. There was nothing that anyone could do. He was tired and wanted to make the most of the time he had left."

Tom spun around, striking Lydia hard across the face.

She stumbled back, a sharp gasp escaping her lips as her hand flew to her cheek. The force sent her reeling into the porch railing, completely caught off guard.

From the far side of the yard, Abril heard the sound—sharp, unmistakable. In an instant, she bounded up the porch steps.

Tom's voice dropped to a dangerously quiet tone.

"Call off your mutt," he ordered Lydia.

"Abril, stay!" she immediately commanded Abril, who heeled in agitated obedience to her human.

"Why did you do that, Tommy?" Lydia exclaimed, tearing, still holding her cheek to quell the sting.

"You just don't get it, do you, Lydia," Tommy seethed, standing over her, the alcohol loosening his tongue. "You're a sanctimonious little bitch in my book who needs to be taken down a notch.

If you were my wife, I'd have you over the table with a paddle coming down hard on your bare butt—and I wouldn't stop until you were so blistered you couldn't sit down for a week!"

Suddenly furious, Lydia demanded, "Is that what you do to my sister, Tommy? Hit her with a paddle until she has blisters? Is that what you do? What kind of evil man are you to do that to your own wife? You aren't a man at all. You're a bully and a coward! And you drink too much!"

He loomed over her, the alcohol on his breath filling her nostrils. "You little bitch!" he hissed. "I finally get your sister to listen the way she should, and then she sees how you are and forgets her place. If you get taken down a notch, she'll listen better..."

Before she could even gasp or cry out, Tom had Lydia's hair in his grip, pushing her head down over the porch rail, her bottom stinging under the palm of his hand, the porch rail digging into her stomach, the weight of his body pinning her to it.

Abril did not lunge but was barking frantically.

From the living room, Simon heard Abril's defense bark. Nearly tossing Jimmy into Anna's arms, he rushed through the kitchen and out onto the porch. Lydia was bent over the railing, her body recoiling with each strike. Tommy's grip was tight in her hair, his hand landing hard. The sound of it cracked through the cold air, needing no explanation.

Simon didn't hesitate.

Grabbing the heavier man by the shoulders, Simon heaved Tommy off of Lydia, throwing him bouncing and rolling down the wooden stairs to the snow-covered ground below. Running down the steps right after him, breathing hard in the cold air, his fists clenched, an enraged Simon stood over his brother-in-law.

"If you decide to stand up," Simon told Tommy through clenched teeth, "go straight to your automobile and drive away. If you try to stay here, I will beat you within an inch of your life. And it's only for Anna's sake, for what she's gone through today, that I haven't already shoved every tooth in your mouth down your throat."

Tom looked up from the ground, furious. He gestured toward Lydia. "You need to keep your little wife in line, Simon. She needed some good old-fashioned correction. It's what a woman's butt is made for, and if you paddled her yourself, someone else wouldn't have to!" He spit out a little blood and got up onto his feet, unsteady but still capable. Glaring at Simon in the darkness, Tom curled his fist into a tight ball.

Simon saw it. His voice was so calm it was frightening. "Don't even think about it, Tom," Simon stated, "I swear to you, I will not hold back... you will not walk away from this, unless you go now."

The two men stared at each other for a tense moment, Tommy growing uncertain that he could take the other man. He really had been drinking too much and knew he was off balance.

"Fine. I'm going," Tom grunted and spit on the ground again. "But I'm tellin' you right now, Simon, this isn't over. Not by a long shot!" He turned and stumbled across the snowy yard to his automobile, slammed the door and drove off down the side street, the Ford weaving slightly into the darkness.

Simon turned, sprinting the distance back to his wife. Reaching Lydia, he pulled her into his arms, holding her close, her sobs muffled against his chest. He didn't speak—there was nothing to say that could soften the moment, nothing that could erase what had just happened.

Abril pressed against his leg, her stance protective, muscles tensed, a low, steady growl rumbling in her throat as she watched the now-empty street.

Lydia was shaking. Simon wrapped an arm around her, guiding her back into the kitchen where, in the light, he immediately saw the bright red handprint across her cheek as well. Simon grabbed the dish towel from its hook and ran back outside to pack it with snow. He returned quickly, carefully holding it to her skin as she trembled on the kitchen chair.

Anna called out from the living room, "Everything okay, Simon?"

"Yes, Mom," he answered back.

"Did Tommy go out? Did I hear the car?"

"Yeah, he had an errand," Simon called back, thinking hard about what he was going to do next. Looking into Lydia's eyes, Simon quietly asked, "Can you make it up the stairs to your room? I'll get Jimmy and come right up."

She nodded, holding the snow-filled towel to her cheek. Lydia went through the dining room to the central stairway, stumbling upstairs to the privacy of the bedroom with Abril on her heels... her bottom on fire. There, Lydia looked at her cheek in the mirror over the bureau. It would fade by morning... all she could think about was Peggy. *She knows her place.* That's what Tommy had said. How long had her sister been living like this?

With Jimmy in his arms, Simon soon opened the door to the bedroom. He placed the baby in the padded dresser drawer they'd made into a makeshift crib, on the floor before examining Lydia's cheek and her eye. "I didn't realize he had followed you out there."

"He was drunk. He really resents us. He said I needed to be 'taken down a notch'. I have to tell my mother something to explain coming up tonight like this," she said tearfully.

"I told her it was time to nurse Jimmy and then you were going to rock him to sleep," Simon assured her. "I'll go back down and figure something out in a minute."

"He's been beating Peggy," Lydia blurted out angrily, "to make sure she knows her place. I wish women had the right to divorce."

"Me, too," Simon agreed. "He's an angry guy. Alcohol and anger never mix. She'd be better off without him. Kids, too. Let me see your bottom." He reached for the hem of her dress.

"No, Simon," Lydia stopped him. She couldn't bring herself to face it yet, past and present colliding. She turned to Jimmy who stirred in his little drawer—a welcome diversion.

"Well, you were right about feeding Jimmy." She leaned over, scooping him up, her cheek throbbing as she bent down. Opening her blouse, she put Jimmy to her breast and felt the milk flowing.

"It's so simple for him. He's hungry and I feed him. He's lonely, and we play with him. He tries to talk, and we shower him with praise. When does it start getting so complicated?"

Simon brushed a lock of hair behind her ear. "Likely the day he gets up and starts exploring on his own two little feet. Then, we start worrying about all the dangers. We start warning him—don't fall, don't run in the street, don't eat that, play nice..."

Lydia caressed the baby's cheek. "I hope he always feels this safe, Simon."

Simon touched her breast gently as she nursed. "He will. He already feels loved, safe, and wanted. He'll never have to be kept quiet and distracted so he doesn't anger his father. I felt terrible for Mary and Steve tonight, tiptoeing around Tom."

"Me, too," Lydia kept her focus on Jimmy.

"I'll be back after I talk to your mother and sister," Simon kissed Lydia's forehead before going back down the stairs.

Lydia soon heard low voices in a discussion that went on long enough that she finally did rock Jimmy to sleep. She carefully tucked him back into the drawer, wrapped snugly in his blanket. Exhausted, she changed into her nightgown before slipping under the covers. Laying there quietly, Lydia thought of her father... feeling the weight of his absence... missing him.

She let down her guard, weeping softly into her pillow.

Returning to the top of the stairs, Simon saw Abril guarding the door to Lydia's room. He stopped to rub her ears. "Good girl," he said, as she thumped her tail on the carpet.

In the softly lit room, he moved with care, mindful not to disturb his wife. As he undressed, an image surged back into his mind—Tom's hand striking Lydia, the sickening sound of it, the way she reeled against the porch railing.

His fury was beyond measure.

Uncertain what to do with his rage, not wanting to wake Lydia... he drew closer to check on her, then he saw them... silent tears slipping from the corners of her eyes.

She wasn't sleeping. She was grieving.

With great resolve, Simon pushed his anger aside, for the time being... it would not serve its purpose just now and Lydia needed him. And for tonight, it seemed Tom would keep his distance, avoiding the reckoning that would eventually come.

Sitting on the edge of the bed, Simon kissed Lydia's forehead, her wet eyes, her sore cheek... the corners of her mouth. He was glad when she reached for him. Simon spent ample time caressing her, before gently pulling up her gown, removing her undergarment, and rolling her over to check her skin. Simon kissed her bottom softly.

He slid into bed beside her, pulling her to his shoulder, his arm around her, stroking her hair until she fell asleep.

Simon couldn't deny it—it had felt so good, sending that man tumbling down the steps. The urge to knock his teeth out had been overwhelming... but Simon's hand had paid the price once before—he thought back to when he'd punched the German commander.

No, let Tom be the only one in pain tonight. Simon's thought.

He wondered how he might protect them from Tom, now that they had seen what he was capable of? He thought of how very deeply they would all miss Andrew Blackwell... but Lydia was restless, struggling to stay out of the trenches, no doubt. She needed to be his focus.

Even before the New Year, Peggy let Lydia know that she had already returned to full-time work in Greensburg, settling back into the familiar routine of the law office where she had worked years before. She didn't mention Tom, and Lydia didn't ask. The incident on the back porch remained unspoken between them.

Simon had done his best to take care of it the night of Andrew's funeral, offering Peggy only as much detail as was necessary, shifting the focus to her safety... and the well-being of the children. Tom's anger, his drinking... it was clear what her priorities had to be. And Peggy hadn't hesitated. She had gathered her children and moved them into her mother's house straight away. For Anna, their presence was a comfort. She loved them so... and Mary and Steve gave her something to hold onto, something to soften the edges of her grief.

New Year's Eve brought Marcus, Suzie, and Nikki to the house on the corner for a welcome celebration. Nikki was excited to sleep in her old bedroom for the night, and after both she and Jimmy were asleep, Marcus popped open a bottle of champagne. He poured a splash of the bubbling fluid into glasses for Lydia and Suzie, but filled Simon's and his own nearly to the top.

Marcus stroked Suzie's rather large belly and raised his glass. "A toast to pregnant, and nursing, mothers!" he exclaimed. "And to Doctor Richard Maloney, who wisely hired the finest medical staff on Earth!"

"Cheers!" Lydia raised her glass, taking the tiniest sip. "And a toast to the best friends and neighbors in the world!"

"May they always be so!" Simon added, clinking her glass before reaching for Marc's and Suzie's.

Suzie remained on the sofa, resting, gently stroking her abdomen. Her baby was turning within her as Marcus sat on the floor just beside them, waiting to feel each surprise movement.

"Feeling the baby moving?" Lydia asked Suzie. "I loved that feeling! I miss it. It's the best part of being pregnant."

"My friends at the club think so, too," Suzie replied casually.

"The club?" Lydia returned. "Is the writing and reading group a club now?"

Suzie nodded. "We've had so many join... it's become quite a social club for aspiring writers. We were meeting weekly, before the flu got so bad... sharing things we'd written... offering critiques. Some of the works have been published. I love it! It's very stimulating. We still get together, in smaller groups, now."

"I'm thoroughly impressed that you're writing! You could be the next Edith Wharton!" Lydia was astonished.

Suzie explained further, "People are writing now, more than ever... about the war, the influenza, social issues... we have poets, storytellers, reporters... all kinds of people."

Marcus lifted his glass yet again. "To all of the writers out there. May you be published and famous, if you so choose."

Suzie smiled. "James says he's going to publish one of my short stories—"

"James?" Lydia asked, curiosity piqued. "Is he one of the group writers?"

Suzie sipped the little champagne left in her glass, smiling to herself. "You could say that."

Marcus studied her carefully over the rim of his glass, his gaze steady. Then, setting his drink aside, he pushed himself up from his seat. "Anybody need anything from the kitchen? Cheese, crackers, salami?"

Simon stood as well. "I'll help you make up a snack for us all. It'll tide us over till midnight. After all, supper was hours ago—I'm hungry."

The two men headed to the kitchen, leaving Lydia and Suzie alone by the crackling fire. Lydia looked closely at her friend.

"Suzie, are you happy… with the baby coming… and with work and all? Or have you picked up writing to fill some other need?"

"Truthfully, Lydia, I do need the outlet," Suzie said, setting down her glass. "Life is okay. We like our work… Nikki is a wonder… the house is nice—but the club is so fun! I like talking to other writers. It's quite stimulating… and James says I have true potential."

"Do you share your writings with Marcus?" Lydia asked. "He's never said much about the writers' club, only that you go."

"No. He's more interested in medical journals… and the religious stuff, which I'm not into… rather than poetry or fiction."

"Give him a chance," Lydia suggested. "Maybe it's just an area of the arts that he hasn't had the opportunity to explore. He might enjoy it! Can I read anything you've written?"

"Sure. Go grab my pocketbook. My journal is the small red book. I carry it because you never know when an idea will come to you. James says a journal helps you capture the moment."

Lydia retrieved the journal as directed, bringing it over to her chair, closer to the firelight. "Anything in particular?"

"No. Turn to any page you like," Suzie offered. "It's all been shared with my club, already."

Lydia gently turned the pages of the journal. Within the lines of neat writing she saw some poetry, small essays, single lines of thought that might later be developed into something deeper. Then, a poem caught her eye. She read it through.

"You have some lovely things in this journal, Suzie. I had no idea you were so talented."

Suzie laughed lightly. "Do you write?"

"Just a collection of little letters to Jimmy, about how Simon and I love him, our hopes for him... or what's going on around him in these early years. Things that he might read later in life and appreciate... I see that you also have a poem in here, to James."

Suzie nodded. "I wrote it for him a month or two ago. He's been so encouraging. He's nice."

"It's rather... personal," Lydia said softly.

Suzie nodded again. "That happens when people share intense thoughts and ideas. Poetry is very personal."

"Yes, I suppose so," Lydia mused. "He sounds gallant... intriguing, in the way you describe him in this poem."

Suzie regarded Lydia calmly. "Now, Marcus has been intrigued, as you say, with lots of women. I don't hold that against him. And there's nothing, with James, to hold against me."

"But not since he's been back. Not since you've been married, Suzie," Lydia protested. "That was the Marcus, before..."

"Hm, well, the fact is we just don't have as much in common as we used to. People don't always grow in the same direction," her friend admitted. "But we can still be compatible, for Nikki's sake... and for the new one, when it comes."

Lydia closed the red journal, returning it to Suzie's pocketbook. "I hope that's enough. You two are very special to Simon and me. I was so glad when you found each other again."

"People change, Lydia," Suzie said softly. "It's a fact of life."

With surgical precision, Marcus stood at the cutting board making precise quarter inch slices of salami while Simon cut matching squares from a brick of cheddar.

"So, this guy, James, wants to help Suzie get her writing out in print?" Simon asked.

"I guess. That's what I hear," Marc nodded dispassionately.

"Think he's on the up-and-up, Marc?"

"Don't know, Simon," Marc admitted quietly. "I've never met the guy."

"Maybe this is just all due to her being close to the end of her pregnancy," Simon offered.

Marc nodded. "Could be... but... when Lydia's dad died last week, Suzie went on and on about how 'life is short'. You know, the get-everything-done-while-you-can thing."

Simon nodded. "I guess the whole 'life is short' thing is hitting a lot of people. Lydia's sister is doing the same thing, after leaving Tommy."

"He still drinking so heavily?"

"Seems so," Simon nodded. "I threw him off the back porch at their mom's house."

Marc's knife paused, mid-air. "You what?"

Simon continued cutting the cheddar. "He was drunk. He was out on the porch and slapped Lydia across the face, started hitting her—I heard Abril barking—"

"Abril never barks!" Marcus stared at Simon, astonished.

Simon continued, his voice low and controlled, feeling the rage rising within him. "Yeah, well, the guy had Lydia bent over the porch rail. Spanking her, with his bare hand. He's been beating Peg too—"

Marcus stabbed the salami, the sharp knife piercing straight through into the cutting board, the knife standing straight up, quivering. His full attention was on Simon. "He what?!"

"So, I threw him off the porch, bounced him right down the steps into the snow," Simon nodded. "Told him to leave before he wouldn't be able to walk away."

Marcus hadn't moved a muscle. "Did he... is she... was Lydia—"

"Left his handprints. Several handprints," Simon said. He set his knife down. "I wanted to draw blood, Marc. But Anna, Peg, Tom's kids... They were all inside grieving, after having just buried Andrew. I just couldn't give them more trouble. So, I threatened Tom and he drove off. But he said it's not over, Marc."

"I won't be taking her back to Greensburg. Peg and Anna can come here instead. I don't want Lydia anywhere near Monroeville, or anywhere Tom is."

Marc hadn't even blinked yet. "Damn it!" he exclaimed under his breath. "The trenches..."

"That's what I thought too, Marcus."

Both men took a moment to collect themselves, before going back into the living room where the women gladly enjoyed their platter of snacks. While Marcus tried his best to act as if nothing was out of the ordinary, wanting everyone to enjoy the holiday... this new information was weighing on him, heavily.

They soon fell into easy conversation and before they all knew it, there was an announcement over the radio and the celebratory music began playing. The new year had begun. As the airwaves fell quiet, Marcus leaned over Suzie, on the sofa, kissing her and her belly.

Simon held Lydia on his lap, her arms around his neck. She held his face in her hands and looked into his eyes, whispering, "I love you, Simon. Happy New Year."

He smiled, whispering in her ear, "I love you. Let's not wait too long to go upstairs. We should start the year off right."

Chapter 18
Premature

The Spanish flu took its toll on the world.

Pittsburgh, like many other cities, saw its headlines shift from battlefield casualties to the growing devastation caused by the pandemic. Obituaries, once detailed tributes, were now trimmed to manage the overwhelming need and limited print space. Appeals for help filled their pages, especially calls to aid orphaned children. The weight of the epidemic was heavy for struggling families already spread thin, as schools and businesses remained shuttered.

Volunteer nurses moved with urgency, visiting the homes of those afflicted. Nancy, Sally, and Lydia were among them. They offered not only care, but knowledge. They taught families how to slow the spread, how to protect one another in the face of this invisible enemy. In a time of great uncertainty, their presence was a lifeline, a reminder that even in crisis, there was still hope to be found. Suzie would have joined them, but she had stepped away from work some time ago, her focus now entirely on the arrival of the baby. Nikki had come early, and she had a feeling that this child would be the same. She couldn't risk exposure.

One bitterly cold afternoon, after her last patient, Lydia picked up Jimmy before stopping at home to wash up. She wanted to go check on Suzie and Nikki. Her hands had only just begun to warm when she bundled them up again to make the familiar trek across the alleyway. As she nudged Suzie's door open, just enough to squeeze inside, Lydia kicked the snow from her boots, leaving them neatly by the entrance.

"Ooooh, cold and snowy out there today!" she exclaimed, settling Jimmy into the playpen. "Good thing you're staying home!"

Suzie was warmly bundled in the living room, playing with Nikki, who had her doll set up for quite the tea party.

"Care to join us?" she called out, smiling as she watched Nikki prepare for another guest.

"Thanks, but first I'm putting the kettle on for some real, hot tea, if you don't mind, and then I need to feed Jimmy."

"Help yourself! You know where to find everything!" Suzie gestured toward the kitchen.

Lydia placed the kettle on the stove and rubbed her hands briskly. They were red and chapped. She needed some lanolin or Vaseline... there would be some in the bathroom. As she walked through the dining room, a small book on the hutch caught her eye. *Through the Kaleidoscope,* was printed on the cover. She picked it up as she continued through to the living room.

"What's this little book, Suzie?" Lydia asked. "Poetry?"

"Essays," Susannah replied "James brought it by. He just had it printed. He has commentary on everything from the Spanish flu and prohibition, to a woman's right to vote!"

Lydia settled into the easy chair, drawing Jimmy to her breast before opening the little book.

"Wow!" she exclaimed. "He's really a social activist, isn't he! Look at this..." Her eyes skimmed some of the pages as Jimmy nursed. "Very pro-women, I can see that!"

Suzie laughed, nodding. "He certainly is! Find the one about why women should be voting."

Lydia flipped through a few more pages. "Here's one on alcohol. Looks like he's against the government limiting it."

"He's against the government limiting anything. Thinks people should be able to make up their own minds. Society of the people, for the people... and all that."

Lydia nodded. "Thomas Jefferson thought so, too!"

Suzie leaned in slightly, studying Lydia. "Do you want the vote?"

Lydia considered for a moment. "I suppose so. A lot of government decision-making now is about social welfare, helping the poor, the sick, widows, orphans. Why shouldn't women have a say in all of that? We do the work for so much of it!"

"You should come to the club, when it's in full swing again," Suzie smiled. "You'd fit right in."

"So they aren't meeting at all now... with the epidemic?" Lydia asked.

"No, that's why James came over to see me and bring me his book. Plus, he knows the baby is coming soon," Suzie explained.

"What does he do for a living?" Lydia asked.

"Publisher, remember? He's going to publish my writings."

"Are you going to use your own name?" Lydia wondered, still flipping through the pages.

"I don't know," Suzie admitted. "I guess I'll let him decide. Sister Edwarda might not want to see my name in print, depending on what's being written."

"That bold, huh?" Lydia teased.

Suzie smiled. "Depends on who you ask. James doesn't think so."

"What did you decide about sharing your writing with Marcus?" Lydia asked, setting the little book aside for a moment as she shifted Jimmy to her other breast.

Suzie leaned back against the sofa, stretching out her legs, relaxing as Nikki busied herself with her doll.

"Not right now," she admitted. "He's too focused on the baby coming early..."

Lydia glanced up from Jimmy's face, her expression softening.

"Can't blame him. He didn't get to be there when Nikki was born, and he sure doesn't want to miss this one! At least if you are early, it'll be a quick ride to the hospital—you are still planning on going inpatient for the delivery."

"I certainly am!" Susannah assured her friend. "A whole week in bed, with a nurse bringing the baby for feedings. Bed rest, sleeping all day, meals delivered to me—no way I'm passing that up!"

Lydia laughed. "You make it sound like a fine vacation! It doesn't always go quite as planned, you know."

Suzie stretched out on the sofa, her expression serene.

"You were an exception—tea kettle's whistling."

"I hope I was a rare exception. Want some?"

Suzie shook her head.

Lydia headed to the kitchen, balancing Jimmy in her arm as she carefully poured a cup of tea, returning with intentional steadiness.

Settling back into the chair, she glanced at Suzie.

"So, how did James get into publishing, I wonder?"

"Family business. Worked his way up and is now the editor of several journals. It's so different from the medical world. He meets with congressmen and heads of companies about their publishing needs. Lots of bigwigs in politics and all. He travels, too, talking to famous writers, getting their books out. Pretty exciting life," Suzie sighed.

"Does he have a family?" Lydia asked, carefully.

Suzie glanced over, catching the tone in Lydia's voice. "Not yet. Wants one."

"Hm," Lydia mused.

Just then, the kitchen door opened and they heard Simon and Marcus stamping the snow from their boots and exclaiming about the freezing temperature. There were the familiar sounds of chairs sliding, boots dropping, and hands being washed at the sink. It wasn't long before the men made their way into the living room to find the two women with the children.

Marcus leaned over Suzie and kissed her forehead before patting her belly. "How's everyone here?" he asked eagerly. "Any pains? Everything still okay? You've got your feet up! Good!"

He scooped up Nikki who reached for him the moment he entered the room.

"How's my little angel?" he asked as she wrapped her arms around his neck.

"Dada!" Nikki exclaimed.

"You betcha!" Marcus grinned. "Nikki!" he added, kissing her forehead.

"Ki-ki," the toddler replied.

"Close enough!" Marcus laughed and tickled her belly.

After kissing Lydia and Jimmy, Simon turned to Marcus and his daughter.

"And who am I, Nikki?" he asked as she reached for his beard.

"Imah..." Nikki giggled.

"That's right... Uncle Simon," he said slowly. "Care to dance?"

Marcus handed Nikki to her self-appointed uncle, and they twirled around the room.

As they passed Lydia in her chair, Simon paused mischievously. "We need to make one of these, my love."

Lydia, happy to see Simon so lighthearted, teased back without hesitation. "Any time you're ready."

Simon spun right back over to his wife, Nikki still in his arms, kissing the top of Lydia's head, again. "Really? Hm. So it's up to me, is it?"

"Jimmy will be one at Easter, so you know what they say... " Lydia smiled. "Oh! How was the surgery today, you two? And when one of you is able to take Jimmy, I'll go make us all some supper."

Marcus quickly obliged, taking the now satisfied Jimmy from Lydia, lifting him up with a knowing grin. "Are you going to spit up on me?"

"My baby would never spit up on his godfather," Lydia admonished.

"Of course he would!" Marcus declared. "And we don't mind at all, do we, Jimmy?"

Simon followed Lydia into the kitchen as she fastened the buttons on her blouse. Gently, he leaned her against the counter, stopping her hands before she could fasten the last one.

"Let me," he murmured, though instead of closing it, his fingers lingered.

"So, you wouldn't be opposed to another baby, beloved? Even after everything you went through with our son?" He studied her expression, cautiously hopeful.

Taking his face in her hands, she made him look into her eyes. "Ancient history," Lydia said firmly. "But the same conditions apply—birth at home, with Sister Anne, and you must go through it with me." She held his gaze. "If you're going to have fun making this baby, you're going to suffer through the delivery of it right alongside me—just like last time."

She still held his face, her touch capable of bringing him to his knees.

He kissed her deeply, then murmured, "I promise you—I will tip the scale to my advantage!"

With a playful sigh, she reached up, taking down a saucepan from one of the hooks to start dinner. "Now, tell me about your day."

"We did rounds... No disasters in the wards. Had a couple of gallbladders and a gangrenous foot. Had to remove a couple of toes, poor guy, and then I helped Mike Franklin with a cesarean."

Lydia glanced at him as she began to sauté some chopped onions. "Did you, now? What did the woman have? Did it go well this time?"

Simon remained leaning against the counter, watching her cook. "It did. She had a little boy—well, figuratively speaking! He was a strapping ten-pound baby if he was an ounce! There was no way she could have delivered that baby on her own."

"Ten pounds! I can't even imagine," Lydia agreed, amazed, imagining carrying such a large baby and trying to deliver it naturally. "How long was she in labor before Doctor Franklin decided on the cesarean?"

"Several hours, but he said he wasn't going to waste her time, or strength, on something he was sure wasn't going to happen... I like his approach. Good man."

She nodded, stirring in tomatoes and chunks of beef to the skillet. "He was very considerate with me."

Simon hesitated. "You know, he could deliver for you, Lydia. Then if there's a problem, he'd be right there with all the proper staff."

Lydia paused. "There won't be any problems, Simon. It's not going to happen twice. I'm sure of it."

Simon hesitated. "I'm just saying..." his voice trailed off, the memory of Lydia bleeding so heavily after Jimmy's birth still haunting him. "And I'm sure I could convince him to let me stay in the room since he let me stay with you in his office for that follow-up exam."

Lydia's gaze remained on the skillet in front of her. "Simon, I do not want to be at the hospital. I want to be home—it's not up for negotiation... or further discussion. And besides, I'm not even pregnant yet."

He stepped up behind her, wrapping his arms around her waist and kissed her cheek in apology. "I'm sorry, my love. End of discussion. We can go back to the having fun part..."

"You know, Suzie got pregnant when she was still nursing Nikki. How does that happen?"

"You want the long, medical version or the short, random chance scenario?"

"I guess 'random chance' will have to do..." She tapped the spoon on the edge of the pan before setting it on the spoon rest. "Because right now, it's time to start setting the table for us. Oh and later, when we're home, remind me to tell you about James."

"Our James? Jimmy?" he asked, opening the silverware drawer.

Lydia shook her head. "No, the other one."

He looked confused, but nodded. *Remember to ask about James.*

Just then, Marcus stepped into the kitchen, ready to help plate the meal.

As Simon shut the drawer, he realized he had forgotten an important update. "Oh! Lydia, I talked to Mike about that other matter... the woman you saw... with the significant cramping."

Lydia quickly set a tray of baked potatoes on the stove before the heat could seep through her potholders, her attention snapping to Simon. "What did he say? Is that really something doctors are doing? Because I'm telling you now, I'm not even considering going to a doctor, not even for a check-up, if that's standard care..."

Marcus glanced up, thoroughly interested. "What are doctors doing now?"

Simon turned to Marcus, "Um, shall we say, therapeutically assisting women... to orgasm in the office... as a treatment for pain during menses."

"Therapeutically assist—" Marc's jaw dropped. "That's utter bullsh—"

"I'm telling you, Simon, if Mike Franklin—"

He shook his head. "You don't have to worry about Mike, Lydia. He said that while some doctors claim that relaxing the pelvic muscles helps ease the pain—and there is some anecdotal evidence to support that, though it's unclear where that data would even come from—Mike was adamant that he does not perform that particular... procedure."

"Well! I should certainly hope not!" Lydia declared, though she was deeply relieved. *So! If I ever do need an obstetrician, Mike Franklin is still safe.*

Marcus, however, was quite bewildered. He caught Simon's eye as Lydia left to set the table. He would have to ask Simon for more information on the subject, later... in private. *Therapeutically assisted...? Unbelievable!*

As they enjoyed their time together over dinner, Simon and Marcus spoke about the hospital—specifically, the student nurses in its two-year training program. Upon completion, the nurses were assured they would be officially placed on the registry.

Simon shook his head. "Honestly, Lydia, it doesn't make sense that you can't work on the wards just because you're married. You do more in the clinic and in patients' homes than any of the student nurses on the wards. Sometimes I think hospitals run these programs just to get free patient care.'"

"Well, I never felt used during my training—I gained so much valuable experience. But I am glad I chose to volunteer overseas. I learned far more from you doctors, than I ever would have if I'd stayed home. Mary Baxter was right when she said our work overseas went far beyond what nurses are allowed to do here, even today. And though we're on the registry, every state has different nursing requirements... no one has figured out a nationwide standard yet."

"Is that coming? Nationwide requirements, like in medicine?" Marcus asked, thinking of Suzie, being out with the baby for an extended leave.

"It will eventually, I think, if they can ever figure out what it is that we nurses actually do," Lydia said, only half joking.

"Is being on the registry enough for you two?" Simon asked. "Will you need, or want, more official training at some point? College classes, maybe?"

Suzie set her fork down on her now empty plate and took a sip of water. "I'd stop nursing and go into journalism or something."

"For me... maybe. I love learning," Lydia answered. "But I prefer learning in the field... not in a classroom."

Marcus took a moment, appreciating these women he knew so well. "You ladies have an uncanny ability to master new skills... and quickly. If there's something you don't know, you're always eager to figure it out. You've both been that way, since we first met you."

Nodding, Simon added, "Marcus, remember on the transport ship, when we were coming home... you asked me what Lydia wanted to do after the baby was born, and I said, 'take care of the baby', remember? And you said, 'that will never be enough for her'... you were quite right, Marc."

Lydia stood, gathering the dishes. "Having a baby has taught me more than I could have ever imagined. I certainly got a college-level education during those nine months—just no diploma."

"Our children are the diploma!" Suzie laughed.

The snow was falling heavily as Simon and Lydia crossed the alley, back to their house on the corner. Simon had tucked Jimmy inside of his coat. It was coming down so hard that they could barely tell where the grass ended and the alley began. Lydia called Abril up to the back porch and invited her into the house. Usually Abril preferred the cold, but this time she came right in. They shook the snow from their coats and left them in the kitchen, hanging on the chairs, to dry.

"If it keeps up like this, no one is going out tomorrow," Simon told her. "Especially not you, walking the streets—there won't be any streets to walk. And Abril won't be able to see over the drifts."

Lydia nodded. "If it keeps up like this, we'll all stay home. Oh, wouldn't that be fun, Simon? To have a snow day in front of the fireplace?"

"Fun for us, definitely! Not fun for the hospital if the doctors can't get in," Simon replied, worried.

"At least the nurses in the residence don't have to travel."

They settled Jimmy into his bed and then changed into their night robes.

Lydia took Simon's hand and said, "Let's go back down and sit in front of a fire, Simon."

"You don't want to get warm under the covers?"

"Not yet," she smiled, grabbing her hairbrush as they headed downstairs.

After building up the fire and starting it crackling, he turned to his wife, "Sit here, on the blanket, and I'll brush your hair."

Following his invitation, she settled in, enjoying the dancing flames as Simon kneeled behind her. He loosened her hair from its bun, and began the nightly brushing routine.

"I lost another patient today," Lydia said quietly. "Influenza again. Still taking its toll. The man had heart disease and then got the flu. It made me think of Dad."

"I'm sorry," Simon replied. "Was he gone before you got there?"

Lydia shook her head. "No, his wife called early this morning and said he wasn't well, so I switched my route around to see him first. He died shortly after I got there."

"Are you okay?"

She nodded. "It's just sad. Second time this week. So many have died. I waited with his wife until the hearse came for him." Lydia felt him pause, kissing her head before resuming his brushing.

"Like you said, 'it's not easy, even if it's inevitable'."

"No, not easy at all. I'll stop by next week and see how his wife is holding up. Oh, I had one of Marc's post-ops today, too. He had repaired an aneurysm for the man. He was doing pretty well... healing. Also saw a family with chickenpox."

"Little bit of everything, sounds like," Simon observed.

She fell quiet under his hands, soothed by his touch.

"Oh, right..." he said, returning to their earlier discussion. "Tell me about this, James?"

"Ah, yes. He came to see Suzie today... to bring her his new book of essays," Lydia reported. "He's from her writing club."

"Oh," Simon said. "That James. She mentioned him once before, at New Year's."

Lydia nodded. "That's the one. I'm beginning to wonder if it's more than a club friendship."

"What makes you think so?" Simon pressed.

"A poem she wrote for him in her journal," Lydia added. "She invited me to read her journal, and I saw it and asked her about it... he comes over to their house often."

Simon said nothing, but the brushstrokes through Lydia's chestnut brown waves slowed a little.

"He comes when she's home alone," she continued. "I get the feeling from her that there may be something, more. And it breaks my heart for Marcus and her."

Simon nodded, weighing this information against Suzie's earlier discussion with him about their differing interests and opinions. Finally, he said, "I think Marc shares your concern."

Lydia looked over her shoulder and sighed. "Oh, Simon."

"Yeh... one hundred." He set the brush aside and sat behind her, stretching his legs out on either side of hers. Simon wrapped his arms around her, leaning her back against him.

"Should we say something to them?" Lydia broke the silence.

He hesitated. "I think it's better to let them work it out for themselves. If they need our advice, they'll ask. If not, then, well... we'll just be supportive."

"But with a baby coming, Simon, "Lydia continued. "Marcus is so excited about the baby. It would be awful to have something happen that robbed them of the joy of welcoming this new child, together."

Simon kissed her head. *Yes, it would be awful,* he thought. He never wanted anything to come between him and Lydia... he thought of their tense conversation in the kitchen.

"My love, I... I'm sorry I upset you earlier," Simon whispered softly into her ear.

"Oh, the delivery thing? It's okay, Simon, really," she re-assured him. "I was just upset... about the man dying this morning, then the whole thing with Suzie and how it would hurt Marcus if she is developing a relationship with this guy. I didn't mean to take it out on you.

"I really do want to have the baby at home though. But I'll tell you what I will consider—just consider—Now that I know Doctor Franklin isn't one of those peculiar doctors, I'd consider, letting him deliver the baby, here. And if—only if, mind you—the baby is in danger, then we could go to the hospital... as long as you stay right beside me."

Simon felt a rush of relief. "Oh my God, Lydia, thank you!" he exclaimed. "It does make me feel better... that you would at least 'consider' it."

She reached her arms up around his neck, a gap in her robe opening up as she did so.

"Did you do that intentionally?" he murmured, appreciating the view.

"What?" she asked, watching the flames leaping and falling. "Take it out on you? Oh my goodness, no, my love. It was unintentional; I was just preoccupied."

"No, I meant this," he said, pulling the edges of her robe even farther apart.

"Oh... oh that..." She had not even noticed. "Simon, how on earth can you find me desirable when you see me breastfeeding Jimmy all the time?"

"Are you kidding? That makes you even more desirable," he murmured. "So very feminine... so womanly... so very soft..."

Simon pulled her robe completely open, letting the warmth of the flickering fire radiate over her exposed skin.

Lydia leaned back against his chest, inviting his hands to wander. Simon relished moments like these, when they had the time to let want build, slowly. He draped each of her legs out over his own, thinking back to the times he'd made love to her in their tent in France, by the small glowing stove... a far cry from their roaring fireplace... and spacious living room floor, so much more comfortable than the narrow cot that had been their bed.

This was heaven compared to the camp.

But tonight, as he laid her back against the floor and felt her welcome him, everything else was the same. This woman was still his alone, as she had been since the beginning, through all of their many trials and tribulations. Simon knew, without a doubt, that Lydia held nothing of herself back from him... and he gave her everything he was, in return.

After heading up for the night, they snuggled in bed, beneath the warm quilt. He rubbed her back as she fell asleep, his hand lingering on her bare bottom. The image of Tommy striking her skin was keeping him awake. The rage resurfacing. He couldn't press charges, but Tom had promised that it wasn't over yet.

Simon wanted, more than anything, to go find the man and truly finish it. With Tom's temper, Simon knew it wouldn't take much for the man to throw the first punch and then Simon could let his rage take over... he could hurt Tom Franklin for what he had done. The man had put his beloved Lydia over a railing and... Simon's muscles tightened, his face flushed in the darkness.

Simon moved his fingers softly over her skin, feeling the scars. Tom likely hadn't noticed them in the dim light of the porch. Tracing the length of the smooth lines, memorials of her trauma, Simon appreciated anew the length of the hard, leather crop.

Suddenly, the first sight of her wounds, when he had washed her in their tent, came back to him. The wounds had been deep, from being reopened several times by the leather. How on earth had she run back to camp that night, with the German soldiers, who had surrendered, saving her, Charlotte and the two sentries...

How had she made it back, in that kind of pain?

He remembered that her undergarment had been stiff with dried blood when he had carefully removed it. He hadn't been able to suture the long gashes for her. If he had, maybe he could have reduced her scarring. Simon knew that the sting of Tom's hand hadn't been nearly as painful as that crop had been, but still, tears fell from Simon's eyes as he lay there.

Lydia whimpered in her sleep—his fingers paused. He waited, not moving, afraid he had triggered memories by tracing the scars. Then Lydia cried out softly and began weeping like a young child.

Pushing up on one elbow, Simon softly kissed her cheek. "It's Simon, beloved. I'm here. You're safe," he whispered. "It's Simon... it's okay now... it's all over now..." He waited.

In Lydia's nightmare, the images of a Commander/Tommy figure holding her over a railing, not a desk, but with a crop, striking her... began to fade. Lydia fought to wake from the dream. Simon's voice was breaking through, telling her that it was over... she realized that she was back in their bed. She rolled over, hugging his chest and feeling his soft kisses on her forehead. He brushed the damp hair away from her eyes.

"You're safe, beloved," Simon whispered gently. "You're with me now. I have you."

Her eyes opened. "Simon? Oh, Simon... cover me. Cover me, Simon."

He rolled on top of her and covered her in his protection, sliding an arm beneath her shoulders. "I'm here," he repeated softly. "Sleep, Lydia. Sleep..."

Her eyes closed again, almost immediately, as he kissed her tenderly. He rested his head beside hers, feeling the warmth of her body and the softness of her skin beneath him.

How could any man ever want to hurt her?

As the snow continued to fall, hearses and ambulances could no longer navigate the city streets. The death count climbed, it seemed, with the rising drifts of snow, now coming up to their back porch. Simon peeked out their front living room window, distressed at what he saw.

He called the hospital to confirm the protocol. Doctor Maloney, who answered, assured him that everyone was to stay put; the clinic and operating rooms would remain closed. There were enough doctors and medical students on-site, to make rounds.

Simon and Lydia stood there in the living room, exchanging a glance—equal parts concern for those who might need help today and the childlike thrill of an unexpected snow day, for them.

"Let's start with breakfast!" Lydia smiled, kissing him quickly before heading into the kitchen.

Simon called after her, "I'll go get Jimmy... we'll meet you in there!"

Simon sat at the kitchen table, playing with Jimmy while Lydia scrambled eggs and fried bacon. Outside, the snow was still coming down, softer now, but still steady. Abril stood at the kitchen door, her tail wagging.

"You'll regret this," Lydia warned, but opened the door anyway.

The dog trotted out onto the porch. Unable to see the steps, she plunged into the snow, taking great leaps, nearly disappearing with each landing.

"I told you so," Lydia called after her, seeing only ears and a blur of fur emerging each time the dog bounded back toward the porch, where she thoroughly shook the snow from her fur before flopping down on the wooden planks beside the swing. Lydia went back inside and turned the bacon, to fry the other side.

Simon read aloud from a medical journal in the singsong voice he often used with Jimmy. "Making a transverse incision, retract the omentum using a..."

Jimmy gazed up at Simon with his curious blue eyes.

Lydia smiled. "You do have Mother Goose in your library, somewhere, don't you?" she admonished.

Obediently, Simon adjusted his material, "And then Mother Hubbard went to her cupboard and fried all the bacon and eggs. And when they were done, Daddy said, I'll have some fun and play with your mommy's long legs."

Lydia rested a hand on her hip while waving the bacon tongs in the other. "You are incorrigible," she said, smiling. "Besides, didn't we do that last night?"

"Ancient history," he said, using her phrase from the day before.

"It won't be long before he understands what you're saying!" Lydia pressed.

Simon turned to his son, smiling at him. "Not for quite a while though, and until then, I will tell Mommy all about her lovely long, silky legs and her lovely round bottom—"

Interrupted by the telephone in the front hallway, Simon scooped up Jimmy, giving Lydia's bottom a playful squeeze as he passed her.

"I'll get it," he offered.

Lydia heard the low murmur of his voice and began plating their breakfast as he returned from the other room.

"Hospital?" she asked as he quickly dug into the pile of bacon and eggs on his plate.

"We have to go across the alley after breakfast. Suzie is in labor."

"Oh no! She's early again." Lydia set the pan back on the stove and poured a cup of coffee for each of them. "And there is no way she's going to make it to the hospital in this snow! How far apart?"

"Marcus said every ten minutes."

"Okay," Lydia said. "We'll eat quick and go—Suzie isn't going to be happy about this at all. I don't suppose you have another medical bag under the bed, do you?"

He looked up, surprised, realizing she'd known about his secret emergency bag since her own delivery.

"No, unfortunately not, only my normal one... but that doesn't mean Marcus hasn't thought of it."

They placed their dishes in the sink, not bothering to wash them. Bundling themselves in a layer of pants, boots, and coats, Simon said, "I'll go first. Follow in my path and hold onto me."

Feeling his way down the steps, Simon pushed through the snow toward the back fence, only to find it wouldn't budge. Without hesitation, he vaulted over it, then turned to lift Lydia and Jimmy—then Abril—over the pickets. They made their way across the alley to Marc's buried back steps, finally reaching the door. Abril dropped onto the porch, content to watch the snow fall from there.

As they entered the kitchen, they heard Suzie cry out from the living room. Quickly shedding their winter layers, Lydia pulled the playpen into the dining room, where she could keep an eye on both of the little ones. Simon washed his hands and went straight to the living room, where he found Suzie on the sofa, holding her abdomen and Marcus on a foot stool beside her, feeling her muscles rising with a contraction.

"I'll get sheets and some newspaper," Simon announced. "How far apart, Suzie?"

"Maybe three minutes," she gasped. "I don't want to do this, Marcus! I wasn't supposed to have to feel this! You were supposed to make sure I was at the hospital—asleep! I'm not supposed to be here!"

Lydia left the children in the playpen to go to her friend. She took her hand, touching her cheek gently. "It's okay, Suzie. The baby will be small. It won't be too hard to push. We've been birthing babies at home for thousands of years."

"Tell my body that!" Suzie groaned. "It thinks this baby is enormous."

"I'll go boil a knife for the cord," Lydia told them. "Unless, Marcus, by any chance—"

He nodded. "I did. Front hall closet."

In the front entry, Lydia found his medical bag on the shelf above the coats. *These two men are so much alike*, she thought! Pulling it down, she looked inside and saw scalpels, gloves, scissors, clamps... everything they would likely need. And a little bottle of ether. Hm. She wouldn't tell Suzie just yet about that, knowing how close her friend was to delivery.

She shook her head, relieved that Marcus had prepared, and brought the black bag back into the living room, just as Simon was coming down the stairs with linens.

"Newspapers?" he asked Marcus.

"Kitchen closet by the icebox," Marcus confirmed, intensely relieved that Simon and Lydia had come so quickly to help.

He took Suzie's hand and stroked her forehead, where her hair was damp from exertion and clinging to her skin. "We'll get through this together," he assured her, kissing her forehead.

"Easy for you to say," she almost sobbed as the contraction subsided and she rested back against the pillows. "You can do it next time! Then let me know how getting through this works out for you!"

Simon returned with newspaper and began layering it for a pad beneath the sheet to spread over the sofa. "Have you checked her dilation yet?" he asked Marcus.

Marcus nodded. "About seven."

"Well on your way, Suzie," Simon said.

He was much less worried about her delivery than he was about how the premature infant would manage when it arrived. He remembered the tiny French baby that Lydia had delivered outside of Nancy... how she had had to help it breathe.

He decided that he should give Suzie the option of Lydia bringing this baby out.

"Do you want me here, Suzie? Or Lydia, who has also delivered babies?"

"I don't care who is here, as long as it's over soon," Suzie gasped, another contraction coming over her. Clutching her stomach, she cried out again.

Lydia returned to the living room with the bag, "Remember you told me to walk, Suzie. Let's walk while they set up the couch. Come on."

As the pain eased, Suzie let her friend help her up, and together they walked through the downstairs—from the living room to the kitchen, then to the dining room, where she reassured Nikki that everything was alright—before circling back to the front door. They made the trip twice before another contraction gripped her. She leaned against the wall.

"Deep breaths, slow and easy," Lydia reminded her. "You gave me good advice, let me return the favor."

"I know," Suzie said, grabbing her hand. "I just... at this point last time, I was already asleep. I didn't have to do any of this, Lydia. It's not fair! Marcus was supposed to get me to the hospital. Everything was planned! This isn't right!"

Lydia nodded. "I know, dear, but we can do this. The second is easier than the first."

"If this is easy, then I'm a....!" Suzie grimaced.

"Keep walking with me," Lydia urged her as the pain subsided.

Marcus watched them disappear from view again as he and Simon spread out the layers of newspaper and then the sheets.

Relieved, Simon noticed the medical bag Lydia had placed by the couch. "Great minds," he commended Marcus, looking through the bag. "Ether?"

"Yes, but I haven't told her," Marcus admitted.

"Ah. Well, so be it. Only if necessary—This baby will be small," Simon paused. "It needs to be able to breathe."

Marcus nodded. He looked absolutely haggard.

"We've been up most of the night. I'm pretty sure she hates me right about now."

Simon couldn't help but laugh. "Of course she does, buddy! That's why we're here! It's not like you planned the snowstorm of the century, she knows that... And hey, you get to see your own baby born after all!"

"But Simon, what if it is too small to...?" Marcus was wracked with anxiety.

Simon placed a steady hand on his friend's shoulder. "Let's not borrow trouble." He looked up as they both heard another cry from the front of the house again. "'That must be a good one.' That's what Sister Anne would say, 'let her do what she has to do.' Sister Anne just sat there knitting while Lydia walked the hall."

"I'll go find my needles," Marcus muttered under his breath. "Thank God we found this house right across the alley!"

"I do thank God... every single day." Simon replied. "Listen, go hold Nikki for a minute. Let her know everything will be okay."

Marcus nodded and headed for the dining room, where he scooped up Nikki, cradling her in a tender hug. He told her that Mommy was going to have a new baby soon—she'd have a new playmate, one very much like her doll. Holding Nikki close to reassure her, he glanced at Jimmy, who was quietly rolling around the playpen, exploring its corners on his hands and knees.

He heard another anguished cry. Fully appreciating how quickly the contractions were coming now, he kissed the top of Nikki's head, took a deep breath and made his way back to the living room.

The two women had also made it back. Suzie headed straight for the couch while Lydia turned to Simon. "Keep the playpen just around the corner there, close but out of sight, and check on them, Simon."

He nodded, his orders clear.

"Lydia! You do this delivery!" Suzie called out.

Lydia quickly washed up and hurried back to the couch. She checked her friend, feeling the baby's head, the fine hair, and the thinning cervix.

"It's soon now," Lydia assured her. "I could feel the weight of the baby and knew I needed to push, but yours is smaller... you might not have the same urge."

Suzie grimaced. "Doesn't feel small at all! I'll let you know... Oh god, there's another one already starting! Marcus! What have you done to me? How could you?"

"Marcus, sit behind her and support her... up against you," Lydia instructed. "It's much easier for her than lying flat."

Marcus took his place on the couch, pulling Suzie back against his chest... her legs over his knees. Lydia steadied herself, ready to receive the baby.

"She's crowning," Lydia told Simon and Marcus, glancing up at them. "It's almost here, Suzie," she reassured, her voice steady. "Almost done..."

Suzie gasped as a series of painful contractions overtook her. "If this is the 'time to push' moment, then here it comes, Lydia!"

Suzie groaned loudly, the pain cresting, and to everyone's astonishment, the tiny infant slipped effortlessly into Lydia's waiting hands.

Moving swiftly, Lydia wiped clear the baby's mouth and nose with a towel, watching intently for that first breath. Simon clamped the cord and severed it as Lydia wrapped the tiny newborn, cradling the delicate bundle.

"Simon?" Marcus asked with a quiet urgency.

They all waited, holding their breath.

"Lydia?" Simon pressed for a response.

She was watching the infant. Just as in France, she put her mouth over the infant's face and puffed repeatedly... small, short little puffs of air. She stopped to watch for chest movement, then repeated the process.

Suzie, still wrapped in her husband's arms, stared, wide-eyed.

"What's she doing?" she cried out to Marcus as Lydia worked. "What's happening, Marcus?"

"Just wait," Marcus replied calmly, masking his own fear, praying frantically... willing the baby to breathe. *Please, God, forgive a sinful man and don't take this baby as my punishment. I swear I will raise it to know you... and do my very best to care for it...*

Softly, calmly, Simon prayed aloud so they all could hear, "Almighty God, please bring the breath of life into this child."

Lydia paused. The tiny infant still limp in her arms.

She began again... steady puffs of air, one after another, after another... willing this tiny baby to live with everything in her being.

Finally, she stopped and they watched yet again.

Waiting.

A thin cry pierced the silence as the lungs finally expanded, drawing their first breath.

Suzie's tears spilled over. "What is it, Lydia? What did I have?"

Lydia worked quickly to clean and warm the tiny baby. "You have another beautiful daughter," she announced and carried the infant to the couch.

"Suzie, put the baby right between your breasts, under this blanket. Let your body warm her. She doesn't have an ounce of fat on her, she's so tiny. She'll get cold fast. Here, put this fleece tight over the both of you, inside your robe. There you go... right where she can hear your heartbeat... that's it..."

Marcus watched his new, spindly little daughter snuggle in between Suzie's ample breasts. They gently pressed the fleece against her, then pulled the robe around both mother and infant until only the baby's little face was showing.

"Marcus, give me a sock," Lydia held out her hand while also reaching for a pair of scissors. Without question, he pulled a sock right off his foot. Lydia cut closer to the toe end of the sock and gently slid the makeshift cap over the baby's head.

Lydia's eyes were filled with tears as she looked up at Marcus, meeting his gaze.

"Thank you, Lydia," he whispered. "How did you learn to do that?"

"Another time," she said softly, positioning herself for the delivery of the placenta. "What will you name her?"

"Hannah," he said, focusing again on his wife. "For Susannah, at least for the first name. What do you think, Suzie? Hannah Lynn, maybe?"

Suzie looked up at Marcus, just as he wiped a tear from his face. "I like Hannah very much," she said. "And I'm sorry I blamed you for everything. I didn't mean it—Ow! I thought these cramps were done."

Lydia was already focused on her next task. "Just getting the placenta out, Suzie. This is the easy part. Over soon."

Marcus cradled his wife in his arms and kissed the top of her head. He gazed down at the tiny face peeking out from her robe, overwhelmed with wonder.

Simon slipped out of the room quietly, soon returning with both Nikki and Jimmy.

"Meet your new little sister, Nikki," he encouraged the toddler, holding her up so she could see the baby nestled against her mother.

Nikki studied the newborn, eyes wide with curiosity. The baby was even smaller than the doll she clutched tightly in her hand.

Marcus reached out, tenderly touching Nikki's face. "This is baby Hannah, Nikki."

"Anna," Nikki repeated.

"Close enough," Marc laughed. "Thank you, God!"

Simon nodded. "Yes, indeed, we do thank you, Almighty God, for Suzie and this new little daughter—"

Lydia arched an eyebrow. "Simon, would you take Nikki and Jimmy to the dining room before this afterbirth comes?"

He nodded, taking the two little ones back to their playpen.

As Lydia received the placenta, Simon returned, laying out some newspaper for her. She placed it onto the paper and handed it to him, watching as he inspected it carefully.

"It sure looks intact to me," he said. "Not that I'm the expert by any means. But it doesn't look at all like yours did, Lydia."

Lydia laughed softly. "I'll take your word for it, my love... I don't remember, but I do remember you being there for me." She took the afterbirth, wrapping it in the newspaper for Simon to take outside.

The snow was still falling. The city seemed to be at a complete standstill. Simon took a moment there, listening to the quiet and patting Abril's head.

He praised the Lord for the safe delivery of the infant and whispered thanks again for his beloved Lydia. He prayed that the baby would keep breathing and would be strong enough to nurse. He prayed for Marcus, that he would be a good father and husband, that he would lead his family with love. And then, he prayed for Suzie's health and that her heart would be fully committed to his friend.

Only then did he step back into the house, ready to celebrate with the rest of them.

With so much to tend to and Suzie needing her rest, Lydia and Simon gladly planned to stay the night. Lydia also knew that the baby would require special care, having arrived so early. She would need frequent, small feedings to survive, and Suzie's milk wouldn't come in for at least a day or two. So, following in the honored tradition of wet nurses, Lydia would offer her own ample supply. In the kitchen, Simon nodded his approval as she proposed her plan.

"That sounds good to me, if you think you can do it," he told her, then turned to grab a towel from the hook. "I'm going to get Abril, though... bring her inside... and cook us something edible."

Relieved, Lydia thanked him. "I hadn't even gotten that far yet. Thank you for thinking ahead, my love."

In the living room, Lydia explained her plan to Marcus and Suzie.

"We'll stay here tonight, to help however we can. I can feed Hannah hourly, just until Suzie's milk comes in. Then we'll take turns every hour, making sure she eats... it's the best way I can think of to help her pull through. We have to make sure she gets enough fluids and nourishment."

Marcus stared at her. "Do you realize what you're proposing? And feeding Jimmy, too? You'll be exhausted, Lydia."

"I don't see another way, Marc. Hannah won't survive without it... and she's far too tiny and weak to get milk from a rubber nipple... and formula wouldn't be rich enough to keep her alive... I think this is the only option." Lydia was adamant.

With a nod from Suzie, as she began to doze off, Marcus ever so gently lifted the tiny infant. He passed her to Lydia, who immediately tucked the baby between her own breasts, securing her snugly within the fleece to keep her warm.

Picking Suzie up in his arms, Marcus carried her up the stairs to the comfort of their bed.

Lydia knew that not everyone would sleep tonight; they would have to take turns to make sure the baby kept breathing. And they'd probably sleep in shifts for many nights to come.

When Simon returned from the kitchen, having toweled the melting snow from Abril's fur, he paused at the sight before him. A tiny face peeked out from Lydia's chest, nestled against her warmth. "What, so they liked the plan?"

"Suzie is sleeping." Lydia explained, nodding. "Hannah is so tiny, Simon, she could stop breathing on the turn of a dime, or if she's squeezed too hard... or someone rolls over onto her. And she won't stay warm enough in the bassinet. I'm going to sit up with her, keep her warm, and try to nurse. Would you run up and find a long-sleeved shirt of Marc's from his closet... and another sock?"

Simon ran up the stairs and returned with a clean sock and a green and black checked, flannel shirt. "I figured you'd want something warm?"

She kissed him. "You think of everything." She gestured to the flannel. "Tie the arms at the ends... we need to make a little pouch to hold her. She's got no body fat at all. This will have to be her womb for a while."

He fashioned a kind of sling to secure the baby against her chest, freeing up her hands.

Her breasts were filling with milk for Jimmy, but she held off nursing him. "The baby clothes Suzie saved from Nikki won't fit Hannah for at least a month! Let's cut another cap from the sock, and then slide that longer part of the sock up over her little body... like a cocoon. I'll see if Hannah is strong enough to nurse. I hope if my milk is really ready to flow, she might not have to work too hard to get some."

"Dear Lord, she's tiny." Simon breathed steadily as he slipped the sock gently over her torso. "Jimmy looks like a two-year-old next to this one. Beloved, you do know this little baby might not make it at this birth weight... despite everything you're trying to do. You might need to prepare yourself for that."

Lydia teared up. "I know," she whispered. "But we have to try. We don't have a feeding tube or incubator for her."

He kissed her forehead. "I support whatever you think makes sense."

"I'll wait to feed Jimmy until after I try to get the baby to take a little. She won't need much, and he'll keep my milk flowing with his appetite," Lydia told him. "How's Marcus doing up there?"

"He's keeping an eye on Suzie's bleeding and comforting her... it really shook them up when the baby was limp for so long," he told her. "Abril is right by the playpen. When I left them, Nikki was showing her the babydoll and telling her that there's another, new doll in the house. I'll take care of Nikki and Jimmy and get that dinner started."

Lydia settled herself into an easy chair in the living room. She could hear Simon as he talked to Nikki and Jimmy in the other room. As her breasts tightened and she heard Jimmy begin to fuss a little from the playpen, her milk began to drip in response to him. Carefully, Lydia adjusted the infant inside of her blouse and positioned her little face to her nipple.

"Come on, dear little Hannah," Lydia whispered. "Try to take it..."

The baby was so weak, but instinctively opened her mouth accepting a drop of the life-giving fluid. "Okay, just a few little sucks now. Come on... you can do it, my dear one..."

Lydia silently rejoiced when the frail infant took her nipple and began to nurse. Thankfully, the baby was not having to work too hard for the nutrition. "Oh, God! Thank you. Thank you, Lord. Help her nurse and give Suzie and me what we need for her to thrive."

Lydia drew a deep breath, feeling immeasurable gratitude, when she noticed that Marcus had come back down the stairs.

Without hesitation, he dropped to his knees beside her. He saw the baby cradled against her, saw the quiet miracle unfolding before him. His cheeks were wet with tears, and he was not ashamed. He cupped his hand around the baby's head, covered in its little sock hat. Her entire head easily fit within just the area of his palm.

"Is she truly taking your milk, Lydia? Is she swallowing it?" he whispered anxiously.

"She is nursing," Lydia reassured him, smiling with pure joy. "This is such a good sign, Marcus. She's a fighter."

"Oh my God, I hope so. She's so tiny!" Marcus exhaled, shaking his head. "You saved her, Lydia, getting her to breathe on her own like that. Is that something midwives are doing now?"

"No. Well, maybe. I don't know. But outside of Nancy, in France, a woman delivered prematurely. Her baby wasn't breathing either, so I tried it... out of desperation... and it worked.

"It could be a couple of days before Suzie's milk comes in, but Jimmy is a good eater... he'll keep me well supplied for both of them. And Hannah is pink, Marc. It's such a good sign that she pinked-up, isn't it? So, now she's just got to eat, stay warm, and grow. I'll feed her as often as she'll take it, every hour if she'll do it."

They watched as the newborn tired quickly but she had completed her first effort at nourishment. Lydia nestled Hannah as close to her heart as possible, both for warmth and so the baby could hear her heartbeat. Once the little one was secure, Lydia's focus turned to Jimmy, whose cries had grown lusty with impatience.

As Lydia stood, Marcus stopped her, taking both of her hands in his own, still on his knees. He looked up at the woman, then dropped his forehead down onto her hands.

"I... don't even know how to say what I want to..." his voice faltered.

Lydia lifted his chin. "Marcus," she said softly. "It's okay. It's what friends do," she added gently.

Simon had stepped out of the kitchen, overhearing the conversation. His look spoke volumes to her. He rested his hand on Marc's shoulder, comforting him.

"We get through things together, Marc," Simon promised him. "Always have. Always will."

Lydia's eyes brimmed with tears as she took her seat again, looking at the two men. "This is going to be touch and go for a while. I want Suzie to sleep as much as she can, until her milk starts to come in. But I need someone, one of you, to help me stay upright in this chair so I don't crush Hannah... or miss a feeding. You have to wake me every hour, if I fall asleep. Help me tonight, please."

The two men nodded. They would take turns staying up with her.

Standing, Marcus moved aside as Simon retrieved Jimmy from the playpen, bringing him to Lydia in her chair. Simon helped to position Jimmy safely below the tiny baby who was up closer to her sternum.

Once Jimmy began nursing, Simon turned to Marc, "Congratulations, Dad. How about a toast?"

Marcus laughed for the first time, drying his eyes. "Yeh, I'd like that!"

"Already poured," Simon announced. "C'mon." The two men headed for the kitchen.

Lydia relaxed in her chair, Jimmy's feeding relieving the pressure from the build up of milk, while tiny Hannah remained safely nestled against her chest.

We can do this, she thought. *There's no other choice. We can do this. Lord, please... please let Hannah live.*

Lydia and Simon stayed with Suzie and Marcus for days. When Suzie's milk came in, the two women took turns staying awake in four-hour shifts, feeding Hannah hourly... always monitoring her breathing. The men took turns helping them stay upright through the nights, the baby cradled inside the shirt sling, keeping her safe and warm.

As it became more certain that Hannah would keep breathing and was gaining strength, they changed to feedings every two hours at night. Even after the city roads had cleared the women stayed home, to care for the children. Simon returned to his daily schedule at the hospital, while Marcus took on an amended routine, leaving early each day to help as much as he could at home.

Simon also hired Mrs. Gilbert, arranging for her to take on housekeeping in addition to caring for Jimmy, as well as Nikki, who began affectionately referring to the woman as "Gibby."

It turned out that Gibby was also an excellent cook. When Lydia returned for half-days, making house calls, she would come home to hot meals and well-tended toddlers, so she could still take shifts feeding Hannah.

Mrs. Gilbert made a fuss over all three children, exclaiming that Hannah was her "precious little darling," Nikki was "the smartest thing I've ever seen," and Jimmy of course, "the baby with the most easy-going disposition in the world."

Even Abril approved of the woman.

Most importantly, with all of this support, Hannah kept right on breathing… and nursing… and growing.

By ensuring Suzie had the time to rest and heal in the comfort of their home—rather than in a hospital maternity ward—Marcus was pleased to see her recover quickly from the birth. Selfishly, he was grateful the snow had created the opportunity for him to share in the whole experience, although he didn't say that to Suzie.

She seemed happy. He often saw her writing in her journal, and though curiosity tugged at him, he knew better than to pry. So, he had been waiting, trusting that when she was ready, she would share her thoughts with him. He hoped the writing was helping her process the early birth of their second daughter.

Eventually, the silence became too much, and Marcus decided to say something. One afternoon, with Lydia downstairs tending to Hannah after a few nearby home visits, he finally had some rare time alone with Suzie. Marcus ran up the stairs and sat on the edge of their bed just as Suzie slowly closed her journal.

"Care to share?" he asked gently.

She smiled, tucking the red journal beneath her pillow. "Not just yet," she said simply, settling back against the pillow.

"How are you feeling, Suz?"

"How am I feeling? Haven't thought about that much, with a five-pound baby who needs to eat every hour?" she teased.

Marcus smiled, drawing her long blonde hair away from her face. "My God, you're a lovely woman, Susannah."

"Haven't washed my hair since the baby. One of these days, I'll have to figure that out," she murmured, pulling a few strands forward, assessing how many more days she could wait.

"How about we get in the tub together and I wash it for you? Not in a full bathtub or anything... it's too soon for that, but I could pour the water over you?" he offered. "I'll bring in the watering can from the garden, and make you a hot shower! Fill the bathroom with roses so it smells like a garden."

Suzie patted his hand. "I appreciate your imagination, Marcus, but honestly, leaning over the kitchen sink every few days might be easier."

"That works too," he smiled, touching her cheek tenderly. He leaned into her, kissing her softly, as she draped her arm around his neck. He continued, "I want you to feel pampered.... I hope she looks just like you, Suzie... a blonde, blue-eyed beauty... Who knows? Maybe she'll become a nurse-journalist just like you, too!"

"You see, Marcus," Suzie said suddenly. "That's what's so great about my writing club. When we write, we can be anyone or anything we want to be. There are no limitations, none at all! No flu, no loss of body tone... no unfulfilled dreams. Anything is possible on the written page. Every dream can take flight, even ones that may never happen in real life."

Marcus brought her hand to his lips, kissing her fingers. "What dreams do you have that need to be filled, Suz? Are there dreams you think will never happen for you, in real life? Let's make them happen for you. I love you… I want you to be happy."

Marcus's gaze was so earnest that Suzie felt her cheeks flush.

"I don't think it's possible… for my dreams to happen," Suzie said, but her voice wasn't bitter or unkind. "It's written somewhere that you can't have your cake and eat it, too. So… maybe… maybe you bake a second cake… one to eat and one to look at…"

Taking in his puzzled expression, she smiled, adding, "See, Marc! I'm basically working on a poem, right now, while we talk! Isn't that amazing how that works? Our imagination is always churning up crazy new ideas that float around, waiting to be put into some kind of rhyme and rhythm. That's why writing is so much fun. It's like traveling the whole world on a hot air balloon, thoughts free and flying high."

He lovingly traced the length of her neck, his hand lingering at her shoulder. "Maybe someday we'll take a trip around the world and see it all, Suzie. Would you like that?"

She exhaled softly. "I think I'd like a nap right now," she said softly. "It'll be my turn with Hannah before I know it. Just pull the shade a little, would you, Marcus? It's too bright for me to sleep."

He crossed to the window and drew the shade, dimming the room. Turning back, he saw Suzie had already rolled onto her side, the covers tucked up over her as her eyes fluttered closed.

"Much better," she sighed. "Thanks."

"Would you like me to stay a little, cuddle?" Marcus said softly, kissing the top of her head. "I love you, Suzie."

"Nap time. Love you, too," she whispered and drifted off into sleep.

Marcus wandered back down the stairs, pausing to kiss Nikki's head, then Hannah's tiny sock cap as she slept against Lydia in the makeshift shirt sling.

Lydia's eyes were closing as well.

With Jimmy and Nikki quietly entertaining each other in the playpen, Marcus picked up the newspaper and got comfortable on the sofa, his gaze drifting now and then to the baby's steady breathing.

He would need to wake Lydia in an hour for the next feeding.

It had taken nearly a week, but at last, the streets were clear, allowing people to venture out... to markets, to work... to something resembling normalcy. For the first time in ages, influenza numbers fell, and with the early February thaw, the city dared to hope that the worst might be behind them.

After a full day visiting patients, Lydia stepped into the kitchen at the house on Beech Street, peeling off her damp boots. Suzie had assured them all that she could manage Hannah's daytime feedings, as long as she could get some rest at night with their help. Back from work and ready to see what was needed, Lydia greeted Mrs. Gilbert before scooping up Jimmy, for a hug and to prepare for his feeding. In the living room, Nikki was quietly playing on the floor with Abril, surrounded by her books and dolls.

"Suzie and Hannah up resting?" Lydia asked.

Mrs. Gilbert glanced toward the stairs. "Yes," she said, looking more than a little troubled.

Lydia started up the stairs, Jimmy in her arms. Not sure why, she stopped midway to glance back downstairs. There was another pair of boots at the front door. Curious, she continued up the stairs and turned right, to the master bedroom. The door was ajar, and a man's voice could be heard inside.

She tapped the door and pushed it open. Suzie sat resting against the pillows in her gown and robe. Beside her, stretched out comfortably on the bed, was a man Lydia had never seen before, reading aloud to her.

Without hesitation, Lydia approached, Jimmy balanced on her hip. "Oh, you must be James!" Lydia declared smoothly.

"James, this is Lydia, the friend who helped deliver Hannah," Suzie said carefully. "I've told her all about our writing club."

The nice-looking, bespectacled man looked up, closing the book from which he had been reading. "Pleased to meet you, Lydia," he said courteously with a slow smile. "I've heard a bit about you."

Lydia held Jimmy with both arms, preempting the man's attempt to reach out and shake her hand. She had no intention of shaking his hand. He had no business stretched out on this bed. Her gaze lingered on them, unwavering.

"Did Hannah nurse well today, Suzie? Did Marcus call at lunch?" Lydia pressed her friend, focusing her on the baby and on her husband. "Do you want me to take her awhile so you can rest before Marcus and Simon get home? Mrs. Gilbert is about to start supper."

She did not offer for the man to join them for dinner.

"About time for me to take off anyway," James looked at Suzie, as he got up from the bed. "I'm glad you enjoyed the readings."

"I certainly did," Suzie told him, smiling up at him. "It was very kind of you to stop in while I'm still confined. I appreciate that, James."

"Any time," he replied warmly. He looked down at Suzie, awkwardly hesitating. Lydia didn't leave the bedside. "Well, I guess I'm off then," he added, heading for the bedroom door in his stockinged feet.

"I'll just put Jimmy in the playpen and then come take Hannah for a bit," Lydia told Suzie as she followed the man down the stairs.

But Lydia handed Jimmy to Mrs. Gilbert and followed him to the door, watching as he retrieved the boots she had noted earlier in the foyer.

"Don't you realize how wrong this is coming here like this?" she asked, her voice quiet, measured.

He pulled on the second boot and reached for his coat. "Why would I?" he asked evenly, pulling it over his shoulders.

"It would be more appropriate to visit when Marcus is home," Lydia suggested. "And when Suzie has had a chance to dress appropriately."

"She looked just fine to me. She's a lovely woman," he continued. "Look, Lydia, I don't play games with people. I like her, and she likes me. Whatever other arrangement she has doesn't concern me."

"But you are playing games," she challenged him. "The other arrangement happens to be a husband and a family who are like blood to me, and I will defend them."

"It's Suzie's choice, Lydia, not yours. She likes seeing me," James said, opening the front door. "Talk to her, not to me."

"I will," Lydia assured him, watching as he sauntered down the walk, his ease in sharp contrast to the tightness in her chest.

She shut the door and pressed her forehead against the cold wood, exhaling slowly.

The walk back up to Suzie's bedroom felt steeper, farther than usual. Lydia tapped on the door and entered. She kept her voice even. "Now, let me take little Hannah so you can rest up a bit before the guys come home for supper."

Suzie lifted the infant from inside of her robe and passed her to Lydia.

"Don't say anything, please, Lydia," Suzie pleaded. "Not to Marcus. I'll... I'll figure this out."

"If I can help, let me know. You're both my friends, and I care what happens to you." She exhaled quietly. "I just don't like keeping secrets."

"I know," Suzie said, now looking sad. "I know I'm asking too much."

Lydia cradled the baby. "I do believe she's gained a little weight, Suzie. And look! She's going to have lots of blonde hair, just like you... she's going to be a beautiful little girl. Close your eyes for a few minutes before everyone gets home."

Lydia took the infant downstairs, nursing her briefly. She was glad to see that Hannah was steadily gaining strength with each nursing.

Mrs. Gilbert regarded Lydia for a long moment, watching her cradle the infant, before speaking.

"Mrs. Finney, I didn't know if I should let that man in when he came calling like that," the housekeeper admitted, wrestling with the guilt she felt, having opened the door to him.

"It is an awkward situation for me, too," Lydia agreed. "I'll talk to Doctor Finney about it, and we'll try to figure it out. Go on home, Mrs. Gilbert. Thank you for making supper for us... and bundle up. Still chilly out there."

Lydia sat quietly, cradling Hannah against her chest, the infant's tiny flannel bunting tucked snugly inside her sweater. She had Jimmy cradled in the crook of her elbow, beneath the tiny infant. With practiced ease, she helped him latch on for his supper. Jimmy's brown hair had grown longer now, his eyes still so strikingly blue. She loved how he gripped her finger with his chubby hand. From the playpen, Nikki glanced up from time to time, her cloth book clutched in her small hands.

"You are the most wonderful children in the whole world," she told them all. "I love you so much."

That evening, Lydia was sitting in Marc and Suzie's living room, helping with Hannah and watching Jimmy sleep in the playpen beside her. Simon had just come in after letting Abril run for a bit outside and took his spot on the sofa, making room for Lydia to lean back against him, between his legs.

"So, what's it feel like to have two to take care of?" Simon asked, one arm resting on the back of the sofa and the other around Lydia.

Lydia rested her head back against his shoulder, gently patting Hannah's tiny backside. "This is a bit of an exceptional situation. With our luck, our next baby will come a month late, not early... and weighing over eight pounds. It won't be the same at all. But I have been wondering, after all of this, if that little baby outside of Nancy ever made it through its first year. Simon, do you think it did? It didn't have two nursing mothers who could take turns, to keep it going."

"If it didn't, it wasn't for lack of trying!" he exclaimed softly. "That grandmother was enthusiastic, more than committed to helping her daughter do everything she could to keep the baby alive."

Simon turned the ring on Lydia's right finger. "This is getting thin, you know. I want you to have another. We can put this one on a chain if you like."

"I suppose it's time. Would I get a ring for this same finger, though? I'm so used to having it there... on my right hand. What do you think? Should I switch to the left like everyone else?"

He laughed. "Lydia, you've never been like everyone else. Wear it on your big toe if you want. I don't care—Just as long as it's not in your nose, like those enormous rings some women wear in other countries."

"Okay," she conceded. "No nose rings. Seriously though, Simon, if I get a new ring, you will need one too, because our rings match. Wouldn't we still want them to match?"

"It's hard to go wrong with plain gold bands, yellow or white, I don't care," he paused. "What about simple gold bands?"

"Maybe engraved inside, though?" she proposed, tracing the veins on the back of his hand with her fingertips.

"We could do that. We can go back over to Feldman's and see what he has. I like this idea," Simon said approvingly. "Hm, what would I want to have engraved in your ring... Not enough space for much. I need to think about this. It would need to be meaningful."

"Short and meaningful. That is hard," she agreed.

Marcus came running lightly down the steps and scooped Nikki up into his arms.

"How's my little angel?" he asked her, hugging her close.

"Dada an Ab do Anna," Nikki told him, quite seriously.

Marcus looked into her thoughtful young eyes. "If you say so! Who loves Nikki?"

"Dada wuv ki-ki," she said, grinning, her small hands reaching up to his cheeks.

Marcus nuzzled her face as she giggled, grabbing for his chin. "That's right, Nikki. Daddy loves Nikki, and Daddy loves Hannah."

"Dada wuv Ab?" she said, looking at the dog who was lying peacefully on the floor still surrounded by Nikki's books and toys.

He laughed. "Yes, Daddy loves Abril, too!"

The child squirmed, eager to be set down. Once balanced on her feet, she ran straight to Abril, fondly throwing her arms around the dog's neck, "Ki-ki wuv Ab."

Lydia watched as the child hugged Abril, the ever-patient dog kindly accepting the embrace. "Anyone want supper? Mrs. Gilbert made some delicious spaghetti. Is Suzie awake enough to eat, Marcus?"

He shook his head, "She seemed to be asleep when I went up. I'm glad. Been long shifts for you girls."

"Not that much different than our shifts in the medical camp," Lydia reminded him. "Getting up every morning at four o'clock to take a shift in the recovery, remember? Except now it's for one tiny little patient, not hundreds, so this is maybe a little better! And, of course, we weren't breastfeeding over there."

"Good thing!" Simon blurted out. "Every wounded man in the war would've been demanding a transfer to our clearing station."

"And the surgeons would have been too distracted to help a single one of them!" Marcus chuckled.

They moved the children into the kitchen and served up the spaghetti and meatballs made by Mrs. Gilbert. Marcus poured a glass of wine for Simon and himself and lifted his glass in a toast.

"I really appreciate everything you two have done for Suzie and me," Marcus shook his head, a little emotional. "Hannah wouldn't even be here if it weren't for the two of you."

Simon raised a hand. "No thanks needed. We're glad to be here for you both... you know that. You're a brother to me, Marcus. I'm just glad you agreed to come back with us... and be our family."

"Simon, you made concessions, too... not dragging me to the hinterlands of West Virginia!" Marcus exclaimed.

Simon laughed. "Yeah, we sure gave up on the Daniel Boone thing. It wouldn't have been so bad. But I think you like teaching the medical students and residents, here. You're great with them in the operating theater, Marc. They're learning a lot."

"Surprised even me! I do enjoy it. Never thought I was the teacher type. It's easier than I thought it would be. Funny how you can spot it... some students will leave that rotation and never enter another operating theater in their life... just isn't for them. But then there are the ones, focused, hands steady, hungry to make a difference. You see it plain as day. They'll be in it for life, no two ways about it."

Lydia sipped her tea, her gaze distant. "I remember the days of nonstop surgery! That part of the war, I miss... working with you men."

Marcus smiled. "You counted the seconds between the sound of a shell and when the tremor would reach our camp. I'm surprised you remember any of that fondly!"

"The war had its moments..." she said quietly.

"Well, I was never happier than when you were able to spend the entire day with me in the surgery," Simon mused. "How did we do it? Ten, twelve hours... non-stop?"

"Stockton never quite figured us out, Simon," Marcus added.

"Yes, he did," Simon countered. "He was just smart enough to let us do what we're good at and stay out of the way."

"Cheers to that!" Marcus raised his glass. "I remember just about passing out one day... right over a patient's open abdomen—"

"I remember that! You were exhausted and starving. Doctor Fortraine had to take over. I didn't even know who he was because he'd just arrived at camp..."

A silence settled in between them, memories of their lives before, flooding back. Little Hannah squeaked, and Lydia felt her body respond instinctively. She shifted Hannah toward her breast, guiding her to latch... grateful when she did.

Marcus watched her tend to his daughter.

"I also remember falling all over you in a drunken stupor... when Suzie left the camp... and me. I'm still so sorry about that, Lydia," Marcus admitted regretfully. "After all you've done for me..."

"You were a mess!" Lydia remembered candidly. "But I knew her leaving would hit you hard. You know, I asked Doctor Stockton to take it easy on you when he gave you that talking-to, after you sobered up."

"I wouldn't say he took it easy on me!" Marcus laughed dryly. "He made sure I'd never forget it—and rightfully so."

He swirled the liquid in his glass, recalling how the senior surgeon had poured a veritable pot of coffee down his throat, while delivering an admonition to never, even remotely ever, let something like that happen again.

Marcus added quietly, "She might leave me again."

Silence fell over the table.

It was Simon who finally broke it. "If that happens, if there is no way to avoid it, Lydia and I will stand with you, Marc... you know that."

Marcus swirled the wine in his glass for a moment longer before bringing it to his lips. "I do know that. Thank you. I wonder... if she leaves... if she would take the girls..."

"What has she actually said at this point?" Lydia pressed gently.

"That we've grown apart... that if she does stay with me, it would have to be an... 'open'... relationship. That's what she calls it. Open."

"What the heck is that?" Simon asked, in disbelief.

"It's when you have your cake and eat it, too," Marcus replied, dryly. "We'd raise the children together, share the house, and come and go as we please—"

"With other people," Simon finished.

Marcus drained his glass. "With other people."

Marcus set his empty glass on the table. "Funny thing is, just a couple years ago, that would have been fine by me. Most of my life, I was happy with... whoever was available. But in the camp, when I was with Suzie—I was only with Suzie. And here, of course, I've only been with her since we were married. So now, it seems the shoe is on the other foot. She's the one who wants to be with whoever's available. Currently, a James... I believe."

Lydia's heart was breaking, she reached across the table to take Marc's hand. "Maybe she's just struggling with all of the changes from the pregnancy... the baby coming early... feeling the demands of having two children. This might just be a temporary thing she's going through."

Simon shook his head. "It's even deeper than that, Lydia. Suzie's struggling with her beliefs, trying to figure out where she fits, in the grand scheme of things. She doesn't have a sense of God's purpose for her yet. And she doesn't approve of Marc finding his. She mentioned that she feels their beliefs are driving a wedge between them."

They considered the ramifications of that for a moment.

Marcus nodded, continuing. "And I don't know that the children and I can give her enough of a sense of purpose to keep her with me. I do know that I don't want another man raising Nikki and Hannah, which will happen if she leaves with this James guy and takes the girls with her. So, if we don't have a future together, I have to at least consider this open relationship idea."

Lydia tucked Hannah, now fast asleep, back into her bunting. She couldn't help but envy the little one... she was cared for, content and would sleep well until her next feeding... a luxury none of the adults in the house would enjoy tonight.

After everyone else had had a chance to get ready for bed, Lydia slipped into the master bedroom, passing Hannah to Suzie for the next shift. It was only after the baby was safely in her mother's arms that Lydia realized just how exhausted she really was. She made her way down the hall to the bathroom, and washed up, barely recognizing the woman staring back at her through the mirror. In the hallway, just outside the room they were using, Lydia took a moment to pat Abril. "You're such a good dog," she whispered.

Closing the door behind her, Lydia noticed that Simon was leaning back against the pillows, waiting up for her. Lydia checked on Jimmy, all warm and cozy in his little crib. He looked so peaceful, his little mouth half open. Reaching for the wall lamp, she dimmed the light. Outside, the streetlights cast a pale white glimmer over the lingering snow. She slipped out of her robe, knowing Simon would want to snuggle, and lifted the covers to join him.

He immediately pulled her to him. "It's been days…" he murmured. "You're tired, I know," he said, kissing the top of her head.

She nodded.

"I feel lousy over this whole situation," Simon said, caressing her hair as she rested against his chest.

Tears welled in her eyes, unseen by him. She nodded again. "Me, too," she whispered.

Simon sighed deeply. Between nursing the babies and working part-time, she was giving so much of herself away. He was just grateful for every warm and loving look she had cast his direction throughout the evening. He struggled with himself… not wanting to be selfish as he breathed in the scent of her, resigning himself to counting sheep… or the number of times a dog barked nearby.

Just then, a jolt of pleasure electrified his entire body. Lydia had run a finger delicately along his unfulfilled wish.

She whispered, "Once before I remember telling you that I loved you, but if you wanted me, you'd have to do all the work—"

"I'll do all the work!" Simon replied eagerly, quickly rolling her onto her back. He kissed her lips, her neck… her breasts… and continued moving down her body without stopping, except to say, "You just lay back, my beloved, and enjoy… I'll do absolutely everything…"

Lydia smiled, she was already half asleep, but awake enough at least to enjoy this, besides, he was very good at doing all of the work.

At four o'clock, Suzie tapped on the bedroom door, rousing Lydia to take her shift with Hannah. Quietly, Lydia slipped out of the bed, pulled on her robe, and gathered the newborn into her arms. Wishing Suzie a good four hours of sleep, Lydia made her way downstairs. The easy chair in the living room seemed to be waiting for her. She put her feet up on a hassock, pulled a blanket up over them, and snuggled the infant against her sternum. Almost immediately, Hannah made a little squeak and Lydia guided her tiny head to her breast.

"Your built-in milk machines," she whispered to the tiny child. "Between your mother and me and by the grace of God, you will grow strong and healthy, dear one..."

Hannah was nursing longer now, her strength improving with each feeding. Lydia felt an overwhelming sense of gratitude—relief in the baby's ability to draw more from her, comfort in knowing her body could keep up without shortchanging Jimmy.

She heard the familiar tap of Abril's nails descending the stairs. The dog plopped down beside her, faithful as ever. Lydia dropped one hand over the arm of the chair, resting it gently against the animal.

Coming downstairs to make breakfast, Marcus found Lydia just like that—Hannah snug against her chest, one hand resting on the dog. His eyes brimmed. Marcus leaned over and kissed her head so softly, but still she stirred.

"Oh!" she said, quickly, checking Hannah. "I drifted off. Oh my. Whew. She's breathing."

"It's okay," he told her. "You're entitled. I'll make something to eat."

"How about a nice bowl of hot oatmeal... with brown sugar?" she requested. "Is Simon up yet?"

"Already left for the hospital," Marc smiled. "I'll go in a little late today, Mrs. Gilbert has an appointment and can't come until ten-thirty.

I'll fix you whatever your heart desires," he added, heading for the kitchen.

Lydia felt a pang of regret—she hadn't said goodbye to Simon or wished him a good day.

Then, she noticed a small piece of paper tucked between her breasts, nestled against Hannah. Curious, she pulled it free and unfolded it, revealing Simon's fine handwriting.

There aren't the right words to explain... I'm just left with "I love you."

She smiled. She would make it up to him later.

Carefully, she rose from the chair, steadying Hannah in her arms. Lydia made her way toward the stairs, ready to hand the baby back to Suzie and dress for her house calls."

Abril's ears perked up and she woofed, before Lydia even heard the tap at the front door. She tightened her robe around herself and made her way to the foyer, opening the door just enough to see James, standing on the stoop.

"What on earth—" she started, staring at the man in disbelief, Hannah still tucked in the bunting inside her robe. "I cannot believe you'd just show up like this!"

James met her gaze, a hint of diffidence, but unwavering.

"She's expecting me," he said and without hesitation, started to push the door open. "What are you doing here?"

"This is wrong, James! You need to leave this house immediately!" Lydia exclaimed. She attempted to shut the door, but he stopped it with his foot.

"Again, it's not for you to say, Lydia," the man insisted, his hand still on the doorknob, pushing against her lesser strength.

"Maybe not. But it certainly is mine." Marcus' voice was controlled and powerful from over Lydia's shoulder. His expression was an even mix of anger and sorrow as he moved Lydia protectively behind him. He smoothly swung the door wide, squaring up to the other man. His fists clenched. "This is my home. And I do say who comes and goes. Do not come back again. Ever."

James looked at Marcus in surprise. It was obvious that he had not expected the husband to be home.

"It's best you go, James." Suzie had reached the lower landing of the stairs. Catching her gaze, James nodded to her.

"Call me," he said boldly as he turned and walked away from the house.

Marcus quietly shut the front door, resting his forehead against it.

Lydia slipped upstairs to dress and feed Jimmy, leaving the couple alone. Below, murmured voices filled the space, low, steady... absent of any shouting. No doubt, some tears, Lydia imagined, fastening her blouse then changing Jimmy's diaper. She prayed, as the hushed conversation continued, wondering when she should interrupt to pass the baby back to her mother. Her answer came when she heard the back door open, then shut, then the hum of the automobile pulling away. Marcus had gone to the hospital, after all, well before Mrs. Gilbert would arrive. Lydia took a deep breath, gathered both babies in her arms, and took a moment to check on Nikki. Still asleep in her bed.

Making her way downstairs, Lydia found Suzie at the kitchen table. Her eyes were red and she held a cup of hot tea in both hands. Without a word, she set down the tea and reached for Hannah, tucking her inside of her own robe. Lydia saw that a bowl of oatmeal with brown sugar, now grown cold, had indeed been set out for her. She sat and ate it anyway, Jimmy balanced on her knee.

"Tell me what to do, Lydia," Suzie begged.

Lydia pressed Jimmy to her side on her leg. "You know I can't," Lydia said. "And you already know what is right and what is wrong."

"I still love Marcus. He's the girls' father, after all," Suzie affirmed. "But, I think I love James, too."

"Is Marcus Hannah's father, Suzie?" Lydia asked point-blank.

Suzie flushed. "Of course, he is. I didn't know James then."

"Then you have a lot of good here that's worth saving, should you choose to," Lydia told her. "I will pray for you all day, Suzie... especially that you find your answer before Marcus comes home tonight. Will you be okay with Jimmy in the playpen until Mrs. Gilbert gets here shortly? I'll be back around two to feed him."

Suzie nodded, wiping her eyes. "I'll be okay."

Lydia nodded, rising to rinse her bowl in the sink before placing Jimmy in the playpen with his toys—including a little stuffed dog he had come to adore. She retrieved her coat and nursing bag from the closet.

"See you in a few hours," she called out to Suzie.

Abril padded at her heels as she stepped outside, the morning air cool against her face. She glanced down the street, scanning the alleyway. *Could James still be waiting somewhere? Watching for her to leave?* The neighborhood seemed quiet though. Lydia pressed forward, focusing her mind on the day ahead.

Chapter 19
Death Warmed Over

A month passed quickly. The arrangement, at the house across the alley, was in a truce of sorts. At least, as far as Lydia and Simon were aware, James had not returned.

Hannah had grown nicely and could now sleep safely in a bassinet beside the bed. She was even starting to fill out a little and had just become the most beautiful little blonde-haired infant. Everyone adored her.

Suzie was still home on maternity leave, and still had Mrs. Gilbert coming to help with the children. But lately, she had started going out on regular errands, always during lunch when Lydia returned to nurse Jimmy. The new routine was suspect, but at least Suzie was keeping things away from the house.

One of Lydia's newer assignments was visiting a home for soldiers disabled during the war. There were five men living there, all of whom had suffered from exposure to the gases in the trenches. They were plagued with chronic illnesses and other challenges, not the least of which were various amputations, making it difficult for them to get out to the doctors' offices or clinics in the city.

One of them, a corporal named Lewis, greeted her at the door.

"Come in, Nurse," he said, leaning on his crutches. "Sister Edwarda told us you'd be stopping by."

Lydia stepped inside, motioning to Abril.

"Is that your dog?" he asked.

She nodded, smiling, "Abril."

"Hey, sounds French. The dog can come in." Lewis said. Then called out to the other men," We don't mind, do we guys?"

The other men began to emerge from their respective rooms. Lydia noted that all of them were either using crutches or walking with sleeves pinned up halfway, to cover missing arms.

"Hello, gentlemen," Lydia greeted them warmly. "I'm Nurse Finney, one of the community nurses from Charity. A pleasure to meet you gentlemen."

Abril happily trotted into the house. Men like these were familiar to her. She immediately went to greet each one, smelling them to get to know them, before following them all into the dining room.

Lewis sat first, leaning his crutches up against the table, and turned to Abril. "Come here, girl," he said and rubbed behind her ears. "So you're the helper today? You sure are a friendly thing."

"She's a war dog," Lydia told the men. "She served right along with us in France... and came home with me."

"Where were you, Nurse Lydia?" one of the other men asked in surprise as he took a seat as well. He offered his remaining hand to her. "I'm Tony."

"Pleased to meet you, Tony," Lydia said, shaking his hand firmly. "France and Belgium... followed the Meuse."

"Wow," Tony exclaimed, sharing glances with the others who were still gathering around the table.

One by one, Lydia met with each man, assessing their medical needs: breathing problems, loss of feeling in their feet from prior trench foot and frostbite, missing toes or tips of fingers, bowel troubles from shrapnel wounds to the abdomen or chest cavities, some with pieces of shrapnel still working their way out through their skin. She listened, devising a health plan for each individual. It would take time, but they would make it through this winter and hopefully feel more whole by spring.

As Lydia left the house, Abril at her side, she felt like she had just left the recovery tent back in Ypres or Verdun. The courage and spirit of these men inspired her greatly.

At two o'clock, Lydia took the trolley back to the house, fed Jimmy, then set out for a few more house calls.

One visit was with a woman who had just had a breast removed. Lydia wrapped a clean bandage around a drain tube and checked the woman for fever. Her next patient was an elderly man with a bladder catheter who, to her trained eye, did not look well. She arranged a doctor's appointment for him the following day before heading back to the house across the alley.

When she opened the door, the house was quiet. Mrs. Gilbert was in the living room, holding Nikki and Jimmy while reading to them.

"Mrs. Lovell is resting in her room," Mrs. Gilbert called out, as Lydia slid out of her coat.

Upstairs, Lydia peeked into the master bedroom and found Suzie fast asleep, Hannah nestled inside her robe. Carefully, she picked up the infant and tucked her inside her own blouse before returning to the living room.

"How did it go today?" Lydia asked the housekeeper.

"Telephone calls all day long, back and forth," Mrs. Gilbert reported. "Noisy thing, the telephone. An intrusion, if you ask me."

"Any messages for Doctor Lovell?" Lydia asked, sitting beside her on the sofa to nurse the babies.

"No, but one from Mrs. Lovell's mother—Vanessa, I believe—who asked her to call once she wakes. If you wouldn't mind letting her know," the woman requested.

"Of course. And no visitors?" Lydia asked.

Mrs. Gilbert rolled her eyes. "No visitors, thank the Lord."

"Good," Lydia sighed, watching as Abril padded in after stopping for a drink and a bite to eat from the bowls set out for her in the kitchen.

Mrs. Gilbert stood. "I'll make some supper."

"It's okay, I stopped and picked up some fresh fish. When the men get home, it'll cook up in no time," Lydia assured her.

Mrs. Gilbert hesitated for a moment before asking, "Why do you and Doctor Finney stay here and help out like this?"

"We all served together, in the war, Mrs. Gilbert," Lydia said plainly. "In the same unit, through the thick of it. It makes for very strong ties. A different kind of kinship but just as powerful as blood relations... maybe even more so."

The woman nodded in understanding. "Ah, I imagine it would. Well, if you don't need me for supper, I'll just settle Nikki in the playpen and go on home."

"That will be fine," Lydia told her. "Thank you for your help, and have a good weekend with your family."

"You, too," the woman retrieved her coat from the closet. "I'll see you Monday, then."

Lydia waved farewell as Mrs. Gilbert closed the door behind her. She finished nursing Jimmy then placed him in the playpen with Nikki.

Needing to use the bathroom, Lydia ran up the stairs, stopping along the way to wake Suzie for supper. The woman's cheeks were flushed. Lydia was shocked by how hot Suzie was when she touched the back of her hand to Suzie's forehead.

"Suzie," she called to her friend.

"Hm... " Suzie mumbled.

"You feel feverish," Lydia told her. "Is your throat sore or anything, Suzie?"

"Just a headache," Suzie said, not opening her eyes. "I'm just tired."

"Rest, I'll keep the kids downstairs," Lydia assured her.

With Hannah in the makeshift sling, Lydia washed her hands carefully before start supper. *Marcus and Simon will be home soon, they'll take a look at Suzie*, she thought, glancing toward the upstairs bedroom. Nikki began fussing in the other room, pulling Lydia from her worried thoughts. She went to tend to the child, then decided to move the playpen into the kitchen so she could more easily watch them play. Abril also seemed to be doing her best to keep them entertained. With everything in place, she began setting the table.

Before long, an hour had passed. With fish in the oven and rice and brussel sprouts nearly ready on the stove, Lydia was relieved to see the men arriving home. As Simon greeted her tenderly, she turned immediately to Marcus. "Suzie has a fever. She's in bed."

Immediately, his clear blue eyes widened. "Okay," he said, tossing his coat over a kitchen chair before bounding up the stairs. Nikki's smile faltered when he didn't pick her up, heading straight for the stairs instead. She fussed, stretching her arms toward Simon.

"Imah up," she called out. Leaning over, Simon scooped the little girl up into his arms. She snuggled against him comfortably, reaching for his beard.

"Where's your babydoll, honey?" he asked the child. She pointed to Hannah, resting against Lydia.

Simon laughed softly. "No, not Hannah. Your other doll. Should we go find it? Is it in the living room? Shall we go see?" He took the child to the living room and found her toy, returning to the kitchen.

"When did it start?" Simon asked Lydia as he settled into a kitchen chair, Nikki perched on his lap.

"She seemed okay when I left this morning... I gave her the baby and everything was quiet. But when I got home this afternoon, she was hot."

Simon looked concerned. "We'll see what Marcus thinks when he comes down." He pulled Jimmy up onto his lap with Nikki. "Good thing I have two knees."

When Marcus returned to the kitchen, he washed his hands well. "I think it's the flu."

The three exchanged a tense glance, their eyes settling on Hannah. The tiny infant wouldn't survive catching influenza. Marc met Lydia's gaze.

"I agree," Marcus said, answering the unspoken question.

After a quiet dinner, Lydia and Simon packed up all three children and, with Abril, returned to their house.

Once back in the house on the corner, Nikki settled back into her old room, Jimmy into his crib in the other bedroom, and Simon placed Hannah's bassinet in their room, close to the bed for nighttime feedings. Mrs. Gilbert would come to their house on Monday, ensuring Suzie had the space and time to recover in her own home with uninterrupted rest... and Marcus seeing to plenty of fluids.

The following day, with the new routine of daily life established, Simon went to the kitchen door, pondering the serious turn of events over at the house across the alley. He knew what this would mean for Lydia, caring for both babies as well as Nikki, and he was worried. Abril remained outside, enjoying a little air in the backyard. As Simon stood watching the dog, he saw the stranger in the alley. A man, leaning against Simon's own fence, staring at Marc and Suzie's house. Without hesitation, Simon strode down the back walk to speak the man he could only assume was James.

"Can I help you with something?" Simon began.

"Uh, no," he answered. "I was just... um—"

"Just wondering if Suzie would look out and see you here?" Simon asked him calmly.

The man nodded, he looked miserable.

"You're James, I assume," Simon said.

"I am," the other admitted. "Look, I'm not trying to cause anyone any trouble."

Simon nodded. "Appreciate that. I don't want any. And I don't want my friends to have any trouble, either. It's best that you go home. This path you're on is leading you in the wrong direction. You'll find no happiness in it, only pain."

"I just wanted her to know I'm not feeling very well and won't be able to meet her Monday," the man said.

Simon nodded. "I think you should go take care of yourself if you aren't well."

"Will you tell her?"

"I'll tell her husband," Simon said. "But only if he asks me. I encourage you, James, to prayerfully think about what you're doing. Choose another path."

"You don't understand," James said miserably. The man shoved both of his hands into his pockets and walked away with his shoulders slumped and head bowed as Simon watched him go. Then, Simon returned to the house to help Lydia with the babies.

At nap time, Simon informed Lydia that he was going over to Marcus' house to check on them and that he would bring her an update.

Marcus was in the living room, sitting in an easy chair. The radio was softly playing classical music, but otherwise, the house was quiet. Simon took a seat.

"How're you holding up? Is her fever down?"

Marcus looked up wearily. He had dark circles under his eyes. "Not yet. She's pretty sick, Simon. But she did drink some. Maybe I should take her over to the hospital for intravenous fluids. It would keep her kidneys working while she fights this off."

Simon nodded. "I'll help you take her."

Together, they bundled Suzie up. Marcus carried her down the stairs and out to the Ford, while Simon held the doors open. They eased her onto the back seat, so she could lay across it. She complained a bit, confused and unsettled by all the movement.

Simon drove around the corner, stopping briefly in front of his own house just to open the door and tell Lydia their plan.

She looked deeply worried. "Be careful," she called after him.

Simon ran back to the car and slid into the driver's seat, wasting no time as he sped across the bridge toward the hospital.

Arriving at the hospital, Marcus carried Suzie inside, laying her on a rolling cart and getting her admitted to the flu ward.

The staff moved with practiced precision, their faces obscured behind masks, their uniforms covered in protective gowns... each step taken in careful defense against the spread of infection.

Simon waited in a chair outside of the ward, silently praying for everyone. He thought of Suzie, Marcus, the children... even of James, who had said in the alley that he wasn't feeling well either... perhaps also under this flu's dangerous grip.

A couple of hours passed before Marc came out, pulling off a face mask, dropping heavily into a chair beside Simon. "They put in the intravenous and are giving her fluids. Her fever is still high. She's not making much sense. Delirium."

"I can stay," Simon offered compassionately.

Marcus shook his head. "Go home, Simon, for Lydia and the children. It'll help Nikki if you're there. Can you find a way to tell her Suzie is sick? And call the Boytons, will you?"

Simon nodded. "Let's pray together before I go, buddy. You can always sleep in the doctors' lounge if you spend the night. And just call me. I'll come back over any time, day or night."

Marcus rubbed his tired eyes. He nodded. The two men bent their heads together as Simon softly prayed for Suzie and Marc before he left the hospital and made his way back home.

Simon parked behind the house in the alley and made his way up to the porch, the weight of the day settling heavily on his chest. Inside, he went straight to the kitchen, scrubbing his hands, arms, and face before heading upstairs to change into clean clothes.

When he came back down, Lydia and the children were gathered in the living room, with Abril watching over them. Lydia, with Hannah and Jimmy slid over on the sofa to make room as Simon joined them, and Nikki wasted no time climbing onto his lap.

"Imah, na ki-ki dada?" she asked, patting his bearded cheek.

"Your daddy is taking care of your mommy, Nikki," Simon told the child. "Nikki, you are going to stay here with Uncle Simon and Aunt Lydia."

"An Immy?" she asked.

"Yes, and Jimmy... and Abril," Simon told her.

Lydia reached out, squeezing Simon's hand. "How is she?" she asked worriedly.

"Started intravenous fluids, but she's delirious," he reported sadly. "I doubt she even knows that Marc is there... or where she is."

"Oh, Simon!" Lydia exclaimed softly. "Poor thing. And how's Marc? Is he spending the night over there?"

Simon nodded. "Yep. Won't leave her. He'll call if he needs us. Oh, I need to call Suzie's parents. Let them know how sick she is. It's a long trip down. I doubt... even if they tried to come..." Simon looked troubled. "I have a feeling she isn't going to make it, Lydia. It's just a feeling, but it's strong. I'm also worried about what that would mean... for you."

Lydia pressed his hand to her cheek, not letting go. The baby was tucked against her chest. If Suzie didn't... Hannah would... Hannah would need her around the clock. There was no question in Lydia's mind what she was prepared to do. She said nothing, just silently sent up a prayer that Suzie would make it through this.

"Lydia," Simon said intently. "There are other ways. We can get her on a bottle... maybe. Hire a nurse."

"I am a nurse, Simon," she said softly, her hand instinctively moving to cradle the tiny baby, who had already become so precious to her.

For the next several days, everyone simply went through the motions. Jimmy was now sleeping through the night with a single feeding before bed. Hannah sometimes made it three-hours between night feedings and was able to sleep in between. Lydia kept the bassinet right next to the bed so she could get as much rest as possible.

The night Marcus had called for Simon to rush to the hospital, Lydia had just finished feeding Hannah around three in the morning. She was tucking the baby into the bassinet when she heard his heavy footsteps climbing the stairs.

Simon opened the door and just stood there. Tears in his eyes.

Lydia pulled him to the bed, and they just lay there, his head on her breasts as she gently ran her fingers through his hair, soothing him until she heard his breathing deepen and he drifted off to sleep lying against her.

She lay awake a little longer, grieved in her spirit that the infant would never get to know her mother. Thinking about this heartbreaking, cruel turn of events, she wondered about the why of it all. All the other 'w' questions had ready answers this time, but once again, she stumbled over the why.

What would you say to this, Doctor Reese? Why does a new mother fall desperately ill and die just when her desperately small infant finally starts to live? Maybe some why questions just don't have answers... because sometimes... life just isn't fair.

Suzie's funeral fell on a day when there was an unexpected mid-winter thaw.

As a toddler, Nikki could not comprehend all the people crowding the house, all wearing black clothing, her grandparents from Rochester included. She clung to Marcus, seeking his comfort. Lydia kept Hannah tucked up against her in the shirt-sling, not permitting anyone to hold her, fearful of exposing such a fragile infant to any sort of illness.

Everyone congregated at the church. Many of the nuns from Charity, including Sister Edwarda, were in attendance. Doctors Peter Martin and Mike Franklin also attended out of respect for the nurse who had brought so much to the clinic. Nancy and Sally came... and Gretha drove in from her farm in Ohio... all devastated by losing one of their own from their unit in the war.

At Marcus' request, Father Henderson performed the service, though he had met Suzie only once, at the baptism of the Finney's baby. From the pulpit, the minister spoke of God's love and His desire to bring all of His sheep into the fold. He explained that everyone, up to and including the moment of their final crossing, has the opportunity to turn to God—that the private thoughts of the soul and its Creator at the time of transition are known only to a fair and righteous God, and the soul itself.

Marcus found comfort in these words. Later, he wouldn't remember much of the sermon, except how it felt... soothing.

Taking comfort in the presence of his friends, Marcus rode in the automobile with Lydia, Simon, and the children over to the cemetery. A late February breeze stirred, carrying the faint warmth of a pale sun. Only the death of his mother, when he was young, came even close to what he was experiencing at this moment.

Theirs was not the only burial at the cemetery that day, though illness continued to decline in the city. Across the grounds, several other small tents had been erected with groups of mourners under each of them, gathered in prayer or placing flowers on coffins in preparation for returning dust to dust.

The line of black automobiles came to a halt behind the hearse. Simon glanced at Marcus.

"We're right beside you," Simon reminded his friend as they got out of the car.

Marcus held Nikki, Simon had Jimmy in his arms, and Lydia kept little Hannah tucked close to her. As they approached the coffin, Marcus clasped Father Henderson's hand once more, waiting as the mourners gathered around.

When the prayers began, Simon rested a steady hand on Marcus' shoulder. And in that moment, Marcus knew he wasn't carrying this grief alone. Lydia stood beside him, taking his hand while Nikki rested securely in the crook of his other arm.

In the quiet, Marcus heard the calls from a small group of geese. He looked up, watching as they passed over the cemetery. No doubt they were heading toward the river, but to him, it felt as if they were bearing Suzie's spirit heavenward.

When his turn came at last, Marcus stepped forward. He lingered for just a breath, then laid a single white rose on Susannah's coffin. Then he turned away, joining his friends and in-laws—her mother, father, sister, and brother—who were weeping quietly, holding on to one another. Not one of them noticed the lone man, leaning against a tree, watching from a distance.

Once back at Marcus' house, Lydia invited the Boytons to peek at baby Hannah. They gushed over her fine blonde hair, marveling at her tiny, delicate features. Lydia took breaks throughout the day to nurse the babies upstairs, while downstairs, Mrs. Gilbert served dishes that had been prepared by the women from the church down the block.

Marcus kept Nikki with him as he quietly spoke with everyone, introducing her to each person, moving from one small group to the next. Vanessa Boyton hovered anxiously, wanting her grandchild, to herself.

When Nancy and Sally approached him, they gave Marcus a quick hug.

"What can we do?" Nancy asked, genuinely concerned.

"I guess nothing," he told them. "I'm not really even sure what we'll need. Maybe in a few weeks, but I don't even know what I'm thinking, right now."

"We're here... if we can help," Sally assured him. "If you need us to help with the girls... or anything... just say something."

Marcus nodded. He shifted his weight as his mother-in-law approached them, again reaching for Nikki.

"Marcus, we can take Nikki to live with us," Vanessa brushed a stray hair from Nikki's forehead. "Wayne and I can raise her, give her a wonderful life."

"That is generous of you, Mrs. Boyton, but I'm more than able to raise the girls... and Mrs. Gilbert has offered to stay on and help," he told them all. "She's been a tremendous help, with Hannah coming so early. I don't know how we would have managed without her... and Nikki feels close to her too."

Nancy recognized the pain in Mrs. Boyton's eyes. "I'm so sorry for your loss, Mrs. Boyton. This is too awful, losing a daughter like this."

Marcus added, "I am glad we were up to visit before the holidays. Suzie loved seeing some of her friends that week and most of the family. At least we have that."

Vanessa nodded sadly. "Yes, it was a good visit, Marcus. I'm glad you came."

Sally jumped in. "Can you take some time off from the hospital, Marcus?"

"I'm sure I could. I don't know, though... maybe I need to stay in a routine... I think I'll just get through today."

"Where's Lydia?" Nancy asked.

"Upstairs, nursing the babies," Marcus glanced toward the stairs.

Nancy smiled at the group. "I'll go up and see how she's doing."

Upstairs, Nancy peeked inside a couple of doors, before finding her in the back bedroom. Lydia was in the rocking chair, Jimmy on her lap and the tiny infant at her breast.

Nancy perched on the edge of the bed, taking in the scene before her. "Who would have ever thought you'd still be nursing Jimmy, when this little one would also need to nurse? I mean, what are the chances?"

"Mothers of twins do it all the time. It's easier now with Jimmy eating soft foods too. Hannah still doesn't take nearly as much as Jimmy does... It's a miracle she's growing. She was so tiny and weak... when Suzie and I... when we took shifts every four hours, nursing her every hour..." she managed tearfully. "I'm really going to miss her, Nancy..."

Nancy exhaled, shaking her head. "Who'd have figured we'd all make it back from the front, only to have Suzie die of influenza. Life doesn't make any sense, Lydia. She had a husband, two daughters, a home. And now she's just gone? It's just not right... It doesn't make any sense."

"No, it doesn't." Lydia moved Hannah from her breast and into the sling over her shoulder, then reached for Jimmy, who was more than ready to nurse. He latched on immediately, likely needing comfort as much as her milk.

Nancy watched in fascination. "And your body simply does all that. All on its own."

Caressing her son's chubby cheeks, Lydia smiled down at Jimmy. "Yes, it does. And by the time little Hannah is ready to take a lot more, Jimmy will be weaned."

Nancy looked at her curiously. "It sounds like you intend to just keep feeding and caring for Suzie's baby?"

Lydia looked up, a bit surprised by the question. "Well, of course!" she exclaimed. "Why wouldn't I?"

"Well, Marcus will likely meet someone else, and she'll want to take over the motherly stuff, no doubt," Nancy reasoned.

Lydia hadn't given that any thought whatsoever. Feeding and caring for Hannah was just the thing to do.

"Well, of course, that's true, he might."

"I mean, after a loss like this, some guys take up with the first woman who shows interest... and a young doctor with two little daughters..." Nancy said. "And he's such a handsome guy. There will be women, eager to offer him help with his girls."

Lydia felt so close to this tiny infant. But of course, Marcus wouldn't remain alone for long; he would need a woman in his life sooner rather than later. Naturally, a new wife would have to establish her own role in raising Nikki and Hannah. Lydia's mind reeled. Of course, she'd be glad if he found someone to love again. And when little Hannah was strong enough to wrap her mouth around a rubber nipple, they could switch her to bottles. She would have to talk to Simon about this. When Jimmy was done, she changed him quickly, eager for her and Nancy to rejoin the group downstairs.

Some visitors had already paid their respects and said their goodbyes to Marcus, but Suzannah's family was staying another night before heading back to Rochester, wanting as much time as possible with the girls, especially Nikki, since Marcus had made it clear he wasn't willing to let them take her with them.

Soon, the house was empty except for Marcus, his in-laws, and Lydia and Simon with the children. In the quiet, the soft music of the radio was a comfort. As Nikki's eyes grew heavy, Marcus carried her up to his bed, tucking her in for the night so the Boytons could have her room.

When he came back down, he headed for the kitchen to pour himself a glass of juice. As he closed the latch for the icebox, Lydia approached him, cradling his face in her hands, studying his face.

He took her hands in his and kissed them. "Trying to figure out my soul, Lydia?" he asked gently. "Tell me when you have it all nailed down."

She held his gaze. "I guess I am," she admitted.

"I'm okay, Lydia. In a strange way... I'm a tiny bit relieved," he assured her. "Suzie was leaving me, one way or the other. Somehow, it's a little easier having her leave me this way, rather than to another man. I know how awful that must sound. But in a way, it's like I was being prepared for her to leave for the last eight weeks, at least emotionally." He hesitated, his fingers tightening slightly on the glass in his hand. "But by the grace of God, she's left the girls with me, instead of taking them to live with another man to be their father... I want to be their father, Lydia. I want to be the best father to Nikki and Hannah. It would have been so hard watching another man take over my role."

"You're already a really great father to the girls, Marcus. Nikki loves you with all her little heart. And so will Hannah."

Marcus looked at his baby girl, tucked in the shirt-sling against Lydia's chest. His daughter would have died without Lydia.

He cleared his throat. "I already owe you everything, Lydia. Everything," Marcus said, his voice gruff with emotion, holding back tears. "I've no right to ask a single thing from you ever again in life—"

"But it looks like you want to ask something. What is it, Marcus?" she asked. "Anything, truly, you know that."

Just at that moment, Simon came in looking for Lydia, seeing the two of them in an intense moment. He approached quietly and wrapped an arm around Lydia's waist.

"Can I help?" he asked them both, concerned about the look in Marcus' eyes.

"Yes, Simon, you can," Marcus said openly. "You're my best friends, and before you say anything, I do realize what I'm asking. And it's okay to say no. But is it too much to ask for you to keep Hannah with you for a while? At least while she still needs to nurse?" He exhaled, rubbing the back of his neck. "I realize what I'm asking, really, I do... I mean, when she's bigger, I can hire someone to bottle-feed her with formula. Or Mrs. Gilbert would probably be willing, since she's staying on with Nikki and Jimmy while we're all at work... I've no right to ask more of you, Lydia, but... I am asking. Would you and Simon see fit to care for Hannah, with Nikki and me until she's stronger and can go without night feedings, anyway?"

Lydia was unable to hold in her tears, as she felt Simon give her a little squeeze of agreement.

"You told me once, Marcus, that you would help raise Simon's baby if God had decided not to give Simon back to me," Lydia reminded him. "And now you give me the gift of being able to return the favor with your own baby? Yes, Marcus. For as long as you need us, we're here."

"Then that will be forever," Marcus said, looking at Simon and Lydia, and his tiny Hannah. "And thankfully, forever is a really long time."

Spring was in the air, not quite arrived, but whispering its promise to relieve them from what had been a long winter. At the end of the alley, a car sat still, engine off, its dark frame partially hidden by some bushes that stayed full all winter. From where he sat, the driver could see the house on the corner.

Hm. There goes Simon... and the other one that lives across the alley? That Marcus friend of theirs, getting into the car. Oh. Who's this?

An older woman walked straight inside, without even knocking. Someone apparently well known to them.

Hm. And that dog running around the yard... no, that dog isn't a problem really. Would go down fast with a bat, or a knife. Yeh, don't have to worry about the dog. Dog's okay.

The dog rolled in the grass and bolted back under the trees chasing something. Then dropped down in the grass and just looked around keeping an eye on things.

What's this? Ah, there you are, Lydia. Got laundry to hang out? Just get it out on the line real nice there, let the wind blow it dry. Just an ordinary day in the neighborhood while the men go off to the hospital. Where's your baby? Leave him inside with the housekeeper, if that's who that older woman is?

His fingers drummed the steering wheel. The best way to get even with the man who ruined his life, was to get to the man's wife. His shoulder still smarted from hitting the stairs, tumbling down and then hitting the frozen ground so hard. He probably broke it.

I told you this wasn't over, Simon. But Lydia is also to blame! Yes, Lydia, your sister listened to you. All your fault she left me! All those ideas you stuffed in her head!

Silently watching, Tommy gripped the steering wheel. What he wanted to do to her, to get even! He'd been thinking about it for some time.

Peggy refused to see him. He'd gone to the schoolyard a couple of times, caught glimpses of Steven during recess. But Peggy was still staying with Anna, and without her, he had no way to relieve his anger, or his want.

Drinking it away only worked some of the time. Most of the time, the fury clawed at him, left him teetering on the edge. He'd almost gotten himself fired, snapping at his boss.

This really was all Lydia's fault. If she had just accepted her correction on the back porch, admitted she had been wrong, and then kept her mouth shut. If she hadn't let that damn dog bark at Anna's house while he was teaching her—none of this would have happened... and he would still have Peggy.

Tommy sat up suddenly, leaning forward. His gaze narrowed. He almost got out of the car, almost slipped behind a tree to get a closer look.

What now? That's a baby against her chest? Isn't her kid older than that by now? This is a little one. What the heck? And right on that back porch swing, behind the rhododendron there. Is she opening her shirt a little? She is! Breastfeeding right on the back porch there! Unbelievable! She is such a whore! Putting it right out there for anyone to see. She does not know how to behave!

Tommy's knuckles were white from gripping the steering wheel so tightly. What he wouldn't give to be able to put her over a table until she learned her proper place... then he'd drag her right to bed.

He had to think this out. Doctors had to be on call, sometimes. Yes, night would work. No housekeeper then or that other nurse from that house across the alley. Just Lydia, at home, alone, where he could take her. He could make this happen.

Revenge is much better than whiskey... or at least tied for first place.

Starting the engine, Tommy carefully backed up the alley before turning to find somewhere to plan. He whispered to himself as he drove off.

"I'm gonna bring you down a notch, Lydia. Give you a lesson you won't be able to ignore." A slow, twisted grin curled at his lips. "And Simon... you'll pay for making me lose my wife. I'll just take yours instead."

FISHING CREEK

Book III of The River Series

... excerpt ...

Marcus cast his line into the open edge of water, glancing at Simon. "Are you talking about things?" he asked quietly.

Simon wheezed, steadying his breath before answering. "Uh-huh... when she can handle it. She knows the house is paid for... the car too. There's the cabin, and money in the bank for her. She said she wants to keep working. I'm putting away as much as I can each paycheck... for her, for the children."

Marcus nodded. "You know I'll make sure she doesn't go without, Simon. For as long as she lives... or I do."

Simon stared into the water. "I'm counting on you. Never thought it would come to this. Not now."

Marcus shook his head. "I just don't understand it."

"I'm going to a good place, Marcus. Remember? In my Father's house are many mansions?"

"Yeh, well, I'm gonna need a reservation—I don't want my mansion to be on the other side of Heaven from you two!" Marcus protested.

Simon chuckled, suppressing a sudden cough.

"Well, there, we may be traveling at the speed of thought. But, since I'm arriving first, I'll put in a proper request. How about right across the alley?" He pulled a fish in from the river with an expert flick of his pole and line.

"I let you have that one."

"No need to compete, you've still got me at chess."

There was a comfortable silence between them.

"This is going to be hard," Marcus exhaled, his breath a white puff that vanished into the cold air.

"I know. I've been writing letters to the children. They won't have a chance to get to know me, so I'm writing to them about growing up, my folks, Doc Albright, how I met their mother. Someda—"

His voice caught. He swallowed hard, composing himself.

"I'll read them the letters, buddy. They'll know who their dad is... I'll make sure of it. But I swear, if you make me cry out here, my eyes will freeze shut... You'll have to lead me back, carrying the fish... and whatever's left of my dignity."

"Good grief!" Simon let out a laugh, despite himself. The deep sadness of the moment broken, Simon reached into his pants pocket and pulled out a handkerchief. "Here. I always have a couple handy now. I cry a lot lately."

Marcus took it gratefully. "You going to tell Becky and Phil this trip?"

"I'd better. We've been given this time to prepare. They should get the same gift."

Marcus reeled in his line, barely noticing the fish thrashing at the end of it. He turned, meeting his friend's gaze, face-to-face. "Is it a gift, Simon? Is it? Or is it actually a burden."

Simon rested his gloved hand on Marcus' shoulder.

"It's a gift to have the time to prepare, Marc. A gift, knowing I can leave Lydia and the children safely in your hands. I'm lucky to have enough time to tell people how much I love them, and I'll say it as often as I can."

He squeezed Marcus' shoulder, "I really love you, buddy."

Marcus choked on his tears, swallowing hard before managing, "Should we like... kiss now, or something?"

Simon laughed out loud, then coughed hard, shaking his head. "Come on, Marc. Let's go eat these fish..."

Acknowledgements

With unlimited gratitude and thanks to my daughter, for her unflagging support, manuscript review, marketing, networking, and middle-man masterminding.

With heartfelt thanks to my mother whose patience was unending as she "red-lined with enthusiasm" each improper use of "lie and lay", de-dangled participles, and flagged typos, while moderating the debate over commas versus semicolons.

With deep admiration for the courageous patients who, over the decades, taught me to never quit, to never lose hope—who showed me the resilience of love and the profound power of healing.

To my family who sometimes went without floors swept or sinks scrubbed because I "can't stop typing now."

With humility toward Almighty God who indeed makes the impossible, possible.

This is a work of fiction, dedicated to the patients who place their trust in our care, and to the nurses and doctors who bring that care where it is needed most, no matter the cost.

About the Author

Rachael Hiatt is an American author and has been a practicing Registered Nurse for over 50 years, with Master's Degrees in both Nursing and Counseling. Her debut work, *The River Series*, is comprised of ten medical historical romance novels which follow a group of exceptional Nurses and Doctors over a 40 year period, starting in WWI. The journey plunges readers into the struggle to find courage, love, faith, and meaning in the throes of the battle between good and evil.

Rachael is a mother of two and grandmother of three. When she sets aside her pen, she finds joy in playing the piano, writing poetry, and observing the migrations of Snow Geese. With heartfelt gratitude to the patients she has had the privilege of serving as well as the practitioners she has worked alongside, to her mother, her most loyal critic, and to God, she humbly offers these novels to her readers.

Also by

Rachael Hiatt

THE RIVER SERIES
The Meuse
~ Three Rivers ~
future releases
Fishing Creek
Elk River
Six Penny Creek
Hot Springs
Tributary
Monongahela
White Water
Frozen Falls

www.ingramcontent.com/pod-product-compliance
Lightning Source LLC
Chambersburg PA
CBHW022248310726
48973CB00001B/5